The Anomaly Crystal

John (a great mate)
Enjoy the Story.
J.Martin

The Anomaly Crystal

Jamie Martin

To order additional copies of this book, contact:
Xlibris
800-056-3182
www.Xlibrispublishing.co.uk
Orders@Xlibrispublishing.co.uk
702448

Acknowledgements

THANK YOU to my family and friends for all the support and encouragement they have given me. I want to acknowledge the value of trust and companionship in the relationships we develop throughout our lives; it's important to stay honest and true to each other. I am dedicating this book to my nan (June Mary Forfar, 29 June 1931–4 August 2005). You will always remain in our thoughts.

Jamie Lionel Martin

LAIR OF DEATH

WASTELANDS

EAGLE FOREST

OPEN VALLEY

SWAMP FIELDS

CADAVER ROCK

REALM OF DESERTED LANDS

THE PLANET

UNDERGROUND DUNGEON

N
W   E
S

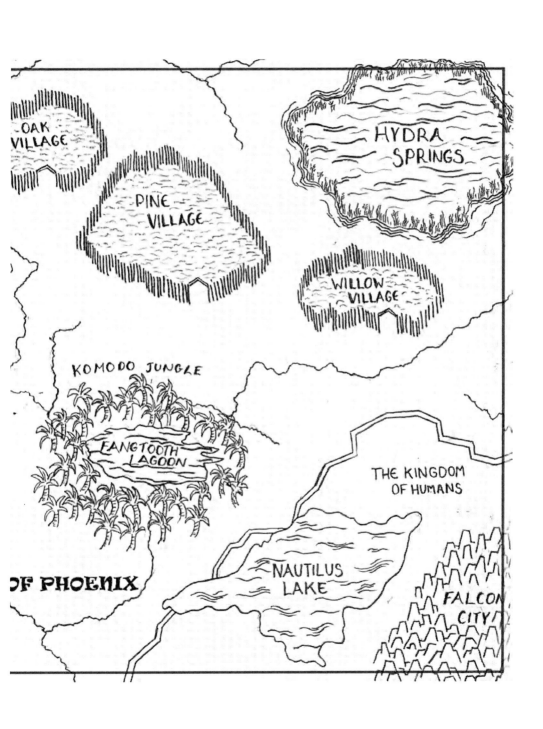

Death is Only the Beginning

One

'OVER 200 HUNDRED years ago, a wise, cerebral, and powerful wizard known as Grackle who had trained in the mastery of fundamental and elemental magic, along with the art of sorcery for hundreds of years, begrudgingly forged a supernatural diamond by depleting all his enchanted powers and life force. Grackle called this supernatural diamond the anomaly crystal. This anomaly crystal possessed magnificent and wondrous magical powers that went beyond all intellectual imagination and something that the Planet of Phoenix's human and creature inhabitants had never experienced before. Grackle sacrificed his own life force and magical capabilities to create the anomaly crystal, as he inadvertently foresaw in the time to come within the next 200 years that evil creatures would enforce a great war in striving to become the rulers over our Planet of Phoenix and would enslave or annihilate all the humans upon it. Whereas in the distant past, all the ancient creatures residing on the Planet of Phoenix were at peace with one another and posed no threat to us humans, now times have drastically changed.

'Before the superlative Grackle sacrificed his own life in aid of creating the anomaly crystal, he spoke of the great war and what would come to be to his most loyal of friends, the sorcerer known as Hake. Grackle and Hake both deliberated for much duration about what would be the best plan to prevent the great war from occurring and to save the humans from an eternity of suffering. Against Hake's appeal, Grackle saw no other alternative but to create the anomaly crystal and got Hake to give the anomaly crystal to his eldest son, Sparrow, to be its protector and also to continue passing the anomaly crystal down the generations of Grackle's bloodline, for when the time would come to wield its elemental powers against the creatures in aid of ending the inevitable great war. Sparrow was a brave and praiseworthy human, and he is your great-grandfather. Sparrow kept the anomaly crystal hidden and secret for all these years by passing it down through our bloodline, which is the admirable bloodline of Grackle, for all our family to protect at all costs, even if it also meant sacrificing our own lives. Although it might be seen as a curse for our family, it's also a commendable blessing to be the protectors of such a remarkable artefact. The story of the anomaly crystal is extensive and has incredible tales of love, honour, sacrifice, and sinfulness within the last 200 years, enabling us to be lucky enough to end up with the anomaly crystal here in my shop, as the last inheritor of Grackle's living bloodline. Here is the anomaly crystal, Raven,' says Barious dramatically to his grandson Raven.

Barious is sixty-seven years old and is Raven's only living grandfather. Barious is small in height compared with other humans living on the Planet of Phoenix. The average height of most humans living on the Planet pf Phoenix is approximately five feet and eight inches, although Barious is quite a bit smaller than this average height. Barious used to be taller but has now started to shrink due to his age. He is one of a handful of humans who has managed to live to this age. Thirty-four years old is the average age of a human living on the Planet of Phoenix due to there being an abundance of disease, famine, and war. Barious has short curly grey hair, brown eyes, a pale wrinkly face, and an average physique. His current appearance is from the hard work and battles in the past that he has endured, but has now made him quite strong for his age. Barious wears old dirty white and grey wool clothing and white overalls as he owns a tool shop in Oak Village and has done so for most of his life. Although Barious has experienced many difficult situations, such as fights against creatures and heartache in his past, like when his son Ruthus and daughter-in-law Jewel were murdered, he remains a very jolly and content character, as he wants to make sure that his grandson Raven whom he looks after has a good upbringing.

Barious starts to slowly pull out a small metal box that glistens in the sunlight brightly shining through his bedroom window. He takes out the metal box which is shaped like a treasure chest from under one of the long but loose wooden floor boards. Barious is in his quaint bedroom on the second floor of his small, old established wooden tool shop in Oak Village. He grabs a small shiny silver key with a golden handle from his white overall pocket, and with this key, he begins to unlock the glistening metal box. After Barious turns the silver key by its golden handle three times in the lock of the metal box, he opens it carefully and slowly takes out a small reflective diamond that is larger in the middle and then shrinks in size towards the smooth points at both ends of it. The anomaly crystal constantly illuminates with every colour of the rainbow along with shades of white and black energetically swirling around the centre of it. The colours of the rainbow; red, orange, yellow, green, blue, indigo, and violet swirl actively alongside one another as well as through each other, which also enables them to change into other colours like pink and brown.

'Wow, that crystal looks incredible, Grandfather,' replies Raven as he looks upon the anomaly crystal in great astonishment.

'Yes, my lad, it certainly is incredible and has been kept in our family for all those generations back from Sparrow and the legendary Grackle himself until the day its virtues will be required to help save our Planet of Phoenix and our fellow humans that live upon it,' explains Barious wearily.

'How does the anomaly crystal work, Grandfather? What kind of magic can be released from it?' Raven asks enthusiastically.

'As far as I'm aware, no one has yet been able to wield the limitless magical powers in the anomaly crystal, but I do remember my father, Trogon, telling me at the same time as he gave the anomaly crystal to me to keep it safe and that the strength and value of emotions from those humans, who only possess the bloodline of Grackle, would be able to unleash cosmic forms of extraordinary powers that are produced intentionally to be most useful in the situation the anomaly crystal holders find themselves in. Due to the prodigious and unusual magical powers of the anomaly crystal, it can also be an extremely dangerous artefact, and even I am still oblivious of what the anomaly crystal can actually do. Unfortunately, in this uncertain and changing environment that our Planet of Phoenix is experiencing, I have regrettably no choice but to take on the role bestowed upon me by our family's bloodline. Raven, the time has come when I have to ask you the most important duties to be undertaken,' states Barious uneasily in a sad manner.

'Of course, Grandfather . . . I will do anything and everything to help you, my ancestors, and our fellow humans,' exclaims Raven boldly.

'Suspicious word has only just come to my knowledge of a malicious evil growing beyond the Wastelands in the highest north-west point of the Planet of Phoenix, far and deep within the frozen Mountains of Doom upon a desolate peak called Crow Mountain. Upon Crow Mountain in a fortress lives a treacherous creature called Lord Scartor, and with his increase in armoured Potorian forces, they seek to find and steal the anomaly crystal in order to cast anarchy and chaos through the Planet of Phoenix. And for those humans who will not be slaves to Lord Scartor, he will brutally and callously kill them.

'Lord Scartor is the purest of evil. He possesses no morals, shame, or remorse and will do anything and stop at nothing to make other humans suffer until he becomes the one and only ruler of the Planet of Phoenix. I now fear some of his Potorian spies have traced the anomaly crystal to being hidden somewhere within our Oak Village. I do not wish to place this burden upon you, my grandson, but I require you to take responsibility of the anomaly crystal and swiftly travel east to Pine Village, where your cousin Parrot lives. Ask for Parrot's help upon my request and hide the anomaly crystal in a safe and protected place in Pine Village for now until more secure plans can be made, when I will seek to consult my good friends, King Exodus of Falcon City and Panther the leader of Willow Village, regarding this crucial matter,' proclaims Barious as Raven listens intently to his cautious words.

Barious slowly places the anomaly crystal in Raven's right hand, and with his own hand, he closes Raven's hand tight around the anomaly crystal.

'Do not speak of the anomaly crystal or the story of Grackle, Sparrow, and Lord Scartor I have just shared with you to anyone, as there are many untrusted creatures and even humans in the Planet of Phoenix. I am unaware of how many of them know of the anomaly crystal and also what they would do if they find out about its inconceivable magical powers. Raven; do not stop for passing strangers when you are riding on the long cobbled roads. I will give you my mighty horse, Felix, to take on this journey, and it will be also beneficial to take any weapons to protect yourself with, which you have kept from when you used to practice taekwondo. Be quick, quiet, and above all safe as I wouldn't be able to live with myself if anything would happen to you because of these duties I have also now bestowed upon you. However, dark times are approaching, Raven, which is what Grackle inevitably foretold. I worry that if the anomaly crystal doesn't remain in the good and pure hands of the bloodline of Grackle, the Planet of Phoenix and the peaceful humans who live in it might perish at the terror and evilness of the abhorrent creatures,' says Barious in an anxious voice, looking seriously at Raven's young and innocent face.

'We will never let anything bad happen to the Planet of Phoenix, Grandfather. Also, it's not your fault that any of this has happened, so please don't feel regret about the knowledge and duties you have just shared with me. I am honoured to be part of the bloodline of the renowned Grackle. I will go to see Parrot in Pine Village straight away and hopefully return before sunset in order to make it back to Oak Village's coronation celebration festival for Wolf's third year as the leader of our Oak Village,' replies Raven optimistically, smiling at Barious's concerned face.

RAVEN PUTS THE anomaly crystal in the right pocket of his brown trousers and flattens the top part of his pocket to conceal it. Barious smiles back at Raven and then kneels down to place the small metal box back underneath the long loose wooden floor board in his bedroom. Raven leaves Barious's bedroom and walks quickly to his own bedroom immediately across from Barious's bedroom in his old wooden tool shop. After Raven enters his bedroom, he grabs his grey coat hanging on a metal hook fixed at the back of his bedroom door. The grey coat has an attached hood and has creased indents over some parts of the coat. Raven kneels on the floor by his bed to grab a pair of old white nunchucks from beneath his bed. Raven had obtained the white nunchucks after achieving his green belt in the discipline of taekwondo that he took up as a hobby for four years under the advice of Barious so that Raven could build up his muscles and fighting abilities. Recently, however, Raven had given up taekwondo as he did not have the time needed to achieve excellence in it, since he wanted to pursue other interests, such as dating his girlfriend Emerald.

While Raven in his bedroom is gathering the essential things that he needs for the journey to Pine Village, Barious leaves his bedroom and walks down the steep pokey wooden stairs that lead into the main section of his wooden tool shop. Barious's tool shop was one of the first buildings to be built when Oak Village was initially developed over 200 years ago by a Pine villager called Hyena. Barious's wooden tool shop was designed to have living quarters above the wooden tool shop, and the first tool shop owner called Buffalo allowed Sparrow's wife Star and his child Trogon to live in the tool shop's bedrooms when they first relocated to Oak Village, as they did not have anywhere else to live, especially since Buffalo had no wife or children of his own. Buffalo was a great tool maker and he also taught Trogon the trade of it so he could help him around the shop, as payment for allowing him and his mother Star to live there.

After Buffalo died of a virus he unfortunately picked up from the poisonous bugs within the Swamp Fields near the Wastelands in the north-west side of the Planet of Phoenix when he was walking through them one day, the ownership of the wooden tool shop was transferred to Star and then on to Trogon when Star died of old age. During the years of living in Oak Village, Trogon married one of the Oak Village farmers' pretty daughters who was named Gem, and later in their marriage they had a son called Barious, whom Star got also to meet just before she died. Trogon taught Barious when he was at an appropriate age on how to make tools and run the wooden tool shop that he also inherited many years later when Trogon died of old age.

Barious returns to the front counter where he was before he decided to tell Raven about the anomaly crystal, and he continues to pack metal tools like hammers, nails, and screwdrivers into small wooden boxes that he will display around the tool shop's wooden shelves.

Back in his bedroom, Raven puts on his grey coat and places the white nunchucks in his brown trouser pocket just before he leaves his bedroom. Raven has just turned eighteen years old; he is also quite small in height like Barious and has a medium-sized and muscly physique that was developed from the four years he trained as a taekwondo student. Raven has short spiked dark blond hair and brown eyes; he has a smooth and clear face that has an innocent look upon it. He is currently wearing brown trousers, a blue shirt, brown boots, and a grey coat with a hood attached to it. Raven is a vibrant and caring person; he has enjoyed learning and socialising at Oakus School and he has just recently left as he has completed his compulsory education during his teenager years and is now also training alongside Barious on how to make tools, supply them via trade, and run the tool shop in order to become the owner of the wooden tool shop when Barious becomes too old to look after it no more. Raven, although friendly and outgoing, is quite reserved and introverted; these particular characteristics Raven had developed during his childhood, due to losing his parents at a very young age.

Raven's father, Ruthus, was the elder son of Barious and Barious's previous wife, Flower; they also had another younger son called Rio, who was Raven's uncle and Parrot's father. Ruthus would have now been forty-six years old; he had short brown straight hair and brown eyes and was a tool, cloth, and farm foods trader. Raven's mother, Jewel, would have now been forty-one years old; she had long, straight blonde hair and brown eyes and had been an intelligent and loving housewife. Both Ruthus and Jewel had also been short in height as compared with the average human upon the Planet of Phoenix as well as having medium-sized physiques and they also had clear skin upon their faces. Raven cherished his parents until Ruthus and Jewel were both murdered by a snake-like creature called Viper eleven years ago. Viper poisoned them both with black venom that he spit from the large pointed white fangs in his mouth; this deadly black poison had the ability to disintegrate human flesh and bones and that was what happened to the physical bodies of Ruthus and Jewel.

On the day of their untimely deaths in their old wooden house in Oak Village that used to be located in the north-west direction not too far from Barious's wooden tool shop, Barious had taken a young Raven at the age of seven for a walk in the Grass Terrain Fields that resided near the enchanted Eagle Forest in the north-west direction of the Planet of Phoenix, along with Ruthus and Jewel's friend, Ruby, her husband, Gaius, and young daughter, Emerald. When they had all returned to Oak Village and gone to leave Raven at Ruthus and Jewel's wooden house, they found the withering remains of Ruthus's and Jewel's bodies upon the wooden floor of their downstairs living room. Barious, Raven, Ruby, Gaius, and Emerald were all distraught and heartbroken to find their beloved Ruthus and Jewel murdered in such a cruel manner. After this horrible incident, Barious took Raven back to his wooden tool shop to live with him, and Barious promised himself that he would bring Raven up as best as he could in honour of his dead son, Ruthus, and daughter-in-law, Jewel. The repressed memories of that dramatic scene ensured Raven never really spoke about his father and mother to anyone due to the deep pain it caused him remembering those traumatic events during his childhood.

After Raven collects his white nunchucks and grey coat with the hood attached to it and puts on his brown boots, he walks out of his bedroom, but he suddenly stops at the top of the steep wooden stairs in Barious's wooden tool shop as he experiences an overwhelming memory that has just came into his thoughts from his past. Raven remembers that when he was very young around the age of a toddler his parents Ruthus and Jewel used to tell him a bedtime story about Grackle and his great-grandfather Sparrow. He remembers his parents speaking about how Grackle was known as the most powerful wizard ever to live on the Planet of Phoenix; his age was unknown, but he used to wear a one-piece long blue cloth that had white wolf's fur padded around the shoulders. Grackle always carried a long, sharply pointed pure white wooden wand with him. Grackle was respected and admired by the Alder villagers who lived near him and his family in the ancient village known as Alder Village that used to be located to the far north-east of the Planet of Phoenix. Alder Village was also situated near the beautiful and exotic scenery known as Hydra Springs.

Grackle used to practice and develop his mastery of spells and potions for many long hours each day and would use his wisdom and knowledge to help the Alder villagers by replenishing their health and physical skills and also creating safety precautions for their homes. His eldest son Sparrow was trustworthy, had moral values, and was similar looking to Raven, which is what Raven remembers his parents saying as they had in turn also been told these stories that were passed down from Ruthus's grandfather Trogon, who managed to live to a grand old age of seventy-three. Trogon also had blond spikey hair and brown eyes. Raven also remembers his parents telling the story of the anomaly crystal to him, just as Barious had done only moments ago, but all this knowledge had been blocked in his memory over the past years, as that information had been repressed along with the memories of his parents being brutally murdered.

Raven closes his brown eyes and breathes deeply until the memories of his ancestors pass from his thoughts. Raven opens his brown eyes again and starts to run down the steep wooden stairs of Barious's wooden tool shop until he reaches the bottom of it, and he walks into the middle of the tool shop that is surrounded by large wooden shelves full of metal tools as well as pieces of wood cut into different lengths, which can be fixed to make shelves and furniture.

'I'll be back shortly, Grandfather,' shouts Raven as he waves at Barious, quickly walking through the wooden tool shop to the front entrance.

'Be careful, Raven,' replies Barious. As Raven approaches the front entrance of the tool shop, the front door opens softly, and a beautiful girl with long wavy red hair and glittering blue eyes, wearing a breathtaking long silk blue dress and purple shoes, also carrying a purple handbag, walks in through the front entrance door and gazes deep into Raven's brown eyes. Emerald's complexion is beautiful and elegant and her soft tender skin is smooth like the water that exists in Hydra Springs. Emerald is also of a similar height as Raven, but is thinner in body size.

'Good morning, Raven, where are you off to in a hurry?' asks Emerald, giggling affectionately. Emerald is seventeen years old and is currently training as a gymnast at Oakus School; although she had also left school when Raven had done early in the year as both of them had finished their compulsory education. Emerald decided to stay helping within the school, specifically to teach the younger children gymnastic skills as well as help her mother, Ruby, when she taught her classes of religious education. Emerald is a kind-hearted and bubbly person; she enjoys and appreciates the environment and animals that surround Oak Village and reside upon the Planet of Phoenix.

Emerald has known Raven ever since they were babies, as her mother Ruby and father Gaius were friends with Raven's parents, Ruthus and Jewel. Emerald and Raven had always played games together when they were younger and had become great friends; their feelings for each other developed more deeply for one another and they became more intimate when they approached puberty and maturity during their teenage years. Emerald and Raven always speak fondly to one another and to their families of the first time when Raven built up the courage and finally kissed her when they were on a walk through the Grass Terrain Fields near Eagle Forest one sunny day; they were both fourteen years old.

'Ah, Emerald, it's you,' stutters Raven, momentarily blinded by Emerald's exquisite beauty.

'Well, of course, it's me. Who else would it be?' giggles Emerald.

'Um, yes, I mean, nothing. Sorry, I have to quickly go visit my cousin Parrot in Pine Village,' says Raven hesitantly.

'Oh, right, will you make it back in time later for our date at Wolf's coronation celebration festival?' asks Emerald.

'Yes, of course, I will, Emerald. Wild beasts couldn't keep me away,' laughs Raven.

'That's good. Well, I guess I'll see you later then, my darling,' says Emerald, while she kisses Raven slowly and tenderly on the cheek. Raven blushes a bright red colour and continues walking out the front entrance door; he begins to run around one of the sides of Barious's wooden tool shop until he reaches the back of it, where in a small grass field surrounded by wooden fences grazes Felix, Barious's big and beautiful black stallion horse who is twenty-four years old. Raven climbs over the wooden fence to enter the small grass field. Felix lifts his head up from eating hay at one end of the small grass field, as he hears the sound of Raven climbing over the wooden fence; he notices Raven and gallops up to him in a fierce but elegant manner, while enduring the heat of the bright sun.

Raven fits Felix with Barious's brown leather saddle that was left in a small wooden shed at another edge of the small grass field, opposite to where Felix had been eating the hay. Raven climbs on top of Felix's strong black back and strokes Felix's thick black hair on the back of his neck. Raven grabs on to the brown rope reins tightly, which are already attached to Felix; as he pulls them, Felix gallops, and they race through the small grass field until Felix jumps high in the air over the wooden fence surrounding the small grass field. As Felix lands on his strong sturdy hooves on the other side of the wooden fence, he continues galloping down the wooden and cobbled paths of Oak Village, which lead out of Oak Village's entrance gate made of thick wood in the east direction and on to the long cobbled road connecting Oak Village to Pine Village. The cobbled roads are bigger pebbled and rocky paths, made of small stones and rocks that had been built over a hundred years ago to connect the surrounding villages to each other.

Oak Village is a very basic and underdeveloped village, as it hasn't existed as long as Pine Village or Falcon City. Oak Village has one tool, clothing, and food shop, a couple of bars, inns, and several small houses and cottages made out of wood, and it's surrounded by farmlands that harvest wheat and vegetables, along with small grass fields that are filled with various farm animals such as sheep, cows, chicken, and pigs. Oak Village also has a small church called Oakus Church with an attached Oakus Graveyard that is positioned on a small grass hill in the south-east direction of Oak Village. There is also a school called Oakus School, and in the middle of Oak Village is a medium-sized open plain square, where every now and again they hold trade events, parties, and festivals. Oak Village was built over 200 years ago by villagers who migrated from Pine Village and the now destroyed Alder Village. Oak Village currently has around 300 villagers living there, accompanied by many animals.

'HOW ARE YOU, Emerald, my dear?' shouts Barious from behind the front counter of his wooden tool shop, while he slowly moves a stack of small wooden boxes in which tools had been placed recently, on the floor below the front counter.

'Yes, I'm fine, thank you, Barious. Is everything all right with Raven? He seemed quite flustered?' asks Emerald.

'Oh yes, everything is fine. I have just sent him on a small errand, but don't worry. He'll be back before sunset for your date to Wolf's coronation celebration festival tonight,' remarks Barious as Emerald smiles softly.

'Is there anything I can help you with, Emerald?' asks Barious.

'Yes, please, my mother needs a hammer and some nails to fix one of our broken cupboards,' says Emerald.

'Ah right, I will get that for you now. How is your mother, Ruby?' Barious asks as he collects a metal hammer and several metal nails from one of the small wooden boxes he had put down on the floor behind the front counter.

'Yes, she is fine. You know my mother. She loves teaching the children at Oakus School, but she is also still a bit sad and lonely due to my father Gaius leaving her two years back. I know it was a while ago now, but he has been her only love, and she is still in love with him. It breaks her heart every day the way he left us both. Time, however, is a healer. I have made sure that I have been there for her to support her during this difficult time, although I am still upset myself about my father leaving me too,' says Emerald quietly.

'Ah yes, time does heal and you both will be fine, I'm sure of it. I'm sorry about your father Gaius leaving you both. He always seemed a loyal man and we had shared many laughs together over the years. Did he say anything why he left you both?' asks Barious softly.

'No, he said nothing to my mother. I knew they had been previously arguing before, and he had left for short breaks to Falcon City every now and again to see his parents at their cloth shop there, as he explained to me that they needed to have their own space sometimes to work through their marriage. But when he did leave, I found a short note upon my bed saying he was sorry as he was leaving, when I was at Oakus School that day and my mother was also teaching children there at the same time. I always expected him to come back though, as he had done many times before, but he still hasn't returned and we have not heard any word from him since. I do hope nothing bad has happened to him and I miss him greatly,' replies Emerald.

'Well, always remain hopeful, Emerald. If we believe in our hearts and trust our instincts anything is possible,' says Barious.

'Yes, it is, but I think this time my father has really gone for good. When I get enough money and supplies together, I am thinking of taking the long journey to Falcon City to see if I can find out what's happened to him. I was going to ask Raven to come with me, but I know he is busy training to take over your tool shop, and I really don't want to leave my mother on her own at the moment either. My parents had been together for over twenty years, so I know she feels lost without him, like a part of her life has been taken away from her. So I don't think she would be able to cope if she didn't see me on a daily basis too,' explains Emerald.

'It is a real shame, and if you ever did make the journey to Falcon City, be very careful as some parts of the Planet of Phoenix aren't as safe as our villages, and even now our villages aren't as safe as they used to be. Of course, I wouldn't mind if Raven undertook the journey to Falcon City with you. I think it would be good for him to come out of his shell a bit more and experience the Planet of Phoenix in more depth, as you never know when knowledge of this planet and its surroundings may be beneficial to you. Besides, I got a few more years yet as owner of this tool shop and you are like family to me, so I want nothing more than to see you both happy,' states Barious.

'Thank you, Barious, for those kind and caring words,' replies Emerald, smiling brightly at Barious.

'You also know, Raven and I are both here for you and Ruby any time if you need help or assistance with anything. I have known your mother for a long time now, due to her being great friends with Raven's parents, Ruthus and Jewel. She is a wonderful and caring woman and will make the best out of any situation, and you are a lovely daughter for helping her through this situation too,' says Barious, reminiscing of good memories from the past.

'That's also very nice of you to say. My mother also still greatly mourns for Raven's parents ever since they were poisoned and murdered by that narcissistic creature Viper. Mother frequently talks about them to me and all the good memories they shared together when they were children at Oakus School and also as they become older when Raven and I were born. I would like to talk to Raven about his parents more and share those great stories with him, but he always seems to shy away from the subject,' says Emerald sadly.

'Ah yes, Raven is a bit of an introvert, but in time I'm sure he will completely open up to you and you two will become soul mates and share many more happy times together too, like Ruby, Jewel, and Ruthus had always believed you would.' Emerald blushes. 'Here you go then, Emerald. Take these items to your mum and give her my best and let her know that I am here to help you both any time,' states

Barious as he passes the metal hammer and nails in a brown paper bag over the front counter into Emerald's hands. Emerald collects some silver coins from her purple handbag and gives the coins to Barious for the items; Barious closes Emerald's hand and smiles.

'Are you sure?' says Emerald.

'Of course, Emerald, take care now and follow your heart,' replies Barious. Emerald joyfully walks back out of Barious's wooden tool shop through the front entrance and gently down the short cobbled path that leads to her mother Ruby's house in the east direction of Oak Village. Along the way, Emerald is warmly greeted by Oak villagers who pass her by.

'Young love,' laughs Barious as he puts his elbow on the front counter and rests his chin on it. Barious stares happily ahead as he stands in his wooden tool shop.

Two

LORD SCARTOR POSSESSES a devious, withered, lost, and empty soul; he has remained living for over a 150 years; no human has ever lived to such an age before. Lord Scartor was born half human and half creature due to a creature gene that was passed down from his father. From a young age, Lord Scartor knew he was different from his brother, but he didn't realise the full extent of his creature powers until he reached maturity. Although Lord Scartor is one of the oldest remaining living creatures still existing upon the Planet of Phoenix, he still retains a resilient and mischievous youth that was generated from an evil and dark magic curse he cast upon himself many decades ago to prolong his life force; however, this corrupt and dark magic curse has rotted his skin, deformed his face, and withered the muscles around his body, which makes Lord Scartor walk in a slow and awkward manner. Thus, in the past three decades of his life, Lord Scartor has not moved around as much as he had done when he was of younger age and orders his army of creatures and minions to do the physical work and fighting.

Lord Scartor has dark grey coloured eyes and short grey ragged hair; he wears a long black cape that covers the whole of his body and black boots, as he is unable to wear any clothes that constrict his body tightly due to the withering of his body's muscles. Lord Scartor also has a grey metal mask that covers his deformed and twisted face except for his dark grey coloured eyes and rough malformed lips. Lord Scartor also wears dark grey coloured gloves to cover his frail hands, in order for him to still be able to hold and carry a long golden sceptre that can shoot magical black laser beams from the two side points of the three pointy trident spikes that reside on the top of the golden sceptre. This golden sceptre was given to him by his father when he was a teenager, but instead of using the golden sceptre for pure and good magic as his farther intended, Lord Scartor's tormented mind and thoughts push him to wield the golden sceptre to employ dark and dangerous magic against his foes.

Lord Scartor developed his nasty, malicious, and devious characteristics and personality during his childhood years due to his humble mother Angelina, who was loved and held in esteem by many of the other villages; she died during Lord Scartor's birth. Because of Lord Scartor's mother dying during his childbirth, thereafter he was bullied mentally and physically by the other children at Alder School in their village that was known as Alder Village, before Lord Scartor destroyed it many years later out of vengeance. On one occasion when the other children bullied Lord Scartor on his way home from the Alder School, one of the children named Condor tripped Lord Scartor's feet, which caused him to follow hard on to the ground and land on a large rock that indented a scar on the right side of his face, thus giving him his name 'Scartor' that the Alder School children taunted him with for many years until Lord Scartor decided to leave Alder Village.

After leaving Alder Village as a teenager, Lord Scartor withdrew to live a lonely and solemn life in the cold icy Mountains of Doom that are located in the far north-west direction of the Planet of Phoenix. Lord Scartor decided to reside upon one of the smaller and not so vigorous mountains known as Crow Mountain. Crow Mountain is a small snowy, icy, and rocky mountain residing amongst the large and treacherous Mountains of Doom; the Mountains of Doom lie past a long Open Valley and the vast Wastelands that are covered with sand and rock debris. Various small nomad tribes are situated throughout the Wastelands due to those humans who form the nomad tribes; they are banished humans from the main villages due to their crimes against the humans in the main villages located in the middle north direction of the Planet of Phoenix.

The Planet of Phoenix is a small planet located in the far region in the Cryptic solar system of the universe, however, the core within the Planet of Phoenix was created from unique elements that mysteriously increase or reduce the mass of the planet at random times. The sporadic change in the Planet of Phoenix's physical shape can alter a journey's distance and travelling time from one location to another. The Planet of Phoenix is a diverse planet, where many humans as well as various different creatures, animals, plants, environments, and terrains are located throughout the different sections of the planet. On the Planet of Phoenix, there are several locations that were named by the original creatures that existed first on the Planet of Phoenix. The names of these locations were given their title when these original creatures initially discovered these locations thousands of years ago.

In the north-west direction of the Planet of Phoenix reside the Mountains of Doom, the Open Valley, the Wastelands, the Swamp Fields, and Eagle Forest. In the south-west direction, the deserted and unforgiving Realm of Deserted Lands is situated. In the Planet of Phoenix's north-east direction reside Hydra Springs and several human inhabited villages known as Oak, Pine, and Willow Villages, and in the middle and south-west direction of the Planet of Phoenix resides another larger forest known as Komodo Jungle. Also, in the far south area is the Kingdom of Humans, where grand Falcon City was built by the humans next to Nautilus Lake. The rest of the Planet of Phoenix areas are covered with rich vegetation land known as the Grass Terrain Fields.

When Lord Scartor was living in a small fortress, he named it Lair of Death, that he built himself using magic from his golden sceptre. This Lair of Death also grew in size later on, due to his Lieutenant Triton relocating there and recruiting an army of Potorians to also live in the Lair of Death. Lord Scartor spent much time further developing his born creature natural abilities in black magic and was able to enhance his skills in the art of magical technology. By designing and developing powerful magical technology like the anomaly crystal device, he aimed to search for the almighty anomaly crystal that he had known about since he was a teenager in

Alder Village. Lord Scartor's life's purpose was to one day wield the astonishing powers of the anomaly crystal to take over the rule of the Planet of Phoenix and kill or enslave all its human inhabitants. After many of long and isolated years, Lord Scartor's hatred intensified and engulfed his entire body and mind due to his unnatural prolonged life and tortured memories because of the unfortunate events and circumstances during his childhood years.

LORD SCARTOR IMPATIENTLY and awkwardly walks around his Lair of Death that stands huge and fixated upon Crow Mountain. Lord Scartor's Lair of Death is now a tall grey brick castle that is dark, creepy, and hollow; it has one large main hall where Lord Scartor usually sits perched upon a big golden throne at one end of it. Lord Scartor's Lair of Death also has a few other gloomy rooms in it, such as the food quarters and sleeping rooms for his Potorian army. There is also a large room where Lieutenant Triton's rhino and the Potorians' horses are kept as well as a couple of torture chamber rooms that have various types of torture items placed in them, where there are sharp metal weapons like knives, iron pokers, whips, and chains and torturing machines such as the Knee Splitter, Cat's Paw, and Head Crusher that are fixed around the torture chambers.

Through the cold cloudy mist in the dark silence of the empty night residing above Crow Mountain outside Lord Scartor's Lair of Death approaches Lieutenant Triton, who is Lord Scartor's lieutenant, accompanied by a small patrol of Potorians that approach the big solid iron gates, the entrance to Lord Scartor's disconsolate Lair of Death that resides near the middle of the blistering Crow Mountain. Lieutenant Triton grabs a big iron key from around the neck of one of the Potorians, and he uses the big iron key to unlock the big iron door to gain entrance into Lord Scartor's Lair of Death; upon unlocking the big iron door, two Potorians also remove a big iron plank that is fixed against the big iron door from the inside. Lieutenant Triton and the small patrol of Potorians walk strong and sturdy in lines through the big iron door and head straight down into the main hall of Lord Scartor's Lair of Death, where he is now sitting due to becoming weakened by his furious paces earlier in the main hall; he is infuriated and aggravated as he stares indignantly from his golden throne at the approaching Potorian patrol with Lieutenant Triton.

Lieutenant Triton is thirty-six years old; he is a large and muscly beast-like creature having dark complexion; he has brown eyes and has a completely bald head. Lieutenant Triton is very tall and larger than nearly all the other humans or creatures that still reside upon the Planet of Phoenix. Lieutenant Triton is hugely built with bulging muscles that possess incredible and immense strength; he wears gold-plated armour to cover his chest and torsos but wears nothing on his thighs or large feet. Lieutenant Triton possesses a weapon in the form of a large solid spiked iron ball at the end of a very long golden chain; the spikes at the end of this iron ball are sharp and big, which are able to crush through bones with great ease.

Lieutenant Triton has always been a bit of a loner from the time he was growing up due to him being isolated from the humans as he had the creature genes. From a young creature, Lieutenant Triton found himself defending himself to survive with regard to food and shelter as he did not have much interaction with other humans or creatures. Lieutenant Triton now worships and admires Lord Scartor as Lord Scartor has given Triton focus and a purpose to follow in his life. He prefers to follow someone's orders rather than make his own decisions and is completely loyal to Lord Scartor and will carry out any duty that is asked of him.

Lieutenant Triton's parents, Taurus and Trudy, abandoned him as a child in the Wastelands as he possessed creature genes. After some time, Lieutenant Triton found it difficult to live in the Wastelands due to nomad tribes constantly fighting against him as they saw Lieutenant Triton as a potential threat to their homes. Lieutenant Triton decided to undertake the long journey to the Realm of Deserted Lands in the south-west direction of the Planet of Phoenix, which was far away from the humans and the main villages. As Lieutenant Triton was born half human with creature genes, it made it almost impossible for his parents to hide this secret from the rest of the humans in the villages, as the creature gene made Lieutenant Triton's appearance to be beast-like.

Although his parents didn't really want to abandon Lieutenant Triton as a child due to him being their only child, whom they had tried for many years to conceive, they knew that he would be imprisoned or killed by some of the other humans in their Pine Village as he was a half creature. Around forty years ago in Pine Village, where Lieutenant Triton and his parents originally lived. The Pine villagers were very intolerant and fearful of creatures due to the stories that had been passed down by their ancestors about previous battles between humans and creatures that occurred in the Wastelands many years ago. Also, the villagers passed down stories to their children about how evil and malicious creatures can be, like Lord Scartor was and all the destruction and malevolent deeds they had previously cast upon the Planet of Phoenix.

After reaching the Realm of Deserted Lands, Lieutenant Triton manages to survive in the harsh dark, cold, and stormy environment by eating the large insects that also existed in this desolated landscape. He spent all his waking hours undergoing tough physical training such as weightlifting large rocks so that he would become even stronger and resilient. Lieutenant Triton is, however, not very intelligent due to having no education and has not learnt much about the surrounding environment or inhabitants that reside in the Planet of Phoenix, but he has learnt practical knowledge of how to survive alone in the wild with no help from others. During Lieutenant Triton's many long years at the Realm of Deserted Lands, he fortunately stumbled across an underground passage way at the furthest south-east edge of the Planet of Phoenix.

The long and narrow passage way that Lieutenant Triton discovered leads below the actual ground and rocky surface of the Realm of Deserted Lands in the Planet of Phoenix and deep down below the rock surface where lava drizzles upwards from the core of the planet. In this underground passage, Lieutenant Triton began building an Underground Dungeon for himself to live in privacy and away from the harsh outside atmosphere of the Realm of Deserted Lands that is covered with dark and furious sandstorms; the construction of the Underground Dungeon took many years for Triton to complete.

During the building of several different-sized rooms out of rock with his bare hands in his Underground Dungeon, Lieutenant Triton stumbled upon pure raw material that was gold, from which he crafted his weapon that is the golden chain with an iron spiked ball at the end of it. Sometimes, Lieutenant Triton also came across other types of creatures roaming around the Realm of Deserted Lands, as they also scourged for food and looked for an isolated destination away from the humans. During these situations, Lieutenant Triton would fight and brutally destroy these other creatures as he didn't want his Underground Dungeon to be discovered or to have any competition for the sparse food located in the Realm of Deserted Lands.

DURING THE TIME that Lieutenant Triton was constructing his Underground Dungeon in the Realm of Deserted Lands; Lord Scartor lived in his Lair of Death in Crow Mountain that he was also building with dark magical powers. These dark magical powers, although, were gifted to Lord Scartor when he was born; due to being a half creature, they were enhanced and developed when he was taught as a boy to learn to master the art of sorcery from the great and ancient sorcerer named Hake.

After Lord Scartor had finished creating his Lair of Death as a fortress for him, he realised that he would need an army of creatures to aid him in obliterating the Planet of Phoenix from its human inhabitants; thus, he began searching over the Planet of Phoenix for more creatures to join under his legion. As Lord Scartor aged, his body was not physically as able as it used to be due to withering of it because of the dark magic curse he used upon himself to prolong his life force. Thus, he was required to use the magical powers from the middle pointy trident spike in between the three tridents on the top of his golden sceptre, which could open small magical portals that were made out of a black cloudy smoke and could view and relocate creatures and humans to different parts in the Planet of Phoenix.

Lord Scartor already knew about the snake-like creature Viper and his army of Serpents that lurked amongst Komodo Jungle in the middle eastern section of the Planet of Phoenix, but Lord Scartor didn't want to join forces with Viper again, due to a previous battle they had endured together when they were in allegiance with one another, but they lost this battle against the humans. Since then Viper had been angry and opposed to Lord Scartor's plans for taking over the Planet of Phoenix, as Viper realised they were currently outnumbered against the race of humans that lived on the Planet of Phoenix. Viper decided to only take control over Komodo Jungle and its surroundings but not any other location remaining upon the Planet of Phoenix; however, Lord Scartor would not stop until he destroyed all the humans, especially those blessed with the bloodline from Grackle.

When Lord Scartor was searching through one of the magical cloudy portals, viewing a part of the vast Realm of Deserted Lands in the south-west direction of the Planet of Phoenix, he noticed a large and muscly beast-like creature that was carrying many large pieces of rock through the Realm of Deserted Lands. Lord Scartor became intrigued by this creature that was known as Triton and continued to observe him with optimism. On several of these occasions, Lord Scartor noticed that Triton would disappear straight through the ground at the furthest south-west edge of the Realm of Deserted Lands in the Planet of Phoenix and would reappear from beneath the ground hours later to feed on the large insects that swarmed around a place called Cadaver Rock or Triton would hunt the occasional large animal that would get lost from the Grass Terrain Fields and stumble into the Realm of Deserted Lands. Lord Scartor admired how Triton was very aware of his surroundings and would keep a careful watch over the Realm of Deserted Lands and would fight and slay any other creatures that would threaten his territory; he noticed that Triton fought fiercely and without guilt, which meant he would do anything to win in a battle or war.

Lord Scartor, after a few weeks of observing Triton in the Realm of Deserted Lands, decided to travel through the magical cloudy portal he created from the middle pointy trident spike on the top of his golden sceptre, and he teleported to the Realm of Deserted Lands to meet with Triton. Lord Scartor located the Underground Dungeon by observing Triton's movements, and he teleported to ground above the Underground Dungeon. Lord Scartor entered into the passageway that led straight into the rocky surface leading to the main room within Triton's Underground Dungeon, where Triton was standing by the side of a large wooden table that he had made himself to place large dead insects on when he needed to eat. Triton's instinctive reaction forced him to run up to and fight Lord Scartor as he saw him as a threat to his Underground Dungeon, but just as Triton was about to attack to him, Lord Scartor quickly cast a dark magical curse upon Triton from the middle trident of his golden sceptre, which made him possessed and wanting to serve Lord Scartor; hence, Triton became Lord Scartor's lieutenant.

Lord Scartor had also used this dark magic possession curse of controlling creatures from his golden sceptre, by which he had also controlled other creatures before, such as the enormous sea lion creature that lived in Nautilus Lake located next to Falcon City in the Kingdom of Humans residing in the south-east corner of the Planet of Phoenix. Over thirty years ago, Lord Scartor had possessed and controlled this sea lion creature to attack the humans who lived in Falcon City; he also planned to manipulate Lieutenant Triton in a similar way. Lord Scartor and his newly made Lieutenant Triton travelled back through the magical cloudy portal to Lord Scartor's Lair of Death back on top of Crow Mountain, taking with them some of the gold that Lieutenant Triton had found in his Underground Dungeon by which he then built Lord Scartor's golden throne from it.

OVER MANY YEARS during which Lieutenant Triton served under Lord Scartor's magical possession curse, Lord Scartor continued to use this possession curse to increasingly brainwash Lieutenant Triton into intensifying his hatred for the humans that lived on the Planet of Phoenix. Together they began building up an army of nomad warriors who resided near Crow Mountain in the Wastelands; Lord Scartor called this army his Potorians. The Potorians were trained by Lieutenant Triton to become skilled and trained in combat and punishment; they wore silver-plated armour covering their entire body and carried a variety of metal swords and axe weapons. The nomad warriors were originally banished or they escaped from imprisonment in their home villages for committing crimes and illegal deeds against other humans such as fighting, rape, and murder or against the village itself such as theft and causing fires.

These nomad warriors were banished from their villages by the village leaders as they were seen as a threat to the harmony of the village; thus, these banished villagers travelled away from the main villages and built small huts made of wood and grass throughout the wide open deserted plain of the Wastelands, thus forming nomad tribes consisting of warriors and clans. Nomad warriors would join with other clans of nomad warriors throughout the Wastelands to build up their tribes and procreate to increase their numbers to defend themselves against creatures of fight against the humans in their home villages. These nomad warriors were mischievous, dirty, and immoral humans and would cause many problems amongst their own clans and other tribes of nomad warriors throughout the Wastelands.

Occasionally, when passing villagers were spotted in the Wastelands or near the Wastelands in the Swamp Fields, the nomad warriors would steal from these villagers or sometimes cause physical harm or even kill them. Although these nomad warriors had no morals, they did have the intelligence to realise that they would not be able to win in a battle against all the villagers in the three main villages that consisted of Oak, Pine, and Willow Village. Hence, the nomad warriors didn't travel too close to the main villages or cause too much harm to all villagers who travelled through or near the Wastelands to reduce the risk of a war brewing between the villages and the nomad tribes. Over several hundred years of the nomad warriors existing in the Wastelands, the number of nomad warriors living in clans and tribes grew to over 300, consisting of men, women, and children.

The Wastelands are located quite near to Crow Mountain as it's just past the Open Valley that connects the two locations together; it was deemed resourceful to Lord Scartor and Lieutenant Triton as they lived in Lord Scartor's Liar of Death on Crow Mountain amongst the Mountains of Doom. Lord Scartor felt it was more devious and relevant to get Lieutenant Triton to kidnap the strong nomad men warriors from the clans amongst the nomad tribes within the Wastelands and bring them to him to become a part of his Potorian army. Although Lord Scartor hated humans and wanted an army of creatures, he understood that there weren't many creatures existing upon the Planet of Phoenix, and it would take considerable more time to raise such an army that would be strong enough and worthy of being able to defeat all the humans in a great war. These captured men nomad warriors were tortured, humiliated, and blackmailed until they pledged allegiance to Lord Scartor, and if they tried to escape from betraying Lord Scartor in anything, these nomad warriors were horribly killed by Lieutenant Triton.

After adding several nomad warriors into Lord Scartor's new Potorian army by Lieutenant Triton training them to be resilient to pain and fighting without honour, it made it easier for Lieutenant Triton to take these small patrols of Potorians with him to capture other male nomad warriors in the Wastelands, and he then also turned them into Potorians, and if they refused or fought back then their wives and children would be killed. Some nomad warriors understood how powerful Lord Scartor and Lieutenant Triton was becoming and willingly travelled across the Open Valley from the Wastelands that leads to the bottom of Crow Mountain; they would then trek up the icy rock and stone trails of Crow Mountain upon entering Lord Scartor's Lair of Death. These men nomad warriors would pledge their allegiance to Lord Scartor and become a part of his Potorian army due to the fear of being captured or having their families killed. Also, for some nomad warriors who were living really rough in the Wastelands due to not being part of a nomad clan or tribe, they thought it would be best to join the newly formed Potorian army, as at least they would get regular food and a warm place to sleep in Lord Scartor's Lair of Death.

In a short period of time, Lord Scartor and Lieutenant Triton managed to build up an army of nearly 200 Potorians, as well as capturing many wild horses and stealing horses from the main villages' farms to also use for their Potorian army. Lieutenant Triton and a patrol of Potorians undertook many trips to the mysterious Eagle Forest that is next to the Wastelands to gather food such as fruit, plants, and wild animals. Lieutenant Trion and the Potorians would, however, only venture in the outskirts of Eagle Forest due to the fear of the unknown that lay deep in the heart of this ancient and mysterious forest.

During one of these trips to Eagle Forest's perimeter, Lieutenant Triton stumbled upon a fierce and powerful black rhino that he managed to capture after several attempts of ambush, during the occasions of which the black rhino charged into several Potorians that killed them. Lieutenant Triton claimed this black rhino for himself and took it back to Lord Scartor's Lair of Death for much taming. Finally after many long awaited bitter years, Lord Scartor recruited his creature lieutenant as well as generated big enough a fearful army of Potorians to unleash his war against the humans on the Planet of Phoenix, in aid of his desperate search to uncover and claim the anomaly crystal.

'WHAT IS YOUR report, Lieutenant Triton?' shouts Lord Scartor intensely, sitting upon his golden throne at the far end of Lord Scartor's Lair of Death, as Lieutenant Triton and the accompanying patrol of Potorians halt in front of Lord Scartor on his golden throne.

'A Potorian using your crystal finding device located the anomaly crystal to be hidden somewhere in Oak Village, Master,' states Lieutenant Triton attentively, looking at Lord Scartor's steel grey mask upon his distorted face.

'At last, finally after all these long cruel years, the anomaly crystal and then the Planet of Phoenix will be all mine! The anomaly crystal is in Oak Village now you say. The bloodline of Grackle must have extended their kin to that puny unprotected village. Whoever has the anomaly crystal has condemned all the other Oak villagers to certain death,' laughs Lord Scartor with passion.

'Lieutenant Triton, gather a large patrol of my Potorians, travel to Oak Village, and burn it to the ground. Kill anyone who tries to stop you from finding the anomaly crystal. The current leader of Oak Village is called Wolf, and he is a brave and gallant leader. That means he will defend his family and Oak Village until he draws his last breath. So you will need to take his life first and quickly, and then the rest of the villagers will crumble easily due to them being lost for direction without their magnificent leader. This is your last chance, Lieutenant Triton, to do your trusted duty as I have entrusted you to find the anomaly crystal for me and you pledged a promise that you will find it and give it to me. You have been a very loyal and helpful lieutenant over the years, and in return I have helped you out with providing purpose to your once worthless life. But if the anomaly crystal is not handed to me by nightfall, you will burn and perish as the rest of the humans will for your incompetence, is that understood?' screeches Lord Scartor.

As Lord Scartor screeches his orders to Lieutenant Triton, he becomes furious and suddenly remembers troubled past memories of when he was bullied and tortured as a child in Alder Village by the other children due to his mother Angelina dying because of his birth. The scar upon Lord Scartor's face on the ride side begins to itch from the memory of him being tripped by another child and landing face first on to a large rock. Lord Scartor stands up in rage and rapidly swerves the golden sceptre in his right hand to hold it out straight in front of him; he magically shoots two black laser beams from the two trident spikes at the sides on top of the golden sceptre. The magical black laser beams shoot across the main hall of Lord Scartor's Lair of Death quicker than the speed of sound and crash into two Potorians who had been in formation in front of Lord Scartor's golden throne. The two Potorians that are shot with the magical black laser beam screech in pain as their body limbs explode in the air of the main hall, leading to blood pouring from the body limbs that land on top of other Potorians, who had also lined up in front of Lord Scartor's golden throne.

Lieutenant Triton and the other Potorians hurriedly stand back in fear and watch helplessly as the limbs of the two dead Potorians fall to the ground and roll along the cold wooden uneven floor in Lord Scartor's Lair of Death.

'Of course, my Almighty and Powerful Lord, your orders will be done. I will stop at nothing to fulfil my allegiance and duty to you. We will retrieve the supreme anomaly crystal from those thieving villagers in Oak Village and return it to you, its rightful master,' grovels Lieutenant Triton quickly at the death of the two Potorians.

'Yes, you will! And finally I can reap my revenge on those pathetic humans and the Planet of Phoenix for all the suffering and misery it's caused me. I will not be denied my true right to rule, for I was blessed with the blood and power of magical abilities that defy all other meaningless humans and creatures. The humans have ruled with spiteful tongues and hands for too long. They caused the Planet of Phoenix to be ruined by their extensive families and territories. All of the humans need to be rid from the Planet of Phoenix and perish deep in the dark places of the afterlife, for they are below us creatures and especially those blessed with magical powers,' exclaims Lord Scartor.

'Yes, Master, the time has now come for you to become the most powerful Lord that has ever existed on the Planet of Phoenix, and then after taking it for your own, the entire Cryptic solar system will bow to your limitless powers!' shouts Lieutenant Triton.

'Stop your grovelling and go, Lieutenant Triton. Do what must be done to those pitiful Oak villagers and kin of the ancient human race. And to my army of Potorians, although you are criminal humans, I have fed and sheltered you and Lieutenant Triton has trained you to become the fierce warriors you are today. I have also given your meaningless lives value, so now it's the time for you to show me your worth and allegiance. For those who demonstrate exceptional talent during the great war, I will let you live after I take over the Planet of Phoenix and will let you do as you will to any of the villager women who manage to survive. However, if you try to escape, betray me, or do not kill as many humans as possible, then I will shoot you with my golden sceptre just like those two other Potorians, but you will experience more agony from the blast, is that understood?' orders Lord Scartor as he waves his golden sceptre in the air and hovers it over the Potorian army in formation in front of his golden throne.

'Yes, of course, our Lord Scartor, who is named the almighty master of the universe!' shout all the startled Potorians at once.

'One more thing, Lieutenant Triton, when you find the anomaly crystal, make sure you kill all the humans of the house or place from where you find it. I want to make sure that all the remaining kin from the bloodline of Grackle are once and for all destroyed and rid from this life so they will pose no threat to me at all in the forthcoming great war to come, due to them also possessing the gifted ability of being able to wield the anomaly crystal's remarkable powers,' says Lord Scartor anxiously.

'As you wish, Lord Scartor, and we will soon rid all the humans from the Planet of Phoenix as it was always meant to be,' replies Lieutenant Triton in a confident tone of voice.

'And the way it will always remain. Now go and retrieve the anomaly crystal!' yells Lord Scartor as he sits back down upon his golden throne.

Lieutenant Triton and the patrol of Potorians, who was in formation when they were talking to Lord Scartor on his golden throne, begin to gather a larger force of Potorians from the other food quarters, sleeping rooms, and chambers in Lord Scartor's Lair of Death where the Potorians have either been eating or sleeping. After only around twenty minutes, Lieutenant Triton and a 187 Potorians gather and start suiting up with their silver-plated armour and weapons of metal swords and axes. Some of the Potorians also retrieve enough wild brown and black horses from the animal's large room in Lord Scartor's Lair of Death to use them for carrying the Potorians quickly on their journey to Oak Village.

Lieutenant Triton grabs his golden chain with the iron spiked ball at the end of it, which is hanging up on the wall on a large metal hook in his personal living quarters, and then he also gathers his black rhino from the animal's large room as no other Potorian has been able to tame Lieutenant Triton's black rhino. Lieutenant Triton along with the 187 Potorians all ride in line formation hastily out of Lord Scartor's main hall in the Lair of Death and exit through the big iron door. As Lieutenant Triton and the Potorians exit Lord Scartor's Lair of Death and approach the edge at the top of Crow Mountain, they begin to trot steadily down the deep and long winding icy rock and stone trails of Crow Mountain, which are covered with snow. After their careful treacherous journey down to the bottom of Crow Mountain, they kick the backs of their brown and black horses and Lieutenant Triton does the same to his black rhino to increase their speed as they travel in the east direction through the Open Valley made of rocks and vegetation, which leads out into the vast and dusty Wastelands covered with red-tinted sand.

After a strong ride through the Wastelands for around thirty minutes, Lieutenant Triton and the 187 Potorians reach the rotten Swamp Fields, where they start getting their brown and black horses to tread carefully to avoid treading into the vile muddy and deep bogs. As they continue through the Swamp Fields, they take the trail which has been known before to be less hazardous than the slippery muddy bogs, but they are still caught up in the tall grass and vegetation that tower high above the ground and are littered with various types of small stinging insects. Eagle Forest would have been a less hazardous path to take around the Swamp Fields to reach Oak Village, but Eagle Forest is avoided as much as possible by Lieutenant Triton and the Potorians due to the mysterious creatures that reside in it. After exiting the foul-smelling Swamp Fields, Lieutenant Triton and the 187 Potorians on their brown and black horses continue for several hours, journeying over the Grass Terrain Fields heading towards Oak Village.

Three

AS RAVEN SITS on Felix's large, sturdy, black hairy back, they ride steadily and swiftly in the east direction down the long cobbled road that cuts straight through the Grass Terrain Fields located between Oak Village and Pine Village. The air in the sky of the Planet of Phoenix is calm with a slight breeze hovering over Raven's and Felix's heads. The sun is shining brightly, warming the grass throughout the Grass Terrain Fields, which enables them to grow quickly. The bright sun's warm heat tickles the back of Raven's neck as he holds firmly on to the rope reins attached to Felix's head while riding towards Pine Village; sweat starts to drip down Raven's face as his mind is filled with thoughts of Emerald's beautiful blue sparkly eyes and tender lips.

Raven also thinks about all the good memories of the dates they've shared together recently, which included them walking through the Grass Terrain Fields and sitting peacefully by the small ponds and trees that are located not too far from Oak Village. They would walk for miles together, and enjoy watching the wild animals such as deer and zebras live their lives in harmony amongst the Grass Terrain Fields. During those walks, Raven and Emerald would not have to care about any negativity or creatures in the Planet of Phoenix; they would walk, holding hands, until they found a quiet place to have a picnic, where they would then spend hours kissing, falling even more in love with each other.

Raven and Emerald had known each other ever since they were born as Raven's parents Ruthus and Jewel had been great friends with Emerald's parents Ruby and Gaius, as they all lived very close to each other in Oak Village and had done for many years. Ruthus was Barious's oldest son, and he and Jewel got together during their teenage years. They had both attended Oakus School together, but due to Ruthus being a couple of years older than Jewel they didn't get much time to interact with one another but they had always given deep glances at each other as they would walk past each other in Oakus School hallway. During one of the yearly Oak Village fairs, they finally ended up having the courage to talk to each other and ended up spending the whole day getting to know one another better. Ruthus and Jewel fell for each other instantly and continued to spend many wonderful times together for many years until they got married in their early adult years and was gifted with a much wanted son that they named Raven.

Jewel and Ruby were also best friends from their childhood as they were of the same age and in the same class at Oakus School; they used to play skipping games and share secrets together in their spare time. Jewel and Ruby were inseparable friends and were always there for each other during difficult times. They saw each other nearly every day of their lives, especially since they both lived quite near to each other within Oak Village. Ruby was Jewel's maid of honour at Jewel and Ruthus's wedding just as Jewel was Ruby's maid of honour at Ruby and Gaius's wedding. During Jewel's and Ruby's early adult years, Ruby was introduced to Gaius by Ruthus. Ruthus worked as a tradesman, and he traded cloth, farm foods, and tools from Barious's tool shop among the three main villages that were Oak, Pine and Willow Village, and then occasionally he would undertake the long journey to Falcon City that was in the kingdom of humans in the far south-east of the Planet of Phoenix, in order to trade with better quality produce, since Falcon City was more prosperous compared with the three main villages.

On one of Ruthus occasional journeys to Falcon City where he journeyed on Felix, which would pull a wooden cart on wooden wheels with various tradable items, he traded wool cloth made from the sheep of the Oak Village farms with a cloth shop owner called Nerolus who had a son of a similar age to Ruthus. Nerolus, after much debate with his wife Tameka about his final decision, offered to pay Ruthus extra money when trading Ruthus's wool cloth for his clothes in his shop, which Tameka made by hand, for offering to take his son Gaius back with him to Oak Village so he could learn to grow up with a better attitude and start working in a trade, as Gaius made it quite clear that he had no interest in taking over from his father in the management of the cloth shop.

During Gaius's teenage years in Falcon City, he had also been getting into minor trouble with some of the other Falcon City teenagers, so Nerolus thought it would be best for him to have a fresh start in a new village away from the arguments and fights he had with the other teenagers. Ruthus agreed to take Gaius back with him and Gaius was also happy to leave Falcon City to explore a new village, and after spending time with one another during the long journey back to Oak Village, they become friends. As the time went on, Ruthus made Gaius a partner in his trading business to aid in expanding it. After meeting Gaius, Jewel decided to set up a double date for herself, Ruthus, Gaius, and Ruby to go on; they went for a meal in Pinus Tavern in Pine Village. On this double date, Ruthus introduced Gaius to Ruby, following which Ruby and Gaius became lovers very quickly and also got married within a couple of years of them being together. Later on, they had a beautiful baby girl who was named Emerald, born not long after Ruthus and Jewel's son, Raven, was born.

AFTER RIDING FOR approximately an hour in the east direction along the long cobbled road, Raven and Felix approach a big village that is surrounded by a big wooden fence, but in the distance Raven can see the village which is covered with beautiful fruit trees, colourful flowers, and big stone monuments of animals. This village is called Pine Village, and it is constantly vibrant and proactive with various villagers from the other main villages trading and working throughout Pine Village. There are also many Pine guards that are the Pine Village leaders, who are called Lynx's personal guards. They continually patrol the outer wooden fences and gates that are made of metal to be lookouts in order to protect Pine Village from any returning banished nomad warriors. Raven climbs down slowly from Felix's big black back, and holding on to the brown rope reins attached to Felix's head, he walks up to the west entrance metal gate of Pine Village. He is quickly stopped by a Pine guard who is wearing metal armour and carrying a sword and shield.

'Good morning, lad. I am not sure I have noticed you in Pine Village before. What business do you have coming here?' asks the Pine guard, whose name is Flame.

Flame is twenty-five years old and has short messy black hair and brown eyes. He is very tall and slim compared with most other humans living on the Planet of Phoenix, and he is also a very serious but competent and friendly human. Although Flame is knowledgeable, he didn't like learning at Pinus School located in Pine Village, as all Flame wanted to do from a young age was become a Pine guard and protect his fellow villagers. As soon as he was of the age to leave Pinus School, which was seventeen years of age, he applied and joined the Pinus guard. He enjoyed that very much and after a long and hard training period, Flame managed to quickly succeed within the ranks of the Pinus guard. During his many years of service as a Pine guard, he became good friends with another Pine guard called Bruce, who was already friends with Parrot, Raven's cousin. Flame and Parrot also became good friends and along with Bruce they shared many laughs and drinking sessions together in Pinus Tavern.

'I have been to Pine Village before, but it was quite a while ago now. My name is Raven. I am the grandson of Barious, who owns the tool shop in Oak Village. I have come on an errand from my grandfather to visit my cousin Parrot, who is a maker of specially made weapons, if that is all right with you, sir,' replies Raven confidently.

'Oh yes, I know Barious from Oak Village. I have visited his renowned tool shop before and I know he is a very kind and wholehearted human. My name is Flame, and Parrot has been a good friend of mine for a few years. He lives in the far east of Pine Village near the Pinus Tavern and is best friends with our Pine Village leader, Lynx. The Pine Village guards are particularly grateful to Parrot due to him providing us with his specially made weapons that you mentioned. He has mentioned his cousin Raven from Oak Village to me a few times, but as I have never met you, I was not sure of what you looked like. Sorry, Raven, but it is my duty to check every passer-by who comes in and out of Pine Village due to the problems we have had with the nomad warriors sneaking into Pine Village in the past. Of course, you can go through to see your cousin Parrot, lad, and you are welcome to stay in Pine Village for as long as you like,' replies Flame happily as he strokes Felix's forehead; at the same time, Felix moves his head around frantically in excitement because of Flame stroking his forehead.

'Thank you, Flame, and it's good to know that you're a friend of Parrot's too. I am most looking forward to catching up with him as it has been too long,' says Raven.

'That's no problem at all, Raven. It's also nice to meet friendly villagers from other villages such as Oak Village and especially family of my great friend, Parrot. Please remember to be careful on your journeys between the villages along the cobbled roads through the open Grass Terrain Fields, Raven, as us humans and villages can't be too careful during these recent times because of the commotion caused by the nomad warriors and their tribes and clans lurking throughout the Wastelands and even because of other unknown creatures that may exist on the Planet of Phoenix, especially some of the stories I've heard amongst the guards,' mutters Flame as Raven enters through the west entrance metal gate of Pine Village while walking and holding on to the brown rope reins of Felix.

AS RAVEN AND Felix stroll contentedly down the cobbled paths of Pine Village, they pass many small and large wooden flats and houses, doctors' clinics, chemist shops, a few farms with farm animals, a school called Pinus School, and a big church and graveyard called Pinus Church and Pinus Graveyard. There are shops selling various items such as tools, food, clothes, jewellery, weapons, and musical instruments as well as bars and inns and the main tavern is called Pinus Tavern where they serve food and ale and have guest rooms to stay over. Also, a small wooden castle is located in the south-east of Pine Village where the Pine Village leader Lynx lives.

Pine Village has 874 villagers living there, which include 300 of Lynx's Pine guards; Pine Village was the first among the main villages to be constructed when humans branched away and relocated from Falcon City, led by the original leader of Pine Village called Woken. Pine Village also has three small wooden towers around the edges of

Pine Village next to the big wooden fence that surrounds Pine Village, similar to Oak Village's surrounding fence. The small wooden towers overlook the perimeter outside the big wooden fence surrounding Pine Village so the Pinus guards can watch out for intruders and enemies such as nomad warriors or creatures from the Planet of Phoenix.

Raven is greeted warmly by Pine villagers who pass by him, as he walks with Felix down the cobbled paths of Pine Village where the sun still shines brightly, but as it moves across the sky, it causes shadows to form upon the cobbled paths. Raven arrives in about twenty minutes from the west entrance gate at Parrot's small wooden flat that is opposite Pinus Tavern in the far eastern direction of Pine Village. Raven leads Felix by his brown rope reins over to a large pine tree near Parrot's small wooden flat on the side of the cobbled path. Raven ties Felix's brown rope reins around the Pine tree tightly and pats Felix on the neck before walking over to Parrot's small wooden flat and knocking on the front door, waiting patiently until Parrot opens it.

'Raven, what are you doing here?! It's very good to see you again, Cousin. It's been way too long,' shouts Parrot, hugging Raven in an enthusiastic manner.

'Yes, it has, Parrot, and of course it's good to see you too,' remarks Raven, smiling at Parrot.

'Well, don't just stand there. Come in, come in, I'll get us some ale and we'll see if you can actually handle your drink now,' chuckles Parrot as he walks through the living room of his small wooden flat towards the kitchen to prepare some ale in cups for him and Raven. Parrot is twenty-three years old. He has short black straight hair and dark brown eye; unlike Raven, he is taller than the average human and skinny, but has similar facial looks to Raven and Barious due to them being related. Barious had two sons, who were Ruthus and Rio. Rio was the younger of the two brothers and was Parrot's father, making Raven and Parrot cousins. Parrot is wearing a thin grey jumper, light-coloured brown trousers, and dark brown boots. He is a friendly, supportive, and courageous human, and he has many friends as he goes out of his way to help people when he can. Parrot is a very comical character and has a determined nature about him.

Parrot didn't enjoy all his time during his education at Pinus School as he preferred to only do practical rather than academic studies; he did, however, appreciate one thing at Pinus School. That was meeting a lovely girl called Sapphire, who also liked Parrot very much, but they didn't manage to become boyfriend and girlfriend as both their closest friends fell out with one another. Unfortunately, Sapphire left Pine Village two years ago to continue her education at Falcon University in Falcon City, although Parrot and Sapphire still keep in contact with each other via letters that are sent to one another by the use of carrier pigeons. Because he was more practically inclined and enjoyed working with his hands, Parrot continued doing what his father Rio did; that was making tools as Barious had taught him to do, but Parrot progressed and extended making tools as his own business by making and selling specially designed and created weapons.

Raven retires to the living room of Parrot's small wooden flat that is connected straight from the front door and is next to the small kitchen, toilet, closet, and bedroom. Raven sits down on a wooden chair in the living room next to a small wooden table, as Parrot fetches Raven and himself the drink of ale from the kitchen. Then he joins Raven in sitting down on a wooden chair in the living room next to a small wooden table that is covered with all kinds of scrap metal and tools such as hammers, screwdrivers, and nails that Parrot utilises when making his specially created weapons.

'I do remember that I was of a much younger age when you influenced me to first drink ale at that Pinus Village fair,' mumbles Raven as he takes a sip of the ale from the cup Parrot has just given him.

'Ha ha, yes, I remember, and you were sick in one of the Pine villagers' stew during the stew tasting competition. No wonder you haven't been back to Pine Village since,' laughs Parrot, as Raven pauses in embarrassment but then laughs also.

'How are your parents Rio and Olivia doing? I haven't seen them in a long time also, especially since they moved to Willow Village,' asks Raven with interest.

'Yes, my parents are doing well and relaxing a bit more in Willow Village from the busier lifestyle of Pine Village. Thus, my father, along with my mother, was happy to not only move to Willow Village for a peaceful retirement but to also extend his tool making business, and working in cooperation with Barious and myself, we all cover throughout the three main villages. But yes, I also haven't seen them recently due to having to now travel to Willow Village to see them, and due to the demand of creating my specially made weapons I don't get much spare time. However, my mother writes letters to me frequently. So what can I do for you, Cousin? Have you come to purchase any of my specially made weapons? My stock has grown and I have all sorts now, ranging from sharp swords to fury raptor throwing stars,' says Parrot enthusiastically.

'No, thank you, Parrot. I've come because our grandfather, Barious, has sent me to Pine Village to hide somewhere secret an old but extremely powerful family heirloom. It's now not safe to be kept in grandfather's tool shop or even in Oak Village. Grandfather asked me to seek help from you to see if we could hide it somewhere safe and secure in Pine village until further plans can be made for it, and he said he would consult with his friends, King Exodus from Falcon City and Panther the leader of Willow Village, but no one else must know about this as this information may become too dangerous,' replies Raven mysteriously.

'This sounds very serious, Raven. Has it got anything to do with the nomad warriors and the unknown evil residing in the Mountains of Doom in the north-west of the Planet of Phoenix, far beyond the Wastelands and Eagle woods?' asks Parrot, intrigued.

'Yes, it has, Parrot. Past the Swamp Fields and Wastelands, upon a smaller mountain amongst the Mountains of Doom called Crow Mountain, lives a dark and evil warlord called Lord Scartor. He and his legions of Potorians and monstrous creatures search vigorously and seek to find this anomaly crystal and use its unimaginable magical powers to cause destruction and terror over our Planet of Phoenix and its human inhabitants,' answers Raven wearily. Raven slowly pulls out the anomaly crystal from his right brown trouser pocket, and as he shows it to Parrot, every colour of the rainbow and shades of white and black swirl sharply, brightly, and rapidly throughout the centre of the anomaly crystal.

'My eyes have never laid upon such an astonishing and remarkable crystal. What magical powers does it behold, Raven?' asks Parrot with captivating interest.

'It supposedly holds many different magical and wondrous elemental powers depending upon the type of emotions the anomaly crystal holder is experiencing at the time in a threatening or anxious situation,' replies Raven inexplicably. Suddenly a loud knocking occurs at the front door of Parrot's small wooden flat. Raven and Parrot both jolt back in their small wooden chairs and look at each other, slightly worried, as Raven quickly puts the anomaly crystal back in his right brown trouser pocket.

'Are you expecting someone Parrot?' asks Raven in a guarded manner.

'No, I don't think so,' answers Parrot. Parrot stands up from the wooden chair and walks cautiously to the front door of his small wooden flat; he slowly opens the front door, while Ravens clenches his hand upon one of the white nunchucks in one of his grey coat's pockets. As Parrot opens the front door, he sees a male stranger who is dressed in all black clothing and wearing a long brown hooded coat.

'Are you Parrot?' asks the male stranger.

'Um, yes,' replies Parrot in a nervous tone.

'Ah, great, I've been looking for your flat for ages. I hear you make specially made weapons. I am looking to purchase some from you. May I have a look at them?' asks the male stranger.

'Oh right, I see. Yes, that's fine, but unfortunately I have a quick family errand to run. If you pop back to my flat in an hour or so, I will be happy to show you what weapons I have then. There is a tavern just opposite across the cobbled path called Pinus Tavern that does a great lamb stew if you find yourself hungry,' says Parrot calmly.

'Yes, food is of much need right now as I have travelled all the way from Willow Village. Am grateful for the information and I will come back see you again later, kind sir,' says the male stranger. The male stranger turns around and begins to walk across the cobbled path over to Pinus Tavern as Parrot closes the front door behind him.

'That was lucky. We must be careful not to trust anyone at the moment,' mentions Raven.

'Yes, of course. Come let's leave here and hide the anomaly crystal quickly. There's an old horse monument statue amongst the bushes and trees at one of the edges in Pine Village. No one rarely goes there now and it is well covered with foliage. We should hide the anomaly crystal there for the time being until further instruction from Grandfather,' states Parrot.

'Yes, that sounds like a good idea and let's do that right away, as the longer I possess the anomaly crystal in my hands, I feel more cagey about dangerous times that might come to be,' answers Raven reluctantly.

PARROT GATHERS HIS thick brown coat from the closet in his small wooden flat and puts on his brown boots, and then they both quickly drink up the last bit of their ale from their cups and place them down on the small wooden table. Raven and Parrot walk through the living room towards the front door of Parrot's small wooden flat. As Parrot closes and locks the front door behind him, he notices Felix tied up by his rope reins to the pine tree near his small wooden flat.

'Felix, that strong and stunning stallion, I haven't seen him since he was a much younger horse at the back of Barious's tool shop in Oak Village. Although older, he's still looking mighty powerful as ever,' comments Parrot in surprise.

'Yes, Felix is and always been a magnificent horse. I know Grandfather values him very much as he has had him for over twenty years now, and my father even used to ride Felix on the long journeys he undertook when trading with Falcon City. Shall we both ride Felix to the horse monument statue as that would be quicker?' asks Raven.

'I think it's best not to as it might draw more attention to us than we want at the moment,' replies Parrot.

'Will Felix be all right left tied to this pine tree though?' Raven asks again.

'Yes, of course, it's not too far, so Felix won't be left here on his own for long. Anyway, the Pine villagers here are very genuine humans and wouldn't steal him or anything. Come let's hurry,' exclaims Parrot. Raven and Parrot walk calmly but quickly down the main cobbled path of Pine Village so as to not draw any attention to themselves, and they smile and say hello to the villagers passing by. Raven and Parrot then change on to another path connected by smaller cobbled paths, which lead to the south-east of Pine Village, until they approach the edge of Pine Village where the horse monument statue is located.

The horse monument statue is built of marble stone; it is large, white, and beautiful, although the colour of the statue has faded due to weather and the length of time it had been placed there; it has been there for over 200 years. Many years ago, marble statues were built originally by the first leader Woken throughout Pine Village to pay homage to the animals that helped them become developed by increasing the demands of crops during the farming seasons. The horse monument statue is also covered with cobwebs and dried-up old leaves and is surrounded by many large green bushes and shrubs, mixed with different trees such as pine, silver bay, and sweet oak trees. The horse monument statue is surrounded by a big metal white fence with various tangled flowers spreading and twisting across the metal bars of the big metal white fence.

Raven and Parrot walk up to a small gate near the middle of the big metal white fence, but then they realise it's locked with a large silver padlock and chain. Raven and Parrot scan with their eyes to look around the big metal white fence for another way in. Parrot sees a small pine tree that can be climbed, whose branches have grown over the big metal white fence. Parrot followed by Raven walks over to the small pine tree, and then they start to climb it by helping one another, by being each other's support in climbing the tree and also using the new tough branches attached to the tree, in order to climb upon the branch that has grown over the big metal white fence. Once on this big sturdy branch, they climb across it to get inside the big metal white fence and drop down one at a time onto the grass floor in the big metal white fence. Both Parrot and Raven land on their feet and begin approaching the horse monument statue, looking over it for a place to hide the anomaly crystal.

As both Parrot and Raven can't see a suitable and safe place to hide the anomaly crystal, they circle around to the back of it after rechecking behind them that no other Pine villager is nearby in the surrounding area. When they are at the back of the horse monument statue, Parrot pulls out a small steel metal chisel from one of his brown boots; he carefully carves a small piece out of one of the horse's long marble legs, which takes a good twenty-five minutes due to the tough marble texture. Parrot then carves into the middle of that marble stone piece a small hole just big enough to fit the anomaly crystal firmly inside it. Raven pulls out the anomaly crystal from his right brown trouser pocket and places it in the middle of the cut-out marble stone piece, and Parrot firmly fits it back in the long marble leg of the big white horse monument statue.

'That took effort to carve that marble, but at least it should be safe for now, hidden away in this horse monument statue,' puffs Parrot.

'Yes, I really hope so as from what grandfather was saying about the anomaly crystal, I'm really worried that Lord Scartor will always continue to search for it. That means our villages and the humans we love in them won't ever truly be safe until Lord Scartor ceases to live upon the Planet of Phoenix,' worries Raven.

'Don't worry, Raven. I will always be here to protect you and our family and friends. Besides, the humans in the three main villages would reunite with one another along with King Exodus of Falcon City and his army of royal Falcon guards, which would mean that us humans would outnumber the creatures throughout the Planet of Phoenix and would thus be victorious if a battle situation was to occur,' says Parrot confidently.

'But even if that was the outcome, how many humans would suffer before an end result is achieved?' Raven mentions gloomily.

'Well, if the anomaly crystal is as powerful as Grandfather said it was, then I'm sure its unimaginable magical powers would be used to save all of us humans from an unfortunate fate,' states Parrot.

'Yes, I hope you're right, Parrot. That is why it's extremely important that the anomaly crystal will never be found by Lord Scartor or any other creature for that matter as they would only use its astonishing elemental abilities to annihilate all the humans from the Planet of Phoenix,' remarks Raven as he glances over the horse monument statue to look for any Pine villagers in the immediate surroundings.

'That will never come to be,' replies Parrot as he puts his arm on Raven's shoulder in a comforting manner.

'Come on, let's go back to see Felix, and I must get back to Oak Village soon to be ready in time for Wolf's coronation celebration festival as I have another date with Emerald to go to,' smirks Raven.

'Ah yes, I've heard many good things about Wolf's coronation celebration festival that occurs every year but have not found the time to attend one of them yet, but there's always next year. My best friend Lynx said Wolf is an honourable leader of Oak Village as well as a noble human, so I hope you all have a magnificent time at the coronation celebration festival. Also, how are you and Emerald getting on? She is a lovely girl and I've always known you have admired her ever since you were small children as you used to always speak fondly about her with such thoughtful words. I'm surprised it took you so long to finally build up the courage and get together with her. Special women like that won't stay alone forever, and one of my biggest life regrets is not asking Sapphire to be with me before she left to go to gain her PhD at Falcon University in Falcon City as by the time she returns home it might be too late for me and her as she might have already found another lucky human to be with,' Parrot states sadly.

'I'm sure she will have been too busy with her studies to think about another guy, and when she returns to Pine Village, you will then have your chance to fall in love with one another,' Raven smiles at Parrot as Raven puts his right foot on to Parrot's cupped hands to jump up on the side of the big white metal fence, where he grabs the strong and sturdy branch of the small pine tree that is next to it. Raven swings his legs up on to the branch and pull himself back around so as to be positioned on top of the branch in order to grab Parrot's hands and assist in helping him to also grab on to that branch of the pine tree. Raven and Parrot carefully climb across the branch and back down the small pine tree to get back on the other side of the big metal white fence. As they both get their feet back on the ground, Raven and Parrot hurriedly walk back down the several smaller cobbled paths until they reach the main cobbled path leading towards Parrot's small wooden flat.

On reaching Parrot's small wooden flat, walking on the cobbled path, Raven unties Felix's brown rope reins from the pine tree and climbs on top of him in the saddle on his strong black back.

'Much gratitude for your help today, Parrot. You are a kind cousin. I will go and seek word with Grandfather later tonight and will come back to Pine Village to see you again in a few days' time to discuss where to relocate the anomaly crystal too,' says Raven positively.

'No problem, Cousin. I'm here for you and Grandfather whenever you need it. You both are family and family is the most important thing in the world. Send my love to Grandfather for me and I hope you enjoy your date tonight with Emerald. Take care and ride safe as sometimes the cobbled roads can also be dangerous and especially now more than ever. Here take this,' exclaims Parrot. Parrot pulls out a small sharp silver dagger from his other brown boot and gives it to Raven.

'Thank you, Parrot . . . but there is no need. I have some of my own nunchucks with me anyways,' replies Raven, as he avoids taking the small sharp silver dagger which Parrots attempts to give into his hands.

'There's every need to be extra safe!' remarks Parrot as he places the small sharp dagger into one of Raven's brown boots and then smacks Felix's backside hard with his right hand. Felix feels the slap of Parrot's hand upon his backside and begins to gallop swiftly off down the cobbled path towards west, leading out of Pine Village's west entrance metal gate, while Parrot humbly watches Raven and Felix ride off in the distance.

Four

IN THE CENTRE of Oak Village resides a medium-sized square that is made from wooden and cobbled paths, and here on the day of Wolf's coronation celebration festival, the Oak villagers have over the past few days specially built and set up many wooden stalls and sections for the Oak villagers to interact with. The Oak Village square now has several and various ale and food stalls like hot dogs, stews, and vegetables and stalls of tradable items such as cloth, tools, and meat, as well as a dancing tent for a party that will occur at the end of the coronation celebration festival. The special corner sections at the edges of the square are occupied with games such as food testing contests and food eating competitions, maypole and country dancing, archery and spear throwing as well as 'guess the weight of farm animal' competitions.

This annual coronation celebration festival revitalizes all the Oak villagers' spirits and bonds everyone together during the coronation celebration festival; the Oak villagers share much fun and laughter with one another. As the sun brightly shines upon the ground, the loud sounds of cheer and laughter come from the Oak villagers, who have now all made their way to the Oak Village square and are enjoying the fun games and activities with each other. The Oak guards are still busy making sure everything is set up ready for the much anticipated start of the coronation celebration festival.

At the east end of Oak Village's square in the centre of Oak Village, the Oak guard has created a big but basic wooden stage that has two separate long red cloth curtains fixed by a metal rail at the top of the big wooden stage, which covers the sides of the stage in order not to reveal the leader of Oak villager who is called Wolf until the coronation celebration festival begins. Placed upon this big wooden stage is a small stone carved monument statue of Wolf who is holding a metal shield and a sword that is fixed upon the stone carved monument statue. There are also other various types of silver knight's armour such as chest and leg armour and royal artefacts of Wolf's ancestors displayed on top of two wooden stands that are on either side of the big wooden stage. The Oak guards have also created a big wooden throne that is positioned in the middle of two smaller wooden throne seats, which are all specifically placed upon the big wooden stage for Wolf, his wife Opal, and son Leopard, especially for Wolf's coronation celebration festival.

Wolf is the leader of Oak Village and has been the leader for three years; he was the naturally proclaimed leader of Oak Village after his father Jackal unfortunately passed away because of fever just over three years ago. The previous leaders of Oak Village had always been from within Wolf's bloodline, covering four generations back to the beginning when Oak Village was first built up and developed by migrating villagers who had left Alder Village and Pine Village just under 200 years ago.

Wolf's great-grandfather Hyena was the first villager to suggest leaving Pine Village to construct and settle at another village since Hyena was a very independent and ambitious human who wanted to become a leader of his own village; as he saw the population of Pine Village continue to grow, he thought it was the perfect opportunity to relocate at another village that he named Oak Village. Hyena discussed this proposition with many Pine villagers who also rallied and agreed with his decision as they too wanted to depart from a fast growing and busy Pine Village. In particular, the migrating Alder villagers began relocating to Pine Village due to the potential threat of creature attacks occurring in Alder Village that was located in the far north-east edge of the Planet of Phoenix, next to the luxurious and spiritual oasis named Hydra Springs.

After a small but progressing Oak Village had begun being built by Hyena and his Pine villager followers, many more villagers from Alder Village decided to journey further than Pine Village and relocate to Oak Village. These circumstances mostly occurred after Alder Village was eventually destroyed by Lord Scartor in a fierce and continuous battle against the Alder villagers, which spanned from the Wastelands and Swamp Fields across the Grass Terrain Fields in the north-east direction and ended up in Alder Village. The battle of Alder Village was the worst battle between creatures and humans to have been witnessed on the Planet of Phoenix since the planet's creation. The battle of Alder Village was atrocious and disturbing due to the entire village being completely destroyed. This heinous act of violence made all the humans throughout the Planet of Phoenix have increased hatred against all of the creature species who lived on the Planet of Phoenix. The strong opinions, hatred, and stories of the Alder Village battle and the malicious deeds of creatures were spread throughout all the human settlements and passed down their generations so that all kin of humans would be cautious and loathed the creatures.

At first, the new Oak Village leader Hyena and the current Pine Village leader called Woken had some resentment toward one another as Woken was dubious about Hyena leaving his rule over Pine Village and taking many of the Pine villagers with him to develop another village not so far from Pine Village. However, Woken decided it would be better to unite with Hyena and Oak Village to strengthen the bond of humans due to creature threats; also, Woken was required to follow the orders of the king of Falcon City at that time, who was King Primus, that is, King Exodus's grandfather. King Primus, who was a knowledgeable and realistic human, decreed that in order to maintain the strong alliance between the humans residing on the Planet of Phoenix and also to increase the trade and development of the villages and Falcon City all the village leaders would need to be civil and responsive with one another.

WOLF IS THIRTY-THREE years of age; he has blue eyes and thick black wavy hair, and his face is clear except for a rough unshaven beard. Wolf is also of medium-sized height or around five feet and nine inches and has a muscly but skinny build. Wolf wears a silver crown with the word 'Oak' written upon it in the ancient Phoenix language in gold across the front middle part of the silver crown; he also wears metal knighthood armour and steel boots. Ever since Wolf was a child, he has been trained and coached by his father Jackal, just as Jackal was trained by his father, Jaguar, as Jaguar's father, Hyena, trained him. Wolf was also trained and coached by his father Jackal's most loyal and capable Oak guards in the techniques of sword fighting, archery, hunting, horse riding, navigation, and educational subjects like Geography, History, English, and Maths.

As Jackal knew his son Wolf would become leader of Oak Village one day, he wanted him to possess the essential skills and characteristics to lead effectively and efficiently due to the threat of the creatures inevitable increase in numbers. Wolf has thus acquired to become a strong, innovative, and prodigious leader; he is also wise, tactful, and talented at generating battle strategies that have enabled him and his Oak guards in previous battles to protect Oak Village against the mischievous nomad warriors from the Wastelands.

Nomad warriors used to be villagers that lived in Oak, Pine, and in recent times in Willow Village, but they were banished from the villages due to their criminal offences such as theft, rape, and murder. These nomad warriors would travel away from the three main villages to the Wastelands but would always have a vendetta against the villages for banishing them and making them fend for themselves against the creatures on the Planet of Phoenix. In the earlier times of these main villages' development, the villagers who committed criminal officers in the villages were sentenced to death by being hanged or shot to death with arrows or spears. However, King Primus of Falcon City decreed that he wanted killing of any human by another human to stop as he did not want the humans to have the same mind-set as the creatures. Thus, King Primus ordered the village leaders to banish the criminal villagers.

These criminal villages at first tried to relocate to other areas in the Planet of Phoenix but ended up getting killed by creatures; thus, after residing in the Wastelands, they decided to train themselves up to become warriors in order to fight back against any creature intruders. Over the many decades, the nomad warriors who were banished to the Wastelands managed to build small tribal huts and shacks, where they then grouped with other nomad warrior clans and tribes throughout the vast plain of the Wastelands in order to share knowledge and trade items with one another. Occasionally alone or in groups, the nomad warriors would attack the main villages for revenge of their banishment or to gather much needed food and shelter supplies for the rest of their clans. In recent times, however, the nomad warriors had attacked the main villages less due to being not only heavily outnumbered by the growing population of humans in the villages but also by the recent battle strategies and resources developed to protect the villages against nomad warrior attacks.

As the noise of the Oak villager crowd grows more vibrant and smell of the food from the food eating contest becomes more fragrant, the eagerly awaited coronation celebration is about to begin. Wolf is currently standing at the back of the coronation celebration big wooden stage with his radiant wife Opal, his young son who is named Leopard, and several of his Oak guards who had also pledged many years of loyal service to his father Jackal before he died three years ago. These Oak guards are currently preparing the staging for the coronation celebration and checking over the speeches for Wolf to read with his wife Opal, as Wolf's attention is distracted by the cheerful and lively noises he hears from the Oak Village crowd near the front of the big wooden stage. Wolf is wearing a long red and black silk robe that is only worn during the coronation celebration ceremonies, which was specially made by the skilful Tameka in Nerolus's prodigious cloth shop located in Falcon City.

Wolf's elegant wife Opal is twenty-eight years old and has long, black, curly silky hair and hazel eyes; her face and skin has a bright and smooth complexion. She also has long black eyelashes and colourfully decorated nails. Opal is wearing a beautiful long blue silk dress that is covered with silver glitter, which matches her bright blue shoes; she is also wearing a sparkling silver diamond ring that Wolf gave to her on their memorable wedding day nine years ago. Opal is a loving and caring human, with a kind and honest nature about her. Opal was originally from Willow Village and was very close to her father Alexis and mother Illumin and was brought up with a very happy childhood, and during and after her education at Willow School, her parents wanted her to be part of the family business that was in their florist shop in Willow Village. Opal enjoyed working with different species and colours of flowers as she enjoyed the beauty and miracles of nature. Wolf and Opal first met just over six years ago when Wolf visited her family's florist shop in the newly developed Willow Village, as he wanted to buy flowers for his mother Amber's funeral and had heard that this florist shop in Willow Village produced the most lavish flowers.

Wolf was very distraught and saddened when his mother Amber died of a terminal virus six years ago, as he was still young, only in his mid-twenties at the time. Both Wolf's parents Jackal and Amber had loved and cared for him dearly and his father Jackal trained him to become a powerful leader. Wolf's mother Amber nurtured him to become an accountable, honourable, and honest leader too. Their family had spent many happy years and times together, and they would travel often to the other main villages and Falcon City to interact with the other humans, including the leader of Pine Village that was Igon and King Exodus of Falcon City. Jackal, Amber, and their son Wolf were admired by all the humans and shared the pain of Wolf when his mother Amber died untimely. Wolf wanted to make sure his mother Amber had the most spiritual send-off to heaven during her funeral; that is why he travelled to Willow Village to get the most appropriate flowers for this unfortunate occasion.

Wolf was served and helped by Opal in her family's flower shop in Willow Village and she found beautiful and brightly coloured roses for his mother's funeral. Wolf and Opal fell in love at first sight, and she comforted Wolf through his mother's death for many of the following months. Wolf and Opal's bond and love developed further for one another, and although Opal's parents were reluctant at first that their only daughter wanted to leave Willow Village, she moved to Oak Village and become Wolf's wife. Within a year of their marriage, to much delight of Wolf's father Jackal and the Oak guards and villagers, Opal gave birth to a marvellous son whom they named Leopard.

Leopard is now four years old and has very short black hair, blue eyes, and the same facial characteristics as his father; he is a very happy and content toddler, and he is quickly learning about his surroundings and gaining the admirable characteristics and traits of both of his parents. Leopard is dressed in a small royal black gown outfit with a small blue hat on his head and small blue shoes on his feet. Due to Wolf being the new leader of Oak Village, the previous Oak guards had pledged their new allegiance to him, and after recruiting other courageous Oak villagers who wanted to become Oak guards, Wolf now has a total of thirty-two Oak guards who wear metal armour and boots and carry metal swords and shields around. The Oak guards have been specially trained in the art of combat and battle strategy by Jackal and Wolf to enable them to protect Oak Village and its villagers in it against any dangerous or potential threats from nomad warriors or creatures.

THE OAK VILLAGE coronation celebration festival is swarming with lots of happy and satisfied Oak villagers of all ages, genders, and trades, who are enjoying the wondrous atmosphere of the festival country music played by villager musicians on animals' horns, drums, and tambourines. Ale beverages and warm meat and stew are filling the stomachs of the villagers, who are cheering loudly while watching the games and competitions, and the colourful decoration of flowers, statues, and the villagers' different types of clothing make the whole of the villagers in the Oak Village square gleam with enthusiasm and spirit.

The hot sun continues to shine brightly down upon Oak Village and the different types of birds like the Red-eyed Vireo and the Brown Thrasher fly over Oak Village and sing and twerp along to the sound of the country music being played. They also swoop down to the ground to try and pick up crumbs dropped by the villagers, who are eating bread. There are many competitive events taking place like country dancing competitions that are only for women Oak villagers as well as archery and arm wrestling competitions that are only for the men Oak villagers. There is much joy and laughter among all the Oak villagers who participate in these competitive events or watch it, as the villagers are very competitive but positive towards one another. The rest of the villagers will spend quality time with their family and friends by chatting and eating with each other.

Emerald, who is wearing her new red dress that she bought especially from Pine Village a few weeks ago for her date with Raven to Wolf's coronation celebration, and her mother Ruby are walking together blissfully through the Oak Village square, while enjoying the heat from the sun and the smiles upon every villager's face. Emerald and Ruby have spent twenty minutes watching the country dancing competition as the school children from Oakus School religious education class where Ruby teaches are involved in it. The country dancing competition was in the north of the Oak Village square. After Emerald and Ruby finish clapping for Ruby's classroom children, who had just finished their country dancing routine in front of Oak villager judges, they decide to walk through the village square in the south-west direction, where they pass the game that was to guess the weight of farm animals. Emerald and Ruby tenderly greet or smile at the Oak villagers passing by and the villagers who are also attentively watching the guessing of the weight of farm animals game, since all the Oak villagers know Ruby very well due to her being a teacher at Oakus School.

Ruby is forty-one years old, smaller than the average height of humans, and she has short dark brown hair, green eyes, and some freckles upon her face. Ruby wears dense glasses over her eyes and is also wearing a long grey dress with black shoes. Ruby is a very friendly, focused, and helpful human and enjoys socialising with her daughter Emerald and the other Oak villagers as well as participating and helping Oak Village provide community and interactive activities for the children, especially since she is a teacher at Oakus School. Ruby had really enjoyed learning religious education at Oakus School when she was a young child and went to school with Raven's mother Jewel, who was her best friend. Later in her life, Ruby decided to become a teacher's assistant after she finished her education at Oakus School, where she achieved very high academic results. That led on to her being trained to become a religious education teacher; however, she stopped teaching for a few years when she became pregnant with Emerald. Ruby has now been a consistent religious education teacher at Oakus School for twenty years apart from the break she took off for Emerald, but when Emerald was old enough to attend Oakus School, Ruby was able to go back to her job again. Ruby wanted teach Emerald at Oakus School, as the humans living on the Planet of Phoenix have different views about religion. Some humans believe that only one God exists and other humans believe that several gods exist. Ruby wanted to make sure that Emerald understood why humans had their own beliefs to allow Emerald make her own judgement in the areas of religion she would like to worship.

Ruby was very happy for many years during her teenage and early youth, especially when she and her husband Gaius would double-date with her best friend Jewel and her husband Ruthus. Ruby was devastated and never properly recovered from the overwhelming situation when Jewel and Ruthus was killed by Viper eleven years ago. Ruby relied upon Gaius to be her support during these difficult circumstances, and for a short while after the long period grief and shock of Jewel's and Ruthus's murders, Ruby was enjoying a happy live with Gaius and their wonderful daughter, Emerald. This happy situation, however, all changed around six years ago when Ruby and Gaius began to argue more often due to spending a lot more time with one another and due to the pressure they put on each other to be each other's support after their friends' deaths. Also, Gaius found it difficult to continue running Ruthus's trade business on his own, which caused him to be stressful and argumentative with Ruby. Thus, Gaius used to spend more time away from Ruby and his home when he was out trading with the other villagers and would more often undergo the long journey back to Falcon City to see his father, Nerolus, and mother, Tamika, in their cloth shop when he and Ruby started having problems with each other. On one occasion upon Gaius's journey to Falcon City, he never returned home to Ruby in Oak Village.

Ruby was devastated that Gaius left her and Emerald as she wanted to work through their problems and stay as a family, especially after all they had been through with regard to losing their close friends, Ruthus and Jewel. Ruby spent many months crying and had to take time off from teaching at Oakus School to cope with the thought that Gaius had left her completely, and it took her a long time to realise that Gaius won't be coming back to her and their marriage. Ruby had tried to get in touch with Gaius to sort out their marriage; she sent letters to his mother, Tameka, and his father, Nerolus, at their cloth shop in Falcon City via a carrier pigeon to find out about what had happened to Gaius and to ask them to tell him to get in contact with her or Emerald, but she did not receive any word back from Gaius, Nerolus, or Tameka. Ruby tried to maintain a strong and supportive attitude for Emerald and also in her role as a religious education teacher at Oakus School, although she felt it hard to cope with continuing her normal personality and attitude towards life many times.

AS EMERALD AND Ruby continue walking past the guess the animal's weight game, they catch a glimpse of Barious at a distance, who is currently at the hot dog eating competition stall. Emerald and Ruby happily walk over to Barious, and upon reaching Barious, Ruby taps him gently on the back.

'Well, good afternoon, my dears,' says Barious as he turns around and happily sees Ruby and Emerald standing elegantly in front of him.

'It's good to see you, Barious! And thank you so very much for the hammer and nails you supplied to Emerald earlier. You are so generous to us and are a very kind man,' replies Ruby humbly.

'You're very welcome, my lady, and it is no trouble at all as you and Emerald are like family to me also. Did you manage to fix the broken shelf up in your home?' asks Barious, smiling radiantly.

'Yes, I did after, and only after an hour or so. I feel very proud of myself for doing it,' laughs Ruby.

'And so you should, my dear, as it can be quite a tricky task. And how are you doing, Emerald, and might I add you are also looking lovely today in your bright red dress?' states Barious.

'I am fine, thank you, Barious, and yes, this is a new dress I bought to wear to this coronation celebration festival for my date with Raven. Do you know if he is back from his errand in Pine Village yet?' asks Emerald excitedly.

'Sorry, Emerald, he has not returned to Oak Village as of yet, but I'm sure he will be here soon as he wouldn't miss your date for anything,' replies Barious reassuringly.

'That's good, as I'm really excited for our date tonight. We are going to go to the late night dancing tent after the coronation celebration festival has finished. You are most welcome to come along with us to that as well, Barious, and maybe you could also convince my mother to come too. They will have the great Oakus band playing again like last year. That was so much fun,' says Emerald enthusiastically.

'I think that will be a bit past my bedtime, ha ha, but hope you and Raven have a grand time together there,' replies Barious happily.

'That reminds me, Barious, when Raven does come to the coronation celebration festival, would it be all right if I tagged along with you as I'm sure Emerald and Raven would want to spend some time by themselves?' says Ruby, winking at Emerald.

'Mother,' laughs Emerald.

'Of course, Ruby, you don't even need to ask. I was meaning to spend some much needed time and share conversation with you anyways as I haven't really seen you around Oak Village much recently,' states Barious sadly.

'Yes, I do apologise, Barious. I have been extremely busy at Oakus School preparing the children for their annual assessments as I want them all to do really well and achieve great results,' answers Ruby.

'Ah right, how are the children getting on? I still remember when Raven and Emerald was at Oakus school preparing for their annual assessments and how Raven used to get really stressed about the pressure of them. That was a bit different to my day,' laughs Barious.

'As do I, but they both did really well and got good results that they should be proud of. And yes, the children at Oakus School are all getting on fine, and it's good that I've been keeping myself busy with helping them at the moment. As it has been two years ago now, I am still quite lonely and sad about what happened with me and Gaius, especially the way he left us both, although Emerald has been a diamond in being there for me not only as a daughter but as a friend,' says Ruby, sad at the thought of Gaius not being a part of her life no more.

'Yes, of course, it has been a real shame for you and Emerald since Gaius left. I remember how upset you were at the time when he left you two years ago, but you have come a long way and are doing really well in being there for Emerald and Oakus School children too. You seem to have got your spark back in your eyes, and of course you know I'm here to help you through anything too,' says Barious softly.

'Thank you, Barious, and yes, you and Raven have been there for us also for many years and through many unfortunate situations. I really do appreciate your friendship very much, especially since Jewel and Ruthus untimely left us from this life on the Planet of Phoenix,' says Ruby with a tear in her eyes as she is also thinking back to all the good times and laughter she shared on their double dates with Gaius, Ruthus, and Jewel.

'Yes, and although it has been over eleven years ago now that Ruthus and Jewel were murdered by that evil creature Viper, it feels just like yesterday we were all going for a pleasant and peaceful walk through the Grass Terrain Fields near Eagle woods. However, I know they are watching over all of us from heaven and would be very proud of the young adults Raven and Emerald have turned out to be and especially now that they have finally got together as partners,' says Barious tenderly.

'Yes, I remember those grand walks and the laughs we all used to share with one another. I miss them both so very much and particularly Jewel, as we've been best friends for as long as I can remember and life is now not the same without her. I know she would have made me feel so much better about myself during the months straight after Gaius had left me. But yes, you are right, Barious. They would have both been ecstatic to see Raven and Emerald together now,' smiles Ruby.

'I am still here you know, Mother,' laughs Emerald, turning away from looking at a man Oak villager quickly eating as many hot dogs as he can in the hot dog eating competition and looking at Ruby.

'Oh yes, sorry, my dear, but I am very proud of you and cherish Raven like a member of my family too. It means the world to me that you have found a great and caring human like Raven to be with, and I hope you both are very happy together for the rest of your lives,' says Ruby softly, thinking again about when she and Gaius had first got together and all the great times they had spent with each other. Emerald notices the sad expression on her mother's face and gives her a firm hug.

'I'm sure you will also find someone else one day who really deserves you, Ruby. I did really like Gaius, but he always seemed to have a rogue nature about him and never seem to be the kind of human who would be content with his life for a long period of time. That has again changed a bit from my day, as generally when you get together with the first person you would generally spend the rest of your life with them,' says Barious, also thinking about his dead wife Flower.

'Yes, he always had a bit of a knack for getting into trouble. That is why his father, Nerolus, sent him away with Ruthus to Oak Village in the first place, in order to sort himself out and become more of a responsible human. He was, however, for a time, especially when Jewel and Ruthus died and also when we first had Emerald. I would always say that he was a great father to Emerald, as he would always spend time looking after her and we would all share many happy memories together and outings together. We had travelled to Falcon City a couple of times with Emerald to meet Gaius's parents, Nerolus and Tameka, who were both lovely city humans and had a wonderful cloth shop there. But then Gaius changed a few years back and I'm not sure why but we would argue more with each other and he would spend more time on his trading away from home, until it just stopped working between us, although I always wanted it too and also wanted it to work between us for Emerald's sake,' explains Ruby.

'Sometimes humans just grow apart from one another or change when they increase in age as they start to look at life and situations differently from when they were younger. Or maybe those humans weren't right for each other in the first place, as I do remember you both getting married very quickly, although I'm sure your relationship was strengthened when you had Emerald,' says Barious naturally.

'Yes, you could be right, Barious, but I fell in love with him the instance I met him, ever since Ruthus introduced us both, when I went on the blind date that was arranged by Jewel when she. I went to meet Ruthus and Gaius at Pinus Tavern in Pine Village after Ruthus and Gaius had done some trading there that evening. Gaius was a very mysterious and charming human, and I remember it being a magical night and I even ended up going back to his flat in Oak Village on the first night we spent with one another, as I knew it was meant to be. But I had noticed as the years went by that he never really seemed settled here in Oak Village. Maybe it was because he grew up in the fast and developed lifestyle in Falcon City,' exclaims Ruby.

'Have you not thought about going to find out what's happened to him in Falcon City so that your mind could be at peace?' Barious asks.

'Yes, of course I have, but it's a long and expensive journey to undertake, especially if I had to go by myself, although I'm sure Emerald would have come with me as I knew she really wanted to go to Falcon City herself to find Gaius. I would also have to consider

Oakus School children whom I teach, as they rely on a consistent teaching style and no other teacher at Oakus School also teaches religious education. That is the subject I specialise in. I had, however, previously sent a couple of letters addressed to Gaius at his father Nerolus's cloth shop in Falcon City via carrier pigeon, but received no reply from either Nerolus or Gaius's mother Tamika, with whom I thought we got on well together.

'I figured Gaius didn't want to be with me no more, and it would thus be a waste of time, money, and energy for me to go physically find him in Falcon City and persuade him otherwise to come back home in Oak Village, particularly as I know he is a very stubborn human. Besides, although my heart hurts every time I think about him, I don't think I can forgive the fact that he not only walked out on me with no contact since, but he also left our wonderful daughter, Emerald. I know it would be awkward between us and I know he may have had his reasons, but you don't just stop being a parent. And for that reason, I don't know if I would want to see him again at the moment, although I'm sure I will feel differently about it in time to come as you can't control the emotion of love,' states Ruby.

ONE OF THE men Oak villagers wins the hot dog eating contest and stands up from his wooden chair at the hot dog stall in excitement; all the other men Oak villagers sitting next to him at a big wooden table put down the hot dogs they had in their hands ready to eat and clap for the man Oak villager who has won.

'And the winner is Roland,' shouts the Pinus Church vicar, who is judging the hot dog eating contest and is visiting from Pine Village to help out in the contests and competitions for Wolf's coronation celebration festival. Barious, Ruby, Emerald, and the rest of the crowd watching the hot dog eating contest clap and cheer for the man Oak villager who has won. Suddenly, a loud high-pitched sound comes from trumpets that some of the Oak guards have started playing, who are standing on the big wooden stage, which sounds the notification for Wolf's coronation celebration to begin. All the crowd at the hot dog eating contesting and the rest of the Oak villagers throughout the square turn in excitement to see and hear the brass trumpets being played by Oak guards on top of the big wooden stage in the south-east direction of the square. The Oak villagers all stop what they are doing and gather with their family and friends and begin to move eagerly towards the big wooden stage.

'Oh good, Wolf's coronation celebration is about to begin now,' says Barious positively.

'Oh, but Raven hasn't returned from Pine Village yet,' says Emerald sadly.

'Hopefully he will be here soon,' says Ruby, placing her left arm around Emerald's shoulders. Barious, Ruby, Emerald, and all the other Oak villagers throughout the Oak Village square now begin or continue to walk over for Wolf's coronation celebration towards the big wooden stage located in the south-east direction of the square. The Oak villagers begin to clap and chant loudly Wolf's name in anticipation of his entrance onto the big wooden stage.

Wolf pulls back the long red curtain from one of the sides of the big wooden coronation celebration stage after hearing his name being chanted loudly by the Oak Village crowd and sneakily looks out at the Oak Village crowd that have started approaching to gather in large groups at the front of the big wooden stage.

'There seems to be a lot of Oak villagers out there, more than I remember,' says Wolf nervously, twiddling his fingers and closing the big red curtain as he turns towards Opal.

'Well, of course, there is, my love. All the Oak villagers and even some Pine and Willow villagers have come here today to see the magnificent leader and protector of Oak Village, who is the perfect human, husband, and father in every way,' says Opal gladly, kissing Wolf on the lips while holding their son Leopard's hand, who is standing on the ground next to her at the back of the big wooden stage.

'Anyways, I don't know why you still get so nervous. You have been in countless battles and killed many dangerous nomad warriors and have also done this coronation celebration ceremony two times before,' remarks Opal.

'I know, but I feel I have to live up to my father, who was a grand human and one of the best Oak Village leaders who had accomplished so much for our village. I just don't want to disappoint you or any one of the villagers who live here,' replies Wolf humbly.

'Always humble and righteous you are, Wolf, and I know Jackal and your mother, Amber, would be very proud of the leader you have become, and they will both be watching over you and all of us today from heaven,' says Opal, smiling brightly at Wolf as well as gazing into his blue eyes.

'Thank you for your beautiful words as usual, Opal. You and Leopard mean the world to me as did my father and mother whom I miss very much and would seek to make them proud on this day,' replies Wolf.

'As do I miss Jackal, and I regret that I never got to meet your cherished mother, but know in my heart that their death by illnesses was far before their time. I also know that they are here with us in spirit and will guide us through today and for many delightful days to come,' states Opal, putting her other hand on the side of Wolf's face; the warm touch of Opal's hand makes Wolf feel calm. One of the Oak guard's walks up to Wolf from behind the big wooden stage and carefully takes the silver crown from his head that he is still currently wearing. This silver crown has been passed down his ancestry bloodline since his great-grandfather Hyena became the first leader of Oak Village just over 200 years ago.

'We shall present this crown back to you along with your sword and shield during the coronation celebration ceremony, Leader of Oak Village,' says the Oak guard as he holds on to Wolf's silver crown in his hands. Another Oak guard at the front of the big wooden stage grabs a sheep's horn from the top of one of the wooden tables on the big wooden stage and blows it hard to make a loud deep sound.

'Yes, that is fine,' states Wolf to the Oak guard, as he hears the deep sound of the sheep's horn.

'The Oakus horns have now been blown and the Oak Village crowd is fervently waiting for you at the front of the wooden stage to praise and appreciate their grand Oak Village leader. The coronation celebration is about to commence. Are you ready, my leader?' says the Oak guard while speaking to Wolf.

'Yes, I think so,' replies Wolf as he looks at Opal's attractive face.

'See you on stage, my love, and don't worry the crowd will love you as much as I do,' says Opal as she kisses Wolf tenderly on the lips, and she walks through the long red curtain at the right side of the big wooden stage to walk on to the front of the big wooden stage, holding Leopard's hand. Some of the Oak guards also follow behind Opal and Leopard through the long red curtain.

As Opal, Leopard, and the Oak guards walk slowly to the front of the big wooden stage, the Oak Village crowd cheer and clap loudly in admiration. Opal and Leopard smile and wave at the Oak Village crowd as they walk across the front of the big wooden stage; they sit down on their smaller wooden throne seats that are next to Wolf's big wooden throne in the middle of the big wooden stage. Wolf waits nervously at the back of the big wooden stage behind the long red curtains, ready to greet the Oak Village crowd at the front of the big wooden stage as soon as he hears Opal introduce him.

Five

RAVEN AND FELIX continue to gallop fast in the western direction down the long and straight cobbled road between Pine Village and Oak Village. This cobbled road lays through many Grass Terrain Fields and over small hills, where the village's crops like wheat, barley, and vegetables are planted, which are currently growing strong in the sun's blazing heat, as well as where the farm animals such as cows, pigs, and sheep graze upon. Raven feels the heat of the sun's rays upon his neck and forehead as he clenches tightly on to Felix's brown rope reins that are made of leather, currently having a rough and dry texture to them.

As Raven and Felix continue galloping over the rocky coble roads for over twenty minutes, Felix's strong and sturdy feet display no sign of weakness due to the power in his thigh muscles because of the healthy lifestyle he has been brought up to have by Barious. Raven's mind wanders back to the time when he was young at the age of seven; he remembers slight and fuzzy memories of his parents Ruthus and Jewel reading bed time stories to him before he would go to sleep at night in their old house in Oak Village as well as the joyful times when Raven's parents would take him for peaceful walks to the different locations across the Planet of Phoenix for them to see the beautiful and diverse environments and nature that Raven remembers enjoying very much.

However, due to being of such a young age at the time, Raven can only remember small bits of the memories he shared with his parents and what they used to look like. Although Raven has happy memories regarding his parents, he tries not to think about them too much as every time he brings these memories back into his thoughts, the great memories turn into negative and upsetting ones. They always come shuddering back to the memory he has retained from eleven years ago on the terrible day when he came back to his parents' house in Oak Village, after he had been out for a walk in the Grass Terrains Fields near Eagle Forest with Barious, Emerald, Ruby, and Gaius.

As Barious entered his elder son Ruthus and daughter-in-law Jewel's house, Raven followed Barious, walking into the main living room of Ruthus and Jewel's house, where they noticed that the main living room had been torn apart in a destructive mess. All the wooden chairs had fallen over and parts of them were broken, as well as the ornaments that were upon the wooden shelves above the fireplace and chimney had fallen to the ground and been smashed into little pieces. Barious and Raven immediately started to panic and quickly ran into the kitchen of the house, where they were distraught to see only the few disintegrated bones and blood remains of Ruthus's and Jewel's bodies lying on the floor in a pile of their clothes that were not, however, disintegrated, as Viper's black poisonous venom was only able to disintegrate living flesh and bone.

The kitchen was also trashed because of the struggle or fight Ruthus and Jewel had with Viper, who was accompanied by a couple of his Serpents, but there was no sign of Viper and his serpents still being in the house since there was complete silence. Barious knew that it must have been Viper that had killed Ruthus and Jewel as he was the only creature on the Planet of Phoenix that possessed black poisonous venom that could disintegrate living flesh and bone, as this happened to Ruthus and Jewel's bodies. He had heard stories of Viper's spiteful and brutal attacks on humans before, but had never seen the outcome of what Viper's black poisonous venom could leave humans remains as. The stories passed between villagers stated that Viper prowled somewhere in Komodo Jungle and never really left that dangerous habitat unless he had to hunt humans for food or have fights against the royal Falcon guards from Falcon City.

Barious also remembered his father Trogon telling him that before Alder Village was completely destroyed just over 200 years ago, Viper had also joined forces with Lord Scartor in a previous battle against the humans, which occurred in the Swamp Fields in the north-east of the Planet of Phoenix, which was near the Wastelands and Eagle Forest. This battle was the worst encounter that the humans of the Planet of Phoenix had experienced with the creatures, and although, the humans were victorious in this battle, hundreds of decent humans were violently killed and the stories of this unbearable battle were passed down the generations of the humans for them to always remember the killed humans in this battle and to always be on their guard against the creatures that resided throughout the Planet of Phoenix.

After Raven saw the disintegrated remains of his beloved and cherished parents' bodies upon the floor of their kitchen, he fell instantly to his knees, covered his eyes with his hands, and began crying in shock and despair. After hearing the loud and heart-breaking cries from Raven, Emerald, Ruby, and Gaius quickly ran through the house to see what had happened to their dear friends. Emerald threw her arms around Raven and held him tightly as his tears streamed down his cold cheeks. Ruby and Gaius were also extremely shocked and distraught on losing their great friends and also had tears rolling down their faces, but understanding how this unbearable situation would be too much for Raven to cope with, so they had to quickly react appropriately to keep Raven calm.

Ruby quickly picked Raven up, and along with Emerald, they hurried to Barious's tool shop further in the south of Oak Village, which was near Ruby and Gaius's house. Ruby asked Emerald to stay and comfort Raven in the spare room of Barious's tool shop while Ruby went back to Ruthus and Jewel's house to gather Raven's clothes together and bring them back to Barious's tool shop as it would now be unsafe for Raven to continue living in that house. While Ruby was gathering Raven's clothes, Barious and Gaius quickly cleaned up Ruthus and Jewel's disintegrated remains as well as also tidied the house and moved the furniture and Ruthus's and Jewel's things in it to Barious's tool shop.

While Barious, although upset, quickly sorted out Ruthus and Jewel's house, Gaius went to explain about what had happened to Jackal, who was the Oak Village leader at the time. Jackal was also deeply upset by the news and quickly ordered his loyal Oak guards to search for Viper and his Serpents throughout Oak Village, and he ordered if they were to find them, they should be killed for the heinous crime they had just committed. Jackal and a few of his Oak guards also went to Ruthus and Jewel's house to help Barious clean it up, and they both agreed that it would be best to board up the windows and doors of the house so that it could not be used as a home again, due to the pain and sorrow it would cause Raven.

After the devastating situation had passed, including the memorial ceremony in which the Oak villagers that were led by Ruby, Gaius, Ruthus's brother Rio, sister-in-law Olivia, including Raven's cousin Parrot, took part for Ruthus and Jewel, Barious realised that Lord Scartor or Viper might have been looking for the anomaly crystal in Oak Village, in order to steal if from the bloodline of Grackle to use against the humans of the Planet of Phoenix. Somehow Viper had found out Ruthus had descended from the powerful wizard Grackle and had also located where he and Jewel lived in Oak Village. Ruthus and Jewel had thought back as best as they could to hide the location of the anomaly crystal and was hence killed for not giving Viper the information regarding the whereabouts of the anomaly crystal. Barious constantly felt confounded and full of grief because of what had happened to his son and daughter-in-law but couldn't tell Ruby, Gaius, or Raven the real truth as he did not want to put them at risk either.

Previously, Barious had told his elder son, Ruthus, who also told his wife Jewel, the whole story about his ancestors Grackle and Sparrow and how the creature Lord Scartor sought to find the anomaly crystal to use against the humans he despised. Barious, however, didn't give Ruthus the anomaly crystal, as he thought it was best to protect the anomaly crystal himself, as Ruthus was now living with his wife Jewel and their son Raven. That is why Barious hid the anomaly crystal underneath the wooden floorboards of his bedroom in his tool shop. Ruthus and Jewel knew that Barious had hidden the anomaly crystal somewhere in his tool shop, but sacrificed their lives to protect the secret of where the anomaly crystal was really hidden so that the creatures wouldn't locate and use it against the humans throughout the Planet of Phoenix.

FROM THE DAY of this family tragedy, Barious had raised Raven and tried to protect him and the rest of his ancestry bloodline of Grackle from knowing about the anomaly crystal as he didn't want to also put them at risk of being attacked by creatures such as Lord Scartor and Viper. This is the reason Barious never spoke about the anomaly crystal to his other son, who was called Rio, the younger brother of Ruthus and also Parrot's father. Due to what had happened to Ruthus and Jewel, Barious realised that he would have to keep the knowledge of the astonishing anomaly crystal to himself and protect it also with his life in order to keep the rest of his family and friends from being put in unforeseen danger.

Barious did his best in raising Raven from the age of seven, and he tried to make him happy again and enjoy the rest of his childhood, although the memory and thoughts he had of losing his adored parents would always stay with Raven and would haunt him for the rest of his life. Ruby was just as upset as Barious and Raven were due to losing her lifetime best friend that was Jewel; thus, she also spent much time in trying to help Barious in taking care of Raven too, but their lives in Oak Village would never be the same again. Raven never really spoke about his parents much due to the horrific memories he would have about finding his parents' disintegrated remains in their old house; he became very quiet and reserved for a long time, whereas earlier he was full of energy and laughter. As Raven continued to go to Oakus School, he did not socialise as much with the other school children due to him still feeling impaired and not like the other children; consequently, Barious and Raven's religious education teacher Ruby began to worry much that Raven wouldn't grow up as he normally would have done if his parents hadn't been murdered by Viper.

Raven, however, did spend a lot of time with Emerald as a child because Ruby would also care and look after him when Barious had other matters to attend to when he would visit Panther, who was leader of Willow Village, and King Exodus of Falcon City. Raven built up a close and personal relationship with Emerald, and they used to play together for many hours and became very good friends. Emerald seemed to be the only person who could make Raven smile and be his usual self again. Barious and Ruby could see the impact Emerald was having on Raven and encouraged their friendship with each other. They used to all go out as a group of four on walks through the Grass Terrain Fields to show Raven and Emerald the peacefulness and beauty of the nature and environment the Planet of Phoenix had.

Raven's and Emerald's feelings developed for each other intimately as they both went through puberty, and they spent much more time with one another at Oakus School as they were in the same classes and also would go on dates with each other after school. They would see each other every day, and every time they saw one another they would both feel the tingly butterfly feelings in their stomachs. Barious and Ruby were very happy that Raven and Emerald had decided to progress from their friendship to start dating, as it brought out the best personality and characteristics of both Raven and Emerald; it was like they were made for each other.

Raven and Emerald spent much time together walking through the Grass Terrain Fields in all directions from Oak Village, where they would see the wildlife or animals and plants throughout the Planet of Phoenix, which were graceful and stimulating. Raven and Emerald would have picnics together near Eagle Forest and would watch the white fluffy and different shaped clouds glide across the vast bright blue sky. They would also have meals with Barious and Ruby, spending time at each other's houses, and they would also go to Oak Village's dances and festivals together as well as visit Parrot in Pine Village, who would take them to Pinus Tavern for drinks and food.

Raven and Emerald shared many treasured laughs and make-believe stories with one another about a planet without pain, suffering, or malicious creatures. Emerald would also help Raven with his educational studies, especially during their annual assessments, as Raven was slow to learn new information sometimes due to his now introvert behaviour. Raven would also watch and support Emerald when she took part in gymnastic competitions that took place at Oakus School or at Pinus School in Pine Village, when the three main villages would compete against one another. Emerald appreciated Raven's support very much as she would be having a tough time since she needed to train hard in preparation for the gymnastic competitions. Raven now started to become more expressive and confident in himself and tried to put the horrible memories of the unfortunate circumstances in the past behind him, but he would still find it difficult to speak about his parents, even with Emerald.

Raven has now been in love with Emerald for as long as he can remember; she is his soul mate and the only person he only ever feels around himself. She has helped him out so much through his parents' death, his education, and in being more social and outgoing again. She has brought happiness and hope back to his life again, after suffering with pain and sorrow for many years. Emerald feels the same as Raven feels for her; she even knew she loved Raven before he loved her, as Emerald had matured more quickly than Raven during their puberty. Emerald loves Raven's company as he is very imaginative, supportive, and compassionate towards her and all she has ever wanted is to become Raven's wife. Raven admires Emerald's ambition and charisma when she trains as a gymnast at Oakus School, and Raven appreciates how Emerald cares for him and makes him feel special. Raven's heart beats for Emerald as much as Emerald's heart beats for Raven; they would be lost without each other, and as every second of every day passes, they are always in each other's thoughts.

AS RAVEN AND Felix approach the perimeter of Oak Village, Raven worriedly sees in the distance two nomad warriors standing upon one of the small hills of the Grass Terrain Fields, looking around the area. Raven notices curiously that the nomad warriors are both wearing silver-plated armour and metal boots and one of the nomad warriors is carrying a steel axe while the other is holding tightly on to a steel sword; it is quite unusual for a nomad warrior to be wearing armour and carrying these weapons as they do not have much resources living as they are in the Wastelands. Raven thinks this is also strange as he has never seen nomad warriors so close to Oak Village, particularly in recent years, although he has heard the stories about the nomad warriors occasionally attacking the villages and villagers for food, clothes, or weapons.

Raven immediately thinks about Emerald, Barious, and Ruby and hopes that they are safe in Oak Village somewhere during Wolf's coronation celebration festival. Raven starts to fear that the nomad warriors might now also have something to do with Lord Scartor and his search for the anomaly crystal, since Barious had just explained to him that Lord Scartor would stop at nothing in order to get his hands upon the wondrous anomaly crystal. Raven's heart skips a beat as he worries more intensely for Emerald's safety in Oak Village, especially after what had happened with his parents being murdered when he was a child. Raven releases one of his hands from the tight grip he has around Felix's brown rope reins and grabs one of his white nunchucks from his grey coat pocket, kicking his heels against Felix's backside to make it gallop faster along the cobbled road so that it heads as quickly as possible towards the east entrance of Oak Village.

Raven holds firmly on to Felix's brown rope reins with his other hand as he swerves Felix from the cobbled road on to the Grass Terrain Fields to take the quickest shortcut route to Oak Village. The normal cobbled road tends to bend around difficult terrain and small hills to make it a steady and suitable path for villagers to walk between the villages. Felix's hooves strongly pound on the tough and unstable ground of the Grass Terrain Fields, as he treads on top of flowers, plants, and crops that grow in the mud. The two nomad warriors watch Raven riding Felix swiftly through the Grass Terrain Fields from a distance and realise that Raven and Felix are coming closer towards them, attempting to head towards the Oak Village's east entrance.

The two nomad warriors sprint rapidly towards a part of the Grass Terrain Field which Raven and Felix will be crossing briefly. The two nomad warriors shout, screech, and wave their metal weapons in the air to attract Raven's attention and to frighten him in order to distract him from riding properly upon the fast galloping and powerful Felix. Raven notices the nomad warriors chasing angrily towards him, and in alarm he steers Felix strongly by yanking on his brown rope reins in another direction in order to change Felix's route back on to the cobbled road. Then he yanks the brown rope reins again to swerve Felix's tough body on to the cobbled road of another Grass Terrain Field, which is opposite to the road from where the nomad warriors are charging. Suddenly, another nomad warrior quickly jumps down from an oak tree that is in the other Grass Terrain Field on to which Raven and Felix have changed their course and are racing through;

without realising, Raven and Felix ride straight into the other nomad warrior that has just jumped down from the oak tree.

The nomad warrior in front of Raven and Felix forcefully pulls out his metal sword from his metal belt and lunges it forward to stab Felix in his big black tough chest. Felix halts his hooves abruptly before getting stabbed by the nomad warrior's metal sword; he uses his immense strength to lift both his front legs up high in the air, narrowly missing the nomad warrior's metal sword, and then Felix kicks the nomad warrior forcefully in the face with the strong sturdy hoofs at the end of his long legs. Raven, in shock, holds securely on to Felix's brown rope reins as he feels the immense strength of Felix kicking the nomad warrior in the face. The nomad warrior feels a large pounding pain in the front of his face and head; the pressure of Felix's kick is so powerful it forces the nomad warrior to fly back in the air with blood pouring out of his now broken nose, feeling a throbbing agony in his face and head, which makes him lose his consciousness. The nomad warrior lands several metres back upon the Grass Terrain Fields' tough ground unconscious with a bruised, broken, and bloody face. Raven grasps hold again of Felix's brown rope reins as Felix lowers his two front legs quickly down, enabling him and Raven to be steady again back on the ground.

Raven breathes deeply in surprise and he gains his stability back on top of Felix. Raven holds firmly on to the brown rope reins as he raises it in the air and kicks both sides of Felix with his shoe heels to continue back on track in riding towards Oak Village; however, by this time the other two nomad warriors who had been sprinting through the Grass Terrain Fields have now caught up with Raven and Felix. One of the nomad warriors angrily charges forward and jumps up high in the air towards Raven and Felix; as he jumps to a height just above Felix's big black body, he manages to push Raven off Felix's black back and follows him as he holds on to Raven's chest. As Raven and the nomad warrior both fly through the air towards the ground from Felix's big black back, Raven unintentionally drops his white nunchuck that he had in his hand and both him and the nomad warrior on top of him crash-land on the ground in a painful thud.

Raven blinks hard and looks up in a daze as he sees the nomad warrior on top of him, swinging his axe down upon Raven's confused and frightened face. Raven's previous training in taekwondo has enabled him to learn quick reflexes, especially in times of dangerous situations; in a split second, Raven quickly grabs the small sharp silver dagger Parrot gave him in Pine Village from one of his brown boots. Raven reaches his arm in front of his chest and stabs the small sharp silver dagger fiercely into the side of the nomad warrior's neck. Blood starts to squirt out from the nomad warrior's neck, and the nomad warrior screeches in horrific pain as he feels the sharp pain of the dagger splitting his arteries and muscles in his neck. Raven, although a bit injured from the fall to the ground off Felix's big black back, manages to find the strength in his hands to push the nomad warrior from top of him. The nomad warrior quickly dies because of the deep stab wound to his neck from Raven's small sharp silver dagger, as he falls to the ground beside Raven in the Grass Terrain Fields.

RAVEN'S HEART IS pounding fast and he is breathing deeply as he has become winded from the fall he had off Felix to the ground; he is also feeling pain in the top part at the back of his head and in his back muscles and bones again because of the fall to the ground from Felix's big black back. Everything seems like a slow blur to Raven at the moment, as he is still dazed from hitting the ground hard, but he is also feeling adrenaline and anxiety as he has never been in a life-threatening situation like this before. Raven looks up at the clear blue sky with small flecks of grey clouds floating across it, as he hears the other nomad warrior screeching and shouting loudly from behind him. Raven, confused and afraid, creates an image of Emerald's beautiful face with her sparkling blue eyes, tender lips, and cheerful smile in his mind, which enables his whole body to be engulfed with feelings of love for Emerald, giving him the energy required for him to attempt defeating the nomad warrior behind him and return to Oak Village for Emerald and his date to Wolf's coronation celebration festival.

The nomad warrior continues to screech and shout while slashing his metal sword from side to side as he draws closer to Raven, who is still lying on his back upon the ground of the Grass Terrain Fields. Raven rolls from his back on to his front and pushes with his hands to help him get up from the grass and mud; he scans his immediate area with his eyes to search for his white nunchuck that he had dropped when he fell from Felix's big black back. After quickly locating the white nunchuck, he picks it up and stands up straight to fight with the approaching nomad warrior.

The nomad warrior comes and stands in front of Raven; he quickly tries to stab Raven in the head with his metal sword. Raven ducks and narrowly misses the nomad warrior's metal sword's blow. Raven stands back up straight and swings his white nunchuck around in front of him, using his skills he learnt when he was trained in taekwondo, and he smacks the white nunchuck at the nomad warrior that hits him rigidly on the head. The nomad warrior becomes momentarily stunned due to the blow from one of the white nunchucks that causes him step a couple of paces back. The nomad warrior becomes angry, and he furiously thrusts his metal sword again at Raven, which spitefully cuts Raven's left arm near his shoulder. Raven yells in pain as he feels his arm's skin being sliced by the metal sword's sharp edge.

Raven quickly composes himself in order to defend himself; he jumps up into the air and kicks the metal sword out of the nomad warrior's right hand, and the metal sword flies promptly through the air and lands upon the ground behind them. The nomad warrior looks at Raven heatedly due to his right hand hurting from Raven's kick. The nomad warrior tries to punch Raven hard in the face, but Raven speedily dashes to the side to avoid the punch from the nomad warrior and quickly pulls out the other white nunchuck from his grey coat pocket and swings both the white nunchucks around his hands and shoulders while continuously hitting the nomad warrior around the face and head. As the nomad warrior is being hit in the face and head by Raven's tough white nunchucks, it makes him stumble back, at which he is finally knocked out due to the consistent blows of the white nunchucks, and he falls backwards hard to the ground.

Raven stops swinging both his nunchucks and bends over in exhaustion, putting his hand across his chest to try and grab his full breath back. Raven looks up in shock to see what he has just done to the nomad warriors, who are all now lying on the ground dead or unconscious. Felix circles around Raven, also huffing with his breath in anger towards the nomad warriors who had tried to attack Raven and him. Before Raven can dwell on what has happened with regard to the fight he just had with the nomad warriors, he suddenly notices small black smoke arising from the big wooden fence that surrounds

Oak Village at the furthest east direction; this small black smoke turns into small grey coloured clouds that start floating across the sky.

Raven begins to fear about what is currently happening in Oak Village, especially since the nomad warriors he has just fought do not appear to be like normal nomad warrior. Raven, without hesitation, quickly puts both his white nunchucks back in his grey coat pockets and runs over to the dead nomad warrior in order to pull out the small sharp silver dagger lodged in the nomad warrior's neck, and Raven places the small sharp silver dagger back in the side of one of his grey boots. Raven runs back over to Felix and climbs back on top of his big black back, who is full of energy and adrenaline. Raven looks up in the far distance and once again glares at Oak Village, where thicker black smoke can be seen rising from the wooden fence in the far east direction.

'Emerald!' anxiously speaks Raven aloud as his heart squeezes at the thought of something bad happening to her or any other villager in Oak Village. Raven firmly holds tightly on to Felix's brown rope reins and kicks both his heels against Felix's side. Felix empowers his strong muscles to lift himself up and holds his hooves high in the air again and makes a loud sound from his mouth; as his hooves hit the ground, he begins to gallop swiftly at his fastest pace across the Grass Terrain Fields, crossing back over the cobbled road and on to the other Grass Terrain Fields to take the shortest route possible towards the east entrance wooden gate of Oak Village.

Six

THE SUN IS gleaming down from the sky upon the vast Grass Terrain Fields in the north direction of the Planet of Phoenix; the wind flows through the sky, moving the faint clustered smoke to form clouds that drift high above Oak Village. The Oak Village crowd in front of the small coronation celebration wooden stage in the south direction of the Oak Village square are unaware of the increasing grey clouds passing by in the sky as they are excited and joyful about Wolf's anticipated entrance upon the small wooden coronation celebration stage. The claps, cheers, and chants from the Oak Village crowd increase in in volume for their honourable leader Wolf to greet the crowd on his third year of being the Oak Village leader. Opal stands up graciously from her small wooden throne upon the middle of the small wooden coronation celebration stage and smiles radiantly at the Oak Village crowd, who begin to quieten to hear Opal's announcement.

'Villagers of Oak, Pine, and Willow Villages, welcome to the third year coronation celebration of Oak's Village glorious leader, Wolf!' announces Opal loudly. The Oak guards, who are holding brass trumpets at the sides of the small wooden stage, start to blow on their trumpets in honour of Wolf.

'Please welcome my husband and your valiant leader of Oak Village, Wolf!' remarks Opal as she turns her head softly to look at the red curtain that is at the right side of the small wooden stage from where Wolf will be entering through. After hearing his name announced by Opal, Wolf takes a deep breath and slowly opens the long red curtain from the right side of the small coronation celebration wooden stage; he proudly walks across it in a stylish manner to his big wooden throne that is placed in the centre of the small wooden stage. As Wolf happily walks across the small wooden stage, he turns to look, smile, and wave at the Oak Village crowd who are chanting and cheering for him. As Wolf reaches his big wooden throne, he stands in front of it for a few minutes alongside Opal and Leopard, both of whom are also standing up smiling and waving at the Oak Village crowd.

Wolf sits down on his big wooden throne followed by Opal and Leopard as the Oak guards stop playing their brass trumpets; the Oak Village crowd continue to roar and cheer with joyfulness and excitement. A couple of Wolf's Oak guards who are also standing upon the small wooden stage begin to gather the various types of silver knight's armour from one end of the stage upon one of the wooden stands and bring them over to Wolf, where they aid him in putting the knighthood armour on. The silver knighthood armour includes Wolf's silver sword and silver shield that had been given to him by Jackal when he was upon his deathbed. He had explained to Wolf at the time that the silver sword and shield had been passed down his family's bloodline since his great-grandfather Hyena who was the first leader of Oak Village. Hyena had the silver sword and silver shield especially made by a master sword smith from Falcon City in honour of him becoming the first leader of Oak Village when it was built over 200 years ago.

Wolf kneels to the floor of the small wooden stage in front of his big wooden throne, and then the Oak guards at the side of the small coronation celebration wooden stage begin to play their brass trumpets again. As the two Oak guards who collected the silver knight's armour from one of the wooden stands at the side of the stage continue to fit them upon Wolf, while one of the Oak guards holds on to the silver sword and silver shield ready to give to Wolf when he stands up, another Oak guard from the back of the stage collects Wolf's silver crown and walks back to the throne where Wolf is kneeling and gives Wolf's silver crown to Opal. Opal stands up slowly from her small wooden throne; she waits for the two Oak guards to move to either side of Wolf after they have finished helping Wolf with his silver knight's armour and walks in front of Wolf, holding the silver crown above his head as he is still kneeling on the floor of the small wooden stage.

'This crown that has been passed down the bloodline of Wolf's ancestors since the development of Oak Village by Hyena many decades ago resembles the hope and glory of our Oak Village and how it has stood the test of time unlike many other fallen villages. This crown is presented to the worthy bloodline my husband Wolf possesses, but more than that, this silver crown is worn by those men who are moral, valiant, and courageous and who have fought for, protected, and ruled our Oak Village for countless years. We are blessed on this beautiful day to once again place this crown on Wolf's head in honour of his three-year coronation celebration and let there be many more coronation celebrations to come for Wolf and the descendants of his bloodline like our son, Leopard,' says Opal humbly, placing the silver crown upon Wolf's head as the Oak Village crowd clap, cheer, and chant for Wolf. Unexpectedly, some of the Oak villagers who are at the back of the Oak Village crowd that is in front of the small coronation celebration wooden stage begin to scream and shout in terror.

'Fire! Fire!' shout some of the Oak villagers nervously. The rest of the Oak Village crowd hears the pleas of the Oak villagers shouting at the back of the Oak Village crowd and abruptly stop their clapping and cheering to quickly turn around to see what all the commotion is about. Wolf, Opal, and the Oak guards standing on top of the small coronation celebration wooden stage also quickly look up in the distance in the north-west direction of Oak Village from where the shouts of the Oak villagers are coming and gaze up in shock to see an immense black smoke cloud thrusting into the air and sky above Oak Village because the big wooden fence below it is covered in an intense bright orange fire with agitated burning flames. The rest of the Oak Village crowd who have now also seen the black smoke cloud and scorching fire start to panic and begin to run frantically around the Oak Village square everywhere, which causes them to bump into each other, knocking not only villagers over to the ground but also some of the small wooden shops, stalls, and coronation celebration items that are displayed throughout the Oak Village square.

Barious, who is standing next to Ruby and Emerald in the middle of the Oak Village crowd, quickly reacts to the situation in order to keep as many of the villagers as calm as possible; so he reaches out with his hands to gather a group of men Oak villagers who are nearby him, which includes the Oakus Church vicar and Pinus Church vicar.

'Come on, Oak villagers, let's get some water in buckets from the wells and put this fire out before any damage is done to our valuable Oak Village!' orders Barious as the group of men Oak villagers nod to show Barious that they understand the situation and quickly start running towards the wells that are near the big wooden fence that is burning. Barious then quickly turns towards Ruby and Emerald. 'Ruby, Emerald, run to the front of the coronation stage and stay close to it and the Oak guards as much as possible. You will be a lot safer there.'

'But what about you, Barious?' exclaims Ruby, having worried thoughts.

'I'll be fine, Ruby. Don't worry about me or this unexplainable fire. Us Oak villagers will put it out without a problem. Now please go quickly to the front of the coronation stage and be careful of the rushing and frantic village crowd,' states Barious as he smiles at Ruby in a comforting manner.

'Be safe, Barious, and make sure you come and find us at the front of the coronation stage when the fire is put out. You're a very brave human,' says Ruby as she gives Barious a firm hug.

'Please be careful, Barious, I don't know how Raven would cope if something bad happened to you also,' says a concern Emerald.

'Everything will be all right, sweetheart. Now go with your mother to a less hectic location. I will come back and find you both shortly,' replies Barious as he puts his hand on Emerald's shoulder and smiles. Ruby smiles back at Barious and then quickly grabs Emerald's hand to quickly hurry through the panicky Oak Village crowd towards the front of the small wooden coronation celebration stage. Barious rushes over towards the burning big wooden fence to rejoin the group of men Oak villagers, including the Oakus Church vicar and Pinus Church vicar, who have quickly gone and gathered wooden buckets from behind the small wooden shops and stalls surrounding the Oak Village square, and then with the other group of men Oak villagers, they begin filling these wooden buckets up from wells located near the big wooden fence in the north-west of Oak Village.

The Oak Village crowd continues to run frantically throughout the Oak Village square, and some Oak villagers accidentally bump into some of the men Oak villagers who are trying to carry the wooden buckets towards the burning big wooden fence, knocking the water from the wooden buckets on to the ground. The group of men Oak villagers finally reach the burning big wooden fence in the north-west of Oak Village that have become more burnt and destroyed by the heated fire. This group of men Oak villagers now quickly form themselves into two lines so that they are able to pass between them the wooden buckets with water in them from the closest wells to the burning big wooden fence. The men Oak villager at the end of the line throw the water inside the bucket on to the fire of the big wooden fence, which aids in decreasing the intense fire slightly.

The heat and smoke coming from the burning big wooden fence cause much discomfort for the men Oak villager closest to it; thus, the men Oak villagers change positions with each other quickly when it is safe to do so. These empty wooden buckets are then passed back down the line of the men Oak villagers towards the wells so that the Oak villager nearest to the well can refill it with water and pass it back down the line of Oak villagers again.

Back on the small coronation celebration wooden stage, Wolf has stood up from kneeling quickly and has grabbed his silver sword and shield from the Oak guard who was holding it.

'Opal, quickly take Leopard and go back to our house. Lock all the doors and hide somewhere safe. Take as many of my Oak guards with you for yours and Leopard's protection,' states Wolf in apprehension.

'No! I'm not leaving you, Wolf,' remarks Opal, clutching on to his hand that is gripped tightly around his silver sword.

'You must. Yours and Leopard's safety is my first priority. If I know you two are safe, it will then help me concentrate on handling this strange situation accordingly and carry out my duty in protecting Oak villagers and its villagers. I'll come back for you both once the fire has been put out and the hysterics of the Oak villagers has calmed down. You and Leopard mean the world to me and nothing will stop me from returning to your arms,' replies Wolf as he firmly hugs and kisses Opal and Leopard reassuringly, and Opal smiles lovingly back at Wolf.

'Please be careful, my love. There's something that just doesn't feel right about this situation,' exclaims Opal.

'Oak guards, take Opal and Leopard back to my house and guard them with your lives, and you other Oak guards come with me to diminish this fire urgently!' shouts Wolf urgently. Wolf takes a deep look for one last time into Opal's beautiful hazel eyes; he strengthens his grip around his silver sword and silver shield, and he and twenty-six of his Oak guards who have just listened to his orders from upon or at the front of the small coronation celebration wooden stage begin to scurry through the core of the panicking Oak Village crowd in the middle of the Oak Village square, after mixing throughout the Oak villagers; they hurriedly make it over to the burning big wooden fence in the north-west of Oak Village, which has now been completely engulfed by large heated fiery flames.

Opal, who had watched Wolf climb down from the big wooden stage and then lost sight of him as he passed through the running Oak Village crowd, quickly picks up Leopard and hurries away along with six other Oak guards. These were the guards who were on top of the small coronation celebration wooden stage, who either played the brass trumpets or gave Wolf his silver knight's armour and weapons; they all hastily run across the small wooden stage behind the long red curtain at the right side of the big wooden stage. After passing through the long red curtain that leads them quickly out of the Oak Village square, as it is built at the very edge of it in the south direction, they all hurry back to Wolf and Opal's big wooden house that is located at the north-east side of Oak Village. As they travelled over one of the wooden paths that is away from the Oak Village square, they pass minimal scurrying Oak villagers, that enable them to avoid being bashed or knocked into. Many of the Oak villagers such as the woman and children will stay within the Oak Village square.

RUBY AND EMERALD after much caution finally make it through the terrified Oak Village crowd, who are running throughout the Oak

Village square, to reach the front of the small coronation celebration wooden stage. Other women and children Oak villagers also wait huddled together, panicking, in front of the big wooden stage while looking up anxiously in the far distance at the burning big wooden fence in the far north-west of Oak Village. Ruby and Emerald join the huddled women and children Oak villagers and smile at them to try and keep them calm.

'Don't worry, everything will be all right and back to normal soon,' says Emerald to one of the small children beside her, who has tears streaming down her eyes. Surprisingly, everyone in Oak Village begins to hear a large thudding destructive bang followed by war cries and chants that pierce through the hearts of all the Oak villagers throughout Oak Village. Lieutenant Triton, who is riding on top of his powerful strong black rhino, smashes viciously straight through the burning big wooden fence in the north-west. Pieces of the burning wood fence fly into the air and land on top of the villagers, causing minor head injuries, or right into Oak villagers, cutting, scraping, or burning some of the Oak villagers in the face or chest.

As Lieutenant Triton, who is on top of the black rhino, breaks through the burning big wooden fence, he tramples its muscular hooves cruelly over some men Oak villagers who are closest to the burning big wooden fence; these men Oak villagers shout and scream in excruciating pain. The black rhino uses its big black horn on top of its head to knock over and stab some of the other men Oak villagers who are using water buckets to put out the blazing fire. These men Oak villagers either fall hard to the ground or are jabbed by the black rhino's black horn, causing a painful wound. When at this point the men Oak villagers are stuck on to the black rhino's black horn, Lieutenant Triton uses his strong hands to grasp their heads and twists them firmly until their necks break, which kills them.

The Oak villagers, attacked or injured by the flaming bits of wood from the big wooden fence, burning through their tender skin, shriek in pain because of excruciating burn marks or when blood pours out from the cuts and piercing wounds. The 184 Potorians on their black horses, carrying metal swords and axes, who have accompanied Lieutenant Triton from Lord Scartor's Lair of Death to Oak Village, also break and charge through other parts of the burning big wooden fence. The Potorians while riding on their horses continue charging deep into Oak Village, slicing helpless and defenceless Oak villagers' heads of with their metal swords or throwing their metal axes into Oak villagers' chests and heads, which kill them because of the painful wounds and injuries.

Another Potorian riding on his horse approaches one of the wells where the Oakus Church vicar is fetching water from the well to fill up the wooden bucket. The Potorians throws his axe from a close distance, which slices through the chest of the Oakus Church vicar, killing him instantly, and as he falls to the ground, his hand releases the grip he has on the wooden bucket. As the wooden bucket drops to the floor, it breaks and the water spills out from it. The whole of Oak Village has in a few short moments turned into chaos and anarchy invoked by the intense frenzied fire and brutal murders caused by Lieutenant Triton and the Potorians as well as the black smoky cloud erupting through the air of Oak Village, which causes darkness due to blocking of the sun rays. Many Oak villagers from among the crowd standing in front of the small coronation celebration wooden stage see and hear the devastation caused by the attack by Lieutenant Triton and the Potorians. The Oak villagers cry or scream terrifyingly and attempt to run from the Oak Village square into their small wooden houses, cottages, and shops in unbelievable fear.

'Find the anomaly crystal. Leave no one alive!' roars Lieutenant Triton to the Potorians who are closest to him near the burning and now semi-broken big wooden fence; the fire has now started to spread across the whole of the big wooden fence that surrounds the perimeter of Oak Village. Barious, who is also near the burning big wooden fence, overhears Lieutenant Triton shouting about the anomaly crystal. Barious quickly realises that this battle has been caused by the evil doings of Lord Scartor and he has to do whatever he can to protect Oak Village and Raven from any harm. Barious anxiously looks around him and sees a long piece of broken wood on the ground, which has sharp burnt edges at one end of it.

Barious scampers over to the long piece of broken wood on the ground while coughing because of the intoxicating black smoke being released from the burning big wooden fence. Barious bends over and grabs the long piece of broken wood from the ground, and as he stands back up, he holds it tightly out in front of him, which causes some splinters from this long piece of broken wood get lodged in his brittle hands. Barious gallantly runs towards Lieutenant Triton, who is still on top of his black rhino, not far from him. Barious swiftly positions the long piece of broken wood so that the sharp burnt edge at one end of it will hit Lieutenant Triton in the chest between the gaps of his metal armour. Lieutenant Triton is attentive and sees from the corner of his eyes a desperate Barious running towards him with the long broken piece of wood held out in front of him.

Lieutenant Triton reacts to this attempted attack by swinging his golden chain with the spiked iron ball at the end of it around his head fiercely; he then whips the chain forcefully to swing it straight at Barious. The spiked iron ball crashes into Barious's chest, which pierces deep into his skin and shatters his rib bones. The force of the spiked iron ball blow sends Barious flying sharply high up into the air for several metres before he crash-lands down into a small wooden cottage. Parts of the small wooden cottage break down to the ground as Barious crashes through it, and large broken pieces of wood from the small wooden cottage land directly on top of Barious, horrifically causing him intense tremor and agony.

Lieutenant Triton laughs loudly at the sight of Barious crashing into the small wooden cottage; he again swings his golden chain with the spiked iron ball at the end of it around his head and hits the spikes attached to the iron ball into many men, women, and children Oak villagers' heads and chests as Lieutenant Triton passes ferociously through Oak Village in the south direction towards the Oak Village square. Pinus Church's vicar who is also near Lieutenant Triton watches on in horror at the helpless Oak villagers getting torn apart by Lieutenant Triton's weapon. The Pinus Church vicar also makes a foolish attempt in trying to stop the spiked iron ball from crashing into a woman Oak villager after Lieutenant Triton directs it towards her, by getting in the way of the attack. The Pinus Church vicar receives the blow of the spiked iron ball through his head and skull, and pieces of brain and blood squirt out everywhere over nearby Oak villagers. These Oak villagers are then also killed by Lieutenant Triton, who swings his golden chain with the spiked iron ball at the end of it around his head, smashing into their faces, shattering their teeth, nose, and eyes, which kills them immediately.

WOLF, ACCOMPANIED BY his twenty-six Oak guards, is hastily
running towards the burning big wooden fence in the north-west of
Oak Village. As they run towards the burning big wooden fence, they
shockingly see the legion of Potorians and Lieutenant Triton causing
havoc throughout Oak Village; they feel sick with grief on witnessing
the horrendous killing of the innocent Oak villagers, which spurs
Wolf on more to quickly take control of the situation and defeat
Lieutenant Triton and the Potorian army in battle.

'Quick! Oak guards, saddle upon our horses and kill these devil
bastards immediately,' shouts Wolf, as he changes his direction to
go retrieve his horse, on realising that he will not be able to defeat
Lieutenant Trion, who is on top of his black rhino, if he also doesn't
fight against him sitting upon his horse too. A group of the Oak
guards also rapidly change direction and run alongside Wolf to
retrieve their horses that are resting close by in a farmer's field in
the north side of Oak Village, while the rest of the group of Oak
guards draw their metal swords from their belts and continue in their
direction, to begin fighting against the Potorians who are currently
slicing the heads of helpless Oak villagers.

As the group of Oak villagers who continue running in the same
direction approach the fighting Potorians, the Potorians stop killing
the helpless Oak villagers, who quickly scamper away on seeing the
running Oak guards. The Potorians begin shouting war cries at the
Oak guards in an attempt to scare and distract them before they
gallop on their horses to charge straight at the running Oak guards.
As the Potorians gallop into this group of Oak guards, they quickly
control their horses to trample upon them or stab the Oak guards in
the face with their metal swords. Within minutes, this group of Oak
guards are slayed brutally by the Potorians on their horses and their
bodies covered in cuts and blood fall dramatically to the ground.

Wolf and the other Oak Guards quickly reach the farm field in the
north. As they hear the screams and shouts of other Oak guards and
Oak villagers getting horribly murdered by the unmerciful Potorians,
they are infuriated by this horrific situation. Wolf and his Oak guards
quickly scramble over the wooden fence surrounding the farm field
and jump upon their horses in order to race frantically back towards
the wooden fence; as they jump on their horses high over it, they
continue galloping to the battle occurring in the north-west and the

Oak Village square among the Oak guards, Oak villagers, Lieutenant Triton, and the Potorians.

A brutal fight continues throughout most of Oak Village, in which many Oak villagers, Oak guards, and some Potorians are killed in cold blood. As Wolf and the group of Oak guards gallop hastily upon their horses across the wooden paths through the darkened atmosphere that has now covered Oak Village due to the burning big wooden fence and thick cloudy smoke, they encounter small numbers of Potorians throughout Oak Village. Wolf and his Oak guards quickly fight against these Potorians in an attempt to protect the nearest Oak villagers who are dashing around Oak Village, looking for places to hide. Wolf and his Oak guards on their horses thrust in front of them and then clash their metal swords with the Potorians' metal axes and swords, who are also on their horses. Wolf and his Oak guards use their shields to protect them against the blows from the Potorians' metal swords and axes. This hesitant fight continues for many minutes, during which Wolf demonstrates his leadership and fighting abilities by rallying his Oak guards around him and forcing an offensive fighting tactic in order to stab the Potorians quickly before they have much of a chance to fight back.

Wolf and his Oak guards quickly kill some of these Potorians by slicing their heads off with their swords and stabbing them through the hearts and chests while adopting their offensive position that cause some of the Potorians to deflect their combat tactics. However, some of Wolf's guards also get stabbed in their heads and faces by the unforgiving Potorians, and unfortunately, they fall from their horses and die before they hit the hard ground beneath them. The horses of the Oak guards or Potorians who have fallen from them panic and indistinctly gallop wildly throughout Oak Village, which cause them incidentally to trample over running Oak villagers, causing more deaths. Wolf becomes overwhelmed with grief at the sight of so many of his Oak guards and Oak villagers getting killed; he shouts in anger and causes more quick and durable blows with his silver sword to the heads of the Potorians he is fighting against.

Throughout the rest of Oak Village, the other Potorians who are on the horses brace further and deeper in Oak Village towards the Oak Village square. As they enter forcefully the Oak Village square by trampling on top of wooden stalls and shops, along with small

Oak village children, the Oak villagers who are huddled together at the front of the small coronation celebration wooden stage begin to scream and cry in terror. The Potorians laugh at the sight of these frightened Oak villagers and kick their heels into their horses' sides, leading them to begin charging at the Oak villagers in front of the small wooden stage. Ruby glances up in fear to see several Potorians on their horses charging savagely towards the Oak village crowd; she instantly grabs Emerald's hand tightly without a second thought and runs along with her out of the Oak Village crowd standing by the small wooden stage, pushing other Oak villagers out of the way.

Emerald and Ruby, holding firmly on to Emerald's hand, both erratically sprint towards their house down one of the wooden and cobbled paths in the east direction of Oak Village after they exited the Oak Village square. A Potorian, who is charging upon his horse at the Oak Village crowd near the east side of the Oak Village square, curiously sees Ruby and Emerald running out of the Oak Village square and down one of the wooden and cobbled paths in the east direction. After momentarily thinking that it could be something to do with the anomaly crystal, the Potorian forcefully steers the rope reins of his horse to change the horse's direction and also gallops out of the Oak Village square, chasing after Ruby and Emerald in the east direction. As the Potorian leaves the Oak Village square, the other charging Potorians charge viciously into the Oak Village crowd and begin killing every single one of them as quickly and inhumanely as possible. The Potorian rapidly approaches Emerald and Ruby; he violently gallops in between Ruby and Emerald in an attempt to separate them, as they are holding each other's hands. Emerald hears the sound of a galloping horse behind them and quickly looks over her shoulder; she is nervous on seeing the Potorian on horseback coming speedily towards her and Ruby, and she decides in a split second to make a difficult but necessary decision.

'I love you, Mother!' shouts Emerald as she pulls her hand away from Ruby's grip and pushes Ruby heavily to one side of the wooden and cobbled path. Ruby in shock loses her balance and falls over to the ground and rolls down a small grass hill that is next to the wooden and cobbled path. Ruby hurts herself on her hip slightly due to the push to the ground, but as she rolls down the small grass hill and loses sight of Emerald, she feels like her heart has shattered into a million pieces. After Emerald pushes Ruby out of the way, she continues running down the wooden and cobbled path to distract the Potorian's attention from Ruby's disappearance down the small grass hill.

As Emerald runs, she decides to confuse the horse that the Potorian is riding upon by doing an arrow spring followed by a row of several backflips across the ground. The horse that the Potorian is riding becomes surprised by Emerald's backflips and reduces its galloping speed; however, the Potorian quickly reacts by yanking on the horse's rope reins to continue its galloping at full speed along the wooden and cobbled path across which Emerald is backflipping. Within a few moments, the Potorian upon his galloping horse catches up with Emerald, and he manoeuvres his long and strong arm to grab Emerald while she is doing a backflip. After grabbing her, the Potorians spins Emerald around by using his sturdy arm and pulls her to be positioned in front of him on his horse. He holds Emerald tightly as he yanks the rope reins again with his other hand to turn the horse around in order to ride back towards the burning big wooden fence in the north-west. Terrified, Emerald attempts to look back over her shoulder, but wretchedly doesn't see any sight of her mother Ruby as the Potorian's horse quickly gallops away from the small grass hill.

Back in the Oak Village square, the Potorians have finished slaughtering all the Oak villagers in front of the small coronation celebration wooden stage and now begin burning and tearing apart and destroying the small wooden stage to search for the anomaly crystal. On not finding any sign of the anomaly crystal in the Oak Village square or by the small coronation celebration wooden stage, they begin to ride through Oak Village to enter the small wooden houses, cottages, and shops, where they fiercely kick through the wooden front doors. Upon entering the small wooden houses, cottages, and shops, they instantly kill the Oak villagers who have been hiding in their homes.

After killing the Oak villagers, these Potorians ransack the small wooden houses, flats, and shops, looking everywhere and anywhere for the anomaly crystal; they even disturbingly request some of the Oak villagers to tell them where the anomaly crystal is before killing them. The frightened Oak villagers say nothing and give no answer regarding the whereabouts of the anomaly crystal as they have never heard of it or seen it before. Hence, the Oak villagers remain silent, cry, or scream that they don't know where the anomaly crystal is, hoping that the Potorians would spare theirs and their families' lives, but the Potorians still cruelly stab them with their metal swords and axes anyways, killing them.

AFTER AN HOUR from the start of the Oak Village battle, nearly all the Oak villagers and Wolf's Oak guards have been brutally murdered in the painful battle. After Wolf kills the Potorians on horses he is fighting against, he quickly gallops on his horse towards the north-west direction of Oak Village, where Lieutenant Triton is still killing the last of the men Oak villagers who are attempting to put out the fire with water buckets. As Wolf approaches, he desperately kicks his heels in the side of his horse in order for it to reach full speed for charging at Lieutenant Triton.

When Wolf is only metres away from Lieutenant Triton upon his black rhino near the burning big wooden fence, he infuriatedly tries to stab Lieutenant Triton in the heart with his silver sword. Lieutenant Triton quickly swerves his black rhino to the side, scarcely missing the sword blow by Wolf. Lieutenant Triton yanks the gold chains he has round the black rhino's neck in order to get the black rhino to do a full circle so that Lieutenant Triton can now charge with the black rhino's big white horn going deep into the back of Wolf's horse. Wolf's horse gets horribly stabbed by the black rhino's big black horn deep in its tough skin; the horse in explicit pain dies while falling hard to the ground. At the same time, Wolf loses his grip on the rope reins of his horse and also falls from the horse and lands on to the ground suddenly in a crushing thud; he receives bruises from the fall, and his silver crown also drops from his head and rolls a little bit across the ground.

Wolf stands up in the midst of the cloudy black smoke, feeling the extensive heat and fumes of the burning flames around him; he looks around to see the mayhem of the last remaining Oak villagers being slaughtered by the Potorians. Lieutenant Triton jumps down to the ground from his black rhino near Wolf and quickly swings his golden chain with the spiked iron ball at the end of it around his head and aims it straight at Wolf. Wolf quickly blocks the blow of the iron spiked ball with his silver shield, but the spikes of the iron ball pierce sharply through the silver shield and scrapes across Wolf's chest, causing it to be cut open, and a part of his intestines pops out from the wound. Lieutenant Triton fiercely yanks the golden chain back towards him with his powerful muscles, pulling the silver shield ferociously from Wolf's hand and forcing Wolf to be pulled over to the ground. Lieutenant Triton crashes the golden chain with the iron spiked iron ball at the end of it hard to the ground so that Wolf's silver shield breaks away and releases the iron spiked ball away from it. Wolf, in pain and shock, quickly uses his strength and determination to pull himself up from the ground; he clenches his silver shield that has been passed down to him from his father Jackal and raises it high in the air, as he sprints towards Lieutenant Triton.

'I'm going to send you to hell!' shouts Wolf loudly.

'Ha ha ha . . .' laughs Lieutenant Triton as he swiftly swings his golden chain with the spiked iron ball at the end of it around his head again and thrusts the full force of it straight into Wolf's horrified face. The spikes of the iron ball pierce through Wolf's eyes, which cause him to lose his sight immediately, as well as the blow breaks his nose and shatters his teeth, which cause him to be killed instantly. Wolf's dead body falls to his knees as blood and bone squirt out from his disfigured face. Lieutenant Triton yanks the golden chain forcefully again, and the spiked iron ball pops out of Wolf's face, leaving Wolf to fall face down to the ground in silence.

Near Wolf and Opal's big wooden house located in the north-east direction of Oak Village, three Potorians who have been searching for the anomaly crystal in houses close by reach Wolf and Opal's house and brusquely break through the wooden front door with their strong horses as the wooden front door is bolted firmly from inside the house. After the wooden front door of Wolf and Opal's house is broken through, the Potorians jump down from their horses and quickly run through the house, killing Wolf's six Oak guards who had stayed near the wooden front door in order to protect Opal and Leopard. These six Oak guards are quickly and horribly killed by the Potorians as they take a sudden offensive tactic and attack the Oak guards with their metal axes several times in the head and stabbing them in the hearts and faces with their metal swords. The quick and painful deaths of the six Oak guards makes Opal panic in fear for Wolf's and Leopard's lives.

Opal locks herself in her bedroom on the second floor of her and Wolf's big wooden house; she quickly puts Leopard underneath her and Wolf's big bed. Leopard starts crying on hearing all the loud commotion and shouting happening on the first floor of their big wooden house.

'Shh, Leopard, you must stay quiet and you'll be safe. Mummy will come back for you, I promise,' whispers Opal quietly as she kisses Leopard on his forehead after she has placed him carefully beneath the bed. Opal then makes sure the white bed quilt that is made of sheep's wool covers the entire part below the bed so Leopard could not be seen. Opal hurries towards the bedroom door and struggles as she tries to move her wooden bedside table from the side of her bed and lodge it as a barricade in front of the bedroom door. After the Potorians heartlessly kill all the six Oak guards on the first floor inside Wolf and Opal's big wooden house, they charge up the steep wooden stairs to search for the anomaly crystal; as they reach the bedroom door, behind which Opal and Leopard are hiding, the Potorians furiously try to kick it down.

'Leave me alone!' shouts Opal nervously.

'Give us the anomaly crystal and we will,' laughs one of the Potorians who continues kicking the bedroom door.

'What is the anomaly crystal? I don't even know what you're on about,' yells Opal in terrifying panic. After continuing to kick the bedroom door strongly with their feet, which doesn't manage to break through the bedroom door, the Potorians start to smash through the wooden pieces of the bedroom door with their metal axes. Opal screams loudly as she sees the sharp edges of the metal axes smash through the wood of her bedroom. Opal quickly moves away from the bedroom door as a big hole is made by the Potorians' metal axes, which gives them the opportunity to put their hands through the door and push the bedside table out of the way. One of the Potorians sturdily kicks the bedroom door again and it opens wide; another two of the Potorians rush through into the bedroom and grab Opal, where they then take her out of the bedroom and start forcing her down the steep wooden stairs.

As the Potorians holding Opal continue to scurry down the steep wooden stairs, they all hear a cry from Leopard in Opal's bedroom, as he hears the screams and shouts of his mother. Another one of the Potorians pushes past Opal, and the two Potorians who are currently on the steep wooden stairs run back up into Opal's bedroom. Opal desperately tries to fight off the other two Potorians who are holding on to her and attempts to climb back up the steep wooden stairs after the other Potorians who have just ran past them towards the bedroom. In Opal's futile escape attempt, she gets hit in the face by one of the Potorians who is struggling to hold on to her, which momentarily stuns her. The other Potorian who had rushed into Opal's bedroom has a quick look around but can't see anyone until he hears some more murmuring from the big bed; he stares at the big bed for a brief moment and walks eagerly up to this bed. He lifts up the bed quilt that is made of sheep's wool and sees Leopard there, crying. The Potorian releases his grip on the bed quilt made of sheep's wool and stands back up. The Potorian lifts his metal sword above the big bed, and without hesitation, he continuously stabs the metal sword deep through the bed, which kills Leopard coldheartedly.

'No!' shouts Opal desperately; the Potorian who is holding her punches her strongly in the face again out of irritation, which now knocks her out and makes her unconscious. The two Potorians continue carrying Opal hastily out of Wolf and Opal's big wooden house and climb back upon their horses, where the other Potorian passes Opal's unconscious body to the other Potorians sitting on his horse. The last Potorian who has just left Wolf and Opal's bedroom after killing Leopard and exited the big wooden house also quickly climbs back upon his horse.

'Finally, now let's get back to Lieutenant Triton,' says one of the Potorians.

'Wait!' says one of the Potorians mischievously as he climbs back down from his horse and runs over to a part of the burning big wooden fence that is located near Wolf and Opal's big wooden house, especially since the original fire has spread. The Potorian brings his axe down onto the burning big wooden fence in order to cut a piece of wood from it that is still in flames; he holds the end of the burning wood and swiftly runs over to Wolf and Opal's big wooden house and throws the burning piece of wood through the front wooden door.

Wolf and Opal's big wooden house quickly catches fire as everything in it is mostly made of wood, and the entire house burns down to the ground, while the Potorians who are carrying Opal now all ride on their horses back towards Lieutenant Triton in the north-west of Oak Village. Also by this time, in the Oak Village battle the fire from the north-west burning big wooden fence has continues to spread around and has now consumed the entire fence surrounding Oak Village.

The rest of the Potorians throughout Oak Village kill off either any Oak guards or Oak villagers who are still alive as they continue the last of the searching for the anomaly crystal in the small wooden houses, cottages, and shops. After hopelessly searching for a while, the Potorians decide to stop searching and leave the small wooden houses, cottages, and shops to mount their horses to ride back over to Lieutenant Triton, who is still by the burning big fence in the north-west of Oak Village. All the Potorians along with the two Potorians that are carrying Emerald and Opal on their horses start circling around Lieutenant Triton in the north-west of Oak Village, who has just finished the last of the Oak guards and Oak villagers in his area with his golden chain and the spiked iron ball at the end of it.

'The anomaly crystal is not here. I haven't been able to locate it at all by the crystal finding device. Interference may be blocking the transmitter signal!' states one of the Potorians on his horse, circling around Lieutenant Triton and fiddling with buttons upon a crystal finding device that had been built by Lord Scartor.

'Lord Scartor will not be pleased at all with this unfortunate news,' remarks Lieutenant Triton as he jumps back on top of his black rhino, and then his attention is drawn to the Potorians who are carrying Emerald and Opal upon their horses.

'Why are you carrying those pretty little things with you, Potorians?' asks Lieutenant Triton suspiciously.

'We've got to have some fun too, ha ha ha. Besides, we could torture these Oak villagers to get information from them or hold them as hostages in exchange for the anomaly crystal,' answers the Potorian who is carrying Emerald, covering her mouth with his strong hand as she squirms to break free from his grip.

'Fine! We have no choice but to go back to Lord Scartor without the anomaly crystal as it will have probably been moved from Oak Village by now. But you're right. At least, we can give the women Oak villagers to him as a gesture of faith that we will eventually find the anomaly crystal by tearing apart every village or even Falcon City if necessary. Let's go, Potorians!' shouts Lieutenant Triton to all the Potorians who are currently circling around him upon their horses.

Lieutenant Triton pulls the gold chain from around his black rhino's neck and starts riding on it through a passage made quickly by the circling Potorians and out of the burning big wooden fence in the north-west of Oak Village. The remaining 151 Potorians who have survived the battle of Oak Village upon their black horses, which include Emerald and Opal who are being carried on the horses by two Potorians, all begin to follow Lieutenant Triton and ride rapidly back through the burning big fence towards Lord Scartor's Lair of Death that resides upon the hazardous Crow Mountain amongst the Mountains of Doom in the far north-west direction of the Planet of Phoenix. Lieutenant Triton and the 151 Potorians including Emerald and Opal will need to pass through the Swamp Fields and Wastelands on their journey to Lord Scartor's Lair of Death, while they leave behind them a burnt-down and massacred Oak Village that now has rubble, broken wood, and dead Oak guards and Oak villagers all over the place.

Seven

RAVEN BREATHES STRONGLY as he continues to hold on firmly to the brown rope reins of the powerful galloping Felix as they head into Oak Village's east entrance wooden gate. The whole of Oak Village has now been covered with thick cloudy black smoke, as burnt wood, rubble, and dead humans lie everywhere throughout Oak Village. Upon entering the east entrance wooden gate of Oak Village, Raven feels the intense heat of the surroundings that has been engulfed by an intense fire, which has now condensed to small fires that are decreasing in size.

Raven in a dreadful panic pulls the brown rope reins of Felix suddenly to bring him to a halt; he jumps down from Felix's large back and looks around Oak Village in shock at the massacre Lieutenant Triton and the Potorians have caused to Oak Village and the villagers in it. Raven coughs as he breathes in the thick black smoke that lingers in the air covering Oak Village; Raven scans his eyes to look down the now dark and smoky wooden paths throughout Oak Village to look for any sign of Emerald, Barious, or Ruby. As Raven frantically looks around in the distance of Oak Village, he hears some faint sounds and murmurs from a few of the injured Oak guards and villagers, who are slowly dying on the wooden paths due to their bloody wounds and burnt bodies.

Raven coughs again because of the thick black intoxicating smoke that he inhales through his mouth into his lungs; he also again feels a sharp and unfamiliar feeling because of the intense heat of the small flames released due to the still burning small wooden houses, cottages, shops, and the last remaining sections of the big wooden fences. Raven in emotional horror scrambles back on to Felix's back and carefully kicks his heels into the sides of Felix for him to start trotting down the wooden paths through the now silent and desolate Oak Village. After steadily trotting down the wooden paths to the north of Oak Village, Raven riding on top of Felix enters the Oak Village square, looking for any Oak villagers or guards who still might be alive to offer an explanation for what had happened to Oak Village and assist Raven in his desperate search to find Emerald, Barious, and Ruby. The silence and occasional soft murmur Raven hears from the dying Oak villagers makes his heart bleed due to the sorrow of what has happened to Oak Village and the villagers he knew that used to live in it.

'Emerald! Barious! Ruby!' shouts Raven frantically in his loudest voice. Raven pulls the brown rope reins on Felix again to quickly make him gallop out of the Oak Village square, as he is not being able to cope with the horrific sight he has just witnessed of the hundreds of dead women and children villagers who are piled upon one another near the semi-broken coronation celebration wooden stage. Raven grips tightly on to the brown rope reins of Felix as he steers Felix towards the north-west edge of Oak Village to the big wooden fence, where Raven had assumed the fire had started. As Raven scans Oak Village, he notices that is the area where most of the Oak guards' and villagers' dead bodies lie still and silent upon the ground.

As Raven sitting upon Felix gallops to the north-west edge of Oak Village, the faint sounds and murmurs of the Oak villagers and guards who are dying begin to lessen. Raven quickly looks in the direction from where he hears the faint sounds of the dying Oak villagers and guards, but he can only slightly see the dead Oak villagers' and guards' bodies through the thick cloudy black smoke; with some of these dead bodies having had their heads and body limbs chopped off, it makes Raven feel sick from inside his stomach.

As Raven continues along the wooden paths in order to approach the big wooden fence at the north-west edge of Oak Village, he again sees many other Oak villagers' and guards' dead bodies lying on the ground just outside the front of their small wooden houses, cottages, and shops. The dead bodies of the Oak villagers are covered in bloody wounds with some metal swords and metal axes still sticking out of the bodies, which makes Raven think back to the fight he has had with the nomad warriors in the Grass Terrain Fields due to them also carrying the same weapons. Raven treads with Felix carefully in order to not trample on any of the Oak villagers' and guards' dead bodies.

'Emerald! Barious! Ruby! Wolf! Is anybody still alive?' cries Raven loudly. In the near distance, Barious hears the soft distressed sounds of Raven's voice.

'Raven, Raven!' coughs Barious quietly, which takes much of his diminishing energy to speak. At the sound of his name, Raven quickly looks around him in the hope of finding someone still alive; he quickly jumps down from Felix's large back and quickly searches the area around him to find the villager who is calling his name.

'Raven, I'm over here,' coughs Barious quietly again. Raven listens carefully to his name being said again, and he swiftly runs towards the direction he hears the sound coming from, leading him to end up in front of a broken-down small wooden cottage where wooden rubble is covering the top of an Oak villager. Raven falls to his knees on the wooden path beneath him, and he starts ripping the wood from the broken-down small wooden cottage on top of the Oak villager, throwing the pieces of broken wood he rips off behind him. In Raven's frantic attempt to rescue this Oak villager, he manages to cut his hands with the broken pieces of wood he is pulling off the Oak villager's covered body.

After a few moments that feels like hours to Raven and Barious who is beneath the broken pieces of wood, Raven is left with a large piece of solid wood that only lies between him and the Oak villager. Raven tries to yank this large piece of solid wood from the Oak villager with all his strength, but the large piece of solid wood doesn't budge even a little bit. Raven feels the pain in his hands and shoulder muscles from attempting to yank this large piece of solid wood again, but it is too heavy for him to lift it, which makes him cry in despair.

Raven quickly pulls out the small silver dagger that Parrot had given him back in Pine Village from one of his brown boots; he lifts it up to the large piece of solid wood and starts to carefully cut some holes in the large piece of solid wood until he uncovers an old face full of scratches and cuts, covered in black dust from the crash fall he has had in the small wooden cottage and from the cuttings Raven has made with his small silver dagger on the large piece of solid wood.

'Grandfather . . .,' cries Raven, on noticing it is Barious underneath the large piece of solid wood.

'It's good to see you again one last time, my wonderful grandson,' says Barious, choking due to the black dust and shredding of wood stuck in his mouth.

'I'm going to get you out of here, Grandfather,' states Raven, struggling again with all his strength to remove the large piece of solid wood from Barious's paralysed body. Barious yelps in agony as the large piece of solid wood crushes his body harder when Raven attempts to remove this piece of wood from Barious's body.

'It's no good, Raven. This wood is stuck and my body has already been broken. Listen to me now as we don't have much time. Lieutenant Triton and Lord Scartor's Potorian army destroyed our Oak village in search of the anomaly crystal. It's now obvious that Lord Scartor will stop at nothing in his desperate search of the anomaly crystal. However, he must not ever find it, for if he does, he will use its magnificent powers to destroy all of the humans living on the Planet of Phoenix and all hope and memory of the human's existence will be lost forever. Is the anomaly crystal safe?' asks Barious, as he coughs and breathes deeply in intense pain and exhaustion. Raven's tears roll down the side of his flustered cheeks as he looks into Barious's squinted eyes.

'Why is Lord Scartor going to all this trouble and horrific cruelty to find the anomaly crystal? Even if he does find its whereabouts, he can't wield its powers, as you said the anomaly crystal would only aid the bloodline directly descended from Grackle himself. I don't understand,' states Raven in confusion.

'Raven, please tell me the anomaly crystal is safe,' coughs Barious, while blood is coming out of his mouth.

'Yes, Grandfather, Parrot and I hid it somewhere secret in Pine Village,' cries Raven at the sight of his dying grandfather.

'Well done, my lad. You and Parrot must now go and retrieve the anomaly crystal from that secret hiding place in Pine Village and seek the help from as many Pine villagers and guards from Pine Village as you can and quickly travel to Lord Scartor's Lair of Death mounted on top of Crow Mountain, amongst the Mountains of Doom beyond the Wastelands and the Swamp Fields in the furthest north-west direction of the Planet of Phoenix, in an attempt to kill them all. Lord Scartor's army has grown fourfold, and along with the immense strength of Lieutenant Triton, they are more powerful than ever. The aid of my lifelong friends King Exodus and his royal Falcon guards, along with Panther who is the leader of Willow Village, would be of much assistance during the great war. But, Raven, I don't know how much time you will have to get word to them of this terrible tragedy. I'm very sorry, but as Lieutenant Triton and the Potorians were leaving Oak Village, I overheard that they had taken Emerald and Opal with them as prisoners,' says Barious as his voice and coughing begin to quieten due to the intense pain he is experiencing throughout his respiratory system.

'EMERALD! WHY DID they take her and Opal back with them? How can I possibly defeat Lord Scartor, Lieutenant Triton, and the Potorian army?' says Raven in a devastated and confused manner.

'Raven, I don't know why they took Emerald and Opal. It was probably to hold them as ransom in exchange for the anomaly crystal. I'm really sorry that Emerald is now also involved in this great war, and I'm very sorry that you have been cursed with this burden being the last descendent of Grackle. That means you possess his bloodline, allowing you the gift of wielding the anomaly crystal. I've tried my hardest for many decades to keep the anomaly crystal safe and hidden since it was passed down to me by my father, Trogon. I continued to carry the burden of the anomaly crystal and didn't want to pass it on to my sons Ruthus and Rio as they had families that meant the world to them. Thus, I kept the anomaly crystal in my tool shop at all times to protect it from the rest of my family being involved with this unfortunate series of events, which has led us to this point in time when the great war will inevitably come to pass. I thought about hiding it somewhere else instead of Oak Village but couldn't trust anyone to keep it safe or die for it as I would have done, and that sacrifice required to be made in order to protect it from the evil creatures such as Lord Scartor and Viper,' coughs Barious more vigorously.

'It's not your fault, Grandfather. You were also unfortunately placed with this burden and did all you could to try and protect the anomaly crystal and all of our family from malevolent events,' says Raven, putting his hand on Barious's forehead in a soothing manner and also to wipe some of the blood from Barious's forehead that was cut open from the large piece of solid wood that had sliced into his skin.

'No, Raven, it is my fault and I will die with a broken heart and soul. I should have done more to protect everyone, especially my dearest loved ones. My elder son and your parents, Ruthus and Jewel, died from the black poison of Viper, as he was also searching for the anomaly crystal due to him being in cahoots with Lord Scartor at that time. I don't know how Viper found out that Ruthus was one of the bloodline descendants of Grackle, but it's my fault for hiding the anomaly crystal in Oak Village, which meant both of your parents died to protect this secret that had then ruined the rest of your life,' sobs Barious, gasping for breath. Raven remains silent for a moment due to the shock of what Barious has just told him.

'You weren't to know anyone would find out about Ruthus being a bloodline descendent of Grackle, and you had also risked your own life keeping the anomaly crystal locked away all the time with you in your tool shop in order to spare the rest of our family from also trying to protect it. My parents' and your son's death wasn't your fault, and although I will never be the same person without my parents, you brought me up just as good as they would have done and I give you my full gratitude for doing the best you could for me,' replies Raven as he smiles at Barious, while tears roll down Raven's cheeks and drop on to the large piece of solid wood that covers the top of Barious's crushed body.

'Your kind words will remain with me forever in the afterlife and I will share them with Ruthus and Jewel when I also reunite with them again in heaven. You are a remarkable human and I have every faith you will find a way to end this great war once and for all, ridding the devil creatures from the Planet of Phoenix. Stay strong and true in your heart and mine. You must find a way to wield the ultimate elemental power of the anomaly crystal to aid you through this terrible nightmare. You will know how to wield its astonishing powers as it's in our bloodline and a part of your soul, Raven. You will need to finally defeat that evil warlord Lord Scartor and banish him, Lieutenant Triton, and his Potorian army to the depths of hell for all the pain and suffering they had caused to the humans for a long time,' says Barious softly, while his lungs tried gasping for air.

'Don't worry, Grandfather. I will rescue Emerald and Opal as well as murder Lord Scartor, Lieutenant Triton, and also Viper one day for all the harm they have caused to my family, Oak Village, and all the humans in the past and the present, who had lived upon the Planet of Phoenix. I will miss you so very much and will remember all the knowledge and characteristics you taught me in order to become the brave human I will need to be to end this great war. Please say to my parents I love them and have missed them dearly as well as that you will all remain in my heart and the Planet of Phoenix will never be the same without you all living on it,' replies Raven, more tears flowing from his eyes.

'Your father and mother loved you with all their hearts to the very end and they died to protect all of our family from a similar fate. They would have been so proud that you have grown up to become a hero just like you great-great-grandfather Sparrow. Please also tell Parrot and Rio that I said goodbye and that I also love them profoundly as I do you,' coughs Barious as he gasps for one last breath and closes his eyes.

'Hold on, Grandfather,' cries Raven desperately as he watches hopelessly Barious take no more breath and die. Raven pauses in disbelief as streams of tears pour from his eyes. Raven kisses Barious on the head through the broken pieces of wood he has carved into the large piece of broken wood with his small silver dagger.

'Goodbye, Grandfather, I will promise to avenge yours and my parents' deaths,' states Raven.

RAVEN SLOWLY STANDS up from the side of the large piece of solid wood; his body feels cold and numb, and he walks wearily back over to Felix who is nearby also, feeling disheartened and irritated because of the strange and unusual surroundings he has been experiencing in Oak Village. Raven slowly and steadily climbs back on top of

Felix's strong black back, and Felix begins to trot towards the south-east direction of Oak Village away from Barious's dead body. Raven tries to compose himself in order to ensure his mind and body are ready for what needs to be done in the great war in order to defeat Lord Scartor and Lieutenant Triton, although Raven is finding this unbearably difficult due to being extremely overwhelmed by Barious's recent death. Raven continues to ride on Felix cautiously in the south-east direction through the Oak Village square towards the east entrance wooden gate of Oak Village. The air present in Oak Village is still covered with now thinner black smoke and dust particles; the burning fire has continued, weakening its ferocious burning of the small wooden houses, flats, shops, and fences and has now all been nearly distinguished.

As Raven leaves the Oak Village square and reaches the top of a wooden path near a small grass hill in the south-east direction on his way to the east entrance wooden gate of Oak Village, he hears deep and heavy breathing from an Oak villager who appears to be somewhere down the side of the small grass hill. Raven quickly looks all around him in hope of finding any Oak villager still alive, when suddenly Ruby appears near the top of the small grass hill from which she has rolled down. She crawls to the wooden path at the very top of the small grass hill and sits down in exhaustion and dismay on top of the wooden path.

'Ruby, you're alive!' says Raven, an unbelievable and happy expression on his face.

'Only barely, Raven, and only because Emerald risked her own life to save mine, and now she's gone. She's been killed by one of the horrible and nasty nomad warriors on horseback,' cries Ruby hysterically, mumbling her words to Raven.

'No, Ruby, don't worry. Emerald's not dead. Barious just told me that Lieutenant Triton and the Potorians took her and Opal back to Lord Scartor's Lair of Death upon Crow Mountain as prisoners, but don't worry. I will save her and Opal!' says Raven in a comforting manner.

'They've taken her and Opal back to Lord Scartor's fortress amongst the Mountains of Doom. God only knows what torture she will have to suffer at the hands of those devil monsters,' sobs Ruby hopelessly.

'Emerald is strong and she will survive through this nightmare for the both of us,' remarks Raven.

'Please save my daughter, Raven. She means the world to me and is my everything. I can't bear to lose her just like I've lost Ruthus, Jewel, and Gaius,' exclaims Ruby while tears of sorrow fall from her heartbroken eyes.

'Emerald loves you very much too and she means the world to me also. She is my heart and soul mate and I would not let anything happen to her,' says Raven strongly with passion. Ruby slowly stands up and grabs Raven's right hand, who is still sitting on top of Felix's big black back.

'Thank you so very much, Raven. Please bring her back home to me safe and unharmed,' says Ruby, smiling hopefully at Raven as he also smiles back at Ruby.

'I must hurry to Pine Village and gain aid from my cousin Parrot and any of the willing Pine villagers there to help defeat Lord Scartor, Lieutenant Triton, and his Potorian army once and for all. Stay here and look for any Oak villagers or guards who may still be alive. Tend to their wounds or make them as comfortable as you can if their lives have to unfortunately come to an end. I will come back here from Pine Village first to bring you assistance from women Pine villagers. After that, I will then travel with Parrot and the men Pine villagers to Lord Scartor's Lair of Death on top of Crow Mountain and kill him in revenge for what he has done to Oak Village, my parents, Barious, and now Emerald,' replies Raven courageously.

'God bless you, Raven. You are a true hero, and yes, now I know that Emerald will come home safely, I will do my upmost to help the Oak villagers and Oak guards as well as clean up the massacred Oak Village. Just promise you will both come back to me safe,' says Ruby compassionately.

'I promise you, Ruby,' replies Raven as he lets go of Ruby's hand and holds on to the brown rope reins of Felix again, as he is about to set off for Pine Village.

'Raven, wait, you said you just spoke with Barious. Where is he? The last I saw of him he went with other men Oak villagers to put out the explosive fire at the fence in the north-west direction of Oak Village,' asks Ruby.

'I did just speak with Barious in the north-west edge of Oak Village. But unfortunately he died while speaking to me due to being trapped under a broken down wooden cottage. I did all I could but . . .,' answers Raven with a tear in his eye and he chokes up on his words as he is trying to explain to Ruby. As Ruby understands Raven's heart-breaking pain, she quickly grabs Raven's right hand again, which is holding on to Felix's brown rope reins.

'Oh my God, I'm so very sorry, Raven. I can't believe he has also now left the Planet of Phoenix. But he loved you so very much and I know he was proud of you just as your parents were, and they will all be watching over us together in blissful peace from heaven,' cries Ruby at the devastating news regarding Barious's death.

'Thank you, Ruby, and they all cared for you and Emerald very much too. Although Barious is now dead, I'm thankful that I got to be with him at the very end and share kind words with another one last time,' sobs Raven as tears roll down his eyes and drop on to Felix's big black back.

'You poor boy, having to go through so much sorrow in such a short lifetime. Why is all this happening to us?' curses Ruby.

'We are put on the Planet of Phoenix for a reason, and although unfortunate events happen that affect our lives tragically, we must keep faith and hope that a purposeful plan is occurring that will one day let us all live in peace and harmony with one another as it should be,' says Raven while remembering these words that Barious used to speak to him when he was confused about life as his parents were killed by Viper back when he was seven years old. Raven smiles brightly at Ruby and lets go of her hand again to hold Felix's brown rope reins again.

'You're a very brave and wonderful human. That is why my daughter loves you so very much,' states Ruby.

'Your kind words and Emerald's love will give me the strength I require to get through this unexplainable situation that is about to happen to us all. I will be back from Pine Village as soon as possible. Take care of yourself Ruby,' says Raven as he nods respectfully at Ruby.

Raven kicks his heels gently into the sides of Felix, and Felix begins to gallop down the rest of the wooden path leading out of Oak Village's east entrance wooden gate. They continue to gallop swiftly across the long cobbled road, crossing over the Grass Terrain Fields leading to Pine Village in the east direction. After Ruby sadly watches Raven riding upon Felix, leaving Oak Village from the east wooden entrance gate, she despairingly looks around at the devastation Oak Village has endured during the battle that has occurred in Oak Village in the last few hours. Ruby takes a deep breath and begins to hopelessly hurry around the wooden paths and small wooden houses, cottages, and shops to check the Oak villagers' and guards' bodies for anyone who is still alive.

RAVEN RIDES UPON Felix's strong powerful back as they speed with haste and emotion across the long cobbled road connecting Oak Village and Pine Village. Raven holds tightly on to the brown rope reins of Felix as he unleashes his ultimate pace in order to reach the Pine Village's west entrance metal gate in just under an hour. Raven is excruciatingly heartbroken and distraught from the catastrophe that has just happened in Oak Village, along with witnessing his grandfather Barious dying painfully before his eyes. In the journey that Raven and Felix have just taken between Oak Village and Pine Village along the long cobbled road, Raven's mind is blank and empty of thought as his mind supresses the tragedy of losing his grandfather and also the knowledge he has just learnt about his beloved Emerald being captured as a prisoner by the evil warlord Lord Scartor and his cruel minions Lieutenant Triton and the Potorians. Raven's body feels cold and numb, and it is lucky that Felix can sense how distraught Raven is so he keeps Raven safely upon his muscular back and gets them both quickly to Pine Village.

Raven rides upon Felix straight past the Pine guard called Flame, whom he had met earlier that day by the west entrance metal gate of Pine Village. Raven continues racing upon Felix without hesitation down Pine Village's cobbled paths, where he barely misses knocking over the Pine villagers who are walking contentedly along the cobbled paths at the time. Flame is surprised by Raven's quick actions in riding on Felix through the west entrance metal gate that have been already opened by him; his immediate reaction is to alert the other Pine guards. Flame realises he has spoken with Raven earlier and that he is the grandson of Barious and cousin of Parrot; thus, he understands Raven may had some emergency in order to travel to

Pine Village and contact his cousin Parrot. So Flame lets Raven continue on his journey onwards into Pine Village, although he is still slightly concerned by the urgency of Raven's movements.

Raven riding upon Felix through the cobbled paths of Pine Village in the east direction tries to cautiously avoid knocking into the Pine villagers passing by as they quickly travel to Parrot's small wooden flat that is opposite Pinus Tavern in the middle eastern part of Pine Village. Raven quickly jumps down from the big black back of Felix right outside Parrot's small wooden house, and he starts banging hard on Parrot's front wooden door. At this moment in time, Parrot is in the kitchen of his small wooden flat making a drink of ale; he unintentionally gets shocked by the loud banging noises coming from his front door. He quickly puts down his cup of ale on the wooden tables around the kitchen and rushes towards the front wooden door, where the banging noises get louder and louder.

'All right, calm down. I'm coming!' yells Parrot, who is only a few meters away from the front wooden door. Parrot swiftly opens the front wooden door and sees a frustrated Raven standing with an empty stare in his eyes, his facial expression one of deep upset along with bruises and dried blood on his cheeks and hands.

'Parrot, you must come with me quick to get the anomaly crystal back from that horse stone monument and use it to save Emerald and Opal from Lord Scartor at Crow Mountain!' says Raven anxiously in a panic.

'Catch your breath, Raven. Come in and tell me what's happened. Don't worry. Everything will be all right as I'm here to help you,' says Parrot in a surprised but calm manner and tone of voice in order to aid Raven in relaxing a bit.

Raven listens to Parrot's relaxing words, and as he has complete trust in Parrot, Raven decides to walk through the front wooden door and sit quickly down on one of the wooden chairs that are in Parrot's main room of his small wooden flat. Raven sits down in silence with a disturbed expression upon his face. Parrot begins to worry about Raven's quick change in emotions; just as Parrot is about to walk into the main room to speak with Raven, he notices Felix wandering around the cobbled paths outside his small wooden flat. Parrot runs outside his small wooden flat and grabs on to the brown rope reins attached to the neck of Felix; he pats Felix on his strong black back and walks him across the cobbled path in order to tie his brown rope reins around a pine tree that is opposite to Parrot's small wooden flat. Parrot also sees that Felix is exhausted and dehydrated too; hence, Parrot gives him another firm stroke on his sturdy black back and brings him some water in a wooden bucket from a nearby well; as soon as Parrot brings the wooden bucket filled with water to Felix, he laps up the water from the wooden bucket with his long tongue without hesitation.

Parrot leaves Felix to drink the water from the wooden bucket and quickly hurries back to his small wooden flat and into the main room where he again sees Raven looking at the wooden floor in distress and anguish. Parrots quickly walks past Raven into his kitchen where he retrieves a cup of water that he gives to Raven when he walks back into the main room. Parrot passes the cup of water into Raven's shaking hands, and Raven hesitantly holds on to the cup of water and takes a sip of it to quench his thirst and calm his nerves.

'Raven, what's happened? I'm really worried about you as I've never seen you like this before,' asks Parrot in a concerned voice.

'Lieutenant Triton and Lord Scartor's Potorian army burnt Oak Village to the ground just over an hour ago. They slaughtered all the Oak villagers without mercy in search of the anomaly crystal. I've just only come back from Oak Village, and I have never seen such a disastrous sight in all my life. The memory of what I witnessed in Oak Village will haunt my dreams forever. I was told by Barious that Lieutenant Triton and the Potorians couldn't find the anomaly crystal, so they took Emerald and Wolf's wife Opal back to Lord Scartor's Lair of Death upon Crow Mountain instead to probably torture them for information or hold them as hostages until the humans give the anomaly crystal to Lord Scartor,' says Raven quickly and quietly with a sick and guilty feeling in his stomach.

'I can't believe it! I've heard stories about the nomad warriors and the evil lurking beyond the Wastelands deep within the heart of the Mountains of Doom, but to come and destroy a whole village in such a brutal massacre passes anything I could have ever comprehended. Is every Oak villager dead, Barious? Ruby? Wolf?' says Parrot in a worried voice, while his thoughts quickly drift to think about all the poor Oak villagers who had just lost their lives in a horrible way.

'After I left you in Pine Village to travel back to Oak Village, I encountered three nomad warriors that I now have reason to believe were a part of Lord Scartor's Potorian army. I luckily defeated them and quickly hurried to Oak Village after noticing a black smoke that was caused by the surrounding wooden fence being set on fire by Lieutenant Triton. I scurried through Oak Village to search for Emerald, Barious, Ruby, and Wolf, but in this hopeless attempt, I saw no other Oak villagers alive. As Opal was also taken as a hostage along with Emerald by the Potorians, I assume Wolf may have also been unfortunately killed. When all hope of finding any human alive seemed lost, I luckily found our grandfather under some wooden rubble as he had crash-landed into a small wooden flat.

'After uncovering his broken body, he told me what had happened to Emerald, Opal, and Oak Village. I tried to remove the large pieces of wood on top of Grandfather and rescue him, but unfortunately it was already too late as Grandfather was already broken inside from the fall through the small wooden cottage. Grandfather died right in front of my eyes, but I was privileged enough to share some kind words with him before he left the Planet of Phoenix forever. On my ride out of Oak Village, I bumped into Ruby, who was lucky enough to survive the attack by Lieutenant Triton and the Potorians in the battle of Oak Village, but she was distraught and confused about what had happened to Emerald. After explaining to her what Barious told me I must do, she agreed to stay in Oak Village to search for any survivors and start cleaning up our destroyed homes,' replies Raven wretchedly. Parrot pauses a moment to take in all the words Raven has just spoke to him. Parrot then puts his hand on Raven's left shoulder to comfort him.

'I'm very sorry about our grandfather, Raven. I know how much he meant to you as he did to me. He was a remarkable human and grandfather to us and will never be forgotten,' says Parrot with a tear in his eye, holding firmly on to Raven's left shoulder.

'Grandfather told me in his dying breath to send his loving thoughts to you and your father and his younger brother Rio and to say goodbye until we all reunite again in the afterlife,' states Raven, who also had a tear rolling down the side of his left cheek.

'Thank you for that, Raven. That message has meant the world to me on such a tragic and never forgotten day. Grandfather was loved not only by his family but also many other humans throughout the Planet of Phoenix, who will miss him profoundly. We were fortunate enough to have been related too and also brought up by such an outstanding and admirable human. I'm really glad Ruby survived the battle of Oak Village, but am deeply devastated about all the poor other Oak villagers along with the leader of Oak Village, Wolf, who were killed in cold blood by these sinful and spiteful creatures. We need to retrieve aid from Pine Village to send help to Ruby to search for any other Oak village survivors. And yes, we must quickly go rescue Emerald and Opal from the malevolent hands of Lord Scartor. We will not let them suffer any harm and will kill these wicked creatures for what they have done to the race of humans this day,' exclaims Parrot in anger.

'Do you think the Pine villagers would be willing to risk their own lives for something that doesn't directly concern them or that they may not understand?' Raven asks.

'Of course,' says Parrot. 'Oak Village is our closest neighbour village and we have had a strong relationship bond in trade and unity for hundreds of years. Also, some of the Pine villagers, along with Willow villagers, would have had families and friends living in Oak Village or who actually attended Wolf's coronation celebration festival, as I know also our Pinus Church vicar was also there. So they would be deeply upset to hear this tragic news and would now like to avenge their lost family and friends who died in the Oak Village battle.

'Pine Village is also a very proud village and would not let these devilish creatures from the Planet of Phoenix cause such devastation to the humans, especially since these creatures may also bring the great war to Pine Village too. Unfortunately, my best friend and Pine Village's leader Lynx is with his Pine guards in Falcon City at the moment to discuss further building permission, extension, and its cost for Pine Village with King Exodus and his royal Falcon guards and advisors, so we would not have enough time to retrieve their aid. We could, however, go to Willow Village and ask for help from the Willow Village leader Panther, who is also Lynx's uncle and if I remember correctly a great friend of our grandfather,' states Parrot, trying to logically generate an action plan for what needs to be done to save Emerald and Opal and destroy Lord Scartor, Lieutenant Triton, and the Potorian army.

'Yes, you're right and that aid would be of much need, but Willow Village is far away in the opposite direction to where we need to go, and as it's already going to be a long and extensive journey to Crow Mountain, I don't know how much longer Emerald and Opal will survive in Lord Scartor's Lair of Death without us going there soon,' says Raven with a worried expression and another tear rolling down the right side of his discoloured cheek.

'OK, we will need to move and get organised quickly then in order to save them. I'll grab us some of my specially made weapons from my closet and then you go and retrieve the anomaly crystal back from the horse monument statue. At the same time, I'll go to Pinus Tavern to speak with all the Pine villagers there for help and support on this legendary and unimaginable quest,' replies Parrot, walking over to the front wooden door of his small wooden flat, where he puts on his brown boots that are on the floor and his brown coat that has many different pockets in it, which is hung up on a hook upon the front wooden door.

PARROT NOW WALKS towards the closet wooden door at one side of the main room in his small wooden flat, and as he opens the closet wooden door, it reveals many and various different silver and metal sharp and stylishly designed swords, axes, spears, daggers, metal knuckle dusters, sharp-edged silver fury raptor throwing stars, and wooden bows and wooden arrows with metal spikes at the end of them.

'I wouldn't be able to get through this nightmare if it wasn't for you, Parrot,' explains Raven in appreciation while looking at the floor of Parrot's small wooden flat again in hopelessness at the thought of losing his grandfather forever and also potentially losing his girlfriend Emerald.

'You're welcome, Cousin, and I will always be here for you any time and through any situation. Besides, I'm certainly going to enjoy making Lord Scartor, Lieutenant Triton, and the Potorian army pay for what they have done to my grandfather and all the other humans in Oak Village. Now what weapons would you like to kill some creature scum with? I think I'll use my favourite fury raptor throwing stars and take a bow with some arrows, as this will give me a long-distance advantage over them,' remarks Parrot as Raven begins to look up at Parrot, who is standing next to the closet at one end of the main room of his small wooden flat.

'Well, I've still got that dagger you gave me this morning. That came in great aid earlier when I was attacked by those three Potorians, and I still also possess both my nunchucks. However, I fear such a battle that we are going to face, I would need something more powerful, so if I could get a sword if you have one spare?' asks Raven in an inquiring manner. Parrot puts several fury raptor throwing stars that are small and has five sharp spiked edges designed in a star shape around a solid silver centre in his various pockets around his brown coat, and then Parrot puts the wooden bow around his neck along with the wooden arrows with the sharp metal spikes at the end of them in a wooden pouch pocket that he has also put round his neck and attached it to his back to hold them.

After Parrot had kitted himself up with the weapons he will require in battle, he starts to fiddle around his closet, looking for a sword to give to Raven. As he shuffles around the closet, some weapons get knocked over and it uncovers the bottom of the closet; for some reason, Parrot's hand draws close towards this special sword that he hasn't thought about or touched for a long time.

'This one is perfect,' states Parrot with a grin on his face. Parrot slowly pulls out from his closet a long, sharp, and magnificent golden sword with a silver handle; it has specially carved scripted writings in silver down the middle of the golden sword written in the ancient Phoenix language.

'Wow! Now that's a phenomenal sword,' remarks Raven, glaring at the golden sword that glistens as Parrot pulls it out of the closet.

'Yes, this sword was uncovered by our great-grandfather Trogon in the Swamp Fields near Eagle Forest many decades ago. He explained to my father Rio, who was his grandson, that he was unexplainably drawn to this sword, almost guided towards it by some kind of mysterious energy. He retrieved it when he was crossing the Swamp Fields towards the Wastelands, when he along with many other Pine and Oak villagers went to fight in a battle against Lord Scartor, Viper, and the Serpents, which was planned to occur deep in the middle of the Wastelands over a century ago. There was no explanation why such a magnificent sword was left and hidden in the Swamp Fields, but my father Rio explained that Lexus said it helped him a lot during that battle and it even caused the winning blow to Viper that injured him badly, which caused him to leave the battle early and Lord Scartor to retreat back to his Lair of Death upon Crow Mountain.

'Trogon gave it to my father Rio before he died as he saw his interest in weapons and tool making, and then my father also passed it down to me as I wanted to continue with our family business in making tools and particularly for me in creating specially made weapons. So I've been looking after it ever since it was discovered. However, it hasn't been used again yet as I wasn't sure what I was meant to do with it or who I was meant to give it too. But just now when I was looking for a sword in my closet for you, I also strangely felt drawn to it for some reason. That I can't explain, but it seems that you were meant to have it, Raven,' explains Parrot, smiling at Raven excitedly. Raven attempts to smile back at Parrot but finds it difficult due to all the strong emotional feelings he is currently experiencing because of the battle of Oak Village. Raven stands up from the wooden chair he is sitting on and looks more closely at the golden sword as Parrot passes it to his hands.

'What do these markings in the middle of the sword say or represent?' asks Raven curiously, while sliding one of his fingers down the middle of the golden sword across the silver carved markings on the golden sword written in the ancient Phoenix language.

'I honestly don't know, Raven. Lexus told my father that he thinks it was from the ancient Phoenix language that was used long ago when the time of magic and sorcery was at its most influential period in the Planet of Phoenix's history. However, neither Lexus nor any human since that have seen this sword could translate what it says,' replies Parrot passionately. Raven holds the golden sword in his right hand firmly and looks at it in astonishment from the handle all the way to the top of its tip; after a moment of glaring at the sword in wonder, Raven turns to walk to the front wooden door of Parrot's small wooden flat.

'I will retrieve the anomaly crystal now and meet up with you again in Pinus Tavern. Thank you for your help again, Parrot,' says Raven as he runs out of Parrot's front wooden door and over towards Felix who is still tied up to the pine tree across the cobbled path from

Parrot's small wooden flat. Raven pats Felix softly on the thick black hair on his back and he unties Felix's brown rope reins from the pine tree. Raven climbs back on top of Felix's large back and instructs him with the movement of the brown rope reins in order to guide Felix to gallop down the cobbled paths and connecting smaller cobbled paths that are attached to the main cobbled path of Pine Village, which changes direction to lead Raven and Felix back towards the horse monument statue in the south-east direction of Pine Village.

Raven quickly gallops on Felix, but also remains cautious not to draw attention to him from the Pine villagers passing by along the cobbled paths. After Raven reaches the horse monument statue that is engulfed amongst the surrounding large green bushes, shrubs, and various trees within a big metal white fence. Raven controls Felix to stop near the small pine tree that has a large strong branch sticking over the big metal white fence. Raven carefully stands up on Felix's black back and uses his back to aid him in climbing up the small pine tree, and Raven climbs across the large strong wooden branch and jumps down to the ground on the other side of the big metal white fence.

Raven quietly walks around the back of the horse monument statue and prudently retrieves the anomaly crystal from one of the legs of the horse monument statue by pulling out the carved piece or marble that Parrot had made earlier by using a small steel metal chisel. Raven holds the anomaly crystal in his hands again and puts it securely in one of his grey coat pockets and refits the small cut-out marble piece back into the horse monument statue's leg. Raven hurries back to the big metal white fence and uses the strength in his thigh muscles to jump high in the air to grab the wooden branch of the small pine tree that is hanging over the big white metal fence; he swings up on the wooden branch to grab it with his feet, and he is then able to turns himself around to be on top of the wooden branch. Raven scurries across the wooden branch to the other side of the big metal white fence and back down the small pine tree on to Felix's large black back again; he controls Felix's brown rope reins and also taps his heels into the sides of Felix in order to instruct him to gallop back across the smaller cobbled paths and then on to the main cobbled path that leads back in the west direction towards Pinus Tavern, where Raven is to meet up with Parrot.

PARROT LEAVES HIS small wooden flat in a hurry after Raven has just left him to retrieve the anomaly crystal from the horse monument statue. Parrot closes the wooden front door behind him and runs across the cobbled path to Pinus Tavern that is nearly opposite to his small wooden flat. Pinus Tavern is a big old wooden building that had been created after the construction of Pine Village over 300 years ago. Pinus Tavern has a big main room where several big wooden tables and wooden chairs are laid out, also a big wooden bar where the ale is kept to be served to the villagers, and it has a connecting passageway to a kitchen at the back of it where the food is prepared. There are also two public toilets, a cellar where stock and supplies are kept, as well as two storeys of floors that have guest rooms and the bedrooms of the owner, Leon, his wife, Lemur, and their children Siva and Sam to stay in.

Pinus Tavern serves to the Pine and other villagers passing by water, basic ale, and food like stew that Pinus Tavern is renowned for throughout the entire Planet of Phoenix, as well as farm animal meat, vegetables, fruit, fish caught from Nautilus Lake in the Kingdom of Humans region near Falcon City, soup and bread, as well as providing spare rooms for villagers to stay in on their long journeys between the main villages and Falcon City. Pinus Tavern is usually crowded with many Pine villagers and other villagers who travel to Pine Village to trade or see family and friends as Pinus Tavern is the only tavern in Pine Village; thus, it's a good place for the Pine villagers to socialise and catch up with the gossip about events and situations in the Planet of Phoenix. Pinus Tavern also provides functions for the Pine villagers such as wedding ceremonies, remembrance services, and village meetings that aid in the communication with the Leader of Pine Village, Lynx, his Pine guards, and the Pine villagers to strengthen their bond and unity with one another.

Parrot hurries over to Pinus Tavern and pushes open the big wooden entrance doors at the front of Pinus Tavern. He walks in through to see a lot of Pine villagers drinking ale, eating food like stew and soup, while gossiping with one another about the black smoke in the sky some of them had witnessed arising in the west direction of the Planet of Phoenix. The atmosphere in Pinus Tavern is responsive, joyful, and vibrant as family and friends enjoy socialising with another. Parrot quickly looks around for a good place to stand on so that everyone will notice him as he requires grabbing their immediate attention. Parrot climbs on top of one of the big wooden tables that has several Pine villagers sitting around it, eating and drinking.

'How rude!' says a woman Pine villager abruptly.

'Hey, get down from there!' shouts Pinus Tavern owner, who at the time had been working behind the wooden bar of Pinus Tavern and had noticed Parrot had climbed on top of one of the big wooden tables that had Pine villagers drinking around it.

Pinus Tavern owner is called Leon; he is forty-six years old and has brown eyes with long brown wavy hair. He has dry skin and a stubble moustache and beard upon his face. Leon is tall in height and has an average body weight for his age; he wears old dirty grey and brown clothes with brown boots. These clothes usually remain dirty because of him working at the bar and in the kitchen of Pinus Tavern, where mess gets created quite easily. Leon is a very practical and friendly person and prefers to work with his hands. His kind humour, communication, and interaction skills with the villagers make him a very popular human, and the villagers really enjoy sharing conversation with him when they come into Pinus Tavern. Leon is also very patriotic and loyal to Pine Village and the Pine Village leader Lynx, as they both get on well with one another and Leon is very happy to let Lynx use Leon's Pinus Tavern for any village meetings or celebrations.

Leon has been the owner of Pinus Tavern since his father Omron died and left Pinus Tavern to him just over seventeen years ago, as Pinus Tavern has been in Leon's ancestors since it was first built when Pine Village was being developed. His mother Hilda died during the birth of Leon as many women did due to the lack of medicine and treatment required during childbirth. Leon was brought up all his life only by his father Omron, and Omron didn't want Leon to attend Pinus School and complete his education as he needed help in running Pinus Tavern, where Leon would work, preparing food in the kitchen and cleaning up the place when it got messy. Although Leon missed socialising with other Pinus school children and felt he wanted to learn more about practical and academic studies, he enjoyed working in the Pinus Tavern and entertaining the villagers who came in it, and he built his relationship building and communication skills.

'Everyone, listen up! I've just had a visit from my cousin Raven from Oak Village and he unfortunately came to me with the most gravest of news. Oak Village was burnt to the ground just over a couple of hours ago and nearly all of the villagers in it were killed by a powerful creature called Lieutenant Triton and an army of Potorians that used to be nomad warriors, who were all commanded to destroy Oak Village by an evil warlord known as Lord Scartor who resides upon Crow Mountain amongst the Mountains of Doom in the north-west side of the Planet of Phoenix,' shouts Parrot sincerely. All the Pine villagers in Pinus Tavern completely stop gossiping and chatting with one another after hearing the shocking news from Parrot. The Pine villagers pause and gasp in disbelief, and some of the women Pine villagers begin to cry at the knowledge of this tragic situation.

'I thought I saw black smoke in the far distance in the west when I was tending to my flock of sheep upon the Grass Terrain Fields earlier, but I didn't think much of it at the time as fires are usually created by the villages to get rid of waste and broken furniture,' says a man Pine villager, looking up at Parrot from one of the big wooden tables near the opposite far end of Pinus Tavern.

'Oh God, my daughter and her friends went to Oak Village to see Wolf's coronation celebration festival today. Are they all right?' cries one of the women Pine villagers. The rest of the Pine villagers either stay seated upon their wooden chairs around the big wooden tables or stand upset, covering their mouths in shock and despondency; the silence in Pinus Tavern sends chills down the back of Parrot's spine as he looks upon the horrified faces of the Pine villagers staring back at him.

'I'm so very sorry. I really don't know and I hope your daughter and her friends are all right. All I know is that we need women from Pine Village to go help an Oak villager who survived the battle of Oak Village. She is called Ruby and requires aid in uncovering and tending to any other wounded villagers who have survived, as well as to also help clean up the destruction of Oak Village that had been caused from a great fire. I then must unfortunately but necessarily ask for the help of any willing men Pine villagers to come with me and my cousin Raven to travel to Crow Mountain amongst the Mountains of Doom, past the Wastelands and the Swamp Fields, and assassinate Lord Scartor, Lieutenant Triton, and his Potorian army in Lord Scartor's Lair of Death for what he has done to Oak Village as well as some of our family and friends,' states Parrot amicably as the Pine villagers listen to Parrot's plea, but remain in silence as they are still in shock due to this catastrophic situation.

'That's a suicide mission! Even if we make it across the treacherous Swamp Fields and vast dangerous Wastelands and be able to climb to the top of the icy rock and stone mountain trails upon Crow Mountain, we would have no chance in heaven in being able to defeat such evil creatures and warlords who can cause such destruction to one of our human villagers within a matter of hours. We will also be greatly outnumbered and . . .,' moans a man Pine villager.

'Yea, yea!' shout most of the other Pine villagers in Pinus Tavern, interrupting the man Pine villager who was speaking at the time. Parrot becomes silent in a confused and despondent manner at the response from some of the Pine villagers, although he understands the way they feel about it, as it is an impossible task to undergo such a journey and defeat these powerful creatures. Suddenly, Raven pushes Pinus Tavern's big wooden doors wide open and walks firmly into Pinus Tavern and stands near Parrot, who is still standing upon one of the big wooden tables. Raven glances at all the Pine villagers staring back at him in disbelief and misunderstanding.

'Those evil creatures have taken hostage the woman I love, who's called Emerald. She is daughter of Ruby, who is Oakus School religious education teacher. They have also captured my Oak Village leader Wolf's wife, Opal. These arrogant creatures killed my grandfather, Barious, without humanity and easily slaughtered all the innocent villagers of Oak Village, many of that you Pine villagers would have known or been related to. These evil creatures will stop at nothing on their path of destruction to annihilate all the humans living upon the Planet of Phoenix. We need to defeat them now before they destroy Pine Village or another village and continue to kill many more innocent humans,' shouts Raven emotionally as some of the Pine villagers continue or start to cry because of the more informative knowledge about the horror that has occurred in the battle of Oak Village, including the news regarding the death of Barious.

'Poor Barious, he was a delightful and tender human,' says Leon, standing behind Pinus Tavern's big wooden bar, while holding his wife Lemur's hand firmly, who had come and stood next to him on hearing the news from Parrot and Raven.

'Why did they destroy Oak Village and kill all the villagers there? It doesn't make any sense as we haven't provoked any of the creatures from the Mountains of Doom!' shouts a man Pine villager in misperception. Raven and Parrot remain silent, being careful not to mention any information regarding the anomaly crystal.

'They didn't attack Pine Village, so they might not come to our village at all,' states a woman Pine villager.

'We cannot take that risk as surely they will continue to kill other humans, especially if they think King Exodus and his royal Falcon guards will retaliate in revenge to what they had done to Oak Village and the villagers who were living there. Think of your children. Do you want them to grow up on our Planet of Phoenix and always be terrified that Lord Scartor and his army of creatures may come at any moment to destroy their homes and take their lives and lives of the humans they love, because their parents didn't attempt to even try and defeat them? What would your children and your grandchildren think of all of their ancestors then?' exclaims Parrot directly in an attempt to gain the support of all the Pine villagers. The Pine villagers in Pinus Tavern become quiet again and sensitively think about Parrot's influential words.

'Why don't we get aid from Panther, leader of Willow Village, or send word of this implausible news to our leader Lynx and King Exodus who are currently in Falcon City?' says another man Pine villager.

'Yes, that would seem the rational action to take, but we won't be able to do all of that in time. Emerald's and Opal's lives hang in the balance of time, and if we do not defeat Lord Scartor, Lieutenant Triton, and the Potorians right now, they will not only kill them, but may also quickly come back and destroy this and other villages while we seek to gather extra help,' explains Raven in a frustrated voice tone at the thought of Emerald being tortured by creatures.

'How can we possibly stand a chance against such power, strength, and numbers? Most of the Pine villagers here are not trained in weaponry and combat. We are only peaceful farmers and tool makers,' says a man Pine villager bleakly.

A LARGE AND muscular man stands up from his wooden chair next to a big wooden table at another end of Pinus Tavern.

'I can swing an axe!' shouts the large and muscular man Pine villager, who is known as Drakus and who is a woodcutter. Drakus is twenty-eight years old; he has green eyes, long blond straggly hair, and rough skin with hair covering all his body, he wears a black T-shirt that has only one shoulder strap, as well as black shorts and thick grey boots. Drakus is one of the strongest villagers in Pine Village due to his father, who was called Walrus as he was also physically built and was strong in muscles and aptitude; he taught Drakus to be a part of the woodcutting trade ever since he was a young child. Drakus also did not attend Pinus School as he possessed low intelligence, so his father Walrus and mother Bella thought it was best for him to learn a trade rather than be educated, as he would struggle and feel insecure about himself. Drakus is a very solemn, introverted, but caring person; unfortunately, his father Walrus was killed by a nomad warrior nine years ago. Walrus was cutting wood on the outskirts of Eagle Forest near the Wastelands, when a nomad warrior killed him viciously in order to steal his woodcutting tools. The death of Walrus was devastating for Drakus and his mother Bella; thus, Drakus trained long and hard to become bigger and stronger in order to avenge his father's death, although he would never know that nomad warrior actually killed his father.

'Here, here!' say a couple of the other men Pine villagers, looking at the strong muscular arms of Drakus.

'I also have quite a few specialised weapons we can use for protection, and if anyone else has shields or weapons or some sort and horses, could we also please use them on this epic quest? We beg of you all, will you help us?' asks Parrot emphatically. The Pine villagers in Pinus Tavern pause for a brief moment.

'Yes, I will come to your aid, as I will have no creature threaten my children, my wife, or the other humans I care about,' remarks Leon firmly from behind Pinus Tavern big wooden bar, while his wife Lemur squeezes his hand resolutely.

'Yes, yes . . . Let's kill some nomad warriors and creature bastards!' roars Drakus as he slams his pint of ale down on the big wooden table he is sitting at, spilling some of the ale. The rest of Pine villagers in Pinus Tavern start to cheer and clap with thoughts of bravery and hope. Parrot turns towards Raven and smiles at him.

'Right, everyone, we need the women Pine villagers to grab any health packs and medicine to help Ruby and aid the poor wounded souls of Oak Village. Any of the men Pine villagers who are brave enough to come with us on this quest must grab any weapons and horses available in Pine Village and say goodbye to their loved ones, for none of us know what we might face upon this remarkable journey,' states Leon, looking at all the Pine villagers from behind Pinus Tavern wooden bar.

'Thank you, Leon and honourable Pine villagers. We can be victorious against this creature threat as long as we believe in each other and protect one another. The men Pine villagers who will come on this journey should come to my flat first just opposite Pinus Tavern so I can give them each some of my specialised weapons. We should then all meet at the west entrance gate of Pine Village and leave within the hour,' remarks Parrot as he jumps down from the big wooden table he is standing upon, while the men Pine village nod at Parrot to show they have understood his instructions.

After a collective effort in getting everyone organised and speaking with one another about what the right plan of action would be, Raven, Parrot, and thirty-eight young and old men Pine villagers including Drakus quickly leave Pinus Tavern through the big wooden entrance doors and cross the cobbled path over to Parrot's small wooden flat. They enter Parrot's small wooden flat in a line, and Parrot and Raven supply all the thirty-eight Pine villagers with Parrot's specialised weapons from the closet, which includes metal swords, daggers, and spears; Parrot especially made sure he gave Drakus his specially made battle axe that is big in size and sharp at the metal points of it.

After being equipped with weapons, the thirty-eight men Pine villagers then leave Parrot's small wooden flat and cross the cobbled path to go back to Pinus Tavern or to their small wooden houses and flats where they live to collect any shields and horses they possess. At the same time, if their families or friends they'd meet didn't already know where they were going due to not hearing the conversation that occurred in Pinus Tavern regarding the battle of Pine Village, then these men Pine villager will quickly explain to their families and friends what has had happened and the circumstances leading them to deciding to go battle the creatures upon Crow Mountain. They would also say a dramatic goodbye to them, with the hope they would return soon and unharmed; however, they fear this may not be the case.

Back in Pinus Tavern, Leon discusses with his wife Lemur about what their thoughts are regarding these unfortunate circumstances. Lemur is the wife of Leon and is Pinus Tavern cook and cleaner; she is forty-two years old and has hazel eyes, short black hair, and is of average size in height with soft petite skin. She wears plain grey and brown clothes. She has been married to Leon for twenty-one years and has only loved Leon right from when she was of a young age. Lemur originally knew Leon as he worked behind the bar of Pinus Tavern when he was working for his father Omron instead of getting his education at Pinus School. Leon and Lemur would share much conversation and laughter when Lemur and her school friends would come and meet their family members in Pinus Tavern after they had finished school for that day, and after a while of Leon and Lemur getting to know each other, they fell in love with one another. After many years of dating and being in a relationship with each other, they decided to get married, and Lemur moved into Pinus Tavern to share a room with Leon.

After Omron died of old age a few years later, Lemur helped Leon to continue to run Pinus Tavern. Lemur is a content and homely person, who got her education particularly in health care and first aid that she learnt at Pinus School; she is very good in caring for villagers when they are ill or injured, although she is not a qualified doctor. Leon and Lemur have two children, a girl who is twelve called Siva and a boy who is five called Sam.

Siva has hazel eyes and long black curly hair and also wears plain grey and brown clothing; she is also medium size in height for her age and looks more like her mother Lemur than her father Leon. Siva is a comical and outgoing girl, and she not only enjoys studies and socialising with her friends at Pinus School, but also likes to help her parents manage Pinus Tavern by working as a glass collector and cleaner in Pinus Tavern. Sam has brown eyes and short black hair; due to his age he is small in height and has the facial characteristics resembling his father. Sam is a happy character and is currently too young to attend Pinus School, so he attends the Pinus nursery instead, which is where women Pine villagers care for and play games with very young children in order that their parents can keep on working.

'I'm really sorry for my decision on the matter without discussing it with you first, but it seemed like the right thing to do in order to rally the villagers to aid Parrot and Raven. Besides, they were right in saying that we can't let those type of evil creatures get away with what they had done to Oak Village,' explains Leon as he kisses Lemur on the lips.

'That is all right, my husband. You did the right thing as always. I just hope nothing bad happens to any of you as I couldn't bear to go through the pain and suffering of losing a loved one like many of the other villagers are having to cope with at the moment due to the outcome of the Oak Village battle,' replies Lemur sadly.

'Don't worry, my wife. Of course, I will come back to you, our children, and our home. Can you please also arrange for women Pine villagers to look after our children and then gather up all the health packs we have in Pinus Tavern along with several other women Pine villagers to go and help Ruby at Oak Village, if you also don't mind?' says Leon to Lemur when they are both behind Pinus Tavern big wooden bar.

'Of course, that is fine. I will do my best to help Ruby and Oak Village out during these tragic circumstances,' replies Lemur, hugging Leon. After their passionate hug, Leon leaves Pinus Tavern's big wooden bar in order to gather his metal spear and shield in his bedroom on the second floor of Pinus Tavern; this metal spear and shield were also passed down to him from his father Omron when he died. At the same time, Lemur also leaves Pinus Tavern's big wooden bar to gather medicines and bandages from the cellar of Pinus Tavern that is underground, and she puts all the health packs into one of her big brown leather bags so that she can carry it all to Oak Village.

After a short period of time, both Leon and Lemur make it back in the kitchen of Pinus Tavern, which is connected by a small passageway from the back of Pinus Tavern's big wooden bar, where their children Siva and Sam are waiting in apprehension. Once they all meet back up in the kitchen, they all hug and kiss each other lovingly.

'Mummy will be back soon, my wonderful children. Stay in Pinus Tavern where you will be well looked after by one of my friends,' says Siva calmly.

'What's happening in Oak Village? Can't I come with you to help, Mother?' asks Siva in a concerned voice.

'Everything's all right, my dear. Your mother and I just need to help out some of our fellow Oak villagers in their time of need. I admire your bravery and compassion that you have acquired from your mother and me, but we need you to stay here to look after your younger brother and we'll be back before you know it. Is that all right, my angel?' says Leon as he hugs Siva strongly again and Siva giggles.

'Sure thing, Daddy. Just don't be too long as the Planet of Phoenix can be a dangerous place,' replies Siva to Leon, as Lemur walks back out of the kitchen and through the connecting passageway to Pinus Tavern's big wooden bar.

'Please, remaining Pine villagers, can you look after my children as I am needed in Oak Village? Lock all the doors and windows in Pinus Tavern and tell all other Pine villagers to do the same in their homes in the rest of Pine Village until this potential threat has passed. Thank you for your help. Stay safe and look after one another. Leon and I will be back shortly,' says Lemur to some of the women Pine villagers, who are sitting in shock at one of the big wooden tables in Pinus Tavern.

'Yes, that's no problem, Lemur. We will stay in here to look after your children as you have always been so generous to us. We hope you all return shortly,' replies one of the women Pine villagers. Leon and Lemur say one last goodbye to their children and leave Pinus Tavern's big wooden entrance doors, and after walking round to a medium-sized field at the back of Pinus Tavern, they both saddle upon Leon's brown horse, along with many other men and women Pine villagers who are also saddled up on other horses in this medium-sized field in preparation to their journey to Oak Village. One by one led by Leon and Lemur on their brown horse, they all leave the medium-sized field at the back of Pinus Tavern and continue to ride on their horses down the cobbled paths of Pine Village in the west direction.

As the sun shines down upon the cobbled paths of Pine Village, some Pine villagers, who are family or friends of the men and women Pine villagers that are leaving Pine Village to aid the survivors in Oak Village or attempt to defeat Lord Scartor and other creatures at Crow Mountain, have already positioned themselves on either side of the cobbled paths and are cheering and throwing pretty flowers like tulips and buttercups on the cobbled paths in honour of these brave men and women Pine villagers.

Leon and Lemur riding Leon's brown horse and the other men and women Pine villagers on horseback reach the west entrance metal gate of Pine Village after twenty minutes; Raven on Felix is already at the west entrance metal gate with Parrot on his black horse, both of them carrying volunteer women Pine villagers on the back of their horses to aid Ruby in Oak Village. Drakus and a few other men and women Pine villagers are also already at the west entrance metal gate, eagerly waiting on their horses for Leon, Lemur, and the remaining men and women Pine villagers to meet up with them.

Drakus is carrying his mother Bella on the back of his horse, who after being told about this situation by Drakus when he returned to their home had also volunteered to help Ruby in Oak Village in the search for survivors and in the cleaning up after the battle of Oak Village, especially since she had known Barious during previous years and was very upset to hear he had been killed. Bella is sixty-four years old; she is one of the oldest living villagers in Pine Village and she has blue eyes and shoulder-length grey curly hair with wrinkly skin, she wears a black woolen jumper and long skirt with grey shoes. She has not shrunk in height from the average size of a human on the Planet of Phoenix. She has lived in Pine Village all her life as all her ancestors had done before; she is a gracious and humble person who loves her son Drakus very much and has mothered him very much, especially after her husband Walrus was murdered nine years ago by a nomad warrior near Eagle Forest. She has only ever been partners with Walrus, and they both got married at a young age and were very happy together all throughout their lives.

Bella had only been a housewife and cared for her husband Walrus and son Drakus, and they shared many happy family times together. Bella was lost and heartbroken without Walrus at first after she found out that he was killed by the nomad warrior, but she found

the strength and determination to keep on living their lives happily
so that Drakus could also cope with his father's death, as Drakus
had a bit of a slow cognitive processing function in his brain, which
made him react differently to emotional situations from how normal
humans usually would.

After all the men and women Pine villagers are united with one
another at the west entrance metal gate of Pine Village, Parrot trots
on his black horse up to his friend Flame, who is still on security
watch after being on his Pine guard duty at the west entrance metal
gate of Pine Village.

'How are you, my friend Flame?' asks Parrot nodding at Flame
happily, as he has not seen him for a few weeks.

'Parrot, my friend, it's good to see you on this sunny day. Yes, I am
fine, and it has been relatively quiet except for a few villagers passing
by, although I was a bit concerned earlier when I saw your cousin
Raven racing through here. What is happening with some of the
Pine villagers upon horseback behind you?' asks Flame inquisitively.

'Yes, apologies for that, but it was an emergency. My cousin Raven
has just told me unfortunate news that had just recently occurred
in Oak Village at Wolf's coronation celebration festival. Oak Village
was attacked by the evil warlord creature Lord Scartor's Lieutenant
Triton and his Potorian army, where nearly all the Oak villagers were
killed as well as most of the village was destroyed and burnt to the
ground. We had no choice but to recruit men Pine villagers from
Pinus Tavern to quickly travel with us to Lord Scartor's Lair of Death
upon the top of Crow Mountain amongst the Mountains of Doom
beyond the Wastelands in the far north-west of the Planet of Phoenix
in order to rescue Raven's girlfriend Emerald and Wolf's wife Opal
from being taken prisoner there, as well as seek revenge upon these
malicious creatures for what they had done to Oak Village and our
fellow humans.

'Due to the urgency of this situation, we did not have enough
time to rally the aid from Panther and the Willow villagers, and
as I knew Lynx along with nearly all his Pine guards are in Falcon
City with King Exodus and the royal Falcon guards, we would not
have been able to consult our plans with him or also ask for their
assistance in this forthcoming battle. Can you please do me a favour
and send word to Lynx via carrier pigeon about what I have just told

you and state that the message was from me and yourself so that he will be aware of what is happening in preparation for the next stages that may unfold in the great war that was pronounced inevitable for many hundreds of years?' explains Parrot sadly at the thought of the recently destroyed Oak Village.

'Yes, of course, I will make Lynx aware of this situation. Thank you for explaining that all to me. But I am completely shocked and deeply disturbed by hearing what these terrible creatures have done to Oak Village and the poor Oak villagers who were living there. I was myself starting to get quite concerned as I had also noticed black smoke arising from the west direction a couple of hours ago. I had spoken with some of the other Pine guards who were on lookout duty upon the wooden tower watch posts, but they also weren't sure where the black smoke was coming from and thought it may have been something to do with burning the wastage or setting a fire in honour of Wolf during his coronation celebration festival. That is why we didn't attempt to take much action regarding these circumstances.

'Why have us humans suffered so much pain and misfortune upon this day and now I only wish that some of the Pine guards and myself could aid you in this quest, but unfortunately we have strict orders to stay at our positions and protect Pine Village as nearly all the Pine guards have travelled with Lynx to meet with King Exodus in Falcon City, due to the growing concern of Viper and his Serpents attacking travellers passing by, when they had to journey near Komodo Jungle where they all reside in order to travel to Falcon City in the far south-east direction of the Planet of Phoenix.

'I pray to the gods in heaven for good luck to be bestowed upon you all and hope that you have a safe journey across the Swamp Fields and Wastelands in order to defeat Lord Scartor at Crow Mountain. If you want my advice, it would be best to avoid travelling through Eagle Forest, although it could be a quicker route. No one really knows what enigmatic creatures lurk in those mysterious woods. Also, in the battle, try your utmost to quickly take the control away from Lord Scartor, as I have heard stories about him retreating in a previous battle that had occurred in the Wastelands after he realised he was outnumbered and wouldn't be victorious. I hope you all return back to Pine Village soon and unharmed,' replies Flame compassionately.

'Thank you for your kind words, Flame, and yes, I understand you and the other Pine guards will need to remain to protect Pine Village, especially in this uncertain time when the creature threat is at its highest. It has been many weeks since Bruce and we have had a laugh over a pint of ale in Pinus Tavern. We all must do so when I return as I am sure we will all need the support from one another during the difficult times we might have to face ahead,' says Parrot warmly.

'Too right, Parrot. It has been much work and hardship for all of us recently due to the forever growing threat of creatures and the extra precautions required to be undertaken in order to protect Pine Village. It will be good for all of us to have a well-deserved relaxation soon. Bruce is currently in one of the watch towers in the south-east direction of Pine Village, but if I see him before you do I will let him know of our drinking plans. Take care, my friend,' replies Flame, nodding at Parrot and the men and women Pine villagers passing by. The sun continues to glisten brightly as the brave forty-one men, including Raven, Parrot, Leon, and Drakus, and twenty-three women Pine villagers, including Lemur and Bella, begin to ride upon their horses led by Parrot, Raven, and Leon out of the west entrance metal gate of Pine Village and continue journeying down the long cobbled road in the east direction leading towards Oak Village.

Eight

LIEUTENANT TRITON AND Lord Scartor's 151 Potorians, including the two Potorians who are still strongly holding a struggling Emerald and an unconscious Opal while riding upon their horses, have continued on their long journey in the north-west direction across the Planet of Phoenix. Along this journey, they enter the vile and malodorous Swamp Fields that are nearby to the mysterious and enchanting Eagle Forest. The Swamp Fields are constructed of deep water and muddy bogs surrounded by long weeds and rotten vegetation, which attracts and is covered with various poisonous insects and bugs such as hornets, mosquitos, and earwigs. The Swamp Fields overflow when it rains, which makes the bogs further deeper and muddier. The Swamp Fields have been a location in the past that have hosted a battle between the humans and creatures, and many of the bodies have been buried underneath the surface of the muddy bogs, which empowers a smell of rotten death lingering throughout the area.

Lieutenant Triton and the Potorians tread cautiously and steadily through the Swamp Fields down a passageway that is not as deep, muddy, and hazardous compared to the rest of the Swamp Fields. This safe passageway through the Swamp Fields is known from some of the Potorians who were previously nomad warriors; this was discovered after many attempted treks back and forth through the Swamp Fields when they required to travel back to the three main villages to steal either livestock from the Grass Terrain Fields surrounding the three main villages for food or clothing and tools from those villagers who ventured too close through the Grass Terrain Fields that were near the unforgiving Swamp Fields and mystical Eagle Forest.

These nomad warriors during their journeys would undergo the perilous excursion through the Swamp Fields to get to the three main villages as they would not dare enter through Eagle Forest that was next to the Swamp Fields and would have been the quicker route to the three main villages. The nomad warriors chose not to enter the mysterious Eagle Forest due to the shadowy stories they had either heard about the happenings in Eagle Forest from their nomad ancestors, which explained how some nomad warriors who had previously entered Eagle Forest had never returned to the nomad warriors' clans and huts located in the Wastelands. Also, occasionally the nomad warriors living in these huts upon the Wastelands that were quite close to the perimeter of Eagle Forest would sometimes hear bird like screeching sounds that were sharp and unusual as well as have glimpses of some weird green flashing lights that would shoot frantically through the dark and eerie tall trees in Eagle Forest.

Over thirty minutes have passed, before Lieutenant Triton and the Potorians cautiously ride on their horses through the Swamp Fields, where they narrowly miss standing on misplaced stepping in the ghastly muddy bogs, and all eventually reach the end of the Swamp Fields area, which brings them to the outskirts of the vast and exposed Wastelands. The Wastelands are made up of wide open red rock plains that spread across the distance in all directions as far as the eye can see in the horizon. The Wastelands are dry areas, where no rainwater is retained, preventing any vegetation from growing. Throughout the Wastelands, large rocks can be spotted that had fallen from the Mountains of Doom during avalanches. Due to the Wastelands not able to be cultivated with crops as they are extremely unfertile, the villages do not tend to branch out their settlements across the Wastelands, as it is lacking in natural resources; thus, the nomad warriors who were banished settled here so as to be far enough from the villages as they would not be under threat from those villages they had committed crimes against, but still be close enough to steal much needed resources to survive.

The nomad warriors who were banished to the Wastelands from the three main villages thus created small wooden huts that they made from the trees in Eagle Forest, which was right next to the Wastelands, leading to small clans of nomad warriors spreading through the vast Wastelands. At present, there are seven different small nomad warrior clans that are situated quite far from each other in the middle and around some of the edges of the Wastelands. The clans had developed separately as these nomad warriors were banished from one of the three main villages due to their heinous crimes at different times over the past 300 years and because the Wastelands are so extensive. These nomad warriors quickly build huts to live in without noticing that other clans of nomad warriors had already been developed at other areas in the Wastelands.

These nomad warrior clans usually keep to themselves and don't look to mixing or associating with the other nomad warrior clans as nomad warriors are known to be not very trustworthy or sociable humans due to their previous criminal offences they have caused against other humans. However, occasionally in present times, the seven nomad warrior clan leaders arrange to meet with one another at the same time in a specified location in the Wastelands to either trade resources, women, and wood or discuss any important events happening on the Planet of Phoenix with regard to humans in the three main villages or creatures like Lord Scartor residing upon Crow Mountain.

The only other reason why a meeting of the seven nomad warrior clan leaders occurs is to settle a feud between one or more of the clans if something happens between the clan members; these feuds are agreed to be settled amicably with either one clan member being killed or a fair trade taking place as they do not want to diminish the harm to the nomad warrior clans as a whole since they could be being vastly outnumbered by the other humans and creatures residing upon the Planet of Phoenix. Rarely there has been any battles of great consequence among all the nomad warrior clans, due to the lack of resources available to aid an efficient attack and also because the leaders of the nomad warrior clans feared if too many nomad warriors were killed, the existence of the nomad warriors might become extinct.

There had been previously more number of nomad warrior clans, but over the years some of the smaller nomad warrior clans joined with some of the other nomad warrior clans in order to increase security and protection within the clan. However, for this to happen the nomad warrior clan leader of the smaller clan would be forced to give his women and children to the bigger nomad warrior clan leader that they are joining with and the smaller nomad clan leader would also be turned into a slave of the bigger nomad warrior clan leader. This sacrifice was made in order to ensure the survival of the whole clan, but generally the nomad warrior clans wouldn't really join with other nomad warrior clans across the Wastelands unless they had absolutely no choice; the pain and suffering of the women and children forced some of the small nomad warrior clan leaders to make this unpleasant decision.

In recent times, no new nomad warriors or clans had been created from the banished criminals of any of the three main villages, as the three main villages' lifestyles were wealthier and more prosperous, enabling resources to be shared easily, as well as the humans were now more harmonious with each other in order to unite predominantly against the increasing creature threat existing on the Planet of Phoenix. The nomad warrior clans that already existed would, however, increase because the women nomad warriors gave birth frequently; however, the nomad warrior clans were also reduced sometimes rapidly due to Lord Scartor and Lieutenant Triton capturing the men nomad warriors and turning them into Potorians.

LIEUTENANT TRITON AND the 151 Potorians, including Emerald and Opal, continue on their long journey across the dusty, sweltering, and deserted Wastelands for over two hours until they approach a passageway of these sandy Wastelands to the Mountains of Doom called the Open Valleys, which is located near the south-west corner of the Mountains of Doom and leads to the foot of Crow Mountain, the smallest mountain amongst the five mountains that make up the Mountains of Doom. They all ride forcefully on their horses to quickly cross the Open Valleys that is made of small grass hills and winding landscapes.

After reaching the foot of the treacherous Crow Mountain, they begin trekking up the steep icy rock and stone paths of Crow Mountain, which takes another couple of hours due to the hazardous environment surrounding Crow Mountain; the ride up Crow Mountain is therefore slow as the temperature is freezing cold with windy blizzards and snow impacting the Potorians' and horses' momentum as they travel up Crow Mountain; the icy rock and stone paths are very slippery and steep. In previous experiences, those Potorians who had fallen over or down the icy rock and stone paths of Crow Mountains generally didn't survive due to the blistering temperatures of the snow, which ended up covering their bodies, or being cut to shreds because of the sharp edged rocks and stones they fell into, which are grounded in Crow Mountain.

Opal is still unconscious from the punch she had received earlier back at her and Wolf's small wooden house in Oak Village by the Potorian that is currently carrying her upon his horse. Emerald has been struggling since the start of the journey to Crow Mountain for the Potorian to release her from the strong grip he has around her while carrying her on his horse, but every time she struggles to break free, the Potorian tightens his grip around her more, which causes her cramps or numbness in her muscles, or he slaps her over the head if she speaks or shouts for help, which makes Emerald quiet and distressed. Lieutenant Triton and the 151 Potorians don't stop, hesitate, or rest on their journey back to Crow Mountain from Oak Village, enabling them to all manage to reach Lord Scartor's Lair of Death upon the top of Crow Mountain in just over three hours.

After making it to the top of Crow Mountain, Lieutenant Triton jumps down from his fierce black rhino in front of Lord Scartor's Lair of Death, which has a big iron door at the bottom of a tall solid rock fortress. Lieutenant Triton opens the big iron door to Lord Scartor's Lair of Death by a big iron key that is placed around the neck of a Potorian, who is also carrying the crystal finding device that he used to locate the anomaly crystal at Oak Village yesterday, but was unable to detect it earlier during the battle of Oak Village.

The crystal finding device is a small black machine that Lord Scartor had built and designed over forty years ago, using the dark magic energy and power from his golden sceptre. The crystal finding device has a glass sphere in the middle of it, which specifically detects energy from magical items. The crystal finding device was created by Lord Scartor for the purpose of finding the anomaly crystal, and it is also able to track the bloodline descendants of Grackle; however, it can only locate the area where the anomaly crystal or the bloodline descendants of Grackle are residing in and not their actual precise location. Lord Scartor had previously allowed Viper to use the crystal finding device eleven years ago to search for the anomaly crystal, which is why Viper had tracked Ruthus, who was with Jewel at their small wooden house in Oak Village. Viper had then killed them both with his poisonous black venom that disintegrated their bodies as they both did not reveal to him where the anomaly crystal was located.

After Lieutenant Triton unlocks the big iron door of Lord Scartor's Lair of Death, two of the Potorians from the inside of the big iron door remove the big iron plank from the large hooks fixed against the big iron door in order to open the big iron door from the inside. Lieutenant Triton climbs back on to the large back of his tough black rhino and rides with the other 151 Potorians upon their horses through the now opened big iron door until they approach Lord Scartor, who is sitting on his golden throne near a huge glass window overlooking the peak of Crow Mountain at one end of his Lair of Death. Except for Lieutenant Triton who remains seated upon his black rhino, all the Potorians quickly jump down from their horses and kneel in front of Lord Scartor on his golden throne, while continuing to hold on to the rope reins of their horses. The big iron door is closed and the two Potorians fix the big iron plank back on the large hooks to hold the door close, but they don't lock the big iron door with the big iron key as Lieutenant Triton is still holding on to it.

At the foot of Lord Scartor's golden throne, Emerald is forced to get down from the horse and is also made to kneel in front of Lord Scartor by the Potorian who had captured her. The Potorian who had taken Opal as hostage holds her in his arms while kneeling in front of Lord Scartor, as she is still unconscious. Lord Scartor gazes fascinatedly at the unconscious Opal; after a brief moment of examining her face, he finds that it reminds him of another girl from his childhood whose name was Veronica. Lord Scartor's scar upon the right side of his face begins to itch irritatingly again, and it casts Lord Scartor's thoughts back to one of his childhood memories.

During Lord Scartor's adolescent period and just before he left Alder Village that was located in the north-east corner on the Planet of Phoenix to relocate to Crow Mountain, he had developed his first and only feelings for a girl called Veronica. Veronica resembled Opal in that her hair was long, black, and curly, as well as she had a bright and smooth complexion with regard to her facial features. Veronica was a gentle and kind-hearted human, and she would spent her time after school helping her parents tend to the less fortunate or unwell villagers that lived in Alder Village at the time. Veronica was very humble and also well liked at the Alder School. Unlike many of the other Alder School children who bullied and ignored Lord Scartor, due to him being different from the other children. And because everyone knew that Lord Scartor's mother Angelina had died during his childbirth, Veronica was the only one who would speak with Lord Scartor and treat him with respect and compassion.

Lord Scartor had no friends for many years, and thus he found it difficult to interact with other villagers from Alder Village, especially since most of the villagers in Alder Village would keep their distance from Lord Scartor due to his unusual characteristics and abnormal scarred face. Lord Scartor felt very isolated and mentally hurt on receiving this treatment from the other Alder villagers; however, Veronica was different and she would always try her best to speak with and include Lord Scartor in the activities that the school children participated in Alder School. Many of the school children, especially one of the school bullies called Condor, were not pleased about Veronica speaking with Lord Scartor, but Veronica didn't care what the other Alder School children thought and continued to treat Lord Scartor like a normal human being.

Lord Scartor felt feelings that he had never experienced before, not just the feelings of friendship and enjoyable communication with another child, but also as he developed through his adolescence, he felt deeper feelings for Veronica. With Veronica in his life as a friend, Lord Scartor felt much better about himself, and this helped him to cope with the distress and torment that he constantly received from the other Alder School children during the time he attended Alder School. If Veronica ever saw Lord Scartor getting bullied by the other

Alder School children, she would stop the bullying straight away or tell a teacher about these actions as Lord Scartor would never speak with the Alder School teachers or his family about the extent of bullying he received.

Lord Scartor never built up the courage to explain to Veronica how he truly felt about her, although the other Alder School children like Condor realised that Lord Scartor really liked Veronica more than a friend. Condor knew how Lord Scartor felt about Veronica by the way he gazed at Veronica and also how he would collect items from her and keep it in his own personal locker in Alder School without her knowing. Condor was outraged by the fact that Lord Scartor liked Veronica, especially since Condor also was infatuated by Veronica's beauty and personality. Condor also understood that Lord Scartor was not only physically, but also mentally different from the other humans in Alder Village, as Condor thought that Lord Scartor possessed creature genes as well. Condor's parents were fanatic about creature hatred and also moulded Condor to share these same views and opinions about the creatures that also lived on the Planet of Phoenix.

Condor wanted to expose Lord Scartor's creature genes to the whole Alder School so that Veronica would find out about Lord Scartor and would not speak to him no more. One normal day, when Lord Scartor was entering the classroom in Alder School, Condor was sitting on his wooden chair, which was in front of his wooden desk, and he stuck his leg out to trip Lord Scartor over as he walked past Condor's desk. As Lord Scartor fell quickly to the floor in front of him, his face landed into a small bucket of cow's faeces that Condor had collected and placed at that spot earlier in the day. After Lord Scartor fell into the cow's faeces, he stood back up again and saw the entire children in the Alder School classroom laughing at him, all except Veronica, who was horrified to see this unfortunate situation.

Lord Scartor was mortified to see Veronica staring back at his face covered with stinking faeces. Lord Scartor turned round to look at Condor in an attempt to finally defend himself against all the bullying he had received from Condor. As soon as Lord Scartor turned around, Condor stood up from his wooden chair and kicked Lord Scartor hard in the belly, and this made Lord Scartor cry in pain. Condor began chanting aloud how much of a freak Lord

Scartor was and how he had killed his mother during his childbirth. Lord Scartor became outraged by this horrible situation he was experiencing, and unintentionally Lord Scartor released one of his dark magic creature powers that he didn't even know he had inside him. Lord Scartor's fury enabled his mind to physically explode all the wooden chairs and wooden desks in the Alder School classroom.

As Lord Scartor caused the wooden chairs and wooden desks to break without even touching them, the Alder School children realised that Lord Scartor was also a creature. As the wooden chairs and wooden desks exploded in the Alder School classroom, it caused many wooden splinters to fly in the air, causing many of the children to be pierced with these wooden splinters, including Veronica. These children ran out of the classroom screaming in fear and pain and went home to explain to their parents about Lord Scartor being a creature. The last time Lord Scartor saw Veronica was when she ran out of the classroom to escape from being pierced by those flying splinters that he had caused by his creature abilities. Lord Scartor did not return back to the Alder School because of these circumstances. Not so long after this situation, filled with hatred, Lord Scartor burnt the entire Alder Village in his attempt to find the anomaly crystal so that he could defeat the humans and rule over the Planet of Phoenix.

'Give me the anomaly crystal now!' shouts Lord Scartor impatiently, as he forgets about his childhood memory of Veronica from Alder Village and his scar on the right side of his face now itches less. A momentary pause and silence fills the surroundings in Lord Scartor's Lair of Death.

'We burnt Oak Village to the ground and slayed all the Oak villagers there, even including the leader of Oak Village, Wolf, and his Oak guards. We searched the entire village, all of the houses, cottages and shops but could not uncover the anomaly crystal anywhere. The crystal finding device picked up no sign of the anomaly crystal being there. Now that was not what it stated yesterday. Maybe the crystal finding device might have picked up some faults to it,' says Lieutenant Triton wearily. Lord Scartor furiously stands up from his golden throne in an absolute rage; he swings his golden sceptre quickly forward and uses its magical black laser beam to shoot at one of the Potorians who is currently next to Lieutenant Triton upon his black rhino. The magical black laser beam shoots out of the two-sided trident spikes on the top of the golden sceptre; it rapidly zooms across the air and hits that Potorian in the chest. His limbs explode into the air while the blood from his body and decapitated limbs falls to the floor, landing on the other Potorians, including Opal, making her very slowly regain consciousness in a drowsy manner, as her forehead becomes wet with the blood of the dead Potorian.

'The crystal finding device is never wrong! No, the worthless Oak villagers must have realised we were coming for the anomaly crystal and irritatingly hid it somewhere else. Go now to Pine Village. Destroy it completely and slay all of its villagers and search there for the anomaly crystal there! And this time don't return without it!' shouts Lord Scartor angrily. Opal starts to regain full consciousness, and as her mind and thoughts return to its normal state, she slowly opens her eyes and hazily looks around to see the grotesque Lord Scartor standing near her. Opal starts to scream loudly in panic, and the Potorian holding her forcefully puts his hand across her mouth to make her quiet.

'What are those disgusting vermin doing in my Lair of Death?' states Lord Scartor with supreme anger.

'We took these women villagers from Oak Village as we thought whoever had hid the anomaly crystal somewhere else would bring it here in order to rescue these measly women villagers. We also thought it would be a good idea to torture these vermin to find out any information about the current location of the anomaly crystal,' answers Lieutenant Triton resignedly, looking down at the Potorians who are holding tightly Emerald and Opal tightly.

'Well, your thick and dull mind can be useful sometimes, Lieutenant Triton. Take both these woman Oak villagers to the torture chambers and do what you must to find out where the anomaly crystal has now been hidden. If we have no new information from these women Oak villagers and if any other villagers have not come to rescue these worthless and disgusting vermin by tomorrow sunrise, then I order you to kill the women painfully and annihilate Pine Village and then Willow Village after until the anomaly crystal is found and placed in my hand as the rightful holder of it,' orders Lord Scartor in a furious manner.

'Yes, of course, Master, your will is my command. Potorians, take these women villagers to the torture chambers and find out where the anomaly crystal is. You other Potorians, go and hide in the Open Valley or the Wastelands. There you can ambush and slay any villagers who might come through that way to attempt to rescue these women villagers. Once you have found the villagers, search them entirely for the anomaly crystal and then murder them all,' states Lieutenant Triton, pointing across at a group of thirteen Potorians who are kneeling in a line in front of Lord Scartor sitting on his golden throne; the thirteen Potorians that Lieutenant Triton points to nod back at him to show that they have understood his orders.

'Yes, of course, Lieutenant Triton. Lord Scartor, our most powerful and miraculous master, we will do whatever it takes to find and retrieve the almighty anomaly crystal for you,' says one of the thirteen Potorians.

'You had better, Potorians, or I will blow your brains out with my golden sceptre and also slaughter all the others members of your nomad families and clans until the anomaly crystal is given to me!' shouts Lord Scartor wrathfully.

LORD SCARTOR SITS back down slowly on his golden throne in an irritated manner. The thirteen Potorians whom Lieutenant Triton demands to go back to the Wastelands quickly stand up from kneeling and run back out of Lord Scartor's Lair of Death; they decide not to ride on horseback in order to make sure they can hide somewhere undetected. The thirteen Potorians continue running out of the big iron door that is opened by the two Potorians on the inside of the big iron door; they unhook the big iron plank and fix it back up again on the large hooks once the thirteen Potorians have exited Lord Scartor's Lair of Death. These thirteen Potorians now continue back down the icy rock and stone paths of Crow Mountain. After their long and careful journey down Crow Mountain's icy rock and stone paths and through the Open Valley, the thirteen Potorians position themselves around the large fallen rocks from Crow Mountain at close by but different locations in the Wastelands, enabling them not to be noticed by any intruders or villagers passing through the Wastelands. Only the Potorians would be able to see them coming.

Back in Lord Scartor's Lair of Death, Lieutenant Triton jumps down from his strong black rhino and walks it by a golden chain around its neck over to a large room where the animals stay in Lord Scartor's

Lair of Death; the other Potorians also stand up from kneeling in front of Lord Scartor and pull the rope reins of their horses in order to take these horses also into that large room, where Lieutenant Triton had just kept the black rhino. All the Potorians put their horses into this large room, except for the Potorians holding Emerald and Opal tightly, who still remain kneeling in front of Lord Scartor, who is currently sitting down upon his golden throne. Emerald and Opal continue to be held tightly by the Potorians, which makes Opal to start crying as she is petrified at the situation she finds herself in and from the thoughts that have come back into her consciousness of her recent tragedy that she has experienced regarding her husband Wolf and son Leopard being murdered during the Oak Village battle.

Lieutenant Triton locks the door of that large room where the animals are kept with the big iron key that he had also used to open the big iron door at the front of Lord Scartor's Lair of Death. Lieutenant Triton hangs this big iron key up along with his golden chain with the spiked iron ball at the end of it upon large metal hooks that have been attached to one of the solid rock walls in Lord Scartor's Lair of Death. After this, Lieutenant Triton begins to shamefully walk away from Lord Scartor's main hall in his Lair of Death towards another big room that is used as the food quarters that is also at another of Lord Scartor's Lair of Death. Annoyed, Lieutenant Triton sits down upon a large wooden table and starts to chomp his way through large amounts of rotten horse meat that has been left spread across the large wooden table.

The remaining 136 Potorians, who had remained in the main hall of Lord Scartor's Liar of Death after securing their horses in the large room where the animals are kept, now return in formation in front of Lord Scartor who is still sitting on his golden throne at one end of his Lair of Death; all these Potorians begin to kneel at Lord Scartor again and will stay kneeling until otherwise ordered to do so by Lord Scartor. The two Potorians who were holding Emerald and Opal firmly now begin to drag them with the aid of two other Potorians to one side of Lord Scartor's Lair of Death, where the gruesome torture chambers are located. Emerald and Opal scream loudly in terror and proactively try to struggle away from the Potorians who are dragging them to the torture chambers. The other two Potorians who are assisting the original two Potorians punch and kick Emerald and Opal in order to make it easier for the Potorians to drag Emerald and Opal into one of the torture chambers.

The torture chamber where Emerald and Opal are dragged into is a medium-sized but confining room. It has different torture machines such as the Knee Splitter, Cat's Paw, and Head Crusher as well as pointy metal tools like hammers, iron pokers, metal claws, nails, and sharp knives lying around the room, with blood stains still over the tools because of the previous torturing that had been carried out. The four Potorians quickly and forcefully tie Emerald and Opal with rough tight ropes down to two dirty and bloodstained big wooden tables in the middle of the torture chamber room. The Potorians gag Emerald's and Opal's mouths with old bloody rags. Emerald quickly tries to bite one of the Potorians' hands as he attempts to put the bloody rag in her mouth; this Potorian swiftly moves his hand away after being bitten by Emerald, and he shouts loudly in pain. He then punches Emerald hard in the face in revenge for the bite she has given him; he then gags her again in the mouth with the bloody rag.

The four Potorians start grabbing various metal pointy and sharp tools, black leather whips, and hot iron pokers and start violently attacking Emerald and Opal with them slowly and painfully by scraping and piercing the metal pointy and sharp objects like knives and nails into their delicate and tender skin. Emerald and Opal try to scream in intense agony and excruciating pain, but then start to choke on the bloody rags that are stuffed firmly in their mouths and held in there by another one of the Potorians' hands. After a good few minutes of quick and nasty torture implementing various harmful techniques, the Potorian pulls the bloody rags out of both of their mouths, as Emerald and Opal choke and cry in terror.

'Where has the anomaly crystal been hidden now?' shouts a Potorian at Opal.

'I don't know!' cries Opal in fear as tears stream down her cold cheeks.

'And what about you, precious?' asks the Potorian, looking at Emerald's innocent and dejected face.

'I don't know either. Please let us go,' shouts Emerald toughly.

'Tell us where the anomaly crystal has now been hidden or that Oak villager has got it with them and then we will let you go,' responds the Potorian.

'We don't know where or what the anomaly crystal is!' yells Emerald.

'Very well. We will continue torturing you until you do know where or what it is,' replies the Potorian as the other three Potorians laugh.

'No, please stop!' screams Opal maniacally. The Potorian stuffs the bloody rags back into Emerald's and Opal's mouths, and they both choke again on the bloody rags unbearably. As one of the Potorians holds both of his hands over Emerald's and Opal's mouths to keep the bloody rags stuffed in them as a gag, all the other Potorians continue to horribly torture Emerald and Opal again in a brutal way, including sexually abusing them as well as burning their skin with the hot iron poker and whipping their chests with black leather whips. The Potorians also stab them slightly or scrape their soft skin with the metal pointy and sharp tools in the torture chamber; this dreadful torture causes Emerald and Opal to suffer throbbing hurt and discomfort that they had experienced before.

Nine

RAVEN, PARROT, LEON, Lemur, Drakus, Bella, and the other sixty-two men and women Pine villagers continue riding swiftly down the rough long cobbled road in the east direction across the Planet of Phoenix's Grass Terrain Fields towards Oak Village. The men and women Pine villagers ride sturdily upon their horses in lines, and spoken words are rarely shared between the Pine villagers due to the growing concern of what atmosphere they will find Oak Village in as well as they forthcoming battle the men Pine villagers will undertake against Lord Scartor, Lieutenant Triton, and the Potorian army at Lord Scartor's Lair of Death on Crow Mountain. As all the men and women Pine villagers led by Raven, Parrot, Leon, Lemur, Drakus, and Bella approach the destroyed Oak Village, they despondently begin entering through Oak Village's east entrance wooden gate to drop off the twenty-three women who have kindly come from Pine Village to help Ruby tend to any survivors and clean up Oak Village after the attack caused by Lieutenant Triton and the Potorians.

The black smoke caused by the fire upon the burning fence that used to surround Oak Village has now thinned out but it still lingers throughout the whole village. The fire that started at the north-east big wooden fence has now burnt completely out, but the thin black cloudy smoke causes the pine villages to cough as it tickles their throats in their mouths and the smell of death of the recently deceased abundant number of Oak villagers begins to spread throughout Oak Village, which is tough for the Pine villagers that are entering to endure. The eerie sound of silence along with the signs of burnt wooden houses, cottages, and shops everywhere unnerves all the men and women Pine villagers as they all cautiously ride down some of the wooden and cobbled paths, and their emotions quickly turn into despair and shock at the sight of the massacre that has occurred during the battle of Oak Village. All the pine villagers gasp or cover their mouths and eyes at the sight of such a horrific sight.

Lemur squeezes her arms tightly around Leon's body as they continue riding on their horse, as they follow Raven and Parrot. Raven consciously looks all around and scans the area for Ruby as they continue riding further down the wooden and cobbled paths of Oak Village towards the Oak Village square, but he cannot see her at present. Raven and Parrot keep pressing forward to lead the other men and women Pine villagers closer towards the Oak Village square where now the Pine villagers see the devastation of the wooden coronation celebration stage that had been mostly knocked over. Most of the Oak villagers' dead bodies lie upon it with their blood splattered all over the ground. Most of the women Pine villagers begin to cry and scream at such an unimaginable sight, as most of the dead Oak villagers would have been their friends or distant family.

As Raven looks further in the distance, he thankfully sees Ruby at one end of the Oak Village square in the north-west direction, where Ruby is carefully picking up the nearby Oak villagers' dead bodies but she is finding this task very difficult. Ruby is trying to put these dead bodies on a big wooden cart fixed upon wooden wheels to which two horses are attached by rope reins in order to pull the wooden cart. This big wooden cart on wheels had been used in Oak Village previously by Ruby's husband and Emerald's father Gaius to carry various trade items like cloth and tools as well as farm meat and vegetables between the main villages and Falcon City, but these wooden carts upon wheels will now require to be used to transport dead Oak villagers to Oakus Graveyard. There are a couple more of these big wooden carts on wheels in Oak Village, but Ruby had been only able to collect one earlier from one of the small fields, where some of the Oak guards' horses stayed behind Wolf and Opal's big wooden house.

Before collecting the big wooden cart on wheels, Ruby manages to find and calm down two rouge horses who have been running wildly around Oak Village since their Oak guards have fallen off the backs of them during the Oak Village battle; she then uses these horses to pull the big wooden cart on wheels to the Oak Village square in order to begin transporting the dead Oak villagers to Oakus Graveyard in the south-east direction of Oak Village. Raven taps the back of Felix with his heels and rides quickly across the Oak Village square up to Ruby in the north-west area of the Oak Village square, and he is followed by Parrot, Leon, Lemur, Drakus, and Bella along with all the other men and women Pine villagers. Ruby's cold dirty cheeks move up to give a slight smile as she first hears and then sees the sight of several honourable Pine villagers coming to her and Oak Village's aid.

'Ruby, it's good to see you again and sorry I have been a while, but now we've brought you help from Pine Village. Have you managed to locate any other Oak villager survivors yet from the battle? Wolf or any of his Oak guards?' asks Raven in hope.

'Thank you, Raven, and all of you Pine villagers for coming to Oak Village's and my aid in this most drastic of circumstances. It's very much appreciated. Raven, unfortunately I haven't found any other Oak villagers who are still alive yet, but I will keep praying to God and hope that we will find some as I haven't managed to search the whole of Oak Village at this moment in time or even been in anyone's homes or shops yet. I have, however, checked through all the bodies in the Oak Village square and near the big wooden fence where the battle all started in the north-west direction of Oak Village and have found no survivors. Even more devastating news that I can barely share with you all is that I found our poor Oak Village leader Wolf dead with his head split into half as well as Barious's broken body stuck underneath all the wood from one of the broken down flats,' cries Ruby, remembering when she had first uncovered the dead bodies of Wold and Barious and how difficult it was for her. Upon hearing this demoralising news, other men and women Pine villagers also start to shed tears from their eyes or cry hysterically at the news of Wolf's and Barious's deaths.

'My daughter had come to Wolf's coronation celebration festival early today. She has long blonde hair and brown eyes with pale skin. She was wearing a bright pink dress and pink shoes that I had made for her only last week. Have you come across my daughter yet? Please tell me she's still alive, Ruby,' cries one of the women Pine villagers.

'I'm really sorry, but I haven't found someone of that description as of yet, but we all must remain hopeful as surely our gods would be merciful upon such a tragedy that has occurred to our humble Oak Village,' replies Ruby softly, as the woman Pine villager begins to cry floods of tears at the thought of her daughter also being brutally murdered.

'In all my years of living on the Planet of Phoenix, I have never seen such a horrific or catastrophic sight,' says Bella in shock, climbing down from the horse that Drakus is riding and which is carrying her on the back of it.

'Don't worry, Mother, we will avenge Oak Village and these poor fallen villagers just as my father had done all those years ago, right, Pine villagers?!' Drakus hollers. The other men Pine villagers sitting on their horses cheer at Drakus's comment in order to ease the women Pine villagers that all these deaths of the humans of the Planet of Phoenix will not be tolerated. The other women Pine villagers who are on the back of the men Pine villagers upon their horses either hug or kiss their husbands or family members sitting on the horses and begin to carefully climb down from the horses. Leon turns around and looks into Lemur's saddened and tearful eyes; he gives her a long soft kiss on the lips.

'Be careful and come back, you hear, my husband? I couldn't bear it if anything would happen to you nor could our children. I have been with only you all my life and you're the only man I've ever loved, and my heart would shatter a million times over if I lose you during this horrible situation we are currently facing with those narcissistic creatures,' says Lemur unhappily.

'Of course, I will come back to you, my love. Don't worry, nothing will keep me away from your arms or that of our wonderful children. You are the most important thing in my life, and that will never change,' replies Leon in a comforting tone of voice.

'Thank you for those kind words and for all the wonderful memories we've shared together over the years. I trust the words I hear from your mouth as they have never let me down before,' states Lemur.

Lemur gives Leon another long adoring hug and climbs down from the horse she is sitting upon; she opens the big brown bag that she has around her back and starts handing medicines and bandages to the other women Pine villagers to heal any of the surviving Oak villagers they would find.

'Take care, my boy, and I will look forward to seeing you upon your return. Make me proud in avenging your father as those Potorians have had this battle long overdue,' says Bella, holding on to one of Drakus's hands as she stands on the ground and Drakus sits on his horse.

'Of course, Mother, these Potorians and creatures will feel the wrath of my axe,' states Drakus.

'Right, everyone, split up into small groups and search all the houses, cottages, and shops for all the poor Oak villagers. We will not rest until we find and help those unfortunate souls who have suffered on this most devilish of days,' says Bella loudly to all the women Pine villagers who have just got down from the back of the horses they were sitting upon on the journey between Pine Village and Oak Village. Bella leads quickly a group of five women Pine villagers in the south-west direction of Oak Village to start searching the small wooden houses, cottages, and shops while the other women Pine villagers also split up into groups of five or six and go quickly in different directions of Oak Village to also search the areas for any Oak villager survivors. Lemur walks up to Ruby and gives her a strong comforting hug and then starts to help her put the Oak villagers' dead bodies on top of the big wooden cart upon wheels pulled by the horses.

'We must go straight away to Lord Scartor's Lair of Death upon Crow Mountain to destroy those evil creatures and bring Emerald and Opal home to Oak Village,' says Raven to Ruby.

'Thank you, Raven and Parrot as well as all of you brave Pine villager men. I pray that Emerald and Opal have not been harmed and I hope that the gods watch over all you and that you will all safely return back home to your women and Pine Village very soon,' says Ruby as she smiles at everyone and then turns to Lemur, holding on to one of her hands. Lemur smiles back at Ruby and then gives a passionate look at her husband Leon.

'Ruby, as you said Barious's body is still stuck under the large pieces of wood at the broken down cottage that is close to the wooden fence in the north-west edge of Oak Village. If it's possible, I would like to bury him properly myself when I return. If you and the other women Pine villagers would be kind enough to retrieve his body and place in Oakus Graveyard ready for me, I will be forever in your debt,' says Raven softly with a tear rolling down his dusty cheeks, as the entire circumstances of his grandfather dying also bring back the memories of his parents Ruthus and Jewel when they were previously murdered by Viper, which makes Raven realise that he nearly has no family left to support or comfort him no more.

'Of course, Raven, you poor boy. Barious thought the world of you, as well as we all do. Barious was also a much loved human and will be dearly missed by all of the humans whether they are in the small or main villages as well as from the grand Falcon City. I will also miss him as much as I do your parents, and life on the Planet of Phoenix will never be the same again,' cries Ruby, and Lemur gives her another firm and consoling hug.

Raven and Parrot give a soft smile to Ruby as she looks at them, while Lemur is hugging her; the other thirty-seven men Pine villagers that are led by Drakus now kick the sides of their horses with their heels and start to gallop along the wooden and cobbled paths through Oak Village in the west direction towards the west entrance wooden gate of Oak Village. As Lemur stops hugging Ruby, Leon pauses for a brief moment to look deep into Lemur's small eyes and gives her an adoring smile, and then Raven, Parrot, and he control their horses with the rope reins in order to gallop off and follow all the men Pine villagers who are led by Drakus and are riding through the thin and lingering black cloudy smoke until they go out of Oak Village's west entrance wooden gate.

RAVEN RIDING UPON Felix, Parrot, Leon, Drakus, and the thirty-seven other men Pine villagers ride upon their horses swiftly in the west direction over the cobbled road that is laid across the Grass Terrain Fields of the Planet of Phoenix. The men Pine villagers continue this journey for about twenty minutes until the cobbled road ends as they reach the repulsive Swamp Fields that are located close to the mysterious Eagle Forest. The Swamp Fields cover a vast area where most of the grass and weeds are tall enough to tower above the average human size, which makes it difficult to plan their journey carefully through the Swamp Fields. One of the men Pine villagers already starts to tread upon his horse through the outskirts of the Swamp Fields, but suddenly his horse's hooves and leg accidentally trod in quick sinking mud and start to sink in one of the muddy vile bogs. This horse starts to frantically panic, and the man Pine village quickly yanks his horse's rope reins tight, which enables the horse to struggle with its hooves with all the muscle power in its legs. Fortunately, he frees its feet back out of the muddy bog and out of the outskirts of the Swamp Field to join back on to the cobbled road with all the other men Pine villagers.

'We're not going through here! We'll all sink into the disgusting muddy bogs before we get to the other side of it and into the Wastelands. Let's journey through Eagle woods. My father told me that it's the quicker way to reach the Wastelands anyway,' says the man Pine villager whose horse is rubbing one of its long legs against the other to wipe the sticky mud from its hooves.

'Yes, it is the quickest way to get to the Wastelands, but Eagle Forest is full of mysterious creatures and dark magic that is unknown to us humans. This is why everyone takes the long way around and even going through the abhorrent Swamp Fields,' states Leon.

'Leon's right. I wouldn't risk us all going through Eagle Forest. Who knows what lies deep in the heart of those black woods?' exclaims Parrot.

'Very well, we have no choice but to go through the Swamp Fields. Just be careful where you and your horses step,' says Raven as he starts leading Felix by his brown rope reins into the Swamp Fields, and all the other men Pine villagers follow him, treading upon their horses long and deep across the Swamp Fields. As they start their cautious journey through the nauseating Swamp Fields, the men Pine villagers keep getting bitten or stung by all spiteful bugs and insects that reside in the tall weeds of the Swamp Fields. The horses or the men Pine villagers also keep getting stuck in some of the muddy bogs, and time is needed to be spent on the man Pine village yanking the rope rein of the horse for it to struggle free from the deep muddy bogs.

All the men Pine villagers eventually make it near the edge of the Swamp Fields after around fifty minutes of gruelling trekking due them needing to take several different passageways through the muddy bogs to find a suitable way through it. At this time, swirls of grey clouds have begun to form high in the blue sky of the Planet of Phoenix; in fact droplets of light rain have started to fall to the ground upon the men Pine villagers and their horses; this eventually lead to heavy rain covering the entire sky. The men Pine villagers start getting incredibly drenched due to the heavy rain and their horses, and they become more covered in sticky smelly mud from the overflowing Swamp Fields.

One of the men Pine villagers is really soaked and feels uncomfortable due to being continuously bitten by hornets and mosquitos; thus, he unintentionally kicks the side of his horse hard in order for it to quickly get out of the Swamp Fields. As the horse starts to gallop through one of the passageways in the Swamp Fields towards the surrounding edges between the Swamp fields and the Wastelands, the horse misplaces its footing and lands abruptly into one of the large muddy holes; the horse and the man Pine villager begin to easily sink right through and down in the swampy mud that is now thicker and overflowing due to the rain storms.

'Help!' shouts the man Pine villager with his feet into the sides of his horses as he gets stuck into the large muddy bog. As his horse sinks more deeply into it, the man Pine villager frantically tries to release himself free from the thick mud, but he gets more immovable and continues to sink even more into the resilient muddy bog. Not far from the sinking man Pine villager, Drakus notices and hears the man Pine villager shouting for assistance. Without a moment's thought, Drakus kicks the sides of his horse hard with his feet, enabling the horse to forcefully gallop through one of the passage ways in the Swamp Fields; they narrowly miss other men Pine villagers along the way as they ride briskly past them.

Within minutes, Drakus reaches the man Pine villager who is sinking in the large muddy bog. Drakus jumps strongly down from his horse on to the side of the large muddy bog. Drakus extends the full reach of his long strong arm in an attempt to grab the man Pine villager's hand to pull him out of the large muddy bog, but unfortunately it is too late as the large muddy bog speedily pulls the man Pine villager and his horse in it. The man Pine villager sinks right through the large muddy bog and dies instantly as his lungs drown in the sloppy and suffocating mud. The rain pours more heavily on to the Planet of Phoenix's ground, and as Drakus wipes the cold wet rain from his bulky forehead with one of his big hands he looks up in sorrow in the distance, and Raven and Parrot see Drakus's facial expression.

'Come on, Pine villagers, we need to get out of these Swamp Fields now!' Parrot shouts. As the heavy rains pours more violently, all the men Pine villagers quickly kick the sides of their horses and scramble frenziedly through the rest of the passageways of the Swamp Fields, still trying to being extremely cautious so that none of them steps in any of the muddy bogs, as it would mean certain death due to the teeming rain causing the large muddy bogs to overflow with sticky and bulging mud. Drakus hurries back on his horse and joins the rest of the men Pine villagers in their agitated actions in getting through the last parts of the Swamp Fields without sinking into the large muddy bogs; finally, they all make it out of the Swamp Fields on the outskirts and on to the red sand debris of the vast Wastelands.

The Wastelands have a wide and humongous open plain covered with red sand debris and all sizes of grey and white rocks scattered across the Wastelands, which had been falling over many years from the Mountains of Doom. Also located in the south-west direction of the Wastelands is the Open Valley that is made of several small hills of sand, grass, and vegetation, which lead to the bottom of Crow Mountain where Lord Scartor's Lair of Death is situated.

A storm of thunder, lightning, and hail starts to pour from the sky of the Planet of Phoenix, as the sun now begins to sets in the west, bringing a darkness that quickly occurs across the whole area of the Swamp Fields, Wastelands, and Mountains of Doom. Raven, Parrot, Leon, Drakus, and the now thirty-six men Pine villagers are worn out and drenched from their careful trek through the Swamp Fields, as they have now become more exposed, feeling the cold due to the hail rain and the sharp stinging pain because of the bites of the insects and bugs, which had bitten them in the Swamp Fields. Raven, grasping his shoulder to ease the pain he is feeling from the wasp bite that had occurred minutes earlier in the Swamp Fields, takes a quick look over the vast Wastelands that continues on for as far as the eyes can see. Raven looks behind him to see the soaked, muddy, stung, and bruised men Pine villagers, which causes him to become upset;

he then turns to Parrot anxiously, who is on his horse standing next to him in front of all the men Pine villagers.

'Something doesn't feel right, Parrot,' says Raven, and just before Parrot can respond to Raven's concerns, Leon abruptly interrupts.

'Come on, Pine villagers, we need to ride across these Wastelands now before we get caught up in the storm, and we will not be able to survive it if we are stuck in the middle of that open plain of debris and rock!' shouts Leon. Leon suddenly kicks the sides of his horse hard again with his strong large feet, which makes the horse to start galloping heavily across the Wastelands, and red sand debris is kicked up from the ground, covering Leon's face. All the other men Pine villagers including Drakus understand Leon's warning and also quickly kick the sides of their horses, which makes them gallop briskly through the Wastelands. Parrot watches as the men Pine villagers charge off through the Wastelands, and then he turns to look at a nervous Raven.

'Of course, it doesn't feel right, Raven. We have never been in this situation before and are nearly approaching Lord Scartor's Lair of Death upon Crow Mountain. Who knows what black magic or creature abilities he has bestowed upon us, but don't worry we're all in it together and will protect each other,' says Parrot honestly.

'No, it's something else. I'm starting to feel some kind of mysterious energy that I haven't experience before. I think it's coming from this golden sword and the anomaly crystal that is now starting to concern me,' explains Raven.

'Don't worry, Cousin, everything will be all right, and the golden sword and the anomaly crystal are items to help you and all of us through this battle. I'll be right by your side too throughout the whole battle. But Leon is right. We need to reach the Open Valley before the storm gets any worse, otherwise we won't make it through the Wastelands and battle with Lord Scartor and save Emerald and Opal tonight,' indicates Parrot.

'OK, Parrot, I trust what you say. Just be careful through these Wastelands,' replies Raven, clutching on to his golden sword with his right hand and rubbing the anomaly crystal that is in his grey coat pocket with his left hand. Parrot nods back at Raven before also kicking the side of his horse with his feet, which enables it to gallop speedily across the enormous Wastelands. Parrot squints at the ground in an attempt to try and follow the trails left behind by the other men Pine villagers' galloping horses. 'Show me the full extent of your speed, Felix,' states Raven as he pulls tightly on to the brown rope reins around Felix's neck, and Felix gallops incredibly fast in order to catch up with Parrot galloping on his horse currently across the Wastelands.

As the men Pine villagers who are led by Leon and Drakus rapidly gallop across the Wastelands, they all swerve quickly from side to side in order to avoid crashing into the big grey and white rocks that they are only able to notice at the last minute due to the rainy storm and dark skies. Occasionally, the horses are too slow at manoeuvring and get cut on their legs by the sharp edges of the big grey and white rocks. Red sand debris also gets kicked up by the horses' hooves and smacks some of the men Pine villagers following behind the horses in the faces, which makes them irritated and causes pain and short stints of blindness in their eyes.

Felix races at his fastest pace across the Wastelands and occasionally jumps in the air over the smaller grey and white rocks, which aids him to continually gallop strong and fast through the Wastelands without hesitation, although Raven and Felix are hit all over their bodies by the cold hail rain that is dropping powerfully from the sky. Felix's continuous fast speed enables him and Raven to catch up with all the other men Pine villagers including Parrot, Leon and Drakus, and Raven and Felix now gallop at the back left side of the whole group of men Pine villagers.

Raven continuous to hold tightly with all his strength on to the racing Felix; however, when Raven looks up and squints in the far distance, through the hammering hail and the darkness, he manages to catch a glimpse of one of the men Pine villagers at the front left side of the group of men Pine villagers suddenly getting his head sliced off by a sword that appears from behind one of the grey and white big rocks; that man Pine villager dies instantly as his headless body falls from his horse on to the sandy ground of the Wastelands.

'Potorians!' shouts Raven at the top of his lungs.

MOST OF THE men Pine villagers become confused and start to panic after hearing what Raven has just shouted loudly to them; the men Pine villagers quickly pull their horses' rope reins tightly to stop the horses from galloping and bring them to an immediate halt, and the horses' hooves slide across the wet and slippery red sand debris of the Wastelands. Suddenly, thirteen Potorians rapidly appear from behind the various big grey and white rocks scattered in the Wastelands; they raise their metal sword and axes in the air and start charging on foot in the midst of the windy and hail storm towards the group of men Pine villagers upon their horses.

Leon sees the angry group of Potorians charging towards him and his fellow Pine villagers; without hesitation, he grabs his spear that is made of wood with a sharp metal spike at the end of it, which is hung to one of the sides of his horse. He lifts his strong arm in the air above his head and launches the spear strongly in front of him. The spear soars through the air, slicing through hail droplets that are falling heavily to the ground; within a few seconds, the spear smashes into one of the charging Potorians in his face. That Potorian gets his face torn apart by the powerful spear, and he falls roughly to the ground and dies instantly.

As the rest of the Potorians reach the group of men Pine villagers, they begin hastily fighting against the men Pine villagers who are still upon their horses, a bit disorientated due to the gusty storm surrounding them. The Potorians attempt to hit and stab the men Pine villagers with their metal swords and axes, while the men Pine villagers quickly try to block these brutal attacks with their metal shields. After blocking the attacks by the Potorians, the men Pine villagers, who have the advantage of being upon their horses, quickly hit downwards at the Potorians' exposed faces with their metal swords. After a couple of minutes of this battle starting, one man Pine villager and two Potorians are killed immediately. Drakus yanks the rope reins and strongly kicks the side of his horse with his large feet to charge his horse powerfully through the battle; with his huge rounded arm, he swings his battle axe around both sides of his horse, which causes him to chop three Potorians' heads clean off from their bodies, and their headless bodies crash-land to the ground.

The battle harshly continues in the hail storm, and thunder along with lightening begins to strike from the thick clouds in the Planet of Phoenix's sky on different parts of the Wastelands' ground, which causes small fires to spark from the red sand debris; also, loud sounds can be heard. A lot of the men Pine villagers are already exhausted and drenched from the journey through the Swamp Fields and the storm they had already experienced until this time, also as they have now endured some bloody wounds and scratches in the battle that is taking place with the Potorians, which makes them become weakened and chaotic in their fighting skills.

One of the Potorians approaches Raven and starts fighting with him; they both clash their swords together, narrowly missing cutting each other's bodies. The Potorian clashes his sword again hard against Raven's golden sword, unfortunately knocking the golden sword straight out of Raven's hand, and it falls quickly to the sandy ground. Raven nervously circles around, sitting on Felix, trying to locate his dropped golden sword on the ground, while also trying to avoid the continuous sword attacks of the Potorian.

Parrot is angry as he sees Raven getting attacked by the Potorian from a distance; he eagerly pulls out one of his fury raptor throwing stars from his big brown coat pocket and launches it straight at the Potorian. The sharp metal spikes of the fury raptor throwing star causes it to speedily fly through the air and hit through the Potorian's cheek; it ends up in his mouth, slicing away at his tongue and teeth. In explicit pain, the Potorian grabs the sides of his cheek and falls to his knees on the ground. Parrot now takes the wooden bow from his back along with the arrows from the pouch tied around his back and starts shooting these wooden arrows with sharp metal spikes at the end of them from his bow in the battle, and he hits two Potorians in the head, which causes them to be killed painfully. Raven continues to anxiously hunt around on the ground for his fallen golden sword; out of the corner of his eyes, he notices the rest of the battle happening between the Potorians and the men Pine villagers in the dramatic storm. Two more men Pine villagers are killed by the Potorians, who carve their metal axes into their chests and hearts. Once the men Pine villagers die, they fall from their horses hard to the ground far beneath them, and the horses of the fallen men Pine villagers in the confusion gallop off into the distant open space of the vast Wastelands.

Raven in annoyance begins to rub his right hand around the anomaly crystal that is in his grey coat pocket; he decides to pull it out and he quickly holds it towards the battle in an attempt to try and unleash the anomaly crystal's astounding powers in order to defeat the remaining four Potorians left. All the colours of the rainbow including the white and black shades frantically start to swirl around the middle of the anomaly crystal, but then after a few moments, the frantically swirling colours begin to slow down again and nothing happens from the anomaly crystal. Raven looks at the anomaly crystal in confusion, but then suddenly a wilful magical energy from the anomaly crystal causes Raven's hands to move and the anomaly crystal points itself towards the ground. He hurriedly jumps down from Felix, and guided by the wilful strong power of the anomaly crystal, it leads him towards his lost golden sword.

In the midst of the battle, Leon swings his metal shield and smacks it straight at a Potorian, which makes him fall hard to the wet and gritty sandy ground of the Wastelands. Leon then pulls the rope reins of his horse back tightly, enabling the horse's legs to lift up in the air, and then the horse drops his legs back down to the ground to trample the Potorian's bruised body with his hooves until he dies. In another part of the battle, a Potorian stabs a man Pine villager in the chest with his metal sword, which causes his liver to be torn apart. Drakus who is nearby sees this happening to the man Pine villager; he screeches furiously at the Potorian and rapidly gallops upon his horse towards the Potorian. As Drakus comes in close contact with the Potorian, he releases his grip from the rope reins and jumps from his horse right on top of the Potorian's back; he uses his huge hands to twist the Potorian's neck quickly until his neck twists so far that it causes his spine to be snapped, killing him promptly.

Another Potorian throws his metal axe through the air, hitting a man Pine villager's face, causing blood to squirt out from his wounded face, and he falls from his horse on to the ground of Wastelands and dies excruciatingly. Raven, who is close by standing on the ground and horrifically watching this man Pine villager being killed, quickly swings his golden sword out in front of him and stabs the Potorian forcefully in the chest; his formidable golden sword slices swiftly through the Potorian's flesh and bone and kills him, splitting his body into half with the two halves of the Potorian's body falling separately to the ground.

The last Potorian in this battle hurriedly attempts to manoeuvre through the rest of the men Pine villagers in order to escape and dash back towards the Open Valley leading to the bottom of Crow

Mountain. As this Potorian manages to remove himself from the group of men Pine villagers upon their horses, trying to attack him with their swords, Parrot quickly loads up another wooden arrow with the metal spike at the end of it in the middle of his wooden bow, and as he pulls the string back in the wooden bow, Parrot accurately shoots the wooden arrow with the metal spike at the end of it into the air, which cuts through rain and hail easily until it sticks into the back of the Potorian who is running away. The sharp metal spike at the end of the wooden arrow cuts right through the body of the Potorian until it reaches the other side and sticks out his chest, killing the Potorian as he falls to the ground. The men Pine villagers watching from a close distance are relieved the battle is over.

'Is everyone all right?' shouts Leon as he gets down from his horse and yanks the blood-covered spear that is lodged into the Potorian that is dead on the ground of the Wastelands.

'Yea!' shouts some of the men Pine villagers as they all pant or catch their breath, while checking their bodies to look at the wounds they have received during the battle.

'There's no time to rest. We must swiftly ride on to Crow Mountain, before Lord Scartor realises we are coming for him!' Drakus exclaims.

'What about the fallen men Pine villagers? We can't just leave them to rest in these cruel Wastelands,' says Parrot, upset.

'I feel your pain also, Parrot, but there's nothing we can do with their bodies at the moment I'm afraid. We are in the midst of a storm, and if we don't get out of it quickly, then all of us will also die,' replies Leon begrudgingly.

'Yes, let's get out of this storm and desolate Wastelands,' says one of the men Pine villagers, as all the men Pine villagers kick their feet in the sides of their horses to get them to gallop towards Open Valley.

Leon, Drakus, and the now remaining thirty-two men Pine villagers are all shattered being emotionally and physically drained from the battle, but they have no choice but to continue riding towards the north-west edge of the Wastelands and then onwards through the Open Valley that is made up of more sand, grass, and vegetation over hills; a small sand and mud path has been built by the nomad warriors to connect the Wastelands to the foot of Crow Mountain. Raven looks at the anomaly crystal in which the colours are now motionless. He still has the anomaly crystal in one of his hands from when he tried using it during the battle; it's now getting covered with rain and hail because of the storm. He quickly puts it back in his grey coat pocket before anyone notices it and climbs back on top of Felix. Raven pulls the brown rope reins of Felix and manoeuvres him to ride alongside Parrot, who has just started riding upon his horse at the back of the group of men Pine villagers, who are led by Leon and Drakus.

'The anomaly crystal did nothing when I tried to use it during the battle,' says Raven disappointedly, as Parrot pauses for a moment.

'I thought you said that Barious said it would only work and release magnificent elemental powers during intense emotions the anomaly crystal holder is experiencing during a threatening situation. So what emotions were you experiencing when you just tried to use it?' asks Parrot inquisitively.

'Well, I was really rather worried about finding that sword you gave me at the time. A Potorian had knocked it from my hand, which made me drop it on the ground, but I was also annoyed about the men Pine villagers suffering during the battle,' replies Raven as rain and hail pour down the sides of his cold cheeks.

'Maybe the anomaly crystal might need a stronger emotion to be experienced by you than worry and annoyance in order to release such astonishing supernatural powers,' states Parrot as he pulls the rope reins of his horse to quickly gallop faster along with the rest of the men Pine villagers; after another half an hour, they finally come to the end of the Wastelands that lead into the Open Valley in the north-west direction. Raven also catches up with everyone after pushing Felix to gallop at his immense speed.

Raven on Felix, Parrot, Leon, Drakus, and the thirty-two remaining men Pine villagers who are riding on their horses now reduce their speed to canter through the Open Valley's path built of sand and mud over the small hills, which enables them all to reach the base of the renowned Crow Mountain amongst the Mountains of Doom in twenty minutes. The sky in the Planet of Phoenix becomes even darker, and it still continues to rain, but the hail, thunder, and lightning decrease.

At the base of Crow Mountain, a man Pine villager kicks the side of his horse with his feet to start climbing up the icy rock and stone trails that lead to the top of Crow Mountain. The man Pine villager on his horse cautiously trots up to Crow Mountain on the icy rock and stone trails, but unintentionally his horse slips and loses its footing as the icy rock and stone trails are now more perilous since they are covered by the recent storm's hail and rain. The horse completely slips over and both the horse and the man Pine villager fall hard on to the ground and slide back down the icy rock and stone trail to the bottom of Crow Mountain and also accidentally bang into another man Pine villager and his horse, which also knocks them on to the ground.

'Be careful where you step, men. Crow Mountain has a treacherous nature about it, and we must be ready to fight quickly when we reach the top of it in order to surprise Lord Scartor, Lieutenant Triton, and the Potorian army if we stand any chance of winning this unforgettable battle,' states Leon as he climbs down from his horse and helps both the men Pine villagers who have fallen over back on to their horses.

Everyone takes a moment to calm and steady themselves upon their horses, before all the men Pine villagers undergo the long and tough climb up Crow Mountain's icy rock and stone trails with much caution. Leon and Drakus trot up the icy rock and stone trails of Crow Mountain, leading at the front, while Raven and Parrot ride at the back of the remaining men Pine villagers. As the long journey up Crow Mountain commences for many hours, the cold windy rain and snow that fall all over Crow Mountain freeze the men Pine villagers' hands and faces, causing sharp pain and numbness throughout their bodies.

Ten

THE BIG SOLID iron door of Lord Scartor's Lair of Death echoes with the large banging noises that Raven, who is sitting on top of Felix, Parrot, Leon, Drakus, and the thirty-two remaining men Pine villagers upon their horses make as they try to kick down the big iron doors with the horses' hooves. The attention of the remaining 138 Potorians, who are still kneeling in front of Lord Scartor on his golden throne in the main hall of Lord Scartor's Lair of Death, is quickly diverted to this loud and constant banging sound. Lord Scartor diverts his gaze towards the big iron doors at the far end of his Lair of Death, and the withered muscles on his face moves slyly as he grins sarcastically. Lieutenant Triton, who is still in the food quarters room, also hears the repetitive sound of loud banging coming from the big iron door in front of Lord Scartor's Lair of Death; without hesitation, Lieutenant Triton puts down the rotten horse meat he is eating and leaves the food quarters and rushes into the main hall to give his battle orders to the Potorians.

'Potorians, get armed with your weapons and kill all those that intrude into our glorious Lord Scartor's Lair of Death. On this day, some of the humans who had taunted us creatures for far too long will have their excruciating comeuppance,' orders Lieutenant Triton.

'Yes, finally my revenge will be bestowed upon those ancestors' descendants who cruelly mocked me all those years ago,' mutters Lord Scartor.

'Potorians by the big iron door and the Potorians also who are in the torture chambers, leave those vile women villagers tied up and lock the door to the torture chamber. You must come join us in destroying these fools!' shouts Lieutenant Triton as he grabs the big iron keys and his golden chain with the spiked iron ball at the end of it from one of the main hall walls, where these items are hanging upon big iron hooks. Lieutenant Triton hurries to unlock the door to the large room where his black rhino and the Potorians horses are kept.

Within minutes, Lieutenant Triton and over half of the Potorian army have retrieved their horses from the large room, along with their metal swords and axes; they climb on top of the horses and position themselves in lines in the main hall of Lord Scartor's Lair of Death, waiting for the orders to readily charge towards the big iron doors and slaughter all the humans who come through it. The two Potorians at the front of the big iron doors and the other half of the Potorians who were previously kneeling in front of Lord Scartor on his golden throne also gather their metal swords and axes, manoeuvring themselves in front of Lieutenant Triton on his black rhino and the Potorians upon their horses, waiting to also charge on foot. The four Potorians in the torture chambers, having heard Lieutenant Triton's orders, quickly stop torturing Emerald and Opal with the pointy and sharp metal torture tools.

'Don't worry, we'll be back to continue this fun,' laughs and smiles one of the Potorians at Emerald and Opal. The other Potorian who had his hands over the bloody rags that he had stuffed into Emerald's and Opal's mouths now releases his grip and also walks towards the door of the chamber room with the other three Potorians.

'It looks like your rescue party has come to foolishly attempt to save both of your insignificant lives. Unfortunately for you, they won't last one minute against us Potorians, our Lieutenant Triton's mighty iron spiked ball weapon, and our magnificent Lord Scartor's incredible dark black magic from his golden sceptre. Your fellow villagers are sentenced to certain death, and it'll be before you will get a chance to see them again!' laughs one of the other Potorians and the other three Potorians join in the laughter; in pain and annoyance, Emerald spits the bloody rag out of her mouth.

'It's you evil beings that should be afraid, for the strength, unity, and love within any of us humans outweigh any power possessed by soulless creatures,' states Emerald as tears stream down her eyes at the thought of Raven being murdered. The Potorians laugh again at Emerald's futile words and quickly lock the torture chamber door; they also gather their metal swords and axes that are placed at one side of the main hall and join the other Potorian group who are at the front of the lines formed by Lieutenant Triton on his black rhino and the other half of the Potorians upon their horses in front of Lord Scartor's golden throne. Emerald and Opal, who have been half tortured to death already and in unbelievable agony all over and in their fragile bodies, turn their heads to look at one another in despair; they begin to cry in hopelessness.

'It's all right, Opal. Whatever happens, I will be here by your side until the end,' remarks Emerald as she looks at Opal's bruised and scarred face.

The loud banging on the big iron gates gets louder and more frequent. Lord Scartor stands up in indignation from his golden throne and grasps tightly in his hands his supernatural golden sceptre.

'Let them come to their inevitable doom and then I will take the colossal anomaly crystal from them!' shouts Lord Scartor in wrath. On Lord Scartor's command, two of the Potorians who had come from the big iron door initially now leave their position at the front of the lines of Potorians on their horses and sprint across the main hall up to the big iron door of Lord Scartor's Lair of Death. These two Potorians run to either side of the big iron door and unhook a big iron plank that has been lodged in the middle of the big iron door on large hooks to keep the big iron door fixed shut from the inside. As soon as the big iron plank is removed by the two Potorians, the men Pine villagers' horses that had been constantly kicking the big iron door with their hooves now manage to push the big iron door inwards, and it opens wide in a matter of seconds.

A man Pine villager kicks his feet in the side of his horse hard, to strongly gallop through the now open big iron door, and upon entering, he forcefully stabs one of the Potorians, who is next to the inside of the big iron door, with his sword in the middle of his heart. This Potorian feels intense pain in the side of his body and dies as the man Pine villager pulls his sword quickly back out of his heart. Drakus, who had also just charged in on his horse through the big iron door, viciously cuts the other Potorian's head off with his hard battle axe. This Potorian's body falls to its knees before the head hits the ground. The Potorians in front of Lord Scartor's golden throne stand in anger as all the men Pine villagers including Raven, Parrot, and Leon enter the big iron door and now begin to charge down through the main hall of Lord Scartor's Lair of Death.

'Attack!' shouts Lieutenant Triton after seeing the two Potorians at the front of the big iron door were killed quickly. The Potorians standing in front of the Potorians on their horses first start to run towards the charging men Pine villagers coming towards them on their horses. Parrot speedily pulls out several of his fury raptor throwing stars from his brown coat pocket and throws them at five Potorians running towards the men Pine villagers. The several fury raptor throwing stars that fly elegantly through the air land into these five Potorians' faces and bodies; the sharp edges cause intense pain and wounds, injuring or killing the five Potorians as they all fall suddenly to the ground due to the shock of the fury raptor throwing stars being lodged in their bodies.

For those Potorians who don't die immediately from the fury raptor throwing stars' throbbing wounds, they quickly get trampled on by the rest of the army of Potorians, who are also running alongside these fallen Potorians towards the men Pine villagers. As Felix encounters Potorians who run up to him and Raven, he uses his large and powerful legs to trample the running Potorians, which causes their brains to be damaged due to Felix's sturdy hooves pounding into the skulls of these Potorians. At the same time, Raven stabs three Potorians powerfully with his golden sword, who are trying to attack him and Felix with their metal swords and axes; the blood of these Potorians who are stabbed firmly by Raven is discharged out of their stab wounds, which squirts in the air as these three Potorians fall to the ground.

In the midst of the battle that is currently occurring between the men Pine villagers on their horses and the Potorians who are on their feet, Leon pierces his long wooden spear with the metal spike at the end of it into the hearts of another three Potorians, as he charges right into them while running around. As the battle quickly gets heated in the middle of the main hall of Lord Scartor's Lair of Death, the other men Pine villagers swing their metal swords, spears, and axes frantically beneath them to attack the running Potorians on foot, which also kills another nine Potorians. Lieutenant Triton becomes furiously angry; he yanks the golden chain around his black rhino, which forces it to start charging towards the men Pine villagers in a rage.

As Lieutenant Triton charges on his powerful black rhino through the battle, he knocks over many Potorians who are on their horses as well as tramples over the Potorians who are running on the ground. As Lieutenant Triton gets in the middle of the battle, he robustly swings his golden chain with the spiked iron ball at the end of it out in front of him, and the spikes of the iron spiked ball smash through one of the men Pine villagers' chest, which breaks his rib cage instantly. Blood squirts out from this man Pine villager's body as Lieutenant Triton yanks the golden chain, releasing the iron spiked ball wedged in the man Pine villager's chest, and he now falls from his horse and hits the ground beneath him in misery. Lieutenant Triton swings the golden chain with the iron spiked ball at the end of it again around his head and launches it to bang straight into another man Pine villager's head; the spikes of the iron spiked ball go right through the head of the man Pine villager; this shatters his skull and teeth that fly out of his mouth in little broken pieces. This man Pine villager is killed within seconds of receiving the blow from Lieutenant Triton's spiked iron ball.

Lieutenant Triton swings his golden chain with the iron spiked ball at the end of it around his head again and uses it to violently kill another two more men Pine villagers, which makes Lieutenant Triton even hungrier to kill more men Pine villagers. The other Potorians also start to charge on their horses to fight against the men Pine villagers near the middle of the main hall; the Potorians' metal swords and axes clash hard against the men Pine villagers' metal swords and shields. As the careful manoeuvring and tactical fighting continue, both the men Pine villagers and the Potorians experience stab wounds on the arms and legs, and seventeen Potorians get killed by the men Pine villagers, but the Potorians also manage to kill four men Pine villagers and injure two more men Pine villagers.

Raven sees a Potorian on a horse charging sketchily towards him. He quickly pulls out one of his white nunchucks from his grey coat pocket; he chucks it into the air in a spinning rotation towards that Potorian. Raven's white nunchuck hits the Potorian hard in the face, which knocks him out, and he falls from his horse, crashing on to the ground. The horse that the Potorian has just fallen from now begins to run wildly confused around the large main hall in Lord Scartor's Lair of Death. Raven rides on Felix while swerving to his left and right sides to avoid the action in the battle in order to locate where Emerald and Opal have been taken to. Raven gallops on Felix towards the far edge of Lord Scartor's Lair of Death's main hall, where he notices some wooden doors that are shut.

'Emerald! Opal!' shouts Raven hysterically at the top of his lungs. In one of the torture chamber rooms, a disheartened Emerald hears Raven's loud voice calling out her name; she becomes astounded at the thought of her love still being alive and coming to rescue her and Opal.

'We're in here!' screams Emerald, banging her hands and feet loudly against the big wooden table that she is currently tied down to. Raven hears Emerald's cries for help from inside one of the shut wooden doors. He pulls the brown rope reins of Felix, and Felix stands up on his two back legs to start brutally kicking the shut wooden doors. Raven and Felix kicks through two shut wooden doors, until he finds the torture chamber room where Emerald and Opal are located.

In the battle between the men Pine villagers and Potorians, Leon forcefully fights his way through this alarming battle and decides to charge towards Lord Scartor, who is currently standing irritated in front of his golden throne at the furthest end of the main hall of Lord Scartor's Lair of Death. As Leon charges through the battle, while dodging the attacks from the Potorians' metal sword and axes, he boldly lifts his wooden spear above his head and sturdily throws it precisely towards Lord Scartor sitting on his golden throne. As Lord Scartor sees the long spear flying towards him, he quickly reacts by using his dark magic creature powers to shoot the magical black beam from the two-sided trident spikes from the top of his golden sceptre. This magical black beam hits the spear and immediately disintegrates it to dust just before it reaches his disfigured face.

Lord Scartor turns furiously towards Leon and shoots another but much bigger and more powerful magical black laser beam from his golden sceptre's two-sided trident spikes, which thrashes through the air like lightning that hits a shocked and oblivious Leon; this powerful magical black laser beam explodes Leon and the horse he is sitting upon into several segments of body parts that fly up high into the air and land back down on top of the men Pine villagers and Potorians who are fighting near Leon. Lord Scartor violently continues to shoot several magical black laser beams from his golden sceptre's two-side trident spikes at other men Pine villagers, which also destroy their horses' body parts and six more men Pine villagers are executed instantaneously.

'Leon!' shouts Parrot despairingly on seeing through the corner of his eyes Leon being blown up maliciously into pieces by Lord Scartor's golden sceptre's magical black laser beam.

Parrot furiously pulls his wooden bow from his back along with the arrows that are located in another pouch attached to his back. Parrot angrily starts shooting these wooden arrows with metal spikes at the end of them at five Potorians who are on horses in the battle; most of the wooden arrows with metal spikes at the end of them fired by Parrot smack the Potorians in the head, causing these Potorians to fall from their horses and die as they hit the ground beneath their horses with a firm thud. The horses of these dead Potorians also begin to run around the main hall and throughout the battle in terrifying panic. As Parrot continues to shoot arrows at Potorians from his wooden bow and Drake keeps swinging his large axe into Potorians' bodies, the other men Pine villagers and Potorians also continue to battle hard and painfully, and eleven men Pine villagers get killed along with another seventeen Potorians.

FELIX CONTINUES KICKING hard with his hooves to knock down the torture chamber room's wooden door behind which are Emerald and Opal. In the middle of the destructive fight between the men Pine villagers and the Potorians, Lieutenant Triton sees what Raven and Felix are doing to one of the torture chamber room's door; he yanks the golden chain around the neck of his black rhino to swiftly change direction in order to charge as he sits on top of his fierce black rhino towards Raven on Felix. The large black rhino viciously knocks the men Pine villagers and Potorians out of the way as it charges right into the side of Felix with its robust white horn; the sudden painful blow to Felix's side bangs him and Raven suddenly over, and they fall, crashing to the ground. Raven falls away from Felix, dropping his golden sword at the same time.

Lieutenant Triton aggressively swings his golden chain with the iron spiked ball at the end of it quickly out in front of him to hit Raven in the chest, but fortunately the iron spiked ball is stopped forcefully by Drakus's battle axe as he has also just managed to sprint over near the torture chamber rooms. Drakus swings his tough battle axe again in front of him to smack Lieutenant Triton in the chest; as the sharp metal battle axe pierces into Lieutenant Triton's thick chest, it gets wedged in it. Lieutenant Triton feels the brutal pain of Drakus's battle axe that is now stuck right inside his chest; he angrily yanks it out with his strong hands, and in a tragic moment, Lieutenant Triton swings the battle axe around and efficiently chops off Drakus's head. Drakus's large and bulky body falls to the ground slowly while his chopped off head flies in the air, and then when it hits the ground a few moments later, its head rolls along the ground towards Raven and Felix, who are still knocked in shock on the ground.

Lieutenant Triton pulls the huge black rhino up in the air by holding strongly on to the golden chain around its neck, and as the black rhino's large hooves lift from the ground and are about to trample Raven to death, Raven quickly grabs his golden sword from the ground nearby him and pushes it compellingly right through the black rhino's tough skin and straight into its heart. The black rhino feels his body tense up as his heart stops the circulation of blood rushing through its arteries; he stumbles back a bit on his back legs and then dies as he falls backwards, crashing hard to the ground. Lieutenant Triton also smacks loudly against the ground behind him as the black rhino falls backwards, which makes the black rhino land with a thump on top of Lieutenant Triton's legs. Triton releases his grip on the golden chain with the iron spiked ball at the end of it, which falls to the ground also. Lord Scartor sees the fight that has just occurred between Raven and Lieutenant Triton from across the main hall, and he suddenly notices Raven's golden sword that he has gripped tightly in his hand after he yanks it back out from the black rhino's heart.

'The sword of Grackle!' says Lord Scartor in astonishment.

'We can't defeat them all!' shouts one of the men Pine villagers in the midst of the battle in the main hall. This man Pine villager begins to swing his metal sword and cuts off another one of the Potorians' head.

'Keep attacking hard. We can win this battle,' shouts Parrot as he gloomily watches one of the men Pine villagers getting axed to death by a Potorian in the distance.

'Bring the women to me, Lieutenant Triton!' orders Lord Scartor, as he has become hungry for the sword of Grackle, which is what Raven is holding. Although Lieutenant Triton is injured from the fall to the ground, after hearing Lord Scartor's orders, he uses all his incredible bodily strength to heave the dead black rhino on top of his large legs, and he manages to roll the black rhino on the ground by the side of him.

Lieutenant Triton now stands up on his bruised legs and then charges into and smashes straight through the half-broken wooden door to the torture chamber, where Emerald and Opal still lie tied to the big wooden tables. Lieutenant Triton rips the dirty ropes from Emerald's and Opal's arms and legs that are tied to the wooden tables, and using his muscular arms, he swiftly carries them both out of the torture chamber room and across the main hall to Lord Scartor, while Emerald and Opal both frantically scream in terror. Raven stumbles to his feet in rage and starts running after Lieutenant Triton while dodging through the battle occurring in the main hall between the men Pine villagers and the Potorians.

'Parrot, I need your help!' shouts Raven at the top of his lungs as he continues to run after Lieutenant Triton, who is holding Emerald and Opal tightly. Parrot quickly kills four more Potorians by shooting the arrows with metal spikes at the end of them from his wooden bow; the Potorians are shot in the head with these arrows and they fall to the ground and die. After hearing Raven's plea for aid, Parrot kicks the sides of his horse with his feet and charges strongly upon his horse, knocking over the Potorians on their feet while galloping through the battle in order to catch up with Raven running after Lieutenant Trion.

At this time during the ruthless and difficult battle, the remaining five men Pine villagers continue battling hard against the remaining eighty-six Potorians in the centre of the main hall. Another seven more Potorians die, but then the rest of the Potorians on their horses surround the remaining five men Pine villagers and eventually slay all of them. As the remaining five men Pine villagers are slaughtered by the Potorians on their horses, twenty-one of the other Potorians on their feet begin to run towards Lord Scartor in order to protect him, where he is still standing by his golden throne at the far side of the main hall.

Lieutenant Triton, who has reached Lord Scartor on his golden throne, now chucks Emerald and Opal roughly on the ground in front of Lord Scartor. Lieutenant Triton uses his big dirty hands to hold Opal by the throat in order to make her kneel in front of Lord Scartor, and Opal begins to choke in horror. Parrot swiftly grabs Raven by his arms as he gallops past him on his horse and uses his strength to swing Raven into the air and on the back of his horse, and then they gallop together upon the horse towards Lord Scartor standing in front of his golden throne.

Raven, who is injured and upset now, begins to become completely overwhelmed by the magical energy from the anomaly crystal; as he feels this strong energetic supernatural force, he pulls the anomaly crystal out of his grey coat pocket, and he now sees all the colours of the rainbow and the shades of white and black frantically swirling around in the middle of the anomaly crystal. As he holds the anomaly crystal out in front of him, the shade of white suddenly becomes the most dominant colour temporarily, releasing the brightest white light from the anomaly crystal, which blinds Lord Scartor, Lieutenant Triton, and the Potorians momentarily.

'Enough!' shouts Lord Scartor angrily, stunned by the brightest white light he has ever seen, as he realises that Raven has just released this magical power from the almighty anomaly crystal. Parrot quickly pulls his horse to a halt with its rope reins, which stops the horse just in front of the golden throne, and Raven jumps down from the horse and looks up to glare at Lord Scartor in fury.

'Let the women go now!' shouts Raven furiously, as he holds the anomaly crystal out in front of him again, now realising that it can provide magical powers to protect him.

'You have the anomaly crystal! Give it to me along with the sword of Grackle and then I will let them go,' states Lord Scartor in a lustful manner.

'We can't trust him, Raven. Once you give him the anomaly crystal, he'll slaughter us and won't stop until he eliminates all the other humans amongst the Planet of Phoenix,' exclaims Parrot in an attempt to persuade Raven not to give Lord Scartor the anomaly crystal. Raven pauses for a brief moment.

'Let the woman and my cousin leave your fortress first and then I will give you the anomaly crystal,' stutters Raven fairly. Lord Scartor ignores Raven's comment and pokes Lieutenant Triton hard in the back with his golden sceptre. On feeling the poke from Lord Scartor's golden sceptre, Lieutenant Triton brutally tears Opal's head clean off her neck with his bare hands, squirting the blood from Opal's headless neck all over Emerald.

'No!' cries Emerald.

'Do not test my patience, you pathetic human. Now give me the anomaly crystal before my Lieutenant Triton kills the other woman!' shouts Lord Scartor furiously as the remaining fifty-eight Potorians, who have just finished killing the remaining five men Pine villagers in the battle in the middle of Lord Scartor's Lair of Death's main hall, make it back near the Lord Scartor's golden throne and begin to circle behind Raven and Parrot, who is still upon his horse, which makes them alarmed.

LIEUTENANT TRTION WHO is still holding Opal's head now releases his strong grip on it and drops it to the ground; he then steps to the side behind Emerald and grabs her neck with his strong hands, and she starts choking as her tearful eyes look up at Raven. Raven becomes engulfed with rage and fury at the sight of Lieutenant Triton strangling Emerald's neck. The anomaly crystal starts to swirl frantically again with all the colours of the rainbow and the shades of white and black, and then the whole crystal turns sharply into a bright flamboyant red in Raven's hand, and a faint violet line also arises across the centre of the anomaly crystal.

Suddenly the anomaly crystal employs its elemental magical abilities and releases an enormous ball of scalding fire that is directed towards Lord Scartor, Lieutenant Triton, and the twenty-one

Potorians standing behind Lord Scartor's golden throne. As the fireball hits everyone at the end of the main hall, a magical violet force field is also quickly released from the anomaly crystal, which mystically covers the whole of Emerald's body, acting as a force field to protect her from the fireball that engulfs everyone else. Lieutenant Triton unintentionally lets go of Emerald's neck and falls back far away from her as he is in agony after being burnt by the fiery flames of the large fireball. Eleven of the Potorians die instantly on being cremated by the fireball, and the other ten Potorians at the back are quickly burnt all over their body, but only endure minor wounds.

The immense fireball, after engulfing everyone and the end of Lord Scartor's Lair of Death, due to its immense heat also starts burning through the solid stone walls and completely shatters the large glass window on the wall behind the golden throne that overlooks Crow Mountain. As the glass shatters abruptly, it begins to pour on the ground outside Lord Scartor's Lair of Death upon Crow Mountain as well as inside the main hall, brutally cutting and slicing some of the Potorians who are standing behind Lord Scartor and the golden throne. As the immense fireball engulfs Lord Scartor, he hurriedly tries to use his golden sceptre's dark magic to also create a magical force field, in order to protect him from the fireball's heated flames, but the gigantic fireball is too powerful and fierce; it disintegrates his force field, along with melting most of Lord Scartor's golden sceptre, which nearly obliterates all its black magical powers. The black cape and mask across Lord Scartor's face is all disintegrated due to the fireball's flames, revealing a rotten old and gruesome scarred face beneath it, along with wrinkly and sagging skin.

Lord Scartor is now sore due to the burns over his face and body; he slowly bends over to pick up the remaining and half-disintegrated top piece of his golden sceptre that still has one middle trident spike at the top of it. With the last of the golden sceptre's dark magical powers, Lord Scartor creates a magical teleportation portal that is generated in the form of a large circle filled with cloudy, grey, bubbly smoke. Lord Scartor turns towards Raven, looking at his honourable face in fury and resentment.

'You haven't seen the last of me, heir to the bloodline of Grackle,' states Lord Scartor as he throws down the remaining piece of his melted golden sceptre on to the ground, turns around, and walks through the magical teleportation portal he has just created. Lieutenant Triton quickly stands back on his feet and runs back over to the torture chamber doors to collect his golden chain with the spiked iron ball at the end of it, which was left on the ground after Triton had fallen from his black rhino. Lieutenant Triton has to force himself to do this as he is still aching and sore from the burns he has just experienced from the immense fireball.

After collecting his golden chain with the iron spiked ball at the end of it, he makes his way back to the golden throne to join the remaining sixty-eight Potorians, including the nine burnt Potorians who have all quickly followed Lord Scartor through the magical teleportation cloudy portal that briefly stays open just long enough for all the Potorians as well as Lieutenant Triton to run through it. Upon entering the magical teleportation cloudy portal, it magically transports Lord Scartor, Lieutenant Triton, and all the Potorians to Lieutenant Triton's Underground Dungeon that resided at a different location in the Realm of Deserted Lands at the far south-west direction of the Planet of Phoenix. After a brief moment, the magical portal that is made from the circle of cloudy grey smoke suddenly disappears within itself.

Raven takes a deep breath and puts the anomaly crystal back in his grey coat pocket with his shaking hands; he quickly rushes over to Emerald who is now led on to the ground, injured as she is from all the suffering she has endured in the torture chambers. After Raven makes it next to Emerald, he hugs her strongly and passionately.

'I'm so glad you're alive as I never thought I would see you again! Emerald, I love you and want to spend the rest of my life with you. I want you to be my wife,' says Raven emotionally with tears in his eyes.

'I love you too, Raven, and of course, I want you to be my husband. You're the only human I ever want to be with. You're my soul mate and hero and I knew you would be the one to rescue me from this awful nightmare,' Emerald cries with joy and emotion. Felix who had been wounded in the chest earlier by Lieutenant Triton's black rhino, which had knocked him over with its white horn, and two other men Pine villagers, who were also wounded in the battle and had also managed to stop, calm down, and climb back on two horses who had been running around wildly, all now hurry back over to Parrot who is currently near the golden throne. Parrot on his horse, Felix, and the other two men Pine villagers on their horses all walk over to Raven and Emerald who are still hugging each other on the ground, still in shock from all the events that have just occurred in a matter of days. Emerald looks up and sees Parrot smiling back at them both.

'It's good to see you again, Emerald,' says Parrot happily.

'You too, Parrot,' smiles Emerald.

'This quest will be a legendary story that will be told to all our ancestors one day,' remarks Parrot.

'Yes, you are right about that, Parrot, and it will never be forgotten. Where did that gigantic fireball come from and how come I was protected from its burning flames? Did you have the anomaly crystal, Raven?' asks Emerald curiously.

'I'm really sorry about everything that has happened to you and all the Oak and Pine villagers, but it's a long and complicated story, so I'll explain everything to you another time when we are safe and out of harm's way,' says Raven softly, upset on looking at the scars and wounds upon Emerald's body.

'OK, Raven, I trust you with my life, and I know none of what has happened was caused because of you. But poor Opal and all the other men Pine villagers. We need to take their bodies back to our villages and give them a proper honourable burial. That is the least we can do since they risked their lives to save ours,' remarks Emerald humbly. Suddenly, the burning fire that has spread throughout the stone walls in the main hall continues to disintegrate its way through more walls in Lord Scartor's Lair of Death, and the entire building now starts to crumble, and large pieces of stone and rock start falling from the ceiling to the ground, narrowly missing hitting Raven, Parrot, Emerald, Felix, and the two men Pine villagers on their horses.

'We need to get out of here quick!' Parrot shouts. Raven hurriedly but carefully helps Emerald up from the ground and they both climb back on top of Felix. Raven pulls the brown rope reins of Felix to start riding hastily towards the big iron door at the front of Lord Scartor's Lair of Death, along with Parrot on his horse and the two surviving men Pine villagers on their horses. Lord Scartor's Lair of Death continues to rapidly burn down due to the extensive fire and flames, and the stone building crumbles more dramatically, causing more larger pieces of stone and rock to fall through the air, slamming hard on to the ground and shattering into smaller pieces, which fly through the air nearly hitting everyone. But as Felix and the other horses gallop out of the main hall, they swerve rapidly to miss broken pieces of stone and rock.

After a few moments, Raven and Emerald on Felix, Parrot on his horse, and the other two men Pine villagers on their horses all barely escape through the big iron door after galloping out of Lord Scartor's Lair of Death in terrifying panic. After leaving Lord Scartor's Lair of Death through the big iron door, Raven, Emerald, Parrot, or either of the two men Pine villagers don't take a moment to glance behind them, and they all quickly begin to carefully ride east down Crow Mountain's icy rock and stone trails. They continue on their long journey east, back across the Open Valley and the vast Wastelands and through the smelly, muddy Swamp Fields, heading towards Oak Village. As their journey home continues, Lord Scartor's Lair of Death collapses in a massive demolition behind them, destroying any of the other remaining horses, along with Lieutenant Triton's black rhino as well as the dead bodies of the men Pine villagers and Potorians that are trapped inside.

Eleven

RAVEN AND EMERALD riding on Felix, Parrot, and the two other surviving men Pine villagers who are riding on their horses all heroically return through the west entrance wooden gate of Oak Village, as the sun begins to rise again in the early hours of the morning. They are all exhausted due to riding the long journey back home through the dark and cold night; also they are wounded and devastated from being in the recent battle at Lord Scartor's Lair of Death upon Crow Mountain, amongst the Mountains of Doom in the north-west direction of the Planet of Phoenix. The early sun rises higher to shine brightly in the sky, which lightens the entire Oak Village; the black cloudy smoke there has now all cleared due the breezy winds that have been recently blowing.

During the night, the dead bodies of the Oak villagers that were scattered upon the wooden and cobbled paths or throughout the many small wooden houses, cottages, and shops have now been carefully placed by Ruby, Lemur, Bella, and the other women Pine villagers on top of the big wooden carts on wheels that are pulled horses. These big wooden carts on wheels had been relocated to be situated near a small grass hill in the south of Oak Village where Oakus Church is located, ready for the dead Oak villagers to be buried in Oakus Graveyard.

Bella had also found another bigger wooden cart with wheels attached to it at one of the few farms in Oak Village; she had tied two more horses to this bigger wooden cart so that they could put more of the dead Oak villager bodies on top of the bigger wooden cart, as Bella and the women Pine villagers had found many more dead Oak villagers when they were searching in the south-west direction of Oak Village, and this bigger wooden cart was also taken to Oakus Graveyard.

Oakus Graveyard is a peaceful graveyard and crematorium that is situated upon a small grass hill behind the small wooden Oakus Church in the south-east direction of Oak Village; Oakus Graveyard has many oak trees and various types of flower beds growing throughout the graveyard, including flowers such as roses, tulips, and daisies. Many of the dead Oak villagers' bodies had already been buried in graves in Oakus Graveyard, families had been placed together in bigger-sized graves, while the more burnt or chopped up dead bodies of the Oak villagers during the Oak Village battle were cremated and then their ashes were sprinkled across other graves in Oakus Graveyard.

Wolf had been buried in a special grave in a small separate section in Oakus Graveyard, which was beautifully decorated with rose flowers and small stone monuments, where only those from the bloodline of the leaders of Oak Village were entitled to be buried. Wolf was buried next to his father Jackal and mother Amber's double graves, who were also buried next to Jackal's father and Wolf's grandfather Hyena's double graves, along with their wives with them. Unfortunately, Wolf was only buried in a single grave by himself as his son Leopard's dead body was disintegrated by flames engulfing their wooden house when it was burnt by the Potorians during the Oak Village battle.

Ruby, Lemur, Bella, and the women Pine villagers hadn't slept all night, and they have now all got back together in the Oak Village square, continuing to clean up the rubble from the broken wooden coronation celebration stage as well as tending to a few Oak villagers who had fortunately survived the Oak Village battle, although these Oak village survivors have incurred severe injuries such as broken bones, stab wounds, or burns from the fire that started at the big wooden fence in the north-west direction of Oak Village.

As Ruby bandages one of the Oak village survivors' burnt legs with cloth, she hears in the distance the faint sound of horses trotting along the wooden and cobbled paths leading up to the Oak Village square. In hope, Ruby turns around immediately to see her beloved Emerald and Raven riding on Felix, alongside Parrot and two remaining men Pine villagers, although she quickly notices that they are all looking completely drained and injured due to the horrifying circumstances they had to endure at Lord Scartor's Lair of Death.

Ruby quickly ties the bandage on the leg of a surviving Oak villager and stands up to sprint up to Raven and Emerald, who have just entered the Oak Village square from the north direction. At the same time, Emerald also quickly climbs down from Felix and runs up to Ruby, and they both meet within a few moments, both giving each other a long heart-warming hug.

'My poor child, I thought I would never see you again,' cries Ruby as she squeezes Emerald tightly while hugging her.

'I'm so glad to be in your arms again, Mother,' says Emerald as tears start to stream down her cold, dirty, and bloodstained cheeks.

'Look at you. What's happened? What have those evil creatures done to you?' cries Ruby, who is upset and shocked, as she strokes Emerald's blonde hair back from her face that is also now covered in dirt and blood.

'It's all right, Mother. My wounds will heal, but unfortunately other wounds won't,' states Emerald, tears pouring out from her soft blue eyes.

Lemur, Bella, and the rest of the women Pine villagers leave the cleaning up of the rubble at the big wooden coronation celebration stage and also hurry over to the few men Pine villagers who have just returned to Oak Village. They look far in the distance but see that most of the men Pine villagers haven't survived, with whom most of the women Pine villagers were either in love with, related to, or friends with for many years. The women Pine villagers start to cry uproariously in sorrow and quickly hug each other for comfort or fall to the ground in despair. One woman Pine villager runs up to one of the young men Pine villagers that have returned to Oak Village, but he is half dead on his horse due to enervation; she hugs him strongly and cries in happiness as if he was her son. The woman Pine villager and other women Pine villagers help this young man Pine villager down from his horse and begin bandaging up a bloody stab wound in his leg.

AFTER LEMUR NOTICES that Leon didn't return to Oak Village, she collapses on to her knees on the ground and starts to cry hysterically. Parrot quickly jumps down from his brown horse and runs up to Lemur and holds her tightly.

'I'm very sorry that Leon did not return home with us, Lemur. My heart really bleeds for you. Leon fought honourably for you and Pine Village, and he killed many of the Potorians during the two different battles we had to endure against these creatures. Leon's strength and courage aided us greatly upon this quest, and without him none of us would have returned home. Leon is a truly remarkable human, someone whom we will owe all a debt to for the help he had provided all of us to during these battles, as well as enabling us to bring Emerald back home to Oak Village,' says Parrot empathetically to Lemur.

'How was Leon killed?' cries Lemur, streams of tears rolling down her face.

'Sadly Leon was killed near the end of the battle by ghastly Lord Scartor when we were in Lord Scartor's Lair of Death upon Crow Mountain,' replies Parrot as Lemur continues to cry hopelessly.

'Drakus? Did he fall as well?' asks Bella with tears accumulating in her eye, as she also kneels down to the ground and hugs Lemur from behind.

'Yes, I'm also very sorry for your loss too, Bella. Lieutenant Triton took Drakus's life during the battle in Lord Scartor's Lair of Death. Drakus was also another brave and bold human, and without both Leon and Drakus, we would never have been able to defeat many of the Potorians and for us few to return back to Oak Village after also saving Emerald's life,' says Parrot humbly to Bella.

'My son was a good lad and I am very proud to be his mother. I will always remember him in my heart and thoughts. Raising Drakus was the best thing that had ever happened in my life, especially when my husband was killed. Drakus was my support and my motivation. Let God help them both rest in peace in heaven together with the rest of our family ancestors,' remarks Bella.

'What about the bodies of Leon, Drakus, and all the other men Pine villagers who were killed this day? Did you not bring their bodies home with you so we could have put them to rest properly inside Pinus Graveyard back in Pine Village?' Lemur asks in disappointment.

'Unfortunately, all the bodies were destroyed back at Lord Scartor's Lair of Death upon Crow Mountain. We regrettably could not bring their bodies home with us as the whole building of Lord Scartor's Lair of Death collapsed to the ground due to an enormous fire that had occurred there at the end of the battle. We only luckily escaped out of the building alive ourselves,' says Raven sadly as he climbs down from Felix and walks over to give Emerald and Ruby a hug who are also still hugging each other.

'Leon's soul can't ever be laid to rest peacefully back in his home village. He promised me that he would never leave me, and now look what has happened. My children and I will never be able to visit his body and mourn over him properly,' cries Lemur in distress.

'What of those bastards Lord Scartor and Lieutenant Triton?' says Bella angrily at the upsetting news regarding Leon's and Drakus's deaths and of their bodies being destroyed.

'We were hugely outnumbered during the battle against them, but we fought bravely and valiantly. There were many decent men Pine villagers who died, along with Opal's life. That was also lost during this most unfortunate battle. We tried our hardest to defeat Lord Scartor and Lieutenant Triton during the battle, but unfortunately we were not successful in this attempt. Both Lord Scartor and Lieutenant Triton and some of their Potorians managed to cowardly escape just in the nick of time,' explains Raven, turning towards Bella and Lemur.

'If the building had collapsed, how did these grim creatures escape?' asks Bella.

'I'm unsure myself of what my eyes witnessed during this battle, but it seemed that Lord Scartor had created some kind of teleportation portal by using his dark magic creature abilities. A cloud of smoke was created from Lord Scartor's now broken sceptre. This cloud of smoke must have relocated them to another destination on the Planet of Phoenix. Where Lord Scartor and Lieutenant Triton are now however, we don't know,' replies Raven with a gutted feeling.

'Poor Opal, she will be missed greatly. Let's hope that she has reunited with Wolf and their son Leopard in heaven now. But those evil warlords are still alive. Are we ever going to be safe from those despicable creatures?' says Ruby as she hugs Emerald more tightly in fear that the creatures might come back to Oak Village and take her prisoner again.

'We will search the entire Planet of Phoenix until we find them! We will not let these vile creatures get away with what they have done to all of us humans and the unfortunate Oak and Pine villagers this day. I will go to Falcon City in the Kingdom of Humans to gather help from King Exodus and the other Pine and Willow Village leaders Lynx and Panther to do whatever it takes to finally destroy Lord Scartor, Lieutenant Triton, and their Potorian army. I promise you all that these creatures will suffer so much pain for all the agony and sadness they have caused the humans these past few days. I will also avenge Barious, my parents, as well as the loved ones we have all lost on this most tragic of days that has occurred in the history of the Planet of Phoenix,' exclaims Raven.

Lemur and the other women Pine villagers continue to cry at the heart-breaking news about the deaths of their loved ones, while everyone who are all close to each other in the north of the Oak Village square also subconsciously take a quiet moment to reflect upon what has happened and to pay homage in honour of the noble fallen men Oak and Pine villagers.

'I hope that Lord Scartor, Lieutenant Triton, and their Potorian army receive the worst possible torture in hell for an eternity for all the harm they have caused us innocent humans lives for no real reason,' remarks Bella.

'Do you think that King Exodus and the Pine and Willow Village leaders will risk their own villages and villagers' lives to battle against such powerful creatures without proper cause?' asks Ruby in a troubled tone.

'Of course, they will help us. For as long as these creatures exist on the Planet of Phoenix, we can't truly be safe and will always be worried that they will come back to attack us again,' states Parrot.

'No, no, surely they won't come back to our villages and attack us again. What about my children?' moans Lemur.

'We won't let that happen. Myself and . . .,' Raven starts to say when he is interrupted by Bella.

'Calm yourself, Lemur. Take a deep breath and everything will be all right,' mentions Bella softly. A moment passes as Lemur catches her breath.

'Thank you, women Pine villagers, for coming to the aid of the Oak villagers in their time of greatest need. Your compassion will not be forgotten by all humans who reside on the Planet of Phoenix,' says Parrot with gratitude.

'I must leave Oak Village now to get back to my poor children. We will not be able to cope without Leon, and what will happen to Pinus Tavern?' Lemur sobs hopelessly.

'Don't worry, Lemur, I will be there to help you with your children every step of the way through these horrible circumstances. I can also move into Pinus Tavern with you to help maintain it in Leon's honour,' says Bella, putting her arm around Lemur again.

'We will all be here to lend a helping hand for those who are in need. Us villagers and humans will unite together stronger than ever and are in debt to those fallen men Pine villagers. I will speak to Lynx when I see him back in Pine Village and he will also feel the same about this situation and along with his Pine guards they will make sure that the families of those fallen men Pine villagers will be supported financially and mentally, along with helping in the rebuilding of Oak Village,' says Parrot humbly as he knows what kind of human Lynx is.

'Were you able to retrieve Barious's body?' asks Raven quietly to Ruby.

'Yes, we managed to free him from the wooden rubble of the broken down cottage. It took many hours and several women Pine villagers to accomplish this. We have placed him in a coffin at the bottom of the hill by Oakus Graveyard. I wanted to wait for you to return before we buried him properly,' replies Ruby with a sad expression on her face.

'Thank you, Ruby, for this,' mentions Raven.

'You're welcome, my dear,' replies Ruby.

'I also would like to show my overwhelming appreciation to Bella, Lemur, the men and women Pine villagers. Your help will never be forgotten by us Oak villagers. Return to your loved ones in Pine

Village, get some rest, and pray for the souls of those villagers who have been untimely taken from us and the Planet of Phoenix,' says Raven humbly.

'We shall return to Pine Village and cope with our losses, but the situation that has just occurred has now changed all our lives forever and that's something that can't be undone. Upon my return, I will also send any able men Pine villagers to come back here soon to continue helping you all with the clean-up and rebuilding of Oak Village,' says Bella.

'Thank you, Bella. Take some of Oak Village's horses for all of your journeys back to Pine Village. I will return at a later time after I see Barious be put to rest in Oakus Graveyard. I will then spend my time back in Pine Village comforting any Pine villagers who need it as well as share many words with Lynx about the catastrophic events that have just recently happened,' says Parrot as he hugs Lemur strongly again and stands back up from the ground along with Bella.

BELLA AND PARROT help Lemur slowly up from kneeling on the ground and steadily puts her on top of the brown horse that Parrot has been riding on. Bella also climbs on to the same brown horse so that both of them can ride back to Pine Village. The other twenty-two remaining women Pine villagers climb on to some other free horses in Oak Village, apart from two women Pine villagers who get on the back of the two other surviving men Pine villagers upon their horses. Due to their not being enough horses to carry all the women Pine villagers, a few of them decide to walk alongside the horses, carrying the other remaining Pine villagers.

As the bright blazing sun sets higher in the sky above Oak Village and all the women Pine villagers attempt to smile back at Raven, Emerald and Ruby struggle with their distraught emotions. They then all begin to slowly and devastatingly leave along the wooden and cobbled paths led by Bella and Lemur until they all exit through the east entrance wooden gate of Oak Village and continue on the journey across the long cobbled road crossing over the Grass Terrain Field towards Pine Village in the east direction of the Planet of Phoenix.

Raven, Emerald, Ruby, along with Parrot who is holding on to Felix's brown rope reins after having watched all the Pine villagers leave Oak Village, then begin to walk through the rest of the Oak Village square and head in the south-east direction of Oak Village over to Oakus Graveyard. Once they reach Oakus Graveyard that is at the back of Oakus Church, Emerald now takes the brown rope reins of Felix and along with Ruby they walk through the entrance to Oakus Graveyard; the entrance is a large archway made of black metal that is tangled together in the shape of flowers.

Emerald holds on to Felix's brown rope reins, and along with Ruby, they continue walking through Oakus Graveyard passing by many newly created graves until they reach halfway up a grass hill. Emerald ties Felix loosely to an Oak tree near an open grave that has been dug especially for Barious to be buried in. Emerald and Ruby now begin to light white wax candles from a box that have already been put near Barious's open grave, and they carefully place them all the way around the edge of the open grave and begin to sing softly in unison couple of Barious's favourite hymns.

Raven and Parrot also walk through Oakus Graveyard entrance over to Barious's wooden coffin that has been placed at the bottom of Oakus Graveyard hill. Raven cautiously opens the lid of the wooden coffin and sees Barious lying inside it motionless and lifeless with his eyes closed; the scars are still over his body because of the pieces of broken wood that had crushed his body.

'Thank you for always being there for me for my entire life, Grandfather, and especially helping me continue growing up to be a decent human after my parents were unfortunately murdered. Tell my parents when you see them in heaven that I miss and love them more every day as I also will for you from now on until we are all reunited again in the afterlife,' says Raven quietly with tears rolling down his cold dirty cheeks. Parrot pats Raven softly on the back to comfort him.

'Our grandfather Barious and your parents, that is, also my uncle Ruthus and auntie Jewel, will always remain forever in our hearts along with the wonderful memories and time we all shared together. We are blessed to have spent time with these most cherished humans and will keep in our minds the life lessons and characteristics that we had learnt from them. But they would now not want you to be sad no more or live your life in sorrow for their untimely loss. They would want you to be happy and marry the love of your life, Emerald, and be a wonderful father to your own children someday. I will be here along with my parents, who are also your uncle Rio and auntie Olivia, whenever you need help with anything. We are your closest family and will look after one another no matter what,' says Parrot caringly, as Raven gives a slight smile back at Parrot. Raven looks at Barious again and closes the lid of the wooden coffin. Raven then grabs the front end of the wooden coffin while Parrot grabs the back of the wooden coffin, and they both slowly pick it from the ground at the same time.

Raven and Parrot carefully carry Barious's wooden coffin through Oakus Graveyard and continue walking up the grass hill until they reach the open grave that is halfway up the grass hill. They tie large ropes to the top of Barious's wooden coffin so that they are able to gradually lower it down slowly into the already dug hole in the muddy ground; after the wooden coffin has been fixed in the bottom of the hole in the ground, Raven and Parrot unhook the large ropes from Barious's wooden coffin. They stand back and look at the wooden crucifix that has already been placed at the top end of Barious's grave. Raven looks back down at the hole in the ground and stares at Barious's wooden coffin for a brief moment; he then slowly walks around Barious's grave to stand next to Emerald, who is standing next to Ruby at the bottom of Barious's grave.

Raven kisses Emerald on the lips and hugs her tightly, as Emerald and Ruby stop singing some of Barious's favourite hymns. Parrot grabs a handful of mud that is near Barious's grave and drops it slowly down on the centre of Barious's wooden coffin; a tear falls from Parrot's eyes as he walks over to some flower beds that had been planted in Oakus Graveyard. He picks four red roses from the flower beds.

Parrot then walks back over to Raven, Emerald, and Ruby at the bottom of Barious's grave and gives them a red rose each. Raven, Emerald, Parrot, and Ruby all stand silently for a moment and look at Barious's wooden coffin in the open grave, and then they turn to one another in sorrow as the sun's beams of light and heat shine down upon them. Parrot drops his red rose first into the open grave, and the red rose lands in the middle of Barious's wooden coffin.

'Goodbye, Grandfather, you were a wise and caring grandfather and human who will be greatly missed by all the other humans throughout the villages and Falcon City. We will avenge your, Ruthus's, and Jewel's deaths along with any other human who had suffered a similar fate because of those atrocious creatures. Until we meet again, rest in peace,' says Parrot sadly, as more tears form in his eyes. Ruby also drops her red rose on Barious's wooden coffin in the open grave; she does this while crying, as she is upset.

'Safe journey to heaven, Barious. Say a warm hello to Ruthus and Jewel for me. Life on the Planet of Phoenix will never be the same without you all sharing it with me, and I terribly miss the days and laughter we all used to share together many years ago,' weeps Ruby.

'Goodbye, Barious, you always made me smile and feel safe. I know you are proud of Raven and would have loved to have seen Raven and I start a family together, although I know you will all be watching over us from heaven,' sobs Emerald, as she also drops her red rose in the middle of Barious's wooden coffin, while holding on to Raven's hand tightly. Finally, Raven drops his red rose on to the middle of Barious's wooden coffin; his red rose slowly falls through the air in a timeless manner.

'Death is only the beginning . . .,' says Raven.

The Death of Our Time

Twelve

NEARLY A YEAR has passed since Emerald was taken away from Raven by Lord Scartor, his Lieutenant Triton, and the Potorian army when the horrific battle had taken place in Lord Scartor's Lair of Death upon Crow Mountain and Raven had first unleashed the magical powers of the anomaly crystal. In the past year, the humans on the Planet of Phoenix had been dealing and coping with the tragic news about what had happened between the creatures and the villagers of Oak Village and Pine Village. Many of these humans would pray and mourn the loss of their loved ones and friends who perished in the battles at Oak Village and at Crow Mountain. The tragic news spread quickly across the entire Planet of Phoenix, and the lives of the killed humans would not be forgotten, but even more importantly, it made the rest of the humans realise that the creatures existing on the Planet of Phoenix are a constant threat to their survival and action must be taken to ensure that such battles don't occur again.

Raven had spent the last year helping to rebuild Oak Village with the aid of Parrot, the surviving Oak villagers, the leader of Pine Village, Lynx, and his Pine guards as well as some Pine villagers who had decided to move to Oak Village, as they wanted to be in quieter surroundings compared with Pine Village's busy lifestyle and also to increase the number of villagers living in Oak Village. Raven had also now become the owner of his grandfather Barious's tool shop due to the tragic loss of Barious's life, which was taken in the Oak Village battle. In the battle, he unfortunately died after coming under a small broken wooden flat on being hit by Lieutenant Triton's golden chain with an iron spiked ball at the end of it during Wolf's coronation celebration ceremony.

Raven not only became the owner of Barious's tool shop, where Raven continued to manage Barious's long-standing business, he also continued to live in his room, and Emerald had also moved into Barious's tool shop in only just a couple of months after she had returned to Oak Village after being captured and taken as prisoner to Lord Scartor's Lair of Death on Crow Mountain. Emerald's mother Ruby was so pleased when Emerald was rescued and brought back home to Oak Village that it caused her to be a bit upset when Emerald wanted to leave home at first, especially after everything that had happened; Ruby wanted to protect her all the time in their home. Ruby, however, understood how much Raven and Emerald were in love and that Raven wouldn't let anything bad to happen to Emerald again; that made her feel better about Emerald leaving home, and also as Barious's tool shop was right near Ruby's house in the east of Oak Village, she was able to see Emerald daily.

Ruby continued teaching religious education at Oakus School; she also helped in restructuring the future of Oak Village along with Lynx, since Ruby was one of the oldest and most intelligent surviving Oak villagers from the Oak Village battle. That meant she possessed a lot of knowledge on how Oak Village was previously and how Oak Village maintained itself. Emerald also continued training as a gymnast at Oakus School; she also decided to teach younger Oakus School children who took an interest in the sport of gymnastics. It was also good that Emerald helped her mother Ruby teach children at Oakus School as all the previous Oakus School teachers had died in the battle of Oak Village. This meant that Ruby was the last remaining teacher in Oak Village, and she became the headmistress of Oakus School, although there were only a few Oakus School children that attended Oakus School, which included the Pine Village children that had recently moved, as all the rest of the Oak Village children were also killed in the battle of Oak Village.

After Raven and Emerald had spent many months living together in Barious's tool shop, Raven explained the whole story to Emerald about what Barious had told him with regard to his great-great-great-grandfather Grackle, who was the most powerful wizard, and his creation of the anomaly crystal in order to protect the Planet of Phoenix from evil creatures who would eventually attempt to destroy all the humans who lived upon it.

Raven continued describing to Emerald the story of the anomaly crystal and how it was passed down from all the ancestors within his bloodline, which was the bloodline of Grackle, until the anomaly crystal finally ended up in Raven's own hands to be its protector. Raven also explained what had really happened with the creature Viper and how Viper killed Raven's parents Ruthus and Jewel when he was only seven years old, which happened because Viper had been trying to uncover the anomaly crystal when he was previously in cahoots with Lord Scartor. Raven finished by telling Emerald the whole situation Raven and Parrot had to go through in their journey with the Pine villagers and battles against Lord Scartor and Lieutenant Triton upon Crow Mountain and how Raven attempted rescuing Emerald and the previous Oak Village leader Wolf's wife Opal.

Emerald was at first shocked to hear all the history of the anomaly crystal and the stories regarding what Raven and Parrot had to endure to rescue her and Opal after they were captured at the battle of Oak Village. Then after many tears, Emerald explained what heart-rending actions actually happened in the battle of Oak Village between Lieutenant Triton, the Potorians, and the previous Oak Village leader Wolf and his Oak guards, which included how nearly all the Oak villagers and Barious were brutally murdered as well as how Opal and Emerald were captured and tortured by the Potorians. Raven and Emerald continued to share many upsetting stories together and comforted each other for many months because of the tragic events that had happened in their lives, especially with regard to losing Raven's grandfather, Barious.

Both Raven and Emerald visited Barious's grave in Oakus Graveyard a number of times to say prayers, sing hymns, and speak to Barious about their current lives, as they believed that Barious was now in heaven with Raven's parents Ruthus and Jewel. Ruby and many other Oak, Pine, and Willow villagers as well as some Falcon City humans who also travelled for many miles and many times throughout the past year visited Barious and other dead Oak villagers' graves that were either buried or cremated, and these humans would light candles, lay flowers, and pay their respects to these unfortunate humans. The news about Barious's death, which occurred in the Oak Village battle, was devastating for all the humans who lived on the Planet of Phoenix, and the other humans became very angry and distraught, especially for Panther, who was the leader of Willow Village, and King Exodus, who was the king of Falcon City, as both of them were good old friends with Barious and had shared many fascinating memories with each other when they were teenagers and young adults.

Shortly after Raven rescued Emerald from Lord Scartor's Lair of Death upon Crow Mountain amongst the Mountains of Doom in the north-west of the Planet of Phoenix and took her back home to Oak Village, he had proposed to her while they shared a romantic meal he had prepared for her in his bedroom in Barious's tool shop, and Emerald accepted his proposal. Raven and Emerald, however, humbly decided to wait several months to have their wedding and celebrate this grand occasion because of the devastation many villagers had suffered due the battles that had recently occurred, leading to much grief to the villagers; also, a lot of physical work was required to be done by the surviving villagers in order to rebuild Oak Village and the lives that had been destroyed.

Eleven months after the battle of Oak Village had occurred, Raven and Emerald got married in Oakus Church, which was located in the south of Oak Village; Barious was buried in Oakus Graveyard along with Wolf and his bloodline ancestors and the many other families of Oak villagers who had also died in the Oak Village battle. Willow Church's vicar married Raven and Emerald as the Oakus and Pinus Church vicars had also been killed by Potorians in the battle of Oak Village. Raven and Emerald really wanted to have the wedding ceremony in Oakus Church as they felt it would be appropriate to have it close to Barious's grave as Barious had always wanted Raven and Emerald to get married and had promised to walk Emerald down the aisle of the church on her wedding after her father Gaius left her and her mother, Ruby, four years ago.

Raven, without having any doubt, decided to have Parrot as his best man and Emerald had Parrot's new girlfriend who was called Sapphire as her maid of honour, while Ruby enjoyed planning and conducting the whole wedding and the after party ceremony for them. It was a beautiful day and the sun fortunately shone brightly and warmly upon all of the villagers who attended the wedding and party ceremony, but it was also sad for Raven, Emerald, and many Oak and Pine villagers including Lynx, along with Sapphire's parents Sirius and Aura who also attended the wedding and party ceremony, as some of their families and loved ones were not alive to finally see Raven and Emerald get married, which many villagers had also hoped for.

After the actual wedding, Raven and Emerald also had a party ceremony in one of the Grass Terrain Fields located in the south of Oak Village, where Ruby had also arranged a variety of delicious food and appetisers to be served along with live instrumental music to be played; the party ceremony continued into the early hours of the night. Much laughter and good memories were shared as well as an enjoyable time was had by all, which many villages really needed after what they had all suffered through in the past year. Raven and Emerald's wedding would not be forgotten by those villagers who attended it. For her wedding present, Raven gave a beautiful Golden Retriever puppy to Emerald, which she loved and cared for instantly, and they both named him Rexus.

AFTER PARROT RETURNED home to Pine Village following the unforgettable events that occurred in Lord Scartor's Lair of Death upon Crow Mountain just under one year ago, he partook in many discussions with his best friend and leader of Pine Village Lynx about what had happened in the battle of Oak Village and the battle at Lord Scartor's Lair of Death upon Crow Mountain. Parrot also explained about some of the information regarding the anomaly crystal and what kind of magical powers it could unleash. They spoke thoroughly about how Pine Village should step forward in helping the remaining Oak villagers of the battles and how to begin rebuilding Oak Village to its previous state; they also considered about what would be the best option for the remaining Pine villagers who had lost their husbands, fathers, sons, and cousins.

After hearing the extensive news Parrot delivered to him, Lynx travelled to speak and also share this tragic news with his uncle Panther, who was the leader of Willow Village. Once they had met and discussed this inconceivable situation, they quickly decided to both return to Falcon City to converse with King Exodus in Falcon Castle about what to do next for an amicable handling of such a delicate situation as well as to prepare how to protect the surviving humans on the Planet of Phoenix from such treacherous and malicious creatures.

King Exodus, in his good nature, offered to give money from Falcon City's treasury to the victims and families of the battles in Oak Village and at Lord Scartor's Lair of Death to help them survive as they did not have presently any other form of income. He also sent some of his royal Falcon guards and Falcon city's resources such as clothes, weapons, and wood to help rebuild Oak Village, which also were aided by Lynx's Pine guards and more resources from Pine Village. King Exodus also made appropriate plans with his royal Falcon council and guards to prepare battle and survival strategies for all Falcon City humans along with the entire Falcon City for a great war that could occur.

In this past year, Parrot had not only spent a lot of his own time helping to rebuild Oak Village along with Raven, Ruby, Oak and Pine villagers and Pine guards, but also Parrot comforted and helped those Pine villagers who had unfortunately lost their families in the battle with Parrot at Lord Scartor's Lair of Death upon Crow Mountain. This included Bella, whose son Drakus was killed by Lieutenant Triton, along with Lemur and her children Siva and Sam, whose husband and father was Leon. Leon was also the owner of Pinus Tavern and he was killed by Lord Scartor using his golden sceptre's magical black laser beam that obliterated his body by the dark magic power in it. Since then, due to these mitigating circumstances, Bella aided Lemur by moving into Pinus Tavern with her, Siva, and Sam and helped continue manage Pinus Tavern with them.

Pinus Tavern continued its business as usual in honour of Leon, although they found it extremely difficult at first due to the much grief they felt for Leon and Drakus; they also received extra income and support from Parrot and Lynx for Leon's and Drakus's bravery in battle. The other women and children Pine villagers who had also lost their families and loved ones in the battle at Lord Scartor's Lair of Death upon Crow Mountain were also distraught because of the unimaginable events that had happened; they also found it hard to continue with their normal lives, but they also received help with regarding money and resources from King Exodus, Lynx, and his Pine guards.

A couple of months on after the battles in Oak Village and at Lord Scartor's Lair of Death, Sapphire who was Parrot's girlfriend briefly in Pinus School also returned home to Pine Village from Falcon City after completing her PhD in ancient language and literature that she had undertaken at Falcon University. Parrot and Sapphire had kept in touch for many years while Sapphire was studying at Falcon University, as they continued to have infatuation for one another; hence, Parrot was filled with much joy and happiness when she finally returned home to Pine Village.

After everything that Parrot had endured himself or witnessed other villagers suffer during the battles with Lord Scartor, Lieutenant Triton, and the Potorians, he felt he should grab life's precious opportunities before time slipped away. Upon Sapphire's return to Pine Village, Parrot quickly told Sapphire how he had always felt about her and found out that had she also felt the same way, and they wishes they had officially got together a lot sooner in their lives. After Parrot and Sapphire finally shared their true feelings for each other, they decided to become boyfriend and girlfriend and they fell in love immediately. Not long after being together, Sapphire moved into Raven's small wooden flat with him in Pine Village, and within a short space of time, Sapphire also became pregnant, and she gave birth to a baby boy that they named Tigra.

AS RAVEN AND Emerald have just recently got married, they are now currently on their honeymoon at Hydra Springs, that is an oasis of luxurious waterfalls, fruitful vegetation, and exotic wildlife in the furthest north-east direction of the Planet of Phoenix. Hydra Springs is in a much warmer and tropical part in the Planet of Phoenix, and it's a calm and peaceful area where nature has been left to itself, undisturbed by either human or creatures. The pure and crystal warm water residing within the springs continue deep down towards the core in the Planet of Phoenix. This water within Hydra Springs consists of unique elements that helps to spread rain throughout the

Planet of Phoenix and makes this planet habitable due to there not being other large sources of water such as oceans.

Raven and Emerald had travelled to Hydra Springs eight days ago with both of them riding on the beautiful black stallion horse Felix, who is Barious's horse, but is now owned by Raven due to Barious's tragic death. The sun is shining luminously, and the air is clear and quiet with an occasional faint breeze of wind fluttering by. Raven and Emerald are presently swimming naked in one of the small lagoons, where the light blue water is hot and crystal clear; various smooth rocks and beautiful plants surround it. Raven swims from the edge of the small lagoon underneath the steamy water until he reaches Emerald in the centre of the lagoon; he slowly arises from beneath the crystal clear blue water and holds Emerald firmly.

'I've never been so happy, especially after everything we have both been through in this past year. You complete me, Emerald. You have made me whole again, where I was broken for a long time. You enable me to take every breath I take,' smiles Raven, kissing Emerald romantically and pressing his wet body against hers.

'I love you too, Raven, and I am also blessed to have initially met you when we were young due to our parents being great friends. It's like it was always meant to be and I believe that the fate created by the Planet of Phoenix has brought us to be united as one together and we will be forever,' replies Emerald, kissing Raven back softly with her tender lips.

'I agree with you, my gorgeous wife. Everything has happened for a reason, although it's a shame we have had to lose some cherished family members along the way. That breaks my heart every time I think about how happy I am with you now, but that's because you have mended my heart. I do wish my parents and grandfather would have also been there on our wedding day though, as they would have been so proud and happy for the both of us,' says Raven sadly with teary eyes.

'They were with us, Raven, in our thoughts and hearts, and I felt them smiling down upon us from heaven. But you're right. It wasn't the same without them or my father. However, our wedding day was blissful, and I've had such a wonderful honeymoon with you. Thank you my hero, saviour, and protector. Sadly, however, our time here has to come to an end soon,' replies Emerald sympathetically.

'Does it have too? I wish we could just stay here together forever. It's so beautiful and peaceful here. It feels like no evil creature could ever harm this spectacular habitat or this special moment we are experiencing together,' remarks Raven.

'It's like heaven on earth and I feel so safe here. But yes, we will have to return to our home soon. I miss my mother dearly, and this is the first time I have been away from here since I was captured by the Potorians and taken back to Lord Scartor's Lair of Death upon Crow Mountain. That made her also very nervous about me leaving Oak Village and coming here to Hydra Springs while the threat of Lord Scartor and Lieutenant Triton still exists. My mother would never want something that bad ever happen to me again, although I convinced her that we wouldn't stay too long away and that you would never let anything bad ever happen to me.'

'Bless your mother. I do understand her concerns, but I would never let any creature ever harm you again,' states Raven.

'Also, your cousin Parrot and Sapphire have just given birth to the handsome Tigra. Thus, I said I would give Sapphire some help with his upbringing, especially in the first few months of his life, as this period can be the most hardest in raising a baby. That is what my mother told me. Also, I can't wait to see our loyal dog Rexus that Parrot and Sapphire have kindly looked after for us while we've been away on our honeymoon,' explains Emerald, smiling at Raven and stroking his back gently with her fingertips, the water from her fingers slowly dripping down Raven's skin.

'Yes, Rexus is a very magnificent dog and I'm glad you loved that I got him for you as a wedding present. I also can't wait to see Parrot, Sapphire, and my nephew Tigra too so that we can all share many catch-up stories with one another and watch Tigra grow up to be a strong and healthy human,' replies Raven.

'It's also now nearly been a whole year since we buried your grandfather, Barious, so I want to lay another bunch of red roses on his grave back in Oakus Graveyard if that's what you want too, Raven?' says Emerald softly.

'Yes, of course, that's fine, Emerald. I think my grandfather would love that and I expect Ruby would also like to do the same in paying her respects. I miss Grandfather very much and think about him every day just like I do my parents,' says Raven sadly as a tear rolls down his wet cheeks from his watery eyes.

'As do I, but I'm sure they're now our guardian angels and will aid in protecting us from harm and evil ways. You don't really talk with me about your parents much, Raven. I know you can't really remember them much as they died when we were both very young, but you must still retain some wonderful memories of them, and I'm sure it will help your pain to talk about them more with me as I want to be here to comfort you. It may also help to speak about your parents with my mother as she will kindly tell you many great and treasured stories they all used to share together for various years, even before we were both born. Your parents and grandfather were all remarkable and wonderful humans and are also missed by many humans on the Planet of Phoenix,' replies Emerald, while hugging Raven tightly as they pause for a moment.

'I appreciate your kind words, Emerald, but I generally don't like to speak about my parents as it hurts too much, since I can't even visit their bodies now at Oakus Graveyard due to that evil serpent creature Viper's poisonous black venom that not only killed them back at their house in Oak Village twelve years ago but also disintegrated their bodies completely,' says Raven with another tear in his eye, holding tightly on to Emerald.

'I know and I'm very sorry we can't visit a resting place for them, but they are all together now with Barious and are blessed in peace in heaven's paradise and will always remain in our hearts,' replies Emerald, as she passionately kisses Raven again on the lips.

RAVEN LOOKS DEEP into Emerald's beautiful blue eyes and kisses her on the nose.

'Thank you, Emerald, and I know I can always count on you for your support. With regard to returning home, I know Parrot, Lynx, and the other Pine villagers have been busy completing the restructuring of Oak Village, but are also having a special memorial service in Pinus Tavern in three days' time, which will be the first year anniversary for the men Pine villagers who were killed by Lord Scartor, Lieutenant Triton, and the Potorians at Lords Scartor's Lair of Death upon Crow Mountain. So I would also like us to go and pay our respect to the lost Oak and Pine villagers,' says Raven.

'I know how you feel, Raven, and yes, we will pay our respects to those brave men Pine villagers who risked their lives for ours. I expect Lemur, her children, and Bella are still feeling very upset after losing Leon and Drakus. I will go to see them also with flowers after we return home and make sure that they are both getting all right from the tragic events that occurred last year,' Emerald states.

Raven rubs Emerald's arms that still have some scars on them from the torture she had suffered from the Potorians in the torture chambers at Lord Scartor's Lair of Death. Raven then touches her hand and pulls it slowly out of the water, water dripping from their hands back into the lagoon. Raven looks at the golden ring he had given to Emerald at their wedding; this ring is made of pure gold and has the anomaly crystal fixed at the top of it. Raven and Emerald both look at the anomaly crystal on top of Emerald's golden wedding ring and become astounded at how the anomaly crystal starts to shine and illuminate brightly with the colours of the rainbow and the shades of white and black swirling frantically in the centre of it.

'We were lucky to have the anomaly crystal to use against Lord Scartor in the battle at his Lair of Death. Otherwise I don't know if any of us would have survived it, which means fate would not have led us to this special day for us. Have I done the right thing in putting the anomaly crystal on top of your wedding ring?' Raven asks.

'Yes, we were blessed to have the anomaly crystal on that horrific day, but I believe it was our destiny to survive. This anomaly crystal is over a few hundred years old and was passed through Grackle's bloodline generation to yours and now my hands today. We were meant to be the anomaly crystal protectors, just as it protected us from the pure evil of Lord Scartor. You will again need to use its astonishing powers to finally defeat Lord Scartor, Lieutenant Triton, and the Potorian army to finally avenge Barious, your parents, Oak and Pine villagers, and any other human soul on the Planet of Phoenix who have suffered at the hands of Lord Scartor and his nasty dominions.

'Lord Scartor should now be powerless without his dark magical golden sceptre, so also when we return home, we must go and speak with King Exodus in Falcon City as he or his royal Falcon guards may now have uncovered the location of Lord Scartor. We will need to find out where Lord Scartor is soon so that we can destroy him once and for all before he finds some other devious way to brutally battle against the humans of the Planet of Phoenix. And yes, I would rather keep the anomaly crystal on my wedding ring so it's with us safe all the time in case we will require using it against such evil creatures. Besides, I have you, Raven, to always protect me and the anomaly crystal too,' exclaims Emerald as she winks at Raven.

'Yes, I have already got plans with Parrot and Lynx to go to Falcon City soon to speak with King Exodus about Lord Scartor's fortress, as we will all make him suffer much deserved agony for what he has done to all of us humans. Although Lord Scartor doesn't have his golden sceptre no more, he is still very powerful in dark magic and sorcery, so we should all be very cautious of him at this uncertain time. Of course, Emerald, I will always be here for you. It broke my heart into sharp pieces when we were taken away from one another last time by Lord Scartor, and I promise that it will never happen again,' expresses Raven firmly.

'Well, whatever happens, one day soon Lord Scartor will get what's coming to him. I can feel it in my blood. But for now I suggest we forget about Lord Scartor and enjoy the rest of our memorable honeymoon,' whispers Emerald quietly into Raven's right ear, as they both begin to kiss each other passionately and sink beneath the crystal clear hot water of the lagoon together.

Thirteen

JUST UNDER ONE year ago, Lord Scartor, Triton, and the sixty-eight surviving Potorians escaped from the battle against Raven, Parrot, and the men Pine villagers at Lord Scartor's Lair of Death, located upon Crow Mountain amongst the Mountains of Doom that are in the far north-west of the Planet of Phoenix, residing beyond the Open Valley, Wastelands, Swamp Fields, and Eagle Forest. Lord Scartor, Triton, and ten of the sixty-eight surviving Potorians were wounded and burnt due to the immense fireball that Raven had fortunately released from the phenomenal anomaly crystal. The burns they had experienced from this supernatural fireball caused lasting scars upon their bruised bodies, as well as an agonising pain lingered upon the burn wounds for many weeks later.

When Lord Scartor, Triton, and the sixty-eight Potorians escaped from Lord Scartor's Lair of Death, they were all transported through a magical teleportation portal appearing in the form of a large circle filled with cloudy grey smoke. This magical teleportation portal was created by the dark magic remaining in Lord Scartor's melted golden sceptre, enabling them all to be transferred through normal space and time to the far south-west of the Planet of Phoenix in Triton's Underground Dungeon, which is located below the ground's surface in a dark and dangerous corner in the Realm of Deserted Lands.

The Realm of Deserted Lands resides in the south-west direction of the Planet of Phoenix and is mostly filled with silent emptiness covering an open rocky plain land for as far as the eye can see. The lands within the Realm of Deserted Lands are made of sharp and spikey rocks, and the air above these rocks is damp, cold, and dismal, preventing any green pastures or fruit to grow. Due to the lack of sunlight reaching the Realm of Deserted Lands in this area of the Planet of Phoenix, the sky above the Realm of Deserted Lands generally stays dark and gloomy, as thick gusts of strong winds covered with tiny rock and dirt particles sweep across these barren lands.

No human can live or dare to venture the Realm of Deserted Lands due to their being no sustainability to sustain their lives; however, occasionally wild creatures and monsters are inclined to lurk throughout the Realm of Deserted Lands, as they avoid contact with the humans located in other areas of the Planet of Phoenix. These wild creatures find it tough to survive in the Realm of Deserted Lands and are lucky if they find the occasional insect meal. The wild creatures and monsters that lurk across the Realm of Deserted Lands will fight to death if they bump into another wild creature, as they would need to kill this opponent for food as well as reducing the competition due to the sparse resources within the Realm of Deserted Lands.

After Lord Scartor, Triton, and the sixty-eight Potorians teleported to Triton's Underground Dungeon, Lord Scartor immediately become even more withdrawn and full of hatred against the humans of the Planet of Phoenix, as he lost the battle against Raven, Parrot, and the men Pine villagers in his Lair of Death. He was also outraged that his Lair of Death that had been his home for over eighty years was now burnt to the ground at the cold, snowy peak of Crow Mountain, and Lord Scartor was quite malevolent due to the fact that he was so close to finally grasping the much desired anomaly crystal and was instead infuriatingly tortured by the anomaly crystal's astonishing elemental magical powers. At first, Lord Scartor would take his fury and rage out on the Potorians by either physically harming or horribly kill them with cruel and evil curses that he would generate and cast upon the Potorians from his knowledge of magical potions and dark sorcery.

Lord Scartor killed a total of twelve Potorians by his conjured evil curses, which included rotting of skins until only the bones remained and confusion curses that would make the Potorians unaware of reality and end up harming themselves until they committed suicide. Triton was also mistreated badly by Lord Scartor, as Lord Scartor fully blamed Triton for losing the battle against Raven, Parrot, and the men Pine villagers at Lord Scartor's Lair of Death, although Lord Scartor tortured Triton with minor curses or sharp pains as he realised he still needed Triton to help him launch the great war against Raven and the other humans on the Planet of Phoenix in order to eventually retrieve the anomaly crystal.

Unfortunately for Lord Scartor, when his golden sceptre was destroyed by the fireball that Raven had created using the incredible anomaly crystal, the dark magical curse of possession that Lord Scartor had bestowed upon Triton many years ago in order to possess Triton's mind into making him want to serve Lord Scartor and become his lieutenant in the first place was now banished, as the dark power of Lord Scartor's golden sceptre was distinguished. Triton's mind and thoughts slowly started to change back to what it used to be like, and he began to realise that he was being manipulated and used by Lord Scartor, and he now started to resent the mistreatment he was receiving from Lord Scartor, although as he was less powerful than Lord Scartor, he decided it was wise not to challenge Lord Scartor's powers and knowledge of dark sorcery.

Triton continued to pretend being Lord Scartor's lieutenant as he was tenacious and resilient, which enabled him to survive through Lord Scartor's foul and devious torture. Triton promised Lord Scartor that if his life was spared, he would make sure that he would rebuild the Potorian army and finally take the anomaly crystal from Raven as well as kill all the humans existing on the Planet of Phoenix, especially those that had defeated them in battle. Lord Scartor accepted Triton's proposal, but made sure that Triton knew what the punishment would be for another failure in this great war.

Within a few days of recovery and settling into their new fortress at Triton's Underground Dungeon, Triton started to quickly begin rebuilding another bigger and better Potorian army, and he would travel back to the Wastelands with other existing Potorians and they would capture more men nomad warriors from the Wastelands again and would bring them on the long journey back to his Underground Dungeon in the Realm of Deserted Lands and force them to be trained into Potorians. This process took many months to execute as it was a three-week journey from Triton's Underground Dungeon in the far south-west of the Realm of Deserted Lands to the Wastelands in the north of the Planet of Phoenix; also, time was needed for preparation in fighting and capturing against the nomad warrior tribes, along with training these savage humans to be strong Potorian warriors.

THROUGHOUT THESE SEVERAL long journeys taken by Triton and some of the existing Potorian army to the Wastelands to capture and recruit more nomad warriors, Triton unintentionally bumped into two wild creatures on different occasions in the Realm of Deserted Lands called Vicious and Vulture; after defeating both of them in battle, he stated that he would spare their lives if they would join him and Lord Scartor in the inevitable great war. Triton hence recruited Vicious and Vulture as his own henchmen to aid himself and the Potorian army in winning the great war against the humans on the Planet of Phoenix.

Triton's new henchman Vicious is thirty-three years old; he has no hair over his entire body and has dark brown eyes and dark skin. He possesses a very large muscly build that enables him to possess enormous strength due to which he can break metal with his bare hands. Vicious can also breathe intense burning fire from his mouth, and when he burps, it releases a large shockwave of intense power that can destroy small brick buildings. Vicious can be a really loyal creature, but he's solemn and .cruel so he hungers for challenging fights in battles as he has done so for many years against other creatures or monsters that roam throughout the Realm of Deserted Lands as well as other humans he has encountered and killed throughout the Planet of Phoenix. Triton's other new henchman Vulture is twenty-eight years old and looks like the bird vulture animal; he can fly because of the power in his big black feathery wings attached to his feathery body and he can also use his creature abilities to grow larger and smaller in size. Vulture has long sharp claws at the end of his black feathery arms and feathery legs by which he can pierce flesh and bone with great ease. Vulture has a very enthusiastic and mischievous personality and likes to be the centre of attention.

During these several journeys between the Wastelands and Triton's Underground Dungeon, Triton was also lucky enough to meet a woman creature who was called Venus; shortly after interacting with one another, they became lovers. Venus is twenty-six years old; she is of Chinese origin and has black long silky straight hair and pure red eyes. Venus is breathtakingly beautiful with smooth and thin skin; she however has very domineering, possessive, manipulative, and seductive characteristics that she exploits by wearing provocative clothing, which includes a purple and red corset with black fishnet tights and high black leather boots. Venus is a Metamorphmagi and Animagi, which enables her to be a witch that uses magical creature abilities to change her physical appearance into other humans as well as animals. Because of also possessing such unique creature genes, Venus has also developed magical creature powers that facilitate her to physically create animals such as creatures and dinosaurs.

Venus, however, has a tormented soul because she knows very little about her parents as she was abandoned in the Realm of Deserted Lands when she was a young child, since her parents Axel and Miranda from Falcon City realised that their daughter Venus was of creature origin and wanted to get rid of her secretly before King Exodus and the royal Falcon guards realised this truth. After being abandoned by her parents, Venus quickly learnt how to use her Metamorphmagus and Animagus abilities in order to help her survive in such harsh conditions in the Realm of Deserted Lands.

As Venus grew older, she decided to investigate and study about the human race, so she would fly over Falcon City in the physical form of a white dove, which she was able to do by using her Animagus abilities that turned her physical body into an actual animal like the white dove. After many years of flying around Falcon City and listening to conversations through the windows of Falcon City humans' brick houses, Venus discovered what had happened to her as a young child and hated the humans for disowning human children with creature abilities. Finally, after Venus had found out who her parents Axel and Miranda actually were, she created a small venomous black spider with a red stripe down the middle of its back using her magical creature abilities, which she released in Axel and Miranda's house, and it bit them both and poisoned them until they were killed.

Triton and Venus had met just over five months ago when Triton was in the Wastelands fighting and capturing men nomad warriors from their small wooden huts and clans in order to turn them into Potorians, ready for when the right time approaches for Lord Scartor to launch his great war against the humans in the Planet of Phoenix. Venus had been flying around and analysing the Wasteland area in her Quetzalcoatlus form, a bird flying dinosaur that she created from her Animagus abilities, which she had managed to master during the previous years.

After watching Triton in action for many days, Venus admired Triton's strength, power, and brute force. After observing Triton fight and capture the men nomad warriors, Venus wanted to make sure that Triton was worthy of her heart. Venus thus waited and finally introduced herself to Triton on his journey back to the Realm of Deserted Lands, Triton was mesmerised by Venus's beauty, flirtatious seduction, and also her interest in him, which is something that Triton had never experienced before with a women. When Venus flew down to the rocky surface of the Realm of Deserted Lands in her Quetzalcoatlus form and used her Animagus abilities to turn back into her human form, Triton was also amazed at her remarkable creature abilities and could see her as a fierce asset in the forthcoming great war.

After a few hours together, during which they journeyed back to Triton's Underground Dungeon in the far south-west corner of the Realm of Deserted Lands, Triton and Venus had become lovers instantly and thereafter shared many passionate nights with each other. Lord Scartor obviously resented Venus when Triton had brought her back to the Underground Dungeon as he didn't want her distracting Triton from his duties in building a bigger creature and Potorian army in order to retrieve the anomaly crystal. Lord Scartor, however, also instantly sensed how powerful Venus's creature abilities were and didn't want to get on the wrong side of her, so Lord Scartor rarely spoke with Venus. Instead, he just ordered Triton to continue on with his normal duties and agreed to allow Venus to also stay in Triton's Underground Dungeon as per Triton's wishes.

Triton's Underground Dungeon is a big underground building made of rock, which is surrounded by hot boiling lava and fire; the Underground Dungeon resides in the darkest part of the Planet of Phoenix deep below the rocky surface in the Realm of Deserted Lands. It had taken Triton many years to construct his Underground Dungeon after he was initially abandoned by his parents Taurus and Trudy when he was a child as they realised a part of him was of creature origin. Triton had then lived in his Underground Dungeon until Lord Scartor found him and brainwashed him with a possession curse so that Triton would become his lieutenant, after which Lord Scartor made Triton leave his Underground Dungeon and relocate back to Lord Scartor's Lair of Death upon Crow Mountain as he wanted him to create his Potorian army from the nearby nomad warriors who resided in the Wastelands at the bottom of the Mountains of Doom. But Lord Scartor also realised that Triton's Underground Dungeon would serve as a good hideout fortress to go into in times of unpredicted emergencies.

Triton's Underground Dungeon has many different sleeping rooms, where Lord Scartor and the Potorians now live along with Triton's new henchmen Vicious and Vulture. Triton's Underground Dungeon also has a torture chamber and a medium-sized main room that has uncovered pits throughout the rocky floor, exposing the Planet of Phoenix's scorching lava. There is also another food preparation room amongst the hallways and sleeping rooms, where Potorians make feasts consisting of meat for Lord Scartor, Triton, Venus, Vicious, and Vulture.

Triton has also now managed to recruit another 141 more Potorians through the past year, with the aid of Venus, Vicious, and Vulture; they have all continued stealing men nomad warriors from the nomad warrior tribes scattered throughout the Wastelands. These captured nomad warriors were turned into Potorians and when some men nomad warriors resisted they were cremated by vicious fire breath. The total number of Potorians has now reached to 197 as it includes the previous fifty-six Potorians who survived the battle a year ago against Raven, Parrot, and the men Pine villagers in Lord Scartor's Lair of Death; also, these Potorians were fortunately not killed by the wrath of Lord Scartor's recent vengeance curses.

TRITON AND VENUS are at present in their profligate bedroom
in Triton's Underground Dungeon; they are facing each other,
intimately conjuring up an evil plan. Triton and Venus's bedroom
is the largest sleeping room in Triton's Underground Dungeon, as
many of the Potorians don't have sleeping rooms and will just sleep
across any free ground in Triton's Underground Dungeon. In Triton
and Venus's bedroom, they have a large bed, with several wooden
drawers, where they keep Venus's provocative clothes and domination
toys. Triton also stores his golden chain with the iron spiked ball at
the end of it underneath his bed.

'Are you sure it's going to kill Lord Scartor, Venus?' says Triton
in a suspicious tone.

'Of course, my lover, this spider will possess the poison of a
thousand scorpions in it. Not only will it end that scheming bastard
Lord Scartor's life in seconds, it will do it before he realises that he
has been betrayed by us. Once Lord Scartor is dead, we must then
quickly drink his blood while it's still fresh as I intuitively detect that
he possesses the bloodline of Grackle in him. Otherwise he would
never have been able to yield the anomaly crystal's elemental magic.
Hence, once we also have the blood of Grackle inside our bodies,
then we will also be able to absorb the magnificent powers and
release them from the anomaly crystal,' laughs Venus profoundly.

In their bedroom, Triton stares eagerly at Venus with strong
passionate eyes that show his love for Venus, as he watches her create
an animal out of thin air with her own petite hands. Venus puts one
hand above the other hand and faces them both down towards the
ground; her eyes slowly turn from red to pure white, and from within
the middle of her hands she uses her magical creature abilities,
enabling her to create a small venomous black spider with a pure red
stripe across the back of it. Venus's eyes now turn back to being their
normal red colour again, and she removes the bottom hand from the
other hand, as the top hand levitates the newly created spider that
falls to the ground slowly.

The small black spider with the red stripe across the middle of
its back scampers quickly out of Triton and Venus' bedroom on the
ground; it dashes through the short and narrow hallways of Triton's
Underground Dungeon until it reaches the sleeping room where
Lord Scartor is currently in. Lord Scartor is unaware and in deep

thought as he is sitting on a wooden chair next to a wooden table; he is using his crystal finding device to try and detect where the anomaly crystal is currently located. Lord Scartor is moving the crystal finding device in the air while examining coordinates on a hand-drawn map for the Planet of Phoenix, but the crystal finding device is not detecting any sign of the anomaly crystal, which is beginning to frustrate Lord Scartor.

As the spider with the red stripe across its back enters Lord Scartor's sleep room, it swiftly crawls up one of the wooden chair legs on which Lord Scartor is sitting, and then the spider runs along the wooden chair until it uses its hairy and sticky legs to attach itself on to the black cape that Lord Scartor is wearing. The black spider with the red stripe across its back reaches the top of Lord Scartor's black cape without him noticing, and then the black spider fiercely pierces its long, thin, sharp fangs into Lord Scartor's wrinkly neck. The spider's deadly poison gushes out of its tantalising fangs, and just like a lightning bolt, the black spider's poison strikes every organ and blood cell in Lord Scartor's old body. Lord Scartor immediately feels intense throbbing and agony that causes his heart to stop beating within seconds. Lord Scartor's gruesome and half-burnt face falls flat upon the wooden table; as he falls upon the wooden table, he drops the crystal finding device that lands on the map of the Planet of Phoenix where Hydra Springs area is drawn.

TRITON AND VENUS slowly enter Lord Scartor's sleeping room, and in gladness, they see his dead corpse lying cold and still across the wooden table.

'It worked! He's finally dead,' grins Triton in amusement, thinking about all the abuse he had to undergo while being Lord Scartor's lieutenant.

'Of course, it worked, my lover. My animal creations never fail me,' expresses Venus as she puts one of her hands on top of the spider with the red stripe across its back. The spider magically levitates up into the air close to Venus's hand; she then puts her other hand below the spider, both hands facing down towards the ground.

Venus's eyes turn from red to a pure white colour as the spider mystically disappears between her hands due to her magical creature abilities. Venus now pulls out a small sharp wooden stick with a pure silver blade at the end of it, which is lodged in her long black silky hair; she yanks Lord Scartor's dead head up from the wooden table and uses the pure silver blade at the end of the small wooden stick to slit across his neck, cutting his wrinkly skin like a knife cutting through butter. Venus quickly grabs a silver cup from the wooden table, and she watches excitedly as Lord Scartor's thin red blood pours slowly from his neck cut open into the silver cup that she holds beneath Lord Scartor's throat. Once enough of Lord Scartor's blood is poured into the silver cup, Venus lets go of Lord Scartor's dead head, causing it to fall suddenly back down on top of the wooden table, making a thud that jolts the crystal finding device a bit and manoeuvring a bit of the map of the Planet of Phoenix to now covering the area where Oak Village is located. Venus starts to gulp Lord Scartor's thin red blood from the silver cup and then passes it to Triton, who smirks vibrantly as he also drinks Lord Scartor's thin red blood from the silver cup.

'You're the leader of us all now, Triton, and together we will rule the Planet of Phoenix with an iron fist. Let's take this crystal finding device and go find that extraordinary anomaly crystal for our time has come to overthrow the humans who dare to challenge our creature existence upon the Planet of Phoenix.'

'With you at my side and the anomaly crystal in our hands, we will be unstoppable,' laughs Triton as he licks Lord Scartor's remaining blood that sticks to the sides of the silver cup.

'Of course, my lover, with my immense creatures that I can create from my hands, we will slaughter every human for all the wrongdoings they have caused us creatures throughout the last thousand years,' remarks Venus as she and Triton smile at one another mischievously.

'But first let's get rid of this stinking and disgusting corpse. Let the insects bite away at his flesh and bones on Cadaver Rock . . . the resting place of dead for lost souls. Vicious! Vulture! Get in here now!' shouts Triton. On hearing Triton's commands, Vulture hurriedly glides in the air, flapping his big black feathery wings through the short and narrow hallways through the Underground Dungeon until he gets to Lord Scartor's sleeping room. Vicious also arrives shortly after, walking from his sleeping room that is near Lord Scartor's.

'Lord Scartor is dead?' exclaims Vulture on glancing at Lord Scartor's corpse laid across the wooden table.

'This useless old soul was dead long ago. I am your leader now and together we are going to take over the Planet of Phoenix and rid it from that revolting human vermin,' declares Triton.

'Yes, yes,' remarks Vulture excitedly.

'Hail our new leader, Triton,' states Vicious as he walks into Lord Scartor's sleeping room and sees this situation for himself.

'As it was always meant to be,' remarks Venus with a huge smile on her stimulating face.

'I never liked that bizarre Lord Scartor anyways,' expresses Vulture, flapping his big black feathery wings hard to hover above the ground of Lord Scartor's sleeping room.

'Our rightful master has now been reborn and united with his women. He will finally lead all of us creatures to victory against the human scum,' states Vicious, punching his large and powerful fist in the air.

'Grab his withered body and take him to Cadaver Rock, where his soul will be tormented for an eternity,' orders Venus. Vulture stops flapping his big black feathery wings to land back on the ground, and he and Vicious both pick up Lord Scartor's corpse from the wooden chair, leaving the map of the Planet of Phoenix and the crystal finding device upon the wooden table in Lord Scartor's sleeping room. Vicious and Vulture now begin carrying the dead Lord Scartor through the short and narrow hallways of Triton's Underground Dungeon with Triton and Venus walking alongside them both; they all approach the last short and narrow hallway that leads out into the main room of Triton's Underground Dungeon, where the 197 Potorians are currently practicing weapon combat training with one another, using their metal swords and axes. The Potorians quickly notice Lord Scartor's corpse being carried by Vicious and Vulture, and they all suddenly stop their combat training with each other, a concerned look on their faces.

'Lord Scartor exists no more. I am the new leader now. Bow to me to show your respect!' roars Triton. All the Potorians hear Triton's announcement and begin bowing on their knees on the ground of the main room in honour of Triton. 'Join us at Cadaver Rock to finally rid us all of the malicious Lord Scartor.'

'Where we shall watch the insects feast upon his corpse. That is exactly what this piece of rotten creature deserves, and you Potorians should all be grateful that Lord Scartor exists no longer to torture you,' states Venus to the Potorians.

'Yes, our new masters! We vow to serve you at your command,' shouts all the Potorians who are still bowing on the ground of the main room. Vicious and Vulture release their grip on Lord Scartor's corpse, and it falls, crashing to the ground.

'You Potorians, grab his corpse!' orders Vicious, pointing at four Potorians.

'Quickly! Quickly!' laughs Vulture, as four Potorians stand up from bowing and hurry over to Lord Scartor's corpse, picking it up from the ground. Triton, Venus, Vicious, Vulture, the four Potorians carrying Lord Scartor's corpse, along with the other 193 Potorians, all start to leave Triton's Underground Dungeon through an enclosed passageway that is connected to one end of the main room, leading above the ground on to the Planet of Phoenix's Realm of Deserted Lands.

EVERYONE WALKS OUT of the passageway that is connected to Triton's Underground Dungeon; it leads on to the top of the sharp, rocky ground. In this area of the Planet of Phoenix, it's covered with dead bones of humans, creatures, and animals of various sizes and shapes, which are scattered everywhere over and through the Realm of Deserted Lands. The Realm of Deserted Lands is made up of a very treacherous terrain, which makes it difficult to walk across. There's always darkness in the sky and the air remains freezing cold, as dusty sandstorms filled with thick gusts of strong winds of tiny rock and dirt particles circle around the area, causing humans and creatures to choke and cough.

Led by Triton and Venus, Vicious, Vulture, and the 197 Potorians, including the four Potorians who are carrying Lord Scartor's corpse, they all continue pacing fiercely for a couple of hours in the north direction of the Realm of Deserted Lands until they reach Cadaver Rock. Cadaver Rock is made up of a mound of large white rocks, where five big wooden crucifixes are fixed on top of the large white rock pile with nothing placed upon them. The mound of large white rocks resides alone in the middle of the Realm of Deserted Lands, and no one knows the origin of where it came from. The stories in the book of curses state that Cadaver Rock was created when the Planet of Phoenix was formed from asteroids colliding with one another millions of years ago. Cadaver Rock is covered with all kinds of big and ferocious insects such as millipedes, ants, scorpions, and earwigs that are thought to be the first creatures to exist on the Planet of Phoenix.

Vicious and Vulture stand in front of Cadaver Rock before Triton and Venus and point at the four Potorians who are carrying Lord Scartor's corpse. The four Potorians walk over to the bottom of Cadaver Rock and drop Lord Scartor's corpse on to the ground at the bottom, straight in front of the mound of large white rocks; the sight of this mysterious landmark makes all the Potorians cringe. Triton points to a couple of the four Potorians, who begrudgingly pick up Lord Scartor's corpse and scurry with it to the top of the large white rock pile, taking only a couple of minutes. A couple of the large white rocks that the Potorians step on crumble and smaller pieces fall through the gaps of the large white rocks, and they drop deep down into the darkness that lies beneath the mound of the large white rocks. At the top of Cadaver Rock, one of the Potorians holds Lord Scartor's corpse up against the middle of the five large wooden crucifixes while the other Potorian quickly hammers nails into both of Lord Scartor's hands against the middle wood of the crucifix, and then the Potorian hammers another nail through both his feet at the bottom wood of the crucifix, enabling Lord Scartor to be secure against this large wooden crucifix.

Lord Scartor's blood starts to drip from his hands' and feet's wounds because of the nails that have pierced through his corpse, and his thin red blood continues to drip down the large wooden crucifix until it soaks through the large white rocks at the top of Cadaver Rock. As the white rocks at the top of Cadaver Rock start to turn a red colour because of Lord Scartor's blood, suddenly within seconds, thousands of insects making loud biting and rustling noises begin to crawl up through the darkness beneath the large white rocks upon the big wooden crucifix, covering Lord Scartor's corpse. These insects that are big and ferocious insects such as millipedes, ants, scorpions, and earwigs quickly hack, tear, and slice away big amounts of flesh and bone from Lord Scartor's corpse.

By this time, the two Potorians have already started dashing down the mound of large white rocks to get off from Cadaver Rock;

however, thousands of big insects quickly swarm all over Cadaver Rock and keep trying to crawl on to the two running Potorians in order to bite through their flesh too. One of the Potorians jumps down over the last few large white rocks to make it to the bottom of Cadaver Rock, while the other Potorian in a panic unintentionally trips on one of the large sharp white rocks; he stumbles and falls flat on his face, covering several large white rocks. This Potorian shouts in brutal agony and screams in immense torture as he is quickly covered and eaten alive by hundreds of those perilous big insects. As the other remaining 196 Potorians watch in horror while that Potorian gets eaten alive on Cadaver Rock by the big insects, Triton glares up at Lord Scartor's corpse upon the big crucifix at the top of Cadaver Rock and watches as Lord Scartor's flesh and bone get torn and shredded to pieces before being eaten completely by the big spiteful insects.

'See you in hell!' exclaims Triton as Vicious and Vulture shout and cheer in honour of Triton. Venus looks at Triton and smiles gently before kissing him firmly on his lips. After watching the rest of Lord Scartor's corpse getting eaten away quickly by the big insects for a few minutes until only the black cloth and cape that covered Lord Scartor's withered body remains either attached to the big wooden crucifix or gets swept away by the swirling gusty sandstorms, Triton and Venus start to leave Cadaver Rock, and they are followed by Vicious, Vulture, and the remaining 196 Potorians. They continue heading across the Realm of Deserted Lands' rocky surface in the south direction back towards to the furthest south-west corner where Triton's Underground Dungeon is located.

Fourteen

PARROT, HIS GIRLFRIEND Sapphire, their new baby boy Tigra, Sapphire's parents Sirius and Aura, as well as Raven and Emerald's dog Rexus are currently sitting and drinking glasses of water and talking with one another in the main room of Parrot's small wooden flat in Pine Village. Sapphire is twenty-four years old; she has long curly red hair and hazel eyes, and she is of medium height but a bit smaller than Parrot. Sapphire has a slim physique and white soft skin with some small brown freckles on her face and moles on her arms. Sapphire is at present wearing a long and unrevealing plain red dress with matching red shoes. Sapphire is a very intelligent, motivated, and driven character, and she enjoys learning academic subjects, the arts, and classical music. Due to Sapphire's academic background, she has acquired strong articulate communication and pronunciation skills as well as the mindset to be able to research and investigate theory of interest to her; she tends to seize the day and makes the most of the wondrous sight that the Planet of Phoenix's environment has to offer.

Sapphire had recently achieved a PhD in ancient language and literature after attending Falcon University based in Falcon City for five consecutive years. Sapphire found it to be the most complex thing in her life to complete all her assessments and exams that were delivered from some of the most intellectual humans who lived on the Planet of Phoenix. Sapphire found that the passion in her and the support from her parents Sirius and Aura as well as from Parrot aided her in achieving her desired goal, which was to obtain her PhD in ancient language and literature. Parrot and Sapphire have now known each other for most of their lives, as they were both in the same age group and therefore in the same class when they attended Pinus School together during their childhood. Parrot and Sapphire had spoken with each other on a regular basis and become good friends straight away; their attraction grew for one another, but unfortunately they were made to drift apart due to their friends having problems with one another.

Parrot has a good friend called Bruce with whom they used to play together at a very young age as their families lived close to each other in Pine Village near Pinus Tavern. Bruce is also now twenty-four years old; he has short, wavy blond hair, hazel eyes, and a roughish look on his face because of the short stubble he has where his moustache and beard used to be. He is smaller than Parrot, but has more of a muscly build and wears sporty, baggy clothes and trainers when he is not on duty as a Pine guard; otherwise he is suited and booted in the proper Pinus guard armour and weaponry.

Bruce was not too fussy about learning standard educational information when he was made to attend Pinus School; he was instead a very direct and comical character as he liked to have a laugh and joke at other Pine villagers' expense. When growing up together, Parrot was led astray by Bruce quite a bit and they both got into much mischief and trouble by playing practical jokes on many of the Pine villagers; for example, they would stick muck and animal faeces on Pine villagers' clothes, so when they put the clothes on they would get dirty and become very smelly.

As Parrot and Bruce grew older, they drifted apart slightly as Parrot's parents Rio and Olivia felt that Bruce was a bad influence on Parrot, as they would indulge in mischievous pranks and get into trouble in Pinus School or with the villagers of Pine Village. Thus, Parrot's father Rio decided to get Parrot to help him out in making household and farming tools in their small wooden flat during Parrot's spare time, which kept Parrot too busy to spend time with Bruce in causing troublesome behaviour. Parrot, however, enjoyed working with his father in making the tools his father made, in order to sell them in Rio's brother Barious's tool shop in Pine Village or to travellers passing by, who stayed at Pinus Tavern when they visited Pine Village. Raven took a particular interest in designing and making specially made weapons, and he extended and progressed his father's business, so when he grew older, he made these specially made weapons and supplied them to the Pine guards as well as the royal Falcon guards from Falcon City.

Parrot still remained good friends with Bruce due to the long history of friendship, but Parrot now tended to associate with Bruce only when they were at Pinus School rather than in the free time in the evenings and on weekends, as Parrot was really busy in generating his specially made weapon creations. During the time that Parrot and Bruce did spend together at Pinus School, they used to talk to and spend time with various girls, and they would hang around with one another and would attend events such as the Pine Village dances together.

Parrot and Sapphire were already good friends and started to like each other more and more during their continuous years of interacting in the same class at Pinus School. Sapphire was happy to spend her time with Parrot, although she found Bruce quite annoying as he kept disrupting their classes by making jokes and playing practical tricks on their teacher Mrs Penelope when they were being given new information in the subjects they had to learn at Pinus School, which included language and communication skills, literature, history, religion, geography, maths, cooking, tool making, farming, sewing, etc.

Sapphire, however, had a best friend and they had known each other since they were babies due to their parents being friends with one another and she was called Nia. Nia was initially drawn to Bruce's good looks and charms after being introduced to him through Parrot, when Parrot would spend time with Sapphire. Nia is also twenty-four years old now and has long brown straight hair and brown eyes; she is also small in height and smaller than Sapphire. Nia also has a slim but normal sized figure. When at school, she mostly wore yellow T-shirts and orange skirts with white shoes and would tend to put purple ribbons in her hair.

Nia also enjoyed her education at Pinus School and treasured her friendship very much with Sapphire, since they had been friends ever since they were born with Sapphire's mother Aura and Nia's mother Apricot also being best friends since their childhood days. Aura and Apricot would spend much time walking through the Grass Terrain Fields with their daughters Sapphire and Nia, gossiping about Pine Village and sharing many happy childhood memories with each other. Nia was a little bit of an introvert and she was a very quiet and sensitive girl who didn't really socialise well with other children; that is why she would clingy on to Sapphire and only wanted her and Sapphire to hang around together without any of the other girls in their class at Pinus School.

Bruce actually liked the way Nia looked, although he found her very shy, but he used his charms and persuasive communication to finally convince Nia to be his date at the last Pinus School's annual dance for the older children who would be leaving Pinus School in Pine Village that year. Parrot was happy for Bruce, but he was also even happier that he got to take Sapphire as his date to Pinus School's annual dance; thus the four of them decided it would be a good and memorable idea to go together to it. Everyone had dressed up in their finest clothes and the parents of the teenagers who were attending Pinus School's annual dance wished them an enjoyable to end their time at Pinus School. Parrot and Sapphire spent a lovely evening together, dancing, laughing, and sharing intimate personal information with each other as they had now become closer not only as friends, but also in a romantic way. Bruce and Nia also enjoyed a wonderful time together, and Bruce really tried hard to make a good impression on Nia, although Sapphire wasn't too convinced about him, but Nia seemed to be happy; that is what Sapphire cared about.

Towards the end of the night, Bruce had persuaded Nia to leave the annual dance early so they could be alone in a quieter place; begrudgingly, Nia agreed without telling Sapphire that she was leaving the annual dance early. Bruce knew of a haystack that was in a barn located near the annual dance; he took Nia there, although according to Nia's understanding they would only be spending some quality talking time talking with one another. Once in the barn, they sat down on the haystack, and Bruce immediately began to kiss and grope Nia. Nia was appalled by Bruce's behaviour and quickly pushed him from her and ran away from the haystack and him as fast as she could. Nia decided it was best not to go back to Pinus School annual dance and tell Sapphire about what had happened tonight as she didn't want to ruin her time she was spending with Parrot; hence, Nia ran quickly home.

The following few weeks after Pinus School annual dance were the last for Sapphire and Nia to spend in Pine Village, as both of them had decided to travel to Falcon City and attend their higher academic studies at Falcon University. The next day after Pinus School annual dance, Nia had explained to Sapphire with teary eyes how Bruce had been about to force himself on her, so Nia now wanted Sapphire to keep her distance from both Bruce and Parrot. Nia explained to Sapphire in depth about how Bruce had been like towards her and felt too ashamed and nervous for her or Sapphire to be around Bruce or Parrot, and she also didn't want anyone else to find out about this; thus, she didn't want Sapphire to speak to Parrot about what Bruce had done.

Although Sapphire was reluctant about Nia's wishes as she really liked Parrot, Sapphire decided to stay loyal to her best friend's wishes and didn't really associate with Parrot during her last few weeks in Pine Village, so the change in Sapphire's behaviour confused Parrot very much. Sapphire then only saw Parrot one time again when she wanted to say her final goodbye to him before she and Nia went to Falcon City and to Falcon University, where Sapphire chose to study ancient language and literature and Nia chose to study her favourite subject history. Parrot was distraught about the diminished relations with Sapphire after the annual Pinus School dance, as he couldn't understand why it had changed between them, and also he was very upset when Sapphire left Pine Village.

PARROT CONTINUED ON a daily basis with his own business of designing and creating specially made weapons, especially since his parents Rio and Olivia had decided to move to Willow Village since this village was newly built compared with Pine and Oak Villages and it was a more peaceful and quiet place where they could enjoy their retirement compared with the busy life of Pine Village. After Bruce left Pinus School, he joined the Pine guards immediately as he didn't want to work in any job that required him to use educational skills.

Bruce enjoyed and excelled during his time with the Pine guards and also made many friends with the other Pine guards quickly, and in particular, he become good friends with Flame, who also later become good friends with Parrot, and the three of them spent many times drinking ale together and going hunting for meat in the Grass Terrain Fields surrounding Pine and Oak Villages.

Parrot never liked another girl in the same way as he had felt for Sapphire, which still left him heartbroken regarding the situation that had occurred between Bruce and Nia and the awkward situation it had left Sapphire and himself in, although when Sapphire was at Falcon University, they both stayed in touch with one another by sending messages that were written on cloth and transported to each other via the use of carrier pigeons. Parrot would write and woo Sapphire by sharing his most intimate feelings with her and continued expressing how much he cared for her. Sapphire in her letters explained to Parrot the truth about why she had been like that just before she left Pine Village because of what Bruce had done to Nia; this explanation enabled Parrot to understand the awkward situation better with regard to their friends falling out, and in return Sapphire wanted to make up for not spending the time she wanted to with Parrot before she left Pine Village. Thus, she would send poems and her deepest thoughts in messages back to Parrot, and over the next five years they fell in love with each other's mind, spirit, and soul, which made them both very happy, until Sapphire finally returned to Pine Village where their physical bodies could be with each other.

Nia also achieved her PhD in history and stayed on at Falcon University to train in becoming a lecturer in the subject of history as she enjoyed teaching others, and although she was upset to see her best friend Sapphire leave to go back to Pine Village to be with Parrot, she was happy that she had found her true love that she deserved. Sapphire had returned to Pine Village just under a year ago, and Parrot's and her love for each other grew and grew each day, in that everyone including Sapphire's parents Sirius and Aura and Parrot's parents Rio and Olivia as well as Bruce and Nia were extremely pleased for them both. Sapphire became pregnant after returning to Pine Village rather quickly with their new son Tigra. He is now a three-month-old baby boy and he has short wavy red hair, hazel eyes, and facial features like his mother Sapphire. Tigra is a good baby as he doesn't cry or whine very much and his enthusiastic personality already shines through in his behaviour. After an awkward situation and long length of time, Parrot and Sapphire are now currently very happy with each other and are looking forward to settling down and bringing up a family together in Pine Village.

Sirius is Sapphire's father and he is fifty-eight years old and average size in height and weight; he is bold and wears old scruffy clothes as his job is of a farmer. He has been a farmer all his life ever since he took over his father's farm, which was called Turtle's farm in Pine Village. Sirius did so at the age of nineteen as his father Turtle died of old age since the life span did not last as long for most humans on the Planet of Phoenix because of unhealthy and unclean lifestyles. Sirius is a very protective and caring father to Sapphire and husband to Aura, and he works very hard to provide and support for his family.

Aura is Sapphire's mother; she is fifty-five years old and has short red hair and hazel eyes. Aura is short in height and a bit plump in weight, and she spends most of her time helping Sirius run their farm in Pine Village, where they keep animals like cows, chicken, and sheep and harvest wheat. Aura also wears plain scruffy clothes as she's a farmer too and she is also a hard and contentious worker, but she is also a very charitable and humble human, as she gives away free milk, eggs, and wool to those Pine villagers who are poor and don't have much resources for themselves. Sirius and Aura have been married for thirty-four years now and have been each other's first and only love, after Aura met Sirius one day when she was a teenager and had gone to his farm to buy wheat from him to take back home to her family. Shortly after meeting and having a relationship with each other, they got married and Aura moved in with Sirius at his farm. Sirius and Aura had been very happy for many years and were ever more so content with life when Aura gave birth to a daughter whom they named Sapphire. They brought Sapphire up to not only be a determined and focused worker in her studies and around their farm, but also taught her humble characteristics such as helping those humans who were less fortunate than they were and also cherish all that life on the Planet of Phoenix had to offer as time forever moves too quickly.

Rexus, who is Raven and Emerald's dog, is a golden retriever and he is nearly two years old. Raven had brought Rexus from an old couple in Willow Village, whose pure-bred bitch retriever gave birth to three puppies. When he had visited the old couple in Willow Village, Rexus immediately jumped up on to Raven's leg, and Raven knew that Rexus would be the perfect dog to give to Emerald as a wedding present, and they both decided upon the name of Rexus. Since then they had taught Rexus many tricks and how to fend for himself as well as spent much enjoyable quality time walking him across the Grass Terrain Fields near Oak Village. They would also take Rexus on many occasions to visit Parrot, Sapphire, and their new baby boy Tigra in Pine Village. Parrot and Sapphire had offered to look after Rexus when Raven and Emerald went on their honeymoon in Hydra Springs; at that time, Rexus and Tigra bonded greatly with each other.

SAPPHIRE BRINGS MORE cups of fresh water and a plate of vegetable sandwiches made from homemade bread and vegetables that Sirius had brought round from his farm, such as onions, carrots, and lettuce. Sapphire places it all on the small wooden table in the middle of the main room of Parrot's small wooden flat for everyone to drink and eat. Aura is currently holding Tigra's little hand as he lies in his small wooden homemade cot next to the small wooden table that Parrot had built for him.

'He's adorable,' says Aura, looking at Tigra who is lying asleep and motionless in his small wooden homemade cot beside her wooden chair.

'Yes, he is, and he's been such a good baby, sleeping through the night already and hardly crying at all,' replies Sapphire, grinning at Tigra.

'He takes after you then, Sapphire, as you were also a very quiet and quick learning baby,' states Aura in a proud manner.

'That she was, my wife, and what a beautiful and intelligent young woman you have grown up to be. We are very proud of everything you have accomplished in your life and are also very happy for you and Parrot for now creating your own family,' says Sirius, starting to eat his vegetable sandwich.

'Thank you, Father. Your kind words mean a lot to me and thank you both for bringing some of the farm's food to us. That was one of the things I missed when I was at Falcon University, your fresh homemade farm meals as well as missing all my family of course,' says Sapphire as she also sits down on a wooden chair and joins everyone at the small wooden table eating their vegetable sandwiches.

'You're very welcome, my daughter,' replies Sirius, smiling at Sapphire.

'Yes, thank you for this kind gesture. How is your farm getting on, Sirius?' asks Parrot as he sips water slowly from his glass.

'It has been going very well in recent times. Due to the expansion of Willow Village, it has increased my trade between villagers, as well as the number of crops and vegetable stock that used to be stolen quite often by the nomad warriors has also reduced in the last couple of years. I've heard the reason for the nomad warriors not raiding our farms as often, was because Lord Scartor and his Lieutenant Triton captured the nomad warriors and tortured them into becoming their slaves,' says Sirius. Everyone becomes silent for a moment as they remember what Parrot had told them all about the horrific battle that he had endured at Lord Scartor's Lair of Death a year ago upon Crow Mountain and all the unfortunate pain and misery suffered by Oak Village and the men Pine villagers, which was caused by those evil creatures.

'How are your parents doing in Willow Village, Parrot?' says Aura quickly, trying to avoid a sensitive subject.

'Yes, they are both doing well and enjoying the peace and quiet there, although I do miss not seeing them as often,' replies Parrot.

'And is your father still doing his tool shop business?' asks Aura.

'Yes, he's still working hard on making farm and household tools much to my mother's displeasure I suppose, as she wanted him to rest during their retirement,' says Parrot.

'Ah yes, a hard-working human your father is, just like me. I had brought many farm tools from Rio in the past, which had been of much use on my farm. How is the rebuilding of Oak Village also going, Parrot?' asks Sirius in interest.

'Yes, it's nearly completed now and all the Pine guards along with Lynx's and King Exodus's help have done an outstanding job in restoring it so quickly. Although it will never be the same as it was before the massacre caused by Lieutenant Triton and the Potorians last year in the battle of Oak Village, but the surviving Oak villagers are rebuilding their lives again there, and villagers from Pine and

Willow Villages have also moved to Oak Village to aid the progression of Oak Village as well as to start fresh lives for themselves,' answers Parrot.

'Those poor Oak and Pine villagers who had to suffer such a tragedy, those humans, and those terrible events that occurred a year ago will never be forgotten in the foreseeable future of the humans on the Planet of Phoenix,' says Sapphire as she puts her arm around Parrot in comfort and Parrot smiles at her.

'Yes, you were remarkably brave in launching an attack against those powerful creatures, which stylishly ended in victory along with the help of Raven and the men Pine villagers, who also risked their lives to protect our human race. I knew Leon very well for a long time due to him being Pinus Tavern owner, poor Lemur, and her children Siva and Sam, who have had to cope with his untimely death. We have all tried to help her out in the last year, and Bella has been great in taking temporary charge over Pinus Tavern to keep the business running for their father,' says Aura in a sad tone of voice.

'Yes, that poor family, and Leon was a valiant human and fought well during those difficult battles we had to face against Lord Scartor and Lieutenant Triton in unknown territory. In respect of this courageous behaviour, Pine villagers are holding a remembrance service in Pinus Tavern tomorrow for Leon, Drakus, and all the other brave men Pine villagers who lost their lives in the battle at Lord Scartor's Lair of Death amongst the Mountains of Doom,' remarks Parrot, thinking back about some of the dreadful deaths he had witnessed when fighting alongside his fellow men Pine villagers in the battles against Lord Scartor and Lieutenant Triton.

'Yes, we will all also go and pay our respects to those men Pine villagers who deserve it, as well as give aid to any of the remaining families who are in need of financial help, due to losing members of their family in these unfortunate circumstances. Raven and Emerald will also be returning tomorrow from their honeymoon too, and Emerald said after they have visited Oak Village to lay flowers on Barious's grave in honour of his death one year ago, they will also come to the remembrance service with us to pay their respects,' says Sapphire, stroking Rexus who is lying on the wooden floor of Parrot's small wooden flat, wagging his tail.

'HOW ARE RAVEN and Emerald? Their wedding was so beautiful at Oakus Church and the ceremony party afterwards in Oak Village's Grass Terrain Fields was just elegant, a night needed by many to cheer everyone up after the tragedy that had recently happened. Poor Barious though. He would have loved to have seen them both get married with each other. He thought the world of them both, and I'm sure Barious, Ruthus and Jewel were watching over them from heaven on that special day,' says Aura respectfully.

'Yes, Barious was a grand old chap and he will be sadly missed by a lot of humans in all of the villages, including Falcon City. I had the pleasure of knowing Barious myself for many years as I used to trade my farm's crops and vegetables in exchange for supplies in his tool shop,' remarks Sirius, as he drinks from his glass of water after finishing his vegetable sandwich.

'Raven and Emerald are doing well and enjoying their honeymoon in the magical Hydra Springs. Yes, their wedding ceremony at Oakus Church and ceremony party in the Grass Terrain Fields of Oak Village afterwards was wonderful and it was a great night for everyone, and even Tigra seemed to enjoy it, although he was only a couple of months old at the time. Emerald's long elegant white wedding dress was remarkable and Raven gave her the most spectacular wedding ring with a diamond crystal attached to it. I felt also very privileged to be Emerald's maid of honour after only knowing her for such a short time, although we have become very close now,' explains Sapphire.

'Yes, it was a glorious day for them both and all of my family, and I was also privileged to be Raven's best man at their wedding. I have been there for him at different stages of his life and have watched him grow up to be a fine young human, especially after all the tragic events he has had to endure from such an early age, like his parents Ruthus and Jewel being killed by that sinful creature Viper as well as recently losing our grandfather Barious in the battle of Oak Village. But on his wedding day, I couldn't have been prouder of him, just as all of our family would have been. Raven had told me afterwards how much he appreciated mine and Sapphire's support through everything that he and Emerald had been through, but my reply back to him was that's what families are for and that we will always be there to help him and Emerald,' says Parrot modestly.

'They deserve some happiness after all they have been through in these past years,' exclaims Aura, stroking Tigra's short red wavy hair as he lies inside his small wooden cot.

'Yes, you are quite right and it will be good to have them both back home again as we are all missing them greatly,' remarks Parrot.

'How has their dog Rexus been with you?' asks Sirius, looking at Sapphire stroking Rexus who is wagging his small, hairy, golden-coloured tail frantically.

'Rexus has been marvellous and he's such a wonderful dog. He has also taken a real shine to Tigra too,' giggles Sapphire as she stops stroking Rexus and walks over to pick up Tigra from his small homemade wooden cot, beginning to rock him gently in her arms. Parrot, Sirius, and Aura all smile at Tigra and then at one another.

'You must be very proud of him,' says Aura.

'Yes, I am. I've always wanted a son. I can't wait till he grows up so I can teach him the art of designing and creating specially made weapons,' laughs Parrot.

'I think not. Our boy is going to become a great scholar or a member of the royal council in Falcon city, someone of importance who will generate promising change and progression for the Planet of Phoenix,' laughs Sapphire also.

'Or he could take over in running my family's farm business,' smiles Sirius.

'That reminds me. Talking about Falcon City, Nia had sent word to me via a carrier pigeon the day before yesterday that she would finally be coming to visit us and Tigra soon in Pine Village,' smiles Sapphire at the thought of seeing Nia again since she has not seen her in a long time.

'Oh yes, that would be nice for you, my dear, as you haven't seen her since you moved back to Pine Village nearly a year ago now. How are things with her?' says Aura, looking at Sapphire rocking Tigra slowly in her arms.

'Nia is doing well and she loves her well-earned job of being a trainee lecturer of history at the grand Falcon University. But yes, I do miss her very much as we haven't not seen each other for this long ever since we were babies,' says Sapphire sadly.

'Yes, you two were inseparable and we had some lovely memories of us three together along with her mother and my best friend

Apricot. Apricot did a marvellous job of raising Nia from a young child on her own, since Nia's father Bear had left them both due to personal issues between Apricot and himself. Poor Apricot, she had quite a difficult time being a single mother, but I helped her as much as I could with raising Nia along with you too. That may be why Nia was an introvert child and relied on you quite a bit with regard to your friendship, but I know also how much she meant to you as she was an excellent and supportive friend to you. Unfortunately again for Nia, when Apricot passed away two years ago due to illness, I expect she was as distraught as I was. However, life can be cruel sometimes,' says Aura with a tear in her eye at the thought of her best friend Apricot not living no more; Sirius puts his arm around her as he knows how much Apricot had meant to Aura.

'Yes, we had some wonderful times, and I also remember fondly those memories of us four spending happy times with one another. And yes, poor Apricot, she was a very nice human and Nia didn't take the news very well when we were still conducting our studies at Falcon University, but I tried my best to support her through this sad circumstance. She was also very gutted that she was unable to make it back for Apricot's funeral at Pinus Church, but I just don't think Nia could have faced it on her own and we were both in the midst of our exams at the time, which made it impossible for us both to make it back to Pine Village during that sad time. But I know you were there to pay respects from all of us to a wonderful women. Due to everything happening at that time, I'm tremendously proud of Nia for not giving up and she continued striving to achieve her PhD. That is what Apricot always wanted her to do,' explains Sapphire.

'Such sad times have been experienced by us all,' remarks Aura sorrowfully.

'When Nia comes back to Pine Village, how will she feel about staying with Parrot and possibly seeing Bruce again?' asks Sirius in an attempt to change the sad subject, to make everyone feel a bit happier by not pondering upon upsetting thoughts.

'That's all water under the bridge now. Nia is very happy for me and Sapphire and our son Tigra. Thus, she will be fine with seeing me again, as we never had any problems at the time or just before she left Pine Village to go to Falcon University in Falcon City with Sapphire. I don't think she would probably like to see Bruce again after what had happened between them both, but I will just try my best to make sure that they don't see each other in the time that Nia will be staying with us,' replies Parrot.

'And what is Bruce doing with himself now? I hope he has grown up a lot and realised that he can't treat woman like the way he had treated Nia,' says Aura in a stern voice.

'Bruce has really changed a lot now, as he has just been promoted from among the Pine guards to becoming one of the watch tower guards,' answers Parrot.

'Well, that's good news to hear,' states Sirius.

'Yes, if it wasn't for Bruce and the way he behaved towards Nia on that night of Pinus School Annual Dance, things may have been a bit different because of the way Parrot and I had left things between us before I had gone to Falcon University,' remarks Sapphire in slight annoyance.

'Yes, you may be right, but all that matters is that you're here and together with me now as it was clearly always meant to be. As well as now we have a beautiful son and a wonderful extended family to grow old with and share much happiness together. Life couldn't be much better for us at this point in time,' says Parrot to Sapphire gladly. Parrot stands up from his wooden chair and manoeuvres over to Sapphire and Tigra sitting on another wooden chair on a different side of the small wooden table, in the main living room of Parrot's small wooden flat. Parrot kisses Tigra on his soft and small head and then he kisses Sapphire emotionally on the lips, and then they smile happily, staring deep into each other's smitten eyes.

Fifteen

SEVERAL MONTHS AGO on hearing the news and stories that had just recently occurred from Parrot and the surviving men Pine villagers, who had battled against Lord Scartor and Lieutenant Triton in Lord Scartor's Lair of Death upon Crow Mountain while attempting to save Emerald's and Opal's lives, Lynx the Pine Village leader had chosen five of his men Pine villager scouts for a special task. These five men Pine villager scouts were the best at navigating trekking across different types of harsh terrain that resided on the Planet of Phoenix; as also, all these five men Pine villager scouts were very skilled in combat as all of them were well trained by Lynx himself and had experience in many previous fights against the nomad warriors from the Wastelands.

Preceding the selection of his best five men Pine villager scouts, Lynx had journeyed to a neighbouring village from Pine Village that was called Willow Village, where Lynx sought to speak with his uncle Panther, who was also the leader of Willow Village. After their initial interaction and conversation, they both decided the best plan of action would be to travel with a handful of their trusted Pine and Willow guards to seek advice from King Exodus and the royal Falcon council in Falcon City in the Kingdom of Humans at the furthest south-east direction of the Planet of Phoenix. Panther and

King Exodus had been friends with Barious for most of their lives and Lynx had been previously King Exodus's royal Falcon captain; hence Lynx and Panther needed to consult with King Exodus before undertaking steps towards the great war, which would affect all the humans residing upon the Planet of Phoenix.

Once Lynx, Panther, and King Exodus had all reunited with one another, King Exodus arranged an urgent meeting to be conducted in Falcon Castle upon Lynx's and Panther's request, where they would be present along with King Exodus's most intellectual members of the royal Falcon council. After much deliberation and reflection upon these recent troublesome events of the battles the Oak and Pine villagers had experienced with Lord Scartor and Lieutenant Triton, King Exodus, along with his royal Falcon council, made plans with Lynx and Panther to rebuild the now destroyed Oak Village as well as prepare relevant plans to reinforce the protection of Falcon City along with the three main villages in the north of the Planet of Phoenix with regard to the forthcoming great war. It was also agreed that it would be necessary to start searching where Lord Scartor and Lieutenant Triton had escaped and relocated to so that there wouldn't be another surprise battle from these evil creatures again, as this was what happened in the Oak Village battle that had just recently occurred and nearly wiped out the entire Oak Village population.

Following this shocking discussion, King Exodus immediately sent a group of his royal Falcon Scouts to leave Falcon City and start searching the southern area of the Planet of Phoenix for Lord Scartor and Lieutenant Triton's new fortress location. Unfortunately, this group of royal Falcon scouts, which consisted of eight humans, were quickly ambushed by some of Viper's dangerous Serpent warriors, who were also snake-like creatures but had scorpion tails. These Serpents ambushed the eight royal Falcon scouts and gruesomely slaughtered all of them just outside the perimeter of Komodo Jungle that resides in the middle of the Planet of Phoenix between the Pine and Willow Villages in the north and Falcon City in the south, which resides in the designated area surrounding it, known as the Kingdom of Humans.

After hearing about the news of this terrible slaughter the Serpents had bestowed upon the eight royal Falcon scouts, in revenge

King Exodus spent the next four months battling hard against those Serpents who had cruelly attacked his eight royal Falcon scouts; this mini battle that happened in the outer perimeter of Komodo Jungle caused not only several Falcon guards to be murdered, but also many Serpents were also killed. Viper's response to King Exodus's attack at Komodo Jungle on his Serpent warriors was to order his Serpents to attack any city humans or villagers travelling between the three main villages and Falcon City, leading to the break in the normal lines of communication, trade, and support between the three main villages in the north and Falcon City in the south. Viper understood that the inevitable great war would be occurring soon, and although, he wasn't fully aware of what his part in the great war would be, he realised that all the humans on the Planet of Phoenix were seen as a threat to him and his Serpents and that Viper had spent decades in spawning his vast Serpent army in the abominable Komodo Jungle.

As King Exodus and his royal Falcon guards were preoccupied during those few months with protecting the humans in the south in the Kingdom of Heaven against the creature threat from Viper and his Serpents as well as also trying to prepare the entire Falcon City for a great war that would take place against Lord Scartor and Lieutenant Triton, King Exodus found it difficult to spare no more time or resources in an attempt to search for Lord Scartor and Lieutenant Triton's new fortress location. King Exodus notified Lynx of his current predicament via a carrier pigeon as Lynx and Panther were returning back to their villagers after their short visit with King Exodus in Falcon City. Lynx thus took it upon himself to gather the best of his men villager Pine scouts, who were humbly willing to risk their lives in favour of all the humans on the Planet of Phoenix, to participate in this important quest instructed by Lynx to locate where Lord Scartor and Lieutenant Triton were now residing on the Planet of Phoenix. The five men Pine villager scouts were rewarded for their bravery prior to venturing on this extremely dangerous quest with money and resources being given to their families in Pine Village in case these five men Pine villager scouts unfortunately did not return back home to Pine Village.

Lynx completely understood the intense situation King Exodus and the royal Falcon guards were involved in while fighting against Viper and his Serpent army from Komodo Jungle. Fortunately, Lynx was able to keep in contact with King Exodus by sending specially trained carrier pigeons from Pine Village to take messages on cloth back and forth between the three main villages in the north and Falcon City amongst the Kingdom of Humans in the south of the Planet of Phoenix as the normal connections of trade and communication were destroyed by Viper and his Serpents from Komodo Jungle. In these messages transported by the carrier pigeons, Lynx explained his plans to King Exodus and his uncle Panther of Willow Village about the quest he had bestowed on his best five men Pine villager scouts to uncover Lord Scartor and Lieutenant Triton's new fortress location, along with the confirmation plans agreed upon with King Exodus and the royal Falcon council for the protection of Pine Village as well as the rebuilding of Oak Village.

AFTER RECEIVING LYNX'S final orders, the five men Pine villager scouts thus leave their homes in Pine Village after saying their last heart-warming goodbyes to their beloved families, and then they undertake this dangerous adventure and travel south-west across the Grass Terrain Fields of the Planet of Phoenix. These five men Pine villager scouts are dressed in the same armour that a standard Pine guard would wear, but it is made of lighter material for them to be able to trek more quickly over vast distances; their body armour is made up of brown cloth, which covers them from head to toe except for their faces, along with strong leather boots.

The five men Pine villager scouts ride a strong tall brown horse each and carry supplies of water, food such as farm vegetables and salted meat, and extra wool clothing in their leather bags, which will aid them in surviving for many months through changing and hostile environments during their extensive and challenging journey across the Planet of Phoenix. They also carry their metal swords and small metal daggers for protection as well as four clever and well-trained carrier pigeons in a small metal cage in order to send messages back and forth to Lynx in Pine Village regarding any information of their current quest. The five men Pine villager scouts are specially instructed to not go anywhere near Komodo Jungle that is located in the middle of the Planet of Phoenix towards the east, due to continuous dangerous Viper and his Serpents are inflicting against the humans of Falcon City in the Kingdom of Humans.

The five men Pine villager scouts have now travelled for many months, which consisted of long and hard treks over the hazardous and risky Grass Terrain Fields and other underdeveloped landscapes across the Planet of Phoenix in search for signs of Lord Scartor or Lieutenant Triton's new fortress location. The five men Pine villager scouts start their journey by heading west towards the Mountains of Doom and then downwards in order to avoid the mysterious Eagle Forest, the vile Swamp Fields, and the vast Wastelands infested with nomad warriors. They travel towards the south-west of the Planet of Phoenix where the Realm of Deserted Lands is located as Lynx had presumed that this undiscovered area by the humans would be the most likely destination for Lord Scartor and Lieutenant Triton to hide and rebuild an army of Potorians and creatures in secret since no humans ever venture into the Realm of Deserted Lands due to its harsh living conditions and perilous inhabitants who are usually lonesome wild nasty creatures.

When Raven, Emerald, Parrot, and the two surviving men Pine villagers on horseback barely escaped Lord Scartor's Lair of Death, which began to crumble after the anomaly crystal released the large elemental ball of fire a year ago, they journeyed back down the steep Crow Mountain amongst the frozen Mountains of Doom and continued back through the Open Valley, Wastelands, and Swamp Fields towards Oak Village. Parrot reported back to Lynx that they had seen no sign at all of Lord Scartor, Lieutenant Triton, and the remaining Potorians after they disappeared through the magical cloudy portal Lord Scartor created using the last of the dark magic from his golden sceptre in Lord Scartor's Lair of Death. Hence, Lynx wisely suggested to the fine men Pine villager scouts to begin searching other areas of the Planet of Phoenix first as Lord Scartor would also be aware that the villagers from the three main villages and the humans from Falcon City would attempt to search and destroy him for what he had done to Oak Village and would more likely attempt to locate him in the north-west perimeter of the Planet of Phoenix throughout the Wastelands and Mountains of Doom since that was the last place they were known to be located at.

Along the endless journey south-west across the Grass Terrain Fields and other landscapes over the Planet of Phoenix, the five men Pine villager scouts endure blistering weather conditions such as cold hail rain, strong gusty winds, sharp frost bites, and dark empty silent nights. They fortunately avoid coming into contact with any wild creatures of the Planet of Phoenix during their journey as they know that they wouldn't be able to survive an attack by a formidable creature that had some kind of special creature ability or unique power, since the five men Pine villager scouts are only in a small group of humans with only weapons to defend themselves as well as they are completely exhausted and their energy sapped due to all the travelling they had to undergo.

Along the five men Pine villager scouts' journey south-west across the Planet of Phoenix, they do, however, manage to hunt and kill some of the wildlife animals, which they cook and eat in order to maintain their strength and energy to bear the rest of the unknown journey. After many months or gruelling travelling and searching, the five men Pine villager scouts find themselves entering deep into the hostile Realm of Deserted Lands that is located in the furthest south-west direction on the Planet of Phoenix.

The five men Pine villagers scouts venture into the Realm of Deserted Lands cautiously as it is covered in silent darkness since this part of the Planet of Phoenix is predominantly hidden from sunlight because of its location on the Planet of Phoenix with regard to how the Planet of Phoenix spins around on its axis to receive sunlight from the sun located in its universe; this overpowering darkness has an impact that no vegetation grows in the Realm of Deserted Lands, which is why the ground is covered by only a rocky surface. The air over the sky of the Realm of Deserted Lands is covered with freezing gusts of strong winds that carry tiny dirt, rock, sand, and grit particles gyrating around in it, and due to the gloomy darkness, it nearly makes it impossible for the men Pine villager scouts to see beyond a few metres of their immediate surroundings.

'What is this lonesome place?' asks one of the Pine villager scouts in apprehension.

'The map that Lynx gave us of the Planet of Phoenix shows it to be the Realm of Deserted Lands, which is located in the far south-west and on the other darker side of the Planet of Phoenix,' explains another Pine villager scout, gulping his breath due to the dirt, rock, sand, and grit particles swirling in his throat.

'Finally after many suffering months, we have survived and made it to this terrible and deserted location. Let's hope we find signs of Lord Scartor and Lieutenant Triton's new fortress hideout soon so we can finally leave this hellish environment and travel back to our homes in Pine Village,' says another of the Pine villager scouts, thinking about his wife and son still back in Pine Village.

'Yes, we all want to finish this quest and go back home to our loved ones, but we swore an oath to Lynx that we will do our duties in finding Lord Scartor and Lieutenant Triton's new fortress hideout before we leave and journey back home again to report their new location in order for all the guards in Pine, Oak, and Willow Villages along with the aid of the royal Falcon guards in Falcon City to conduct the great war upon these malicious creatures rather than wait Lord Scartor to launch the great war in a startling manner such as what happened to the unfortunate Oak Village a year ago. Now, Pine villager scouts, stay together in formation and watch our close surroundings at all times. We must be prepared to fight and defend one another against any creatures we might unfortunately come across during this journey throughout the perilous Realm of Deserted Lands,' states a Pine villager scout in a confident tone of voice.

THE FIVE MEN Pine villager scouts tread carefully and guardedly as they ride upon their five brown horses across the bumpy and sharp rocks littered all across the Realm of Deserted Lands that extends for miles on end. The rocky ground is also covered with large bones of the creatures that had died here long ago, at a time when most of the large creatures roamed the Planet of Phoenix and they would fight horrifically with one another to mark their territory. The five men Pine villager scouts stay very close together as they continue treading on their horses over the rocky ground across the Realm of Deserted Lands; they move onwards much more slowly than they did when they moved across the continuous Grass Terrain Fields of the Planet of Phoenix.

The five men Pine villager scouts are utterly exhausted and hungry; they are also frightened during the intense moments when they are passing through the Realm of Deserted Lands. In their subconscious thoughts, the five men Pine villager scouts fear that they will not survive this quest and make it back home to Pine Village to see their families and friends again. The five men Pine villager scouts continue treading and occasionally trotting south-west on their horses over the vast and hostile rocky Realm of Deserted Lands; they become very cold and their hands start to turn red and sore because of the frost bite of the cold gusty winds. They still also find it very difficult to see in the space in front of them due to it being constantly dark, and their vision is also blurred because of the gusty winds as they continue to strongly blow around the area that chucks dirt, rock, and sand and grit particles into the faces of the five men Pine villager scouts.

As the five men Pine villager scouts continue treading and trotting on their horses slowly and carefully over the sharp and spiky rocks of the Realm of Deserted Lands, loud moans of sound not too far from them suddenly reach their cold ears.

'Did you hear that?' says one of the men Pine villager scouts quietly.

'No, I didn't hear anything. Stop trying to scare us. You're just imagining it,' says one of the other men Pine villager scouts nervously. There is another moan and it is again heard throughout the vast empty space in the Realm of Deserted Lands.

'What was that?' shouts one of the other men Pine villager scouts.

'See, I told you that I heard something. What do we do?' says the man Pine villager scout in a troubled manner.

'I don't know. It could be anything or anywhere within the Realm of Deserted Lands as the gusty winds might have carried the sound to our ears from far away,' states a man Pine villager scout hopefully. But the noisy and unusual sounding moan is heard again by the five men Pine villager scouts, and this time the sound is much louder and seems to be much closer.

'Quick, let's ride onwards out of this hostile area!' shouts one of the man Pine villager scouts in alarm. The five men Pine villager scouts quickly kick their heels hard into the sides of their horses, and the horses yelp as they gallop swiftly forward. As the five men Pine villagers gallop on their horses agitatedly across the rocky surface through the gusty winds under the dark sky, they hear another much louder moan, and in the distance, the dark outline of a large round figure appears.

'Stop! I see something!' shouts one of the Pine villager scouts as he pulls the rope reins of his horse to stop the horse instantly, and the other four men Pine villager scouts speedily do the same and they stop dead still upon their horses, crowding round each other in the open and silent Realm of Deserted Lands.

'What is it?' asks one of the man Pine villager scouts.

'I don't know, but it's huge and gruesome. Hurry, let's turn back the other way,' states the man Pine villager scout as he squints and sees a very large round figure coming closer towards them. Just as the five men Pine villager scouts grasp the horses' rope reins hard and yank them quickly to turn and gallop the other way, the large round figure appears suddenly through the dirt, rock, sand, and grit particles swirling around in the fierce gusty winds. The large round figure is a troll creature; he is over twenty feet tall and around ten feet wide. The troll creature is covered with thick and long black hair all over his body. He has large yellow teeth pointing out of its mouth; he is a male and he is wearing no clothes except a large brown dirty cloth that covers the bottom part of his body. The troll creature is slow and not very intelligent, but he's starving as he has not eaten anything in weeks. The troll creature dribbles slime from his large putrid mouth and he quickly swings his large bulky hand in the shape of a fist and bashes it against one of the man Pine villager scouts, who falls briskly from his horse and crashes on to the sharp rocky surface, landing with a hard thud, bruising his hip.

'Leave us be!' shouts another man Pine villager scout as he kicks his heels into the side of his horse, and the horse gallops away at the kick of this man Pine village scout; the man Pine villager scout guides the horse by holding tightly its rope reins and he charges towards the troll creature just in front of them. The man Pine villager scout on his horse reaches near the troll creature's huge plump belly quickly undetected as the troll creature is not able to see much with his big eyes because of the gusty winds that are laden with dirt, rock, sand, and grit particles. The man Pine villager scouts thrusts his metal sword out in front of him and into the wide filthy belly button of the large troll creature; the sword slices through the troll creature's belly burton like a knife cutting into butter.

The troll creature groans loudly in agony because of the sword that has just entered his obese stomach. The troll creature in temper slowly pulls the man Pine villager's metal sword out of his belly button with his large fingers; he drops the metal sword on to the rocky ground and flops his body over in front of him, which enables him to roll his gigantic round body into a ball-like shape, using this ball-like shape creature ability to roll along the rocky ground, and he completely squashes the man Pine villager scout and his horse in front of him before they have a chance to move out of the way. As the troll creature rolls his large ball-shaped body over the man Pine villager scout and his horse, he squashes and snaps the bones in their bodies, killing them both instantly as they become flattened like pancakes, their dead bodies spreading across the rocky surface of the Realm of Deserted Lands.

'No!' shouts another man Pine villager scout as he pulls out his small metal dagger from one of his brown boots and quickly throws it straight at the rolling troll creature. The troll creature is currently spinning along the bumpy and rocky ground now towards him as he sits on top of his horse. The small metal dagger flies through the air and fortunately hits the troll creature in his large round head as he is rolling his ball shape; the small metal dagger pierces deep within his brain, causing brain damage and stopping the flow of blood from being circulated to the rest of his huge body. The troll creature quickly flops out of his ball-like position and his huge body unfolds outwards on to the sharp and rocky ground in the Realm of Deserted Lands as he dies promptly. The man Pine villager scout, who was knocked on to the ground first by the troll creature, now stumbles to his feet, slightly dazed from his hard fall to the rocky ground; he hurriedly climbs back on top of his horse and controls the horse to begin galloping off in another direction of the Realm of Deserted Lands, as he is dazed and not sure if the troll creature is actually killed or not.

'Wait!' shouts the man Pine villager scout who had thrown his small metal dagger at the troll creature and killed it; however, the sound of this man Pine villager scout's plea falls on the deaf ears of the other man Pine villager scout who continues to gallop off into the distance.

'Quickly, we must go after him!' shouts another man Pine villager scout. The three remaining men Pine villager scouts gather their composure and kick the backs of their horses, manoeuvring their rope reins to gallop upon their horses in order to follow the other man Pine villager scout. Within about seven minutes, the three men Pine villager scouts rapidly catch up with the other dazed man Pine villager scout who had galloped off speedily on his horse.

AFTER LOSING THEIR bearings due to the attack they faced from the troll creature, the four surviving men Pine villager scouts divert from their initial direction and gallop frantically on horseback constantly in a panic for over an hour across the Realm of Deserted Lands in the east direction until they reach an area that is covered with large white rocks known to the creatures as Cadaver Rock. At this point, the three men Pine villagers manoeuver their horses in front of the other dazed man Pine villager scout in order to halt all their horses together, causing all the horses to stop galloping.

The four men Pine villagers begin to catch their breath, feeling terrified and guilty about the death of the other man Pine villager scout, which had been caused by the troll creature. They look at one another in silence with dampened spirits before they slowly trot on their horses to the bottom of the large white rock pile and carefully climb down from their horses to investigate this unseen landmark. The four men Pine villager scouts all look up in astonishment to see the almost eaten remains of Lord Scartor's corpse upon a large wooden crucifix fixed at the top of Cadaver Rock, with giant millipedes, ants, scorpions, and earwig insects are still crawling all over and throughout Lord Scartor's corpse, tearing away at his rotten flesh.

As the four men Pine villager scouts look more closely at Cadaver Rock, they notice in shock that millions of these giant malicious insects are crawling over the entire large pile of white rocks. They quickly step back away from Cadaver Rock; as they look further down the large pile of white rocks, they notice another dead body whose flesh remains are being torn away by the giant insects. The four men Pine villager scouts panic and quickly run back to their horses far from the pile of large white rocks to avoid any contact with those giant spiteful insects.

'Unless I'm mistaken, that's Lord Scartor's corpse fixed upon that crucifix at the top of that rock pile, apart from the fact he is half eaten by those horrible vile insects. My eyes have never lain upon any giant insect creature like those before. I know his body was devoured, but he does look like the drawing that Parrot had drawn for us to recognise Lord Scartor,' says a man Pine villager scout, looking closely and squinting through the dark gusty winds at a piece of sheep's wool with a red drawing of Lord Scartor on it, which Parrot had painted with sheep's blood and given it to the five men Pine villager scouts before they left Pine Village several months ago.

'Yes, you're right, it's definitely a resemblance of him,' says another man Pine villager scout, also squinting at the piece of sheep's wool with the drawing of Lord Scartor on it.

'We need to send word of this situation quickly to Lynx. If Lord Scartor is now dead, it could mean that this nightmare of a war is finally over and we can at last go home back to our families,' says the man Pine villager scout happily, who is holding on to the piece of sheep's wool with the picture of Lord Scartor drawn on it.

'Or it could mean that Lieutenant Triton has murdered Lord Scartor due to him being a slave to Lord Scartor for far too long now, because Parrot had explained to us that Lieutenant Triton would be cruelly mistreated by Lord Scartor. Maybe he has now taken over the Potorian army and is currently planning to take over the Planet of Phoenix in the great war that had been foretold for centuries would inevitably happen between the humans and the creatures upon the Planet of Phoenix,' replies another men Pine villager scout, thinking about the tales of a great war his father used to tell him about when he was a young boy.

'You have no proof of that. Maybe Lord Scartor just died naturally and Lieutenant Triton has abandoned the plans for launching the great war on the Planet of Phoenix against the humans,' states the other man Pine villager scout nervously.

'If that was true, then why is Lord Scartor fixed upon a crucifix and made to suffer a revolting decease such as being ripped apart by giant insects? Even in the afterlife, his body will be dismantled and his soul will remain lost for ever to darkness and evil. It looks like one of the Potorians' body was also eaten by the big insects near the bottom of the pile of large white rocks. That makes me think that Lieutenant Triton had ordered that Potorian to fix his body upon the crucifix, knowing fully well what the big insects would do to his body,' says a man Pine villager scout.

'Something just doesn't feel right about this. I'll send word of what has happened to Lynx now and let him decide about what this all means and what we humans should do next. Whatever the circumstances, we need to get out of this godforsaken environment quick,' exclaims another man Pine villager scout. Upon this man Pine villager scout's words, one of the other men Pine villager scouts hurriedly pulls out a small piece of cloth and a small wooden stick with animal's blood on it from his brown coat pocket and he writes a small message to Lynx, which states that Lord Scartor has been crucified in the Realm of Deserted Lands and that the humans might need to prepare for an unexpected attack from Lord Scartor. The man Pine villager scout rolls the small piece of cloth up and attaches it to one of the feet of a carrier pigeon that had been resting in a small cage attached to one of the horses' backs.

It is the last of the carrier pigeons from the four carrier pigeons that they had originally set out from Pine Village with, as one of the pigeons had died due to the cold weather and also as they had previously sent messages to Lynx via the other two carrier pigeon regarding their whereabouts; none of those two carrier pigeons had managed to return back to them as the five men Pine villager scouts always had to keep changing locations during their quest in seeking the new fortress hideout of Lord Scartor and Lieutenant Triton.

The man Pine villager scout releases the last remaining carrier pigeon into the air, and it struggles to fly into the sky in the gusty winds of the Realm of Deserted Lands that is covered with dirt, rock, sand, and grit particles. The carrier pigeon, however, continues to fly across the vast Planet of Phoenix in the north-east direction until it will eventually return to Lynx's small wooden castle in Pine Village, which it had been trained to do. The surviving four men Pine villager scouts eagerly watch the carrier pigeon fly into the air until they lose sight of it amongst the gusty winds full of dirt, rock, sand and grit particles in the Realm of Deserted Lands.

Sixteen

TRITON, VENUS, VICIOUS, Vulture, and the remaining 196 Potorians continue marching for a couple of hours over the sharp and unstable rocks upon the ground of the Realm of Deserted Lands, enduring through the gusty winds that swirl around the Realm of Deserted Lands, which are filled with tiny dirt, rock, sand, and grit particles. They are all now back in the main hall of Triton's Underground Dungeon that resides below the rock surface in the far south-west direction of the Realm of Deserted Lands located on the Planet of Phoenix.

Triton, Venus, Vicious, and Vulture are all now perched on big wooden chairs surrounding a big wooden table in the middle of the main room of Triton's Underground Dungeon, where the 196 Potorians begin to practice their weapon combat training with one another in the main hall but away from the big wooden table. All the Potorians practice fighting hard with each other with their metal swords and axes as well as with their fists in order to prepare themselves for the great war; all the Potorians continue attacking and defending each other except for five Potorians who are ordered by Triton to make food in the food room of Triton's Underground Dungeon, which is just outside the main room. After preparing a meal for their masters, these five Potorians bring it to the big wooden table in the main room, along with ale in large cups for Triton, Venus, Vicious, and Vulture to feast upon.

The food is usually meat of wild animals such as horses, deer, and warthogs that had been violently hunted by the Potorians in the Grass Terrain Fields just outside the perimeter of the Realm of Deserted Lands in the east direction. After these wild animals were killed, their carcasses were chopped into smaller pieces, and this meat was then carried for many miles back to Triton's Underground Dungeon in the Realm of Deserted Lands. Vicious and Vulture begin scoffing down the bloody meat that the Potorians have just brought them upon the big wooden table, while Triton accompanied by Venus is looking at the map of the Planet of Phoenix that has been laid out across the big wooden table. This map of the Planet of Phoenix had been drawn by Lord Scartor many years ago while he was attempting to search for the anomaly crystal. Lord Scartor had used his dark magic from his golden sceptre to view the different locations of the Planet of Phoenix by creating cloudy teleportation portals and was then able to draw on specially made brown paper that he had also created from his golden sceptre.

Triton is currently trying to use the crystal finding device that he had taken earlier from Lord Scartor's sleeping room to analyse the coordinates on the map of the Planet of Phoenix in order to try and detect where the anomaly crystal's location presently is. Triton holds the crystal finding device in his large bulky hands up in the air and swings it around and above the map of the Planet of Phoenix; however, the glass sphere in the middle of the crystal finding device remains blank and doesn't react to any of Triton's hand movements above the map of the Planet of Phoenix.

'This stupid machine, it's broken!' says Triton angrily, throwing the crystal finding device down on top of the big wooden table. As the crystal finder device thuds on top of the big wooden table, it causes the big wooden table to jolt slightly, rattling the jugs of ale that had been placed on the big wooden table by the Potorians and stopping Vicious and Vulture from enjoying eating their meat and looking up at Triton in annoyance.

'Calm down, let me have a look at it, my lover, and I'll see if I can get it to activate,' says Venus confidently. Triton's anger quickly calms down with Venus's words; he then picks the crystal finding device back up from the big wooden table and passes it to Venus. Venus examines all over the crystal finder device intriguingly for a moment, while Vicious and Vulture put their heads back down to continue stuffing their faces with the raw horse, deer, and warthog meat that is continually being brought over to them from the food room by five of the Potorians. 'No, it doesn't look broken or faulty. Lord Scartor had initially made this device with dark magic. That means it would be durable for centuries. However, because this device has been generated from such dark magic, maybe the anomaly crystal might currently be in a harmonious and spiritual location somewhere upon the Planet of Phoenix, which would then cause it to be hidden from this sort of black magic.'

'Let's just tear apart all the main villages along with the wretched Falcon City until we find this anomaly crystal,' chuckles Vulture, chewing a piece of raw meat covered with blood, which is spat back out of Vulture's mouth on to the big wooden table as he grinds the meat in his mouth vulgarly. There are a few silent moments as Triton, Venus, and Vicious look at Vulture tearing apart the raw meat with his sharp and jagged teeth in disgust.

TRITON PICKS UP a raw piece of horse meat that is attached to a horse's large leg bone; he lifts it to his mouth and bites a big chunk of the flesh.

'Don't be a fool, Vulture. We don't have enough Potorian warriors or creatures on our side yet to achieve victory against all the main villages in the north and the grand Falcon City in the south-east at the same time. That is why we need the anomaly crystal's supernatural powers to aid us during the great war and finally take back the Planet of Phoenix from those putrid humans along with any creatures who stand against us,' states Triton assertively.

'You mean like those mysterious creatures that lurk within Eagle woods, that I have only managed to catch glimpses of from time to time while flying over Eagle Forest when I was researching the Planet of Phoenix during my younger years?' remarks Venus.

'Yes, that's right, my love. Lord Scartor had explained to me previously about an almighty sorcerer known as Hake and his cloned Hawk Tribe that live deep within the heart of Eagle Forest. Lord Scartor explained that these Hawks never really meddled with any good or bad situation that occurred outside the bounds of Eagle Forest. However, they wouldn't hesitate to attack and kill any creature or human who dare enter their territory within Eagle Forest,' explains Triton.

'What creature abilities do these Hawks possess?' asks Venus curiously.

'I am not sure about the full extent of their creature abilities. Lord Scartor never told me how he knew these unidentified creatures existed, but he did state that they might be a threat to us creatures if we were to take over the whole of the Planet of Phoenix during the great war as they would understand that their precious Eagle Forest may also become a target of ours to abolish,' replies Triton.

'I could easily kill hundreds off puny humans or Hawk creatures with my fire breath and incredible burp shock waves,' boasts Vicious just before he picks up his large cup and gulps down litres of ale rather quickly.

'Why don't we just leave these weird creatures to themselves within Eagle Forest? If they're not likely to interfere with our plans at present, we don't need to worry about them,' says Vulture; his sentences are broken up in between chewing mouthfuls of raw meat.

'No, you stupid bird! If we are going to conquer the entire Planet of Phoenix, we cannot risk leaving any territory that may cause a threat to Venus's and my rule, whether it is now or in the future. The humans and creatures that don't serve or follow us after we win the great war will perish immediately, but if another army of creatures get involved against us during the great war, we don't have the legions of forces required to defeat such a resistance from mystical creatures such as the Hawk Tribe,' states Triton, putting the large horse leg bone back down on the big wooden table, all the meat on which have been eaten by Triton.

'The monstrous creatures I am blessed with creating from using my magical creature abilities should be able to slaughter Hake and his Hawk Tribe,' grins Venus.

'Yes, we do all retain great creature powers and abilities ourselves and especially you, Venus, that are indeed going to be very useful when we enforce the great war against the humans. But Hake is also an extremely powerful sorcerer who possesses unlimited magic and preserves vast knowledge of the Planet of Phoenix. He should not be underestimated and I believe he will be the biggest threat to us on our quest to be triumphant during the great war. This is why we need to find the anomaly crystal, and with it, we can generate unstoppable plans that will enable us to destroy Hake and his Hawk Tribe in Eagle Forest before they can cause us any resistance in the great war,' explains Triton with wise judgements.

'Triton's right. We need to plan a surprise attack carefully so we will have the upper hand against all the humans and good creatures left, who pose against us. Although we all our powerful in our own way, we are outnumbered still by the human race and Hake's unknown sorcerous powers and numbers of Hawks may be very challenging along with the humans that also possess resilient weapons in battles,' remarks Venus, remembering some of the battles she has witnessed while flying in the sky above conflicts between King Exodus's royal Falcon guards and Viper's Serpent warriors that emerged in the Kingdom of Humans.

'Hake should just join us who are his own creature race and not assist in helping those repulsive humans,' remarks Vicious.

'Hake is neither friend nor foe to the humans or us creatures, but I feel he will do what is necessary in order to protect the survival of the overall nature and environment of the Planet of Phoenix,' answers Triton.

'Why don't we get that Viper creature to join with us instead as he has loads of his Serpent warriors at his command?' states Vulture.

'I will only join with Viper if we have no other choice. He's just as likely to betray us as we have done to Lord Scartor. Viper's and the Serpent's life spans are a lot longer than most of us creatures and the humans due to them being part reptilian. I was told by Lord Scartor that Viper had previously joined with him in a battle long ago in order to steal the anomaly crystal from the humans, but they weren't victorious and were unable to find the anomaly crystal. Viper doesn't like to lose, especially against his enemies, the human species. Thus, he broke the allegiance he had with Lord Scartor and returned to his home in the dark and dangerous Komodo Jungle. Viper will now be very much out for himself against the humans and any other creature, but once we possess the astonishing powers of the anomaly crystal he will have no choice but to serve under me too as everyone eventually will,' says Triton lustily.

'Yes, Yes!' laughs Vulture hysterically.

'Hail Triton, the new master of our universe!' shouts Vicious, slamming his fist down on the big wooden table, also jolting the half empty big cups of ale.

'We should send groups of Potorians to attack the smaller villages and huts that are scattered around the Grass Terrain Fields over the Planet of Phoenix, which I have noticed while flying around when researching the various environments. We must kill these small groups of human villagers first so they won't have the chance to join and unite with the bigger main villages, which will cause their numbers to increase when the time of the great war inevitably arises. Vicious and Vulture, you should go to Willow Village and search for the anomaly crystal there. Raven would not be stupid enough to hide the anomaly crystal back in Oak Village or in Pine Village as he knows that would be the first place that we creatures would search for it. Once one of his neighbouring villages is being brutally destroyed, he will have no choice but to try and use the anomaly crystal against us, and when that situation happens, we will then steal it from him,' cackles Venus, smiling heartily at Triton, sitting back down on her wooden chair next to the big wooden table.

'Ha ha!' laughs Vulture loudly.

AS VENUS ALSO laughs along with Vulture, she suddenly experiences a strange and innate animal sensation running deep in her blood, which gushes through the veins of her petite body; her eyes instinctively start turning pure white as she uses a part of her Animagus powers that enable her to connect with other evil creatures throughout the Planet of Phoenix. Venus's Animagus abilities paranormally scan the surrounding area, which allows Venus to connect with one of the big insects that is a scorpion, who is eating savagely at the flesh remains of Lord Scartor's corpse fixed upon the big wooden crucifix on Cadaver Rock. The scorpion's eyes also turn pure white as Venus begins to connect with it. Venus's Animagus powers now permits her to see through the eyes of the scorpion, and she notices out of the corner of its eyes the four remaining men Pine villager scouts who are standing just away from the bottom of the large white rock pile at Cadaver Rock. Venus stands up from her wooden chair in a rage and pushes it quickly from her, causing the wooden chair to fall with a loud thud on to the ground behind her.

'Vermin!' shouts Venus Furiously.

'What is it, Venus?' asks Triton quickly, mystified, in response to Venus's sudden actions.

'I detect humans in the Realm of Deserted Lands, where they are currently at the bottom of Cadaver Rock staring at Lord Scartor's corpse,' says Venus crossly, as her pure white eyes now turn back to their normal red colour, which stops her Animagus powers, causing her to lose the connection and sight from the scorpion's eyes, which is crawling around Lord Scartor's corpse that is fixed upon the big wooden crucifix at the top of Cadaver Rock.

'We must murder those inferior humans before they have a chance to let any other humans know the news of Lord Scartor's death. If this information is uncovered now, it will change their strategies and plans for the forthcoming great war,' states Vicious.

'Yes, yes, and we will lose all our surprise tactics,' mentions Vulture.

'Potorians! Quickly go find and slaughter these pathetic humans before they share with anyone else what has happened to Lord Scartor,' states Triton as he shouts this order across the main hall to the Potorians in Triton's Underground Dungeon.

'Quick! Quick!' shouts Vulture.

'No, those stupid Potorians won't reach the humans in time. Besides, I have a better idea,' remarks Venus deviously.

Venus takes a breath and begins to use her magical creature abilities; she puts both her hands out in front of her; one hand is above the other hand and both of them are facing down towards the ground. Venus's eyes now turn to a pure white colour again, and in between her hands within a few moments, she magically creates a furious sabre-toothed tiger. The sabre-toothed tiger is small at first as it remains between Venus's hands just in front of her body; Venus then removes the bottom hand from out front of her and puts it back by the side of her body. Venus applies the other top hand to levitate the small sabre-toothed tiger down towards the ground; it levitates down to the ground in a slow motion. Venus then moves her top hand higher into the air, which now turns the sabre-toothed tiger to a very large size with strong and robust muscles.

The sabre-toothed tiger is covered in short fur that is a yellow and brown colour. It has a long furry tail that swings wildly from side to side as well as many sharp claws on all four of its feet. The sabre-toothed tiger also has two pointed sharp white teeth that stick out in the front of its mouth; these two pointed sharp white teeth are so big and powerful that they're able to slice into the flesh of any animal or creature that resides on the Planet of Phoenix. The Potorians, who are watching Venus mould her magical creature abilities, all stand back in shock and gasp at the furious sabre-toothed tiger that Venus has just created.

'Feast on those humans flesh and bones!' orders Venus assertively as Triton, Vicious, and Vulture laugh in gratification. Venus maintains her eyes to be white in colour so that she will be able to see through the sabre-toothed tiger's eyes while hunting the men Pine villager scouts in the Realm of Deserted Lands. The sabre-toothed tiger roars forcefully, which sends a loud echoing noise through the whole of the main hall in Triton's Underground Dungeon. The sabre-toothed tiger scratches its sharp claws across the rocky ground, making deep scratch marks on the rocky floor of Triton's Underground dungeon; it then rapidly runs out of the main room, and the Potorians who are close to it swiftly dive out of its way in fear of getting attacked by this monstrous beast. The sabre-toothed tiger sprints at a high speed out of the main hall and along the short passageway that leads up to the rocky surface of the Realm of Deserted Lands that is above Triton's Underground Dungeon.

The sabre-toothed tiger continues racing across the rocky terrain of the Realm of Deserted Lands, led by its strong sense of smell of human flesh towards the four men Pine villager scouts, who are still at the bottom of Cadaver Rock in the north-west direction in the Realm of the Deserted Lands. The sabre-toothed tiger sprints at a fast pace, dodging through the gusty winds filled with tiny dirt, rock, sand, and grit particles, but it's not slowed down by this atmosphere due to the power and speed that the sabre-toothed tiger is travelling at. When the sabre-toothed tiger reaches large piles of sharp rocks that would be an obstruction to most other creatures and humans, the sabre-toothed tiger uses the strong muscles of its hind legs and leaps high up in the air until it passes these sharp rocks so that it can continue sprinting towards the four men Pine villager scouts who are currently unaware of this charging sabre-toothed tiger coming towards them.

After only twenty minutes, the sabre-toothed tiger approaches the four men Pine villager scouts' precise location by using its acute sense of smell. The sabre-toothed tiger now gets excited due to the strong scent of human flesh filling in its nostrils; the sabre-toothed tiger roars wrathfully in eagerness of a bloody meal.

'Can you hear that?' says one of the man Pine villager scouts in a worried manner, as he hears the faint sounds of roaring in the distance.

'Hear what?' asks another man Pine villager scout as he attempts to squint into the dark distance, but he can't see anything except swirling particles of tiny dirt, rock, sand, and grit in the gusty winds.

'Don't start worrying again. I think we have endured enough drama for one day,' replies another man Pine villager scout as he starts preparing to saddle back upon his horse.

'I don't know what it is, but there's definitely something moving very quickly in the distance,' says the man Pine villager scout as the other three men Pine villager scouts quickly look all around them in desperation.

'I can't see anything in this thick gusty wind and fog,' states one of the men Pine villager scout as he now hears a large and terrifying roar that echoes throughout the Realm of Deserted Lands. The four men Pine villager scouts panic in terror and grasp their metal swords tightly that are currently attached to their waists; one of the men Pine villager scouts shakily holds his metal sword out in front of him as he sees a dark figure moving quickly in the distance towards them.

'Over there,' says the man Pine villager scout as he points towards the south direction in the vast open space in the Realm of Deserted Lands.

As the other three men Pine villager scouts squint through the gusty winds in the south direction the other man Pine villager scout is pointing towards, suddenly in complete surprise and shock to the four men Pine villager scouts, they encounter a large and ferocious sabre-toothed tiger that leaps high up in the air as it ascends through the gusty winds and lands forcefully on top of one of the men Pine villager scouts. The sabre-toothed tiger lifts one of its front huge paws that has long sharp claws at the end of it and starts slashing the man Pine villager scout's chest and face viciously, causing squirts of blood to spray out of the man Pine villager scout and splatter the other three men Pine villager scouts who are standing by helpless to defend this atrocious attack. The man Pine villager scout who is being sliced to pieces by the sabre-toothed tiger is killed instantly due to the intense wounds and pain caused.

The horses that are near the three remaining Pine villager scouts begin to run wildly away from Cadaver Rock as they are frightened by the large sabre-toothed tiger creature after witnessing it tearing apart one of the men Pine villager scouts. The other three men Pine villager scouts shout in horror and panic immensely on seeing this monstrous creature tear apart one of their fellow Pine villager scouts; the three remaining men Pine villager scouts also begin to rapidly run away from the sabre-toothed tiger in opposite directions from one another. The sabre-toothed tiger roars loudly in excitement, sending a shattering pain in the ears of the three remaining men Pine villager scouts who are attempting to flee.

The sabre-toothed tiger applies immense power in its hind legs and jumps from top of the dead men Pine villager scout upon the rocky ground, and guided by its acute sense of smell through the darkness, it pounces in the air and quickly lands on another man Pine villager scout, tearing this man Pine villager scout's head off in the blink of an eye by using its two long sharp and pointed white teeth in the front of its mouth. The man Pine villager scout's headless body flops to the ground with blood squirting out from the empty and headless neck, while the sabre-toothed tiger crushes the skull and brains of the man Pine villager scout's head that is still in its mouth with the rest of its teeth in its jaw. As the man Pine villager scout's head gets crushed by the powerful jaws of the sabre-toothed tiger, the blood that pours out from the man Pine villager scout's head stains the sabre-toothed tiger's teeth a red colour.

The sabre-toothed tiger roars loudly again on getting the taste of human flesh and blood, and it now begins to chase after another man Pine villager scout who is running in the west direction of the Realm of Deserted Lands. The man Pine villager scout begins to scream in fear as he rapidly tries to escape, but before he can comprehend what to do next, the sabre-toothed tiger leaps into the air, jumping far across the Realm of Deserted Lands and digging its claws into the side of the running man Pine villager scout's body. The man Pine villager scout feels excruciating pain and dies quickly as the sabre-toothed tiger rips his limbs into several pieces from his body, using the strong and destructive power of sharp claws attached to all four of its large yellow and brown coloured legs.

The last man Pine villager scout is still running frantically away in the opposite east direction of the Realm of Deserted Lands; he quickly looks over his shoulder while continuing to run, but sees nothing except dark gusty wind in the air with the tiny dirt, rock, sand, and grit particles swirling in his eyes. The man Pine villager scout's eyes become red and itchy as he keeps trying to see all around him through the gusty winds; he can hear the terrifying sounds of the screams of the other men Pine villager scouts who have just been horribly slaughtered by the sabre-toothed tiger.

The last remaining man Pine villager scout briskly stops running and stands still and alone as he runs out of breath, grabbing his chest with his hand while panting frantically. The sabre-toothed tiger without warning surprises the man Pine villager scout by suddenly turning up directly in front of him through the darkness and gusty winds of the Realm of Deserted Lands. The sabre-toothed tiger releases another ferocious and territorial roar; it savagely pounces on to the front of the man Pine villager scout's chest and starts eating away at his flesh and bone. The sabre-toothed tiger tears limb from limb effortlessly as the last remaining man Pine villager scout experiences a painful and bloody death from this monstrous beast.

WHILE VENUS'S EYES were still pure white, she had used her magical creature abilities to connect with the sabre-toothed tiger's eyes and had been enjoying watching as the sabre-toothed tiger had mutilated all the men Pine villager scouts. She now connects with the sabre-toothed tiger using her creature magical abilities in a different way to mentally control the thoughts of the sabre-toothed tiger to order it to return back to Triton's Underground Dungeon. After receiving the mind control from Venus, the sabre-toothed tiger quickly gulps the remains of the man Pine villager scout it has just killed and instinctively races swiftly off in the south-west direction over the sharp rocky surface through the Realm of Deserted Lands back towards Triton's Underground Dungeon.

Along the journey back to Triton's Underground Dungeon, the sabre-toothed tiger can smell one of the man Pine villager scouts' horses that had initially run wildly away. In thirst for blood, the sabre-toothed tiger doesn't hesitate to strongly leap up into the air and crashes down on top of the large back of one of those horses that is passing while sprinting through the Realm of Deserted Lands; the sabre-toothed tiger brutishly tears apart the thick meat from the horse's body and then continues back on its journey to Triton's Underground Dungeon.

Now after around twenty-five minutes, the sabre-toothed tiger returns to Triton's Underground Dungeon in the far south-west direction of the Realm of Deserted Lands; the sabre-toothed tiger sprints beneath the ground opening in the Realm of Deserted Lands through a rocky passageway until it reaches the main room of Triton's Underground Dungeon. The sabre-toothed tiger stops sprinting as it enters the main room; it begins roaring at the Potorians near the sides of the walls through the main room, while the Potorians tremble at the sight of the sabre-toothed tiger's bloodstained teeth. The Potorians all stand back close against the rock walls of Triton's Underground Dungeon's main hall as they watch in terror as the sabre-toothed tiger prowls around the main room. The sabre-toothed-tiger decides to sit in front of one of the Potorians against the rock walls. The sabre-toothed tiger sniffs the Potorian intensely and begins to lick the Potorian's left cheek of his face with its long slimy tongue; the Potorian begins to sweat in a panic at the thought that he is about to be eaten by this monstrous creature.

Venus makes her white eyes turn back to their normal red colour; she begins to laugh naughtily as she walks confidently over to the sabre-toothed tiger, who is currently sitting in front of the Potorian against one of the rocky walls of the main hall. Venus puts one of her hands facing down towards the ground above the sabre-toothed tiger's large head, and she employs her magical creature abilities to make the sabre-toothed tiger begin shrinking to a much smaller size, where it then levitates slowly up into the air near her hand. Venus now puts her other hand facing towards the ground underneath the bottom of the now small sabre-toothed tiger, and she continues to use her magical creature abilities to make the sabre-toothed tiger disappear supernaturally in between both her hands.

The Potorians takes a deep breath and relaxes at the sight of the sabre-toothed tiger being made to disappear magically. Venus's eyes turn back to their normal red colour as she walks back over towards Triton at the big wooden table on the opposite side of the main room in Triton's Underground Dungeon.

'There you go, my lover. No more sneaky humans spying around the Realm of Deserted Lands,' grins Venus, pleased with herself. Triton pauses for a moment in astonishment at what Venus had managed to create from her creature abilities. Triton gives Venus an envious grin as he lusts over her creature powers and wants to force his body upon her seductive beauty. Triton now turns towards the Potorians who are standing against the surrounding walls of the main room in Triton's Underground Dungeon.

'Potorians, leave the Realm of Deserted Lands now in large groups and burn any of the smaller villages within the Grass Terrain Fields across the middle lands of the Planet of Phoenix. Kill all of its human inhabitants. Once you have completed this mission, journey towards Pine Village where you will then kill every single Pine villager who exists there. Vicious and Vulture, go to Willow Village and destroy it while searching for the anomaly crystal there. If the anomaly crystal is not located there, regroup with the Potorians to finally launch a disastrous attack on Pine Village,' orders Triton.

'Yes, of course, Master,' says Vulture in an excited manner, standing up from his wooden chair against the big wooden table.

'We will destroy those weak and pathetic humans once and for all!' shouts Vicious confidently. On hearing Triton's orders, the 196 Potorians suit up in their metal armour, swords, and axes that are located around the rocky walls of the main room; they then start marching in formation up the rocky passageway and out of Triton's Underground Dungeon. After a couple of hours of strong marching across the rocky ground against the gusty winds littered with tiny dirt, rock, sand, and grit particles, they finally leave the Realm of Deserted Lands' borders on a mission of destroying the smaller villages throughout the Grass Terrain Fields across the middle lands of the Planet of Phoenix. Following this direction will take their journey through the centre of the Planet of Phoenix in the north-east direction to eventually meet up with Vicious and Vulture near the perimeter of Pine Village.

After the 196 Potorians leave Triton's Underground Dungeon, Vicious chews his last portion of raw warthog meat and stands up from his big wooden chair against the big wooden table. Vulture flaps his large black feathery wings attached to the back of his body, which enables him to hover above the ground in the main hall of Triton's Underground Dungeon. Vulture manoeuvres his body by flapping his large black feathery wings to fly slightly above Vicious so he can grab Vicious's muscly and broad shoulders with his clawed feet. Vulture while holding firmly on to Vicious's broad shoulders now flaps his black feathery wings very hard, enabling him to make both him and Vicious fly out of the main hall and up through the rocky passageway leading to the ground surface of the Realm of Deserted Lands. Vulture flies high up in the sky, where he experiences resistance because of gusty winds filled with tiny dirt, rock, sand, and grit particles that circle throughout the Realms of Deserted Lands. Vulture strains his large black feathery wings hard in trying to keep him and Vicious stable while flying across the Realm of Deserted Lands, after which they eventually exit from its borders and continue in the north-east direction of the Planet of Phoenix towards Willow Village in the far north-east area.

Triton walks vibrantly around the big wooden table in the main hall of his Underground Dungeon towards Venus, who is now at the other end of it. Upon reaching Venus, Triton grabs her strongly in his large muscular grip and kisses her forcefully on the lips, sticking his tongue deep into her throat, while Venus also responds back to Triton in a seductive manner.

'We must wait here with the crystal finding device. I'm sensing a strong feeling that it will show us where the anomaly crystal has been hidden soon, my love,' says Venus, pushing Triton away from her in a playful fashion.

'Of course, Venus . . . I have no doubt now that the Planet of Phoenix will soon be ours to command!' suggests Triton, as he pushes Venus over the big wooden table and begins to passionately fornicate with her.

Seventeen

LYNX IS TWENTY-SIX years old and he has been the leader of Pine Village for four years now. Lynx has shoulder-length brown straight hair and brown eyes; he has smooth skin on his face with stubble on his chin. Lynx has a medium-sized nose and pointy shaped ears. Lynx wears a sliver crown with the word 'Pine' written in gold in the ancient Phoenix language in the front middle part of the silver crown; he also wears silver-plated knight armour and chainmail clothing with steel boots. Lynx is of a muscular build and average size in height; he is quick in reflex with his arms and legs during battle situations as he has been highly trained in war combat.

Lynx's characteristics are that he is intelligent, hardworking, and considerate; he has always sacrificed his time to put the needs of others before him. He is a very humble, caring, and honourable human due to the similar nature of his ancestors, who were also admirable humans, along with the title and status that Lynx presently holds as the Pine Village leader with him being currently the youngest human to ever be deemed a leader of a village on the Planet of Phoenix. Lynx was trained in leadership skills and learnt how to plan, organise, and conduct battle tactics as well as protect the humans and their homes by his father Saber, who was a previous royal Falcon captain to King Exodus, just as was his father and Lynx's grandfather,

Sharkus, who was another royal Falcon captain to King Exodus's father, King Zunus.

Sharkus who was Lynx's grandfather was born and raised in Falcon City, where he was also trained as a formidable leader and warrior from a very young age. Sharkus with only a handful of other fortunate humans attended the royal Falcon class as they had a prestigious or royal family bloodline running through their ancestors. The royal Falcon class was a small school for royalty and wealthy humans, and the royal Falcon class was located in Falcon Castle. Sharkus was given the privilege to attend the royal Falcon class as his father Dominous was King Zunus, main councillor for safety and defence of Falcon City and the city humans who lived in it. Also, Dominous's wife who was Sharkus's mother and was called Cosmika was King Zunus's cousin, meaning that Sharkus and now Lynx had distant royal Falcon blood in them.

Sharkus fortunately attended the royal Falcon class with King Exodus, who was the son of King Zunus and Queen Rainbow and the bloodline descendent of King Primus and Queen Solar, who was initially alive during the same time as renowned wizard Grackle. Although King Primus and Queen Solar resided on the Planet of Phoenix along with Grackle, they were in completely different locations as Grackle lived in the now destroyed Alder Village and King Primus and Queen Solar were developing the beginnings of Falcon City, which made them both unaware of the phenomenal situation with regard to the anomaly crystal. This meant that King Primus and Queen Solar or any other human living in Falcon City in the far south-east direction of the Planet of Phoenix had any knowledge of Grackle creating and giving the mystic anomaly crystal to his eldest son Sparrow, who when the time came also passed the anomaly crystal to his wife Star, who in turn gave it to their son Trogon, who was Barious's father. When Barious became old enough to become the protector of the anomaly crystal, his mother Star explained the entire situation to him of Grackle and the anomaly crystal and how it was the most important duty to protect the anomaly crystal from the evil war lord creature named Lord Scartor.

At the beginning of his rule of Falcon City, King Primus was a strong believer in uniting all the humans that resided on the Planet of Phoenix, in order to protect their species against the evil creatures they were aware of that also lived on the Planet of Phoenix, such as Viper and his mother Mamushi, who attacked and killed humans that journeyed past the enigmatic Komodo Jungle in the middle east area of the Planet of Phoenix. King Primus was the reason behind originally settling the early dispute between Pine Village and Oak Village when Hyena, who was Wolf's great-grandfather, separated away from Pine Village and its leader Woken and strove to create a village of his own that became known as Oak Village. When King Primus and Queen Solar were blessed to have their son, who later became King Zunus, he was also brought up and wisely taught to maintain the alliances with all the humans and the various villages that were located throughout the Planet of Phoenix.

During their time at the royal Falcon class, King Exodus and Lynx's grandfather Sharkus became great friends after spending much time helping each other, learning their academic and practical studies that were specifically designed and implemented by Falcon University lecturers to condition highly intellectual and developed humans to progress the future of Falcon City's supremacy.

After many years and changes later, when King Exodus was proclaimed king of Falcon City due to his father King Zunus passing away because of very old age, he trusted Sharkus with his life and valued his much developed warrior skills and knowledge and made Sharkus his royal Falcon captain. During those decades, King Exodus's mother Queen Rainbow also passed away due to old age, and King Zunus and Queen Rainbow were buried together in the royal Falcon Tombs, and just like King Zunus's father King Primus and his wife Queen Solar would always be remembered for the development of Falcon City along with uniting all the humans together throughout the Planet of Phoenix.

Sharkus had two sons from his wife Melody, whom they named Saber and Panther. Sharkus also brought up Saber and Panther to be trained as leaders and taught them to fight creatures and protect the human species from this threat at all costs. Both Saber and Panther also had the grand opportunity of being taught at the royal Falcon class, where they were also taught by the best Falcon University lecturers of their time in the most important knowledge, skills, and abilities required to become great leaders just as all the kings of Falcon City were taught.

After Sharkus's unfortunate death that was caused by an unusual and painful illness following an infection of a battle wound, King Exodus made Saber the royal Falcon captain at his father Sharkus's last wishes, since he wanted Panther to be made Saber's main royal Falcon guard. Saber was devastated by his father Sharkus's death, which fuelled him with motivation to make him proud by being the best royal Falcon captain to King Exodus that he could be. During his growing up years and the many years of service as the royal Falcon captain, Saber fell in love with a beautiful woman called Lunar, who was the daughter of a prestigious Falcon University astronomy lecturer called Abravis. Saber and Lunar spent many happy years together and was much admired by the rest of the city humans in Falcon City and even more so when Lunar gave birth to their son Lynx.

LYNX WAS NOW also fortunate enough to be taught and trained at the royal Falcon class; that was where he met King Exodus's daughter, Princess Petal, and they both became great friends with each other and got more intimate with one another as they grew in age. Although Lynx was a few years older than Princess Petal, they formed a great bond with each other. King Exodus was already married to an attractive and honourable woman called Eclipse; they had initially met during their childhood when they were both taught education together at the royal Falcon class due to Eclipse being the daughter of one of the chief advisors to King Exodus's father Zunus with regard to the finance and treasury for Falcon City. King Exodus and Eclipse fell in love at an early age and got married as soon as they both turned teenagers, and King Zunus was very happy to unite the couple in holy matrimony. King Exodus and Queen Eclipse remained loyal and happy together for many years until unfortunately Queen Eclipse died of a virus infection shortly after giving birth to Princess Petal.

Viper was the narcissistic snake-like creature who had for numerous years constantly attacked the humans in Falcon City just like his mother Mamushi had done during the reigns of King Primus and King Zunus until Mamushi was finally killed by Lynx's father Saber. Now Viper spawned his Serpent warriors, who were also snake-like creatures but had scorpion tails. Viper, in vengeance of his mother's murder, took many years to spawn an army of Serpents; one day, when Lynx was only eighteen years old, Viper launched a surprise attack on Falcon City, which enabled the Serpents to actually break into Falcon City's big iron portcullis gates. Viper and his Serpents killed many humans of Falcon City in that awful and horrific battle; amongst those victims were the royal Falcon Captain Saber and his wife Lunar, who were Lynx's parents. Viper killed Saber and Lunar by spitting black poisonous venom from his large white fangs, and this venom was so toxic it disintegrated all the flesh and bones from their bodies. King Exodus and Panther along with many of the royal Falcon guards managed to force Viper and his Serpents back out of Falcon City, but the damage had already been done. Along with Panther and King Exodus, Lynx was distraught to get the knowledge that his parents were pitilessly murdered while he was still so young.

King Exodus naturally made Lynx the new royal Falcon captain in honour of his father Saber, to which Panther also agreed as he decided he now wanted to leave Falcon City due the tragic events that had happened with regard to him losing his brother and sister-in-law. King Exodus was sad to see one of the best royal Falcon guards leave Falcon City, but bestowed on Panther for his many years of service the honour of him becoming leader of a new village that was being developed in the far north-east, as ordered by King Exodus due to the increase in human population; this new village was west of Pine Village and was called Willow Village.

King Exodus was happy to trust Panther with being the leader of this new village but was also unhappy to see him leave his royal Falcon guards. Lynx wanted to honour King Exodus, his father Saber, and uncle Panther by being a remarkable royal Falcon captain and protect Falcon City and its city humans, which he achieved s in many dangerous and continuous battles against Viper and his Serpents that lived in Komodo Jungle that was to the north of Falcon City. Lynx desperately wanted to kill Viper and rid him from the Planet of Phoenix to avenge his father Saber and mother Lunar, although unfortunately after numerous battles, Lynx's attempts to kill Viper were unsuccessful.

Two years later, Igon, who was leader of Pine Village and great-grandson who had descended from the first and previous leader of Pine Village known as Woken, was killed in an attack by dozens of nomad warriors from the Wastelands in the far north-west of the Planet of Phoenix, and as Woken had no wife or kin, Pine Village was left without a leader. Although Lynx was a splendid and dedicated royal Falcon captain and was also very close to Princess Petal, he felt the pain of being in Falcon City too much, due to what had happened with his father Saber and mother Lunar when they were killed by Viper.

Lynx asked King Exodus if he could now become the new leader of Pine Village, as he also wanted to relocate closer to his uncle Panther, who was presently the leader of Willow Village; again after much persuasion against this request, King Exodus granted Lynx's wish out of appreciation for his service as the royal Falcon captain. Lynx suggested one of his greatest royal Falcon guards called Clang to take his place as royal Falcon captain in his place; King Exodus trusted Lynx's opinion and knighted Clang as the new royal Falcon captain. Princess Petal was very upset at the news of Lynx relocating to Pine Village and decided that she also wanted to go to Pine Village with Lynx; however, King Exodus would not allow this to happen until Princess Petal had finished all her academic studies in the royal Falcon class, as eventually she would be the queen of Falcon City and would need all the capabilities and knowledge required to rule Falcon City accordingly.

Lynx thus left Falcon City after a heartfelt goodbye to Princess Petal, and he then undertook the long journey north across the Planet of Phoenix to Pine Village upon his white horse that he was given by King Exodus when he was made the royal Falcon captain. On Lynx's travels to the far north-east, he made sure that he avoided the perimeter of Komodo Jungle so he wouldn't face confrontation with Viper or the Serpents due to him currently being outnumbered, but he vowed one day that he would kill Viper to avenge what Viper had done to his parents.

Along the way to Pine Village, Lynx visited his uncle Panther in Willow Village, who was extremely happy about the news that Lynx had been made the new Pine Village leader, as he felt it would be good for them both to be close to each other as both of them had lost their family members Saber and Lunar. After a long catch-up with his uncle Panther, Lynx undertook the last part of his journey to Pine Village, where he was warmly welcomed by Jackal, who was the leader of Oak Village at the time, his son Wolf, and Wolf's wife Opal, along with his Oakus guards and all the Pine villagers, who were made aware of this news by King Exodus sending his decree on cloth messages via carrier pigeons to Jackal to let him know about his wishes.

Jackal was a great aid to Lynx in helping him settle into his new role as the Pine Village leader, but sadly, Jackal died of fever a year later, after which Wolf was made the new Oak Village leader and Panther helped Lynx in employing his new rule over Pine Village, and the three leaders in the main villages in the north united strongly in trade and defence with one another against the creature threat that lingered in the Planet of Phoenix. Lynx continued to stay in contact with King Exodus and Princess Petal by sending cloth messages via carrier pigeons, and Princess Petal was happy for Lynx and excited about seeing him again as soon as she finished her educational studies.

Shortly after Lynx was made the leader of Pine Village, he started getting used to the villagers and how the trade systems, farming, and extended village development would operate, and Igon's Pinus guards helped him in his duties, especially the Pine guard Flame who was of great assistance to Lynx, as he was a vigilant and determined Pinus guard that he had already been for a couple of years. Lynx had a tendency to gallop on his white horse alone round the outskirts of Pine Village to get used to the perimeter of Pine Village and begin generating new plans for battle defence systems of Pine Village with regard to the inevitable great war. On one of these rides around the perimeter of Pine Village, Lynx came across another man Pine villager being attacked by two nomad warriors in the middle of one of the large Grass Terrain Fields; they were trying to kill the man Pine villager and steal his belongings.

Without hesitation, Lynx kicked his heels into the sides of his white horse and charged gallantly up to the two nomad warriors and sliced both their heads clean off with his silver sword just before they nearly killed the man Pine villager. Lynx jumped down from his white horse and helped the man Pine villager to his feet, who explained what had happened and that his name was Parrot. After that, Parrot and Lynx became best friends as they shared much in common with regard to their personalities and their characteristics and how they would both stand by one another in times of need. Parrot felt he owed a debt to Lynx for saving his life that day during the attack by the nomad warriors; this was why he started supplying his specially made weapons for free to the Pinus guards, although Lynx had emphasised many times that Parrot didn't owe him any debt and that he valued his friendship.

LYNX LIVES IN Pine Village in a small wooden castle where he lives with some of his Pine guards, including Flame, and a couple of women Pine villagers who are his maids and cook and clean in the small wooden castle. The castle has a few rooms where Lynx's Pine guards and maids sleep; it also has a medium-sized dining room, a kitchen, a couple of toilets, and storage rooms as well as a big main room where Lynx hosts his meetings with his Pine guards. Lynx's small wooden castle used to be the previous Pine Village leader Igon's castle, just as it had been passed down to Igon from his great-grandfather Woken.

This small wooden castle is located at one of the edges of Pine Village in the south-east area, and it has a small wooden watch tower attached to the small wooden castle, which overlooks the big wooden fence that surrounds Pine Village, just like another three small wooden watch towers that are also located around the other three edges of Pine Village's surrounding big wooden fence. Lynx and his Pine guards are currently sitting at a big wooden table in the big main room of Lynx's small wooden castle; they are all discussing and deliberating plans of finishing the rebuilding of Oak Village following the battle of Oak Village that had occurred a year ago.

Another one of Lynx's Pine guards who is at present walking around a small courtyard and garden that is located outside the front of the small wooden castle notices a carrier pigeon swerve quickly above him in the bright blue sky, as he gazes up, squinting due to the sunlight shining brightly upon the Pine guard's eyes. The carrier pigeon is exhausted and lands down quickly upon the short cut grass in the small wooden castle's front garden; the Pine guard sees that the pigeon has a piece of cloth tied to one of its feet, and he swiftly hurries across the garden and grabs the carrier pigeon before it flies off again. After picking up the pigeon from the grass of the garden, the Pine guard holds the carrier pigeon tightly in his hands and rushes from the small wooden castle's front garden, along the courtyard, until he opens the small wooden castle's main front wooden door; the Pine guard runs promptly down a hallway that leads towards the big main room, where Lynx and the other Pine guards are currently sitting around the big wooden table.

'Lynx, this carrier pigeon had just flown down on to the castle's front garden. It looks like one of those carrier pigeons that the five men Pine villager scouts took with them on their quest across the Planet of Phoenix in search for Lord Scartor's new fortress,' says the Pine guard, panting to catch his breath while holding the carrier pigeon out in front of him.

'Bring it here, please, Pine guard,' says Lynx eagerly. The Pine guard quickly brings the carrier pigeon over to Lynx, who stands up from his wooden chair next to the big wooden table. Lynx takes the carrier pigeon from the Pine guard and carefully unhooks the piece of cloth that has been tied by string to one of the pigeon's feet. Lynx let goes of holding on to the carrier pigeon, and it flies to the other side of the big main room; the carrier pigeon then flaps its short grey feathery wings to perch upon a wooden shelf fixed upon one of the walls in the big main room. This wooden shelf is covered all over with flower seeds; that is the food for the carrier pigeons and it's used to train the carrier pigeons to return back to Lynx's small wooden castle in Pine Village. He opens up the small piece of cloth carefully and notices the writing in red blood that is written across the middle of the piece of cloth. Lynx reads the writing on the piece of cloth in a curious manner. 'You're right. It was from one of the five men Pine villager scouts. It states that Lord Scartor has been murdered and we should prepare for a surprise attack from Triton.'

'Triton's killed Lord Scartor?' remarks another Pine guard, confused.

'Looks that way. Those evil and mischievous creatures can never be trusted, not even within their own ranks,' states Lynx uneasily.

'Do you think that Triton and the Potorians would really come and attack Pine Village as we don't even have the anomaly crystal hidden here?' says another Pine guard, who is concerned for his family that live in Pine Village.

'Yes, you are correct. The anomaly crystal is not currently located in Pine Village, but I won't take any chances, particularly after the massacre that occurred in the Oak Village battle a year ago. Although the anomaly crystal is not here in Pine Village, it doesn't mean Triton won't come looking for it here or any of the other villages that exist upon the Planet of Phoenix. Triton and the creatures upon the Planet of Phoenix will never leave us humans alone, as all they want to do is dominate or kill the entire human race. Let's just hope Triton doesn't ever join forces with Viper and his Serpent army, otherwise us humans will really be in a state of misfortune and unfortunate circumstances.

'You, my Pine guards, must stay here and prepare Pine Village for an attack that might occur. Secure both the gates at the east and west entrances. Put word out to the patrolling Pine guards at these entrances to check anyone whom you don't recognise that comes in or out of Pine Village. Gather the other Pine guards throughout Pine Village and rally any able-bodied men Pine villagers who will also be able to fight in the case of a surprise battle. I will ride swiftly to Willow Village now to warn my uncle Panther of this knowledge. That will also facilitate him to start preparing Willow Village for battle, in case that village is also attacked too. We will need both villages along with the collaboration of Falcon City, if we humans are to have any chance in defeating Triton and his creature army,' pronounces Lynx.

'Today all the Pine villagers will be in Pinus Tavern for the remembrance service. Is it a good idea to worry them about another battle on such a day like today? Are you also going to seek aid from King Exodus in Falcon City and his royal Falcon guard?' asks one of the Pine guards sitting around the big wooden table in the big main room of Lynx's small wooden castle.

'Yes, I am aware and understand that today is an extremely overwhelming day. As I have been friends with the previous Oak Village leader, Wolf, his wife Opal, and son Leopard, who were all devastatingly killed during the Oak Village battle, along with my uncle Panther and King Exodus who had been great old friends with Barious, who had been brutally murdered too, along with nearly the entire Oak Village population, it was such a horrific tragedy for us humans that will never be forgotten. However, I will not let an epic tragedy like that ever occur to us humans again. No child should endure the sorrow of losing his or her parents, whatever their age may be. So yes, I would like the whole of Pine Village warned and prepared for an attack, but please do be careful in delivering this news to the fragile Pine villagers who are attending the remembrance service at Pinus Tavern today. I will also visit Parrot before I leave for Willow Village, to make him aware of this situation we just found out regarding the death of Lord Scartor, and I will also ask Parrot if he can keep everyone in Pinus Tavern secure and calm if a battle was to occur in Pine Village. The journey to Falcon City is too long to undertake in person as I may be required to protect Pine Village doing a battle, but yes, I will send word to King Exodus in Falcon City via a carrier pigeon once I have journeyed to Willow Village and warned Panther about this imminent danger,' replies Lynx.

'Would you like some of us Pine guards to accompany you to Willow Village, Lynx, as the cobbled roads between the main villages can sometimes be dangerous due to wandering nomad warriors?' says one of Lynx's Pine guards.

'Thank you for the offer, but I will be fine as I am well trained in combat and dangerous situations since I was the captain of the royal Falcon guard where I had to defend myself alone on numerous occasions. Besides, I will need all of you who are my finely trained Pine guards to defend Pine Village and the villagers in it against any creature foe. Who knows what dark and precarious times we all might need to undergo in the build-up to the great war? Can one of you Pine Guards make sure you first warn Bruce at the Pine Village east entrance gate and Flame in the north-east watch tower of this news and battle preparation? Both of them will know exactly what to do in order to defend these important areas in Pine Village,' Lynx speaks directly as he nods at his Pine Guards who are sitting on wooden chairs around the big wooden table. Lynx and all his Pine guards then pause in quiet silence for a brief second about the thoughts of danger that is coming forth to Pine Village. 'I will try and be back here before nightfall, my honourable Pine guards. We have been trained to protect the innocent lives of humans. I believe we will all be victorious if an attack occurred here as long as we all stay united together and never give up in times of fear. Take care, my loyal Pine guards.'

LYNX STANDS AND begins to walk away from the big wooden table in the big main room of his small wooden castle situated in the south-east of Pine Village; he grabs from the big wooden table his silver sword and silver shield with the crest of the royal Falcon captain symbol upon it, which is a picture of a crown on top of a falcon bird. Lynx makes his way out of the big main room and walks down a hallway to the back of the small wooden castle; his white horse is kept and fed in the back gardens amongst the other Pine guards' brown and black horses.

One of Lynx's maids is currently waiting by his white horse and is placing the white leather saddle upon the white horse as well as making sure that the white horse's rope reins are secured and tight. Lynx smiles at his maid and climbs on top of his white horse; he kicks the sides of the white horse with his feet and rides out of the small wooden castle's back garden and through a wooden gate that is quickly opened by another one of Lynx's maids. Lynx then rides swiftly down the cobbled paths of Pine Village towards Parrot's small wooden flat.

Lynx's Pine guards also get up from their wooden chairs next to the big wooden table and suit up in their full metal knight amour, swords, and shields that have been left on the floor around the sides of the big main room. This group of Pine guards split up into smaller groups, and after hurrying around Pine Village to speak to other Pine guards, they organise and position patrols of Pine guards around Pine Village in the various different small wooden towers that are located near the entrance metal gate of Pine Village in the east and the west in order to watch out for any forthcoming danger. This group of Pine guards also share the news of what has recently happened with regard to the death of Lord Scartor with other Pine guards around Pine Village, such as Flame who is standing guard at the east entrance metal gate of Pine Village and Bruce who is keeping watch over the outskirts of Pine Village from the south-west small wooden watch tower.

Following this surprising news, Flame and Bruce quickly prepare their areas for battles by positioning other Pine guards and making sure these areas are secured and equipped with resources that may be useful in times of battle. The group of Lynx's Pine guards that had come from Lynx's small wooden castle also tell all Pine villagers passing by that they see during their movements throughout Pine

Village to prepare their families, along with their wooden houses, flats, or shops, for a pre-emptive battle.

After about five minutes, Lynx reaches Parrot's small wooden flat quickly, which is opposite to Pinus Tavern in the east direction of Pine Village. Lynx jumps down from his white horse and then ties the white horse to the Pine tree that is near Parrot's small wooden flat. Lynx hurries back and knocks on Parrot's front wooden door, which is opened by Sapphire.

'Lynx! It's lovely to see you again. Are you coming with us to Pinus Tavern for the remembrance service?' asks Sapphire as she smiles at Lynx after opening Parrot's front wooden door.

'Sapphire, you're looking radiant as always. But unfortunately with much regret, I have to say I can't make it to the remembrance service with you all today as I have other pertinent duties that require to be carried out at Willow Village immediately. I hope the day goes as best as it can though for all the Pine villagers who attend the remembrance service at Pinus Tavern. I have come here first as I wish to speak with Parrot before I go to Willow Village,' says Lynx, smiling back at Sapphire.

'Oh, it sounds quite serious. I hope everything is all right,' replies Sapphire.

'Don't worry, Sapphire, it will all be fine,' remarks Lynx.

'Parrot, Lynx has come to see you,' says Sapphire, while turning around and speaking to Parrot, who is currently in the living room of his small wooden flat. Parrot happily walks towards the front wooden door past Sirius and Aura, who is holding Tigra and stroking Rexus sitting upon the floor.

'Lynx, it's good to see you, my great friend. How are you and the Pine guards coping on this saddest of days? Have you come to speak about the rebuilding plans for Oak Village?' asks Parrot, standing next to Sapphire at the front wooden door.

'I am fine, my friend. However, we need to speak in private, if that is all right with you, Sapphire?' asks Lynx graciously.

'Yes, of course, I will leave you men to your discussions,' says Sapphire as Parrot steps out of the front wooden door of his small wooden flat. Sapphire closes the front wooden door behind Parrot and walks back into Parrot's small wooden flat to also stroke Rexus while smiling at Tigra, who is being rocked in Aura's arms upon her lap.

'WHAT'S THE MATTER, Lynx?' asks Parrot mysteriously, as the sun shines brightly in his eyes while he looks at Lynx's troubled facial expression.

'I have just received word from one of my five men Pine villager scouts who have now reached the Realm of the Deserted Lands in the Planet of Phoenix, in the far south-west region where no human ventures to go there. The message received via carrier pigeon explained that Lord Scartor has now been killed by Triton and we should prepare for a surprise attack . . .,' says Lynx apprehensively and quickly.

'Lord Scartor is dead and that beast Triton has taken command of the Potorians. This is not good news at all. But are we sure that Triton and the Potorians will attack Pine Village? The anomaly crystal I had told you about is not anywhere near any of the main villages at the moment,' states Parrot.

'That is true, Parrot, but I will not take any risks after what you all suffered through the battles with Lord Scartor and Triton last year. Besides, Triton doesn't know where the anomaly crystal currently is, so he's bound to come and search here and all the main villages at some point in time. We've been lucky in this previous last year that none of the main villages have been attacked as we all thought Lord Scartor would have taken some sort of revenge out on you, Raven, and Emerald for escaping with the anomaly crystal and destroying his Lair of Death upon Crow Mountain. I am going to see my uncle Panther in Willow Village to warn him about this urgent and unfortunate message as well as gather support from him for both Pine and the newly built Oak Village in case of a surprise attack. I've come to you first to ask if you could also keep the Pine villagers in Pinus Tavern safe and calm if anything was to happen to Pine Village,' requests Lynx.

'That sounds like a good idea to unite the villages in times of battle. You are a valiant leader and so is your uncle Panther. I appreciate you telling me this situation, but you must not waste your time. Willow Village is a bit of a journey and they will need to be notified immediately. What about Oak Village and Falcon City? Yes,

I will do my best to keep everyone safe and calm in an emergency. Do you want any of my specially made weapons to assist you on the journey?' Parrot asks.

'Much gratitude for the offer, but I will be fine with my trusted sword and shield that have served me well in many difficult battles I've faced against Viper and his Serpents. I will notify King Exodus in Falcon City via carrier pigeon from Willow Village. I am very doubtful that Triton will attack Oak Village again as they will not be aware that we have rebuilt it, but yes, I shall also send a carrier pigeon from Willow Village to Oak Village to let Ruby and the remaining villagers there also know about this news. I have ordered my Pine guards to patrol the surrounding areas of Pine Village and keep every villager safe, if an attack were to occur. They would also sound the alarm and get any able-bodied men Pine villagers to help defend Pine Village too as we will need all the help we can get in protecting us humans if the great war begins to happen. So your specially made weapons may come in handy at that point in time,' remarks Lynx.

'Of course, Lynx, you don't even need to ask. Me and Sapphire will do whatever we can to help Pine Village,' replies Parrot.

'Listen to me, Parrot. If anything happens to Pine Village, you must get Sapphire, Tigra, and the rest of her family out of harm's way. Nothing must happen to your loved ones. I have a hidden and very secure hatch in the cellar of my castle . . . You've seen it before. They will be safe in this secure hatch and there are also plenty of supplies for them to survive down there unnoticed for weeks if need be,' says Lynx.

'Thank you for your help and sanctuary offer, but don't worry. I will defend my family with my life,' states Parrot as he begins to walk with Lynx towards the pine tree, where Lynx's white horse is tied too.

'You are like my family, Parrot. We haven't known each other too long, but you are my truest and most trusted friend. Let the gods watch over your family and all the Pine villagers in their time of need. I hope to return here soon to aid Pine Village with regard to its battle defences,' says Lynx as he unties the rope reins of his white horse from the pine tree. Parrot and Lynx firmly grab each other's forearm as a sign of respect for one another, and then Lynx climbs on top of his white horse.

'Safe journey, Lynx. Would you be able to send word to my parents Rio and Olivia in Willow Village to also stay safe if something were to happen and to also come visit us and Tigra in Pine Village when this threat has passed? Please apologise to them for me that Sapphire and I haven't been to see them yet due to Tigra currently being too young to undergo the journey to Willow Village,' asks Parrot politely.

'Yes, of course, your parents are also like family to me now, and it will be good to see them too. I will speak with them after I have shared words with my uncle,' replies Lynx as he begins to ride off on his white horse down the cobbled paths of Pine Village that lead out of the east entrance metal gate. Lynx continues galloping fast on his white horse through the breezy winds down the long cobbled road that heads towards Willow Village in the far east direction.

'See you soon!' shouts Parrot as Lynx rides off in the distance.

Parrot takes a deep breath after hearing the news Lynx has just shared with him; he notices in the distance patrols of Pine guards hurrying around the cobbled paths of Pine Village and speaking with Pine villagers passing by about the disturbing creature news. As soon as the Pine villagers passing by hear about this news from the Pine guards, their facial reactions are one of shock and worry, which makes Parrot feel sick deep in his stomach. The Pine villagers passing by then run off either towards their homes to barricade the doors and windows or to find their families and friends so that they would do the same in protecting themselves in their homes. Parrot thinks back to the anarchy and tragedy of the battles that had occurred last year in Oak Village, the Wastelands, and at Lord Scartor's Lair of Death upon Crow Mountain, where he dejectedly remembers all the pain and suffering many humans endured, which included some of his family members like Barious.

Parrot walks awkwardly back into his small wooden flat through his front wooden door and sees Sapphire, Sirius, and Aura drinking cups of water around the small wooden table in the living room of his small wooden flat. Parrot has another sick feeling in his stomach and begins to fear that something bad might happen to his loved ones.

'Is everything all right, my dear?' asks Sapphire, noticing Parrot's facial expression has changed since he has shared words with Lynx.

'Yes, I hope so,' remarks Parrot as he shuts and locks the front wooden door of his small wooden flat; he enters the living room and gives Sapphire a false smile, from which Sapphire realises that something isn't right with Parrot, but doesn't say anything out loud as she fears it might worry her parents. Parrot walks over to the small wooden table and strokes Rexus firmly, who is sitting on the floor and wagging his tail quickly from side to side. Parrot then sits down upon a wooden chair next to Sapphire, who is now holding Tigra in her arms. Parrot hugs and kisses Tigra and Sapphire profoundly, as Sapphire remains silent, still pondering about what news Lynx had just shared with Parrot.

Eighteen

RAVEN AND EMERALD had unwillingly left the beautiful and spiritual Hydra Springs in the furthest north-east direction on the Planet of Phoenix just one day ago, and they are currently riding together upon Felix's sturdy back, journeying across the spacious Grass Terrain Fields in the west direction towards Oak Village. Raven and Emerald ride on Felix through the Grass Terrain Fields upon the north-west trails that are muddy paths, located slightly north of Willow Village and Pine Village; they decide not to take the long cobbled road that passes through these villages as they don't have the time at present to stop in these villages as it's a two-day journey from Hydra Springs to Oak Village.

Raven and Emerald both decide to take the far north-west trail through the Grass Terrain Fields as it is the quickest route back to Oak Village, and they both need to get back home quickly to visit Ruby and then Barious's grave at Oakus Graveyard. Thereafter they will both travel to Pine Village to meet up with Parrot, Sapphire, Sirius, Aura, Tigra, and Rexus in order to go to the remembrance service at Pinus Tavern where they desire to pay their respects and say their prayers for the fallen men Oak and Pine villagers who had lost their lives in the battles against Lord Scartor, Triton, and the Potorians one year ago today.

During Raven and Emerald's long pleasant journey upon Felix that carries them steadily west over the north-west trails, cutting through the Grass Terrain Fields in the far north in the Planet of Phoenix, Raven and Emerald share much laughter and childhood stories with one another about how they used to play make-believe games together. They express their deep feelings to one another about how much they always admired each other for as long as they had known each other; this delightful conversation and scenery of the beautiful environment of the tall grass and passive wild animals that they pass upon their journey makes it an enjoyable experience for Raven and Emerald following their departure from Hydra Springs.

Raven and Emerald eventually arrive at the east wooden gate of Oak Village, as the bright sun glistens behind them and shines across Oak Village, making the newly rebuilt Oak Village appealing in the eyes of Raven and Emerald, as they try to supress the awful visions of memories they had endured during the battle of Oak Village a year ago. As Felix trots merrily through the east entrance wooden gate of Oak Village, Raven and Emerald see and wave at some of the few men and women Oak villagers who had survived the massacre of the Oak Village battle, which was caused by Lieutenant Triton and the Potorians; these men and women Oak villagers wave back at Raven and Emerald and smile brightly at their return to Oak Village following their honeymoon.

These surviving men and women Oak villagers are currently assisting the men Pine guards and Pine villagers who have been instructed by Lynx to finish rebuilding the wooden houses, cottages, and shops in Oak Village, which had unfortunately been destroyed by the blazing fire in the battle of Oak Village. The large Oak Village square in the middle of Oak Village has now also been rebuilt back to how it looked before, except for the small coronation celebration wooden stage that was completely destroyed during the Oak Village battle. The remaining wooden pieces of the coronation celebration wooden stage had been dismantled and removed from the Oak Village square not only as a sign of respect but also to help the surviving villagers of the battle of Oak Village forget the awful violence that had been witnessed during the Oak Village battle, in particular with regard to the fallen leader of Oak Village, Wolf, and his family Opal and Leopard who were killed by Triton and the Potorians.

Also, a lot of various wooden houses, cottages, and shops that were destroyed during the fire that took place on the big wooden fence surrounding Oak Village and burnt down many wooden houses, flats, and shops during its fury were not yet rebuilt due to lack of Oak villager humans now living in Oak Village to occupy them; thus, Lynx had instructed to rebuild the most important and maintainable wooden houses, flats, and shops first. Raven and Emerald smile back at the Oak and Pine villagers as they pass by them while trotting down the wooden and cobbled paths in the north direction of Oak Village towards Ruby's house.

'Raven, Emerald, it's good to see you back in Oak Village safe and sound. How was your honeymoon in that magnificent Hydra Springs?' asks one of the women Oak villagers who is called Edna, and she has just bumped into Raven and Emerald who are riding upon Felix as the woman Oak villager walks out of one of the newly finished florist shops, holding a small bunch of marigold flowers in her arms. Edna is small in height due to her old age of fifty-six years; she has short grey hair, blue eyes, wrinkly skin and wears a long plain grey cloak that is made of sheep's wool and covers her from head to toe.

'Good day to you too, Edna, and yes, our honeymoon at Hydra Springs was spectacular. Thank you very much,' replies Raven, e thinking back to all the breathtaking moments Emerald and he had shared together at Hydra Springs when they were on the honeymoon.

'Yes, it was. We really needed that break away and I have never seen such an elegant and divine place in the Planet of Phoenix as what Hydra Springs has developed to be,' smiles Emerald, wrapping her arms around Raven's back as they both sit on top of Felix.

'Yes, Hydra Springs is a remarkable place and it's very renowned for its wonder, transcendence, and pureness. I have never seen Hydra Springs myself yet, not many humans actually have. So you two are very lucky for the opportunity to go there, although you both did deserve a very special honeymoon that you experienced there, especially after what you both had to unfortunately endure last year during those terrible and unforgettable battles,' says Edna sadly, looking in the distance of Oak Village and noticing a lot of the wooden houses, flats and shops that are still broken or burnt.

'Yes, we feel very blessed to have gone to Hydra Springs and made sure we cherished every moment of our time there. Although we suffered in abundance last year, many other innocent humans did too and we are still in regret and sorrow for what had happened to those poor men, women, and children Oak and Pine villagers who untimely lost their lives during the battles against those horrible creatures. It's most upsetting for their surviving family and friends who have to continue their lives without their loved ones sharing it with them,' says Emerald, squeezing her arms tight around Raven's back as she remembers the moments when she was kidnapped by Lieutenant Triton and taken prisoner back to Lord Scartor's Lair of Death upon Crow Mountain; those short moments in her life had felt like an entire lifetime to her due to her being torn away from Raven and her mother Ruby, and she feared that she would never see them both again.

'Of course, those poor souls who had been killed, but the gods will now be caring for them in the afterlife, and one day they will be reunited in blissfulness with their family who will pass over into heaven when it is their rightful time to do so, as it will also be for me when I will gladly get to see and be with my husband Harcus again, who was also killed by a Potorian in the battle of Oak Village last year,' replies Edna sadly with a tear in her eye, which slowly trickles down her wrinkly cheeks.

'I'm very sorry for your loss, Edna, and yes, you will be reunited with your husband Harcus again in heaven as you have a good heart and have lived a pure life, unlike Lord Scartor and Lieutenant Trion, who will burn for an eternity at the bottom of hell for the pain and suffering they have caused all of us humans,' remarks Raven heatedly.

'If you need any help with anything, Edna, just let us know,' says Emerald in a comforting manner.

'You're very kind, my dear, and I really appreciate your offer. I am very grateful to the Pine guards who had come from Pine Village and help rebuild my flat and restore some of Oak Village to what it used to be. Bless them and the leader of Pine villager for helping those in their time of need,' says Edna appreciatively.

'Yes, Lynx and the Pine guards along with my cousin Parrot and other Pine and Oak villagers have done a magnificent and honourable job in restoring Oak Village, and their grand kindness will always be remembered by us surviving Oak villagers,' says Raven supportively, stroking Felix on his long, hairy black neck as he is getting a bit agitated due to him being tired from the long journey back from Hydra Springs in the heated sun.

'I am on my way now to Pine Village to pay my respects at Pinus Tavern remembrance service, which is why I had just spent the last hour finding the prefect marigolds to take in honour of those brave men Pine villagers who were killed by those devilish creatures. During that hour, when I was in this florist shop, I saw your mother Ruby when she was buying some roses. We shared kind words with one another. That is when she told me about your honeymoon at Hydra Springs and how she had missed you both dearly,' says Edna, smiling at Emerald.

'Yes, those marigold flowers are very beautiful, and that's very nice to hear about my mother speaking fondly of us. We have missed her loads too. We are on our way to her house to see her now. It was nice to share words with you, Edna, and we shall see you in Pinus Tavern remembrance service later today,' replies Emerald.

'Yes, take care,' says Raven as he flicks the brown rope reins slightly, which are attached to Felix's strong neck, to continue trotting upon Felix along the wooden and cobbled paths in the north direction of Oak Village towards Ruby's house.

'And you both also take care too,' says Edna as she also continues walking down the wooden and cobbled paths towards the east entrance wooden gate of Oak Village, which leads on to the long cobbled road connecting Oak Village to Pine Village.

'It's so good to be back to Oak Village again,' says Emerald to Raven, releasing her arms from the back of Raven's back and kissing the back of his head as Felix trots towards Ruby's house in the north-east direction of Oak Village.

RAVEN AND EMERALD both continue trotting on Felix down the wooden and cobbled paths until they shortly arrive at Barious's small wooden tool shop of which Raven is now the owner, and he and Emerald are currently living together in Raven's bedroom above the small wooden tool shop. Raven and Emerald have both been living together in Barious's small wooden tool shop for nearly a year now and are very happy with waking up in the mornings and seeing each other the first thing in the morning. Emerald helps Raven in continuing to maintain Barious's small wooden tool shop running, as they receive tool supplies from Parrot in Pine Village and Raven's uncle Rio in Willow Village, which they sell to Oak villagers as well as travellers from other villages. Emerald had managed Barious's small wooden tool shop very well, especially when Raven was also helping Parrot, Lynx, and the Pine guards in rebuilding the wooden house, flats, and shops in Oak Village during this past year.

Raven and Emerald trot upon Felix around the back of Barious's small wooden tool shop to reach the small field surrounding by a small wooden fence; this is where Felix is kept. Raven helps Emerald down from Felix's large back, and he also then climbs down from Felix and leads him by his brown rope reins into the small wooden gate of the small field at the back of Barious's small wooden tool shop. Raven accompanied by Emerald walks Felix over to the small wooden stable across the small grass field, where Emerald and he give Felix hay and water and a strong pat on the back as thanks for Felix carrying both Raven and Emerald on their journeys to and from Hydra Springs.

Raven and Emerald now leave the small grass field while holding hands; they shut the small wooden gate behind them and both walk down the short cobbled path in the east direction leading to Ruby's house. Ruby's house is one of the biggest wooden houses remaining in Oak Village, and Ruby has decorated the outside of the house with various gnomes, ornaments, and flowers that attract bees and wasps, which enjoy collecting nectar and pollinate the flowerbeds. Emerald knocks on the front wooden door of Ruby's big wooden house and an ecstatic Ruby opens it quickly.

'Emerald! Raven! It's so wonderful to see you both. I have missed you very much. Come in, come in,' exclaims Ruby joyfully as she hugs Emerald and Raven tightly just outside the front wooden door.

'It's great to see you too, Mother,' replies Emerald as she smiles at Ruby happily.

'Yes, good to see you, Ruby. We have both missed you too,' says Raven gladly.

Raven, Emerald, and Ruby walk into the front wooden door and down the hallway to the medium-sized kitchen of Ruby's house, which has many wooden cupboards, a sink to wash cutlery in, and also a stove that enables food to be heated on fire by making in a wooden container that is placed beneath cooking pans. Ruby gets Raven and Emerald a drink of water in cups as well as makes them both a vegetable sandwich, which is made of onions, carrots, and lettuces in between homemade bread. Raven and Emerald sit down on wooden chairs at the wooden table, which is also in Ruby's kitchen. Ruby brings the cups of water and vegetables sandwiches over to Raven and Emerald who are sitting exhausted at the wooden kitchen table.

'Eat up. You both must be starving after your long journey home. Did you enjoy your honeymoon at Hydra Springs?' asks Ruby as she walks back over to the kitchen and starts washing up the utensils that she has just used to make the vegetable sandwiches.

'Yes, it was magical and I had the best time,' replies Emerald thankfully.

'Hydra Springs was a remarkable place to go for a honeymoon. Much gratitude for suggesting it to us, Ruby,' states Raven, beginning to eat his vegetable sandwich.

'You're most welcome, and it was where I and Emerald's father Gaius went for our honeymoon and I thought you both would like it as much as we had done,' explains Ruby, feeling a little sad at the thought of not being with Gaius no more, as he had left her three years ago now.

'Yes, I remember you saying that both of you had a good time on your honeymoon at Hydra Springs. I wish my father would have been at mine and Raven's wedding though,' says Emerald, upset.

'Yes, I'm sorry about your father. We lost contact when he left me three years ago, and I do not know where he is currently and no one else seems to know either. It's a shame he didn't at least stay in contact with you though, Emerald,' says Ruby angrily.

'Father had left Oak Village before I had come home from my gymnastic competition at Oakus School that day. He left a note on my bed in my bedroom, but all he said was that he was sorry and that he loved me,' answers Emerald. Raven puts his hand on Emerald's knee to comfort her.

'We can finally begin to search for him if you want,' asks Raven.

'Why should I? He isn't bothered about us, and besides, my mother is all the parent I need,' replies Emerald sternly as Ruby smiles brightly at Emerald's comment about her.

'Are you too staying in Oak Village for good now? I would be very happy to spend more quality time with my lovely daughter every day. We also need to do much work in restoring the rest of Oak Village back to what it used to be like before that atrocious battle. We also need to get Oakus School, shops, and farms back up and running again. That will bring the life back to this unfortunate village,' stated Ruby.

'Yes, we will be permanently living here in Barious's tool shop, and we also want to make Oak Village a great village again. But first we need to go to Pine Village very soon for the remembrance service at Pinus Tavern and see Parrot and Sapphire with their son Tigra and collect Rexus from them. We will then require meeting with King Exodus in Falcon City to seek the new location of Lord Scartor and Lieutenant Triton to finally destroy them once and for all. We can't rest or live our lives properly knowing that those vile creatures are still alive and a threat to all of us humans upon the Planet of Phoenix,' states Raven firmly.

'Oh, those poor Pine villagers who had lost their loved ones last year in those horrific battles. I hope Bella, Lemur, and her children are doing all right. I understand what you say, Raven, but I don't want you both to put yourselves in any kind of danger ever again, especially after what you both had to withstand last year. Besides, I hear Lynx has sent his best Pine villager scouts to seek the whereabouts of Lord Scartor as we speak. Leave the fight against the creatures up to the village leaders and their guards,' remarks Ruby.

'Thank you for your concern, Mother, but even the village leaders and the guards will need all the help they can get in defeating Lord Scartor and Lieutenant Triton. Besides, we want revenge for what happened to us, Barious, and all of the humans and villagers who suffered last year because of those evil and monstrous creatures,' replies Emerald in a frustrated tone as she remembers the pain she had experienced when she was tied to the wooden table in the torture chambers at Lord Scartor's Lair of Death upon Crow Mountain. Ruby becomes silent for a moment at the strong words of Emerald when responding to Ruby. Emerald now takes a bite of her vegetable sandwich, and Ruby looks over at Emerald and sees that her cheeks are a red colour. Ruby tries to understand what Emerald might have experienced when she was taken prisoner by the Potorians back to

Lord Scartor's Lair of Death, as Emerald had never fully told Ruby the whole truth about what torture she had suffered.

'Poor Barious, he was such a grand old chap and I miss him so much. I have a bunch of red roses each for us to put on his grave in Oakus Graveyard today,' says Ruby sadly, changing the subject.

'Much gratitude for the flowers you got us, Ruby. We must go and see Barious's grave soon. Then we will just have enough time to travel to Pine Village for the remembrance service in Pinus Tavern,' says Raven, leaving his hand on Emerald's thigh and smiling at her and Ruby in a heartening manner.

ON THE OTHER side of the Planet of Phoenix in the far south-west area where Triton's Underground Dungeon resides, Triton and Venus are still making passionate love on top of the big wooden table in the main room of Triton's Underground Dungeon. Suddenly, the crystal finding device makes a faint beeping sound and a red dot magically appears on the map of the Planet of Phoenix in the glass sphere on the middle of the crystal finding device. Venus hears the beeping sound noise of the crystal finding device; she quickly pushes Triton forcefully from inside her, and he rolls over the big wooden table and falls to the ground, and she manoeuvres herself from the top of the big wooden table to stand beside of it. Venus rushes round the big wooden table to the crystal finding device that is placed at the other end of the big wooden table; Triton also begrudgingly picks himself up off the ground in a foul mood and follows Venus to the other side of the big wooden table.

'Yes, the anomaly crystal has reappeared in our sight,' states Venus ecstatically.

'Where is it now, my lover?' asks Triton excitedly. Venus looks closely at the red dot on the map of the Planet of Phoenix in the middle of the glass sphere on the crystal finding device and compares it against the larger map of the Planet of Phoenix that has been laid out across the big wooden table.

'Those fools, it's back in Oak Village again,' laughs Venus wickedly.

'We must go travel there and retrieve it together,' says Triton.

'No! I must go and get it now before we lose it from our sight again,' exclaims Venus firmly.

'By yourself? But what if you find yourself outnumbered and captured or worse by the humans?' states Triton in concern for Venus.

'I can take care of myself, lover, and I have done so for many years. Don't worry. No human is a match for my Animagus and creature abilities. I will return back here with the anomaly crystal soon,' says Venus as she kisses Triton powerfully on the lips.

After kissing Triton, Venus puts the crystal finding device back down on the big wooden table; she stands away from the big wooden table and her red eyes begin to turn a pure white colour. Venus concentrates for a moment and uses her Animagus powers, due to which her whole body slowly starts to change into a Quetzalcoatlus form; the Quetzalcoatlus is the biggest of all the Pterosaur dinosaur species. After turning into her Quetzalcoatlus form, Venus screeches through her large beak and Triton stands quickly back from Venus's powerful screeching and ear-piercing sounds.

Venus flaps her large scaly Quetzalcoatlus wings that are enormous in side and are attached to a large but thin body; Venus also has sharp claws on her feet now. Venus flaps above the big wooden table and quickly flies out of the main room of Triton's Underground Dungeon that leads through the narrow passageway and out above the ground over the Realm of Deserted Lands; her power and scaly wings make it easier for her to manoeuvre through the gusty winds filled with tiny dirt, rock, sand, and grit particles in the Realm of Deserted Lands, and Venus continues to fly through the darker skies in this area and hurries across the Planet of Phoenix in the north-east direction towards Oak Village.

BACK IN OAK Village, Ruby collects Emerald's and Raven's empty glasses and plates after they finish eating the vegetable sandwiches. Ruby walks over to the kitchen and pours water from a jug over the empty plates and the glasses in the kitchen sink, making the cutlery clean again. Ruby walks into the hallway that is just outside the kitchen room and turns towards a small compartment that is underneath a wooden staircase connecting the upstairs bedrooms to the downstairs rooms. Ruby opens this compartment wooden door and retrieves from the cupboard her long purple coat and green boots which she wears. Ruby walks from the hallway into the main living room, where she picks up the three bunches of red roses and another bunch of blue lily flowers that are lying on a wooden chair in her living room. Ruby then walks back into the kitchen via the hallway and gives a bunch of the red roses each to Raven and Emerald.

'Ah, these flowers are beautiful. I'm sure Barious would have really appreciated these,' remarks Emerald. Raven and Emerald also put their shoes back on, and along with Ruby, they all walk through the hallway and leave Ruby's house together, continuing to walk in the south direction towards Oakus Graveyard that is located in the far south-east corner of Oak Village next to Oakus Church.

Oakus Graveyard has now been completely filled with all the Oak villagers who had died last year in the battle of Oak Village; many of the graves still haven't been covered with fresh grass. Some Oak villagers were buried either on their own or with their families who had also died during the Oak Village battle; if that was the case, the families were all buried together in bigger plots. Some Oak villagers were also cremated due to being severely burnt by the huge fires during the Oak Village battle and their ashes were either kept in urns with the surviving family members or placed in a designated part of Oakus Graveyard, with the urns being placed in the grass amongst different types of flowers such as lilies, tulips, and marigolds.

Among the graves is the previous leader of Oak Village Wolf's grave, who is buried in the special section of Oakus Graveyard, where only the leaders of Oak Village, including their blood descendants and wives, are buried together. Wolf's father Jackal, his grandfather Jaguar, and his great-grandfather Hyena are all buried in this special section of Oakus Graveyard; they had all been buried in double graves along with their wives. However, Wolf is only buried on his own as his wife Opal and son Leopard's bodies were completely disintegrated in the fire that the Potorians had caused on their big house during the Oak Village battle. All the graves in Oakus Graveyard also now have small wooden crosses or planks of wood at the head of the graves with writings of the names of the humans who were in the graves carved on them and pretty flowers were placed on all of the graves throughout Oakus Graveyard.

Raven, Emerald, and Ruby walk slowly through Oakus Graveyard large archway made of black metal and continue walking up the small grass hill until they reach the grave where Barious is buried, which is halfway up the small grass hill. Raven ponders for a moment in silence about what had happened in the battle of Oak Village a year ago today and how he had found Barious dying underneath a broken down small wooden flat; he had to sadly endure the sight of his grandfather dying before his eyes. Raven sheds a tear for his grandfather, and the tear rolls timelessly down his cold cheek; he squeezes Emerald's hand for comfort to which Emerald responds by lifting Raven's hand to her mouth and kissing it softly. Raven now bends over and lays his bunch of red roses down first on the grass in front of Barious's grave; he gets back up again and walks over to the wooden cross at the head of Barious's grave, putting one of his hands on the wooden cross that reads:

> Barious was a kind and happy soul. He will be greatly missed by Ruthus, Jewel, Raven, and all the humans throughout the Planet of Phoenix.

'Barious's grave looks very graceful and peaceful,' says Ruby, also bending over and placing her bunch of red roses on the grass of Barious's grave in front of the wooden cross. Emerald pauses a moment and also does the same as Ruby.

'I miss you very much, Grandfather, and I wish you were here with us today, but I know you, my father, and mother are all smiling from heaven upon us like guardian angels would,' says Raven with another tear created in his eyes. Emerald walks over to the wooden cross and the head of Barious's grave and hugs Raven tightly as the sun shines brightly above them, but with a cold breeze of wind circling in the air.

'Life's not the same without you, Barious. You will always remain in our hearts and your humour and life lessons will never be forgotten,' states Emerald.

'Bless you, Barious, for all that you had done for your family and my family in your lifetime. For that we are forever thankful for,' remarks Ruby. Raven, Emerald, and Ruby stand for a moment around Barious's grave in silence, looking down at it and thinking happy thoughts of the time they had all spent with Barious as well as Ruthus and Jewel. Ruby now walks over to Raven and Emerald at the head of Barious's grave and gives them both a hug at the same time.

They all remain in a hug with each other for a minute while they all shed a tear for their loved ones who are not alive no more. After Ruby stops hugging Raven and Emerald, they all begin to slowly make their way back down Oakus Graveyard small hill, looking sadly at the numerous other newly made graves of Oak villagers who had also died in the Oak Village battle. After leaving Oakus Graveyard through the black metal archway, Raven, Emerald, and Ruby head back towards the north-east direction, walking over the wooden and cobbled paths of Oak Village leading to Barious's small wooden tool shop. After reaching Barious's small wooden tool shop, Emerald and Ruby walk round the back of it and retrieve Felix from the small field, where he is currently resting in his small wooden stable, while Raven uses his key and enters through Barious's small wooden tool shop's front wooden door.

Raven hurries through the middle of the shop and towards the back, where he climbs the narrow wooden stairs leading to his and Emerald's bedroom. Raven enters their bedroom and he collects his sword from underneath his bed, which Raven still does not know is the sword of Grackle; also, Raven collects Parrot's small sharp silver dagger that Parrot had given to Raven last year back in Pine Village. Raven also notices his pair of taekwondo white nunchucks, but decides to leave them underneath the bed this time. Raven hurries out of the bedroom and back down the wooden stairs towards the front doors of Barious's small wooden tool shop; he leaves and locks the front wooden door behind him. As Raven comes outside the front of Barious's tool shop, he sees Ruby hugging Emerald thoughtfully, standing next to Felix, who is also now outside the front of Barious's small wooden tool shop.

'You're a wonderful daughter, Emerald. I love you so much. Please come back to me safe and sound as I couldn't bear it if I lost you again. Can you also take these flowers to Pinus Tavern for the remembrance service and send my apologies that I can't make it there today as I am currently needed here in Oak Village to help some of Pine guards by guiding how a part of Oakus School requires to be rebuilt?' says Ruby as she passes Emerald a bunch of blue lily flowers.

'Thank you, Mother, for your loving words and don't worry yourself. You will never lose me again. Yes, of course, we will take these flowers to Pinus Tavern remembrance service for you and will also pass on your loving thoughts,' replies Emerald. Raven now walks over to Emerald and Ruby, standing next to Felix, and Ruby notices Raven is carrying his sword in one of his hands.

'Why have you got your sword with you, Raven? Lord Scartor and Lieutenant Triton aren't located over these parts of the Planet of Phoenix no more and surely you won't experience any trouble upon your journey to Pine Village,' says Ruby, confused.

'Yes, you could be quite right, Ruby, but I will take no chances in protecting Emerald's life,' states Raven. Emerald and Ruby smile at each other warmly. Raven helps Emerald climb back on top of Felix, and then Raven also climbs on to the back of Felix's large and strong black hairy back as Ruby grabs Emerald's hand.

'Hurry back home, you two,' says Ruby tenderly.

'We will do. Love you, Mother,' replies Emerald as Raven gently kicks the sides of Felix with his feet, which enables Felix to begin trotting down the wooden and cobbled paths of Oak Village towards the east entrance wooden gate. By this time, it has been three hours since Venus has left Triton's Underground Dungeon from the Realm of Deserted Lands and swiftly flown high up in the sky; she quickly reaches Oak Village while physically being in her Quetzalcoatlus form. She now glides lower to the ground above Oak Village and fortunately sees the interaction that has just taken place between Emerald and Ruby outside Barious's small wooden tool shop. Venus notices with her acute Quetzalcoatlus eyesight Emerald's wedding ring that has the anomaly crystal fixed upon it. Venus is about to swoop down and kill Emerald with her huge claws and powerful beak in order to steal the anomaly crystal when she also sees Raven coming out of Barious's small wooden tool shop with the sword of Grackle in one of his hands.

Venus is concerned about the sword of Grackle, due to what she had heard about it having a deleterious impact if creatures were cut with it, making her decide not to attack Emerald and continue circling around high up in the sky, enabling her to go unnoticed by the humans below in Oak Village, including Raven, Emerald, and Ruby. Venus then waits patiently for Raven and Emerald riding on Felix to leave Oak Village through the east entrance wooden gate. Ruby watches Raven and Emerald riding on Felix leave from her sight before walking back into her big wooden house that is close to Barious's small wooden tool shop; she goes inside to collect the building plans for Oakus School, which she was going to bring with her to Oakus School, where a few of the Pine guards were currently waiting for her to help in rebuilding it.

Venus now takes the opportunity to fly down from the sky swiftly on to the ground just outside Ruby's big wooden house. As Venus lands on to the ground, her eyes turn from being pure white back to their normal red colour again; she then utilises her Animagus abilities to enable her physical body to turn back into what Venus naturally looks like. Venus walks over to Ruby's front wooden door and knocks on it. Ruby on hearing the knocking on her front wooden door decides to turn around suddenly from the hallway and opens the front wooden door.

'Hello, can I help you?' asks Ruby, surprised to see a woman of Chinese origin whom she had never seen before.

'Yes, you can, my dear,' replies Venus as she quickly pulls a small sharp wooden stick with a silver blade at the end of it from between her long silky black hair and forcefully slashes it across Ruby's tender throat; the sharp silver blade splits apart Ruby's delicate neck, causing blood to squirt all out down Ruby's chest. Ruby attempts to scream but loses her voice as she chokes and falls to her knees on the floor of her hallway just behind the front wooden door. Ruby dies quickly because of the large amount of blood she loses from her slit throat. Ruby's last thoughts are of her beloved daughter, Emerald, of whom she envisions in her brain just before her eyelids close and all her thoughts and memory leave Ruby's mind forever.

Venus smiles mischievously and quickly enters through Ruby's front wooden door of her big wooden house, swiftly dragging Ruby's dead body into the small compartment in the hallway underneath the wooden staircase. Venus then collects some water from the kitchen sink and scrubs hard to clean up any bloodstains that are left on the floor of Ruby's big wooden house, after Venus drags Ruby's dead body across the hallway.

Venus walks into the main living room of Ruby's big wooden house and empowers her red eyes to turn pure white again as she focuses on using her Metamorphmagus powers, enabling her physical body to turn into the shape of what Ruby's body physically looked like, including the same clothes and glasses; also, her eyes change into the same green colour as Ruby's had been. Venus's Metamorphmagus powers also permit her voice to change into the same sound as Ruby's voice. Venus had mentally recorded what Ruby sounded like when they had spoken with one another moments ago at the front wooden door of Ruby's big wooden house.

After turning into a duplicate of Ruby's physical body, Venus then puts one hand above the other with both hands facing down towards the floor, and she uses her magical creature abilities to magically create a small white dove in the middle of her hands. Venus now levitates the small white dove to the floor by moving her bottom hand away from the other upper hand, lifting the top hand up into the air, which enables the white dove to grow to its normal size as it lands on the floor of Ruby's main living room.

Venus writes a message in red, using the bloodstained small wooden stick with a sharp silver blade at the end of it on to a small piece of grey cloth that she has torn from the bottom of her long grey dress she is wearing, which is currently the same as what Ruby had worn. The message written upon the small piece of grey cloth by Venus asks Emerald to return home quickly and is signed with Ruby's name. Venus grabs the white dove from the floor and attaches the small piece of grey cloth with the message upon it to one of the dove's small feet via a small piece of cotton string. Venus walks over to the window in Ruby's big wooden house's main living room, and she lets the white dove fly out of the window. Venus watches the white dove fly up in the sky in the east direction towards Pine Village. Venus closes the window and waits patiently for Emerald to return back to Ruby's big wooden house with the anomaly crystal fixed in her wedding ring.

Nineteen

LYNX RACES SWIFTLY on his white horse across the narrow but long cobbled road that had been laid across the large and vast Grass Terrain Fields between Pine Village and Willow Village in the far north-east of the Planet of Phoenix. The enormous sun's hot rays brightly shine upon Lynx's forehead, causing him to sweat as he continues riding hard on his white horse with determination with the challenge of getting to Willow Village as fast as he possibly can, because of the knowledge he has regarding the growing danger of Triton and his creature army residing in the Realm of Deserted Lands.

As Lynx's white horse begins to slow its pace down slightly due to him becoming drained from the sweltering heat of the sun, the white horse stumbles a little upon some of the larger cobbles that are littered all over the cobbled road. Lynx realises his white horse's slowing pace, so he pats him on his long white and wavy hair on the back of his neck in order to show his appreciation to the white horse for his strong effort in riding very fast. Lynx, having confidence in his white horse's abilities, taps his heels gently into the sides of his white horse, enabling the horse to find the energy in himself to continue galloping and now at an increased pace.

As Lynx holds firmly on to the rope reins of his white horse, as it glides swiftly across the narrow and long cobbled road in the east direction towards Willow Village, Lynx's mind wanders back to the past, thinking about how Viper had killed both his parents several years ago in Falcon City. Unfortunately, Viper and his Serpents had managed to force their way through Falcon City's big iron portcullis by inflicting a surprise attack upon Falcon City, since there were not enough royal Falcon guards present at the big iron portcullis to stop Viper and the Serpents from entering Falcon City's inner stone walls.

Lynx takes a slow and overwhelming breath and briefly closes his eyes, as he promises himself that he will not let no more human lives be so easily taken by the hands of creatures, due to the humans not having the appropriate numbers, knowledge, or defence systems to effectively defend against a surprise attack or substantial battle. Lynx whips the rope reins of his white horse in fortitude, causing the white horse to gallop even faster upon the narrow and long cobbled road; within only two hours, Lynx galloping on his white horse ends up approaching the west entrance wooden gate of Willow Village.

Willow Village is a very small and basic village that had only been built just over eight years ago, which was ordered by King Exodus due to the increase in population of humans emerging in Pine Village. King Exodus also felt that where Willow Village was built, just north of Falcon City, it would make the communication and trade routes much easier to transport goods between the three main villages and Falcon City. At present, Willow Village only has around 132 villagers living there, including the Willow Village leader Panther, who is Lynx's uncle, and thirty-nine of his trained Willow guards.

Willow Village is surrounded by a small wooden fence just as Oak Village and Pine Village are, although the wooden fences at Oak Village and Pine Village are much bigger and sturdier than Willow Village's surrounding wooden fence. Willow Village has a couple of basic food and tool shops as well as a florist shop, a guest house for passers-by to stay when journeying between Falcon City and the three main villages, storage facilities for trading, a small Willows Church and Willows Graveyard, along with a school called Willows School. Willow Village is mostly built up of farmlands, where farm animals such as sheep, lambs, chickens, cows, and pigs graze. Willow Village has several small wooden flats and basic shops such like cloth, farm foods, trading, and storage shops as well as two bigger wooden houses where Panther lives, and opposite in the other bigger wooden house is where the majority of his Willow guards live.

Willow Village is very beautiful and elegant and has many fruits such as apples, plums, and pears, along with different willow trees such as the Salix alba and Black Maul willow trees that are scattered around Willow Village as well as several small willow shrubs like Salix phylicifolia and Salix viminalis and small stone carvings of animals throughout. Many of the older generation Pine villagers moved to Willow Village from Pine Village around eight years ago, and since then Willow Village had been established for escaping from the busy and hectic lifestyle of those that resided in Pine Village.

Lynx now enters through the east entrance wooden gate of Willow Village and nods at the Willow guard who is standing next to the west entrance wooden gate; as Lynx quickly rides through it, the Willow guards quickly realise that it is Lynx the Pine Village leader and nephew of Panther riding on his white horse, so they nod and smile back at Lynx. Lynx gallops shortly down the grassy paths of the quiet and peaceful Willow Village until he reaches Panther's big wooden house that is located in the middle and slightly towards the north direction of Willow Village. Lynx jumps down from his white horse after causing him to stop by pulling on his rope reins. He stands next to the horse and pats the white horse again on the white and wavy hair on the back of his neck, before he ties the rope reins of the white horse around a Salix alba willow tree that is planted in the ground near Panther's big wooden house. Lynx runs up to the front wooden door of Panther's big wooden house, and he knocks hard upon it until Panther answers the front wooden door.

'Nephew, it's good to see you! To what do I owe this great pleasure?' asks Panther on realising it is Lynx standing and panting at his wooden front door because of the long and quick journey Lynx had just undertaken from Pine Village.

Panther is sixty-three years old, and he has been the leader of Willow Village for just over eight years now ever since Willow Village was first created due to the decree by King Exodus. Panther has shoulder-length white and wavy hair and green eyes; he is tall, slim but muscular and is a very respectable and principled human. Panther has never married or been blessed with any children of his own; he has had girlfriends during his early adulthood, but none of those relationships developed into marriage and a family. Panther wears a silver crown on his head with the word 'Willow' written in gold in the ancient Phoenix language in the front middle part of the silver crown. He also wears silver knighthood clothing and carries a silver sword and shield that were given to him by King Exodus when he was the main royal Falcon guard, to his brother Saber who at the time was the royal Falcon captain and also Lynx's father.

Panther and Saber's parents Sharkus and Melody were very much involved with the council and royalty in Falcon City due to Sharkus being the royal Falcon captain, because he had been a courageous warrior and also childhood friends with King Exodus when they received their education together at the royal Falcon School located at Falcon Castle. Sharkus was permitted to attend the royal Falcon School due to Sharkus's father Dominous being the main councillor to King Exodus's father King Zunus for many years during his rule over Falcon City. Sharkus naturally taught Panther and Saber how to be respectable and honourable humans as well as how to fight in battle and become efficient and valiant leaders as Sharkus wanted one of his sons to be his replacement when the time would come for Sharkus to not be the royal Falcon captain no more, when he would have to undergo the journey to the afterlife in heaven. Although Panther was elder, to Sharkus, Saber had a more natural talent in being a leader, since he was able to make contentious and tough decisions when difficult situations and circumstances arose, which he had demonstrated numerous times in the various battles Sharkus, Panther, and Lynx had experienced against the Serpents of Komodo Jungle.

Panther and Lynx's mother Melody sadly died of an infectious disease a few years earlier before Sharkus also became ill due to old age. At this time of his life, Sharkus deliberated with King Exodus to proclaim Saber to be the new royal Falcon guard and permit Panther to be his main royal Falcon guard as both his sons demonstrated the required talents for this position in the ranks of the royal Falcon guards. King Exodus respected his great friend and loyal royal Falcon Captain Sharkus's well-thought decision. Panther was also happy to abide by this judgement as he also realised and admired his younger brother Saber's ability to lead the royal Falcon guards as well as his innovative skills in the knowledge of battle attack and defence tactics.

AT AN EARLIER time, that is a generation before King Exodus's rule, when King Zunus was the current king of Falcon City at the time, the leader of Oak Village was Jaguar, who was Wolf's grandfather, and he would undertake the vast journey to Falcon City and meet with King Zunus and his wife Queen Lunar in order to strengthen the humans' alliances amongst the three main villages with Falcon City, just as his father Hyena had done with King Zunus's father, King Primus. Jaguar and King Zunus would discuss and aim to seek solutions regarding the consistent threats from Viper and his Serpents of Komodo Jungle, along with the dangerous and criminal nomad warriors from the Wastelands that were located in the west direction of Oak Village in the far north-west of the Planet of Phoenix near the Mountains of Doom.

During his many travels to Falcon City from Oak Village, Jaguar would take his most trusted Oak guards; his main Oak guard was called Trogon, who was Barious's father. Trogon was the only son of Sparrow and his wife Star; Star had escape to Oak Village just before Alder Village was destroyed by Lord Scartor, which used to be located in the furthest north-east direction of the Planet of Phoenix near Hydra Springs. Sparrow, who was also the son of the prodigious wizard Grackle, knew that he would have to go to war against Lord Scartor in order to stop him from seeking to uncover the hidden location of the wondrous anomaly crystal and enslave all the humans residing throughout the Planet of Phoenix.

Grackle had given the anomaly crystal to Sparrow to protect upon his death, which was actually caused because of creating the anomaly crystal, who in turn then gave the anomaly crystal to his wife Star to take it far away from Alder Village so that Lord Scartor would not be able to find it there in the place that it was originally created. In an epic battle in the Swamp Fields, Lord Scartor sneakily killed Sparrow and then travelled straight afterwards to Alder Village, where he burnt the entire village to the ground in his desperate search for the anomaly crystal, as he became furious to discover that the anomaly crystal was no longer hidden in Alder Village.

At her husband Sparrow's firm request, Star regrettably agreed to leave Alder Village, as also many other Alder villagers did due to the increasing threat from Lord Scartor. Star took her and Sparrow's young son, Trogon, and fled to the safety of the recently developed Oak Village in the east direction of the Planet of Phoenix, which was adjacent to Pine Village. Hyena who was Jaguar's father had recently starting developing Oak Village after his decision to leave Pine Village to become his own village leader.

As the years continued on, the memory of Alder Village and the anomaly crystal started to cease from the next generation of human's minds and thoughts, although all of the humans throughout the Planet of Phoenix were still aware of the immoral creature Lord Scartor and his growing forces of Potorians upon Crow Mountain amongst the Mountains of Doom in the far northwest of the Planet of Phoenix. Star had spent many months waiting for Sparrow to return to Oak Village to reunite with her and their son Trogon, as he had promised her to make her leave Alder Village, but she never saw him again; she had no other choice but to comprehend that Lord Scartor must have murdered Sparrow. Star kept all those cryptic secrets to herself and waited until Trogon was old enough to explain everything that had happened involving their bloodline that descended from the powerful wizard Grackle; on her deathbed, she then gave the anomaly crystal to Trogon to keep it safe among their family descendants.

Trogon became outraged on finding out what had happened to his father Sparrow, because of which he became a strong and gallant soldier who was made the main Oak guard to the recently crowned Oak Village leader Jaguar after Hyena also died due to old age. Trogon for many years protected Oak Village in the frequent battles of Jaguar and his Oakus guards against the nomad warriors from the Wastelands located in the north-west direction of the Planet of Phoenix. Many of the battles faced against the nomad warriors would occur in the Wastelands or in the Swamp Fields, which was where Trogon was drawn to and he uncovered the lost sword of Grackle that Sparrow had dropped in one of the muddy bogs of the Swamp fields when he was slain by Lord Scartor.

After a few of years of being the main Oak guard, Trogon fell in love with a lovely human called Pluto, who worked as a gardener in Oakus Graveyard built next to Oakus Church, which was where Trogon and Pluto ended up getting married; they spent many happy years when they then became blessed by a son, whom they named Barious. Trogon explained the whole story of Grackle, Sparrow, Lord Scartor, and the anomaly crystal to his son, Barious, as his mother, Star, had described to him. Due to these circumstances, Trogon thus felt it relevant to take Barious with him on his journeys with Jaguar and the Oak guards to Falcon City when they visited King Zunus, in order to make Barious known amongst the royalty within Falcon City, in case Barious ever needed aid from the royalty of Falcon City if Lord Scartor were to ever return from Crow Mountain and begin attacking the humans again in search for the anomaly crystal.

During those visits to Falcon City from Oak Village, as the years continued on, an older Barious was introduced to the new King Exodus, in that they became great friends; in later years after these continuous and enjoyable visits, Barious and King Exodus became trusted associates with the royal Falcon captain at the time called Sharkus and his sons Panther and Saber. King Exodus, Sharkus, Panther, Saber, and Barious all shared many important conversations and life events with one another, which strengthened their friendships; these life events included marriages such as King Exodus's marriage to Queen Eclipse and Barious's marriage to Flower, the birth of their children such as King Exodus and Queen Eclipse's daughter Princess Petal and Barious and Flower's sons Ruthus and Rio along with the birth of their grandchildren such as Barious's grandsons, Raven and Parrot. These life events unfortunately also included the deaths of their parents such as King Exodus's father, King Zunus, and mother, Queen Rainbow, Barious's father, Trogon, and mother, Pluto, also Panther and Saber's father's, Sharkus, and mother's, Melody, deaths as well as the death of their wives such as King Exodus's wife Queen Eclipse and Barious's wife Flower.

Other life events with each other included many gory battles against the creatures of the Planet of Phoenix, such as those against Viper and his Serpents as well as the sea creature from Nautilus Lake, which was a monstrous sea lion creature that had killed countless humans from Falcon City, until it was eventually exterminated by the joint forces of arms between King Exodus and his royal Falcon guards, including Panther and Saber, along with their now great friend Barious, who travelled with Wolf's father and the present leader of Oak Village at the time called Jackal and his Oakus guards to aid in the battle against the monstrous sea lion creature. Amongst some of the bluest life events experienced with one another included the royal Falcon captain Sharkus dying of illness and later on his son and Panther's brother, Saber, and wife, Star, were executed by Viper. At this gloomiest point in time, Panther, Barious, and King Exodus who were only a few of the surviving humans from their recently deceased ancestors offered grand support to each other, strengthening their friendships furthermore.

As the decades of existence drifted away, along with many other deplorable events and circumstances occurring, such as Barious and his wife Flower's younger son, Ruthus, along with his wife, Raven's mother, Jewel also being untimely exterminated by Viper, as well as the rest of the bloodline of Grackle's older generations of ancestors all now having passed over to the afterlife in heaven, Barious found himself giving the anomaly crystal to the last descendent to the bloodline of Grackle and his younger grandson, Raven, in order to continue protecting the anomaly crystal, along with his elder grandson Parrot, who was also his elder son Rio and wife Olivia's son Parrot and cousin of Raven.

Until Barious's death that occurred in the battle of Oak Village a year ago, his alliance remained strong with Panther and King Exodus, although he never divulged the information regarding the entire situation and truthful location of the anomaly crystal in order to protect them and their families from the burden of the anomaly crystal, which was indeed created by his great-grandfather Grackle. A similar alliance was also formed by Panther in being the new and only leader of Willow Village under King Exodus's rule of Falcon City, in which he would watch over and assist his nephew Lynx's new leadership over Pine Village as Panther had much admiration and respect for his nephew Lynx.

LYNX CATCHES HIS breath by taking a deep gasp of air; after a moment he answers Panther.

'It's good to see you too, Uncle! Unfortunately, I visit you with disturbing news during these uncertain times,' replies Lynx.

'That unsettles my nerves. Come in and tell me what has happened,' says Panther in concern as he hugs his nephew Lynx quickly and ushers him into his big wooden house through the front wooden door. Panther and Lynx enter through a hallway that leads into the living room of Panther's big wooden house, where Lynx and Panther seat themselves on wooden chairs at one side of the living room. One of Panther's maids, on hearing that Lynx has entered Panther's big wooden house, collects cups from a wooden shelf in the kitchen, which she fills up with water from a large jug and brings them to Panther and Lynx, as they both get comfortable on their wooden chairs in the living room of Panther's big wooden house.

'Thank you, Berta. Now leave us please,' says Panther to his maid Berta.

'Yes, of course,' replies Berta as she leaves the living room of Panther's big wooden house.

'The five men Pine villager scouts I had sent out to search the Planet of Phoenix for Lord Scartor's new fortress several months ago have just sent me word only hours ago, informing me that Lord Scartor has been murdered in the Realm of the Deserted Lands at the far south-west corner of the Planet of Phoenix. They assume that Lord Scartor's murderer was Lieutenant Triton and that we should now prepare for a surprise attack in foresight of the great war by Triton and whatever soulless creatures he's now in league with,' explains Lynx, distressed.

'Oh dear, you were right, Lynx. That's not good news at all, especially after what those poor humans had suffered during the Oak Village battle last year. If this knowledge of Triton executing Lord Scartor is certain truth, it might mean that Triton has joined forces with other creatures on the Planet of Phoenix like that fiend creature Viper. We humans will have to defend and survive not only against Triton and his remaining Potorian army, but maybe also against Viper and his gruesome Serpents in the great war that was indeed foretold in the ancient Planet of Phoenix writings stored in the scripture room of Falcon University. King Exodus and I had spoken on many occasions when the great war was likely to occur. However, it doesn't make the news of these circumstances any easier to deal with. Have you heard from the men Pine villager scouts since? Do you know how long we have to prepare?' asks Panther abruptly, thinking back to the battles he had faced in the past against creatures like Viper and his Serpents and how he had dejectedly watched so many great humans get killed, such as his brother, Saber, and Saber's wife, Lunar.

'No, I have not received no word from the men Pine villager scouts as of yet. I rode here as soon as I found out this news to share this knowledge with you for us both to prepare battle strategies and defences to protect our villages from harm,' replies Lynx.

'Much gratitude for this knowledge, and yes, it's best not to take any risks, especially after the events we have both suffered through in the past. Now that all the humans are united upon the Planet of Phoenix against our foes the creatures, we must depend on one another if we are to have favour in winning the great war of our history. I have several Willow guards here in Willow Village who are masters at archery, and they will be extremely proficient in killing creatures from a safe distance. Apart from that, Willow Village hasn't developed the modern technology that Pine Village and Falcon City have for such a battle as the great war will potentially turn out to be. How is Pine Village currently preparing?' asks Panther.

'I have left my most trusted Pine guards to keep watch over the perimeter of Pine Village at present, and we will recruit as many able-bodied men Pine villagers to help us battle against this evil creature threat,' states Lynx, taking a sip from his cup of water.

'That's a good tactic, Lynx. Have you also told King Exodus and his newest royal Falcon Captain Gaius of this disturbing news? Or shall I send word now to King Exodus in Falcon City in order to aid us during a battle?' asks Panther.

'No, I haven't as yet as I wanted to speak with you first, but please send a carrier pigeon to Falcon City from Willow Village to let King Exodus know what might begin to happen. Hopefully the carrier pigeon will make the long journey to Falcon City in time, and even if King Falcon is able to send royal Falcon guard reinforcements to our villages, it will take a long time for them to undergo the extensive journey north to reach our villages and help us. We must prepare as best as we can ourselves in case of a surprise attack, like what occurred in the Oak Village battle last year. I will send you a couple of hundred men Pine guards and men Pine villagers from Pine Village to help you also defend Willow Village,' says Lynx kindly.

'Yes, you are correct about how long it would take to receive help from Falcon City. That is a shame. That's most kind of you, my nephew, about sending your men to help us, and it's very much appreciated by all of Willow Village and me. I will also speak to my Willow guards about them preparing the security for Willow Village immediately,' thanks Panther.

'Unfortunately, I can't stay with you much longer as I must swiftly return to Pine Village to assist my Pine guards with our battle preparation. But before I go, I promised my best friend Parrot that I would speak with his parents Rio and Olivia personally about what has happened and give them a message from him too. Do you know where they live?' asks Lynx.

'Ah, Rio, he is my good friend's son, but sadly my good friend is now no longer with us upon the Planet of Phoenix and he was called Barious. And yes, Rio's wife Olivia I also know. Yes, of course, I can tell you where they live and they are very nice and caring Willow villagers indeed. Rio and Olivia live in the small wooden flat near the west entrance gate that is opposite a farm food shop,' answers Panther as he also dejectedly remembers how Barious was killed in the battle of Oak Village last year.

'Thank you, Uncle. Good luck in any trouble you might receive from treacherous creatures and don't hesitate to call for aid from Pine Village or myself at any time. It's been good to see you again today, if only for a brief time,' states Lynx.

'Oh yes, time is one thing that doesn't stop for any human or creature. You will understand this more when you reach my old age. All the best to you too, my nephew, and remember I am always here for you. Also, I promised your parents and my brother, Saber, and his wife, Melody, if anything were to happen to them I would always be here to support you. Both of your parents would have been extremely proud of you for what you have accomplished at such a young age, especially by being not only the previous royal Falcon captain but also now a leader of Pine Village too,' emphasises Panther proudly.

'Thank you for your heart-warming words. I always wanted to make my parents feel proud of me, especially my father who was such an inspiration to me,' replies Lynx, his expression one of sadness, as he realises his parents will never see him become the leader of Pine Village.

Lynx and Panther grab each other's forearm as a sign of respect for each other. Then Lynx stands up from his wooden chair, and he leaves via the hallway and through the front wooden door of Panther's big wooden house. He walks over and unties his white horse from the Salix alba willow tree that is located near Panther's big wooden house; he rides swiftly back along the grassy paths in the west direction towards the west entrance gate of Willow Village, where Rio and Olivia's small wooden flat is located opposite a farm food shop.

After Lynx leaves Panther in his big wooden house, Panther quickly retrieves the items he needs in the living room to write a message in sheep's blood on a piece of cloth, which he securely attaches to the foot of one of his carrier pigeons that is stored in cages in the living room of his big wooden house. Panther then carefully releases the carrier pigeon out of the window of the living room of his big wooden house in order to send that message to King Exodus in Falcon City about the knowledge of Triton and Lord Scartor that Lynx has just shared with him.

Panther hurries out of the living room and quickly leaves his big wooden house to go see some of his Willow guards who live in another big wooden house just across the grassy path from his big wooden house. Panther opens this big wooden house's front door with a metal key he has in his pocket, and he walks firmly into this big wooden house to see the Willow guards currently eating bread with chicken and lamb soup in the communal kitchen of this big wooden house.

'Willow guards, I have just received word from my nephew Lynx that Willow Village might be attacked by Triton and his creature army. We need to prepare Willow Village quickly for this imminent danger. Tell all the other Willow guards to suit up with their bows and arrows and surround the fences of Willow Village, as they must protect all the Willow villagers at all costs. Also, speak to any Willow villagers you see during this task and tell them to hide securely in their flats and shops or indeed help us defend this village from devastation. Please tell them not to worry or panic though as everything will be all right in our village as Lynx is also kindly sending us 200 of Pine guards and men Pine villagers to also protect us from a battle,' explains Panther directly to his Willow guards, as he does not have much time to clarify the situation more amicably. The Willow guards are immediately shocked on hearing Panther's orders and stop eating their freshly cooked chicken and lamb soup.

'Yes, of course, Panther, we will carry out your orders straight away,' says one of the Willow guards, as he stands quickly up from his wooden chair against a big wooden table in the middle of the communal kitchen.

'May the gods protect us all against the malicious creatures that might seek to destroy us. Whatever the outcome, don't fear as our souls will be spared and will spend the rest of eternity in the virtuous heaven,' says another Willow guard in a calming manner.

'Our human attributes like strength and loyalty should be enough to spare us humans from extinction from the Planet of Phoenix, but a little help from the gods would be graciously appreciated during this haunting great war,' states Panther.

The rest of the Willow guards also quickly stand up from their wooden chairs and suit up in their metal armour and collect their wooden bows and arrows from the weapons closet in that big wooden house, while Panther leaves that big wooden house and returns to his own big wooden house across the grassy path; he hurries up the wooden staircase into his personal bedroom to also suit up in his own and notable knighthood armour accompanied by his silver sword and silver shield that he has been equipped with in a number of previous battles against creatures during his time existing on the Planet of Phoenix. As Panther suits up in his silver knighthood armour, he also prepares his mind to be mentally strong and confident in preparation of being victorious in a battle that may occur in the peaceful Willow Village.

LYNX TROTS ON his white horse towards the west entrance wooden gate of Willow Village; there he notices the small wooden flat opposite a farm food shop, which Panther had explained was Rio and Olivia's small wooden flat. Lynx halts his white horse by pulling the rope reins; he then jumps down from the white horse and ties the white horse up again to the nearest Black Maul willow tree that is by the side of the farm food shop. Lynx strides across the grassy path and knocks on the front wooden door of Rio and Olivia's small wooden flat.

Rio is forty-nine years old and he has short wavy brown hair with brown eyes on a wrinkled face; he is short in height and of average build in body mass and muscles. Rio wears old scruffy grey clothes that include a top and baggy trousers covered over by a white overall. Rio has always generally been a quiet and soft-spoken human, and he projects introverted characteristics that are the complete opposite to how his brother Ruthus had been when they were growing up. Rio is a tool maker; that is why he also wanted to teach his son Parrot the tool making trade, until Parrot altered and modified this ancient craft to make his own specialised weapons. Rio used to supply tools to his father Barious in order for them to be sold in Barious's small tool shop back in Oak Village; this arrangement became quite profitable for Barious and Rio until Barious died a year ago in the battle of Oak Village. Rio's wife Olivia is forty-seven years old; she has short black straight hair and brown eyes. Olivia is presently wearing dark and old-fashioned woollen clothes in the form of a long dress with a buckled belt at her waist. Olivia has a very slim and petite build, which makes her not as physically strong as other women humans on the Planet of Phoenix. Olivia's characteristics are that she's a very calm, collected, and family-minded human.

Rio fell in love at a very young age with a very kind and humble Pine village girl called Olivia; they originally met each other one time in Pine Village when Flower, who was Barious's wife, took her sons Ruthus and Rio to visit her friend Salamander, who lived in Pine Village and had a daughter of a similar age, called Olivia. For many years, Rio would travel with his mother Flower to Pine Village when she visited her good friend Salamander so that he could spend more time with Olivia; it made Flower and Salamander very happy that their children really liked one another. After six years of getting to know each other, Rio left his home in Barious's small wooden tool shop and moved in with Olivia at their own home in Pine Village in a small wooden flat opposite Pinus Tavern. After many happy years of living in Pine Village, Olivia gave birth to their son Parrot, and Rio brought Parrot up to learn to become the tool maker in order to continue their family trade.

Later in life, Rio and Olivia decided to move to Willow Village when it had been established for a few years, which made it became a bit more developed; although Rio and Olivia didn't want to leave

Parrot alone at Pine Village, they felt they wanted to move to a more quieter and peaceful village compared with the hectic lifestyle of Pine Village to enjoy their old age; also, they both were not very sociable humans. After Parrot pleaded with his parents for him to not have to leave Pine Village and move to Willow Village as he liked the exciting lifestyle of Pine Village as well as had good friends such as Bruce and Flame still in Pine Village, Rio and Olivia decided to leave their small wooden flat to be owned by Parrot; they knew he would be safe living there.

As Rio was emotionally preoccupied with Olivia from an early age, Barious didn't want to place the knowledge and burden of the anomaly crystal upon Rio and his girlfriend Olivia; that is why he only told his younger son Ruthus about these mystical circumstances, but before Barious could pass the anomaly crystal over to Ruthus in order to be the new protector of it, Ruthus and his wife Jewel were killed by Viper at their house in Oak Village. Thus, Barious had no other option but to pass the anomaly crystal on to his grandson Raven, who was still living with him in Oak Village, when the time was right.

'Oh hello, Lynx, I nearly didn't recognise you for a second there. It's been quite a while since we have last seen you. Please do come in,' says Olivia gracefully as she opens the front wooden door of her small wooden flat to Lynx. Lynx enters through the front wooden door into the living room of Rio and Olivia's small wooden flat, where Rio is currently sharpening some of his tools, which included metal chisels, saws, and nails, at a small wooden table in the living room of his small wooden flat. Olivia shows Lynx the way to the small wooden table in the living room and then walks into the kitchen adjacent to the living room. 'I'll get us some drinks.'

'Lynx, what do we owe the pleasure of this visit?' asks Rio while continuing to sharpen the chisel tool he has presently in his warm hands. Lynx sits down upon a wooden chair next to the small wooden table and puts his silver sword and silver shield on the floor in the living room of Rio and Olivia's small wooden flat.

'It's good to see you both again, but I have come with unfortunate news that I had just received from some of my men Pine villager scouts that I had sent on a quest many months ago. Willow Village, along with Pine Village, may be under threat of attack by an evil warlord called Triton and some sort of creature army. I had come to

Willow Village to speak with my Uncle Panther regarding this most disturbing news. We are now both proactively making preparations for battle in order to protect and defend our villages and the villagers residing in it. I wanted to tell you both quickly about this news so you can also prepare your safety by starting to barricade your home in case of an emergency,' says Lynx delicately and softly to try and not worry Olivia, who is overhearing this conversation from the kitchen.

'That's truly most disturbing information, and it's very kind of you to use your precious time to warn us of this forthcoming danger, Lynx. Yes, I remember Parrot telling us about that beast Triton and the chaos and anarchy he had inflicted last year back at the Oak Village battle, in which sadly my father Barious was killed,' says Rio gloomily. Olivia quickly walks back in the living room with glasses of water, and on hearing Lynx's and Rio's alarming conversation, she puts the two glasses of water upon the small wooden table and wraps her arm around Rio's shoulder in comfort.

'Oh dear, us humans can't suffer no more devastating news from those evil creatures that reside upon the Planet of Phoenix. Are Willow Village and Pine Village about to undergo an attack like what happened to Oak Village last year?' says Olivia worriedly, as she also starts to think about her son Parrot, daughter-in-law Sapphire, and her grandson Tigra that are currently living in Pine Village.

'Please try not to worry, Olivia. It will not be similar to what had happened last year in the Oak Village battle. That was a surprise attack. Since then, King Exodus, Panther, and I along with all our well-trained guards have been preparing to battle against Triton and any other creatures again ever since he and Lord Scartor along with a few of their Potorians magically escaped from Raven, Emerald, and Parrot at Crow Mountain amongst the Mountains of Doom a year ago. Panther and I maintain strong alliances and support systems with all the human villages along with King Exodus and the royal Falcon guards at Falcon City. This time round, Triton will be defeated by us humans and he will undoubtedly pay for all of his evil doings and for all of those innocent human lives he has killed since he was born. For these crimes, Triton and similar creatures will be banished to the deepest darkest depths of hell,' exclaims Lynx firmly.

'I will protect us, Olivia. It's been a while since I used a spear that my father taught me how to use in the days he used to face in battle with King Exodus and Panther, but I bet I could still throw it through the heart of a creature,' states Rio as he kisses one of Olivia's soft hands that are still wrapped around his shoulders.

'I will send Pine guards and men Pine villagers back to Willow Village as soon as I get back to Pine Village so they can also be of help here in order to protect Willow Village,' says Lynx generously.

'That's most kind of you, Lynx, as well as those brave Pine guards and villagers to lend us Willow villagers to aid us in our time of need,' replies Olivia.

'That's no problem and there will be nothing to concern you both about. Also before I go, Parrot has sent a message with me for both of you. He really apologises hat he hasn't been to visit you both yet with Sapphire and his new boy Tigra, but they didn't want Tigra to undertake that journey between Pine and Willow Village at such an early age of his life. If possible, he wishes for you both to visit them in Pine Village as soon as this creature danger has passed,' says Lynx as he remembers what Parrot had told him to say to Rio and Olivia.

'Such a sweet boy, our Parrot. Yes, we have unfortunately not been able to make that journey between our villages either to see him as yet, as I had not been feeling well enough these past few weeks to even really leave our home. Yes, if you could please pass on a message to him, whenever you next see him. If you could tell him that we will come and see all of them as soon as it will now be safe to do so. We miss him very much and are much looking forward to seeing Sapphire and Tigra for the first time too. You have made my day by bringing me this wonderful message from my beloved son. This is much appreciated, Lynx,' replies Olivia with a large smile on her face.

'You are very welcome, Olivia,' says Lynx.

'Also, Lynx, when you see Parrot back in Pine Village, please say how much Rio and I love them all dearly and pray to the gods for their safety, if any battle is to occur. We wouldn't bear it if we lost another family member like we had to deal with Barious's death last year,' sobs Olivia with teary eyes, as Rio clenches her hand that is still around his shoulders for comfort.

'Yes, I will pass these messages on, but try not to worry both of you. They will be fine as well as all of the other humans living in Pine and Willow Villages,' says Lynx reassuringly.

Twenty

RAVEN AND EMERALD who are still riding upon Felix's sturdy back, continue to gallop across the long cobbled road between Oak Village and Pine Village, travelling in the east direction. The steaming sun shines clear light over the tall strands of grass within the vast Grass Terrain Fields adjacent to the long cobbled road. The sweltering heat also rises and causes Felix to become slightly dehydrated as he continues dashing over the rough pebbles and cobblestones that are the foundations that have created the long cobbled road. As Felix gallops steadily, he is drawn to a small puddle of water that resides within a ditch embedded within a part of the Grass Terrain Fields located very close to the long cobbled road; fortunately for Felix, this puddle had not yet evaporated from the remaining rain puddle that was created by a downpour of rain that occurred over Oak Village a day ago.

Felix intentionally halts his stride near the puddle of rainwater next to the long cobbled road and lowers his head; he sticks it out and uses his big tongue to gulp large mouthfuls of rainwater to quench his thirst. As Raven realises Felix is dehydrated, he lets Felix drink as much as rainwater from the puddle as Felix requires to rehydrate himself; at this moment, Raven and Emerald tenderly pat and stroke Felix's long black and wavy hair upon the back of his neck to show their affection and appreciation of Felix putting in his great effort in transporting both of them between Oak Village and Pine Village within a short space of time.

As Felix continues to drink the rainwater from the puddle at the side of the long cobbled road, Raven turns around and smiles at his beloved wife Emerald, gazing deep into her sparkling blue eyes, which makes Emerald begin to blush.

'What is it, my remarkable husband? Is there something on your mind?' asks Emerald as she smiles delicately back at Raven.

'Apart from the fact that you get more radiant every time I look at your beautiful eyes, I was just thinking about what you were saying about your father Gaius to Ruby at her house in Oak Village,' replies Raven softly.

'What did I say that made you ponder upon it?' asks Emerald inquisitively.

'Well, I remember the day your father left Oak Village, Ruby, and yourself a few years back. We walked home together from Oakus School that day. That was actually later than usual due to you competing in the annual after-school gymnastic competition, where you competed against Pinus School and Willow School, and that was the year it was due to be held in Oakus School. I remember telling you on the walk home how proud I was of you for achieving the highest score and winning first place from your floor routine that was the final score to enable Oakus School gymnastic team to be victorious against the other villages' school gymnastic teams for the second year in a row,' says Raven.

'Yes, I remember that moment. I was very happy that we won the annual competition again that year as it was the first year I was made Oakus School gymnastic team captain, and we have always received strong competition by Pinus School gymnastic team,' says Emerald.

'Yes, I remember that being a very tough competition for all of Oakus School gymnastic team members, where you did brilliantly in supporting your team members and barley making any errors on your gymnastic routines. Ruby also stayed late after the gymnastic competition had finished in order to help the other schools' teachers pack away all the gymnastic apparatus. So she also didn't get back to her home until after us. I remember that your father Gaius was unable to attend that gymnastic competition, saying that he had an important meeting to go to with another human within Pine Village regarding a large trading of cloth,' Raven continues speaking.

'Thank you, Raven. You are very kind for saying those nice things and always supporting me during my gymnastic competitions. Yes, I remember being sad that my father couldn't make that competition, but I understood the reasons why he couldn't attend, where I was then even more excited to get back home and tell him how it went and that Oakus School won the gymnastic competition. But when I got home, he was not there and after looking all around the house for him, I found a note on my bed that only said that he was sorry and that he loved me. That made me feel so empty inside,' says Emerald sadly while thinking of this memory and recalling how upset she had been when she read that note from her father.

'And after you read that note from Gaius, you ran back to find me in Barious's tool shop, where I was in the tool shop by the till sharing words with Barious about how the gymnastic competition finished. He enjoyed the first half of the competition very much, but had to leave before the end of it as he had an urgent errand to run. When you ran frantically through the front doors of Barious's tool shop, my heart sank to see you crying hysterically. Barious was shocked to see you in such a state, and I was very worried about what had happened to you. I sprinted over to you and held you tightly within my arms. You were crying so much that you couldn't even speak the words about what had happened, but after you showed me the note, I realised why you were so upset.

'I helped you up the stairs and to my bedroom, where shortly after Barious brought us some hot vegetable soup and bread to help calm you down. After you had no more tears left to shed, you told me how devastated you where and how much you wanted to see your father again and would do anything to find him. You even said that you wanted me to go with you that night to search for him and asked Barious if we could borrow Felix in order to travel between villages to find Gaius. Barious rightfully explained that we were too young to be searching around the Planet of Phoenix for Gaius, due to there being sightings from the Pine guards within the watchtowers of Pine Village of dangerous creatures lurking around the perimeter of Oak Village and Pine Village. For a few years you continued to speak constantly with me about getting the necessary resources together in order to begin searching for your father throughout the Planet of Phoenix, and I thought this plan had never changed from your mind. But earlier when you were speaking to Ruby and I mentioned about finally beginning to search for Gaius, you said that you now have no more interest in locating his whereabouts and finding him. That made me think about what has now changed for you to not want to find your father no more?' Raven asks curiously.

'Yes, you're right, Raven. I remember more vividly now all of those dramatic moments and emotions I felt when my father left me and my mother on that initial happy day for me. I remember how I had to break the unfortunate news about my father leaving to my mother that night when she finally came home from packing up at Oakus School, and telling my mother that my father had left her as well as me was one of the worst moments in my life. Barious kindly offered to tell Ruby about the news himself, but I felt it best coming from myself as I knew my mother would not be able to cope. That is why I wanted to be there through every stage of this situation in order to help my mother get through it appropriately. My mother traditionally only loved my father from since they had first met. That was initiated by your parents Ruthus and Jewel introducing them to each other. Mother used to tell me how she fell in love with my father from the very moment she laid her eyes upon him due to her subconsciously being drawn to his rouge appearance and boisterous attitude. He still remains the only man my mother has ever loved or had physical interactions with.

'It wasn't uncommon knowledge that they had been arguing for a few years prior to my father finally leaving, where my father had sometimes taken long breaks away from us and Oak Village to see his parents at their cloth shop in Falcon City. These frequent breaks made me get used to him being away from home, along with his job that required him trading all sorts of goods between the main villages and Falcon City as well as some of the smaller villages that are scattered in faraway places from Oak Village. My mother always told me, however, that she and my father were made for each other and they would sort things out with each other to stop the consistent arguing that they usually did, but only for a brief while. And on that day when my father left us and Oak Village behind, it broke my mother's heart and my heart. I felt very helpless as I couldn't do anything about my mother suffering emotionally until this very day. She will never be able to get over the fact that my farther just left her without any word, not even a note like he had left me. She didn't deserve to have no respect bestowed upon her, especially after everything they had experienced within one another in the past.

'As you said, for many years I did want to find my father, and he's probably somewhere within Falcon City now as he was born there and that is the location of his father Nerolus's cloth shop. I justly did want to find my father and attempt to bring him back to his home in Oak Village and to be with my mother again or at least get him to explain to me why he left us the way he did. But recently, especially after what happened to us last year in the battles against Lord Scartor and Lieutenant Triton, I've realised that my father is a coward for leaving us like he did, whatever his reason for it, and also that he will never return or support us even in dire situations. You and my mother were there for me when I most needed it, and you both will always be there for me for whatever happens in the future. I truly appreciate that and love you both so much. Thus, if my father can't be bothered to watch me grow up into the woman I'm becoming, then why should I care about his life either?' replies Emerald sternly.

'I understand why you now feel the way you do about your father. It's a shame Gaius left Oak Village in the first place and put you and Ruby through a situation like that. You're also right that we will always be there from you, no matter what the situation or circumstances are, where now you don't ever have to worry again about anyone you love ever leaving you,' states Raven as he kisses Emerald gently on her smooth, tender lips. As Raven and Emerald continue kissing, Felix lifts his head up quickly and shakes his head to move the rainwater that had gone upon his face from when he was gulping it from the puddle. Raven and Emerald stop kissing and jolt against each other from Felix's fast head movements. They both laugh merrily together at what Felix had just done. Raven turns back around and shakes Felix's brown rope reins, causing him to begin galloping once again across the long cobbled road, leading in the east direction towards Pine Village.

A WHITE DOVE flying from above in the bright and breezy clear blue sky suddenly drops down and lands upon Felix's black head as he gallops swiftly along the long cobbled road in the east direction towards Pine Village. As the white dove lands upon Felix's head, it surprises Raven, which causes him to quickly pull tightly on Felix's brown rope reins until he jolts to a quick and abrupt stop upon the long cobbled road. Raven calms Felix for his hasty stoppage by patting him on the back. Raven now looks at the white dove as it moves its small, white, feathery head quickly from side to side, and he notices the white dove has a piece of torn grey cloth tied to one of its petite feet. Raven holds the white dove with one of his hands, and with the other hand, he quickly unties the piece of grey cloth from the white dove's feet and reads it with curiosity.

'Emerald, it's a message from Ruby. She writes that she wants you to return home quickly. I'll turn Felix around, and we'll both ride back to Oak Village to visit Ruby again,' says Raven as he releases his hand that was holding on to the white dove, where the white dove just remains on top of Felix's head while not being bothered by Raven just holding on to it.

'No, Raven. That's all right. You go on ahead to Pine Village as we're closer to Pine Village than Oak Village now, and I don't want you to be late to Pinus Tavern for the remembrance service. Could you please explain to Parrot and Sapphire, along with Bella and Lemur, why I've got held up and that I will come along to Pinus Tavern remembrance service shortly? I will swiftly ride Felix back myself to Oak Village to see my mother as she's requested, and I will catch up with you all as soon as I find out what my mother wants,' replies Emerald.

'Are you sure you don't want me to travel with you, Emerald, as I never like leaving your side? I don't mind being late too, as I'm sure Parrot and Sapphire will understand and explain that our absence would be due to a good reason,' Raven says while turning around and looking at Emerald, who is sitting at the back of him upon Felix's back.

'Honestly, it's fine, Raven, but thank you for caring for my well-being as you promised you always would. Mother just probably forgot to tell me something, and, although, it's a slight inconvenience, I better go find out what it is,' mentions Emerald.

'All right then, as you wish. I will now walk the rest of the way to Pine Village and go with Parrot and Sapphire to Pinus Tavern's remembrance service. It won't take me too much longer to the walk, so we should be able to make it in time,' says Raven.

'OK, could you please say hello to everyone for me and tell them how I have missed them while being on our honeymoon? Also give Rexus a stroke and a hug from me. I expect he will be ecstatic to see you. I will be back in your arms before you've even noticed I've gone,' smiles Emerald while looking at Raven's loving face. Raven kisses Emerald on the lips passionately just like the first kiss they ever experienced together, which was also in the Grass Terrain Fields just outside the perimeter of Oak Village. Raven and Emerald both stop kissing after a couple of minutes, and Emerald hugs Raven affectionately, before he climbs down from Felix's big black back as Raven has reached the cobbled road beneath him. He then grabs his sword of Grackle from Felix's back where Raven had placed it when he was riding upon Felix. As Raven climbs down from Felix's back, the white dove now suddenly flies off Felix's head and vanishes from their sight into the wide open blue sky amongst the floating fluffy clouds.

'Ride safe, my perfect wife. I love you,' says Raven, blowing a kiss at Emerald as he is standing by the side of Felix.

'I love you with all my heart too,' replies Emerald as she smiles radiantly at Raven again and kicks the sides of Felix with her feet gently. She pulls on the brown rope reins in order to turn him around and gallops back towards Oak Village going in the west direction across the long cobbled road. The blue lily flowers that Ruby had given to Emerald earlier to take to Pinus Tavern remembrance service were also still slotted between one of Felix's brown rope reins. Raven stands extremely still as he watches Emerald riding quickly upon Felix along the cobbled road in the west direction. Raven keeps watching Emerald riding upon Felix until the sun's rays in the distance shine too brightly in his eyes and cause Raven to look away and enables Emerald and Felix to disappear from his sight.

As Raven loses sight of Emerald, his body tingles and his heart sinks deep within his stomach as he can't stand to be apart from Emerald. Raven looks again at the grey cloth with the message from Ruby written on it. He feels a strange feeling in his mind that something about the message from Ruby seems a bit odd as she knew that they were both in a hurry to get to Pine Village to attend

Pinus Tavern remembrance service. Raven, without having much choice, regrettably turns around and walks speedily towards the west entrance wooden gate of Pine Village. He continues walking down the connecting cobbled paths through Pine Village towards Parrot's small wooden flat, which is located near Pinus Tavern.

Emerald continues to gallop upon Felix in the west direction across the long cobbled road back towards Oak Village; after thirty minutes of fast-pace riding, Emerald and Felix enter through the east entrance wooden gates of Oak Village and continue riding across the wooden and cobbled paths until she eventually reaches Ruby's big wooden house again in the north-east direction of Oak Village near Barious's small wooden tool shop. On approaching Ruby's big wooden house, Emerald pulls the brown rope reins attached around Felix's black and hairy neck, and Felix comes to a stop just outside Ruby's big wooden house. Emerald climbs down carefully from Felix's large black back and pats Felix warmly on his long nose and leads Felix closer to the front door of Ruby's big wooden house. Emerald lets go of Felix's brown rope reins and knocks on the front wooden door of Ruby's big wooden house.

'Mother, it's Emerald. I received your message attached to the dove and have now come back home. What's the emergency?' shouts Emerald. Venus, who now looks and sounds like Ruby would have normally done, walks ruthlessly towards the wooden front door of Ruby's big wooden house through the connecting hallway and opens the wooden front door; she smiles at a tired Emerald.

'I'm sorry to call you back home, my darling, but I forgot about this earlier, and I couldn't wait another moment before showing you something. Come in quickly,' replies Venus, her voice sounding like Ruby's voice.

'OK, Mother, it must be something of great importance if it couldn't have waited another couple of hours when Pinus Tavern remembrance service would have finished,' replies Emerald. Emerald obliviously walks through the wooden front door and into Ruby's big wooden house. She follows Venus into the living room, still thinking it is her mother Ruby. Upon entering the living room, Venus grabs a small wooden bottle from the wooden shelf fixed above the fireplace.

'A few days ago, I brought this from a shop in Willow Village that produces and sells special kinds of liquids and potions. This particular liquid is supposed to shine up jewellery so that it's the most clear and sparkly jewellery that it can be. Along with this cleansing feature, it's also meant to keep jewellery from withering over time. I bought it for you, and I wanted to shine up your wedding ring for you now so that you can show it off when you see the other villagers during your time in Pine Village today,' says Venus.

'That's very thoughtful of you, Mother, to buy this liquid all the way from Willow Village, but there's no need to really use it at the moment. My wedding ring is brand new and already glistens with beauty,' smiles Emerald, looking at her wedding ring on the finger of her left hand.

'It will look even better now though. Can I please have your wedding ring so I can give it a proper shine quickly as I brought this liquid especially for it?' remarks Venus and smiling happily at Emerald.

'Well, all right then, Mother, but yes, please be quick as I really need to get to Pine Village soon to meet up with Raven, Parrot, and Sapphire as Pinus Tavern remembrance service is about to start,' says Emerald as she quickly takes off her wedding ring and passes it to Venus.

Venus takes a white cloth from the wooden shelf fixed above the fireplace and pours a little bit of the liquid from the small wooden bottle on to it and begins to wipe the cloth over Emerald's wedding ring that currently has the anomaly crystal fixed on it. Venus suddenly drops the white cloth on to the floor and uses both her hands to snap the anomaly crystal from being fixed at the top of the wedding ring.

'Mother!' says Emerald as she is quickly shocked by Venus's actions with regards to breaking her wedding ring. Venus smiles suspiciously as her green eyes of Ruby's physical form unexpectedly turn to pure red as Venus enables her Metamorphmagi powers to magically turn her physical body back into what Venus normally looks like.

'You pathetic fool! You should have never been trusted with such an overpowering artefact like this anomaly crystal,' laughs Venus furtively. Emerald stands speechlessly and is in shock on seeing the human who she thought was her mother Ruby magically change her physical appearance into another woman that was now Venus. After a few seconds of intense shock, Emerald starts panicking obsessively at the situation she finds herself in.

'What have you done with my mother?' cries Emerald in confusion.

'I slit her throat, and now it's your turn, my dear!' snaps Venus.

'No!' Emerald shouts Emerald in horror as she dashes out of the living room and frantically heads through the hallway towards the wooden front door of Ruby's big wooden house.

VENUS STARTS BECOMING extremely astounded, and she is full of greed and desire as she finally possesses such magical powers that the anomaly crystal holds. Venus holds the anomaly crystal out in front of her and wields its uncontrollable powers as the colours of the rainbow, including the shades of white and black, begin swirling frantically around the middle of the anomaly crystal, where a jolted yellow stripe is formed at the middle of the anomaly crystal as the rest of the swirling rainbow colours and shades of white and black disappear. Suddenly, the anomaly crystal releases an electrifying bright yellow lightning bolt that shoots magically across the living room and smashes against the window attached to one of the walls at the same side as the wooden front door within Ruby's big wooden house.

As the electrifying lightning bolt sparks against the wall with the window attached to it, half that side of Ruby's big wooden house becomes completely obliterated because of the extreme power of the lightning bolt; it also blows small pieces of shattered glass and broken wood that fly sharply through the air. Fortunately, most of the shattered glass and broken pieces of wood barely miss Felix and Emerald, who have just escaped outside the wooden front door of Ruby's big wooden house before the lightning bolt was released from the anomaly crystal by Venus; however, some pieces do indeed scrape and cut parts of Emerald's and Felix's bodies, which causes them to feel spiteful pain.

The force of the explosion caused by the lightning bolt also knocks both Emerald and Felix off their feet, and they both fall to the hard ground beneath them. As Felix falls to the ground, the blue lily flowers slotted on his back within one of his brown rope reins break apart as they get crushed on the ground. Felix makes a loud noise in his pain and shock from the destruction that had just been caused from the lightning bolt released from the anomaly crystal. Venus lets out a loud, scary, high-pitched, shrieking laugh as Emerald and Felix continue to feel throbbing and soreness from the cuts they received upon their bodies due to the shattered pieces of glass and broken wood. Felix quickly scampers back to his hooves and makes more panicky and angry noises.

Emerald is now slightly disorientated from her sudden fall to the ground; she quickly focuses her mind and pulls herself up from the ground in order to run and jump on to the back of Felix. As Emerald lands partly on Felix's large back, she pulls the rest of herself on top of him, and frantically she whips the brown rope reins at the same time as kicking her feet into the sides of Felix. It causes him to rapidly gallop in frenzy down the wooden and cobbled path of Oak Village that leads them both out of Oak Village's east entrance wooden gate.

Emerald experiences strong emotions of fright and devastation from the news of her mother's death as well as from having had the anomaly crystal stolen from her by Venus. Tears stream down Emerald's red and bruised cheeks as she subconsciously realises that the anomaly crystal is now in the hands of this evil creature woman that is probably in league with Lieutenant Triton. As Emerald holds on tightly while riding on a frantic Felix, she also whips his brown rope reins again to make Felix gallop as fast as he possibly can across the long cobbled road that leads in the east direction towards Pine Village, where she will seek comfort and help from her husband Raven.

The loud and disturbing noise caused from half of Ruby's big wooden house exploding in to thousands of small and broken wooden and glass pieces is heard throughout Oak Village by several Oak villagers and Pine guards, who were presently rebuilding wooden flats and shops along with Oakus School. These Oak villagers and Pine guards are shocked by the noise of the loud explosion and begin to fear that another battle is about to commence within Oak Village. That makes some of the women Oak villagers scream and run back to their homes in a nervous panic. Some of the men Oak villagers and Pine guards hastily run down the wooden and cobbled paths towards Ruby's big wooden house in the north-east direction, where they heard the loud and destructive noise coming from, in order to see what has happened or prepare to fight against the creatures that they think might come to battle against them again.

As these men Oak villagers and Pine guards approach Ruby's now half-broken big wooden house in the north-east direction of Oak Village, they are surprised to see a seductive and petite woman, Venus, walking pleasingly across shattered glass and broken wood; she had walked directly out of the broken wall at one side of Ruby's living room. Venus laughs loudly again and grins intensely; her eyes now turn to pure white again as she utilises her Animagus powers that permit her to turn her whole physical body back into her Quetzalcoatlus form. Venus in her Quetzalcoatlus form now flaps her large and scaly wings rapidly to begin flying up into the air as she screeches loudly in a very high-pitched tone that painfully pierces the men Oak villagers' and Pine guards' eardrums to the point of the eardrums, causing blood to dribble out of their ears ad down the sides of their heads. The Oak villagers and Pine guards feel penetrating agony from their ears and fall to ground upon their knees as they place their hands to cover both of their ears in an attempt to reduce the pain.

The men Oak villagers and Pine guards have just witnessed Venus's inconceivable actions regarding what she had just done to Ruby's big wooden house as well as how she supernaturally changed her physical body into a flying dinosaur, and they become unbelievably confused and petrified. They are also agonised by suffering from what they have just experienced within Oak Village. Venus in her Quetzalcoatlus form swiftly flies high up in the air above Oak Village and continues flying across the wide open skies of the Planet of Phoenix in the south-west direction towards Triton's Underground Dungeon located deep within the ground within the Realm of Deserted Lands.

Twenty-One

AFTER TWENTY MINUTES of walking quickly down the cobbled path, going in the east direction of Pine Village, Raven is now approaching Parrot's small wooden flat. While walking along the cobbled path, Raven notices many Pine guards who were fully suited in armour and running throughout the village, talking to other Pine guards they bumped in to. Because Raven himself also was in a rush, he didn't stop to ask the Pine guards why they were hurrying about; however, Raven had witnessed the Pine guards preparing for battle drills before. He just assumes that it may also be another battle drill. Raven is, however, concerned about the worried and surprised expressions upon the Pine guards' faces. That makes Raven feel rather uneasy and a bit queasy in his stomach due to the battles he had faced against the creatures last year as well as losing his grandfather Barious within the Oak Village battle.

Raven passes Pinus Tavern that is located just before Parrot's small wooden flat on the left as he walks down the cobbled path in the east direction through Pine Village. He sees many Pine villagers and their family members, who are all dressed in the best church clothes and are walking into Pinus Tavern's big front wooden doors. They are all looking very gloomy due to Pinus Tavern remembrance service commencing today. Raven quickens his pace as he passes by

Pinus Tavern in order to reach Parrot's small wooden flat due to it nearly being time for Pinus Tavern remembrance service to begin. As Raven reaches the front of Parrot's small wooden flat, he knocks on the front wooden door quickly.

Parrot, Sapphire, Sirius, Aura holding Tigra in her arms and Rexus are all still sitting in the main room, waiting patiently for Raven and Emerald to meet with them. Now they hear the knock on the Parrot's small wooden flat's front door. Parrot smiles at Sapphire as he stands up from his wooden chair and walks out of the main room and over to the front wooden door.

'Raven! It's good to see you, my cousin. How was your honeymoon at Hydra Springs?' says Parrot while hugging Raven just outside of the front wooden door in a joyful manner.

'Yes, it's also good to see you too, Parrot, and mine and Emerald's honeymoon was magnificent. It was like a dream that I never wanted to wake up from,' replies Raven, smiling at Parrot as Parrot releases his arms from hugging Raven.

'I bet it was like a dream as you're a married man now. Come in and tell us all about it,' laughs Parrot. Raven and Parrot walk through Parrot's small wooden flat front wooden door that connects straight into the main room where Sapphire, Sirius, Aura, Tigra and Rexus are presently resting.

'Raven! What a pleasure it is to see you, but where's Emerald?' asks Sapphire, looking around Raven to see if Emerald is behind him. Raven follows Parrot into the main living room, where Raven then places his sword of Grackle at one edge of the wooden table away from everyone's cups of water.

'And it's good to see you, Sapphire, too, although, it's a very sad day today with regards to Pinus Tavern remembrance service. Unfortunately, Emerald had to hurry back to Oak Village as she was requested by her mother Ruby. Emerald and I were halfway to Pine Village while riding upon Felix, when Ruby sent a dove with a message tied to one of its feet for Emerald to return home urgently. Emerald should be back here though, in time for the remembrance service at Pinus Tavern, and she said to apologise and that she will now meet us in there,' replies Raven, kneeling down on the floor to stroke Rexus. Rexus wags his tail frantically and then jumps up to lick Raven on his face; Parrot and Sirius Laugh.

'Aw, that's a shame. Well, I guess we will catch up with Emerald later on. Did you not go back to Oak Village first to see Ruby on your journey home from Hydra Springs first then?' asks Sapphire curiously.

'Yes, we did as we also wanted to lay flowers on Barious's grave in Oakus Graveyard due to it also being one year today since his death that occurred in the battle of Oak Village. We saw Ruby and had a good chat with her at her house in Oak Village before we visited Barious's grave, so I'm not really sure why she requested Emerald to return home again. However, it must have been important as Ruby knew Emerald and I were going to Pinus Tavern remembrance service with you all today,' explains Raven while continuing to stroke Rexus.

'Yes, poor Barious, he was such an exultant and friendly human. He will also be sadly missed by many humans throughout the Planet of Phoenix, no matter where they are located. How are you doing, though, Raven? I hope you enjoyed your honeymoon at Hydra Springs. I've heard it's a very beautiful and spiritual place,' asks Aura, smiling at Raven stroking Rexus.

'Yes, Emerald and I both enjoyed it very much and are very grateful that we got to see Hydra Springs as it's indeed a place beyond all imagination,' replies Raven. He stops stroking Rexus and stands back on the floor and walks over to Aura. He holds on to Tigra's little hand, who was wrapped in Aura's arms.

'I'm glad you enjoyed your honeymoon, Raven. Yours and Emerald's wedding that occurred only a few weeks back was also a grand spectacle that all the villagers attended and enjoyed very much, and I feel it was much needed for them due to all of the pain and suffering the Oak and Pine villagers have experienced within the last year. You and Emerald deserve to have a great start to your lives together, especially after what you both had to endure with Parrot last year in the battle against Lord Scartor and Lieutenant Triton at Lord Scartor's Lair of Death upon that treacherous Crow Mountain,' says Sirius. Raven pauses a moment at what Sirius has just said, and then he subconsciously thinks about Emerald not being by his side presently and also suddenly remembers that Emerald still has the anomaly crystal fixed in her wedding ring.

'I know when Parrot told us that awful story about what happened to him, you, Emerald, and the other brave Oak and Pine villagers last year, I couldn't sleep for days thinking about how horrible it must have been for you all. In all my years of living on the Planet of Phoenix, I've never heard such devastating or traumatising news. And to go through all of that last year, shortly after also losing your parents at a very young age, I don't know how you have managed to cope. You're certainly a very remarkable and heroic human, just like Parrot is,' explains Aura, smiling at Raven, Parrot, and Sapphire.

Raven appreciates what Aura has just said about him; unintentionally he stares blankly at Tigra in Aura's arms, who was currently quiet and content due to him being half asleep. Raven doesn't reply to Aura's remarks due to him thinking about what Sirius and Aura were speaking to him about and how he would never be able to share words with Barious and his parents again in this lifetime. This makes him upset. He also realises how he wouldn't have been able to cope through any of these tragic situations if it hadn't been for Emerald helping him through everything, but at present Emerald was not with him. This made Raven begin to worry.

'Thank you for your kind words, Aura and Sirius, and we all miss Barious, Ruthus, and Jewel very much, but I'm sure their everlasting spirits are watching over us and will protect us against evil creatures and harmful situations. I know they would have been very pleased that Raven and Emerald have finally got married now as well as the new family I have started with Sapphire,' remarks Parrot as he puts one of his hands over Raven's shoulder to comfort him. This enables Raven to stop wondering worrying thoughts and bring his concentration back to the conversation Aura was having with him.

'How's Tigra doing then? He has grown so much already since I last saw him. That was only a few weeks ago, and it looks like he's going to grow up to be a very honourable and strong human just like his father and grandfather,' says Raven.

'Yes, Tigra has been an absolute pleasure, no trouble at all. Yes, you are right, Raven. He will become a very respectable human as he will have his remarkable father and diligent uncle to guide him, although Parrot and I have already agreed that Tigra is going to be an academic like his mother and not a soldier,' laughs Sapphire as she smiles at Raven and Parrot, who look at one another; everyone else also begins to laugh.

'Pinus Tavern remembrance ceremony is nearly about to start. We should really be making a move over to Pinus Tavern now if that's all right with you, Raven?' Sirius asks as he places his cup of water down back on the wooden table in the main room within Parrot's small wooden flat, and he stands up from his wooden chair.

'Yes, that's all right. Emerald said it was fine for us to go on ahead and she will meet us in Pinus Tavern when she arrives in Pine Village, hopefully soon,' answers Raven. Parrot, Sapphire, Sirius, and Aura all stand up from their wooden chairs and start to put on their coats and boots that Sapphire passes to everyone. She had collected the coats and boots from the wooden closet within the main room of Parrot's small wooden flat as Aura was holding on to Tigra. After Sapphire puts on her purple coat and boots, she begins to put Tigra's small grey coat on him and then takes Tigra from Aura while Raven strokes Rexus some more again before leaving him alone in Parrot's small wooden flat as they all attend Pinus Tavern remembrance service.

'We'll be back soon, buddy,' says Raven to Rexus as he strokes him one last time. Rexus wags his tail frantically from side to side while not really understanding what Raven has just said to him. Raven, Parrot, Aura, Sirius, and Sapphire while holding Tigra in her arms, all now walk out of the main room and the connecting front wooden door of Parrot's small wooden flat and then continue walking across the cobbled path to Pinus Tavern. Rexus begins to bark as Raven leaves Parrot's small wooden flat and closes the front wooden door.

MOST OF THE men and women Pine villagers within Pine Village, which included Bella, Lemur, and her children Siva and Sam, are presently in Pinus Tavern, except for Lynx's Pine guards, who are patrolling the perimeter of Pine Village and are currently preparing for a surprise attack that is still unknown to most of the Pine villagers. The Pine guards discussed with the other Pine guards they saw on their movements throughout Pine Village not to warn the Pine villagers that were attending Pinus Tavern remembrance services unless it was completely necessary to as they didn't want the remembrance service being ruined or disrespected; otherwise, the Pine villagers who were killed last year when they battled against Lord Scartor and Triton would have died in vain.

The Pine guards who are preparing for a surprise attack that may occur within Pine Village, had suited up in their full armour and weapons, had barricaded the weak areas of Pine Village's big wooden fence, and had informed all the Pine guards about where they should be positioned within Pine Village. Parrot's good friend Bruce is currently keeping watch in the north-east small wooden watchtower, whereas Flame is with twenty-seven other Pine guards at the west entrance wooden gate of Pine Village, discussing plans for barricading the west entrance wooden gate in a more durable design.

All the Pine villagers in Pinus Tavern are sitting on wooden chairs around wooden tables throughout the whole room next to the bar and kitchen on the first floor of Pinus Tavern. All the Pine villagers have glasses of water or jugs of ale to drink, but no one is eating any food. None of the Pine villagers are speaking with one another, and the atmosphere in Pinus Tavern is dismal and quiet due to all the Pine villagers mourning the loss of their loved ones. At the far side of Pinus Tavern opposite to Pinus Tavern's big wooden entrance doors, space has been made for a big wooden table, which is covered in white wax candles and various kinds of coloured flowers such as lilies, roses, and tulips. Above this big wooden table, in the wooden wall the names of the men Pine villagers who lost their lives last year in the battle against Lord Scartor and Triton at Lord Scartor's Lair of Death upon Crow Mountain have been carved. Among these carved names are Leon and Drakus.

Lemur is sitting on a small wooden table that is the nearest to this big wooden table that is covered with candles and flowers. Lemur is sitting with Siva and Sam next to her. Lemur is holding Siva's hand tightly, and she is very upset, just as the other men, women, and children Pine villagers who lost their family and friends last year, and these villagers are also sitting on small wooden tables that are closer to the big wooden table that is covered with candles and flowers.

Like most of the other men and women Pine villagers in the Tavern, Lemur, Siva, and Sam are dressed in their best black and grey church clothing. Bella also is wearing a long black elegant dress with black shoes accompanied by a large black hat. Bella is currently standing in front of the big wooden table at the far side of Pinus Tavern, where the big wooden table is covered with small white wax candles, along with flowers such as lilies, roses, and tulips upon it.

Bella had organised and was made in charge of the remembrance service due to the Pinus Church vicar being killed by Triton in the battle of Oak Village last year when he had attended Wolf's coronation celebration festival in the middle of the Oak Village square.

Bella begins to sing an old Pinus Church hymn softly in her high-pitched and inspirational voice; the rest of the Pine villagers in Pinus Tavern join in the singing with Bella in honour of the now deceased men Pine villagers from last year's battles. Raven, Parrot, Sapphire holding Tigra, Sirius, and Aura now enter in Pinus Tavern while everyone is singing the old Pinus Church hymn. They quietly sit down on empty wooden chairs near the entrance of Pinus Tavern and also join in with the singing. The old Pinus Church hymn continues for several minutes until it finishes, and several of the women Pine villagers begin to cry in sadness. Bella sings the last verse of an old Pinus Church hymn by herself as she picks up a wooden stick and lights it with a fire that was made earlier and burning within a metal pan upon the big wooden table.

'We light these candles in honour and memory of our family, friends, and dearly beloved who were untimely taken from their lives on the Planet of Phoenix a year ago today. We pray that their souls have reached the blissful afterlife to be with their ancestors, and we also hope that they are now at peace. We will always keep the fond memories we have of them forever in our hearts and cherished thoughts,' says Bella softly. Lemur starts to cry at the thought of Leon being killed last year; other women Pine villagers are also crying due to the deaths of their family, friends, and loved ones.

'Family members who have lost those brave men Pine villagers, please come up and light a candle for their spirits to remain bright for eternity.' Bella now lights the first candle with her burning wooden stick in memory of her son Drakus, who was killed by Triton at Lord Scartor's Lair of Death upon Crow Mountain. Lemur, who was sitting opposite the big wooden table, now stands up and holding on to Siva's and Sam's hands; they all walk over to the big wooden table first. Siva lets go of Sam's hand and picks up a white wax candle and lights it from Bella's already burning white wax candle that she was still holding in both her hands. Siva and Sam also do the same as Lemur, and they all put the white wax candles back down upon the big wooden table.

'These candles that we have lit are for you, Leon. The love of you will remain in our hearts until we are all reunited again in heaven. We have missed you every day since you were taken from the Planet of Phoenix and will not rest or give up until Lord Scartor has been sent to hell for what he has done to you, our family, and all the other humans on the Planet of Phoenix,' angrily sobs Lemur. Siva gives her mother Lemur a hug and holds her hand tightly as they all sit back down on their wooden chairs.

Other men and women Pine villagers, who were related or close friends to the men Pine villagers who were killed in the battle at Lord Scartor's Lair of Death upon Crow Mountain one year ago, now also begin to slowly walk up to the big wooden table; they pick up the white wax candles and light them from Bella's already burning white wax candle that was still cupped within Bella's hands. These men and women Pine villagers say a few words or prayers for their loved ones and then put their white wax candles back down upon the big wooden table.

After a few of the men and women Pine villagers have gone up to the big wooden table, lit a white wax candle, and said some words or a prayer for their loved ones who had died, Bella begins to sing another but newer Pinus Church hymn, where other men and women Pine villagers who weren't lighting white wax candles join in with the singing; this also includes Parrot, Sapphire, Sirius, and Aura. After a few minutes during the Pine villagers softly singing the new Pinus Church hymn, Emerald suddenly bursts through Pinus Tavern big wooden entrance doors.

Emerald is devastated, exhausted, and depleted. She has cuts all over her face and arms from the broken wood and glass of Ruby's big wooden house that was blown apart from the lightning bolt Venus had created and released from the anomaly crystal. Emerald is crying frantically, and she quickly falls to the wooden floor of Pinus Tavern and lands hard upon her bruised knees. All the Pine villagers within Pinus Tavern are shocked by Emerald's dramatic entrance, and Pinus Tavern goes completely silent as the Pine villagers stop singing the new Pinus Church hymn. Bella and Lemur look across Pinus Tavern and are shocked to see the state that Emerald is in.

RAVEN JUMPS QUICKLY out of his wooden chair almost instantly after seeing Emerald entering dramatically into Pinus Tavern and falling to the wooden floor on her knees. Raven runs over to Emerald and wraps his arms around her lovingly.

'Emerald, are you all right? What's happened?' says a concerned and worried Raven. Emerald continues to cry tearfully as she tries to speak, although her words become all mumbled and it doesn't make any sense to Raven. Raven holds Emerald tightly and begins to breathe deeply until Emerald also does the same.

'This evil woman in Oak Village killed my mother and stole my wedding ring from me. She took the anomaly crystal from my wedding ring and then tried to kill me with it. Felix and I barely escaped, but my mother didn't as she is now dead,' loudly cries Emerald. The Pine villagers in Pinus Tavern, who have heard what Emerald has just said to Raven, shockingly gasp or also begin to cry at the thought of another battle with the creatures occurring against the humans within the villages.

'Poor, poor Ruby,' says a shocked and upset Sapphire, while she gives Tigra to Aura for her to hold him now. Then she quickly rushes over to also hug and comfort Emerald.

'I'm very sorry about your mother, Emerald. We will find this evil woman and also kill her for what she has done to your mother,' states Raven furiously. Emerald continues to cry hysterically. Sapphire hugs her and Raven sincerely. Parrot also hurries over to Raven, Emerald, and Sapphire.

'Raven, Lynx had just recently told me that Lord Scartor was killed by Triton a few days ago in the Realm of Deserted Lands. Sorry, I just told you about this now, but it's been the first chance I've had,' explains Parrot quietly to Raven. Raven stands up and pulls Parrot to one side away from Emerald and Sapphire, who was still hugging Emerald as she was crying and breathing heavily in futility.

'Lord Scartor is dead! Does that mean Lieutenant Triton is no longer a lieutenant and now the new leader of the Potorian army and may be in league with that evil woman who has just stolen the anomaly crystal from Emerald? Emerald also said that evil woman used the anomaly crystal to try and kill her with it. How can she possibly wield the powers of the anomaly crystal as it's only our bloodline, that is the bloodline of Grackle's, it can unleash the elemental powers of the anomaly crystal?' says an anxious and confused Raven.

'I don't know how this woman used it against Emerald, but yes, I suspect this woman's also now in league with Triton,' says Parrot attentively. Raven turns back towards Emerald.

'How did this woman steal the anomaly crystal from you, Emerald? I thought you were going back to Oak Village to share words with Ruby?' asks Raven intently.

'I thought this woman was my mother as she looked and sounded exactly like her. She asked to clean my wedding ring with some special kind of liquid that is meant to sustain it from withering over time. Without suspicion I gave it to her as I thought she was my mother, and then surprisingly this woman broke the anomaly crystal from the wedding ring, and then all of her physical body and voice mysteriously changed completely into another woman of a different origin to us villagers in here now. I've never experienced or ever heard of this kind of creature magic in my life,' replies Emerald, who has difficulty speaking again due to her intense crying. Raven and Parrot look at each other in disbelief and wonder about the creature with such extraordinary abilities.

'Poor thing, she's in shock for what has happened to her mother. We need to get her some rest,' whispers Sapphire to Raven and Parrot.

'No! I know what I saw, and I want to kill this woman with my bare hands for what she has done to my mother!' shouts Emerald.

'What's going on? Is everyone all right?' asks Bella from the other side of Pinus Tavern, who presently couldn't hear the conversation occurring between Raven, Emerald, Parrot, and Sapphire. Although, Bella had noticed some of the Pine villagers who were closer to Raven, Emerald, Parrot, and Sapphire and the back of Pinus Tavern also becoming emotional and beginning to panic.

'Are we going to be attacked by creatures again?' shouts a worried woman Pine villager; the other Pine villagers in Pinus Tavern react frantically to what this women Pine villager says, and they start to hug their children closely.

'No, we're not under attack. Do not worry yourself!' says Parrot loudly in a calming manner.

'We need to get out of here quick before things start get out of control. We should get aid from Lynx and his Pine guards immediately,' says Raven quickly to Parrot.

'Lynx has gone to see Panther in Willow Village to give him the news about the death of Lord Scartor. Lynx had already ordered the Pine guards in Pine Village to begin battle preparations in case of a surprise attack,' replies Parrot quietly to Raven.

'What about King Exodus and his royal Falcon guards then?' asks Raven.

'There wouldn't be enough time to seek assistance from King Exodus in Falcon City either,' states Parrot nervously.

'A few years ago when I was at Falcon University, I read in an ancient book that had been written in the ancient Phoenix language about a lost creature tribe called the Hawks that are assumed to live deep within the heart of Eagle Forest. This ancient book remarks that this Hawk Tribe are peaceful creatures and protect all nature on the Planet of Phoenix from any evil deeds. If we could find these Hawks and gain their trust and aid, we could lure Triton and this mysterious woman away from the three main villages to keep all of the humans here safe. If we had the Hawks fight with us, then hopefully we could destroy Triton and any other evil creature once and for all,' exclaims Sapphire, thinking back to the information she remembered reading about in this ancient book when she was studying at Falcon University in Falcon City.

'Yes! We must do whatever it takes to seek revenge,' states Emerald after hearing what Sapphire said. She tries to stand up from the wooden floor of Pinus Tavern but finds it difficult due to her body feeling depleted; she eventually stumbles to her feet and walks strongly out of Pinus Tavern big wooden entrance doors. Raven follows her quickly out of the big wooden entrance doors, while Sapphire rushes back over to Sirius and Aura, who still has Tigra in her arms and is becoming very concerned about some of the information they hear Raven, Emerald, Parrot, and Sapphire speak about.

'You and Father need to come with me back to Parrot's home quickly. We need to speak about this unexpected situation in private please,' says Sapphire, grabbing Sirius's and Aura's hands and pulling them out of Pinus Tavern's big wooden entrance doors.

'Sorry to have disrupted everyone during the remembrance service. We have an important family matter to currently deal with, but it's nothing for anyone else to worry about. Please continue with the remembrance service and please accept our sincerest apologies for the interruption,' states Parrot as he also rushes out of Pinus Tavern big wooden entrance doors after Sapphire, Sirius, Aura, and Tigra who were hurrying back to Parrot's small wooden flat across the cobbled path from Pinus Tavern. The Pine villagers in Pinus Tavern remain silent and are concerned by what has just happened with Emerald. Bella, who was not fully able to hear the conversations of understand the situation regarding Raven, Emerald, Parrot and Sapphire, decides it is best to start singing the rest of the new Pinus Church hymn again in order to calm some of the panicking Pine villagers down and continue with the rest of the remembrance service.

OUTSIDE PINUS TAVERN'S big wooden entrance doors, Raven tries to grab on to Emerald, who was running over to Felix who had just been left untied outside of Pinus Tavern. Raven finally grabs Emerald's hand and pulls her to change direction in order to follow Parrot, Sapphire, Sirius, and Aura who was holding Tigra in her arms; they were all going back to Parrot's small wooden flat across the cobbled path from Pinus Tavern. After reaching Parrot's small wooden flat, they all walk into the front wooden door, and Raven, who was the last one in, quickly closes the front wooden door behind him. Rexus quickly runs up to Raven and Emerald while barking and wagging his tail in excitement due to seeing them both again. Raven strokes Rexus firmly to stop him barking, while Emerald stands still due to her still being in shock from her mother Ruby's death.

'Listen, Emerald's mother Ruby was killed by an evil woman back in Oak Village just moments ago. This evil woman has also now stolen from Emerald a powerful artefact called the anomaly crystal that has unearthly magical powers. We're now worried that creature Triton we told you about and this other creature woman may be working together where they could potentially come back to our villages and destroy it along with all the humans by using the powers of the anomaly crystal. We have no choice but to go to Eagle Forest now and seek help from an ancient creature tribe called the Hawks to help us defend the villages against Triton and this cruel woman. Sorry to bombard you with all this shocking information, but we don't have the luxury of time at the moment,' explains Sapphire.

'Oh dear, what is happening?' asks a flustered Aura while hugging Tigra tightly and looking at Sapphire's concerned emotions upon her face.

'It's all right, my dear,' says Sirius, putting his hand on one of Aura's shoulders.

'Don't worry, Aura and Sirius. Please stay here and lock all of the doors. We won't put ourselves or yourselves in any danger, but we really need to seek help from this Hawk Tribe within Eagle Forest before circumstances really do develop further,' says Parrot soothingly.

'We will then come with you. We can help in protecting you four as well as the rest of human race on the Planet of Phoenix from these creatures,' replies Sirius decisively.

'No, I appreciate you looking out for all of us, but please stay here where it's safe, and we also need someone we trust fully to look after Tigra and Rexus and protect them from any forthcoming danger. We will be back home as soon as we can,' says Sapphire, hugging both Sirius and Aura adoringly and then kissing her baby boy Tigra on the forehead. During the conversation between Sapphire, Sirius, and Aura, Parrot opens his weapons closet at one side of the main room in his small wooden flat. Parrot now puts several fury raptor throwing stars in the various pockets in his brown coat and then he pulls out of the weapons closet and puts his wooden bow and wooden arrows with sharp metal spikes at the end of them around his neck and back. Raven also picks up his silver-and-gold handle sword that is the sword of Grackle, which he had left on the wooden table in the main room of Parrot's small wooden flat before going to Pinus Tavern remembrance service.

Emerald continues to cry while now kneeling on the floor, hugging and kissing Rexus, who begins to lick the tears from her face. Parrot now pulls out of his weapons closet a small silver dagger, which he passes to Sapphire. Parrot also pulls out of his weapons closet a small sharp silver sword. He closes his weapons closet and walks over to give the small sharp silver sword to Emerald. Emerald quickly gives Rexus one last kiss on the head, and then she takes the small sharp silver sword from Parrot and quickly walks out of the front wooden door of Parrot's small wooden flat in a determined manner, swinging the small sharp sword from side to side. Raven strokes Rexus firmly to say goodbye to him, and then he also follows Emerald outside of Parrot's small wooden flat.

'Please be careful, all of you,' sobs Aura, hugging Sapphire with Tigra still in Aura's arms.

'Please take care of our daughter, Parrot,' remarks Sirius, hugging both Aura and Sapphire at the same time.

'I will. Don't worry. I won't let anything happen to her or any of my family. Both of you stay here, no matter what, and you'll be fine. If there are any creature battles or problems within Pine Village, I have spare specially made weapons in my weapons closet that you are welcome to use. Do whatever it takes to defend yourselves. In the worst-case scenario, if my home is destroyed, Lynx has explained that he has a secret hatch within the cellar of his castle that is unknown to any creatures and will have supplies in there for you to all be locked away from being discovered and survive for many weeks if need be,' says Parrot, kissing Tigra on the forehead. Aura is still holding Tigra tightly to comfort her after she stops hugging Sapphire.

'I love you both very much. Lock the door behind us, and don't open it to anyone, except only us when we return back to Pine Village soon,' says Sapphire as she kisses Sirius, Aura, and Tigra once each on their cheeks. Sapphire, who is now holding on to her small silver dagger, accompanied by Parrot, who is carrying the wooden bow and wooden arrows with sharp metal spikes at the end of them around his neck and fury raptor throwing stars in his brown coat pockets, also now quickly leaves Parrot's small wooden flat. As soon as Parrot and Sapphire leave Parrot's small wooden flat, Sirius locks the front wooden door straight away; he then walks back into the main room of Parrot's small wooden flat and firmly hugs Aura, who is still holding Tigra; Rex runs circles around all of them, barking and wagging his tail, unaware of the situation that has just occurred with Raven, Emerald, Parrot, and Sapphire.

Emerald has already saddled upon Felix across the cobbled path near Pinus Tavern, and Raven strokes Felix's head to greet him before saddling upon him again. Parrot runs across the cobbled path and continues running to the small field behind Pinus Tavern. He jumps over the fence and into the small field; he grabs a brown horse and climbs on to it. Parrot kicks his feet into the side of the brown horse, and the brown horse gallops quickly through the small field; it jumps over the fence and gallops round to the front of Pinus Tavern.

Raven is now saddled at the front of Felix, and Emerald is holding on to Raven's sides with her hands as well as holding on to her small sharp silver sword and Raven's sword of Grackle. Parrot runs quickly to the small field behind Pinus Tavern, where he retrieves a brown horse and rides it round to the front of Pinus Tavern near Raven and Emerald who are sitting upon Felix. Parrot sticks his arm out in order to help Sapphire at the back of him on top of the brown horse he is riding. The sky begins to darken as the sun sets due to the time of evening it now is. As the sky becomes darker, a cold and nippy breeze fills the air. Raven and Emerald riding upon Felix, along with Parrot and Sapphire riding on another brown horse begin to gallop hastily west down the cobbled paths of Pine Village towards the east entrance wooden gate. After ten minutes of fast riding along the cobbled path, with both Raven controlling Felix and Parrot controlling his brown horse, they narrowly miss the Pine guards and Pine villagers passing by along the cobbled paths of Pine Village due to the fast speed they are riding at; they now approach the east entrance wooden gates of Pine Village. Parrot looks ahead and sees in the distance his good friend Flame with other Pine guards starting to barricade the east entrance wooden gate with large pieces of broken-up wood from recently cut pine trees.

'Flame, wait!' loudly shouts Parrot. Flame quickly looks around as his name is shouted, and he sees Parrot galloping hurriedly on a brown horse with Sapphire at the back of him, along with Raven and Emerald galloping on top of Felix, towards the east entrance wooden gate of Pine Village.

'Pine guards, stop!' shouts Flame as he quickly pulls the large piece of pine tree wood to one side that would have closed the last gap to allowing humans in and out of Pine Village. Flame's actions also make the other five Pine guards, who were also holding on to this large piece of pine tree wood, manoeuvre themselves to follow Flame's movements. Within the past year, all of the metal gates within Pine Village where replaced with wooden gates due to the metal from the previous metal gates being used to make more weapons in preparation for the great war. Raven and Emerald, riding upon Felix, gallop past Flame and twenty-seven Pine guards, who had just stopped barricading the last gap of the east entrance wooden gate, and they continue charging out of the east entrance wooden gate and along the long cobbled road in the west direction of the Planet of Phoenix, heading towards Eagle Forest. Parrot and Sapphire, riding upon the brown horse, gallop up to the east entrance wooden gate where Parrot pulls the rope reins of the brown horse tightly to make it halt right next to Flame.

'Parrot, what's going on? Is everything all right?' asks Flame in a concerned voice after seeing Raven and Emerald gallop swiftly on Felix straight past him.

'Yes, everything is all right, my friend. Continue preparing Pine Village for a battle as Lynx commanded. Raven's mother-in-law and Emerald's mother Ruby was killed in Oak Village within the last hour, by what appears to be an evil woman creature that possesses some kind of creature ability no human has ever experienced before. Sapphire and I need to follow Raven and Emerald to seek aid from ancient creature tribe called the Hawks who resided deep within Eagle Forest in order to have any chance in defeating this creature woman who may have also joined forces with Triton,' explains Parrot quickly and directly.

'No need to explain yourselves, Parrot. You are a good friend of mine, and I trust your judgement. Do you need any Pine guards to assist you in this ambiguous quest?' asks Flame in a concerned manner.

'You are very kind in trusting me and offering Pine guards for our aid, Flame, but you will need all the Pine guards you have, when needing to protect Pine Village and against a battle that might unfortunately occur,' says Parrot sadly.

'My parents, our baby boy Tigra, and Raven and Emerald's dog Rexus are currently hiding back in Parrot's home opposite Pinus Tavern. If possible, could you please watch out for their safety, Flame?' asks Sapphire politely.

'Yes, of course, Sapphire, I will do my utmost in protecting them and every other villager that lives within Pine Village. I also wish the best of luck to you all on your expedition,' replies Flame.

'One last thing, Flame, before we must go, when you next see Lynx, could you please tell Lynx about what I have just told you as it's best that he also knows what our intentions are as well as this unheard of evil women creature? Let us all hope that we see each other in this lifetime again and that we all don't suffer any torture by the hands of any creatures. We will return as soon as we can and will then help defend Pine Village if the great war indeed commences,' states Parrot as he and Flame grab each other's forearms as a sign of respect for each other. Parrot kicks his heels into the side of the brown horse, which causes the brown horse to use the strong muscles in the back of its thighs to begin riding hastily out of the last not-barricaded gap at the east entrance wooden gate of Pine Village; they continue to swiftly gallop down the long cobbled road connecting to Oak Village, where they attempt to catch up with Raven and Emerald, who are riding rapidly upon Felix ahead of them.

'Come on, Pine guards, let's get this last gap of the entrance gate barricaded!' shouts Flame as he and the other five Pine guards manoeuvre the large piece of pine tree wood to barricade the last gap of the east entrance wooden gate of Pine Village; the other remaining twenty-two Pine guards who are also presently at the east entrance wooden gate start checking that all the large pieces of broken pine tree wood they have placed are securely fixed and unmovable.

Twenty-Two

VULTURE HAD BEEN carrying Vicious by holding on to his large and bulky muscles with his clawed feet. Because of the huge body mass of Vicious, Vulture had agonisingly flown in the north-east direction through the wide-open skies of the Planet of Phoenix. At the beginning of their journey, Vulture's large black feathery wings had to be flapped furiously in the air that covered the Realm of Deserted Lands due to the freezing gusty winds that carried tiny dirt, rock, sand, and gristle particles that circle around this environment causing much friction against Vulture's flying abilities especially while carrying Vulture's massive muscle body that weighed over two tons. After leaving the air above the Realm of Deserted Lands, Vulture continues to carry Vicious while flying but needs to rest due to the weight of Vicious being too much for Vulture to bear. So they flew to the ground to briefly rest upon the Grass Terrain Fields that are located just outside the perimeter of the Realm of Deserted Lands.

During Vulture's and Vicious's brief rest within these Grass Terrain Fields, they could hear and see in the far distance many wild animals such as horses, deer, warthogs, and zebras swiftly moving locations from where they usually grazed, like they could sense danger of an obnoxious battle approaching. Vulture took a big gasp and flapped his large black feathery wings again that were attached to his back. This enabled him to hover about the ground and grab on to Vicious's hugely built shoulders, and they both continue to fly in the north-east direction in the sky of the Planet of Phoenix, towards Willow Village.

While Vulture is flying through the sky travelling in the north-east direction of the Planet of Phoenix, he purposely decides to take a detour when approaching the middle section of the Planet of Phoenix in order to avoid the perimeter of Komodo Jungle which Viper and his Serpents are currently occupying. Vulture and Vicious think it is not worth the risk being spotted by a Serpent from a distance; otherwise Triton and Venus's plans could be ruined. The journey from the Realm of Deserted Lands to Willow Village takes over six hours for Vulture to get there; that is longer than usual as he has been carrying the robust and heavy Vicious.

As Vulture approaches the air within the outskirts of the perimeter of Willow Village, Vicious notices a carrier pigeon that is presently flying through the air; this carrier pigeon is the same carrier pigeon that had been sent by Panther from Willow Village with a message to King Exodus in Falcon City, which had been written on cloth and tied to the carrier pigeon's foot.

'Vulture, quickly fly towards that carrier pigeon!' shouts Vicious angrily as he assumes it is a human carrier pigeon that transfers messages between the villages and Falcon City.

'As you wish,' puffs Vulture as he forcefully flaps his large black feathery wings to change direction; he now manoeuvres in the air until he comes close to the slow flying carrier pigeon. Vicious releases a large, loud burp from his mouth that projects one of his creature abilities, which is a powerful shock wave. This shock wave is full of a stunning energy force that ripples through the air and clashes into the carrier pigeon; the impact of this shock wave breaks the small wings of the carrier pigeon and makes the carrier pigeon become unconscious instantly. The carrier pigeon is now wingless and unconscious, and the body of the carrier pigeon plummets downwards from the air and falls quickly down towards the ground. Upon impact on to the Grass Terrain Fields within the outskirts of Willow Village, all the remaining bones with in the carrier pigeon become shattered.

Vulture and Vicious laugh nastily at the sight of the carrier pigeon being dismantled. Vulture flaps his large black feathery wings again to manoeuvre back on course straight towards Willow Village. Vulture flies quickly while carrying Vicious with his claws; they reach Willow Village in only a few more minutes. Vulture circles above the cold and shady, darkish sky above Willow Village; due to the setting of the sun, light has now passed.

As Vulture circles above the air of Willow Village, looking for a suitable place to land upon the ground, they are spotted by a few of the Willow villagers below on the ground who are walking along the grassy paths in the west direction of Willow Village. These Willow villagers hear faint noises above in the air, and as they look up and see a flying creature carrying another alarming creature, the Willow villagers all start to panic hysterically. Some of Panther's Willow guards who also notice Vulture flying in the air while carrying Vicious above Willow Village, already start sprinting throughout Willow Village to alarm the Willow villagers that Willow Village is about to be attacked by creatures.

Vulture suddenly releases Vicious from his clawed feet near the west entrance wooden gate of Willow Village. Vicious falls rapidly and strongly on the ground beneath him and crash-lands into a small wooden flat. Due to the size of Vicious, with his hugely built muscles that are as tough as solid rock, he smashes straight through this small wooden flat, and the wood of the small wooden flat breaks into hundreds of smaller pieces that fly up into the air and land in all directions of Willow Village. As Vicious crashes into the small wooden house, he also instantly kills two old Willow villagers who were a married couple and were at present living in this small wooden flat. The loud and terrifying sound of this small wooden flat with two Willow villagers within it being crushed and destroyed is heard throughout the entire Willow Village; most of the Willow villagers immediately run out of their small wooden flats or wooden shops to see what has happened and where the loud noise has come from.

Vicious forcefully lifts his huge arms up and stretches them out to knock away any of the wood that is currently surrounding him from when he crashes into the small wooden flat. Vicious then stomps over all the other pieces of broken wood from the small wooden flat that is now beneath his huge robust feet. Vicious notices Willow villagers running around Willow Village in the opposite direction from him, and he also sees other men Willow villagers running out of their small wooden flats and wooden shops with wooden spears and metal axes. These men Willow villagers start running towards Vicious in attempt to protect Willow Village as well as their family and friends from being attacked.

Vicious smirks, and then he opens his mouth and releases a large breath of fire that engulfs the air in front of him. This specific creature ability discharges an enormous intense ball of bright blazing fire, which Vicious breathes across several of these running men Willow villagers and other small wooden flats close to him. This causes the men Willow villagers and the small wooden flats to instantly burn, killing the Willow villagers inside, and within minutes, these small wooden flats scorch completely to the ground. Lynx, along with Rio and Olivia, was still inside of Rio and Olivia's small wooden flat near the west entrance wooden gate of Willow Village and is also shocked to hear the loud breaking sound of wood and screaming from Willow villagers from the outside of Willow Village.

'Oh no! We're being attacked!' screams Olivia horrifically.

'Don't panic, stay in here, and lock all your doors quickly. I will go and protect you as well as defend Willow Village,' states Lynx, rapidly standing up from his wooden chair and hastily picking up from the floor his silver sword and silver shield that has the crest of the royal Falcon captain symbol on it. Rio also stands up from his wooden chair that is near the small wooden table he was sitting on; he grabs a large metal hammer from his tools that are placed upon the small wooden table.

'I will defend Willow Village with you,' says Rio firmly, looking at Lynx.

'No, please stay here with me. I couldn't bear if I died without you by my side,' cries Olivia, quickly grabbing on to Rio's hand that didn't have the metal hammer grasped within it.

'It's OK, Rio, I'll be fine. Protect Olivia and yourself. You won't die this day, Olivia, I promise you that,' says Lynx, dashing out of the main room and through the front wooden door of Rio and Olivia's small wooden flat.

'Be careful, Lynx!' shouts Rio as he lets go of Olivia's hand and also rushes to the front wooden door to lock it as soon as Lynx leaves the small wooden flat. Rio then runs back over to Olivia and kisses her strongly on the forehead.

'I won't let anything happen to you, Olivia,' says Rio emotionally.

'I love you with all my heart,' sobs Olivia, hugging Rio tightly.

LYNX DASHES OUTSIDE of Rio and Olivia's small wooden house. He sees the terrified Willow villagers running desperately around Willow Village, trying to avoid the intense burning flames from Vicious's fire breath that has singed various parts of Willow Village already. Vicious continues to release scalding fire from his breath that burns the small wooden flats and shops that surround him until these small wooden flats and shops are completely destroyed. The burning wood from the small wooden flats and shops releases deep and thick, black cloudy smoke that rises up into the air above Willow Village. Lynx cringes at the sight of the helpless Willow villagers being mercilessly disintegrated in their once-peaceful homes.

Opal's father Alexis and mother Illumin, who are at present in their florist shop in Willow Village, also hear the loud noise from the wood breaking from crushed small wooden flats and agonising screams from Willow villagers that have been burnt from Vicious's fire breath. Opal's father Alexis is fifty-two years old, and Opals' mother Illumin is forty-nine years old, and they both own the florist shop in Willow Village. Wolf had first met Opal just over seven years ago when Willow Village was being newly developed. Alexis has short black hair and hazel eyes; he is of a medium height and build. Alexis is quite a serious character and another hard-working Willow villager. Alexis wore old black clothes because of working in a flower shop. He had initially taken over the business from his father Farrow and mother Opal.

Alexis's father Farrow and mother Opal were killed by Serpents when they ventured on a walk too close to the perimeter of Komodo Jungle in the south-east direction on the Planet of Phoenix; this horrible tragedy occurred just under nine years ago. Farrow and Opal initially had the florist shop business at Pine Village, but after their untimely murder by the Serpents, Alexis and Illumin decided to relocate to the newly developing Willow Village that was ordered by King Exodus eight years ago. Illumin has long black hair and green eyes and also wears old grey-and-black clothes; she is a nature-loving and spiritual human who fell in love and married Alexis at an early age after they interacted with each other while both originally lived in Pine Village.

Alexis and Illumin gave birth to a daughter they named Opal in honour of Alexis's mother who was also named Opal. Alexis and Illumin's daughter Opal married the old leader of Oak Village Wolf after he met her in their florist shop just over seven years ago, when Wolf visited this florist shop to buy flowers for his mother's funeral. Alexis and Illumin, although reluctant at first to agree to this quick marriage, were happy that Opal had found her soulmate and also treated Wolf like a son to them.

Alexis and Illumin rush towards the front of their florist shop and begin to panic from all the commotion and smoke they nervously see outside the glass window of their florist shop. They think back to how their daughter Opal and grandson Leopard were killed one year ago in the battle of Oak Village with Potorians by being burnt to death within their own home.

'Quick, Illumin, go hide in the underground cellar in the back of the shop. I'll barricade the front door,' states Alexis as he kisses Illumin strongly on the lips.

'No, I'll help you barricade the front door as well,' replies Illumin as she hurriedly begins to grab baskets of flowers and empty clay pots from the floor and quickly stacks them against the front wooden door. Alexis quickly grabs her and hugs her firmly.

'Please go hide now. I won't lose you to these evil creatures, like what happened to Opal and Leopard last year. Please go hide in the back. I'll be able to work quicker on my own. Knowing that you're safe is all that is important to me,' remarks Alexis emotionally.

'OK, but come back and join me as quickly as you can. I love you,' reluctantly replies Illumin as she begins to run frantically towards the back of shop. As she runs through one of the aisles of their florist shop where the aisle is covered with flowers on wooden shelves either side of her, Illumin feels a sharp and intense burning pain of fire that rushes through her entire body and engulfs the entire florist shop. It burns the shop dramatically to the ground and kills both Alexis and Illumin suddenly and painfully.

On another side of Willow Village, after also hearing the commotion within Willow Village, Panther realises what is currently happening and runs sturdily out of his big wooden house in the centre of Willow Village, carrying his previous royal Falcon-crested silver sword and silver shield.

'Willow guards, attack!' shouts Panther to nine of his Willow guards, who are already outside just near him upon the grassy paths of Willow Village. Panther and these nine Willow guards all begin to sprint down the grassy paths, holding their swords and spears out in front of them to where Vicious is standing currently, breathing fire. Lynx also charges towards Vicious from the other side of Willow Village that is near the west entrance wooden gate where he had just came out of Rio and Olivia's small wooden flat.

Suddenly Vulture flaps his large black feathery wings to manoeuvre and fly down quickly to the ground; he lands on the grassy path near the west entrance wooden gate of Willow Village. Vulture screeches loudly from his long beak and enables his creature ability that enables him to physically grow big and tall. Vulture now turns into a humongous giant that towers high above the small wooden flats and shops of Willow Village and is the largest living creature that any Willow villager has ever seen in their lives before.

Vulture, in his giant form, lifts one of his massive clawed feet slowly up into the air and stamps it firmly upon the small wooden flat where Parrot's parents Rio and Olivia are still within the main room, hugging each other. Vulture's massive clawed foot demolishes the small wooden flat immediately and easily kills both Rio and Olivia; their bodies and bones shatter instantly as they are flattened along with their small wooden flat within the ground of Willow Village. The Willow villagers begin to scream and cry hysterically from witnessing Vulture growing into a powerful giant and crushing a small wooden flat within Willow Village with his large clawed feet. Lynx despairingly hears the sounds of breaking of wood and loud screams of Willow villagers; he quickly turns around in desolation after seeing what Vulture had just done to Rio's and Olivia's lives by stamping on their small wooden flat.

Without hesitation and with no thought for his own life, Lynx sprints furiously towards Vulture. Being a giant, Vulture doesn't notice Lynx running towards him from the grassy path beneath him as Lynx is not in Vulture's line of sight. Lynx raises his silver sword and courageously stabs it deep within one of Vulture's massive clawed foot; blood seeps out of this clawed foot, and Vulture releases an intense ear-piercing screech again from his gigantic beak, which is even louder than his screeches when he is in his normal physical form. In pain, Vulture looks down at his large clawed feet and sees Lynx, who is holding on to his silver sword that is still lodged within one of Vulture's clawed feet.

Vulture angrily swings one of his large, sharp clawed hands, and with it he knocks Lynx flying up high into the air; Lynx is still holding on to his silver sword; he now removes it from Vulture's clawed foot, and still holding on to his silver shield, Lynx flies through the air for numerous metres. He lands far back from Vulture near the west entrance wooden gate of Willow Village. Upon Lynx's landing on the ground, he hits into three running Willow villagers upon the grassy paths and knocks all three of these Willow villagers off their feet and on to the grassy paths beneath them. Lynx unintentionally breaks some of their shoulder and leg bones, and unfortunately, one of these running men Willow villagers' back becomes completely paralyzed.

Vulture screeches sharply again from his large beak and starts trampling on more small wooden flats and shops with his massive clawed feet. This awful deed kills several of the Willow villagers who were hiding inside these small wooden flats and shops; one of these unfortunate buildings that is trampled upon by Vulture's large clawed feet includes Willow Church, and that also kills the Willow Vicar. Pieces of broken wood and wooden objects fly all over the place throughout Willow Village and hit the Willow villagers running on the grassy paths and cause cuts and concussion in these Willow villagers that are hit from these pieces of flying broken wood. Vulture also continues to swipe many Willow villagers from the ground and high into the air using his large, sharp, clawed hands, these Willow villagers die instantly by the piercing scrapes from Vulture's large, sharp clawed hands or from the long fall back down to the ground they experience.

Panther and his Willow guards, who are still running towards Vicious, now see in the distance Vulture as a physical giant who is knocking many Willow villagers high up into the air and killing them. Vicious also notices Panther and his Willow guards forcefully charging towards him. Vicious now turns to face them head on and releases his intense scalding fire breath that disintegrates four of the

Willow guards who were, unluckily, in front of the charging Willow guards. These four Willow guards burn to ashes instantaneously; the powerfully generated heated fire fortunately misses Panther narrowly as he is near the back of the charging Willow guards.

WILLOW VILLAGE IS bursting with loud screams and cries from the scared Willow villagers as well as the small wooden flats and shops that are continuously being burnt from Vicious's fire breath, which results in thick black clouds covering Willow Village with a deep and suffocating thick black smoke. Burnt and disfigured dead bodies of numerous Willow villagers already lie across the grassy paths and within the broken small wooden flats and shops. Eight of Panther's other Willow guards who were at present near the west entrance wooden gate of Willow Village quickly hurry towards Vulture's huge legs and clawed feet. These eight Willow guards circle around both of Vulture's massive clawed feet quickly while other Willow guards courageously climb on top of roofs from small wooden flats and shops located near the west entrance wooden gate of Willow Village. These small wooden flats and shops have fortunately not already been burnt or destroyed.

After these Willow guards manage to climb on top of the small wooden flats and shops, along with the eight Willow guards surrounding Vulture's large clawed feet, they all quickly start shooting many sharp wooden arrows from their wooden bows, these wooden arrows are launched and stick into the massive clawed feet and giant body of Vulture. The plentiful wooden arrows pierce through Vulture's huge but tender bird-like skin and get stuck inside of him; blood sprays out of Vulture's body and drips down his black feathers, and red bloodstains appear across his body.

In a rage from the pain of the wooden arrows sticking into him, Vulture lifts his massive clawed feet swiftly up in the air and stamps them forcefully back down, squashing and killing five of the Willow guards who had been circling his large clawed feet on the ground. One of the Willow guards who had climbed on top one of the wooden roofs from a small wooden flat accurately positions his wooden bow and shoots a sharp wooden arrow high up in the air by utilising his well-taught accuracy and precision techniques. This wooden arrow released from the Willow guard's wooden bow flies accurately through the air swiftly and pierces through Vulture's wide left white eye. This causes Vulture's vision to be destroyed in the left eye due to the wooden arrow penetrating straight through the left eye, which damages the iris and makes Vulture lose sight. Vulture screeches excruciatingly and then loses his coordination immediately from the disorientation and confusion that makes him stumble backwards, and then he falls over backwards, crashing hard to the ground on top of several small wooden flats that were behind him. The large broken pieces of wood from these small wooden flats cut and slice through the back of Vulture.

Vicious shockingly sees the gigantic Vulture fall compellingly to the ground behind him and unintentionally stops his fire breath out of surprise at this situation; at the same time, Panther, along with the three remaining Willow guards, is charging towards Vicious and is close to coming in contact with him. Panther quickly picks up a wooden spear from the grassy path that one of the dead Willow guards had dropped when they were burnt to death. Panther launches this wooden spear into the air, and it hits into Vicious's muscly chest. Vicious feels slight pain from the wooden spear that has just lodged into him, but he quickly knocks it back out from his chest. Vicious now realises that he is outnumbered against several Willow guards and Willow villagers because of Vulture's disastrous fall to the ground.

Vicious decides to run from this fight and continues jolting down the grassy paths in the west direction leading out of the west entrance wooden gate of Willow Village. Panther and his Willow guards continue to chase Vicious and persistently throw wooden spears at him; another wooden spear also hits into the back of Vicious and gets stuck into his muscly skin. Vicious's back becomes sore and painful from the second wooden spear that pierces his rough and tough skin. Vicious increases his speed and runs around to Vulture's huge body that is now lying on the ground. Vulture is screeching in agony from his blinded eye.

Vicious irritatingly reacts to his pain caused by the wooden spear by breathing his intense fire flames at the Willow guards or Willow villagers along with using his huge and powerful fists to punch and knock out any of the Willow guards or Willow villagers that are in his running path as he retreats out of Willow Village. Along the way,

Vicious kills four Willow guards and dozens of Willow villagers in his rage of losing this battle as well as not being able to locate the anomaly crystal for Triton and Venus. Vicious keeps charging as he leaves through the west entrance wooden gate of Willow Village; he crosses into the deep corn fields within the perimeter of Willow Village that are adjacent to the long cobbled road that connects Willow Village and Pine Village together in the west direction, on the Planet of Phoenix. The total number of Willow guards who have been killed during the battle of Willow Village is thirteen, along with eighty-five Willow villagers who have also been killed by Vicious and Vulture in the Willow Village battle, leaving only forty-seven Willow villagers and twenty-six Willow guards still alive in Willow Village.

By this time, Lynx manages to hobble back from his fall to the ground and back over to Vulture's giant body that has fallen over. Lynx has many cuts and bruises over his body as well as a sprained ankle from the hard fall he had to the ground caused by Vulture. Lynx looks disturbed at Vulture's gigantic fallen body that is currently wriggling in agony. Lynx begins to compellingly stab his silver sword into Vulture's large head; the sword pierces deep through his large skull and into his tender brain. Panther also dashes over to where Lynx is standing and also does the same action as Lynx with his silver sword while other Willow guards continue to shoot wooden arrows into the face and chest of Vulture's gigantic body. Vulture eventually gets killed from the horrific wounds caused by all the piercing stab wounds to his head and from the wooden arrows that were launched at his face and chest.

'Are you all right?' Panther asks Lynx as they both breathe deeply because of their wounds and energy used during the Willow Village battle.

'Yes, I'm fine, but very gutted that we were not able to defeat both of these vile creatures sooner and save more innocent Willow guards' and villagers' lives,' replies Lynx despondently, puffing and holding on to his sprained ankle with one of his hands.

'Panther, what do we do about the burning flats and shops? As well as the guards and villagers that are injured?' asks a Willow guard who has just caught up with Lynx and Panther after returning from chasing Vicious out of Willow Village.

'Gather all the remaining Willow guards and any surviving villagers you find, send out small groups of guards and villagers in formation to firstly put out the burning flats and shops with water buckets from the wells closest to you. Regarding the injured guards and villagers, locate any of the women villagers who are trained at wound dressing and send them to tend the wounds of those who are injured,' orders Panther quickly. The Willow guard nods at Panther and then begins telling the other Willow guards and Willow villagers of Panther's imminent orders.

'I need to get back to Pine Village quickly before Vicious or Triton attacks there too,' states Lynx, releasing his hold around his sprained ankle with one of his hands and contemplating the devastation that has just been caused within Willow Village in only a matter of minutes.

'Do not delay, my nephew, go now quickly back to Pine Village and send those vile creatures to the depths of hell,' states Panther, patting Lynx on his back as a sign of encouragement for what requires to be done. Lynx nods at Panther, and then without hesitation, Lynx tries to run as best as he can with his sprained ankle in the west direction down the grassy paths towards the west entrance wooden gate of Willow Village, while holding tightly on to his silver sword and silver shield.

Along the grassy path to the west entrance wooden gate, Lynx passes many dead or injured Willow guards and Willow villagers, who were screaming on the ground in intense agony in the thick black cloudy smoke that had been released from the burning fire of the small wooden flats and shops. Lynx reaches near the west entrance wooden gate of Willow Village, where he grabs his white horse that he had tied to the Black Maul willow tree earlier, which was opposite the grassy path from Rio and Olivia's broken small wooden flat. Lynx quickly climbs on top of his white horse and feels intense sadness at the sight of Rio and Olivia's destroyed small wooden flat, knowing that his best friend Parrot's parents have been killed. Lynx's face heats up as sweat drips down from his forehead; he kicks his heels into the sides of his white horse, which permits it to gallop swiftly out of Willow Village west entrance wooden gate and along the long cobbled road in the west direction back towards Pine Village.

AT THE SAME time as the Willow Village battle was occurring, Triton was continuously pacing back and forth throughout the open space within the main room of his Underground Dungeon positioned underneath the rough and gravelly surface of the Realm of Deserted Lands in the far south-west of the Planet of Phoenix. Triton now strides determinedly while circling around the big wooden table within his Underground Dungeon that's positioned amongst hot rock that is filled with fire and lava. Triton is currently waiting impatiently for Venus to return to him from Oak Village, and he's desperately hoping that Venus will return unharmed and with the anomaly crystal. In a silent moment of desperation Triton hears the faint noise of footsteps in the distance that echoes throughout the underground rocky boulders. Triton becomes immediately excited at the thought of Venus's return.

Thirty Potorians who were depleted and injured with cuts, bruises, and blood all over their bodies, unexpectedly march swiftly across the hard rocky and rough surface of the Realm of Deserted Lands until they are at the foot of a small dark passageway that leads them down deep below the rocky ground, where they continue trooping for another ten minutes, walking through the dark and hot unnerving ground until the passageway leads out into the big main room of Triton's Underground Dungeon. As the thirty Potorians march exhaustedly into Triton's Underground Dungeon, Triton becomes dissatisfied on realising that the faint sound of footsteps he heard was from the injured Potorians and not his lover Venus. The Potorians stand in lines but far back from Triton, who was currently at the opposite side of the big main room within his Underground Dungeon.

'What are you Potorians dong back here? Shouldn't you be destroying the smaller villages throughout the Grass Terrain Fields of the Planet of Phoenix?' asks Triton angrily as he continues to pace furiously around the open space within his Underground Dungeon, where he misses stepping into the lava-filled pits scattered throughout the big main room.

'Well, um . . .' One of the Potorians who was covered with dried human blood all over his face hesitates.

'Um, well, what is it!' Triton shouts impatiently.

'We burnt down all the small villages that we found humans within that were located around this south side of the Planet of Phoenix. We cruelly slaughtered all of the villagers and left no traces of human development existing,' says another one of the Potorians quickly who is standing near the back of the line formation the Potorians are currently standing in.

'Although that pleases me slightly to hear this news, due to the fact that these smaller villages of humans will now not be able to unite with the main villages and aid the humans with numbers in the great war to come, it doesn't answer my question about why you are back here, and where is the rest of my Potorian army? Were any Potorians incompetently killed by human scum?' asks Triton irritably.

'No, we lost no other fellow Potorians during these small battles, and the other 166 Potorians are still marching as ordered towards Pine Village as we speak, where they will now destroy this village and the puny humans who live within it too. We regrettably returned back here to recuperate as we have been injured during these smaller village battles and thought it was best to tend to our wounds so that we are at full strength ready for when the great war commences,' wearily replies a Potorian.

'How stupid and weak are you measly Potorians to let humans be able to wound you during battle, especially from untrained and unskilled humans. We are the dominant species now and should receive no threat from any humans ever again,' states Triton loudly.

'Our greatest apologies to you, Master, who is soon to be the only ruler of the Planet of Phoenix. It was foolish of us to be injured like this, although, the humans are weak, they are superior in numbers and intelligence that enables them to sneakily achieve blows against us during battles,' explains another one of the Potorians whose arm was broken by a group of men villagers from one of the battles within the smaller villages located in the far south of the Planet of Phoenix.

'There should be no excuses. If you were injured during these smaller village battles, how will you ensure that we creatures will be victorious in the great war that will incorporate many more numbers of humans who will possess better weapons and be more intelligent in enforcing preparation plans of battle defences?' moans Triton.

'Again our deepest apologies. We will not let nothing stand in your way of fulfilling your destiny in becoming the most powerful creature to ever rule the Planet of Phoenix, who will once and for all rid these pathetic and devious human inhabitants from this life,' says one of the Potorians who is standing at the front line of the thirty injured Potorians who are still facing Triton from a distance within his big main room in his Underground Dungeon.

'And another thing, even though you were pathetically injured, why have you returned here? You should have followed your brethren to Pine Village and faced the battle alongside them. I order you to return at once to Pine Village and aid the rest of the Potorians in the battle of Pine Village, as the winning species of this battle will cause a significant turning point for the great war between creatures and humans that has inevitably come to be,' orders Triton.

AS TRITON WAS just about to shout at his injured Potorians some more, Venus in her physical Quetzalcoatlus form swoops briskly into the narrow passageway that goes beneath the rocky terrain surface of the Realm of Deserted Lands, leading into Triton's Underground Dungeon. Venus screeches loudly from her long scaly beak, which pierces the ears of the injured Potorians, who quickly look all around them in fear of what they cannot yet see. The screams get unexpectedly louder and echo throughout Triton's Underground Dungeon. Venus suddenly enters forcefully into the big main room of Triton's Underground Dungeon. She flaps her large scaly wings over the Potorians' heads, which makes some of the Potorians crouch quickly to the ground in freight, while other Potorians run hurriedly to the rocky sides of the big main room in order to move away from this beast of a creature that is indeed Venus in her Quetzalcoatlus form.

Venus screeches loudly again and now flaps her large scaly wings to fly away from hovering over some of the crouched Potorians; she manoeuvres herself over to the other side of the big main room where Triton is standing anxiously by the side of the big wooden table. Venus flaps her large scaly wings again but in an alternative motion to enable her to glide slowly down to the ground, and as her pure white eyes turn back to their normal colour of red, she uses her Animagus abilities. Venus's physical body paranormally turns back into what Venus normally looks like, which shocks the Potorians who are watching her eagerly from a distance. Venus flicks her black silky hair over one of her petite shoulders and smiles cunningly at Triton; she opens one of her hands in front of Triton and shows him the anomaly crystal, which shines luminously with every colour of the rainbow and the shades of white and black; the colours frantically swirl around the middle of the anomaly crystal from within its diamond exterior.

'You managed to steal the anomaly crystal?' says a surprised and ecstatic Triton, remembering all the miserable years of being Lord Scartor's lieutenant and their many failed attempts of trying to locate and take the anomaly crystal for themselves.

'Well, of course I did, my love. Didn't I tell you I would retrieve it for us?' replies Venus shrewdly as she places the anomaly crystal into Triton's large strong hand. Triton looks deep into the anomaly crystal and stares at it for a moment in bewilderment.

'Yes, you did, my love. You always deliver the outcomes of your promises, and you're by far the most competent and specialist creature that has ever existed on the Planet of Phoenix. This is how orders are properly executed!' shouts Triton, turning around sharply and looking fiercely at his Potorians, who are now positioned back in their lines at the other side of the big main room. The Potorians look down to the ground as they try to shy away from Triton's angry gaze.

'Yes, Potorians, you will not fail my lover ever again, or you will have to face the wrath of my creature abilities,' states Venus as the Potorians gulp at the thought of the beasts and creatures they have seen Venus create as well as physically become herself.

'Ha-ha,' laughs Triton in amusement.

'I'm glad you are pleased, my love, but we must not linger,' states Venus.

'What do you mean? Now that we possess the anomaly crystal, we are invincible,' greedily replies Triton.

'You're correct. We are invincible, but we should act quickly before any devious plans develop in an attempt to try and stop us during the great war. I flew back here with the anomaly crystal to make sure it was at least safe in our possession. As we now possess the anomaly crystal with the blood of Grackle flowing within our bloodstreams, we have become privileged to unleash the mysterious powers of the most extraordinary magical artefact to have ever been created throughout the whole universe.' Venus grins.

'I can't wait to see what unworldly powers I can release from the anomaly crystal,' smirks Triton.

'I have already unleashed one of its many astonishing magical elements. The overwhelming feeling of such ultimate power was something that I've never experienced before, and all I want to do now is have a small taste of that feeling I experienced again,' favourably replies Venus.

'You are amazing. What was the power you generated from the anomaly crystal?' intriguingly says Triton.

'I created with my own hands an almighty and devastating lightning bolt that obliterated half of Raven's wife Emerald's mother's house back at Oak Village in an instance. But as I said, we should not waste time now as opportunities of hope by the humans will being generated as their hope will be the only thing to keep the humans united during the great war,' suspiciously says Venus.

'You seem disturbed, my love?' quickly says Triton.

'Yes, that is because, although, I did manage to kill Emerald's mother and steal the anomaly crystal from Emerald's wedding ring, I didn't manage to destroy Raven or any other humans as I wanted to make sure that there was no risk of losing the anomaly crystal back to the descendants of Grackle,' explains Venus.

'Don't ponder or worry about that, my woman. Now as we have the anomaly crystal, we're unstoppable and can kill as many humans as we desire to with the anomaly crystal. Those humans, including the descendant of Grackle, have lost all faith in beating us creatures during the forthcoming great war,' ecstatically mentions Triton as he slowly touches and rubs his fingers across one of Venus's cheeks.

'Wait, my love, you are indeed very strong and powerful and possess outstanding leadership traits, but there are also numerous sorcerous powers and items you do not understand. When I saw Raven back in Oak Village, I was shocked to see that he has the sword of Grackle in his possession,' describes Venus, looking deeply into Triton's eyes.

'The sword of Grackle? I thought Lord Scartor mentioned once to me that this sword was lost long ago in a battle that occurred within the Swamp Fields between creatures and humans,' answers a confused Triton.

'It probably was lost, but now it has reappeared and found its way into the hands of none other than the last remaining blood descendant of Grackle. Although we have the anomaly crystal to ourselves, this sword also possesses a great risk to creatures as I've heard a stab wound from this particular sword into a creature's body causes the blood, tissue, skin, bone, and organs to dissolve painfully from within. We must kill Raven quickly and take the sword of Grackle from him, before he has an opportunity to use it. I left a dove creature that I created back in Oak Village, which is currently circling around the main villages' perimeter in the far north of the Planet of Phoenix.

'When I was travelling back here, I used my Animagus abilities to connect with this dove creature, and through its eyes I saw Raven and Emerald along with two others, who I believe one of them to be Raven's cousin Parrot and, therefore, is also another blood descendant of Grackles. This Parrot was also riding with another woman accompanying Raven and Emerald, travelling towards Eagle Forest. I believe they are going to seek aid from that old sorcerer Hake and use him and his Hawks to fight against us in the great war. This will cause great resistance to our persistently separating creature forces,' states Venus intuitively.

'Will that stupid old fool Hake help them?' asks Triton in an irritated manner.

'Hake doesn't usually get involved with anything beyond his realm of Eagle Forest. However, I fear if he sees us now being a threat to Eagle Forest and his Hawks, then yes, he will possibly help Raven and his friends. That will make him a powerful creature in opposition to us. We do possess the anomaly crystal, but he is also a great sorcerer too. His understanding and manipulation of sorcery is nearly as close to what the legendary Grackle's was like when he was alive. I suggest we go to Eagle Forest immediately and defeat Hake, his Hawk Tribe, along with Raven and his friends before any of them can prepare for this great war,' exclaims Venus as Triton ponders a moment upon what Venus had just said.

'Potorians, bandage your wounds up now. You can come with us to aid in this long-awaited battle against Hake and the Hawks. Prove your worthiness to me once and for all. We march to Eagle Forest immediately!' orders Triton loudly.

'Of course, your wish is our command, our most powerful masters!' shout a couple of the injured Potorians who were more alert than those Potorians who had got back into their line formations and were still startled form the freight of Venus in her Quetzalcoatlus form.

'WAIT A MOMENT, Venus. What of Vicious and Vulture? Obviously you found the anomaly crystal in Oak Village and stole it from Emerald, but have they also destroyed Willow Village, or they're still searching for the anomaly crystal? Maybe they could be getting ready to attack Pine Village and search for the anomaly crystal there?' asks Triton.

'I don't know of their current location, but I will find out for you, my love,' replies Venus lovingly. Venus stands still just in front of Triton and concentrates as her red eyes turn to pure white, and as she uses her magical creature abilities, she is able to connect with the white dove's eyes that she had created earlier and left flying around the main village's perimeter. The white dove's eyes also now turn to pure white as Venus connects with the white dove, which enables Venus to see through the eyes of the white dove, just as the dove would have seen through its normal vision. The white dove creature flaps its small white feathery wings and circles high up in the sky, which has now turned darker from the recent setting of the sun. At present the white dove is flying around the perimeter of Willow Village in the north-east direction of the Planet of Phoenix. 'I see Willow Village in the far distance, and it is burning in flames. Destroyed homes and dead Willow villagers are scattered everywhere.'

'Virtuous!' laughs Triton. Venus continues using the white dove's vision to search around the areas of Willow Village with a more in-depth sight.

'That idiot beast! I now see Vulture. He is currently in his large form but is dead on the ground within Willow Village, nearby where the Willow villagers are putting out the fires of their homes. Willow Village seems to not have been completely destroyed, and I can't see any sign of Vicious yet,' explains Venus.

'He better not have betrayed me!' states Triton. The white dove's brain is manipulated by Venus's thought, which causes the white dove to manoeuvre to the ground and circle lower around more of the outer perimeter of Willow Village. After several minutes of searching lower to the ground, Venus sees through the white dove's Vicious, who is at present running through one of the corn fields in the south-west direction away from Willow Village.

Venus angrily uses her Animagus abilities to control the white dove's brain again and makes the white dove fly swiftly towards Vicious. The white dove flies abruptly and stops straight in front of Vicious. That startles him and causes him to stop his running pace immediately. Venus uses her Animagus abilities again to control the white dove's linguistic part of the brain, enabling her to be able to speak out aloud in Triton's Underground Dungeon, and causing the white dove to also speak Venus's words to Vicious.

'Why are you running from Willow Village? Vulture has been killed, and there are still humans alive?' states Venus to Vicious, who is shocked for a brief moment at a dove speaking to him. Until after a moment he realises that it is Venus speaking to him via the white dove.

'Vulture was stupidly killed. That made me outnumbered. I thought it was best to regroup with the Potorian army and attack again for a higher chance of winning a battle at Willow Village. I will also continue searching for the anomaly crystal there,' says Vicious wearily to the white dove, holding on to his injured back to comfort it.

'You are a warrior creature and one of the strongest that exists on the Planet of Phoenix. You will never be outnumbered by the likes of the weaker human species,' states Venus snappishly.

'Tell him how disappointed I am at his failure,' interrupts Triton, but Triton's words are ignored by Venus.

'Never mind. It doesn't matter now as we have the anomaly crystal. Triton and I are going to Eagle Forest to kill Raven and his friends as well as also destroy Hake and the Hawk Tribe there too. As we speak; 166 Potorians are marching towards Pine Village. Meet up with them immediately on the south-west side within the Grass Terrain Fields of the perimeter of Pine Village. Meet them quickly before they start attacking Pine Village. You are to lead the Potorian army in the battle of Pine Village. You will prove yourself to us now by destroying Pine Village. Burn it to the ground with your creature abilities and obliterate all of its villagers who exist there. This is your last chance, Vicious. Do not fail us again, or you will experience the rage and full power of the anomaly crystal!' Venus shouts as she controls the white dove, making it flap its small feathery wings in order to fly quickly up high into the sky and out of sight from Vicious's vision.

Vicious watches the white dove fly up into the sky until he sees it no more; he then hurriedly races through the corn fields in the direction towards to the south-west side of Pine Village to regroup with the Potorian army in the Grass Terrain Fields within Pine Village's perimeter. Venus uses her Animagus abilities to disconnect with the white dove's brain, and her eyes now turn back to pure red again.

'Another failure by one of my henchman,' says an annoyed Triton.

'It doesn't matter now, my love. We have the anomaly crystal and are soon going to be the most powerful rulers the inhabitants of the Planet of Phoenix have ever seen. We will then expand our rule across the whole universe and will experience the pleasures of our victory. We can punish whoever we like and however we desire to, but only after we have secured our position as the main rulers. You will soon understand that all good things come to those who wait for it and most truly yearn for it. First we must destroy Hake and his Hawk Tribe in Eagle Forest, and then we will enforce the great war against King Exodus and Falcon City. But I think that we should gain the help of Viper and his Serpents, who will be a great help in defeating the royal Falcon guards and hence diminish the last remaining threat that the humans residing on the Planet of Phoenix hold against us,' exclaims Venus.

'Although, I don't trust Viper, I trust your knowledge, and I agree that this will be the best plan to move forward with. I couldn't have done any of this without you, my love. You will always remain at my side as the queen of the Planet of Phoenix and then the universe,' says Triton, leaning inwards to kiss Venus passionately on her tender lips. During this conversation between Triton and Venus, the thirty Potorians had bandaged most of their cuts and wounds. They are now currently standing near the passageway that leads out of the big main room of Triton's Underground Dungeon. The Potorians are patiently waiting for Triton's and Venus's orders. Triton bites Venus's lip before he stops kissing her. He then collects his golden chain with the spiked iron ball at the end of it that had he had placed under the bed in his and Venus's bedroom in another part of his Underground Dungeon.

'It will take weeks to get to Eagle Forest on foot,' says an exhausted Potorian to Venus as they all wait for Triton to return to the big main room.

'No need to concern yourself with such matters. I have that taken care of.' Venus laughs and flickers her eyelashes and walks towards the Potorians near the passageway in the big main room.

After ten minutes, Triton returns to the big main room of his Underground Dungeon; he walks alongside Venus out of the passageway at one side of the big main room of Triton's Underground Dungeon. This passageway leads up to the rocky surface of the Realm of Deserted Lands. The thirty Potorians also quickly follow Triton and Venus to the ground above them. Venus stands upon a big rock that is laid upon the rocky terrain covering the Realm of Deserted Lands. She looks behind her and sees the thirty Potorians reach the top of the passageway. Venus smiles and then concentrates briefly until her eyes turn pure white, and she uses her Animagus abilities to turn her whole physical body into a very huge and muscly dinosaur called Argentinosaurus. The Argentinosaurus is the biggest dinosaur from the Sauropod family. It is massive and the biggest dinosaur that Venus has ever turned herself into. The height of the Argentinosaurus is thirty-seven meters, and it's length stretches to an incredible fifty-one meters. The thick skin of the Argentinosaurus is so tough that it can't be penetrated, and its tough feet can walk across or crush any living being or environmental terrain beneath it.

The Potorians stand in bewilderment as Venus's fragile and beautiful body turns into this massive dinosaur; the Potorians have never seen a creature this big on the Planet of Phoenix before. Venus, as her Argentinosaurus physical form, swings her large tail from side to side and roars noisily just as this dinosaur would. Triton laughs and uses his strong and powerful legs to jump up high on to the back of the Argentinosaurus; he holds on to the anomaly crystal and his golden chain with the iron spiked ball at the end of it. The Potorians hurry to one of the front legs of the Argentinosaurus and begin to help each other climb on to the back of Venus in her Argentinosaurus form where Triton is currently sitting.

After all the Potorians manage to climb on top of the Argentinosaurus's back, Venus walks quickly with her large feet that cover large distances easily. She is unharmed and unaffected by the gusty winds that swirl around the Realm of Deserted Lands that are filled with tiny dirt, rock, sand, and gristle particles, but Triton and the Potorians have to cover their faces to prevent these particles from getting stuck in their eyes. Venus travels in her Argentinosaurus form in the far north-east direction through the Realm of Deserted Lands and the Swamp Fields towards Eagle Forest.

Twenty-Three

RAVEN AND EMERALD, who were riding on the sturdy black back of Felix, along with Parrot and Sapphire, who were riding close by on the back of another brown horse, had galloped the quickest way to Eagle Forest from Pine Village, where they had taken the direct south-west route leading straight across the vast Grass Terrain Fields without passing through Oak Village in order to save them precious time. They gallop swiftly and ride hard over the rough, springy, and immense Grass Terrain Fields for a couple of hours through the dark sky. They now end up reaching the outskirts of the extensive and secluded Eagle Forest.

As Raven approaches the outskirts of Eagle Forest first, he pulls firmly on the brown rope reins of Felix to make him halt to a stop; shortly after Parrot does the same to his brown horse. Raven and Parrot have both stopped their horses in front of the numerous tall and wide trees of various types. Raven, Emerald, Parrot, and Sapphire have never seen such types of trees before. These tall and wide trees illuminate slightly with the colours of brown, red, green, and orange; they stand fixed into the ground at the boundaries of Eagle Forest. Although they are solid in their posture, these mysterious wide and tall trees also move very slightly and slowly in a rippling effect. These trees are so tall that the leaves and vegetation at the top of the trees cannot be seen from the ground. Raven, Emerald, Parrot, and Sapphire gaze for a moment into the deep and dark space within Eagle Forest. This is a place and environment that they have never been to before or know of any villager that had.

Within Eagle Forest, however, the area is littered with many other different types of tall trees that include oak like myrtle and live oak, pine like longleaf and pond pine, willow, kapok, hawthorn, elm, sea grape, and fiddlewood trees, some of the trees residing within Eagle Forest have survived here for over thousands of years. Various nuts and berries also grow upon the trees within Eagle Forest. Many different types of shrubs, bushes, plants, and flowers grow here and nurture and feed the numerous wild animals that take safe haven within the protective boundaries of Eagle Forest when they are escaping away from the nomad warriors who try and hunt these wild animals within the Wastelands or the Swamp Fields.

'Where is the Hawk Tribe located in Eagle Forest?' asks Parrot, baffled.

'I'm not sure. I've never been in Eagle Forest myself before,' replies Sapphire.

'Not many humans have,' states Raven.

'I had read about the mysterious Eagle Forest in the ancient book that had been written at the beginning of time that is written in the ancient Phoenix language. Only this one ancient book remains. It's over hundreds of years old and contains secret information of the past with regards to the forever lasting conflict between humans and creatures. This ancient book resides in our most safe and cleansed room located at Falcon University within Falcon City as the information contained within this precious book cannot be lost from the human's knowledge. I think it's best if we head for the centre of Eagle Forest first. The Hawk Tribe will probably find us by that point anyway,' says Sapphire wearily.

'Let's hope they're friendly,' states Parrot as he jumps down from his brown horse and then also helps Sapphire down from it. Raven and Emerald also do the same and climb down from Felix, being careful with the weapons they were all carrying in their hands and around their bodies. Raven pats Felix strongly on his large back as a sign of appreciation for galloping fast on their journey to Eagle Forest. Raven now holds the brown rope reins of Felix, just as Parrot does with his brown horse as they now all begin walking cautiously and steadily throughout the trees in the secretive Eagle Forest. They all walk for many miles within Eagle Forest where they continually head in the same direction from what they had started walking in. As they continue deep within the middle, which is also known as the heart of Eagle Forest, the air becomes misty and a strange silence lingers except from the occasional soft sounds and noises that are made by the trees, plants, and animals hiding somewhere from within Eagle Forest.

Raven, Emerald, Parrot, and Sapphire are very exhausted from their long journey and are also currently nervous from the environment they are walking through, but still they remain walking and continue passing in between several trees, shrubs, bushes, plants, flowers, and passageways through Eagle Forest They see countless different types of trees, plants, and small animals; many of that they have also never have seen before or have ever heard about from any other humans, although Sapphire remembers some information that was written in the ancient book at Falcon University regarding the enigmatic trees, plants, and animals that reside within Eagle Forest. Raven, Emerald, Parrot, and Sapphire occasionally see glimpses of diverse and big animals that are located high up in the treetops; they can also hear tiny noises made by these scurrying animals moving around from tree to tree. They experience an eerie feeling that they are being closely monitored as they look all around them for signs of the Hawk Tribe.

'We have been walking for ages, and we haven't found any sign of the Hawk Tribe yet. Are you sure they are still in existence?' says Emerald, who is still deeply upset and devastated from Ruby's death that occurred only hours ago. This overwhelming knowledge was the only thing that had been on Emerald's mind since she found out that Venus had maliciously killed her back in Oak Village. It has now ruined her life forever.

'I really do think that Hake and the Hawk Tribe do still exist on the Planet of Phoenix as these creatures are immortal and can only die if they are killed by another human or creature. But the ancient book I read at Falcon University was very old, so I suppose the Hawk Tribe could have moved from Eagle Forest by now. I'm sorry but I really don't know,' replies Sapphire despondently.

SUDDENLY, FOUR SMALL dwarf bird-like creatures with pure green eyes and small brown beaks for mouths glide down from the very tall trees, using their brown feathery winged arms, and once they gently land upon the ground of Eagle Forest that is covered with grass, twigs, and dirt, they quickly surround Raven, Emerald, Parrot, Sapphire, Felix, and the other brown horse. These four Hawks have light-brown skin, with wrinkly faces, hands, and feet that they don't cover with any shoes or clothes upon their bodies. The four Hawks speedily point their wooden spears they had been carrying in front of them at everyone they are surrounding, except not at Felix and the other brown horse.

'What are you doing in our Eagle Forest?' asks a Hawk quickly and begrudgingly in a very stern and crocked voice.

'We come in peace. We have come with urgency to speak with your tribe leader Hake to ask him for his help in these forthcoming dangerous times,' quickly replies Sapphire while worriedly looking at one of the wooden spears a Hawk had lunged in front of her face.

'Our leader Hake and the Hawk Tribe don't concern ourselves with those troubles of others beyond Eagle Forest,' states another one of the four Hawks again in a crocked voice with distorted speech that meant he couldn't pronounce all his words accurately.

'Once Triton has taken over the Planet of Phoenix, he will not leave Eagle Forest to itself, and by that time you will have no other allies to aid in defending this long-standing forest with,' snaps Emerald.

'We are capable of protecting Eagle Forest ourselves and have done so for countless years. We are gifted with a great creature ability that permits us to shoot powerful laser beams from our eyes, and our tribe leader Hake is the most powerful master at sorcery that now exists on this Planet of Phoenix. He can defeat any threatening foe, especially that beast man Triton,' remarks another one of the four surrounding Hawkes impatiently, sticking his wooden spear in Emerald's face.

'We mean no disrespect. It's just that unfortunately Triton has the anomaly crystal in his possession now, and there's an evil woman who seems to be some sort of witch. She also possess dark powers unlike we have never experienced or heard of before,' says Raven as one of the four surrounding Hawks interrupt him while lowering his wooden spear from Raven's and Emerald's faces.

'Triton possesses the anomaly crystal? How has the bloodline of Grackle failed in protecting this most precious crystal?' asks another one of the four Hawks angrily as he also lowers his wooden spear from Sapphire's face, wanting to find out more information regarding the anomaly crystal.

'We were protecting the anomaly crystal and have done so for many years, but we were roguishly deceived by this evil witch. She killed my mother Ruby and turned into her physical body. She had the same voice and looked exactly like her. How was I supposed to have known that it wasn't my mother?' cries Emerald hysterically at the thought of her mother's death.

'She's a Metamorphmagi?' answers one of the Hawks.

'This is very bad. You don't hear of any Metamorphmagi still existing on the Planet of Phoenix. We shall take you to our tribe leader Hake immediately. Follow us quickly, humans,' says another one of the four surrounding Hawks who completely lowers his wooden spear and hurriedly runs in a rather strange but quiet manner across the ground of Eagle Forest in a different direction to where Raven, Emerald, Parrot, and Sapphire were initially heading. The other three Hawks also quickly run, following the other Hawk, and Raven, Emerald, Parrot, and Sapphire, along with Felix and the brown horse, also quickly follow the Hawks through the interlinking and twining passages residing within Eagle Forest.

THE AIR IS still misty, but it's somehow still transparent in the middle of Eagle Forest. The faint but bright line of sunlight glistens through this misty air that helps to light up the generally dark Eagle Forest due to the very tall trees covering the sky and shadowing the sun rays that shine down upon Eagle Forest. After around forty minutes of running at a steady pace in a direction of Eagle Forest different from the one Raven, Emerald, Parrot, and Sapphire were originally walking in, they, along with Felix, the brown horse, and the four Hawks eventually reach the Hawks' Tribe Camp.

The Hawks' Tribe Camp is developed from several small wooden huts built up at different heights and fixed upon some of the tall and wide trees, along with a few of these wooden huts also being built and located upon the ground of Eagle Forest. These small wooden huts have been built from the wood of those trees that fall naturally to the ground as the Hawks would not chop down any trees to build their homes with; also the large branches and leaves that fall to the ground from the tall trees have been used for the roofs of these small wooden huts. The many small wooden huts have connecting ropes that interlink between all the huts, enabling food and objects to be passed between the Hawks within their small wooden huts. Also in the Hawks' Tribe Camp, the Hawks have created very small wooden huts specifically developed within the inside of the tall and wide trees that are used to keep the new smaller animals' offspring warm and safe. The Hawks also assist the other animals of the forest in caring for and raising their offspring.

There's a bigger wooden hut amongst the Hawks' Tribe Camp that is located on the ground. It's made of thick and sturdy wood, large branches, potent leaves, and colourful cloth. This bigger wooden hut is fixed in front of the biggest and oldest Kapok tree located precisely in the exact middle of Eagle Forest; this bigger wooden hut is home to the Hawk Tribe's leader Hake. The four Hawks swiftly lead Raven, Emerald, Parrot, Sapphire, Felix and the other brown horse through the centre of the Hawks' Tribe Camp; the other seventy-six Hawks eagerly watch these humans from their small wooden huts located against and around the tall trees as they all pass beneath them through the Hawks' Tribe Camp, and several of these Hawks murmur whispers to one another regarding the humans, which makes Parrot and Sapphire feel a bit uneasy.

Two of the four Hawks currently walking on the ground tie Felix and the other brown horse carefully to trees within the Hawks' Tribe Camp, while other members of the Hawk Tribe quickly climb down from the tall and wide trees and begin to fetch water and vegetation food for these horses in order to refuel them both form the long journey they had recently been on. The other two of the four Hawks continue to lead Raven, Emerald, Parrot, and Sapphire into the bigger wooden hut against the Kapok tree where Hake lives; the entrance to this bigger wooden hut is covered with a thick colourful cloth made in the colours of brown, red, green, and orange. The two Hawks hold up the colourful cloth and permit Raven, Emerald, Parrot, and Sapphire to walk into the big wooden hut.

Hake is a small dwarf bird-like creature with large pure green eyes like the eyes of an owl, and he has a small red beak for a mouth. Hake has lived for over a thousand years and now has long grey hair that covers his entire body except for the red and brown feathers that cover his small arms and legs. Hake has a wrinkly face and wrinkly hands and feet that he never covers with shoes, nor does he have clothes upon his body; his skin is dark brown in colour. Hake also has the ability to rotate his whole head around his neck without moving his body, just like an owl does.

Hake is currently sitting cross-legged on the ground at the end of his big wooden hut; he's facing in the direction opposite to the entrance that is covered with the colourful cloth. Hake has his eyes closed, and he's murmuring the ancient Phoenix language to himself that Raven, Emerald, and Parrot had never heard spoken before, but Sapphire slightly recognises this ancient Phoenix Language due to having her PhD in ancient language and literature as well as from reading and studying the writings in the ancient book that had been written in the ancient Phoenix language. In Hake's big wooden hut, there's a black cauldron that is made from stone and placed in the middle of the big wooden hut. The black cauldron has hot green liquid bubbling inside; there are also various candles, magic potions, and enchantment and sorcery books placed upon wooden shelves that had been fixed against the sides of this big wooden hut.

'Hake, leader of the Hawk Tribe, we have come in peace to humbly ask for your help in our most urgent time of need,' says Sapphire humbly as she walks into the big wooden hut and notices Hake sitting cross-legged on the ground at the opposite side of the big wooden hut. Hake becomes silent and stops murmuring the ancient Phoenix language; he stays in the same cross-legged sitting position but mystically manoeuvres his whole body slowly around on the ground without using his wrinkly hands or turning his head around at the same time. After a moment's pause, Hake also manoeuvres his head to turn around his neck to face the entrance of his big wooden hut. Hake, however, keeps his eyes closed. Sapphire looks at Raven, and then Emerald and Parrot, in confusion.

'You're a very intelligent woman and will be greatly relied upon before this uncertain time has renewed itself. Sapphire, I believe your name is,' murmurs Hake in a deep voice that causes Sapphire to stand in astonishment and speechlessness as Hake now opens his eyes and looks at her intuitively. Hake then slowly turns his head towards Emerald and gazes with his large green eyes upon her and speaks.

'Emerald, you must free your mind from the recent tragedy that has now unfortunately happened to your mother Ruby. Otherwise, it will be the death of you also.' Tears start to drip down Emerald's cold and dirty cheeks. Hake slowly moves his head a bit, and he now faces towards and looks proudly at Parrot.

'Parrot, a loyal friend you are and an honourable father and soon-to-be husband. Look after your loved ones closely for I feel much loss has already come to your ancestors.' Parrot looks puzzled, and as he is just about to ask a question about what Hake had said to him regarding his ancestors, Hake now focuses his attention and turns to face Raven, He notices the sword that Raven carries with him and is gripped tightly within one of Raven's hands. Hake reads the ancient Phoenix language markings carved in silver writing down the middle of this gold sword with an attached silver handle.

'Blessed be the bloodline of Grackle . . . Raven, you are holding the legendary and specially created sword of Grackle. You and Parrot possess the prevailing blood of Grackle within you. How honoured I am to be in the presence of the last remaining relations to the most extraordinary wizard that has ever existed upon this Planet of Phoenix,' murmurs Hake thankfully.

'We have travelled many hours to meet you here to plea for your help against . . .' speaks Raven sympathetically as Hake interrupts him.

'I know why you all have journeyed against your logic and trepidations that has now led you deep into Eagle Forest for the purpose of seeking the help of the Hawk Tribe along with mine. But yet you already know that we don't pursue to involve ourselves with the territory and anarchy beyond the realms of Eagle Forest. However, you also know in your hearts that we will indeed aid you against Triton and his evil woman, who is known as Venus. These treacherous creatures possess the almighty anomaly crystal and are already on their way to Eagle Forest with the intention of destroying us all,' states Hake as his voice deepens.

RAVEN, EMERALD, PARROT, and Sapphire begin to panic due to what Hake has just said; Raven turns and kisses Emerald softly on the cheek as Parrot also hugs Sapphire strongly.

'How are you able to know what is happening beyond Eagle Forest? How do you possess the knowledge of who we are?' asks Raven curiously as he turns back towards Hake and holds on to Emerald's hand firmly.

'I see all that occurs beyond Eagle Forest via my magical sorcery from this black caldron that I have generated. I know all about you and what is happening on the Planet of Phoenix as I have been watching over it for an eternity. I knew you were coming here to visit me and why. I know what question you are about to ask me next, but unfortunately there's nothing I could have done to stop all that has happened to everyone with regards to their pain and suffering up until this point due to a vow I made long ago not to interfere with the lives of humans or creatures outside of Eagle Forest. But now I feel my time is also coming to an end. We will help you now and be on the humans' side during this great war against the creatures, mainly Triton and Venus. I will attempt to retrieve the anomaly crystal from them at all costs and give it back to the bloodline of Grackle where it belongs.

'Raven, it's time for you to find out your ancestral past and the truth behind your inevitable destiny. I have known Grackle for many centuries, as we constantly practised peaceful and white magic together in a time where kind and wondrous nature lived in harmony with one another all across the lands over the Planet of Phoenix. We all lived in peace with the creatures. Grackle and I resided in a small and beautiful place known as Alder Village that used to be located near the spiritual Hydra Springs.

'Due to circumstances beyond our control, something happened that we never expected to occur. Over 200 years ago, Grackle's wife Angelina unfortunately died during childbirth. She gave birth to the eldest twin Sparrow, who is your great-great-grandfather, and she then also gave birth to the youngest twin. But during the second birth, there were unexpected complications that scarred the child for life and also killed Angelina during the birth of this child. Grackle was devastated at the loss of his beloved wife Angelina as they were connected together in body, heart, and soul for many decades.

Grackle tried to treat both of his sons equally but unintentionally neglected the youngest twin due to his birth causing the death of his soulmate Angelina. I thus helped Grackle in the twins' upbringing and trained them both to be protectors and lords of the Planet of Phoenix, just as Grackle and I had done for an eternity.

'Sparrow found himself born to be a resilient unique leader and physical fighter, which is why Grackle used his ultimate magical powers to forge the superior shield and sword of Grackle to give to Sparrow. The sword of Grackle has now found its way into your hands, Raven. The youngest twin found himself born to be a master of sorcery. Hence Grackle forged a golden sceptre for him in order to enhance his magical powers. The youngest twin was an introvert and was regrettably teased about his scarred face and causing the death of his mother Angelina during his birth by the other school children from the Alder School that was located within Alder Village. Sparrow used to protect his younger twin brother from these human bullies, but due to the torture the youngest twin received from the other Alder School children and from this torment that he constantly experienced within his mind with the knowledge of his birth killing his mother, the youngest twin became twisted with hatred and evil against humanity.

'As time passed, the youngest twin left the home of his father Grackle. He relocated from Alder Village and ended up residing upon Crow Mountain amongst the Mountains of Doom. Grackle was now aware of the threat from his youngest son with regards to the dark powers he now possessed, along with the other creatures developing upon the Planet of Phoenix who would join forces with his youngest son and would one day enforce a great war against the humans. Recognising this terrible future, Grackle unwillingly created the anomaly crystal to protect the Planet of Phoenix from obliteration.

'Grackle sacrificed himself and was required to use all of his life force in order to be able to transfer all of his magical powers, knowledge, and wisdom into a crystal that he had crafted from the raw materials that were located at the bottom of one of the hot springs within Hydra Springs. By giving this crystal every part of Grackle's soul, it made the crystal have extraordinary elemental powers. Grackle named this crystal the anomaly crystal, and it was supposed to be utilised in times of great misfortunes. Grackle forged the anomaly crystal so that only his bloodline could wield the anomaly crystal's magnificent powers. Although, this also meant that his youngest son could also manipulate the anomaly crystal if he indeed managed to get his hands upon the anomaly crystal too. Grackle left the anomaly crystal with me with instructions to give it to his eldest son Sparrow. I had to explain to Sparrow the reasons why Grackle had sacrificed his life in order to create the anomaly crystal as well as then continue to make sure that this knowledge was passed down through Grackle's descendants about how important it was to guard the anomaly crystal with all of their heart and love.

'After my great friend Grackle sacrificed himself, I felt alone in Alder Village. This is when I used my own sorcerous powers to clone myself. I created eighty Hawks resembling my creature abilities and hence began my own Hawk Tribe. I also relocated to Eagle Forest where I felt I could live secluded in peace with my children for as long as possible. During this time, the youngest twin sensed with his black magic that the anomaly crystal had now been forged by his father Grackle. Along with his lieutenant and his newly gathered army of nomad warriors, he declared hostility against Sparrow and the Alder Village humans. A series of horrible battles continued for a long time between the Alder Village humans and these creatures, where Viper and his Serpents also involved themselves in the desired search for the renowned anomaly crystal. Both human and creature sides killed countless from the opposing enemy along with destroying each other's homes and environments. Eventually, the youngest twin completely destroyed the entire Alder Village along with most of its human inhabitants. the surviving Alder villagers who escaped Alder Village took refuge at either Pine Village or Oak Village that were being newly developed at the time.

'The younger twin's desperate search for the anomaly crystal forced him to kill his elder twin brother Sparrow using his dark magic black laser beam created from his golden sceptre in a great battle that took place in the Wastelands and the Swamp Fields, where the sword of Grackle was also lost in the depths in one of the muddy bogs existing there. The younger twin was furious to find that Sparrow did not have the anomaly crystal on him at the time of his death as earlier that day Sparrow had given the anomaly crystal to his wife Star, who in turn, passed it to their son Trogon. Sparrow had convinced his wife to leave Alder Village and seek refuge in one of the other villages existing on the Planet of Phoenix, and they eventually decided to settle in Oak Village.

'The younger twin, Raven, as you may have probably guessed by now was Lord Scartor, and he continued his search for numerous years to find the anomaly crystal so that he could inevitably wield its astonishing powers by possessing the blood from his father Grackle in attempt to become the one ruler over the Planet of Phoenix. It seems now that before he could take the much-wanted anomaly crystal for himself and fulfil his upmost desires, he was betrayed by his Lieutenant Triton and his woman Venus,' explains Hake thoroughly as Raven stands shocked and in disbelief at the information he has just heard from Hake.

'I'm glad that horrible and malicious Lord Scartor was betrayed! But I've seen that Venus woman use the anomaly crystal. How can she wield it if she's not related to Grackle?' asks Emerald impatiently.

'I'm aware that Venus and Triton drank Lord Scartor's blood after they murdered him, which means they now also possess the bloodline of Grackle within them, enabling them to have the gift of being able to wield the anomaly crystal's elemental powers. You must all be extra careful of Venus. They do indeed have the anomaly crystal in their possession, but she also has dark powers beyond any other creature on the Planet of Phoenix,' cautiously says Hake cautiously.

'I don't believe all of this is happening and all the family and loved ones we have tragically lost along the way, and will continue to lose many more humans due to the past mistakes of some of our other ancestors in the past,' says Raven, confused.

'I'm sorry that this is happening to you all, but we must prepare quickly as there's not much time left before danger comes this way. Hawks, prepare the Hawks' Tribe Camp for battle. We must defend Eagle Forest and the Planet of Phoenix with our last breath. Do whatever it takes to reclaim the anomaly crystal from these evil creatures,' states Hake immediately to the two Hawks currently within the big wooden hut that were standing next to Raven, Emerald, Parrot, and Sapphire. These two Hawks nod at Hake and quickly rush outside the big wooden hut through the colourful cloth. They proactively share Hake's commands with the other seventy-eight

Hawks residing within the Hawks' Tribe Camp to prepare for battle against Triton, Venus, and the Potorians forthcoming.

All the Hawks begin to grab their wooden spears and position themselves at different locations high up in the tall and wide trees throughout Eagle Forest.

'We will help defend Eagle Forest with you. What do you want us to do?' asks Parrot.

'Gather your horses and protect each other from harm's way. We will have a unique part to play in this battle and the inevitable great war that will become clear to us all in due course,' replies Hake. Raven, Emerald, Parrot, and Sapphire now also leave Hake's big wooden hut through the colourful cloth. They hurriedly grab Felix and the brown horse that were attached to one of the trees. Raven and Emerald climb on top of Felix as Parrot and Sapphire also climb on top of the brown horse; they nod proudly and affectionately at each other in hope and then quickly position themselves at different locations within the Hawks' Tribe Camp; each of them carries their weapons close to their bodies, ready to protect themselves and one another.

Hake now stands up from sitting on the ground within his big wooden hut. He begins to take a few different coloured potions from the top of the wooden shelves fixed upon the wooden sides of his big wooden hut and begins to pour them into the black cauldron. The green bubbling liquid inside the black cauldron interacts with the new coloured potions that Hake has just poured into it, and it magically creates an invisible but transparent mirror-like ball that suddenly hovers above the black cauldron, portraying the visual images of Triton and the thirty Potorians on the back of Venus as her Argentinosaurus form. All are swiftly travelling across the Swamp Fields and coming ever closer to Eagle Forest. Hake watches these visual images through this magical invisible mirror-like ball with concern.

Twenty-Four

VICIOUS CONTINUES SPRINTING in the direction he had been running in towards the south-west side perimeter of Pine Village with the purpose of regrouping with the recklessly approaching Potorian army of 166 men marching across the Grass Terrain Fields within Pine Village's perimeter. The sky high above the Planet of Phoenix continues to turn darker as it's now the time of late evening to early night, where the immense burning and bright sun has further settled beautifully upon the west horizon. As the last orangey glows and reflection from the sun's light fades slowly away into darkness, thick clustered clouds that had been accumulating within the air start realising droplets of cold rain that fall quickly down to the ground. These droplets of cold rain mix with the gusty and strong winds, enabling the cold rain to scatter across the Potorians' faces as they march strongly through the Grass Terrain Fields, approaching the south-side perimeter of Pine Village.

Vicious raises his large and bulky head as he continues to sprint swiftly, where in the far distance he sees an army of Potorians marching in formation across the Grass Terrain Fields that have become muddy due to the rain. The Potorians are marching with tenacity and are holding their metal swords and metal axes out in front of them, ready for battle. Vicious increases his speed to quickly meet the marching Potorians and come in close proximity with the front lines of the Potorian army. Just as Vicious reaches the Potorian army, he stops in front of the Potorians and catches his breath as all the Potorians now stop marching.

'I have just spoken with Venus and have now been ordered to lead this Potorian army in the battle against Pine Village,' states Vicious directly and confidently while breathing heavily form all the sprinting he has just done from Willow Village.

'As you command, Vicious, we will follow yours, Triton's and Venus's orders. In this battle of Pine Village we will do as you command where you will lead us all into victory so that we can return to Triton with such glorious news,' says one of the Potorians in response to Triton.

'Kill all the humans for Triton and Venus!' shouts another Potorian; the other Potorians cheer and shout as the rain starts to pour heavier upon their heads and faces.

'Where is Vulture? Is he flying over Pine Village as we speak?' asks another Potorian from the back of the Potorian army, looking high up in the dark sky for Vulture.

'Vulture was stupidly killed back at Willow Village, which caused us to lose that battle. We must attack Pine Village quickly and hard, before Pine Village can receive any help from Willow Village. Attack Pine Village now while these pathetic humans are unprepared for battle!' shouts Vicious as he punches his crunched fist up in the air; he turns around and without hesitation charges towards the west entrance wooden gate of Pine Village. Vicious is instantly followed by the Potorian army, where they all run in anger and rage across the sticky mud of the Grass Terrain Fields, where the now firmer rainstorm starts thrashing water hard over their bodies.

'What in hell is that?' shouts Bruce in a concerned voice as he gazes far into the distance from the south-east small wooden watchtower that was positioned at the south-east corner of Pine Village.

'What can you see, Bruce?' nervously replies a Pine guard who was standing next to Bruce on watch duty upon this the small wooden watchtower.

'Do the gods not show us humans any mercy? It's a creature army approaching the east entrance gate of Pine Village!' bellows Bruce as he quickly turns to another side of the small wooden tower in the south-east corner of Pine Village to blow hard into a ram's horn that had been displayed in this wooden watchtower in order to send a loud and alarming sound that is now heard throughout the whole of Pine Village.

The ram horn's deep sound is a warning signal against creature attacks. Most of the Pine Villagers were already in Pinus Tavern for Pinus Tavern remembrance service; they suddenly hear this ram horn's sound and begin to panic and hold their loved ones in fear of a creature attack. The 300 Pine guards remaining in Pine Village, who were positioned throughout Pine Village in different locations, also hear the loud displeasing sound of the ram's horn. These Pine guards quickly race through any of the small wooden houses, flats, and shops along the cobbled paths throughout Pine Village to sprint towards the east entrance wooden gate of Pine Village in an effort to join Flame and the Pine guards already positioned there. They will attempt to defend Pine Village against Vicious and the fast approaching violent Potorian army.

The Pine guards running through Pine Village are also joined by another 200 able-bodied men Pine villagers who had been gathered during the day by the Pine guards to aid them in the Pine Village battle as requested by Lynx. These 200 men Pine villagers carry wooden spears and kitchen and farm tools, whereas the Pine guards carry their metal swords and shields, along with thirty Pine guards also saddled upon on horses. Now all are getting closer to the west entrance wooden gate of Pine Village, ready for battle.

AS VICIOUS, ACCOMPANIED by the Potorian army, charges furiously close towards Pine Village's west entrance wooden gate and the big wooden fence surrounding the perimeter, the Pine guards within the small wooden watchtower at the west entrance wooden gate begin to shoot the Potorians with wooden arrows with metal spikes at the end of them from their wooden bows. These wooden arrows fly through the air, piercing through the heavy and cold rain that now covers the whole of Pine Village. The wooden arrows puncture sharply into the fleshy necks and faces of Potorians and kill several of them quickly. They fall to the ground and are then unintentionally trampled over by the rest of the Potorian army that is advancing forward in a scurrying manner. As Vicious hastily approaches the west entrance wooden gate of Pine Village, he sees the big wooden barricade that had been constructed in front of the west entrance wooden gate to stop him and the Potorians from breaking through.

Vicious swiftly halts his running pace to stand at the front of this big wooden barricade and laughs; he takes one deep breath to release a large gush of burning fire from his mouth. Vicious uses his intense fire breath to set the big wooden barricade on fire; the Potorian army and Vicious patiently stand still while shouting war chants as they watch the big wooden barricade quickly burn to black ash. The black cloudy smoke caused from the burning of the big wooden barricade is now forced up by the gusty winds and quickly covers the west and south side of Pine Village, making it difficult for the Pine guards in the south-west wooden watchtowers to be able to shoot their wooden arrows at the Potorians as they can hardly see them through the black cloudy smoke.

As the rest of the Pine guards and Pine villagers see this black cloudy smoke spread throughout Pine Village like a plague of rats, they begin to panic about what will happen next and quickly try to prepare themselves mentally for a ghastly fight against the creatures. Vicious loses his patience, and along with the Potorian army, he charges and strongly barges into this burning big wooden barricade. Vicious and the Potorians push forcefully straight through this burnt and damaged wood, and, although they are slightly burnt by the big wooden barricade, it's easily forced out of the way to allow Vicious and the Potorian army to enter into Pine Village in a violent manner. They begin to fight a bloody battle with the Pine guards and men Pine villagers at the west entrance wooden gate.

Many of the men Pine villagers at the west entrance wooden gate are killed quickly and easily by the Potorians as they use their sharp metal axes to slice their heads and limbs off their fragile bodies. The Potorians also stab the men Pine villagers through the chest and faces with their metal swords. The Pine guards who carried metal shields and armour and had been better trained at fighting manage to block some of the metal sword and axe attacks from the Potorians and are able to defend themselves. The Pine guards that blocked the attacks from the Potorians quickly position themselves and luckily inflict stabbed attacks at the Potorians. They stab the Potorians continuously until they die upon the cobbled paths of

Pine Village in the black cloudy smoke. The painful and agonising screams of men Pine villagers and Potorians being killed, along with the piercing sounds of metal weapons clashing against one another, are heard by other Pine villagers throughout Pine Village. After hearing such terrifying noises, the rest of the Pine villagers scamper throughout Pine Village, frantically looking for a place to hide. These Pine villagers begin to barricade the front wooden doors of their small wooden houses, flats, and shops.

'Pine guards, attack and send these creatures far away from Pine Village!' shouts Flame as he charges with dozens of Pine guards towards Vicious and the Potorian army, who had just barged their way through the big wooden barricade at the west entrance gate of Pine Village. Flame, along with many Pine guards, sprints upon his feet towards the Potorian army, and as soon as they come face to face with these Potorians, Flame and the Pine guards lunge their metal swords at them, causing stab wounds in the arms and necks of the Potorians. The Potorians that aren't stabbed too excruciatingly fight back heatedly; they block the constant stabbing attempts by the Pine guards with their metal swords, and then the Potorians either grab the Pine guards by the neck with their hands or stab them in the face with the Potorians' metal swords and axes.

The Pine guards keep running towards the Potorians; the Potorians bend forwards, supporting them to throw the Pine guards over their shoulders. These Pine guards land on to the hard cobbled path and also drop their metal shields and weapons from their hands at the same time. The Potorians then quickly slice the Pine guards who have fallen to the ground. The other Pine guards attempt to help the fallen Pine guards, but are also stopped and killed by other Potorians who are fighting harshly against them in the midst of the black suffocating cloud that is also being penetrated by the heavy rain pouring form the thick clouds in the sky.

Flame swerves out of the way to narrowly miss some Potorians' metal sword and metal axe blows; he also uses his metal shield to block these blow attempts or to smack some Potorians in the face. That does cause them also to fall to the rough, wet cobbled paths or become momentarily stunned. While these Potorians are dazed from the metal shield blows delivered by Fame, it permits enough time for other close-by Pine guards and men Pine villagers to use their

metal weapons to quickly kill them by causing harsh and bloody stab
wounds. The Pine guards, who were upon horses that were just at the
back of this brutal battle in front of the west entrance wooden gate
of Pine Village, now kick their feet hard into the sides of their horses,
which makes them charge quickly through the destructive battle. The
horses trample over some of the Potorians' bodies; that causes them
to be killed from the strong power of these horses' leg muscles.

Vicious grasps what the Pine guards upon their horses have done
to some of the Potorians. It has a negative effect on their formation
during their battle against the Pine guards and men Pine villagers
upon the cobbled paths of Pine Village as it causes the Potorians to be
out of sync, and now they begin to be overpowered by the Pine guards
and men Pine villagers. In fury, Vicious charges forward through
the middle of the battle, where he pushes past any Potorians, Pine
guards, and men Pine villagers.

At a closer proximity, Vicious now charges toughly into these
Pine guards mounted upon their horses. Vicious's immense power
within his huge body gives him the strength to knock the whole horse
over to the ground by shoulder barging into the horse with the Pine
guard on top of it. After knocking several Pine guards and their
horses over to the cobbled paths within Pine Village, Vicious also
runs and jumps off the ground into the air. He uses his large fists
to punch in the face the Pine guards who were sitting upon the top
of the horses. This thrashing punch from Vicious's big and durable
fists sends the Pine guards flying through the air, and as these Pine
guards fall towards the ground from being on top of their horses,
Vicious spits out his scalding fire breath that incinerates these Pine
guards' bodies instantly.

Blood and dead bodies begin to mount up from both the Pine
guards and men Pine Villagers along with the Potorians during
the battle of Pine Village, where these dead bodies now lie upon
each other over the cold and wet cobbled paths of Pine Village. The
blistering rain continues to belt down hard to the ground along with
the gusty cold winds spreading the ash clouds from the burning of
the big wooden barricade throughout the rest of Pine Village. As this
intense battle continues, some Potorians manage to break through
the lines of the Pine guards and men Pine villagers that had been

trying to maintain the battle at the west entrance wooden gate of Pine Village.

As the Potorians filter through the battle in this location, they begin to run throughout the rest of Pine Village in order to savagely kill any other Pine villagers living within Pine Village. The horrific screams and cries of women and children Pine villagers are heard by the Pine guards in the midst of the Pine Village battle as the Potorians who had filtered away from the battle smash through the front wooden doors of other small wooden houses, flats, and shops throughout Pine Village to kill these defenceless women and children Pine villagers in a brutal and unmerciful manner. The Pine guards that heard these awful screams of dying women and children Pine villagers feel intense and unbearable emotions that cause them to lose their concentrations. The Potorians who were attempting to attack them fortunately achieve a direct blow to these Pine guards and slay them.

The Pine villagers who were still within Pinus Tavern due to the remembrance service being held there when the initial battle of Pine Village begun had understood what was happening and were directed by Bella to start moving the big wooden tables and wooden chairs within Pinus Tavern and place them against the big wooden entrance doors of Pinus Tavern, which would make an obstruction to any Potorians that would try to enter.

'Quick, everyone, we need to put all the furniture against the entrance doors. I will not have those creature bastards enter this place, especially today of all days,' says Bella as she and other men and women Pine villagers currently within Pinus Tavern continue to help each other move the last of the wooden tables and wooden chairs against the big front wooden doors inside Pinus Tavern.

'Mother, I'm scared,' says a worried Sam to Lemur with tears in his eyes.

'Don't worry, my baby, Siva and I will protect you,' replies Lemur as she grabs both Siva's and Sam's hands and quickly moves to the opposite side of Pinus Tavern, away from the Pine villagers who were moving all of the wooden tables and wooden chairs in the main ground floor of Pinus Tavern.

'Stay by me, Sam, and we will all be reunited with our father together,' remarks a realistic Siva as she hugs Lemur and Sam strongly.

'I don't want to die!' cries Sam.

'It's all right. I won't let anything happen to you,' says Lemur calmly to Sam.

As the Potorians spread through Pine Village, some of them approach the middle section of it, where Pinus Tavern was situated. Now several Potorians try to bang their way through the barricaded big wooden entrance doors of Pinus Tavern, which causes the Pine villagers within the Pine Tavern to frantically panic, and another two of the Potorians decided to sprint across the cobbled path to enter into other Pine villagers' homes. These two Potorians approach the front of Parrot's small wooden flat, where they hear faint noises of human voices from inside of it. Without hesitation, one of the Potorians barges several times into the front wooden door of Parrot's small wooden flat with his shoulder; on the third shoulder barge, the front wooden door is unhinged, but the front wooden door fortunately still remains standing due to it being locked from inside with a metal bolt. The other Potorian now uses his metal axe to chop through the front wooden door until it eventually breaks the metal bolt, and the two Potorians now crash through the front wooden door. Upon entering Parrot's small wooden flat and the main room, they see and hear Aura yelling loudly in terror as she holds on to Tigra tightly within her arms.

Without thinking, Sirius attempts to protect Aura; he runs towards the first Potorian quickly and attacks him straight away with a small metal dagger. Aura stabs the Potorian sternly in his neck, which causes blood to squirt out all over the main room as the Potorians falls to the floor, dropping his metal sword, and then he dies quickly because his heart stops beating due to the loss of blood drained from the artery in his neck as it was slit apart. The other Potorian, who had also just entered into Parrot's small wooden flat and seen what had happened to this Potorian, quickly swings his metal axe around firmly and smacks it into the middle of Sirius's face. The metal axe blow to Sirius's whole face causes his face to be chopped in half, and Sirius falls to his knees; his eyes pop out from his half-split face with the metal axe still fixed within his face.

Aura screams loudly and the sight of her husband being brutally killed; she quickly puts Tigra safely in his small wooden cot in the main room of Parrot's small wooden flat. Aura now tries to protect

Tigra by also running towards the Potorian. She holds her hands in the air in an attempt to attack him; the Potorian quickly picks up the other Potorian's metal sword that was dropped upon the floor when he was killed. The Potorian lunges this metal sword in front of him in a split second, which stops Aura from running any closer to him as the metal sword slices easily through Aura's upper body until it pierces through the middle of her heart, causing Aura to die quickly. The Potorian pulls the metal sword out from Aura's body, which makes her falls backwards to the floor behind her.

The Potorian now walks smugly over to Tigra who had been placed in his small wooden cot and has now started crying because of all the commotion that had been occurring within the main room of Parrot's small wooden flat. The Potorian lifts his metal sword in the air, and just as he is about to stab Tigra with his metal sword, Rexus quickly runs out from the kitchen and jumps riotously up on to a wooden chair and then jumps again from the wooden chair and lands on the Potorian's face. Rexus starts to bite his sharp teeth into the Potorian's face. In shock and pain, the Potorian falls backwards and crashes on to the floor behind him. He quickly tries to pull Rexus away from his face, but Rexus bites his sharp teeth more firmly into the Potorian's face. Rexus then kills the Potorian by tearing his face from his head by biting him consistently with his sharp teeth.

IN THE MIDST of the Pine Village battle upon the cobbled paths near the west entrance wooden gate of Pine Village, Vicious continues using his intense and destructive fire breath to annihilate numerous more men Pine villagers and several Pine guards upon their horses, which causes the battle to be swayed back in favour of the Potorians. As the thick, black cloudy smoke gets blown in various directions by the gusty winds, the Pine guards within the small wooden watchtower near the west entrance wooden gate are able to see the battle a bit more clearly; they quickly direct their shooting of wooden arrows with metal spikes at the end of them towards Vicious. These wooden arrows with metal spikes at the end fly through the air, and the arrows that reach Vicious pierce into his tough skin, causing these arrows to stick out of Vicious's arms and back. In retaliation due to the pain Vicious experiences from these wooden arrows with the metal spikes at the end of them, he turns swiftly around to look up at the Pine guards on top of the small wooden watchtower.

After taking an extended gasp or air, Vicious releases a huge ball of fire from his breath that travels energetically in less than a second directly to the small wooden watchtower; upon impact, the huge ball of fire burns the small wooden watchtower along with the Pine guards upon it rapidly. The wooden watchtower's wooden structure breaks from the burring fire and crashes down towards the ground. It lands on top of other Pine guards, men Pine villagers, and Potorians, resulting in an atrocious sight with many casualties and deaths.

Flame has now been bruised and wounded from the hard battle he has experienced so far with many Potorians; he devastatingly notices the immense destruction Vicious has just caused to the small wooden watchtower along with many Pine guards and men Pine villagers. Flame perceptively understands that Vicious's focus is now slightly distracted from the main battle; in anger, Flame sprints towards Vicious with his metal sword lunging out in front of him; this was the same metal sword that Parrot had specially created for Flame and had Flame's name carved at the top of the sword's silver handle. Just as Flame attempts to stab his metal sword deep into Vicious's bulky neck from the direction Flame was running towards him, Vicious hears and sees out of the corner of his left eye an angry Flame running towards him.

Vicious promptly turns to his left side and releases a large and disgusting burp that creates a powerful force in the form of a shock wave that thrashes into and through Flame's injured body. The impact from this epic shock wave breaks most of Flame's bones and sends him flying back up in the air where he drops his metal sword and then crash-lands inwards of the burning small wooden watchtower that had just fallen to the ground. As Flame lands and breaks through the small wooden watchtower upon the ground of Pine Village, the heated fire engulfs Flame entirely and not only kills him painfully and quickly but also disintegrates his whole body.

The battle of Pine Village continues for nearly another hour. The battle continues moving throughout the cobbled paths of Pine Village. The battle and smaller fights head towards the west direction of Pine Village. Vicious keeps ordering and shouting at the Potorian army to keep pushing and moving forward deeper into Pine Village, while

Vicious utilises his disparaging fire breath to obliterate countless numbers of the small wooden houses, flats, and shops within Pine Village. As this wrathful and bloody battle continues within Pine Village, the constant loud noises of clashing weapons and painful shouts from all kinds of Pine villagers propel deleterious effects all through Pine Village. The heavy rain continues to pour down upon Pine Village as the thick, black cloudy smoke engulfs the atmosphere above Pine Village. All kinds of Pine villagers, several Pine guards, horses, and animals, along with many Potorians, get injured or killed brutally.

Back in the middle section of Pine Village, some of the Potorians have now managed to violently break their way through the big wooden entrance doors of Pinus Tavern as well as the big wooden tables and wooden chairs that were lodged against it. These Potorians enter the tavern and quickly and forcefully kill many of the innocent men, women, and children Pine villagers who were currently inside of Pinus Tavern. The Potorians are, however, attacked back by some of the men and women Pine villagers in an attempt to protect one another. These men and women Pine villagers throw wooden chairs, glass cups, and other kitchen equipment such as knives, cooking pots, and pans at the Potorians to injure or slow down their attacking.

Some of the men Pine villagers within Pinus Tavern briskly climb on top of the big wooden tables and jump off these big wooden tables on to the Potorians to make the Potorians' lose their balance and knock them over to the floor of Pinus Tavern. Once these Potorians are brought down to the floor, other men and women Pine villagers including Bella hit these Potorians repeatedly in the face with their fists or kitchen equipment until they are killed.

At the centre of all the commotion within the ground floor of Pinus Tavern, Lemur panics for her children's safety; she snappishly grabs Siva's and Sam's hands tightly and attempts to run with them out of Pinus Tavern big wooden entrance doors in order to get away from this horrendous fight within Pinus Tavern. As Lemur manoeuvres Siva and Sam via their hands to dodge past by many Potorians fighting against the Pine villagers within Pinus Tavern, they are unexpectedly stopped by a tall, muscly, and ugly Potorian who was fighting near Pinus Tavern's big wooden entrance doors. This Potorian notices these Pine villagers attempting to escape; in annoyance he swings his metal axe in the space in front of him, and before Lemur could hurriedly manoeuvre Siva and Sam out of harm's way, this Potorian ferociously cuts Lemur's, Siva's, and Sam's fragile bodies up into many pieces with his large and sharp metal axe. At a glance Bella despondently sees what the Potorian had just done to Lemur, Siva, and Sam. Bella cries out loudly in despair and terror at what is currently happening to Pine Village.

WHEN ALL HOPE has been lost for the Pine villagers within Pinus Tavern, fortunately by this time, during the battle of Pine Village, Lynx had travelled swiftly upon his white horse from Willow Village along the long cobbled road back to Pine Village through the east entrance wooden gate. Upon entering the east entrance wooden gate, he is coincidently encountered by Bruce, who has been in small fights with the Potorians that had ventured into the south-east side of Pine Village, where Bruce was positioned following his descent form the south-east watchtower.

Bruce had killed the Potorians in the south-west area, where unfortunately, the Pine guards he was with had been killed by the Potorians. Bruce shares a brief explanation of what he saw at the top of the south-east watchtower with Lynx to inform him of the chaos that has been caused during the Pine Village battle. Bruce is welcomed to climb upon Lynx's white horse by Lynx, and they both gallop on the white horse down the cobbled paths in the west direction, towards the west entrance wooden gate of Pine Village, where the main battle between the humans and the creatures is happening. Lynx is holding on tightly to the rope reins of his white horse, but both Bruce and he swing their swords to chop off the heads of any running Potorians they come across along their way to the middle section of Pine Village.

Upon approaching the middle section of Pine Village, Lynx and Bruce pass by Parrot's small wooden flat and Pinus Tavern, where they hear fighting and screaming sounds occurring within Pinus Tavern. Lynx quickly swerves his white horse to the outside big entrance wooden doors of Pinus Tavern. Bruce and he jump down from Lynx's white horse, although Bruce had to help Lynx hobble into Pinus Tavern's big entrance wooden doors due to Lynx's sprained ankle from his hard fall in the Willow Village battle.

Lynx and Bruce both fight heroically and passionately against the Potorians who were still fighting the Pine villagers within Pinus Tavern. Lynx fights strongly but could only manage to hobble with one foot, although he still manages to kills a couple of Potorians and protect the Pine villagers by using his powerful silver sword. Bruce also courageously stabs the rest of the Potorians in the head and chest with his metal sword, although Lynx and Bruce also got sliced with cut wounds in the arms and legs by some of the Potorians swinging metal swords and axes. After a short but unbearable time, along with being injured and pushed to their mental and physical limits during this fight within Pinus Tavern, Lynx, Bruce, Bella, along with the other men and women Pine villagers, eventually kill the rest of the Potorians by any means necessary within Pinus Tavern.

The Pine Village battle continues intensely and violently over the cobbled paths in the interlinking streets of Pine Village, along with many smaller fights occurring within the plentiful small wooden houses, flats, and shops that were attacked and destroyed during the battle of Pine Village. Both the Pine villagers and Potorians have lost countless members on their sides during this battle; the numbers have decreased so much that the battle could be won by either side now. Some of the Pine guards manage to regroup together back on their horses near the middle of the violent battle near the west entrance wooden gate of Pine Village; they agree to make their final charge at Vicious.

Vicious is now exhausted from all of the many hours of fighting he had done in the Willow Village and Pine Village, but he still has plenty of determination within him to be victorious in this battle as ordered by Triton and Venus. Vicious sees some the remaining Pine guards charging upon their horses through the middle of the battle straight towards him; he reacts quickly by burning them all with his intense fire breath that he releases from his mouth instantly. The Pine guards upon their horses get horrifically burnt by Vicious's fire breath, and some of them fall straight to the ground and die; however, a few Pine guards still manage to continue galloping upon their horse and get close enough to trample over Vicious and eventually knock his muscly body over to the ground.

The burnt Pine guards who had knocked Vicious over to the ground quickly jump down from their horses in agony and join in with the Pine guards and men Pine villagers who had quickly surrounded the fallen Vicious. All these humans repeatedly stab Vicious in the head and heart with their metal swords, shields, and spears as also, wooden arrows with metal spikes at the end of them are still being shot at Vicious and other Potorians over a long distance from Pine guards who were still in the north-west watchtower. This stabbing attack continues fiercely upon Vicious, and he receives various bloody wounds. He draws one last breath but due to his exhaustion, he has no fire that can be released from his breath. Vicious is now slaughtered to death by the Pine guards and the men Pine villagers.

The Pine guards and men Pine villagers manage to outnumber the Potorians now, and after an epic struggle, they finally use their depleted energy and combined strength to kill the remaining Potorians so that all the 166 Potorians are now no more. Although, 100 Pine guards were killed along with 543 Pine villagers, dozens of horses, and many other livestock animals, as well as many buildings were destroyed in the Pine Village battle.

After the Pine Village battle concludes, Lynx and Bruce, along with the remaining 200 Pine guards and the 331 remaining Pine villagers throughout Pine Village, begin to scurry across Pine Village in order to help tend to the wounded Pine guards, villagers, and animals where required. The gusty winds have now calmed, and most of the black clouds have dispersed or left the perimeter of Pine Village's air. The Pine guards and Pine villagers also quickly extinguish many of the burning fires caused by Vicious; the heavy rain has also aided in causing some of the fires not to spread too widely across Pine Village's buildings. The heavy rain begins to slow down to just a drizzle as many of the Pine guards and Pine villagers start to clean up the dead bodies, broken wood, and littered weapons throughout Pine Village, which takes the whole village numerous hours to complete.

Bella, who was still in Pinus Tavern and distraught from the horrific deaths of Lemur, Siva, and Sam, quickly thinks how Parrot, Sapphire, Sirius, Aura, and Tigra left Pinus Tavern earlier due to the commotion regarding Emerald and Raven. Bella quickly runs out of Pinus Tavern and across the cobbled path directly over to Parrot's small wooden flat. Bella walks cautiously and upsettingly into Parrot's small wooden flat through the half-broken front wooden door; she luckily finds Tigra, but he is crying loudly in his small wooden cot in the main room. Rexus is still biting the dead Potorian's face upon the floor of Parrot's small wooden flat.

Bella is shocked and devastated to see Sirius and Aura also dead on the floor. She becomes afraid that Tigra will be emotionally damaged from the sight of his dead grandparents upon the floor of Parrot's small wooden flat; thus she quickly picks up Tigra from his wooden cot and also grabs Rexus's collar. She takes both of them back across the cobbled path to Pinus Tavern, where she will look after them until Raven, Emerald, Parrot, and Sapphire return back to Pine Village. Bella was concerned that She did not find them at Parrot's small wooden flat with Tigra and Rexus.

Twenty-Five

TRITON AND THE thirty Potorians who were holding firmly upon Venus's back as she is currently in her Argentinosaurus physical form have all rather quickly managed to travel in the north-east direction from the Realm of Deserted Lands, across the mucky Swamp Fields and have now reached the renowned Eagle Forest situated in the north of the Planet of Phoenix. Venus as her Argentinosaurus form is very huge and massive, which can make her slower in her physical reactions; however, the powerful and large feet of the Argentinosaurus has allowed her to cover large distances across any kind of terrain at quite a fast pace that enables them to arrive at the faraway Eagle Forest within just under six hours. Also during this time, the Planet of Phoenix's core mysteriously changed in mass, causing the Argentinosaurus's journey to Eagle Forest faster than it normally would have taken.

Triton and the thirty Potorians energetically jump down from the Argentinosaurus's huge back, and as soon as they land on to the ground just at the outskirts of Eagle Forest, the Potorians gather themselves into their standard battle formation. This battle formation consists of six lines of five Potorians in each line, where they hold their metal sword and axe weapons in their hands out antagonistically in front of them, ready for battle. Triton also positions himself at the front of the Potorians battle formation. Triton holds the anomaly crystal in one of his strong hands, and in the other hand, he grips his golden chain with the iron spiked ball at the end of it. He's readily determined to lead the thirty Potorians into the mysterious Eagle Forest. Venus concentrates briefly until her eyes turn from pure white back to their normal red colour again, which permits her to utilise her Animagus abilities so that her whole physical body can now turn back into her normal physical form as a woman again.

Venus now joins her lover Triton at the front of the Potorians' battle formation, and without hesitation, together they lead the thirty Potorians by entering strongly within the tall and peculiar trees of Eagle Forest that are illuminated slightly with the colours of brown, red, green, and orange. Triton waves the anomaly crystal out in front of him in confidence. Venus rubs her hands together slowly, thinking of what beasts to create to fight against Hake and his Hawk Tribe, along with Raven, Emerald, Parrot, and Sapphire, while the Potorians are banging the metal swords and axes together to make a clanking sound that echoes throughout the darkish Eagle Forest.

Triton, Venus, and the thirty Potorians all pace assertively through and between the plentiful and diverse trees, shrubs, flowers, and plants residing within Eagle Forest; however, Triton, Venus, and all the Potorians make sure that they keep their eyes wide open and alert for any Hawks who might be lurking up high in the tall and thick trees. The other animals within Eagle Forest that immediately hear the loud high-pitched sounds of the Potorians clanging their metal swords and axes together speedily run far away from the immediate surroundings and hide somewhere deep within the darker sections of the infinite Eagle Forest. Only after twenty minutes of quickly marching in the north direction through the vast Eagle Forest, Triton becomes irritated and impatient.

'Where's Raven and his friends and that unfaithful Hawk Tribe?' states Triton angrily, looking high up in the seamless never-ending tall and thick trees.

'Don't infuriate yourself, my love. We will come across those pathetic humans and Hake's creature clones soon enough. Your thirst for blood will be fulfilled this day, my future ruler of the Planet of Phoenix,' replies Venus, touching one of Triton's strong muscly arms in a seductive manner.

'And you, my woman, will enjoy all the riches, spoils, and human blood that the Planet of Phoenix has to offer us,' laughs Triton while increasing his pace. The rest of the Potorians also quicken their pace through Eagle Forest. Many of the small plants and shrubs are trampled upon, and Triton also uses his forceful and robust arm muscles to push a few of the smaller trees' roots out from within the deep soil of the ground and over on to the ground as he passes by these smaller trees.

IN THE MIDDLE of Eagle Forest, at one side in the north direction of the Hawks' Tribe Camp, Raven and Emerald are currently sitting on top of Felix's back. Raven is holding his sword of Grackle, and Emerald has laid her small silver sword that Parrot had given her earlier upon the large back of Felix. As the echoes vibrate through the endless Eagle Forest, Raven, Emerald, and Felix begin to hear the faint sounds in the distant spaces of Eagle Forest caused by the beautiful trees falling over to the ground, animals scurrying throughout Eagle Forest, and the clanging of the Potorians metal swords and axes banging together. Emerald places her dirty and bruised arms around Raven from behind to hug him tightly and lovingly.

'I'm very sorry about what has happened to Ruby, Emerald. She will always remain in our hearts and minds. She will be watching over us from heaven along with my parents and grandfather while we avenge all of their untimely deaths this day,' says Raven softly, gently kissing Emerald's petite cold and dirty hands that were now wrapped around his torso.

'I still can't believe my mother is not with us no more. She had always been there for me and did so well in looking after me when my father left us both. Even though her heart was terribly broken from his disappearance, she still tried her hardest to make sure I would still have the best upbringing she could provide me. I feel lost without her now as she was more than a mother to me. She was also my friend and my inspiration. I don't know how I'm going to cope without her and her guidance. It feels like all my family has gone, and my life is fallen apart. We haven't even had chance to bury her body properly and spiritually. I assume her body is still somewhere in her house, if that evil bitch Venus ha left her body in one piece that is,' sobs Emerald with tears dripping down her miserable face.

'Once we obliterate Triton and Venus today, where we will send them to the darkest and dangerous depths of hell for all of their malicious and deceitful behaviour they have inflicted against us and the rest of humans throughout the Planet of Phoenix, we will return to Oak Village straight after and give Ruby a memorable burial. That will help her admirable soul to now rest in peace, and she will join my parents and grandfather also. We have both lost so much and I also feel lost without my family too, but we will always have each other, Emerald, no matter how many tragedies we may have to face throughout the rest our lives. I promise I will always be there to protect and support you. I love you, Emerald, with all my heart, and I would give my life before I let anything hurt you ever again,' states Raven, gripping on to Emerald's hands around his waist in a comforting manner.

'I love you too, Raven, but I wouldn't want you to give your life for me as I really wouldn't be able to cope in this lifetime if I lose you too. You are my world now, and without you being by my side, I really couldn't continue on living,' replies Emerald, kissing with her soft lips on the back of Raven's smooth neck.

'Don't ever ponder on such thoughts, Emerald. Nothing will ever separate us from being in each other's arms, minds, and souls,' remarks Raven as he now turns round to look at Emerald in her beautiful but teary eyes. Emerald attempts to give Raven a slight smile back.

'How do you feel about what Hake told us regarding your family ancestors' history and their past actions? Especially for Grackle, Sparrow, and Lord Scartor?' asks Emerald, looking back at Raven's troubled expression upon his face.

'I still can't believe I am related to Lord Scartor after everything he had previously done to us both, my family, and Oak Village during that horrific battle last year. It has been an absolute shock to acknowledge and realise that we are now a part of something bigger and consequential that will either protect or abolish the current life of humans as we know it existing on the Planet of Phoenix. It's a real frightening feeling to have been previously unaware of everything that had already occurred in the distant past that has now been destined to involve us within it to this very day,' says Raven uneasily and transparently.

'Let's hope we manage to protect the Planet of Phoenix against all of those evil creatures who try to destroy it, for the Planet of Phoenix belongs to us humans and those good creatures like Hake and his Hawk Tribe, who seek to preserve the Planet of Phoenix's peaceful and harmonious environment,' says Emerald. Raven smiles back gently at Emerald and kisses her passionately and softly on the lips for several minutes; they both experience deep emotions for one another just as it was on their very first kiss they shared together. Raven then turns back around and pats Felix happily on his long black neck hair to show his appreciation for Felix. Raven looks up into the far distance where the sounds of trees falling and marching upon the ground throughout Eagle Forest becomes louder and closer towards the Hawks' Tribe Camp.

Parrot and Sapphire are positioned at the opposite and south side of the Hawks' Tribe Camp to where Raven and Emerald are positioned. Parrot and Sapphire are presently standing next to their brown horse and are holding each other's hands, both looking deep into the distance of Eagle Forest in order to locate any danger forthcoming as they also hear the sounds or enemies quickly approaching. Parrot has his wooden bow and wooden arrow with metal spikes at the end of them attached around his neck and back; he also has several fury raptor throwing stars placed within the pockets of his brown coat pocket. Sapphire holds on to her small dagger in one hand and her other hand is holding on to Parrot's firmly.

A dozen Hawks have stayed at the Hawks' Tribe Camp to be in close proximity of Hake in order to provide extra protection for him as required, and the rest of the Hawks have now positioned themselves within the outskirts of the Hawks' Tribe Camp in attempt to stop Triton, Venus, and the Potorians from trying to actually entre within the Hawks' Tribe Camp to kill Hake. Hake has subconsciously decided to stay within his big wooden hut, where he is currently preparing potions and remedies as a defence mechanism during this imminent and abysmal battle. The sky has now completely darkened as the sun has completely set, which makes it very difficult to see through and within Eagle Forest due to the tall and thick trees causing the environment to be very enclosed. Fortunately Hake and the Hawks have fairly good vision and sight in darkness.

The cold wind breezes throughout the Hawks' Tribe Camp, causing fallen leaves to be blown around. Some of these leaves fall over Parrot's and Sapphire's bodies.

'Promise me we will survive this battle, Parrot? I couldn't bear it if we didn't see Tigra or my parents again,' says Sapphire worriedly. She is not able to see too far ahead of her due to the darkness.

'Of course we will survive. Just stay by my side, and I won't let anything happen to you or myself. I have my fury raptor throwing stars ready at hand, along with my specially designed arrows that will protect us now as they also protected me in the previous battles I have had to endure against the Potorians at the Wastelands, along with Triton at Lord Scartor's Lair of Death upon Crow Mountain until it was destroyed. Before you know it we will both be back in Pine Village safe and sound along with Raven and Emerald. You will be holding Tigra in your arms, and we will all be having cold drinks, warm food, and a good old chat with Sirius and Aura. We will all continue to share many more happy memories together in the future, once the threat of these malicious creatures has finally passed,' describes Parrot in a reassuring manner and tone of voice, looking at Sapphire, who was standing right beside him.

'I hope you're right, Parrot, as there's nothing I want more right now, apart from being with you, Tigra, and all of our family and friends, where we are all safe and enjoying life,' replies Sapphire while also turning to look at Parrot's face. She turns back around to look out in front of her while clenching on to her small silver dagger in one of her hands.

As TRITON, VENUS, and the thirty Potorians continue marching swiftly through the dark Eagle Forest and begin approaching the outskirt perimeter of the Hawks' Tribe Camp, the Potorians are suddenly and quickly attacked by the numerous Hawks who had positioned themselves high up in the tall and thick towering trees. The Hawks begin to shoot hundreds of their powerful green laser beams from their green eyes directed at the Potorians upon the ground of Eagle Forest, while also throwing their wooden spears at the same time. The wooden spears pierce through some of the

Potorians' bodies, which cause blood wounds and broken bones mostly on the arms and legs of the Potorians, and these Potorians shout out loudly in pain.

The powerful green laser beams from the Hawks' pure green eyes possess toxic chemicals that facilitate these powerful green laser beams to produce small stinging holes that blow straight through the Potorians' flesh and bone of their bodies. The Potorians who are shot by the Hawks' powerful green laser beams feel excruciating pain, and as the open holes are created in their bodies, blood quickly starts to seep out these open holes, and the Potorians fall to the ground. Some of those shot by the Hawks' powerful green laser beams in the head or heart die.

As the Hawks' powerful green laser beams are continuously shot out via the Hawks' pure green eyes, the illuminating green laser beams light up Eagle Forest, creating a glowing atmosphere in the immediate surroundings. These green luminous lights are perceived by the other Hawks who were positioned in the same location but within various different trees and shrubs. In the midst of this shocking and dangerous situation, Triton and Venus quickly dash behind two very large and thick trees that were nearby each other in an attempt to try and cover themselves from being shot and hit by the Hawks' powerful green laser beams. During these brief moments of energetic reactions to the Hawks shooting their powerful green laser beams from the trees of Eagle Forest, they manage to kill twelve Potorians and injure many more of the Potorians.

The remaining eighteen Potorians also attempt to quickly seek cover from the Hawks' powerful green laser beams by running behind other large trees in the immediate area of this section within Eagle Forest. One of the Hawks who was high up in one of the tall trees predictably shoots his powerful green laser beam from his pure green eyes that flashes speedily through the air and aims into the back of the large tree that Venus was hiding behind. This powerful green laser beam instantaneously incinerates a small hole right through the middle of this tree's wooden bark as the powerful green laser beam quickly goes straight through and comes out the other side of the tree's bark, which also creates a small but painful open wound hole through Venus's left shoulder. Venus screeches suddenly in intense pain due to her shoulder having a wound created through her flesh.

Triton disturbingly turns to look at Venus. He is alarmed to see thick red blood starting to pour out of Venus's left shoulder.

In a furious rage, Triton swings his golden chain with the spiked iron ball at the end of it around in the air and forcefully smacks it into one of the tall and thick trees where two Hawks were currently in it and still shooting their powerful green laser beams from their pure green eyes. The forceful blow from the iron spiked ball crashing into this tall and thick tree breaks and rips the roots from the bottom of the tree that were sticking in the soil; this tall and thick tree slowly leans over to one side from its roots being destroyed and released from the ground, and the entire tree now falls over, crashing down to the ground beneath it, squashing the two Hawks that were stuck within this tall and thick tree.

Before Triton swings his golden chain with the iron spiked ball at the end of it around his head again into another tree, he gets abruptly shot in his forearm by another Hawk's powerful green laser beam. The powerful green laser beam that hits Triton immediately scorches straight through Triton's forearm, and he also shouts loudly in agonising pain. Venus is still trying to cope with the sting from being shot in her left shoulder, and she uses her other hand to cover and put pressure on this open wound. Now she sees what has happened to Triton. She becomes infuriated at Triton's pain. Venus quickly lets go of her shoulder. She turns her eyes from their normal red colour into pure white and then puts one hand above the other hand with both of her hands facing down towards the ground.

Venus utilises her magical creature abilities to create within the middle of her hands a small Spinosaurus dinosaur; she hastily levitates the small Spinosaurus to the ground beneath her hands and then moves her top hand up into the air, which permits the Spinosaurus to grow suddenly to its normal large size with a furious temperament. The Spinosaurus screeches from its large rounded mouth that has many sharp piercing teeth within it. The Spinosaurus whips its large and stiff tail around in the air, which easily knocks over a couple of smaller weaker trees to the ground as its tail smashes into them. This also causes other Hawks to fall out from these trees, but they manage to use their feathery arms to help them glide to the ground safely and not get squashed by the fallen trees.

The ferocious and dominant Spinosaurus charges on its two hind legs and big clawed feet through the interlinking pathways between the various tall and thick trees of Eagle Forest. As the Spinosaurus charges on a wild rampage throughout Eagle Forest, it knocks many of the tighter and sturdier thick trees over to the ground with its huge and colossal body mass and smaller front arms that have claws for its hands. As many more large trees are being destroyed and felled to the ground by the frenzied Spinosaurus, the Hawks who were still up in some of the tall and thick trees now stop shooting their powerful green laser beams and begin to jump out of the trees and glide to the ground by flapping their feathery arms in order to avoid the wrath of the charging Spinosaurus.

As these Hawks land upon the ground of Eagle Forest, the remaining Potorians now run out from hiding behind some of the large trees and begin fighting against these Hawks. The Hawks are surprised by the rapid attack of the Potorians, but they quickly react by using their wooden spears and powerful green laser beams from their eyes to fight back against the Potorians. These Hawks, however, mostly get killed by the Potorians due to their superior combat skills as these Potorians had been efficiently trained to react accordingly against opponent's weapon attacks as well as swiftly employing their metal swords and metal axes to kill their enemies by causing snappish and horrific stab wounds.

The Hawks that were stabbed and cut by the Potorians lose many of their tender limbs; their large brown and now bloody feathers fly in the air away from their bodies as the Hawks fall to the ground and die in excruciating pain. Venus's eyes were still in their pure white state; she again uses her enchanted creature abilities to create another monstrous beast within the middle of her hands that were now both facing down towards the ground. The monstrous beast Venus visualises to create is a small Tyrannosaurus rex dinosaur. She quickly levitates this Tyrannosaurus rex to the ground beneath it and then moves her top hand up into the air, permitting the Tyrannosaurus rex to grow to its normal gigantic size. Venus stands back away from the rapidly expanding Tyrannosaurs rex as her eyes now turn back to their normal red colour again.

The Tyrannosaurus rex releases a terrifying and ear-shattering roar that can be heard by any human, animal, or creature throughout the whole of Eagle Forest. The Tyrannosaurs rex manoeuvres its strong and dominant back legs and large impenetrable body with muscular long tail to start charging into the tall and thick trees throughout Eagle Forest. By using its big and powerful head with numerous severe and sharp teeth within its mouth, it easily dismantles and eats the Hawks that it finds and snaps them up from either hiding upon the some of the large branches of the large trees or hiding on the ground behind the tall and thick trees. The Tyrannosaurs rex chomps its sharp teeth furiously and effortlessly crushes the bones and flesh of the Hawks as they are fixed within the Tyrannosaurs rex's now bloodstained mouth. The Tyrannosaurs rex also uses its huge and strong feet with claws at the of the feet to stamp on top of some of the Hawks that have fallen to the ground from when they were escaping from the falling tall and thick trees; in this short rampage, the boisterous Tyrannosaurus rex quickly kills loads of Hawks.

The Spinosaurus also screeches again because of the loud noise and commotion it had witnessed the Tyrannosaurs rex causing within Eagle Forest. The Spinosaurus decides to charge in the north direction, which leads it closer to the Hawks' Tribe Camp. Raven and Emerald are still sitting upon Felix at one side of the Hawks' Tribe Camp, while Parrot and Sapphire are with their brown horse at the opposite side, along with the remaining dozen Hawks that are still waiting at the Hawks' Tribe Camp. No matter their location, Raven, Emerald, Parrot, Sapphire, and all the Hawks hear the loud thudding sound upon the ground of Eagle Forest that the Spinosaurus's powerful clawed feet are making as it charges towards the centre of the Hawks' Tribe Camp. They all stand firm and alert, as they mentally prepare to fight against the unexpected monster that is quickly approaching them.

Hake is at present within his big wooden hut against the big and old Kapok tree located in the direct middle of the Hawks' Tribe Camp, and he quickly grabs different types and colours of the potions that were placed upon the wooden shelves fixed up against the sides of his big wooden hut. Without hesitation, Hake pours these various potions into his bubbling black cauldron while quickly scanning over the text written in the ancient language of Phoenix from an old sorcerous book of curses.

The Spinosaurus now briskly enters into the Hawks' Tribe Camp by crashing into the tall and thick trees as it is not able to see too clearly in the dark near the south-side location, where Parrot and Sapphire are currently standing in shock at the sight of an outline of such a gigantic monster when they were standing next to their brown horse. The Spinosaurus continues charging frantically onwards, trampling down more tall and thick trees along its path. The Hawks who were upon the ground within the Hawks' Tribe Camp quickly scarper towards the charging Spinosaurus while shooting their powerful green laser beams from their eyes and also throwing wooden spears at the Spinosaurus face and body in an attempt to stop its terrifying charge. The Spinosaurus screeches loudly as it gets shot by some of the powerful and toxic green laser beams; instinctively in retaliation, it tramples its solid clawed feet on top of the Hawks brutally, which kills them instantly. The Spinosaurus again lifts one of his large and strong legs up in the air, near where Parrot and Sapphire are standing. Parrot and Sapphire narrowly dash out from the way of the Spinosaurus's clawed feet booming towards the ground; unfortunately, it stamps upon and squashes their brown horse.

The Spinosaurus squeals forcefully again in excitement as it whips its long and stiff tail around at the back of its large body, which now smacks into Parrot's back as he attempts to run away. The force of the Spinosaurus's thick and powerful tail throws Parrot high up in the air, and he crash-lands on to the ground in another section of Eagle Forest that was not too far from the Hawks' Tribe Camp. Unknown to Sapphire at the time, Parrot is luckily caught in the air by a Hawk who sees Parrot flying towards him as the Hawks' eyesight is good in the darkness. Thus the Hawk flapped its feathery arms to hover above the ground and caught Parrot, preventing a disastrous fall. Sapphire screams upsettingly on seeing Parrot being thrown up in the air, which could have potentially killed him; she changes direction to frantically run towards Hake's big wooden hut at the middle section of the Hawks' Tribe Camp, Sapphire has difficulty seeing while she is running due to the luminous glow from the Hawks shooting their powerful green laser beams at the Spinosaurus.

As Sapphire sprints towards Hake's big wooden hut, her scent is sensed by the Spinosaurus because of its strong sense of smell, and it begins to quickly chase her while swooping its head towards the ground to try and bite Sapphire; fortunately, it couldn't manage to grab her with its sharp teeth. Sapphire desperately rushes over to Hake's big wooden hut and the colourful cloth that covers the entrance of Hake's big wooden hut; upon entering the hut, she sees Hake reading from a big old curse book. He's reading aloud in the ancient Phoenix language, which causes the black cauldron to bubble and change from the original green liquid into a turquoise colour.

Sapphire begins to panic hysterically as the Spinosaurus has been charging after her in the middle of the Hawks' Tribe Camp and is now about to trample its solid clawed feet on top of Hake's big wooden hut. Within a brief second of being about to be squashed and killed, Hake finishes the enchanted spell he was reading from the book of curses written in the ancient Phoenix language. It supernaturally releases a magical and very ancient sorcerous power that causes the Spinosaurus to suddenly disappear completely from Eagle Forest, and it now physically ends up flying through outer space in a distant fragment of the universe.

VENUS SUBCONSCIOUSLY FEELS through her magical creature abilities that the Spinosaurus has now been vanquished from her sensation and awareness within Eagle Forest; she becomes confused and hostile about what has happened to the Spinosaurus that she had created. Venus turns towards Triton, who was still in slight pain from his open hole wound to his forearm; she grabs the anomaly crystal quickly from Triton's hand. While feeling bellicose emotions, Venus holds the anomaly crystal out in front of her. The colours of the rainbow and the shades of white and black fanatically swirl around it, and the colour within the anomaly crystal turns sharply into a grey colour that spins and whirls around the whole of the anomaly crystal in a frenzied manner.

Shockingly, a great gush of thick grey wind that forms into a large and dangerous twirling tornado is mysteriously released from the anomaly crystal; this magical wind now flies in to the air and begins to swerve throughout Eagle Forest in an agitated way. This forceful and destructive tornado expeditiously tears the tall and thick trees' sturdy roots fixed deep within the soil beneath the ground of Eagle Forest. The tornado lifts these thick and tall trees completely from the ground and in the midst of the swirling tornado's thick, gusty, strong winds; several Potorians holding on to their metal sword and metal axe weapons as well as numerous Hawks who were either still on the ground or had been positioned back up within the tall and thick trees are also lifted by the tornado. These Potorians, their metal sword and metal axe weapons, the Hawks, and the thick and tall trees that were dragged into this fierce and uncontrollable tornado, all fly through the air in the midst of the gushing strong and feisty winds of the tornado.

The Potorians and the Hawks feel immense pressure against their bodies and within their heads from the powerful twirling winds within the tornado; also some of the Potorians and Hawks painfully crash into other Potorians, Hawks, and the thick and tall trees as they swirl into one another within the tornado. After being battered and bruised from the colossal power of the spinning wind from the tornado, the Potorians and Hawks are thrown back out of the tornado and fly through the air into another section of Eagle Forest, where they are killed instantly as they fall from a great height to the hard ground or from smashing into the sides of the large and hard wooden trees as they fall towards the ground throughout Eagle Forest.

'Oh my God! Triton and Venus must have used the anomaly crystal's powers to create that horrible tornado,' wails Emerald while faintly seeing through the darkness several Potorians, Hawks, and the tall and thick trees being flung out of the tornado high up in the air and crash-landing back down to the ground into other parts of Eagle Forest, which included the area quite close to the north side of the Hawks' Tribe Camp where Raven and Emerald are still positioned, unaware of all the other fights that have already occurred within Eagle Forest.

'We must stop them before any further harm is inflicted upon us!' states Raven as he brusquely kicks his feet into the sides of Felix's strong back and pulls the brown rope reins tightly, which enables Felix to gallop off quickly with his full speed that is faster than any other horse can gallop. Felix heads swiftly through the Hawks' Tribe Camp in the south direction towards the epic tornado that they can barely see in the distance but can feel breeze over their bodies. While travelling through the middle of the Hawks' Tribe Camp, Emerald notices that there has been some destruction caused and fears for Parrot's and Sapphire's safety.

Raven and Emerald, riding on top of Felix's strong black back, now approach the outer edge of the swirling tornado, where the wind is very strong and causes Felix to partly lose his balance. Raven holds tightly on to Felix's brown rope reins and manoeuvres him strongly around the sides of tornado, and they now see Triton and Venus behind it and grinning at the destruction the tornado is causing throughout Eagle Forest. Emerald also catches glimpses of Venus's face, which makes Emerald furious at the thought of her killing her mother earlier in the day and stealing the anomaly crystal from her wedding ring. Raven feels Emerald shuffling at the back of Felix after they see Triton and Venus. Emerald also quickly places her small silver sword, which she was holding in one of her hands, into her pocket.

'Stay with me, Emerald!' shouts Raven, getting nervous at Emerald's recent movements at the back of him while riding upon Felix.

'No! I can't! I must avenge my mother,' replies Emerald angrily as shuffles her body quickly into a position that allows her to lift herself up and stand on Felix's back while holding on to Raven's shoulders. Raven attempts to get Emerald to sit back down upon Felix, but he can't release his grip from Felix's brown rope reins; otherwise, they would all be knocked over by the gusty and strong winds being released from the overpowering tornado. As Felix, while being controlled by Raven, continues to circle around some of the passageways amongst the tall and thick trees of Eagle Forest, Emerald times it right and does a backflip off the back of Felix's back and lands on top of an unsuspecting Venus as Felix gallops past her. Surprised, Venus falls over hard to the ground from the Emerald's whole body slamming against hers; the anomaly crystal also drops out of Venus's hand and rolls a few times across the ground.

'This is for my mother, you bitch!' screams Emerald furiously as she quickly turns her whole body around to now face Venus's face following the position her backflip on to Venus had left her in. Emerald quickly starts to continually punch Venus harshly in the face, which causes Venus's nose to start bleeding. Before Raven had the time to react to what Emerald had just done, Felix gallops forcefully into Triton, who does not see Felix charging into him due to his attention being diverted to Venus being knocked over to the ground by Emerald. Felix's charge into Triton causes Triton, along with Raven and Felix, to be knocked over to the ground beneath them from the harsh impact that was caused between Felix's and Triton's muscular bodies.

Felix quickly stands back on his feet and lifts his head underneath Raven's body to aid him in rolling him over on to his feet also. With the help of Felix, Raven quickly stands up on his feet and tries to stab the sword of Grackle into the head of a stunned Triton, who had just fallen completely over to the ground. Triton regains his focus on what had just happened and rolls out the way of being stabbed by Raven and also stumbles to his feet. Triton grabs his golden chain with the spiked iron ball at the end of it from the ground where he had dropped it when Felix had charged into him, and he swings the golden chain with the spiked iron ball at the end of it around his head and tries to hit Raven with it. Raven swiftly jumps up in the air and out of the way from the heavy blow of the iron spiked ball being swung by Triton. Raven takes a deep breath and prepares to battle against Triton.

THE HAWKS WHO were now on the ground, having fallen from the thick and tall trees when they were attacked by the Spinosaurus and Tyrannosaurs rex, now continue to fight with the Potorians upon the ground of Eagle Forest. The fight is now in the Hawks' favour as most of the Potorians' have lost their metal weapons in the gushing winds of the tornado or have been injured by the tornado itself after it threw the thick and tall trees out of the tornado and back down to the ground, and the trees had crashed upon some of the Potorians.

The Hawks fortunately manage to kill all the remaining Potorians upon the ground by continually shooting at them their powerful green laser beams from their pure green eyes; however, during these smaller fights, the Potorians also kill many of the Hawks by beating them to death before they were killed themselves. Also, the catastrophic tornado continues to lift some Potorians and Hawks up into the air by the power of its twirling winds, and it throws them back to the ground, where they die from the fall in other parts of Eagle Forest.

Back in Hake's big wooden hut in the middle of the Hawks' Tribe Camp, Sapphire is now curiously watching Hake as he reads another spell in the ancient Phoenix language from the book of curses as well as puts other types of coloured potions into the already bubbling turquoise liquid within the black cauldron. Sapphire listens carefully to the words Hake speaks in the ancient phoenix language; she is able to understand parts of what he is saying as she remembers the information she had learnt about the ancient language of Phoenix while studying her PhD in ancient language and literature at Falcon University within Falcon City.

The hot, bubbling turquoise liquid within the black cauldron now bubbles uncontrollably and suddenly turns a purple colour. As Hake finishes speaking the rest of the spell he was reading from the book of curse, it supernaturally releases an outstanding magical sorcerous power that manages to send an invisible power in the form of a blanket that disintegrates the strong and twirling gusty winds of the tornado that was made from the anomaly crystal. The invisible blanket contains and decreases the large tornado to a smaller size; it also causes the grey winds of the tornado to be sent back within the anomaly crystal.

Further in the north direction and quite near to the Hawks' Tribe Camp, the Tyrannosaurus rex continued charging while crashing through the thick and tall trees within Eagle Forest. During this vicious charge, the Tyrannosaurus rex murders several of the Hawks nearer to the Hawks' Tribe Camp by eating them brutally with its sharp and spikey teeth or trampling on them to break their bones and crush their bodies with its large feet with sharp claws at the end of the feet. Parrot is now close by to the Tyrannosaurus rex due this earlier fall to the ground in this direction caused by the Spinosaurus's stiff tail; he was luckily saved from crash-landing to the ground by being caught by one of the Hawks.

Parrot sees almighty power that the Tyrannosaurs rex possesses, and he intuitively starts shooting several of his wooden arrows with metal spikes at the end of it from his wooden bow at the Tyrannosaurus rex. These wooden arrows with the metal spikes at the end of them quickly fly through the air and hit into the Tyrannosaurus rex's large and thick body along with its bulky head. The Tyrannosaurus rex feels the metal spikes of the wooden arrows entering into its skin and roars loudly in pain. The nearby Hawks that were up in the tall and thick trees also start shooting their powerful and toxic green laser beams anxiously from their green eyes; upon impact on the Tyrannosaurs rex, these powerful green laser beams make agonising holes straight through the Tyrannosaurus rex's thick skin. The Tyrannosaurus rex now becomes very mad and crazy from experiencing the blistering holes caused by the powerful green laser beams. In rage, the Tyrannosaurus rex whips its strong and long tail into the tall and thick trees, where these Hawks shooting their green laser beams from their eyes were positioned. This now causes the Hawks to lose their balance and fall from the tall and thick trees, and as they crash to the ground beneath them, their bones shatter into several broken pieces.

Parrot quickly looks around him; he sees a smaller and climbable tree near the outraged Tyrannosaurs rex, and he sprints over to this smaller and climbable tree; he rapidly climbs his way up the tree via the tough wooden branches that were in abundance upon this smaller tree. Parrot applies all of his energy to climb up this smaller tree quickly until he reaches high enough to tower over the Tyrannosaurs rex's large and broad body. Without a pause, Parrot jumps from one of the strong wooden branches that he was standing upon attached to this smaller tree, and as he glides through the air from the smaller tree, he lands on top of the large back of the Tyrannosaurs rex.

Parrot now breathes deeply upon realising that he is still alive from the jump off the smaller tree and on to the Tyrannosaurus rex's back. Parrot quickly pulls himself across the Tyrannosaurus rex's large and broad back and hurries to reach the tough neck of the Tyrannosaurus rex. Parrot now pulls two of his specially designed fury raptor throwing stars from one of his brown coat's pocket; he forcefully slices the two fury raptor throwing stars deep into the Tyrannosaurus rex's tough neck with the sharp silver points of the fury raptor throwing stars going inwards first. The two fury raptor throwing stars' silver sharp spikes manage to cut through the tough neck of the Tyrannosaurus rex where a lavish amount of thick blood begins to squirt out. More blood continues to pour out as Parrot makes several more harsh slits into the Tyrannosaurus rex's tough neck with his two fury raptor throwing stars.

Parrot puts the two fury raptor throwing stars back in one of the pockets of his brown coat and then grabs three wooden arrows with sharp metal spikes at the end of them that were fixed within the wooden pouch next to his wooden bow around his back. Parrot plunges these three wooden arrows with sharp metal spikes at the end of them deep within the open slits that he had made within the tough neck of Tyrannosaurs rex. These three wooden arrows with the sharp metal spikes at the end of them get shoved weightily deep within the tough neck attached to the gigantic body of the Tyrannosaurs rex. It makes the heart of the Tyrannosaurus rex to receive much pressure and stress and causes it to stop beating that now kills the Tyrannosaurus rex. The newly dead Tyrannosaurs rex loses its balance from its large feet with claws at the end of its feet and falls over to one side and crashes heavy upon the ground of Eagle Forest that causes a large thudding sound to be heard along with many of the trees in the immediate area being shaken about by such a powerful impact upon the ground.

As the Tyrannosaurus rex falls heavily to the ground, Parrot quickly jumps off from the large and broad back of the Tyrannosaurus rex; he also lands upon the ground on to his knees, where he stays down upon the ground breathing deeply in exhaustion. Fifty-four Hawks were killed in the battle within Eagle Forest, and the remaining twenty-six Hawks, along with Parrot, are all now injured and their energy depleted from the battle. After a short period of time contemplating what had happened during the fight against the Potorians and the Tyrannosaurus rex, Parrot leads the Hawks near him to make their way back to the Hawks' Tribe Camp, where they will again continue to fight in order to protect Hake and Sapphire from the remaining creatures that they assume are only Triton and Venus now.

Back in the southern outskirts from the Hawks' Tribe Camp within Eagle Forest, Venus also feels with her magical creature abilities the death of the Tyrannosaurus rex that she had created, while she is being punched in the face by Emerald. In fury, due to the feeling Venus experiences because one of her east creatures has been killed, Venus forcefully scrapes her sharp and pointy fingernails across Emerald's face, which slits one of Emerald's cheeks and blood begins to dribble out. Emerald stops punching Venus due to her cheek being in pain; she then hurriedly grabs the small silver sword she had placed in her pocket and tries to stab it into Venus's bruised face. Venus swiftly stops the small silver sword just before it can pierce into her own face by strongly grabbing on to Emerald's hand with both of her hands in a hard grip to stop Emerald's hand getting any closer to her face with the small silver sword.

Both Emerald and Venus struggle with their hands that are now both attached to the small silver sword in front of Venus's face; for a brief moment, both Emerald and Venus are unable to move from this position, until Venus manages to push Emerald from being on top off her by kicking her right knee hard into Emerald's chest. Emerald rolls off Venus and now rolls over on to the ground beside Venus in pain, which causes her to drop the small silver sword upon the ground as Emerald uses both of her hands to grab her chest that was now in pain from Venus kneeing it. Now that Emerald was not on top of Venus no more, Venus rolls over and pushes her hands against the ground to stand back on her feet; she stumbles over to the anomaly crystal that was not too far away from where she was lying on the ground.

Venus quickly picks up the anomaly crystal from the ground. Emerald notices what Venus is doing and forgets the pain within her chest and also stumbles on to her feet and faces Venus. Venus gives Emerald an evil smirk, and just as she is about to release another one of the anomaly crystal's astonishing elemental powers against Emerald, Venus sees from the corner of one of her eyes that Raven barely misses a powerful hit by Triton's golden chain with the spiked ball at the end of it. Raven manoeuvres out of its way and now manages to stab Triton forcefully in his strong muscular right thigh with the sword of Grackle. Triton loses his balance after experiencing the intense pain caused from the sword of Grackle's blow, which also releases a mystical power that creates an infection within his right thigh. Triton now falls to the ground upon his knees in agony as his blood pours out of the wounded right thigh.

Without hesitation, Raven lifts the sword of Grackle quickly in the air in order to swing it in front of him and finally cuts off Triton's head to end the great war. As Venus glumly notices what is happening to Triton, she experiences feelings of intense loss and sorrow at the thought of Triton being killed, and she also enviously realises Raven's love for his wife Emerald.

'Raven! say goodbye to your wife!' hollers Venus to distract Raven's attention. Venus holds the anomaly crystal quickly out in front of her;

the anomaly crystal frantically swirls with the colours of the rainbow and shades of white and black until unexpectedly, the anomaly crystal turns a pure black colour. Suddenly the anomaly crystal releases a thin but deep black smoke that leaves the anomaly crystal in a peculiar manner and swiftly covers Emerald's entire physical body. This thin pure black smoke goes in and out of Emerald's whole body, and it sucks her life force and soul from her human self; the thin pure black smoke, along with Emerald's soul, is now quickly transferred back into the anomaly crystal. The anomaly crystal releases a slight scream that was from Emerald's soul as the colours of the rainbow and the shades of white and black begin to swirl around the anomaly crystal in a frantic manner again. Emerald's physical dead body falls slowly to the ground beneath her.

'No!' yells Raven as he instantly leaves Triton kneeling on the ground in front of him and desperately races over to Emerald. He drops his sword of Grackle and is just able to catch Emerald within his arms before she hit the ground. Venus momentarily laughs at Emerald's death, and then she quickly makes her red eyes change back into the pure white colour as she applies her Animagus abilities that enable her to turn her physical body back into the Quetzalcoatlus form.

While holding the anomaly crystal within the Quetzalcoatlus's beak, Venus flaps her large scaly wings to lift the body of the Quetzalcoatlus to hover above the ground. She now flies over to Triton who was still kneeling upon the ground, and she grabs his large broad shoulders with the Quetzalcoatlus's clawed feet. Venus flaps her large scaly wings rapidly in order to fly her and Triton, who was still holding on to his golden chain with the iron spiked ball at the end of it. Venus now flies them both high up in the dark sky between the thick and tall trees until they eventually reach the very top of the largest Kapok trees' foliage, which leads them both out of Eagle Forest. Venus flies them both swiftly back towards Triton's Underground Dungeon in the far south-west location of the Planet of Phoenix. Raven cries and shouts loudly in misery and disbelief as he holds tightly on to Emerald's body within his weakened arms and kneels on the ground of Eagle Forest. Raven glances into Emerald's empty beautiful blue eyes and sees a lifeless Emerald staring right through him.

The Curse of Death

Twenty-Six

THE EARLY MORNING sunlight shines through the cold, soundless, vast, and mystical Eagle Forest. The brisk and cold wind flickers across the leaves of the numerous broken and fallen tall and thick trees throughout Eagle Forest, where bodies of several Hawks and Potorians lie still and dead upon the muddy ground. Most of the Hawks' and Potorians' bones were either broken or shattered from the immense power of the tornado that was released from the anomaly crystal, or the bodies of some Hawks and Potorians were decapitated by the extensive rage of the Spinosaurus and Tyrannosaurs rex that Venus had created using her magical creature abilities. Other wild animals that also lived within Eagle Forest, such as foxes, dears, badgers, hedgehogs, squirrels, and various types of birds now start to cover the bodies of dead Hawks and Potorians with fallen dried leaves or begin digging big holes within the soil for burying these dead bodies.

Raven, who is at presently located just south of the Hawks' Tribe Camp within Eagle Forest is still kneeling upon the ground in absolute shock and is crying continuously while holding Emerald's dead body in his bruised and muddy arms. Raven squints his eyes through his heartbroken tears upon Emerald's beautiful face but only sees the glare of Emerald's bright blue eyes staring back at him without any signs of emotion or movement.

Felix now lowers his big and strong muscular legs to kneel upon the ground next to Raven and brushes his wavy black hair upon the back of his neck against Emerald's body, hoping to gain a reaction from her, but again Emerald makes no movement with her body. Raven's head and eyes start to become all blurry, and his body feels all numb at the sight of his newly-wed wife and soulmate being untimely murdered and now taken away from him. Raven's mind hopelessly wanders into deep and dark places thinking of nearly all his family being dead. He will now be alone for the rest of his life and will also be all by himself in the remaining great war against Triton and Venus. The time for Raven seems to last for an eternity as he can't take his eyes away from Emerald, who rests motionless in his arms upon the ground of Eagle Forest.

Parrot and Sapphire are reunited, after Parrot along with several Hawks, hurries back to Hake's big wooden hut in the middle of the Hawks' Tribe Camp following the fight they just experienced with the Tyrannosaurus rex where Parrot was fortunate enough to kill it. After Parrot reunites with Sapphire, they leave Hake's big wooden hut and quickly run fin the south direction through the winding and bending passageways between the tall and thick trees of Eagle Forest, hoping to locate Raven and Emerald and if necessary help them defeat Triton and Venus in the battle of Eagle Forest that had lasted for a couple of hours during the night. After around twenty minutes of both Parrot and Sapphire anxiously running and searching for Raven and Emerald within Eagle Forest, Parrot and Sapphire now see in the distance the back of Raven's body; Felix is next to him, where they are both kneeling upon the ground.

As Parrot and Sapphire come closer to Raven, they despondently realise that Raven is holding Emerald's body in his arms. Sapphire immediately begins to cry emotionally, but she quickly wipes her tears away from her cold cheeks as she tries to compose herself in an attempt to support Raven. Parrot and Sapphire walk slowly up to Raven, and they end up standing next to Raven and Felix. They both look in despair and wretchedness at Raven holding Emerald's dead body in his arms. Raven doesn't look up at Parrot and Sapphire standing next to him; he just continues to keep staring into Emerald's empty and lifeless beautiful blue eyes. Parrot gently puts his left hand upon Raven's right shoulder and pauses for a moment; at the same time, Sapphire notices Raven's sword of Grackle left upon the ground near Raven. Sapphire leans over and picks up the sword of Grackle, and then she also strokes the long black hair of Felix's neck gently. She then carefully grabs his brown rope reins in order to help Felix stand back upon his large legs and strong hooves.

'I'm really sorry about Emerald, Raven. I don't know what to say,' says Parrot softly.

'I can't find any words to express how deeply devastated we are to see this sight before our eyes,' remarks Sapphire with tears still rolling down her cheeks.

'There's nothing that either of you can say or do that will make this situation any better,' Raven tries to say but finds it difficult as he is crying and is choked up by Emerald's death. Parrot and Sapphire look hopelessly at each other.

'Raven, I know all hope seems lost at the moment, but we must hurry back to the Hawks' Tribe Camp as it's still too dangerous for us to be out in the open like this within Eagle Forest without protection. We don't know where Triton and Venus are and if they have no more monstrous surprises for us,' explains Sapphire quietly but in a concerned manner while looking behind her, but all Sapphire can see is silent and motionless movement throughout the tall and thick trees of the endless Eagle Forest.

'It doesn't matter as I don't care what happens to me now; without Emerald in my life, I don't want to live no more,' sobs Raven, still looking at Emerald's soulless face.

'Don't say something like that, Raven, and surely you don't mean it. Sapphire and I are here to look after you and help you through this terrible situation. Emerald would also want you to continue living and fighting in honour of her,' says Parrot in a comforting tone.

'Besides, Triton and Venus have escaped Eagle Forest like cowards, and the Hawks have killed the remaining Potorians . . . Actually, wait, I do still want to live, so I can inflict so much pain and misery upon Triton and Venus that they wish they would have never been born on the Planet of Phoenix,' curses Raven angrily with thoughts of vengeance. Parrot and Sapphire look again at each other in concern on hearing Raven's dark thoughts.

'Come on, Raven, let's go and seek Hake's advice. He'll know how to deal with all that's happened this past night,' states Sapphire.

'What could Hake possibly do to make this situation any better?' asks Raven in a pessimistic way.

'It's all right, Raven, I promise you that we will all help you through this difficult time. You just need to trust me,' says Parrot confidently. Parrot now moves his hand from his shoulder and places both of his hands slowly on to Raven's arms to release his grip that he had around Emerald's dead body. With the help of Sapphire, Parrot gently picks up and takes Emerald's dead body away from Raven's arms, which still feel very numb to Raven. Raven and Sapphire then place Emerald's dead body carefully back down upon the ground next to Raven. Parrot and Sapphire each hold one of Raven's arms, and they apply the strength in their arms to help Raven get up from the ground and stand upon his feet. After a moment of making sure that Raven can sustain his balance upon his feet, Parrot and Sapphire help Raven climb on to the strong back of Felix. Raven does climb on to the back of Felix, but he does this very slowly as he feels unaware of his bodily movements.

Parrot and Sapphire make sure Raven is sitting firmly upon Felix's large back, and then they both carefully pick up Emerald's dead body from the ground and gently lay it over Felix's black back. They now gently take Raven's hands and place them back on Emerald's dead body, which is now on top of Felix. Parrot walks slowly around to the front of Felix and grabs Felix's brown rope reins, while Sapphire holds on to Raven's sword of Grackle in one of her hands. Parrot and Sapphire begin walking gradually across the ground where they lead Felix with Raven, who is holding Emerald's dead body, upon his back in the north-east direction towards the Hawks' Tribe Camp. As they walk back to the Hawks' Tribe Camp, Sapphire holds Parrot's other hand tightly while Raven looks hopelessly into the thin air out in front of him rather than looking back down at Emerald's dead body that is now resting in front of him on the back of Felix.

Raven is holding Emerald's dead body while sitting on the back of Felix. Parrot and Sapphire are walking across the ground, and Parrot is holding on to Felix's brown rope reins to guide him to the Hawks' Tribe Camp; they reach this destination in just under an hour. As they all walk into the middle of the Hawks' Tribe Camp, Parrot and Sapphire notice the twenty-six remaining Hawks have started to rebuild their semi-broken-down Hawks' Tribe Camp. They see plenty of pieces of broken wood from the wooden hut homes of the Hawks, fallen tall and thick trees, and various destroyed plants everywhere.

A few of the Hawks have also begun collecting the dead bodies of Hawks that were residing around several different directions within Eagle Forest. After locating the dead bodies, these Hawks will bury the dead Hawks' bodies in the big holes of the soil that the wild animals of Eagle Forest had dug earlier. The Hawks that were within the Hawks' Tribe Camp cleaning up the area now watch in silence and sorrow as Raven, holding Emerald's dead body upon Felix's back, along with Parrot and Sapphire, passes through the middle of the Hawks' Tribe Camp.

RAVEN WAS HOLDING carefully on to Emerald's dead body on top of Felix's large back while being led by Parrot, who was holding on to Felix's brown rope reins along with Sapphire. They all now approach the outside of Hake's big wooden hut in the middle of the Hawks' Tribe Camp next to the very old and very large Kapok tree. Two of the Hawks presently near Hake's big wooden hut help Parrot and Sapphire to safely remove Emerald's dead body from being led across the back of Felix, and they carefully take her through the colour cloth that covered the entrance to Hake's big wooden hut; they all place Emerald's dead body softly upon the floor within Hake's big wooden hut.

Raven now also slowly climbs down from Felix and walks through the colourful cloth into Hake's big wooden hut as another Hawk collects Felix and ties his brown rope reins to a nearby tree. Other Hawks bring Felix a wooden bowl of water and some fresh apples. Upon entering through the colourful cloth of Hake's big wooden hut, Raven stands next to Sapphire and takes the sword of Grackle back from her. Hake is currently sitting down at the opposite end to the entrance within his big wooden hut; he is sitting upon the floor within his big wooden hut with his eyes closed. Raven, Parrot, and Sapphire look at Hake with devastated expressions about their bruised and muddy faces.

'Much sorrow has come to us all on this most cursed of days. I'm very sorry for all of your loss that you have had to endure, especially you, Raven,' says Hake soothingly and collectively. Raven pauses briefly due to his immense grief; he then looks at the black cauldron that is positioned within the middle of Hake's big wooden hut, and he sees a green liquid that bubbling inside following its change back from the purple colour that Hake and momentarily turned it into when he disintegrated the tornado during the battle of Eagle Forest.

'I thought you could see all that is happening on the planet of Phoenix from your sorcerous cauldron? Why didn't you do anything to stop Emerald's death?' asks Raven curiously and angrily, remembering that Hake had told them about Triton and Venus coming to battle against them at Eagle Forest from what he had seen thorough his magical black cauldron.

'Raven, calm yourself,' interrupts Parrot.

'Unfortunately, Emerald's fate was beyond my control. However, I did try to warn her when I explained that she needed to let the grief of her deceased mother free from her thoughts. Otherwise, it would also destroy her too, but unfortunately she didn't adhere upon my warning,' answers Hake as Raven looks gloomily towards the floor and sees Emerald's dead body lying there.

'Is there nothing you can do, Hake? You are the most powerful sorcerer alive on the Planet of Phoenix. Surely some kind of magic could help Emerald?' pleads Sapphire as Raven sharply looks back up at Hake in hope. Hake pauses a moment as he is in deep thought; he then opens his brown eyes slowly to look transcendentally at Raven, Parrot, and Sapphire.

'There's but only one sorcerous spell that could be of any help in this situation. It's called the curse of death, and it's an ancient type of black magic that is very dangerous and may possess unforeseen circumstances,' replies Hake in a titillating manner as Raven interrupts.

'You mean we could bring Emerald back to life? I don't care what it takes. I'll do anything,' states Raven in desperation. Hake pauses again for a moment as he slowly stands up from the floor; he walks steadily over to grab the large and old book of curses from a wooden shelf fixed upon one of the wooden sides of his big wooden hut. The book of curses is a medium-sized book that has a plain wooden front and back cover and copious black pages inside of it; the curses upon these black pages were written in various animals blood in the ancient

Phoenix language by Hake, Grackle, and other mystical creatures like a preternatural green lizard-like creature called Mamushi, a white unicorn, a red tiger, a blue sea lion, and a black dragon.

The book of curses was written over thousands of years ago when the beginning of magic and sorcery originated and was practised by these mystical creatures, where pure and good as well as dark and evil magic interacted with each other in a distinctive but harmonious manner. Hake slowly turns the black pages within the book of curses until he reaches a page that has a small magical curse written in lamb's blood in the ancient Phoenix language upon the middle of the page; surrounding this written cruse were pictures of various dead mystical creatures.

'As far as I'm aware this curse has never been practised properly before upon a human. At the time of its creation, myself, Grackle, and the other mystical creatures who also aided in writing this book of curses felt that this particular curse was too problematic to practise upon a living human, but we all felt that this curse was required to be generated as a last resort if all other hope was lost for the humans living upon the Planet of Phoenix. There is much unknown about the exact nature of this curse, but I believe you will need a magical catalyst to transfer the soul of another living being when replacing the soul of the dead victim,' explains Hake questionably.

'Where would we find a magical catalyst?' asks Sapphire intriguingly.

'The anomaly crystal is worthy of being a magical catalyst. The anomaly crystal has taken Emerald's soul, so you will need to retrieve the anomaly crystal from Triton and Venus in order to perform this curse or death. You will also need to sacrifice another life in exchange for Emerald's soul as well as to also get Emerald's dead body to drink a specially designed blue healing potion before the written curse of death is read aloud in the ancient Phoenix language.

'The blue potion will aid in extracting Emerald's soul back from the anomaly crystal at the same time as another soul is also being sacrificed. You must get the life of another that you want sacrifice to also drink the blue potion at a similar time too,' Hake enlightens them as he starts to pull all kinds of ancient different coloured magical potions and herbs residing upon one of his small wooden shelves at one of the sides within his big wooden hut. Hake now begins making the blue healing potion in the black cauldron. Hake adds the other different coloured magical potions and various kinds of dried herbs to the green liquid in the black cauldron; the hot liquid begins to bubble uncontrollably and quickly changes to a bright blue colour.

'I'll do it! I'll drink this blue healing potion and sacrifice my soul in exchange for Emeralds,' remarks Raven with a slight hope in his voice at the thought of Emerald being brought back to life.

'No, Raven, you can't, and besides, I know Emerald, and she wouldn't be able to live with herself if she knew that you sacrificed your life for hers,' states Sapphire in a worried manner.

'Why don't we sacrifice that wicked creature witch Venus who took Emerald's soul in the first place,' crossly says Parrot.

'Yes, that she-devil doesn't deserve to live for her crimes against the humans,' declares Raven.

'You must perform this curse of death soon as it can only be conducted within seventy-two hours of the initial victim dying due to the body deteriorating to a point beyond return after this time limit. You will also have to overcome another problem. The curse of death like all the other curses written within this book of curses is only written in the ancient Phoenix language, and as I am unable to come with you on this final quest, you will need someone to read the ancient Phoenix language aloud,' states Hake.

'Why can't you come with us? We will really need your superior sorcery to finally defeat Triton and Venus, especially as they now possess the anomaly crystal,' asks Parrot in a troubled reaction.

'I have to stay here and protect the fragile and important life, along with the spiritual environment within Eagle Forest for as long as I possibly can. This will be my last and final gift that I am able to offer to the Planet of Phoenix, my time existing here upon the Planet of Phoenix is unfortunately coming to an end. Hence, I regrettably won't be accompanying you all at the specific time you will need to perform this curse of death,' replies Hake unhappily. The two Hawks in Hake's big wooden hut become dejected with regards to what Hake has just said about his life coming to the end of its time on the Planet of Phoenix.

'I think I can read the ancient Phoenix language as I practised it within my PhD in ancient language and literature,' says Sapphire, remembering how Hake read the curses from the book of curses when he used it's magical sorcery to make the Spinosaurus disappear from Eagle Forest as well as to disintegrate the tornado that had occurred during the battle of Eagle Forest.

'Yes, I always knew you could read the ancient Phoenix language, Sapphire, but I needed you to realise that you do indeed possess the knowledge to do so. However, you will require to focus, concentrate and most importantly understand the words you read, for these most powerful curses must be read accurately and precisely otherwise the magic creature could turn out to be beyond perilous,' remarks Hake as he now passes Sapphire the book of curses along with the blue potion that he places into a small glass container from the black cauldron.

'Parrot, you will need to stay strong for Raven and Sapphire as they will require the energy from your strength and heart for what you are all about to find out and inevitably endure during this final great war of our time,' says Hake wisely.

'Of course, I will always be there for my family,' replies Parrot as he holds on to Sapphire's hand firmly at the thought of what they might have to face when the great war inevitably comes to be. Hake nods at Parrot with respect and then turns towards Raven.

'Raven, I have one last thing to give you,' says Hake as he carefully lifts a small wooden handle from the floor that lifts up the mud that covered it to uncover a wide and deep hidden compartment. Raven's expression becomes one of surprise as the hidden compartment appears from the floor within Hake's big wooden hut. Hake bends over and reaches down deep within in the mud and pulls out a big and shiny silver shield designed in an octagon shape that has gold writing down the middle of the shield, which is also written in the ancient Phoenix language. This writing down the middle of the silver shield reads . . .

Blessed to the bloodline of Grackle.

'What is this shield?' asks Raven, mystified, as Parrot and Sapphire also curiously stare at the silver shield with great interest.

'This is the shield of Grackle. I have kept it hidden in this compartment for hundreds of years as I promised Grackle that I would keep it safe when he originally gave it to me just before he sacrificed his own life to create the anomaly crystal back in Alder Village. I kept the shield of Grackle hidden here within the spiritual Eagle Forest for the precise time I was bestowed with the honour of giving it to the youngest and last remaining bloodline of Grackle,' smiles Hake enthusiastically.

'The shield looks very strong and tough,' says Raven in amazement, looking at the shiny silver shield of Grackle.

'This shield is the most durable shield that has ever been created on the Planet of Phoenix and along with the sword of Grackle that you also possess, it will protect you from boundless evil in your greatest time of need,' elucidates Hake.

'Let's hope none of us will ever find ourselves in our greatest time of need,' mentions an upset Sapphire, looking at Emerald's dead body still on the floor of Hake's big wooden hut.

'The strength, love, and knowledge of the humans are resilient and will remain that way in the afterlife. All of your ancestors will be watching over you and will help in providing you with the courage and guidance through these darkest of times forthcoming. I'm glad that I got to play my supernatural role on the Planet of Phoenix one final time. It has also been a grand honour to meet the bloodline of Grackle once again as Grackle foretold me about this very day. These encounters with you all have brought me back many blissful memories of Grackle and Alder Village from a time long ago, but not forgotten. I bless hope upon you humans and wish you well on your journeys and lives on this most wonderful and beautiful Planet of Phoenix within this universe. I also want to bless you now, Raven, with regards to your future bloodline descendant of Grackle,' says Hake.

'My future . . . ?' says Raven confusedly as Hake interrupts.

'You must unfortunately all leave Eagle Forest quickly and seek help from other allies of your human race that you will need to assist you against Triton and Venus and many other evil creatures during the great war. Believe in yourselves and one another, for you will all face many difficult challenges yet to come. You all have the purest of souls that will guide you through this uncertain time,' states Hake as he nods one last time at Raven, Parrot, and Sapphire. Hake walks over to Raven and passes him the shield of Grackle. Hake makes sure that Raven grasps it tightly in his other hand before Hake releases his grip from the shield of Grackle. Hake looks at Raven, bursting with pride at the sight of him holding on to the sword and shield of Grackle. Hake then walks around the black cauldron; he closes his brown eyes and sits back down slowly to the floor of his big wooden hut at the opposite end to the entrance.

'Thank you, Hake, for your words of wisdom and for helping us during the great war,' says Sapphire as Raven and Parrot move towards Emerald's dead body on the floor. One of the Hawks within Hake's big wooden hut holds his brown feathery arms out for Raven to give him his sword and shield of Grackle, which he carries outside of Hake's big wooden hut for Raven. Raven and Parrot now carefully pick up Emerald's dead body and steadily walk outside of Hake's big wooden hut through the colourful cloth. Once outside Hake's big wooden hut, Raven and Parrot carry Emerald's dead body over to the nearby tree that Felix was tied to, and they carefully place Emerald's dead body back on top of Felix's strong black back. Raven quickly unties Felix's brown rope reins from the tree he was tied around and then climbs on top of him to hold Emerald's dead body securely; the Hawk hands him back his sword and shield of Grackle.

'We must go seek aid from Lynx and his Pine guards. Hopefully, he will have returned back to Pine Village by now,' says Parrot to Raven and Sapphire, just as the other Hawk walks out of Hake's big wooden hut through the colourful cloth and walks up to Parrot and points in the east direction within Eagle Forest.

'Go straight through the passageways between the trees down this east route, and it will lead you the quickest way out of Eagle Forest towards the human villages,' murmurs the Hawk as he gave Parrot his wooden bow and wooden arrows with metal spikes at the end of it along with his fury raptor throwing stars that they had found scattered through Eagle Forest. This Hawk also gives to Sapphire her small silver dagger that she had also dropped during the battle of Eagle Forest that was against Triton, Venus, the Potorians and Venus's dinosaur creatures she had created.

'Thank you, and yes, we don't have much time now. The curse of death that will hopefully bring Emerald back to life will expire in now less than seventy-two hours,' says a troubled Raven, looking at the Hawk.

'We must hurry then,' remarks Sapphire. Sapphire hugs the Hawk who gave her the small silver dagger, much to the Hawk's surprise.

She then begins to run out of the Hawks' Tribe Camp and through the passageways amongst the tall and thick trees in Eagle Forest in the east direction. Raven, who was holding tightly on to Emerald's dead body, still manages to ride upon Felix. Parrot also runs and quickly follows after Sapphire, who has started running out of Eagle Forest in an attempt to get back to Pine Village as quickly as possible.

Twenty-Seven

VENUS IS STILL in her Quetzalcoatlus dinosaur physical form, and she is currently flying swiftly through the infinite cold and damp skies across the Planet of Phoenix. Venus flaps her large, scaly, and powerful wings frantically to enable her to quickly travel vast distances in a short period of time to achieve her destination at Triton's Underground Dungeon located at darker south side of the Planet of Phoenix. Venus manages to reach this location in just over two hours; she now approaches the air of the Realm of the Deserted Lands that is covered with gusty winds that consist of strong winds carrying tiny rock and dirt particles. Venus finds this environment harsher to fly though, but due to her resilience and determination, she keeps flying quickly until she reaches Triton's Underground Dungeon that is constructed below the Planet of Phoenix's rocky surface in the furthest south-west part of the Realm of Deserted Lands. During their journey from Eagle Forest, which they left just over two hours ago, Venus has the anomaly crystal fixed within her mouth, and she is holding firmly on to Triton's large and muscular shoulders with her sturdy and clawed feet.

Triton is still in intense pain and agony due to the injury he incurred back in Eagle Forest from when Raven stabbed the sword of Grackle deep into his right thigh. The open wound is still bleeding, and the sword of Grackle magically inflicted a deteriorating curse that spreads through the blood of the bodies of evil creatures such as Triton. Triton is also now mentally quite weak and woozy sometimes, as he has to close his eyes to rest, but then he is quickly jolted back to being alert again, because of the sharp and excruciating pains that he experiences spontaneously in various different parts of his body due to the wound caused from the almighty sword of Grackle. Triton is also still holding on to his golden chain with the iron spiked ball at the end of it as Venus carries him while flying through the skies of the Planet of Phoenix, but as the journey continues, Triton's grip upon the heavy golden chain with the iron spiked ball at the end of it became looser, and he finds it difficult to keep holding it towards the end of their journey back to Triton's Underground Dungeon.

Venus is aware of Triton's condition and knows what the sword of Grackle can inflict upon evil creatures if they are unluckily stabbed by it. This is why Venus has exhausted all her energy in flying back to Triton's Underground Dungeon from Eagle Forest. Venus now reaches the area and decides to quickly fly directly down to the ground through the gusty winds with tiny rock and dirt particles within it. Venus maneuverers her Quetzalcoatlus form to continue flying down within the underground passageway that connects to Triton's Underground Dungeon at the far south side from the rocky surface of the Realm of Deserted Lands. Venus now carefully but swiftly flies straight through the underground narrow passageway and then continues into the main hall of Triton's Underground Dungeon; she quickly serves through the other twining hallways until Venus reaches Triton and Venus's bedroom within Triton's Underground Dungeon.

Upon entering into Triton and Venus's bedroom, Venus releases the grip of her clawed feet upon Triton's large muscular shoulders above their large bed. Triton flops down on top of the large bed, and the jolt of the landing upon the large bed causes more intense throbbing within Triton's thigh. The sudden shock of this pain makes Triton release his weak grip on his golden chain with the spiked ball at the end of it that now drops upon the floor of Triton and Venus's bedroom. Venus opens her sharp teeth which were holding on to the anomaly crystal in her beaked mouth, and she drops the anomaly crystal on to their large bed. Venus hovers her Quetzalcoatlus body slowly to the floor until she touches the floor with her clawed feet; she then concentrates strongly to apply her Animagus abilities, where her physical form as the Quetzalcoatlus dinosaur supernaturally turns back into her normal physical body, and her eyes also turn back to their normal red colour again.

VENUS LOOKS AT Triton, an upset expression on her face, as she witnesses and understands the suffering and grief he is enduring from the wounded thigh.

'Are you all right, my love?' asks Venus sympathetically, placing one of her hands on Triton's bulky chest.

'No! I'm not all right. This is the worst pain that I've ever experienced. The wound from that deceitful sword of Grackle has inflicted its magical influence upon my thigh, and now it feels like this wound's soreness is dissolving all of my body from within inside of me,' moans and groans Triton while holding and gripping on to his right thigh with both of his strong large hands.

'Yes, I've heard rumours that the sword of Grackle does indeed have a magical essence about it. Upon its stab wound, it's meant to wither away evil things such as creatures that are mistakenly deemed to be evil, such as ourselves,' replies Venus in an annoyed manner.

'I don't care about the history of that blasted sword of Grackle. I just want to get rid of this terrible pain from my thigh,' hollers a cantankerous Triton.

'I'll bandage it up tightly for you now, and hopefully that will slow the pace of the painful magical essence that has been injected and travelling throughout your body,' replies Venus as she quickly hurries over to some wooden draws in the corner of their bedroom. Venus ruffles her petite hands through these wooden draws that are filled with her provocative clothing, until she finds one of her white netted tights; she rips the white netted tights apart in order to create a long piece of white material that she will be able to tie around Triton's right thigh where the wound from the sword of Grackle had been received. Venus now runs back to Triton, who is still vulnerably laid on their bed; Venus tightly wraps the newly made white material around Triton's right thigh where the cut wound is located, and she then ties her white netted tights into a tight knot as Triton yells in discomfort at the same time due to his dark skin being clenched together.

'I'm sorry my love, but that's the best I can do for you at the moment to relieve your pain,' says Venus softly as she moves back a bit from Triton, who is currently wriggling in agony. After a few moments of feeling intense pain, Triton leans up from the bed and grabs Venus's head with his long arm and pulls her towards his face to give her a passionate kiss on the lips so that he can forget about the throbbing pain he is presently experiencing.

'Thank you, my love. You have been great, and as long as you are by my side, I will get over this ridiculous wound. But I can't believe I managed to let that puny human Raven stab me in the thigh with his sword of Grackle,' says Triton angrily, still holding on to the back of Venus's head with his large hand.

'You shouldn't blame yourself, my love. There were loads of situations happening during the battle of Eagle Forest that were distracting for all of us, and those humans can be mighty sneaky sometimes, especially since Hake and his Hawks joined forces with Raven and Raven's friends against us. Besides, I have indeed made Raven suffer by ultimately taking away his wife from him,' states Venus as she looks at the anomaly crystal, pondering upon what has happened to Emerald's soul that was sucked into it.

'You're right, my woman, and I was more concerned about your life than mine anyways. You were also brilliant in destroying that disgusting wife of Raven's that he deserved to have lost for what he has now done to me,' says Triton cruelly.

'I'm just wondering though if he will either break down because of his loss for his soulmate or return to face us again with vengeance,' mentions Venus.

'Well, in that case, we should be expecting to fight with him again in the great war then, as if he kills you, I will stop at nothing to make sure that he suffers the most pain that can ever be experienced,' explains Triton as he kisses Venus again on her tender lips.

'As I would also do the same for you, my warlord,' replies Venus as she now leans away from Triton and grabs her entire left shoulder, feeling a painful twinge from the hole that had been created by one of the Hawks shooting its powerful and toxic green laser beam through a wooden tree that had gone straight through into Venus's left shoulder during the battle of Eagle Forest.

'How are your wounds from those pathetic bird creatures shooting their laser beams at you?' asks Triton with a furious tone to his voice.

'My shoulder does still sting something rotten, but I am more concerned about your wounded thigh as I'm not entirely sure how much damage the sword of Grackle will continue to inflict upon you,' says Venus worriedly as she places her hand exactly over the small wound she has in her shoulder and then presses it tightly with her fingers, which causes blood to spill out, but this blood will then dry around her skin and cover the open small wound in her left shoulder.

'That traitorous Hake should never have got involved with the humans against us in this battle and the great war between creatures and humans. He will suffer greatly for getting his Hawks involved and also for what they have inflicted upon your beautiful body,' says Triton angrily as he places his hand on Venus's hand over her wound in her shoulder.

'Thank you for showing your love for me, and when we both go back to Eagle Forest to make Hake and his Hawk Tribe suffer intensely. I will also force him to explain to me how I can remove that cursed wound from your thigh. I also have some other bad news though, that I haven't told you about yet, my love,' mentions Venus.

'What is it now?' asks Triton irritably, still feeling sharp pain in his right thigh.

'When I was flying back here from Eagle Forest, I connected again with that white dove that I had created earlier. The white dove was flying high above Pine Village, where I could perceive that Vicious and the Potorian army weren't victorious in the battle against Pine Village, and they are now all dead,' explains Venus in a disappointed tone.

'Goddam that Vicious. Now due to Vicious, Vulture, and all of the Potorians being pathetically demolished during those battles with the humans, I don't see we have any other choice but to seek aid from Viper and his Serpents. We must also do this immediately before Raven has the chance to regroup with the other villages who have also probably been trying to gain the help from King Exodus and his royal Falcon guard within Falcon City. Raven will probably stop at nothing now to avenge Emerald as we both would do the same for one another. If this is the case, then we will be outnumbered along with having to face this great war against all sides and locations of humans across the Planet of Phoenix,' remarks Triton.

'Unfortunately, I do agree with you about requiring the help of Viper and his Serpents during the great war as they will all be very useful against the royal Falcon guards of Falcon City. But first we need to wait here until you have fully recovered from your wound as I won't tempt fate and lose you to death in this forthcoming great war. I can send my monstrous beast creations to recruit Viper and his Serpents as well, and they can also kill all the remaining villages and human within it over the entire Planet of Phoenix,' states Venus cunningly.

'Don't concern yourself. I'll be fine for now unless the pain within my thigh spreads any further to the rest of my body. Besides, Viper won't join allegiance with us unless he sees us in front of him, with the anomaly crystal in our grasp. These kinds of doubts will be racing through Viper's mind due to his failed experiences that he endured with Lord Scartor in the past battles and attempts they had pursued to retrieve the anomaly crystal from the descendants of Grackle but never succeeded. We must then go ourselves to Komodo Jungle and show the anomaly crystal to him and also try to convince him that it will be worth his while to join with us during the great war, but I will only be satisfied with his allegiance if he also follows my command,' explains Triton.

'Don't worry. I can be very persuasive to the likes of spineless creatures like Viper. I will also do as you command and abide by your plans that will come into action now,' replies Venus in an unconvincing manner.

'Your powerful beast creations will be of great use to us during this great war, but we still need to gather as many forces as possible by ourselves to make sure that the humans will not be any threat to us in their collective numbers,' comments Triton, beginning to move his body to one of the sides of Venus and his large bed.

'And what of Hake and the Hawk Tribe, who are probably at present still within Eagle Forest attempting to rebuild their camp?' asks Venus.

'We cannot trust that Hake will stay within Eagle Forest now, especially if he witnesses the humans starting to lose the great war.

We must go destroy Hake and the remaining Hawks, but after we have recruited Viper and his Serpents first for extra back-up in case of unforeseen circumstances,' states Triton as he uses his muscular arms to help him stand up from the large bed upon the floor of his bedroom, but Triton still feels the ache from his wound in his right thigh.

'Of course, my ruler, I shall look forward to sending that meddling sorcerer away from this world just as he did to my beast creations back in the battle of Eagle Forest,' says an annoyed Venus as she also manoeuvres her body to stand upon the floor in front of hers and Triton's large bed.

'Quick, Venus, fly us both to Komodo Jungle now where we will finally meet with Viper and his Serpents,' orders Triton. Venus nods at Triton and then concentrates her energy for a moment; as her eyes turn from red to pure white again. Venus utilises her Animagus abilities, which causes her entire physical body to magically change back into her Quetzalcoatlus form. Triton picks up the anomaly crystal from the large bed but leaves his golden chain with the iron spiked ball at the end of it still upon the floor of their bedroom. Venus flaps her now large and scaly wings to lift her body up in the air and hover in their bedroom. She moves her sturdy clawed feet to grab on to Triton's muscular shoulders. After holding tightly on to Triton, Venus begins to fly out of their bedroom and continues flying through the empty and small hallways and the main hall of Triton's Underground Dungeon until she reaches the narrow passageway that connects upwards to the ground upon the rocky surface of the Realm of Deserted Lands in the south-west corner of the Planet of Phoenix.

HOLDING ONTO TRITON'S broad shoulders tightly with her Quetzalcoatlus clawed feet, Venus swiftly continues flying across the sky above the Realm of Deserted Lands, strongly flapping her large and scaly wings to move briskly through the dirt, rock, sand, and grit particles that are constantly swirling around in the fierce, gusty winds. Venus in her Quetzalcoatlus form carries Triton for numerous miles with difficulty due to the obstructive atmosphere they are traveling through, until they leave the borders of the Realm of Deserted Lands and then continue journeying across sky above the Grass Terrain Fields in the north-east direction of the Planet

of Phoenix. Venus and Triton continue flying high in the sky of the
Grass Terrain Fields located in the middle section of the Planet of
Phoenix for just under three hours; they now both see below them in
the distance the immense and lethal Komodo Jungle.

Venus cautiously swoops down from the sky to enter into the
perimeter of Komodo Jungle. Venus controls and manoeuvres
her Quetzalcoatlus body innovatively, which enables her to fly
expeditiously between the passageways of the large and diverse trees
that reside within Komodo Jungle, while holding Triton. As they
continue through Komodo Jungle, which is a location they have never
experienced before, Venus and Triton see the rest of Komodo Jungle
covered with all kinds of other large wild trees that are withered and
covered in thorns with poisonous and lethal plants twisting around
these wild trees.

As Venus and Triton fly deeper into the different sections of
Komodo Jungle, they notice through the foliage and witness fights
in the open spaces of other ferocious animals like scorpions, snakes,
spiders, crocodiles, tigers, lions, hyenas, and cheetahs. Venus and
Triton hastily continue flying deep into the dark and creepy Komodo
Jungle; they are particularly careful not to come in contact with any
of the poisonous plants wound around the large wild trees. They now
find themselves approaching near the middle part of Komodo Jungle.

Venus and Triton keep flying suspiciously as they are in an
unknown area. Venus and Triton end up reaching a wide, murky, and
misshapen green-coloured swamp lake that is known as Fangtooth
Lagoon. Fangtooth Lagoon is mysteriously covered with a white
cloudy mist that resides just above the green-coloured water of the
lagoon and makes it difficult for animals or creatures above the lake
to see through this misty fog. Fangtooth Lagoon is also littered with
oversized insects that bite painfully such as mosquitoes, hornets,
and resilient army ants as well as many poisonous and dangerous
plants like the Venus flytrap. Triton gulps slightly as Venus in her
Quetzalcoatlus form decides to fly over a section of Fangtooth
Lagoon until she finds a relatively safe spot to land upon the muddy
and grassy ground away from any of the poisonous plants and insects
strewn across Fangtooth Lagoon.

Venus now positions herself to gently place Triton upon the
muddy and grassy ground next to the noxious and contaminated

Fangtooth Lagoon. She releases the grip of her clawed feet from Triton's broad shoulders and then flaps her large scaly wings in a specific fashion to approach the ground beneath her. As she comes closer to the muddy and grassy ground, she uses her Animagus abilities to magically turn back into her normal physical body again, where her eyes also turn back to their normal red colour. As Venus changes into her normal physical body again, she positions herself to stand next to Triton, who is currently looking oddly far across the murky mist of Fangtooth Lagoon.

'This seems like a good place to find that slimy creature Viper,' remarks Venus, covering her nose from the stench of Fangtooth Lagoon.

'Viper, show yourself! I am Lord Scartor's lieutenant, Triton. We need to share words with each other urgently!' shouts Triton loudly. After Triton's shouts echo across the mist of Fangtooth Lagoon, nothing happens immediately except for a slight noise from the poisonous insects scurrying around. Triton and Venus stand in silence for a moment, waiting and watching eagerly for Viper or any other creatures to show themselves from wherever they are currently hiding.

After around four minutes, first Viper's head and then the rest of his scaly body appears slowly out from the cold and murky green swamp-like water of Fangtooth Lagoon. Viper peculiarly walks out of Fangtooth Lagoon at one of its sides in the shallower parts of Fangtooth Lagoon; he continues to walk towards where Triton and Venus are standing patiently at present. Viper has a dark-green-coloured snake-like appearance with scaly skin all over his body. He has pure black eyes, an extended snake-like forked tongue, and two long and very sharp white fangs within his wide mouth, as well as webbed claws for his feet and hands.

Viper is tall in size and physically tough with resilient scaly skin, and he's able to spit black venom from his two sharp white fangs within his wide mouth. This black venom possesses the power of disintegrating any human or creature flesh and bone completely. Viper can also swim and breathe under water as he can also breathe and walk on land; he feels comfortable in whatever environment he finds himself in. As Viper is half a reptilian creature, he ages at a very slow rate, which makes his current age to be 235 years, but for this age, he is still at his prime in both physical strength and mental intellect.

Viper is a very impatient and mischievous creature, who is also very selfish and hates losing at anything due to his ill-tempered nature. Viper was born within Fangtooth Lagoon where his mother, who was called Mamushi, was also a special mystical creature who had lizard-like appearance with dark-green scaly skin, along with webbed hands and feet. Mamushi had given birth to Viper after having mated with a very powerful and boisterous ancient anaconda; this anaconda had also developed other creature abilities due to living within the contaminated environment of Fangtooth Lagoon. This adapted creature ability was two sharp, white, poisonous fangs that could spit black venom. That is where Viper also got these creature features from.

Due to the scarceness of food within Komodo Jungle, Viper's mother Mamushi ate the anaconda father of Viper after she had mated with him; hence, Viper was never able to know his anaconda father. Mamushi was also killed after being hunted down by the older generation of royal Falcon guards from Falcon City, because Mamushi constantly killed any humans from Falcon City that entered the perimeter of Komodo Jungle when they came to search for special mephitic plants and insect poison in an attempt to make medicine from it.

After many failed attempts, Viper's mother Mamushi was eventually brutally hunted and murdered by the royal Falcon guards that were initially ordered to do so by King Primus, who was the grandfather of King Exodus. Viper developed a long-standing vendetta against all the humans who lived upon the Planet of Phoenix. Viper collated an army of his Serpent warriors, who had also been created abnormally from another two of Fangtooth Lagoon's mystical creatures. These mystical creatures were an ancient titanoboa snake and a large scorpion that had mated with each other for several years and created numerous Serpents with abnormal creature features that are possessing both male and female genitalia. The ancient titanoboa snake and large scorpion eventually died of natural causes.

As the years went by, Lord Scartor became aware of Viper's relentless battles against the royal Falcon guards from Falcon City towards the south direction of Komodo Jungle. To aid Lord Scartor's heated vengeance, also against the humans from the Planet of Phoenix, Lord Scartor sought to recruit Viper and his Serpents to join with him in his passionate search for the bewildering anomaly crystal.

After Lord Scartor met with Viper and explained the astonishing powers of the anomaly crystal to him, Viper was also very intrigued and power-hungry in seeking to retrieve the anomaly crystal from the bloodline descendants of Grackle and use it to wipe out all the humans on the Planet of Phoenix. After many failed attempts in battle with Lord Scartor, trying to steal the anomaly crystal from the humans residing at the main villages located in the north section of the Planet of Phoenix, Viper decided to stop joining his forces with Lord Scartor and return back to his initial habitat at Fangtooth Lagoon within Komodo Jungle due to his displeasure from losing against the humans in battles.

After his return to Komodo Jungle, Viper forced his Serpent warriors to fornicate with one another in order to create more Serpents. This enabled Viper to generate a large army of Serpents as he was striving to launch an epic attack within the great war between humans and creatures, where Viper's focus would be to annihilate all the humans who lived within Falcon City in the Kingdom of Humans in the far south-east location within the Planet of Phoenix.

AS TRITON AND Venus suspiciously watch Viper walk sluggishly out of Fangtooth Lagoon and over towards them both on the muddy and grassy ground at the side of Fangtooth Lagoon, suddenly hundreds of Viper's Serpents also very slowly and mysteriously appear out of the cold, misty, and murky green-coloured water within Fangtooth Lagoon. As hundreds of these Serpents' heads appear followed by their reptilian creature bodies, Triton and Venus stand firm in case of a surprise attack by the Serpents, but the Serpents just stand behind Viper, waiting for his orders. The Serpents look very manly and aggressive, buy they do indeed have both male and female genitals, enabling them to procreate with one another. This mutilation was caused from the original creature titanoboa snake and scorpion interspecies mating with each other in the toxic Fangtooth Lagoon.

The Serpents are brown coloured and have also a snake-like appearance with scaly skin. Just like Viper, they also have pure black eyes, but have normal tongues unlike the snake-like forked tongue with the split in the middle at the end of the tongue. The Serpents are tall and thin but physically tough, and their scaly skin is very durable. the Serpents' creature features are large, and they have sharp scorpion-like powerful claws, along with having a poisonous stinging scorpion tail with a sharp pincer at the of the tail that can inject a toxic poison into enemies and stop the hearts of the victims from pumping blood around the arteries. Also like Viper, the Serpents have webbed claws for feet and can swim and breathe in water as they can walk and breathe on land; although, their large scorpion claws make the Serpents not as fast as Viper in swimming under water. Viper eagerly looks at Triton and Venus, while his long tongue pokes out of his snake-like wide mouth and tastes the particles in the air with the forked split at the end of his textured tongue.

'Why should I help Lord Scartor again? I lost faith and respect for him after he made us lose in the battle at the Wastelands and Swamp Fields in his desperate search for that mysterious anomaly crystal over a hundred years ago,' hisses Viper with his forked tongue still poking out of his wide mouth.

'We have killed Lord Scartor due to his previous incompetence. And now we both possess the extraordinary anomaly crystal. We have come to Komodo Jungle to gain your allegiance in joining with us loyal creatures and once and for all enforce the great war that will obliterate all the humans residing on our Planet of Phoenix,' states Triton confidently.

'The great Lord Scartor betrayed by his own followers, ha-ha. I have searched for that inconceivable anomaly crystal for many years myself and have even killed some of Grackle's own bloodline descendants. I believe their names were Ruthus, and his wife was called Jewel, but even then I still couldn't locate the anomaly crystal. I thought the anomaly crystal may have after all been a myth, but now you creatures before me state that you now possess the phenomenal powers of the anomaly crystal? Let me see it!' says Viper excitedly. Triton waits a moment and then holds the anomaly crystal firmly in one of his strong hands but out in front of him to show it briefly to

Viper. Viper glares at the anomaly crystal curiously and lustily, until Triton quickly closes his hand with the anomaly crystal within it.

'What do you say, deadly Viper? Will you join with us and take back the Planet of Phoenix from those menacing humans?' asks Venus to Viper.

'And what do I get in return for my Serpent warriors and myself fighting alongside you creatures in this long-awaited great war that I have heard faint whispers of for hundreds of years?' Asks Viper while hissing with his long snake forked tongue again and moving his webbed clawed hands out in front of him in an unusual fashion.

'Once we have obliterated all the living humans. I will leave you to rule over a quarter of the Planet of Phoenix in whatever way you want to rule over it, and with no interference from us or any other creature,' answers Triton.

'I want to rule over half of the Planet of Phoenix,' hisses Viper snappishly. This makes Triton angry, and just as he is about to speak rudely back to Viper, Venus quickly grabs his strong muscular arm and smiles at him mischievously.

'Fine! You can control half of the Planet of Phoenix, Viper, but not the area over the Realm of Deserted Lands. Return with all your Serpents and us now to Triton's Underground Dungeon in the far south-west, deep within the Realm of the Deserted Lands. There you will find a passageway that will lead beneath the ground and to entrance of our Underground Dungeon. Once you arrive there with your army of Serpents, we will plan our strategy together for launching the great war. Our unity will allow us to attack the humans with full force. It will be unlike nothing they would have ever experienced before.' Venus cackles.

'That seems a bit of a long journey for us to undergo before the great war. Why don't we just attack the humans at Falcon City now from Komodo Jungle?' snarls Viper, still moving his webbed clawed hands bizarrely out in front of him.

'We will not attack Falcon City now in broad daylight, because King Exodus will be expecting us to recruit you in the great war and thus expect an attack directly from Komodo Jungle, due to it being just to the north of the great Falcon City walls. I foresee King Exodus focusing his royal Falcon guard's forces to protect the Nautilus Lake as that is the weakest area within the perimeter of the

Kingdom of Humans and will, therefore, be our entry into Falcon City. Upon entering Falcon City through Nautilus Lake, it will allow us to overthrow the city form the inside of its great stone walls, because we will not be able to tear down the wall effectively.

'Although we have the anomaly crystal and are able to wield its astounding and destructive elemental powers now, we are still outnumbered by the humans and their allies, along with their plenteous weapons. For these reasons, we must launch a surprise attack from the Realm of Deserted Lands against King Exodus and his royal Falcon guards at Falcon City from the south-east direction, so there will be confusion and no chance of their predictable battle preparation and strategies aiding them in winning this only and final great war between the creatures and humans. We will discuss further plans for attack back in my Underground Dungeon at the Realm of Deserted Lands, and we all must hurry about it as we also have another meddling creature to slaughter first before he causes us creatures no more hindrance in the great war,' explains Triton directly.

Before Viper can ask more questions regarding Triton and Venus's plans for the great war, Venus operates her Animagus abilities that turn her normal red eye colour into a pure white colour and magically starts turning her entire physical body back into her Quetzalcoatlus dinosaur form. Venus screeches loudly from her pointed beak and flaps her large scaly wings hard to start flying in the air above the muddy and grassy ground. Venus flies her body above Triton and then grabs both of his strong muscular shoulders with her sturdy feet claws and then flies him quickly high up into the sky and completely out of Komodo Jungle, where they continue in the south-west direction across the Grass Terrain Fields and the Realm of Deserted Lands and eventually fly back into Triton's Underground Dungeon.

'Clever trick for a woman creature. Arise, all my Serpents! The time has finally come for us creatures to rid the Planet of Phoenix from those vermin humans!' shouts and hisses Viper as he punches his green webbed claw fist in the air. Hundreds more Serpents now hear the loud hissing words of Viper from all over Komodo Jungle and begin travelling towards where Viper is located. Viper and the Serpents from Fangtooth Lagoon now start marching directly through Komodo Jungle, where they are then joined from the other

Serpents upon their quick march out of Komodo Jungle directly in the west direction.

After around forty minutes, Viper leaves the perimeter of Komodo Jungle in the west direction, where Viper is now joined by an army of 800 Serpents. Viper and his 800 Serpents continue marching quickly on the long journey for many hours in the south-west direction across the Grass Terrain Fields over the middle section of the Planet of Phoenix. After they pass across these Grass Terrain Fields, they endure their travels through the dirt, rock, sand, and grit particles within the gusty winds of the Realm of Deserted Lands as they head towards Triton's Underground Dungeon in the furthest south-west corner beneath the ground of the Planet of Phoenix.

Twenty-Eight

A THIN, CLOUDY greyish smoke escalates above Pine Village through the bright and sparkling sunlight that begins to shine all across the Planet of Phoenix. This bright and striking sunlight is projected from the rays of the heated sun that rises gradually in the east as the time of early morning approaches; the remaining darkness within the sky also now fades away from shadowing Pine Village. The remaining flames, which had been burning violently throughout the night during the Pine Village battle that were created from Vicious's fire breath, also now start diminishing, especially since the remaining Pine guards and Pine villagers had been scurrying around Pine Village with wooden buckets of water and throwing this over the flaring fires to stop them from causing more destruction to the small wooden houses, flats, and shops.

Unfortunately, most of Pine Village had already been severely damaged, especially in the south-west location of Pine Village, where the battle of Pine Village originally began. The small wooden houses, flats, and shops residing in Pine Village's south-west area had been horrifically and completely destroyed of broken by the destructive attacks caused by the Potorians as well as the roaring fire Vicious released from his fire breathe.

All of the 166 Potorians who were involved in the shocking battle of Pine Village were eventually killed by the Pine guards and men Pine villagers. Vicious was also finally killed towards the end of the Pine Village battle, and Vicious's large, muscular, and tough body still remained upon one of the cobbled paths across the south-west direction of Pine Village.

During the battle of Pine Village, 100 Pine guards were also killed along with 543 Pine villagers including men, women, and children Pine villagers; also countless livestock and farm animals were now also dead, including dozens of horses that participated with the Pine guards directly in the Pine Village battle against the Potorians. Fortunately due to Pine Village winning the battle, many animals did indeed survive this terrible attack that was instigated by Vicious and the Potorian army. Also 200 Pine guards and 331 Pine villagers along with Lynx, Bruce, and Bella also managed to live through this shadowy night to see the morning sunrise.

Lynx directed Bruce to be the main Pine guard in charge of the clean-up of Pine Village following the horrendous battle attack and fights that lasted through the entire night. Bruce and the remaining Pine guards as well as numerous men and women Pine villagers continued for many hours to help each other in the clean-up of the broken pieces of wood, metal weapons, and dead bodies of humans and animals that were still littered all over the cobbled paths of Pine Village as well as in various wooden houses, flats, and shops and amongst the farm's barns and crop fields located throughout Pine Village.

As the Pine villagers and Pine guards saw one another again during their clean-up duties and tasks within various areas upon the cobbled paths and wooden buildings within Pine Village, these humans greeted one another with much happiness, but also sorrow and sincerity when they offered their condolences for those Pine guards and Pine villagers who had lost many of their family, friends, and loved ones during the Pine Village battle. Many of these Pine villagers, especially the women and children, were still extremely distraught and devastated from losing their husbands, fathers, and brothers, and they were unable to help with the cleaning up of Pine Village at the moment because they were crying frantically and hopelessly for their now ruined lives.

Lynx also ordered other Pine guards to gather all of Pine Village's resources and provisions together to be able to provide food, water, medicine, and shelter for those families who had either lost their homes or shops during the unforgettable battle of Pine Village. These Pine guards also offered support to any Pine villagers who needed help in cleaning up their homes or shops as well as these Pine guards assisted the women Pine villagers who were specially trained in stitching up wounds of the injured Pine guards and Pine villagers. These women Pine villagers washed and cleansed the wounds and bandaged broken bones; for more severe wounds, these women Pine villagers had to remove the limb of an injured Pine guard, which caused the injured Pine guards excruciating agony and discomfort.

For many hours these injured Pine guards and Pine villagers who were wounded during the Pine Village battle suffered unbearable pain from their injuries, and not all of these Pine guards and Pine villagers were lucky enough to survive till the morning, due to their injuries being too severe and beyond being healed and restored. Many of the injured Pine guards and Pine villagers were taken into the nearest wooden house, flat, or shop for them to rest and recover upon other villagers' beds, or if these humans were too injured to be moved from their current location, then these women Pine villagers attempted to help mend the wounds with the help of some Pine guards where the injured humans lay upon the cobbled paths throughout Pine Village.

The battle of Pine Village lasted for several hours through the dark night. This battle completely depleted and exhausted all of the Pine guards and Pine villagers throughout Pine Village, as these humans were either directly involved in the terrifying and tough battle fights or were busy cleaning up the abundant remains of Pine Village, along with tending to the poor injured Pine guards and Pine villagers. Other Pine villagers also lost all their energy and motivation for survival, as they were not able to have any sleep or rest during this night; they were hysterical and frightened for their lives and the lives of their loved ones throughout the Pine Village battle. Many of these Pine villagers had never been in a battle or fight before and had never witnessed another human be brutally killed or mutilated; although there were some lucky Pine villagers who managed to survive this horrific and terrifying battle of Pine Village, many of these Pine villagers will be forever scarred emotionally, mentally, and physically for the rest of their natural lives upon the Planet of Phoenix because of what they had seen or endured during the Pine Village battle.

DURING THE CLEAN-UP of Pine Village, the bodies of the dead Potorians were thrown pitilessly on to big wooden carts on wheels that were pulled by two horses, and these two horses, while being guided by Pine guards, transported the dead Potorians' bodies through either of the entrance wooden gates of Pine Village to newly dug mud pits in the ground of the Grass Terrain Fields. These newly dug mud pits were made by the men Pine villagers, and once the Potorians' dead bodies were dropped in these mud pits, all the Potorians' dead bodies were set on fire and burnt to ash. This process was continued several times until all the Potorians' dead bodies from Pine Village were no more. This process of transporting out of Pine Village and being burnt to ash in one of the newly dug mud pits was also done to Vicious's dead body, but due to the strong muscular build of Vicious, he had to be chopped up into pieces by Pine guards before they threw the body parts of Vicious on to a wooden cart with wheels, which was pulled by two horses, due to Vicious's body as a whole being too heavy for the Pine guards and men Pine villagers to pick up from one of the cobbled paths of Pine Village.

The dead Pine guards' and Pine villagers' bodies were also placed on to the wooden carts with wheels pulled by two horses, but instead of being taken to one of these newly dug mud pits, these humans were taken to one of their surviving family members' homes upon request of the family members for them to bury their loved ones within the gardens of their own homes. Alternatively, the dead bodies of the Pine guards and Pine villagers were taken to Pinus Graveyard that was located next to Pinus Church in the north-east direction of Pine Village. Within Pinus Graveyard, the dead Pine guards and Pine villagers were respectfully buried near their previous deceased family ancestors, where mini funerals were conducted briefly by the surviving family members of the newly dead Pine guards and Pine villagers. These burial services continued for many hours in the morning sunshine.

Due to Pinus Graveyard now being overfilled by the huge amount of dead Pine guards and Pine villager's bodies that had filled up the majority of the remaining Pinus Graveyard's original space, some of the newly dead Pine guards' and Pine villagers' bodies had to be cremated, and then the ashes were kept in brass urns with the family members in their homes or placed within another special part of Pinus Graveyard, which was the crematorium section. The cremation of bodies was conducted upon the newly dead Pine guards and Pine villagers only once it had been discussed with their surviving family members; however, if there were no surviving family members to ask permission of this first with, then the dead bodies were required to be cremated due to the lack of space remaining within Pinus Graveyard.

The animals, which also included the horses that were killed during the battle of Pine Village, were either cremated or stored to be kept as food resources, because many of the shops that had stocks of food supplies were now destroyed within the Pine Village battle. The dead Potorians' metal sword and axe weapons that were left across the cobbled paths when the Potorians were killed had now been picked up by the Pine guards or Pine Villagers during their clean-up duties. These metal weapons were also kept and stored within shops, where these metal weapons could be used again by the Pine guards in another battle or these metal weapons could be melted down to their raw material, and craftsmen like Parrot could produce other metal weapons, objects, or machinery that Pine Villagers might require.

After several hours of cleaning the cobbled paths and moving dead bodies of humans and animals from the area located in the south-west direction of Pine Village, where the battle of Pine Village had peaked at its worst, the Pine guards and Pine villagers now began branching out to other areas throughout Pine Village to either move the dead bodies located in these areas, clean up the cobbled paths and broken wooden houses, flats, and shops, or assist with the aid of any wounded or injured Pine guards and Pine villagers.

Many of the men Pine villagers who possessed the particular skills in trades or crafts such as building, tool-making, and farming also now started trying to fix the broken wooden houses, flats, and shops that were burnt or destroyed during the Pine Village battle. They also attempted to restore the large wooden fence that surrounded the perimeter of Pine Village, where parts of it had been burnt or broken during the battle of Pine Village. Many of the wooden houses, flats, and shops, however, were unfortunately unfixable due to there being too much damage caused from fire on these wooden buildings; thus the broken-down pieces of wood and rubble from these destroyed buildings were removed from Pine Village and also placed and burnt within the newly dug mud pits beyond the large wooden fence of Pine Village.

The Pine guards and Pine villagers who had lost their wooden homes or shops during the Pine Village battle had to now seek surviving family members or friends to stay with; although, if none of their family members or friends had survived, then special wooden shelter homes that had been developed within Pine Village for times of war emergencies could be used for the homeless Pine guards or Pine villagers to stay within until their homes were rebuilt. Many of the Pine villagers had not only just lost their loved ones and homes, but also all of their cherished objects and memorabilia within their homes were demolished. These precious items held special meanings for these humans from their childhood memories or had been passed down to them from their ancestors.

BRUCE HAD A crucial role in organising the clean-up and recuperation of Pine Village; he gave precise orders where required, besides providing hands-on help. Bruce helped Pine Village with regards to removing the dead bodies of Pine guards and Pine villagers from the cobbled paths of Pine Village. Bruce also found the time to assist the wounded humans and their remaining family members with support as well as gave advice during the construction of the broken-down wooden houses, flats, and shops that required to be rebuilt within Pine Village.

At this present time, that is several hours later since that Pine Village battle had come to an end, Bruce along with another Pine guard is now approaching the broken and burnt-down small wooden watchtower that resides in the south-west direction of Pine Village. In the rubble and ashes, Bruce stumbles upon a metal sword with a silver handle attached to it on the cobbled path. Bruce stands and stares at this metal sword momentarily before he disturbingly bends over to pick it up. Bruce feels his heart sinking within his chest as he notices that on the silver handle of this metal sword is some carved writing that states the name of Flame upon it, which Parrot had initially and made for him specially a few years back. A tear slowly drops down the left side of Bruce's cold, dirty, and bloody cheeks. He holds the metal sword firmly in his hand and swings it around out in front of him in anger. After a moment of frustration, Bruce then stands motionless in shock and silence.

'Are you all right, Bruce? What's going on?' asks the Pine guard in confusion as he is standing next to Bruce and looking at his devastated facial expressions.

'This is my good friend Flame's sword. I wondered what had happened to him during the battle as I was unaware of his presence in the midst of it. But I just thought that was because we were at different locations within Pine Village at the time the battle of Pine Village started and our positions within the fight continued until then end of this horrific battle. I had just hoped that he was somewhere within Pine Village during the clean-up of Pine Village. As I had ordered many other Pine guards to clean up the dead bodies from the cobbled paths, I assumed that Flame had received these orders passed by other Pine guards. But now I know that he must have been killed as I haven't heard from him since and know his special sword is lying in the ashes. Argh! Those vile and evil creatures!' shouts Bruce as he angrily swings Flame's sword out in front of him again. The Pine guard quickly stands back, and then as Bruce stops swinging Flame's sword around in frustration, the Pine guard puts one of his hands firmly on Bruce's shoulder to calm him down.

'I'm sorry about Flame. He was a loyal and honourable Pine guard. He was one of the best among us,' says the Pine guard respectfully.

'Yes, and he has been a great friend of mine and Parrot's for many years. Flame was the first Pine guard that I had the pleasure of working with and fighting alongside when I initially joined the Pine guards. He really helped me in my training, not only in how to fight but also how to be obedient and controlling my previous temper and boisterous behaviour. I always looked up to Flame, and I really appreciated him spending his time helping me to become the man that I now am today. Before Flame's guidance, I was reckless and uncontrollable in my attitude, which led me to get into quite a bit of trouble when I was of a younger age.

'Flame even gave me that push that I needed as well as mentioning good words about me to Lynx, which aided me in getting promoted to becoming one of the watchtower guards. Although, I was very happy with my promotion and the new responsibility that was bestowed upon me, I was sad that I didn't get to work closely on guard duty with Flame no more, but both got on so well, and where good, we would always make sure that we would go for a pint of ale in Pinus Tavern or go out hunting in the Grass Terrain and Swamp Fields at least once a week. On many of those stimulating occasions, my childhood friend Parrot would also come along with us, and the three of us would share many jokes and laughs together,' sadly says Bruce as he holds Flame's sword out in front of him and looks at his name carved upon the silver handle of the sword; the Pine guard now releases his hand from Bruce's shoulder.

'Yes, I had also previously been on duty with Flame on many occasions. I knew that he had been a Pine guard ever since he left Pinus School, especially as his farther Owl was also a Pine guard for many years to the previous Pine leaders of Pine Village, so he wanted Flame to follow in his footsteps. Flame was a good fighter, passionate about his duties, and enjoyed being one of the Pine guards. He took his role seriously and was willing to go that extra mile to make sure that the villagers of Pine Village were safe and protected from any creatures or human criminals like the nomad warriors. I know Flame will be sadly missed by many of us Pine guards,' explains the Pine guard steadily.

'Thank you for your kind words with regards to Flame, and he will never be forgotten from my memory. I don't know how Parrot is going to handle this tragic news as well. So much pain has come to us humans recently from those ghastly creatures. I won't stop fighting the creatures until they are all made extinct from the Planet of Phoenix. Only then will Flame along with many other humans' lives be avenged by the blood debt of those creatures that have caused or been a part of so many human deaths and destruction of villages,' states Bruce firmly.

'Come now, we should try and find Flame's body amongst the dead Pine guards. I think he would like to be buried beside his father Owl and mother Laurel within Pinus Graveyard. I knew that Flame missed his father very much after he died of that creature disease a few years back, along with his mother who died of natural causes just before his father. So I feel that he will rest in peace knowing that he has been laid to rest next to his parents, since he never married or had children of his own,' says the Pine guard.

'That's if there's any space left within Pinus Graveyard to bury him there,' murmurs Bruce. Bruce and the Pine guard now started using their bare hands to search for Flame's body through all the rubble of broken and burnt wood, amongst the destroyed wooden houses and wooden flats right near the broken-down small wooden watchtower in the south-west area of Pine Village. After several minutes, another couple of Pine guards pass by Bruce and the Pine guard while they were still searching amongst the rubble and ashes; these Pine guards were currently carrying Potorians' metal swords and axes that they had found upon other cobbled paths of Pine Village. These Pine guards also still had their own weapons like the wooden bow and wooden arrows that were placed around their necks and back.

'Don't suppose either of you Pine guards know what has happened to Flame's body? It seems that he was killed during the battle, but I don't know how or what has happened to him?' asks Bruce to one of the Pine guards passing by.

'I'm really sorry, Bruce. I did see what happened to Flame when I was shooting my arrows from one of the small flats during the heat of the battle, but it's not good news, I'm afraid,' stutters one of the Pine guards, turning and looking towards Bruce.

'What is it? Tell me please as I need to know,' states an upset Bruce. 'Flame fought valiantly as he had always done. He had already slayed many Potorians during the fight, and due to his bravery, he attempted to charge at and kill Vicious by his own sword in an effort to try and end the battle of Pine Village. But that monstrous creature Vicious used some kind of shock wave power against Bruce. Vicious had roguishly created this shock wave creature ability from burping. Upon impact, the powerful shock wave sent Bruce flying high up in the air, and he crash-landed backwards into that broken-down watchtower at the same time as when it was burning from the fire that was also caused from Vicious's mouth. I'm really sorry, but no human could have survived that terrible incident, and now I fear that Flame's body would have turned to ash by now.' The Pine guard spoke softly to Bruce.

'That despicable creature Vicious. I hope he suffers an eternity of agony and torture in hell for his evil-doings upon the Planet of

Phoenix. Now I can't even bury Flame's body in Pinus Graveyard or indeed avenge his death by killing that Vicious creature by my own hands,' says Bruce angrily.

'I'm sorry for the loss of your friend Bruce. I also feel your pain as Flames was a friend of mine too. We will all need to grieve and honour Flame appropriately, along with the other fallen Pine guards and Pine villagers as it should be done. However, we don't have the luxury of that time at present. We need to finish the cleaning up and also secure the rest of Pine Village, just in case Triton inflicts another surprise attack against our village. Flame would rather you help those in their time of desperate need and then after the great war has finally ended, we can conduct the respectable burial ceremonies and share all the happy memories we had spent with our fellow Pine guards. Although, it feels like now that it was such a long time ago, but those significant memories will never be forgotten by any of us,' mentions the other Pine guard as he nods at Bruce, and then both of the Pine guards passing by continue walking along the cobbled path to one of the wooden shops that was at present being used for storing the weapons found from the battle. Bruce was still gripping tightly on to Flame's sword, and along with the Pine guard next to him, he continues cleaning up and disposing of the broken wood that they had come across upon the ground from the broken-down wooden houses, flats, and shops.

BELLA IS PRESENTLY in Pinus Tavern with other men and women Pine villagers who had luckily survived the attack from the Potorians that occurred in Pinus Tavern during the Pine Village battle. The men and women Pine villagers are all currently working hard to clean up the broken wooden chairs, tables, and glasses that were used as a weapon against the Potorians as protection or actually destroyed by the Potorians during the fight within Pinus Tavern. Some of the men Pine villagers are also carrying the Potorians' dead bodies on to the cobbled path just outside Pinus Tavern's big wooden entrance doors, in order for these dead Potorians' bodies to be collected by the big wooden cart with wheels pulled by two horses that was led by other Pine guards throughout Pine Village to transport the Potorians' dead bodies to the newly dug mud pits not far from the perimeter of the large wooden fence surrounding Pine Village.

The dead bodies of the Pine villagers that also included Lemur, Siva, and Sam, were indeed the first dead bodies to be carefully carried out of Pinus Tavern and buried or cremated within Pinus Graveyard next to Pinus Church, located in the north-east direction of Pine Village. Lemur's, Siva's, and Sam's dead bodies were, however, cremated due to their bodies already being chopped up by one of the Potorians during the fight within Pinus Tavern; their ashes were all collected together in a big brass vase and placed in the special crematorium section of Pinus Graveyard.

In Pinus Tavern, Bella is comfortingly holding on to Tigra within her arms; Tigra is now crying because of all the commotion that he had witnessed in Parrot's small wooden flat, where his grandparents Sirius and Aura were heartlessly killed by two Potorians. Bella is also looking after Rexus, where at the moment Rexus is running around frantically within Pinus Tavern due to also being confused by some of the situations he had to experience during the battle of Pine Village, such as Rexus having to violently bite to kill one of the Potorians in order to protect Tigra from also being murdered.

Bella now stares hopelessly across the semi-damaged Pinus Tavern, thinking deeply about poor Lemur, Siva, and Sam now being dead. Bella also thinks about how the Pine Village battle had ruined the ceremony of Pinus Tavern remembrance service that had initially been created in honour for the men Pine villagers including Lemur's husband Leon and her son Drakus who were also killed over a year ago following the battle of Oak Village. Bella thankfully sees an exhausted and gloomy Lynx walking through the big wooden entrance doors of Pinus Tavern, although Lynx was still hobbling a bit from his bruised and injured leg caused from his hard fall to the ground during the battle of Willow Village earlier in the evening of yesterday.

'Bella, are you all right? I'm sorry I have just managed to come back here as I've had a lot of organising to do with my Pine guards to control an efficient clean-up of Pine Village following the tragedy that occurred last night,' pants Lynx as he hobbles over towards Bella who is by the wooden bar in the middle of Pinus Tavern.

'That's all right, Lynx. I understand you have many important duties to carry out in attempting to repair and rebuild all that was taken from us this night. I'm still shocked and really upset about seeing Lemur, Siva, and Sam being violently chopped up by a Potorian in front of me. Especially after what we all suffered and endured from the events of the battle of Oak Village and fights against Lord Scartor last year, I never thought I would experience no more heartbreak after that, but I was obviously wrong. And to think of all those humans who will also have to now endure so much sorrow and misery on this most saddest of days. Take Sapphire, for example. How can I explain to her that her beloved parents Sirius and Aura were killed by Potorians only hours ago at Parrot's flat, where their dead bodies still lie lifeless upon the floor . . . I just don't know what to do,' sobs Bella.

'You and the other villagers in Pinus Tavern did great in defending our village and now helping with restoration of it. By all of the humans pulling to together in our utmost strength and love, we will prevail in this great war against the creatures. Yes, poor Lemur and her children. They shouldn't have been made to undergo such a horrible end to their life's after all they had previously suffered, but their souls will now join with Leon's in heaven. Due to that family being pure and kind humans, I'm sure they will all live happily and peacefully together for an eternity in heaven.

'Oh no, I can't believe it. I didn't realise Sapphire's parents are dead as well? Parrot and Sapphire will be distraught to hear this tragic news, especially as Parrot's parents Rio and Olivia were also killed back in the Willow Village battle. We will both have to be extremely supportive and compassionate when we break the news of their parents' deaths to both Parrot and Sapphire and will need to make every effort to be there for them during these devastating grievances. We should go and collect the bodies of Sapphire's parents from Parrot's flat immediately. We can then put Sirius and Aura into coffins up in the guest rooms of Pinus Tavern as I'm sure Parrot and Sapphire would like to say their goodbyes properly to them before they are to be buried within Pinus Graveyard,' says Lynx in devastation while holding on to one of Tigra's hands, who is still currently being held by Bella.

'Poor Rio and Olivia also. I don't know if I can bear no more tragic news. Bless Tigra as now at such a young age that was similar to what had happened with Raven, he will have the subconscious knowledge of some of his family members being killed and taken from the Planet of Phoenix before their time was supposed to have ended. It just breaks my heart so much, and I will do all I can in the future to make sure that Tigra isn't emotionally damaged from these disturbing circumstances. Yes, I will come with you now to collect Sirius's and Aura's bodies from Parrot's flat before Parrot and Sapphire return home,' replies Bella with tears falling down from her cheeks. Bella carefully gives Tigra and Rexus to another woman Pine villager within Pinus Tavern to look after for a while as Lynx and Bella now leave Pinus Tavern big wooden entrance doors and hurry to collect some recently made wooden coffins.

Lynx and Bella retrieve two wooden coffins from a tool-maker who was at present standing on one of the cobbled paths near Pinus Tavern crafting wooden coffins from the broken pieces of wood from the destroyed wooden houses, flats, and shops. This tool-maker would then give the recently built wooden coffins to Pine guards and Pine villagers for them to place the dead Pine guards and Pine villagers within before they buried these dead Pine guards and Pine villagers within Pinus Graveyard.

Lynx and Bella take one wooden coffin at a time from this tool-maker and cautiously walk back into Pinus Tavern and up the wooden stairs to the first floor, where they place the wooden coffin in one of the guest rooms located within Pinus Tavern. After Lynx and Bella have placed two wooden coffins into one of the guest rooms within Pinus Tavern, they both quickly walk across the cobbled path to Parrot's small wooden flat and now enter through the broken-down wooden front door. Upon entry to Parrot's small wooden flat, Bella becomes even more devastated on witnessing the sight of Sirius, whose face was chopped in half, along with the view of Aura's dead body, which was lying cold upon the floor of the main room within Parrot's small wooden flat.

'God have mercy on these poor humans,' remarks Bella. Lynx and Bella take a moment to cope with the situation they both experience; they take a deep breath and then slowly pick up Sirius's dead body first as he was closest to the front wooden door. Lynx and Bella carry Sirius carefully across the cobbled path and back into Pinus Tavern, and after walking up the wooden stars into one of the guest rooms, they place Sirius in one of the wooden coffins. Lynx and Bella now also go back to Parrot's small wooden flat and carry Aura's dead body back to the guest room within Pinus Tavern. After Aura's dead body was carefully placed within the other wooden coffin next to Sirius, Lynx and Bella stand above both of the wooden coffins, looking at Sirius's and Aura's dead bodies in utter misery and depression.

'Why do bad things happen to such wonderful people?' asks Bella as she begins to cry, holding her hands over her face.

'Because we live in a world where vile and evil creatures exist, and I fear more bad things are about to happen to us humans before this great war is over,' sadly states Lynx.

Twenty-Nine

THE WILLOW VILLAGERS are currently still in a complete state of exhaustion and confusion from the battle of Willow Village that had only just occurred during the night, where the ghastly creatures Vicious and Vulture brutally and maliciously destroyed half of Willow Village along with killing numerous Willow guards, Willow villagers, and farm animals. Most of the small wooden flats and shops within Willow Village are either destroyed or burnt from the battle of Willow Village by Vulture's large, crushing, clawed feet or from the intense and destructive fire breath that was released by Vicious.

All these fires upon the small wooden flats and shops caused from Vicious's fire breath have now been extinguished due to the heavy rain that had fallen throughout the night; however, the grey cloudy smoke caused by these fires still resides in the sky above Willow Village. The blazing sun now starts to rise from the east and begins to shine brightly over the remains of Willow Village, accompanied by a calm but breezy wind.

After barely surviving the battle of Willow Village, the remaining forty-seven Willow villagers and twenty-six Willow guards, along with the Willow Village leader Panther spent the rest of the night as well as the early morning attentively healing or tending to the wounded Willow villagers and Willow guards. Many of the women Willow villagers who were not injured during the Willow Village battle also spent a lot of their time helping cleaning up the damaged and broken-down small wooden flats and shops. The Willow guards who had regained their strength from their depleted bodies or injuries spent their time carefully lifting up from the grassy paths and transporting the dead eighty-five Willow villagers' and thirteen Willow guard's bodies, where they were aided by one horse pulling small wooden carts with wooden wheels attached. The Willow guards would ride the horse pulling the wooden cart with wooden wheels to Willow Graveyard that resides in the north-east edge of Willow Village.

These dead Willow villagers were then either buried alongside their ancestors who also rest within the Willows Graveyard, or these dead Willow villagers were buried in newer sections of the Willows Graveyard that had no graves yet. These spaces were for the dead Willow villagers who have no previous family buried within this Willow Graveyard due to some of the Willow villagers having relocated originally from Pine Village or Oak Village. It was a custom for the dead Willow guards that were killed during battle to be cremated; their ashes would then be placed in large urns made of animals' horns, and these urns would be displayed within the Willow guard's crematorium section of Willow Graveyard. The Willow guards' crematorium section was decorated with solid stone memorial statues of previous battle items or features such as weapons, machinery, and armour, along with long woven tapestries that presented pictures and text of previous war stories that had occurred upon the Planet of Phoenix by the humans and the creatures.

The farm animals that were killed during the battle of Willow Village were also transported from the ground and then stored in the butcher shops to be kept as meat that could supply the Willow villagers with food during the difficult and harsh times that may follow due to several of the crops and fruit fields within and just outside of Willow Village being ruined by the mass fires created from Vicious's fire breath.

'Guards, please gather the rest of the Willow guards to start regrouping by Vulture's huge dead body. It's going to need the help of all of us to chop up that body and finally remove that awful creature from my village,' orders Panther to a small group of Willow guards who are at present standing near him, by one of the large clawed feet of Vulture's large dead body that is currently still in its giant physical form and lies still upon the grassy paths and small broken-wooden flats and shops of Willow Village.

'Yes, my leader, we will gather the rest of the able-bodied Willow guards right away,' reply a couple of the Willow guards to Panther. These Willow guards now begin running quickly throughout the rest of Willow Village in order to collect the surviving Willow guards. They explain to them to go to gather with all the other Willow guards at Vulture's dead body that lay near the east entrance wooden gate of Willow Village.

'Also, I will require you to go and recruit any of the non-injured men Willow Villagers and those men Willow villagers who aren't already helping any wounded Willow villagers and ask them to you in digging a deep and wide ditch in the far north-west corner of Willow Village just outside of this village's fences, where it would be viable for us to burn the chopped- up pieces of Vulture's body to ash,' orders Panther.

'Don't worry, Panther. I will complete this order for you now,' replies another one of the other Willow guards who is standing next to Panther.

'Thank you, and can you also supply these men Willow villagers with the digging tools they will need to dig a large-sized ditch?' mentions Panther.

'Yes, of course,' replies the Willow guard as he sets off to collect digging tools and recruit men Willow Villagers to begin digging a large ditch outside of Willow Village to dispose Vulture's large dead body within it.

Panther is the first to start hacking away at Vulture's dead body with his powerful silver sword. The Willow guards standing next to him also begin to help Panther to chop up Vulture's large body, which would make it easier for them to transport Vulture's heavy body pieces to the deep and wide ditch that the Willow villagers have just started digging outside of Willow Village. These Willow guards all use their metal swords, axes, shields, spears, and hammers to hack away at the tough flesh and large bones of Vulture's giant body; the process of chopping up Vulture's entire body takes several hours.

Panther and the Willow guards are also joined by the remaining Willow guards who have just run to Vultures' dead body from other parts of Willow Village, while the rest of the healthy men Willow villagers who were just made aware of Panther's orders continue digging the small in width, but deep in length ditch outside of the north-east fence of Willow Village.

Once Vulture's giant body has been chopped completely up into smaller pieces, these smaller pieces are more manageable to pick up, but it still requires a couple of Willow guards to pick up some of the heavier pieces of Vulture's dead body. All of Vulture's body pieces are carried by the Willow guards and then thrown on to the wooden carts with wooden wheels on them, pulled by one horse that is ridden by a Willow guard. The Willow guard leads the horse to transport the large dead body pieces of Vulture upon the wooden cart with wooden wheels along the grassy paths and out of Willow Village's north entrance wooden gate to the deep and wide ditch located in the north-west direction. The smaller pieces of Vultures' dead body are removed from the wooden cart with wooden wheels by the Willow guard and men Willow villagers, and these pieces are dropped into the deep and wide ditch.

Once the deep and wide ditch is mostly full from Vulture's large chopped-up body pieces, the pieces are burnt by fire created by the men Willow villagers utilising stones and flints that they rub together to set hay and wooden sticks on fire with the aid from the hot sun. The hay and wooden sticks are placed on top of Vulture's large body pieces that lie inside the deep and wide ditch, where the fire quickly burns through the hay and wooden sticks and causes Vulture's large body pieces to burn quickly until they are turned to ash. The transportation of Vulture's large chopped-up body pieces from Willow Village to the deep and wide ditch where the large body pieces are disintegrated continues many times over several hours. The smell of burning rotten flesh caused from the intense burning of Vulture's chopped-up large body pieces generates a nauseating smell that is caught up in the breezy winds and passes over the sky above Willow Village.

The remaining forty-seven men, women, and children Willow villagers who were lucky enough to survive the battle of Willow Village are still either depleted of energy, devastated from the murder of their family and friends, or injured themselves from the ruthless attack that occurred in Willow Village battle less than one sunset ago. Some of these Willow villagers also lost all of their livestock, their family, their friends, and also their small wooden flats or shops, which will cause a detrimental impact for the rest of their futures living upon the Planet of Phoenix.

Within the last fifteen hours, the surviving Willow villagers remaining within the village have either helped in the cleaning up of broken wood throughout Willow Village that required to be mostly done in the small wooden broken flats and shops or they helped in transporting and sadly burying the dead Willow villagers and Willow guards within Willow Graveyard. Also these surviving Willow villagers have tried tending to the wounded and injured villagers by putting them to rest within their homes in bedrooms and guest rooms, along with washing and bandaging up the wounded villagers' cuts, wounds, and broken bones as well as bringing them hot food, fresh water, and any suitable and available medication or herbs to ease their pain.

A MOTHER NAMED Roxanne and daughter named Faith are currently in their small wooden flat in the north-west of Willow Village. They are both looking after the mother's husband and daughter's father named Harold who had unfortunately be badly injured by Lynx, when Lynx accidentally landed on top of him when Lynx was knocked high up into the air by Vulture's powerful clawed hands during the battle of Willow Village. Harold has a broken back and is now paralyzed from this accident, and he is at present resting in his bed at his small wooden flat. Roxanne is sitting beside Harold in their bedroom and is feeding him chicken soup with a wooden spoon, when suddenly a loud banging upon their wooden door is heard.

'What's that banging?' says Roxanne, startled by the loud noise.

'It's our door. I'll go check who it is. It's probably one of the Willow guards with new orders from Panther,' replies Faith as she rushes from her parents' bedroom that is located on the ground floor of their small wooden. Faith heads through the hallway towards the front wooden door as the banging still continues. Once Faith opens the front wooden door, she instantly sees a man Willow villager holding a women Willow villager within his arms. The man Willow villager has streams of tears rolling down his bruised eyes, and the women Willow villager is badly burnt throughout her whole body, and she can barely breathe.

'Please, you must help. It's my wife. I thought she was dead when I couldn't find her after the Willow Village battle, but after many hours of searching, I've finally found her beneath burnt rubble that was near the west entrance gate of Willow Village. She keeps coughing and can't speak, I don't know what to do?' cries the man Willow villager to Faith.

'Quick! Bring her in my room. It's just down the hallway. Mother, I need your help, hurry!' shouts Faith. Faith helps the man Willow villager carry his burnt wife towards her bedroom just down the hallway that was next to her parents' bedroom. Roxanne stops feeding Harold and puts the bowl of chicken soup down upon their bed that Harold was lying in. She then quickly runs out of her bedroom and shockingly sees just entering into Faith's bedroom the man Willow villager holding his burnt wife.

'Oh dear God! I will get some water and towels,' says a stunned Roxanne as she hurries to the kitchen. Roxanne quickly retrieves a bowl of water and towels that were made of sheep's wool, and she rushes into Faith's bedroom. The man Willow villager places his burnt wife carefully down upon Faith's bed as Roxanne starts dabbing the burnt women Willow villager's head gently with a wetted towel.

'Please, Pippa, stay with me. My life would be meaningless without you in it,' cries the man Willow villager as he holds on to his wife Pippa's badly burnt and damaged hand.

'I don't know what to do to help her,' says Faith as she helps Roxanne bathe the burnt wounds of Pippa with their towels that were made of sheep's wool and were dipped in cold water. Pippa starts to cough frantically as she feels the intense pain of her burns engulf her entire body.

'It's all right, my dear. God will make sure you are looked after and safe in heaven,' says Roxanne as she slowly closes Pippa's eyelids, just as Pippa draws her last deep breath and dies painfully.

'No!' shouts the man Willow villager as he sinks his head into Pippa's chest upon Faith's bed and cries loudly and emotionally.

'I'm really sorry we couldn't help her.' sympathised Faith as she puts her hand upon the man Willow villager's shoulder. A tear also falls down from Roxanne's eye as she looks helplessly at the man Willow villager resting his head upon Pippa's dead chest. After a few upsetting moments, Roxanne collects the bowl of water and towels that were made from sheep's wool, and she walks slowly back to the kitchen to place the items back where she retrieved them from. Roxanne makes her way back out of the kitchen and into her bedroom, where she continues to feed Harold with the chicken soup. Roxanne requires holding Harold's head forward due to his paralysis, and then she puts the wooden spoon with chicken soup upon it into his mouth.

'Thank you for the soup, my dear. What happened in the other room?' asks Harold, mystified.

'A man's wife has just died in front of him from her severe injuries from the battle of Willow Village. It's such a shame that so much devastation has been caused upon us innocent humans this night,' replies an upset Roxanne.

NEAR THE WEST entrance wooden gate of Willow Village where Panther and some of his Willow guards are still finishing the cutting and chopping up of Vulture's gigantic dead body, Panther and his Willow guards see in the distance thin greyish smoke arising high in the breezy air in the far west direction.

'Look over there! That smoke looks like it's coming from where Pine Village is located,' says a concerned Willow guard.

'Yes, it sadly looks like that's the case. That must mean that cruel fire-breathing creature must have trekked over to Pine Village and attacked there after he cowardly left Willow Village. I only hope that Lynx managed to ride back to Pine Village in time to be victorious in their battle and finally slay that evil creature,' states Panther in an apprehensive manner.

'Those poor Pine villagers. I hope no other villager suffered no more unnecessary pain or suffering this night just like us Willow villagers has. All of the human populated villages have had to endure and fight against these treacherous creatures in a time that is usually peaceful and harmonious,' remarks another Willow guard who is very disturbed by seeing this grey cloudy smoke in the sky coming from the west direction as he was friends with some of the Pine villagers who lived in Pine Village.

'Unfortunately existing with other creatures on the same planet means that nothing will ever stay peaceful forever,' wisely remarks Panther.

'How do you mean?' asks one of the other Willow guards who is placing the last chopped-up piece of Vulture's dead body on to a wooden cart with wooden wheels that was just about to be pulled and transported to the deep and wide ditch outside of Willow Village by a horse.

'I have been involved with many battles during my time existing on the Planet of Phoenix. I've witnessed numerous horrific and cruel deaths by creatures who us humans originally once thought were peaceful creatures,' says Panther, thinking back about many battle situations he had found himself in during his lifetime.

'Are you talking about that ancient monstrous sea lion creature that used to live within Nautilus Lake in the Kingdom of Humans next to Falcon City?' Inquisitively asks one of the Willow guards inquisitively.

'Yes. That was one of the situations I was pondering on. When I was the main royal Falcon guard to my brother Saber, who was the royal Falcon captain at the time when we used to live in Falcon City, we were aware of the sea lion creature that had lived in the grand Nautilus Lake for over thousands of years as that's what the legends passed down to us humans had states. The sea lion creature used to feed on the fish and small mammals that existed around Nautilus Lake. Thus this creature posed no threats to us humans located within Falcon City, and this creature had never attacked any of the humans before.

'My brother Saber and King Exodus had many discussions about whether to kill the sea lion creature or leave it be. The father of King Exodus, who was the remarkable King Primus, had warned King Exodus about the potential threat of this sea lion creature. King Primus believed that if a creature didn't attack the humans now, then it might do one day due to the scarcity of food. Or another theory King Primus had was that if they could tame this wondrous creature, it could indeed be useful in aiding the humans during the inevitable great war. However, if this ancient sea lion creature was against the humans during the great war then it would be too much of a risk to let this creature live within Nautilus Lake at the present time.

'Regardless of all these assumptions, King Exodus decided to leave the sea lion creature to live its peaceful life, until unexpectedly one day, this sea lion creature just emerged from the depths of Nautilus Lake and forced its way into Falcon City through the lake entrance that connected Falcon City to Nautilus Lake to enable Falcon City boats to travel from Falcon City to Nautilus Lake for fishing purposes and to also watch out and guard against any other possible creature danger that was mostly like to come from Komodo Jungle just north of Nautilus Lake. This once harmonious sea lion creature just attacked Falcon City with such rage and passion. It killed hundreds of Falcon City humans and royal Falcon guards as well as destroyed a good section of Falcon City due to the size and weight of its powerful flippers. The battle against this sea lion creature was long and brutal. Saber, King Exodus, another good friend of mine Barious, and I fought extensively and hard, and eventually we succeeded in killing this sea lion creature. This battle against the sea lion creature was one of the toughest battles I have ever had to undergo. After the sea lion creature was dead, its body was dismantled and used as meat to feed the horses.

'It was a very miserable time for Falcon City humans as they had to bury many of their family members who were killed by the sea lion creature, and it also took many years to rebuild the destroyed sections of Falcon City. King Exodus's royal Falcon council discussed with the top Falcon University lecturers for many hours about why they thought that this sea lion creature suddenly attacked the humans within Falcon City. The truthful answer of this phenomenon was never uncovered, but from the inevitable word of a great war approaching, it made us humans think that the creatures from the Planet of Phoenix might have also innately been aware of this great war between humans and creatures, where they would also be forced to choose either to fight with the humans against the other evil creatures residing on the Planet of Phoenix or join with the creatures against the humans. It appears to be what the sea lion creature did,' explains Panther.

'That's a real shame that the great war has already affected and will affect so many of both humans and creatures that had once already lived in amity for countless years on the Planet of Phoenix,' says one of the Willow guards.

'It was always going to be that way as humans and creatures are not meant to coexist with one another,' states another Willow guard in an angry manner as he continues to look at the rising grey cloudy smoke from the east direction.

'What about the stories of the mysterious creature tribe who live within Eagle Forest? They are rumoured to be creatures who are harmonious with nature and not harmful to any of us humans,' says the other Willow guard.

'Maybe, but you don't see them helping Willow Village or Pine Village in these battles against this giant creature and that fire-breathing creature from last night,' remarks the angry Willow guard.

'I fear that the time has come where we humans will face the worst of our fears and nightmares. We will all need to be fierce and strong in protecting our lands and loved ones, whatever creature or challenge we will be forced to face in due time.' Panther interrupts the two bickering Willow guards.

'We must quickly seek aid from King Exodus and his royal Falcon guards in Falcon City before we are attacked again, especially since Viper and his Serpent creatures exist not too far from Willow Village in their uninhabitable Komodo Jungle,' says another concerned Willow guard.

'We have no conclusive information that Viper and his Serpents have joined forces with Triton in the great war, but yes, you are indeed right. We must travel to Falcon City and meet with King Exodus soon in order to prepare for the fast approaching great war. We should all quickly clean up the rest of Willow Village, along with making sure that all the surviving villagers are healed and safe following what will come next for us Willow villagers and indeed all the humans residing upon the Planet of Phoenix,' gloomily comments Panther.

'We will protect our fellow Willow villagers and especially our dearly loved families at all costs. I will not have any other human suffer again from the evil creatures,' states another Willow guard.

'I'll also need to wait as long as possible for Lynx to return back here to Willow Village as I feel it would be significant for him and his Pine guards to travel with us to Falcon City. I predict that's what his plans will be also, after the Pine guards and Pine villagers have finished protecting Pine Village. As Lynx has been the previous royal Falcon captain and is also friends of King Exodus just like me, King Exodus will take our wisdom and knowledge of the villages into consideration, when the royal Falcon council and himself begin devising plans for the protection for all of the humans living on the Planet of Phoenix during the time of the great war. I want to leave six of you Willow guards here to do your best in barricading all of the Willow Village' entrance wooden gates as soon as we have left Willow Village on our journey to Falcon City so that no creature can break through and attack Willow Village again.

'It will be best for the surviving Willow villagers to take all supplies and resources necessary and locate themselves together in one part of Willow Village, that can be more easily protected and defended if the great war also finds itself involving the main villages and villagers in the north of the Planet of Phoenix. I will then require fourteen of you Willow guards to travel with me, Lynx, and his Pine guards to Falcon City where it will be our duty and honour to help defend Falcon City during the greatest war of our time,' says Panther. The Willow guards beside him all nod and understand Panther's orders.

PANTHER NOW ALSO leaves his Willow guards at the west entrance wooden gate and begins to walk back to his big wooden house near the middle section of Willow Village. After only about ten minutes, Panther quickly enters through his big wooden house, and after reaching his big bedroom he makes sure that all of his armour is securely fixed upon his body. Then he prepares the essential weapons and supplies that he will require for the long journey to Falcon City as well anything that might be useful to him in the great war.

As Panther starts collecting the essential items he needs as well as packing some of his valuables and paperwork away in case he doesn't return form the great war, he suddenly has a memory enter into his pondering thoughts; this memory is of a battle that occurred in Falcon City eight years ago. In the early morning sunrise, Panther was training Lynx to fight at Falcon City Castle in the battle training yard that was located at the back of the castle. The battle training yard was made of grass, stone, or sand, depending on what terrain would be required to train upon on a particular training session. Panther could sometimes train Lynx a bit too harshly, due to Lynx's father and Panther's brother Saber really wanting Lynx to be resilient and smart enough to become the royal Falcon captain one day.

Without warning, a surprise attack by Viper and his Serpents began at the front of Falcon City. The surprise attack occurred when the big iron portcullis at the front of Falcon City was opened by the royal Falcon guards to permit tradesmen from Pine Village to enter. Viper and his Serpents sneakily charged through the now opened big iron portcullis, where they swiftly killed the entire Pine Village tradesmen and royal Falcon guards at the front of Falcon City before the big iron portcullis could be closed again. Viper and his Serpents continued their surprise and spiteful attack within Falcon City's large stone walls, where they slayed as many Falcon City humans and royal Falcon guards as they could.

The royal Falcon guards who had regrettably seen this surprise brutal attack from the various high watch posts located throughout Falcon City quickly sounded the battle alarm by blowing through an antelope's horn that released a deep and loud sound, causing the rest of the royal Falcon guards and Falcon City humans to realise that Falcon City was currently being attacked. Lynx, Panther, King Exodus, and an abundant number of royal Falcon guards had quickly run out of Falcon Castle and charged with passion down the long stone paths towards Falcon City big iron portcullis entrance at the middle north of the city, where they sought to fight against Viper and his Serpents.

By the time Lynx, Panther, King Exodus, and the royal Falcon guards reached the main fight upon the stone streets of Falcon City, the fight was already at its peak. Viper had also managed to sneak into a big stone house in the north-west of Falcon City. This big stone house was where Lynx's father Saber and mother Lunar lived. Saber and Lunar were currently in the bedroom of their home and were taken by complete surprise by Viper; before Saber got a chance to defend Lunar and attempt to attack Viper, Viper projected his venomous black poison from his white sharp fangs, and the venomous black poison sprayed all over Saber's and Lunar's bodies; the lethal poison disintegrated both of their bodies quickly to nothing. The main fight between the royal Falcon guards and the Serpents continued for many hours upon the stone paths of Falcon City, until Viper realised that he had lost many of his Serpent warriors due to them being killed by the royal Falcon guards. Thus he hastily decided to leave Falcon City and retreat back to Komodo Jungle.

After this rancorous fight had ended, Lynx, Panther, and King Exodus quickly realised they didn't see the royal Falcon captain Saber during the fights and rapidly ran towards his home in the north-west location of Falcon City. Upon entering his parents' big stone house and discovering the death of Saber and Lunar, Lynx became immediately distraught for several days, and during this time he wouldn't even speak to the humans closest to him, which included his uncle Panther and King Exodus's daughter Princess Petal for many days. Lynx would never feel or act the same after his parents' untimely death. These horrible circumstances also changed Panther's life forever.

As Panther finishes gathering the items he requires for the journey to Falcon City and locks the front wooden door of his home, he pauses for a moment and stares at his big wooden house. Panther remembers again that devastating fight within Falcon City where his brother Saber and sister-in-law Lunar were unmercifully killed by the creature Viper, and from that day, Panther had vowed to do all within his power to protect any other humans from such an atrocious fate. Panther now walks back across the grassy paths in the west direction of Willow Village, where he rejoins the rest of the Willow guards upon the grassy paths near the west entrance wooden gate. These Willow guards have also gathered the necessary items that they will need for the long journey to Falcon City.

During the wait for Lynx and his Pine guards to return to Willow Village, Panther, his twenty Willow guards and forty-six remaining Willow villagers throughout the whole of Willow Village continue to work hard to clean up the rest of Willow Village and keep attempting to heal any of the wounds from the injured Willow villagers. Some of the Willow guards, especially those six who were remaining at Willow Village to protect it, begin making the wooden barricades around the selected wooden flats and shops of Willow Village in the north-east section, where they presumed this would be the best location to protect the remaining forty-six Willow villagers who will stay at Willow Village during the time of the great war. These Willow guards also work very hard to make these wooden barricades large, strong, durable, and more stable so that if Willow Village is attacked by creatures during the great war then these creatures would find it difficult to break through these wooden barricades unless they had some extraordinary creature ability.

Thirty

RAVEN IS CURRENTLY riding upon Felix's large muscular black back while still downheartedly holding tightly on to Emerald's dead body. Parrot and Sapphire are still running on the grassy ground because the brown horse they were previously riding on was killed by the Spinosaurus that Venus had created during the battle of Eagle Forest. Raven, riding upon Felix, along with Parrot and Sapphire, continues to hurry, racing across the Grass Terrain Fields in the north-east direction of the Planet of Phoenix. After a couple of hours of exhausting travelling in the blistering weather, they all return to the perimeter of Pine Village. From a distance, Parrot and Sapphire disturbingly notice shady black smoke rising from the air above the Pine Village's wooden buildings. They also see some of the small wooden watchtowers located at the western side of Pine Village which had been half burnt and broken down.

Parrot and Sapphire become extremely anxious and concerned for their family, which makes them sprint faster towards the west entrance wooden gates of Pine Village. Sapphire, followed by Parrot and then Raven as he held Emerald's dead body firmly on top of Felix's back enter through the broken and burnt west entrance wooden gate with the extra barricades that were placed there by Flame and some Pine guards the day before.

Upon entering into the Pine Village west entrance wooden gates, Parrot and Sapphire quickly come across many injured Pine guards and Pine villagers that were still either helping to carefully remove dead Pine guards and Pine villagers from resting upon the cobbled paths or were continuing to clean up no more broken pieces of wood from the small wooden houses, flats, and shops that had been destroyed during the Pine Village battle. Parrot and Sapphire now begin to panic more for the safety off Sapphire's parents Sirius and Aura along with their son Tigra. Parrot and Sapphire followed by Raven, who was riding Felix, pass by one of the Pine guards who was holding on to a medium-sized wooden box that was full of metal weapons such as swords and axes that this Pine guard had found when he was searching for survivors within some of the broken wood rubble from the fallen-down small wooden watchtowers, houses, flats, and shops that now lay spread cross the numerous cobbled paths throughout Pine Village.

'What has happened to Pine Village, Pine guard?' asks a concerned Sapphire quickly, gasping deeply for breath after the long journey she had just undertaken from Eagle Forest.

'At the beginning of last night, Pine Village and its villagers were unfortunately attacked by a monstrous fire-breathing beast creature who was leading an army of armoured men. This unforgettable battle was fierce and devastating for everyone who lived within Pine Village. The battle continued for many painful hours during the cold night. This horrible creature and his armoured legion have annihilated half of the Pine Village population along with destroying most of the village's buildings,' states the Pine guard, looking sadly down into the metal weapons that were still covered in blood in the medium-sized wooden box he was carrying.

'That fire-breathing creature must have been one of Triton's new henchmen, and the armoured men are called Potorians. These Potorians used to be the criminal nomad warriors from the Wastelands, until they were captured and indoctrinated by Lord Scartor and Triton and forced to fight against the human race,' murmurs Raven, looking at the Pine guard from where he was sitting upon Felix and holding tightly on to Emerald's dead body.

'Where is Lynx? Is he still alive?' asks Parrot in shock after hearing the devastating news regarding the battle of Pine Village.

'Yes, Lynx is still alive. Fortunately for us, he audaciously led Pine Village to victory during the latter part of the night when all hope of our Pine Village survival seemed to have been lost. Lynx has now also done an excellent job in maintaining the Pine villagers' calmness following the unpleasant battle of Pine Village, along with organising and assisting everyone with helping cleaning up the semi-destroyed Pine Village. I believe Lynx is currently helping out some of the Pine villagers in Pinus Tavern as there was also a mini battle within Pinus Tavern, as well as the surrounding homes nearby it,' says the Pine guard as Sapphire immediately interrupted.

'Father, Mother, Tigra!' cries Sapphire. Without a second thought, Sapphire rapidly sprints past the Pine guard and hurries as quickly as she can down the cobbled path of Pine Village in the east direction towards Parrot's small wooden flat that was located opposite Pinus Tavern.

'Sapphire, wait!' shouts Parrot loudly as he quickly chases after her. Raven nods at the Pine guard and then also controls Felix to follow Parrot and Sapphire. As Sapphire and Parrot continue sprinting down the cobbled paths of Pine Village, they swiftly dodge around some of the Pine guards and Pine villagers who were still busy cleaning up the cobbled paths. The urgent reactions of Parrot and Sapphire surprise some of these Pine villagers.

At the same time, Bruce, who was holding his sword, along with Flame's sword, walks outside of one of the wooden shops that are now being used to store the metal weapons from the battle of Pine Village. He understands that the human that was running quickly was his friend Parrot. Bruce also then sees Raven, who was still holding on to Emerald's dead body upon Felix's back, as he also trots down the cobbled paths of Pine Village behind Sapphire and Parrot. Bruce decides to follow them and begins jogging down the cobbled path in the east direction towards Pinus Tavern.

As an exhausted and heavily panting Sapphire now makes it to the outside of Parrot's small wooden flat that was across the cobbled paths from Pinus Tavern, she immediately realises that Parrot's front wooden door had been broken into. Sapphire snappishly pushes through the front wooden door of Parrot's small wooden flat in apprehension, but she is very surprised and shocked to see within the main room of Parrot's small wooden flat that there were two dead Potorians upon the floor, but no sign of her parents, Tigra, or Rexus. Sapphire quickly rushes over to Tigra's small wooden cot that was at one side of the main room of Parrot's small wooden flat; she looks into Tigra's small wooden cot but becomes very confused on finding that the small wooden cot is also empty. Sapphire walks back outside Parrot's small wooden flat in misconception just as Parrot now makes it up to the front wooden door of his small wooden flat, running after Sapphire down the cobbled paths heading in the east direction of Pine Village.

'No one but two dead Potorians are in there. We told my parents to stay within your home if Pine Village was attached by creatures. Do you think that they are still all right and alive?' asks a confused Sapphire hopefully.

'I'm sure they are fine, Sapphire. They've probably just left my home after the battle and have gone to help out Lynx and Bella clean up the remains within Pinus Tavern,' says Parrot nervously.

'But why are two dead Potorians in there? Let's go to Pinus Tavern right away,' replies Sapphire quickly.

PARROT TIGHTLY HOLDS Sapphire's hand as they both rush across the cobbled path towards Pinus Tavern; at the same time, Raven, who was riding on top of Felix, also reaches outside of Pinus Tavern's big wooden entrance doors.

'Is everyone all right? Did you also find Rexus?' asks Raven delicately.

'We're hoping that Sapphire's parents along with my son Tigra and your dog Rexus are in Pinus Tavern as Sapphire found nothing but two dead Potorians left at my home,' states Parrot. Just as Sapphire was about to enter Pinus Tavern through the big wooden entrance doors, they all hear a deep voice shouting at them from the distance.

'Parrot, Parrot!' shouts Bruce as he quickly runs up to the front of Pinus Tavern, where Parrot, Sapphire, and Raven, holding Emerald's dead body on top of Felix, are currently positioned.

'Bruce, it's good to see you, and I'm glad you're all right,' says Parrot as he hugs an out-of-breath Bruce that just stopped running in front of Parrot.

'Yes, Bruce, it's really nice to see that you are not injured. Don't suppose you have seen my parents Sirius and Aura along with our son Tigra?' asks Sapphire in a troubled manner.

'Unfortunately, I haven't seen any of them yet. I'm sorry, I couldn't have been of more help, Sapphire. I was mostly positioned in the south-east watchtower until I joined with Lynx in the fight against the Potorians within Pinus Tavern. I remember that your parents weren't in Pinus Tavern when it was being brutally attacked by the Potorians. And since the battle of Pine Village, I have been on clean-up duty near the west entrance gate of Pine Village.'

'You must fill me in on everything that happened during the Pine Village battle Bruce, but first Sapphire and I must find our family,' says Parrot.

'Of course, Parrot. But the reason why I ran after you is I have to tell you some most devastating news that I regrettably need to tell you myself,' sadly says Bruce.

'Oh really, what is it, Bruce?' replies Parrot in a concerned manner.

'It's our good and honourable friend Flame. He didn't survive the battle of Pine Village,' says Bruce sensitively with a tear in his eye as he shows Parrot the sword that he had specially made for Flame with his name carved upon the silver handle. Parrot takes a small step back in shock and desolation to hear the news about his good friend Flame being killed during the night. Parrot pauses a moment in disbelief as he looks at the sword Bruce is currently holding.

'I'm really sorry about Flame, Parrot. Flame seemed a really admirable and respectable human,' says Raven, trying to comfort his cousin Parrot.

'That he was, Raven. Flame was also a mighty fine Pine guard and friend to us both during these past few years,' states Bruce. Parrot now slowly takes Flame's sword from Bruce's right hand, and after grabbing Flame's sword, Parrot holds it just in front of him and stares upon Flame's sword with an empty heart.

'Yes, I have some fond memories of us three hunting and drinking together on many occasions. I'm going to miss those times and Flame very much. Life just couldn't get no worse at the moment. First Emerald and now Flame, I, I . . .' stutters Parrot as Sapphire puts her hand upon Parrot's left shoulder in a comforting manner; Parrot takes a deep breath.

'What of his body? I would like us to bury him together with his parents in Pinus Graveyard, that's if any of the other Pine guards haven't already buried him,' says Parrot as he now passes Flame's sword back to Bruce for him to hold on to it due to the pain it was causing Parrot while holding on to Flame's sword.

'I'm really sorry, Parrot, but Flame's body has not been recovered. It appears that he has been killed and his body has been burnt and disintegrated because of one of the falling small wooden watchtowers by the west entrance gate when that fire-breathing creature released his fire breaths upon the watchtower in the midst of the Pine Village battle,' explains Bruce unhappily.

'One of Triton's henchmen! Triton will suffer for this!' says Parrot furiously.

'That he will and along with that witch Venus,' states Raven sternly.

'I'm so very sorry, Parrot and Bruce. We will all grieve for Flame properly together, but I'm really worried about my parents and son, and I really must find them to set me mind at rest,' softly says Sapphire during this hearty exchange.

'That's no problem, and I certainly understand, Sapphire, and I hope your family is safe and unharmed. I must continue helping with the cleaning up of Pine Village now and also prepare for the great war, where I will then be able to get my vengeance for what has happened to Flame and all those other poor humans who were made to suffer by those evil creatures during the night,' says Bruce as he hugs Parrot and then Sapphire, before jogging back down the cobbled path, holding on to his and Flame's swords. He continues jogging towards the area near the west entrance wooden gate of Pine Village, it being one of the main areas to be cleaned and repaired following the battle of Pine Village.

Sapphire watches Bruce jog off in the distance, and then she pushes through and walks straight inside Pinus Tavern's big wooden entrance doors. Parrot sheds a couple of tears on the news of Flame's death, and then he carefully helps Raven lift Emerald's dead body from resting upon Felix's back. Parrot holds Emerald's dead body firmly upon his shoulder on the cobbled path, while Raven climbs down from Felix's large black back. Parrot now sensibly passes Emerald's dead body back into Raven's arms again and takes Felix's brown rope reins where he wisely ties Felix's brown rope reins around the Pine tree that was near Pinus Tavern.

Parrot also makes sure that he has taken all the weapons that were secured upon Felix, and he now carries everyone's weapons, including his wooden bow and wooden arrows with the metal spikes at the end of them, fury raptor throwing stars, Sapphire's dagger, and Raven's sword and shield of Grackle. Parrot walks alongside Raven as they both enter through the big wooden entrance doors of Pinus Tavern.

As Raven and Parrot enter into Pinus Tavern, they see the Pine villagers the remaining within Pinus Tavern, who were presently cleaning up the broken wood and glasses that were smashed during the gruesome fight that had occurred within Pinus Tavern against the Potorians during the battle of Pine Village. Sapphire frantically looks around Pinus Tavern to locate if any of her family among the Pine villagers. As she quickly looks around Pinus Tavern, Sapphire notices a woman Pine villager who was sitting in one of the corners of Pinus Tavern. This woman Pine villager was sitting upon a wooden chair, holding on to Tigra and had Rexus secured between her legs resting upon the floor. Sapphire rushes through Pinus Tavern and over to the woman Pine villager, where she quickly picks up Tigra with both of her hands.

'Thank God!' remarks Sapphire as she hugs and kisses Tigra strongly and tenderly. Tigra also expresses happy emotions while recognising that Sapphire was his mother and that she has returned to him. Rexus squirms his way out of the woman Pine villager's legs; he barks and runs up to Raven while wagging his tail frantically. Raven gently lays Emerald's dead body upon a big wooden table near the corner of Pinus Tavern where the woman Pine villager was sitting. Raven kneels down and pats Rexus firmly as he is very pleased to see him. After being stroked a few times by Raven, Rexus senses the smell of Emerald with his sensitive nose. Rexus turns around and jumps up on to a small wooden chair and then climbs up on to the big wooden table that Raven had placed Emerald's dead body upon. Rexus carefully climbs over Emerald's dead body and begins to lick Emerald upon her face. Rexus quickly becomes confused and distressed, and he stops wagging his tail because Emerald was not reacting to him.

'Where's Lynx?' asks Parrot politely to the woman Pine villager as he walks towards the corner of Pinus Tavern, where Raven, Sapphire, Tigra, Rexus, Emerald's dead body, and the woman Pine villager were. Parrot also kisses Tigra upon his forehead and places all of the weapons he was carrying upon the big wooden table next to Emerald's dead body.

'Oh, um, Lynx is upstairs in one of Pinus Tavern's guest rooms. I believe he is currently with Bella at the moment,' replies the woman Pine villager softly.

'What about my parents Sirius and Aura?' asks Sapphire, still kissing and hugging Tigra tightly. She now places the book of curses and the blue potion in a small glass container that she had been carrying from Eagle Forest upon the big wooden table next to Emerald's dead body.

'I'm sorry, my dear, but I'm not sure where your parents are. Bella just quickly gave me Tigra and Rexus to look after,' answers the woman Pine villager.

'Thank you so much for looking after them both. I'm so glad to be holding Tigra back in my arms again,' mentions Sapphire, smiling vibrantly.

'We must go speak with Lynx and Bella urgently. Would you mind staying with my wife Emerald's body and my dog Rexus a bit longer please?' asks Raven to the woman Pine villager.

'Of course I will, Raven. I'm also very sorry to see that Emerald is no longer with us on the Planet of Phoenix,' sadly replies the woman Pine villager as she gazes upon Emerald's dead body upon the big wooden table. The woman Pine villager stands up from her small wooden chair and picks up Rexus, who was still trying to cause a reaction from Emerald by constantly licking her on the cheek.

Raven nods back at the woman Pine villager and then, along with Parrot and Sapphire, who was still holding on to Tigra, he begins to walk and makes his way up the wooden stairs located near the bar and kitchen wooden counters of Pinus Tavern. Raven, Parrot, and Sapphire holding Tigra continue walking up the wooden stairs to the guest rooms upon the first floor of Pinus Tavern.

Emerald's dead body is still left upon the big wooden table along with all their weapons that Parrot had placed also upon the big wooden table. Sapphire had also put the book of curses along with the blue potion in a small glass container upon it. The woman Pine villager makes sure she has Rexus within her arms firmly, and then she sits back down upon her wooden chair while stroking Rexus in comfort.

AS SAPPHIRE CONTINUES walking up the wooden stairs of Pinus Tavern, she hears faint voices from one of the guest rooms. As Sapphire is the first one to arrive at the top of the wooden stairs and on to the first floor, she pushes the guest room door open that she had heard voices from within, and as soon a she walks into the guest room, Sapphire sees in the middle of this guest room Lynx and Bella standing over two dead bodies that had been placed within two separate wooden coffins with the wooden coffin lids left open. In disbelief, Sapphire runs over to the two wooden coffins and sees her parents Sirius and Aura lying dead within these two wooden coffins and their faces and bodies being covered with cuts and wounds from the fight they had with the two Potorians at Parrot's small wooden flat during the Pine Village battle. Sapphire falls immediately to the floor on to her knees and covers her face with one of her hands, as she was also holding on to Tigra with her other arm. Sapphire bursts into emotional and hysterical tears at the sight of her dead parents.

Parrot realises what has happened to Sapphire's parents after entering into this guest room, and he quickly races over to Sapphire, who was kneeling on the floor. He puts his arms around her and Tigra firmly in a comforting manner. Raven, who has now just entered into this guest room following the responsive cries from Sapphire, also walks over to Sapphire and puts his hand on her right shoulder as she continues to cry loudly in Parrot's arms. Raven then walks up to and puts his right hand on one of the wooden coffins that Aura was placed within. Bella also has tears running down her eyes at the sight of Sapphire's reaction. Bella walks slowly up to Sapphire and gently takes Tigra from Sapphire's arms so that Sapphire can continue to cry into Parrot's arms and chest. Parrot holds her tightly and tries to calm her down.

'Where's Emerald, Parrot?' Bella asks quietly while kissing Tigra's forehead after picking Tigra up from Sapphire's arms.

'Emerald has been killed in Eagle Forest by Triton's mistress who is a witch creature called Venus,' remarks Raven gravely with a tear rolling down his right cheek as he now places his left hand on to Sirius's wooden coffin and stands between the two wooden coffins that has Sapphire's dead parents placed within them.

'Please spare us from this nightmare, our almighty God in heaven. My greatest condolences and sympathy for you, my dear Raven. That poor girl had so much good within her heart, just like her mother Ruby, and they will never be forgotten by many of us Pine villagers. I'm also very sorry about your parents, Sapphire. We were unaware of what had happened to them during the Pine Village battle until it was too late.' Bella speaks softly as Sapphire continues to cry into Parrot's arms and chest, not really mentally processing anyone who was speaking in the guest room.

'Thank you, Bella, and yes Emerald's death feels like my heart has been broken into a million pieces. We are also deeply devastated by what has happened in Pine Village during the battle and are also very sympathetic to those Pine villagers who have also lost so many cherished family members and friends this night. I know this is not really a convenient time due to these unfortunate circumstances, but, Lynx, we have come to ask for your help. Hake, who is a powerful sorcerer and the leader of the Hawk Tribe that resides within Eagle Forest, has just told us a few hours ago that there may be a unique way to bring Emerald back from the dead.

'For this impossible act of hope, we need to find Triton and Venus as they now possess the anomaly crystal that had been originally created by Grackle. One of us will have to kill either Triton or Venus with a curse of death spell chanted from the ancient book of curses. If this deed is conducted precisely, then it should enable us to bring Emerald's soul back from the afterlife. I think Triton and Venus must have a hideout somewhere within the Realm of Deserted Lands as Parrot says that's where your Pine villager scouts found Lord Scartor's dead body crucified upon Cadaver Rock,' explains Raven.

'Don't worry yourself, Raven, as over the years I have learnt that there will never be a perfect time for anything. Yes, of course my Pine guards and I will aid you. We will do whatever we can to help bring Emerald back to life even if there's the slightest possibility of this deed becoming a reality. However, we have regrettably already endured another terrible misfortune at Willow Village last night. I will need to return there with my Pine guards and men Pine villagers very soon to join with my uncle Panther and his Willow guards where we will seek to gain support from King Exodus and his royal Falcon guards at Falcon City before ourselves or any other humans existing on the Planet of Phoenix are attacked by the creatures again.

'At this time, I fear we will be outnumbered in battle especially as Viper and his Serpents might now have also joined sides with Triton. If this is the case, none of us human villagers, even if we are fully united, will stand a chance in surviving against these evil creatures during the great war. But certainly after we have gained support from King Exodus and his royal Falcon guards, we may stand a chance of surviving this most darkest of times in the history of the Planet of Phoenix. I promise you though, after I have united the main villages with Falcon City, we will all travel to the Realm of Deserted Lands to meet up with you, where we will destroy that treacherous monster Triton and his creature woman once and for all,' replies Lynx, looking sadly upon Sapphire being held by Parrot upon the floor of the guest room.

'Viper! That despicable creature who killed my parents many years ago? Where is he?' Raven asks probingly.

'We think Viper lurks deep within the contaminated Komodo Jungle, but we are not entirely sure for certain,' answers Lynx. Parrot gently releases his arms from around Sapphire and stands up to look at Lynx after realising what Raven and Lynx were talking about.

'What's also happened to Willow Village, Lynx?' Parrot asks, as he starts feeling sick inside his stomach.

'I'm really sorry, Parrot. I don't know how to tell you this, my best friend, but when I was visiting Panther in Willow Village yesterday to share the news of what my Pine villager scouts had discovered with regards to Lord Scartor's murder within the Realm of Deserted Lands, there was a surprise attack by two of Triton's cruel and powerful creatures on Willow Village. These creatures destroyed half of Willow Village because one of the creatures possessed a creature ability to grow physically into a giant. In its giant form, this creature trampled and crushed several wooden shops and flats. Unfortunately, one of these flats was your parents' home . . . I'm truly sorry, Parrot, but your parents did not survive this attack,' gradually mentions Lynx while putting both of his arms on to Parrot's shoulder. Parrot takes a brief moment to hear the shattering words spoken by Lynx. Parrot then begins to cry slowly, and he kneels back down to the floor and continues to hug Sapphire again. He becomes even more devastated to hear the news regarding his parents' deaths.

'Words just can't express how much I would want to take all this pain that you're both experiencing right now away from you, but you must take comfort from the fact that in life both of your parents were lovely and kind humans and lived good and long lives. They will now live for eternity in peace with your ancestors in heaven, where they will wait for you both to reunite with them again in the distant future,' says Bella softly while looking into Tigra's impressionable eyes as she holds him tightly within her arms. Raven also walks over and kneels to the floor of the guest room to put both of his arms around Parrot and Sapphire as they both remain speechless due to the overwhelming and distressing news they are both experiencing and feeling with regards to their parents' untimely deaths.

'This is a very disheartening moment for as all and indeed all humanity that remains upon the Planet of Phoenix. Let's hope we will live to see a better and renewed time in the not-too-distant future. I must regrettably go now to round up my Pine guards and any of the able-bodied men Pine villagers. We will leave for Willow Village immediately and then from there go straight on to Falcon City as none of us know how much time we have left before the great war begins. Why don't you all come with us on this journey to Falcon City? Afterwards we can all search for Triton within the Realm of Deserted Lands, and once found, we will fight and kill Triton together after we have gained the allegiance with King Exodus and the renowned royal Falcon guards?' says Lynx.

'I appreciate your wisdom, Lynx, and respect your decisions. But unfortunately, we can't come with you as the curse of death will only have the ability to work within seventy-two hours of a human's soul being taken from their physical body. Thus Emerald's lifeline is rapidly decreasing, so we must continue on this quest without diversion to the Realm of Deserted Lands and hunt down Triton and Venus, who retain the anomaly crystal, as soon as possible,' replies Raven as he stands up from having his arms around Parrot and Sapphire and looks at Lynx's eyes. Lynx nods courteously at Raven and walks over to Parrot and Sapphire, who are still kneeling on the floor, crying together. Lynx hugs both Parrot and Sapphire strongly.

'Both of your parents are with their beloved family in heaven now, and they will be watching over us all during this difficult time. They will guide us and aid in providing the strength and courage that we will desperately need during the great war. After this unforgettable situation has passed, they would want you not to mourn them, but be happy together with your son Tigra for the rest of your futures as you were loved by both of your parents very much, and for a parent, there is nothing better than seeing your children happy. You will always have Raven, Bella, and I, along with many other friendly villagers if you need any extra help or advice during this very difficult time. But don't worry. We will get our revenge against Triton and Venus for the pain and suffering they have caused us all.

'I wish you well in your journey and pursuit, my valued friends. I hope to meet up with you again at the Realm of Deserted Lands as soon as I can, but until the time where the great war has finally ended and our vengeance is attained, my heart bleeds for all your overwhelming losses,' states Lynx as he finishes hugging Parrot and Sapphire. 'Raven, here is a map of the Planet of Phoenix that one of my Pine guards has hand-drawn from his vast knowledge of the Planet of Phoenix's geography. This map can guide you to the Realm of the Deserted Lands and through its stormy and ghastly winds,' says Lynx as he gives Raven a map of the Planet of Phoenix from his armoured pocket; Lynx then grabs forearms with Raven as a sign of respect for each other.

'Take care of yourself, Bella,' says Lynx as he hugs Bella. After a short moment, Lynx leaves the guest room but takes one more look behind him at the devastated Parrot and Sapphire still kneeling on the floor. In determination and rage after what he has just witnessed, Lynx strongly walks down the wooden staircase; upon entering the ground floor, he dejectedly sees Emerald's dead body lying still upon the big wooden table in one corner of Pinus Tavern. Lynx sheds a tear from his left eye and walks quickly through Pinus Tavern. He pushes his way out of the big wooden entrance doors. But as soon as leaves Pinus Tavern, strong feelings of anguish and sorrow pierce through Lynx's body like a wound from a sharp sword. Lynx grabs his chest and leans back against the big wooden entrance doors of Pinus Tavern, and in frustration he bangs his head against the big wooden entrance doors.

AFTER A FEW moments of grief, Lynx looks down the cobbled paths, and in the far distance, he sees that Pine Village has now been considerably cleaned up from the Pine Village battle and that nearly all of the dead bodies have been either burnt if they were Potorians or buried within Pinus Graveyard if they were Pine guards and Pine villagers. Lynx also notices that nearly all of the broken wood, rubble, and metal weapons have also been removed from being littered upon the cobbled paths. Lynx feels a fire burning within his heart and the strength building up in his muscles; he quickly sprints from Pinus Tavern and heads over to the majority of his Pine guards who were assisting some Pine villagers with essential resources on one of the cobbled paths near Lynx's small wooden castle in the south-west direction of Pine Village.

'Pine guards!' shouts Lynx loudly, while running towards them across the cobbled path. 'Gather most of the remaining Pine guards and any able-bodied men Pine villagers and suit up in your armour and ready your horses immediately. Ask some of the Pine guards to remain here in Pine Village to protect the Pine villagers from any more creature attacks. Now is the time we head for Willow Village and then on to Falcon City for the great war of our time. Say goodbye to your loved ones for we know not when or if we will even return back to Pine Village. Please also make sure to gather enough food, water, and medical supplies to take with us on this dangerous venture. One of you Pine guards must find Bruce first to explain my orders and tell him that I would like him to lead these duties. As soon as these orders have been carried out accordingly, we will reunite near the east entrance gate of Pine Village and will leave without no more hesitation, for I will not wait another minute until I get the chance to destroy and send the creature Triton and his evil mistress Venus to the deepest and darkest most painful depths of hell.' Lynx passes by the group of Pine guards after shouting his orders, and then he continues running through the garden entrances into his small wooden castle.

Upon entering into his small wooden castle, Lynx swiftly proceeds to his bedroom on the second floor of his small wooden castle; he grabs all his old royal Falcon captain armour, sword, and shield that were created from the finest and strongest silver. Lynx suits himself up in this prestigious armour; he grabs tightly on to his silver sword and shield and leaves his bedroom. He continues down the stairs to the hallway that leads out into the small grass field that is located at the back of his small wooden castle to collect his white horse that had been recuperating in this small grass field following the battle of Pine Village.

Lynx saddles upon his white horse and pats it firmly on the long strands of white hair upon its muscular neck. Lynx kicks his heels into the sides of his white horse, which causes it to gallop quickly out of the small grass field and around a grassy passageway that leads alongside the small wooden castle to the front of it. Lynx manoeuvres his white horse to continue galloping down one of the cobbled path of Pine Village that leads directly towards the east entrance wooden gate.

Meanwhile, the group of Pine guards had also completed Lynx's order and gathered up most of the remaining Pine guards, which included Bruce and some men Pine villagers who were not injured. As ordered by Lynx, some Pine guards remained in Pine Village to protect the surviving Pine villagers. The Pine guards had requested these men Pine villagers to come and join with Lynx in their journey to Falcon City to fight in the great war between humans and creatures; many of these men Pine villagers were happy to comply with these orders due to them wanting revenge for what had happened to their family members and Pine Village.

The Pine guards and men Pine villagers just had enough time say goodbye to their family members, along with some of their surviving friends. Afterwards, they were helped by their family members or friends to suit up in their Pine guard armoury, except for the men Pine villagers who didn't possess any armour of their own. These men Pine villagers were, however, given metal swords and axes by the Pine guards who had kept the metal weapons in some of the shops taken from the dead Potorians during the clean-up following the battle of Pine Village.

An ample amount of food, water, and medical supplies were also collected by some of the men Pine villagers with the aid from some of the women Pine villagers, and these supplies were placed in leather bags of boxes to make it easier for these supplies to be transported on the long journey to Falcon City. All the remaining horses from within and around the perimeter of Pine Village were also collected by men and women Pine villagers and brought to the east entrance wooden gates of Pine Village. These horses would be required to carry Pine guards and men Pine villagers to Falcon City.

Due to many horses having been killed during the battle of Pine Village, some more horses were offered by farmers from the farmlands in the perimeter of Pine Village. These horses would also be used for the Pine guards and men Pine Villagers to ride to Willow Village and then to Falcon City. After all the horses were gathered, there were still not enough horses to carry all the Pine guards and men Pine villagers. That meant some of the men Pine villagers had to share their horses with one another.

Bruce and a total number of 200 Pine guards, including the able-bodied men Pine villagers all now regroup together equipped with their armour, metal weapons, and resource supplies saddled upon their horses on the cobbled paths of Pine Village. Bruce leads this patrol of Pine guards and men Pine villagers as they all ride in the east direction down the cobbled paths of Pine Village towards the east entrance wooden gate. As they all ride across the cobbled paths of Pine Village, other Pine villagers who were the family members and friends of either the Pine guards or the men Pine villagers that were going to the fight in the great war, begin to shout chants loudly, wave, or throw various kinds of colourful flowers such as tulips, lavenders, and lilies upon the ground in front of these brave humans as a sign of hope and admiration.

Some women and children Pine villager's begin to cry as they say their final goodbyes to their husbands, fathers, brothers, and children who had been recruited with the Pine guards and are now starting to partake in the long journey to Falcon City with the intention of fighting an army of creatures in the inevitable great war. Lynx greets Bruce silently but warmly as Bruce leads the patrol of Pine guards and men Pine villagers to meet him at the east entrance wooden gate. The sun starts to shine intensely as Lynx, Bruce, and the 200 Pine guards and men Pine villagers all begin riding on their horses quickly out of the east entrance wooden gate of Pine Village, led by Lynx and Bruce. They all now gallop swiftly across the long cobbled road that lay over the Grass Terrain Fields in the east direction of the Planet of Phoenix, heading towards Willow Village.

RAVEN, PARROT, AND Sapphire are still within one of Pinus Tavern's guest rooms upon the first floor, along with Bella, who is holding Tigra comfortingly in her arms. They are all still mourning Sapphire's parents Sirius and Aura with much heartache. Bella stares down at the two wooden coffins in which Sirius and Aura lay still and breathless; a tear is created from Bella's watery emotional eyes, and it rolls down the side of her cheek and drops on to Tigra's half-bald head. Raven slowly walks up to and kneels down next to Parrot and Sapphire; he puts his arms tenderly around them as they are still crouched upon on the floor of the guest room. Parrot and Sapphire are holding each other tightly and crying together at the overwhelming realisation of their parents' tragic death.

'We have all lost so much love, hope, and cherished humans these past few days. Our fond memories of our family ancestors will never be forgotten though, but our hearts will also never be mended. We must draw strength from one another in order to help us through these harshest of times within our lives,' softly says Raven while hugging Parrot and Sapphire supportively.

'You were all loved and cherished greatly by your parents. Know that they are in the glorious and blissful heaven now and watching over us. Their spirits will guide and protect you through this atrocious great war so that one day in the future you will be able to live peacefully and happily again as they would have always wanted you to live your lives,' says Bella. She kisses the top of Tigra's forehead and rocks him gently within his arms as he closes his eyes slowly and falls asleep.

'Let us promise to make sure Triton and Venus will suffer as much as possible for what they have done to us as well as the unforgettable impact they have caused upon our families' lives as well as the other humans that exist on the Planet of Phoenix,' says Raven while slowly removing his arms from around Parrot and Sapphire; he stands back on his feet and holds gently on to one of Tigra's little hands.

'Yes, Triton and Venus will pay for their deeds and their hatred against all of us humans. We will send them to an afterlife of horrific pain and torture for an eternity,' strongly states Parrot as he takes a deep breath to compose himself. He lets go of Sapphire and wipes the tears from his face. Parrot stands up on his weakened legs, and with the assistance of Raven, they both begin to help lift Sapphire up from the floor. Her entire body is also numb from the shock of the recent murders of her parents and Parrot's parents.

'I will make those immoral and malicious creatures suffer for what they have done to all of our families and friends,' mumbles Sapphire due to her streaming tears as she looks over at her father and mother lying still within the wooden coffins. Bella stands next to Sapphire and wipes the tears away from her cheeks with a small piece of white cloth that she had in one of her pockets.

'I will go downstairs with Tigra and look after Rexus to give you all a moment with your parents alone,' says Bella to Sapphire as she gracefully leaves the guest room and walks down the wooden stairs of Pinus Tavern. At the bottom of the wooden stairs, Bella looks around and sees some of the Pine villagers cleaning up the last pieces of broken wood and glass upon the floor of Pinus Tavern.

Bella now walks immediately over to the big wooden table in one corner of Pinus Tavern, where Emerald's dead body lay next to the woman Pine villager, who is still holding on to Rexus. Bella gasps for breath and covers her mouth in shock with one of her hands at the sight of Emerald's dead body that is bruised and covered in blood and mud. Bella cries emotionally and places her hand on to Emerald's dead hand that rests upon the big wooden table. The woman Pine villager next to Bella attempts to say something comforting to Bella but finds herself speechless at the distraught sight of Bella's reaction to Emerald's death.

'I will wait downstairs with Bella for as long as you need, Sapphire. I wish there was something I could say to make you feel better, but words just can't take the pain away as I know how you must be feeling,' says Raven quietly as he also slowly walks out of the guest room and down Pinus Tavern wooden stairs to the ground floor.

As Raven walks to Pinus Tavern's ground floor, he sees several devastated Pine villagers hugging their families and friends in honour of Emerald as they had now all finished cleaning up the last remaining broken parts of Pinus Tavern that was destroyed during the Pine Village battle. These Pine villagers walk gradually over to Raven and offer him their condolences. Raven nods at these Pine villagers and shakes their hands as he passes by them on the way to Emerald's dead body upon the big wooden table, where Bella, Tigra, Rexus, and the Pine Village women were currently waiting in silence.

Some of the Pine villagers now leave Pinus Tavern through its big wooden entrance doors as they seek to continue helping the rest of the Pine villagers throughout the whole of Pine Village to clean up or mend more of the broken-down wooden houses, flats, and shops that were destroyed during the Pine Village battle. Also these Pine villagers continue to heal and support the wounded Pine guards and Pine villagers. During the duties of cleaning up Pine Village or aiding the injured, some of the Pine villagers take a brief break to visit their families and friends who were killed and buried at Pinus Graveyard; during these visits to Pinus Graveyard, the Pine villagers light candles, say prayers, and place beautiful flowers upon the graves of their loved ones.

BACK IN PINUS Tavern, Raven walks around the big wooden table and places both of his hands gently on to Emerald's shoulders, and watery tears begin to drip down his cold and muddy cheeks at the thought of Emerald not being with him no more. She would usually help comfort him during these times of hardship like what Parrot and Sapphire were currently experiencing.

'That she-devil creature Venus took our Emerald's life. Her soul should be the one that replaces Emerald's from within that troublesome anomaly crystal when that curse of death spell is conducted as you mentioned in the guest room,' states Bella in misery from Emerald's death.

'Yes, you are right, Bella. Venus definitely deserves to have her soul separated from her earthly body. I just hope we have enough time to find Triton and Venus on the Planet of Phoenix as the curse of death's time limit is quickly ticking away. I fear even if we eventually find them within the vast Realms of Deserted Lands, Venus's creature abilities would be far beyond any of our human skills such as my tae kwon do fighting, Parrot's innovative weapon practices, and Sapphire's intellectual mind. Venus somehow created two powerful and monstrous dinosaurs during the battle of Eagle Forest that annihilated almost all of Hake's Hawk Tribe and numerous sturdy trees within Eagle Forest. I never thought something as extreme as this kind of creature ability would ever be possible,' explains Raven as he looks up at Bella's concerned face.

'How did Venus take Emerald's innocent life?' asks Bella, looking back down at Emerald's dead body upon the big wooden table.

'Emerald was enraged with vengeance from what Venus had done to Ruby earlier that day. Both of us were riding upon Felix through Eagle Forest to fight against Triton and Venus, but before I knew it, Emerald departed from Felix by herself and furiously attacked Venus with all her might. I wanted to aid Emerald, but found myself in battle with Triton, and just as I was about to kill Triton by a swing from my sword, Venus struggled free from Emerald's attack and wielded the astonishing powers of the anomaly crystal that magically took Emerald's soul from her body. There was nothing I could do at this point, and then Venus and Triton cowardly escaped from Eagle Forest. I thought all hope was lost and that I would not be able to continue living without Emerald in my life, until Hake explained to us back in his hut about the curse of death and how it could be employed to bring Emerald's life back from the dead. Slight visions of hope appeared in my mind which will now fuel my energy to do whatever I can to bring Emerald back to the world of the living again,' states Raven as he releases his arms from Emerald's shoulders and bends over to stroke Rex again, who was currently being held by the woman Pine villager while sitting on the wooden chair.

'I could never imagine such sorcery and power existing on this spiritual planet we live on, but I suppose if we have never been exposed to this phenomenon before, we would have no idea about it all. Poor Ruby as well, I was unaware at the time of Pinus Tavern remembrance service what had actually happened to Emerald when she burst through the doors of Pinus Tavern in shock. Let the gods bless you all during the great war, along with aiding you in the final destruction of Triton's and Venus's lives, which will also hopefully bring the beautiful Emerald back to the Planet of Phoenix again. There's nothing that I will pray more than for this to happen,' replies Bella as she bends over the big wooden table to kiss Emerald gently on the forehead.

IN ONE OF Pinus Tavern's guest rooms, Sapphire despondently gazes at her parents within the wooden coffins again.

'They were such good parents to me, and I know I was loved very much as I also loved them with all my heart. My mother said it was the hardest thing for them when I left Pine Village and moved to Falcon City in order to further my studies at Falcon University. We sent each other letters frequently as you and I did, but due to not being easily able to travel back home and seeing them during the time I was at Falcon University, along with being their only child, my mother expressed that she and my father found it very difficult living without seeing me often as they had always done when I was a younger child.

'They were, however, proud of me for wanting to accomplish my degree as I was the only family member in our bloodline to have done so. They were very pleased to see me be awarded with my PhD at the end of my studies in a Falcon University ceremony, when they came to visit me in Falcon City for this occasion and which was the only time they had physically seen me in four years. After I completed my PhD, I travelled back home to be with my family again. I was very sad to leave my best friend Nia there though, as she decided it would be best for her to stay on and train to become a lecturer of history at Falcon University. My heart and instinct told me to come back home to be closer to my parents as well as due to our feelings for each other developing. I also wanted to be nearer and be together with you. Looking back now, I guess I was fortunate to come back home and spend this remaining time with my parents before the gods wanted to reunite my parents with the rest of my ancestors in heaven,' sadly says Sapphire while hugging Parrot tightly.

'I know how you feel, Sapphire. I always knew how much your parents cherished you, and for me personally, I really appreciated them treating me as a part of your family and the help they provided us with raising Tigra. My biggest regret is not getting to introduce my parents to Tigra within these past few months. They mentioned several times for us to come and meet with them in Willow Village, as my mother had been too ill recently to travel to Pine Village. I had wanted to go and see them many times, but due to Tigra being too young for such a journey, along with the increasing creature threat being impacted upon us humans, we just didn't manage to get to see them again with Tigra, and now it's too late,' says Parrot with much despair regarding these unfortunate circumstances.

'I want my revenge upon Triton and Venus, so my parents, your parents, your grandfather Barious, Emerald's mother Ruby, and any other human who has suffered the atrocities of these creatures can finally rest in peace, knowing that their innocent deaths will have been avenged,' remarks Sapphire as she puts her hands on both of her parents' wooden coffins. Then after a moment, she tenderly kisses both of her parents on the forehead. Sapphire takes one last look at her parents in the two wooden coffins; she closes the lids to the wooden coffins gently and then holds Parrot's hand tightly as they both leave this guest room and continue walking down the wooden stairs to the ground floor of Pinus Tavern, where Raven, Bella holding Tigra, Rexus and the woman Pine villager are standing next to Emerald's dead body upon the big wooden table.

'Bella, would you please take care of Tigra and Rexus for a while longer as we have the most important and pressurised mission to complete in support of returning Emerald's soul back to her human body in the hope of bringing her back to life. After this task has been done, we will all return back to Pine Village together, and I would then like to bury my parents properly within Pinus Graveyard, if this can be made possible for me please,' asks Sapphire politely.

'Yes, of course, my dear. Don't worry about Tigra or Rexus. I will make sure that they are well looked after until you all return home safely. Yes, I imagined burying your parents is something you would want to have done personally. That is why I collected their bodies in the wooden coffins and placed them in Pinus Tavern's guest room until the appropriate time,' remarks Bella, looking at Sapphire's demoralised face. Raven smiles when he strokes Rexus again as he wags his tail; Sapphire now gently takes Tigra from Bella's arms, and Sapphire and Parrot hug him strongly together.

'Bella, we will require another horse for our journey. Is there another spare horse near here?' asks Parrot.

'I believe Lynx and his Pine guards took most of the Pine Village horses with them to Willow Village in their preparation for the great war, but there may still be one or two horses left in the field at the back of Pinus Tavern,' replies Bella.

'I'll go check now, much gratitude for helping us all, Bella, during this uncertain time, just as you had also done during the battle of Oak Village a year ago. You are truly a wonderful woman, and we will forever be in your debt,' says Parrot as he stops hugging Tigra and quickly jogs out of Pinus Tavern's big wooden entrance doors and continues running around the back of Pinus Tavern, where he

seeks to retrieve a horse from the small grass field located behind
Pinus Tavern.

'You all will never be in my debt as I value you as my friends,
and our help and compassion for one another is what sets us apart
from those wicked creatures. I'll quickly go and gather some much-
needed supplies for you to take on your long journey to the Realm
of Deserted Lands,' says Bella to Raven and Sapphire. Bella leaves
this corner of Pinus Tavern and hurries to the back room of Pinus
Tavern's front bar, where she enters through a wooden door into a
medium-sized kitchen. Bella quickly gathers a few bottles of water
and food rations such as bread, fruit, and vegetables. Bella packs the
bottles of water and the food rations into a big brown leather bag
with an attached back strap to it. After a few minutes, Bella comes
back out of the kitchen and goes over to the corner of Pinus Tavern,
where she gives the big brown leather bag with the water and food
ration supplies to Sapphire to carry. Sapphire places the big brown
leather bag over one of her shoulders, and then she kisses Tigra softly
on the side of his cheek, which causes Tigra to open his eyes slowly
as it wakes him up.

'Mummy loves you very much. She will be back soon to look after
you and give you many more happy memories with myself and your
father just like my parents had given to me,' says Sapphire as she looks
into Tigra's innocent eyes before passing him back over to Bella, who
rocks him slowly again to sleep.

'We can't thank you enough, Bella. I don't know what we would
have done without you being here to support us through this hurtful
time,' humbly mentions Sapphire.

'Just make sure you all come back home safe and soon. We will
all be waiting for you. I will also try to make sure your parents are
left to rest in peace within the guest room of Pinus Tavern until you
return to give them a well-deserved and praiseworthy burial. I will
pray that no harm comes to any of you during this quest and for
Emerald's soul to be reunited with her body as I would want nothing
more than to see the four of you return back here again,' says Bella
with much sincerity.

'Thank you for your kind and thoughtful prayers, Bella. We hope
they help us during the great war,' says Raven, smiling respectfully
at Bella.

'Safe journey to you all,' says the woman Pine villager who was still holding on to Rexus while sitting in the small wooden chair. Sapphire now picks up the book of curses and the blue potion that was in the glass container and which Hake had given to her back in Eagle Forest. She places them carefully within the brown leather bag around her shoulder.

PARROT LUCKILY FINDS one remaining black horse with an attached saddle that was still left resting in the small grass field at the back of Pinus Tavern. Parrot jumps over the wooden fence that surrounds the small grass field, and he cautiously approaches the black horse. Parrot strokes the black horse firmly so that it starts to trusts him. Raven then gently holds on to the black horse's rope reins and begins to walk with this black horse to lead it out of the small grass field behind Pinus Tavern, and Parrot continues walking it back around to the front of Pinus Tavern. Parrot leaves the black horse outside the front of Pinus Tavern, where he ties its rope reins next to Felix around the pine tree that is located very close to Pinus Tavern.

Parrot leaves the two horses momentarily and pushes open the big wooden entrance doors of Pinus Tavern and hurries back over to the corner where Raven; Sapphire; Bella, who was now holding Tigra; and the woman Pine villager who was holding on to Rexus were waiting. Parrot smiles at everyone, before grabbing his wooden bow and his wooden arrows with the metal spikes at the end of it from the big wooden table on which Emerald's dead body lay. Parrot positions the wooden bow upon his back; he places the wooden arrows with the sharp metal spikes at the end of them into a small wooden pouch that he also attached around his back. Parrot also checks to make sure that he still has some fury raptor throwing stars left within the pockets of his big brown coat that he was wearing around his body.

Parrot now picks up Raven's sword of Grackle and the shield of Grackle from the big wooden table. Raven carefully picks up Emerald's dead body; he places her over his shoulder and carries Emerald's dead body outside Pinus Tavern's big wooden entrance doors and gently places her on top of Felix's back as he was still tied against the pine tree near Pinus Tavern. Raven also still has the small silver dagger fixed in his brown boots that Parrot had given him over a year ago, along with the map for the Planet of Phoenix secured in his brown coat pocket that Lynx recently gave to him in the guest room of Pinus Tavern. Sapphire also carries one of Parrot's small silver daggers that she had just picked up from the big wooden table and places it in the brown leather bag, where all the other weapons will be carried by Parrot.

'We will be back for Tigra and Rexus as soon as we can,' says Parrot to Bella as he touches her shoulder with his arm. Sapphire kisses Tigra's little hand gently. Parrot and Sapphire now walk towards the big wooden entrance doors of Pinus Tavern; they both look gloomily behind them at Bella holding Tigra, who was sleeping firmly in her arms, before they both exit Pinus Tavern together. During this time, Raven had untied Felix and the other black horse from the pine tree located near Pinus Tavern's big wooden entrance doors.

Raven climbs on top of Felix's back and now holds Emerald's dead body carefully in front of him. Parrot and Sapphire leave Pinus Tavern's big wooden entrance doors and walk over to the pine tree, where Parrot helps Sapphire to climb on to the black horse's back. He gives the sword and shield of Grackle to Sapphire to hold, before climbing on to and at the front of the black horse. He holds its rope reins tightly as Sapphire secures herself comfortably behind Parrot. Raven holds on firmly to Emerald and kicks his heels into the sides of Felix to make him canter, just as Parrot and Sapphire also do on their black horse. They pass by Pinus Tavern quickly and then continue down the cobbled paths towards the west entrance wooden gate of Pine Village.

As Raven, Parrot, and Sapphire canter on both of their horses down the cobbled paths of Pine Village, the remaining Pine villagers who were still cleaning up some of the wooden rubble amongst the cobbled paths from the Pine Village battle now notice the horses cantering past them. They smile and cheer for Raven, Parrot, and Sapphire. After around twenty minutes of cantering across the main cobbled path, they reach the west entrance wooden gate of Pine Village that was burnt and half destroyed from the battle of Pine Village. Raven pulls Felix to a halt, and this action is copied by Parrot on his black horse. Raven and Parrot stop for a brief moment so that Raven can examine the map of the Planet of Phoenix that he pulls out of his pocket and unfolds. Raven studies the map of the Planet of

Phoenix to see the quickest route towards the Realm of the Deserted Lands in the far south-west corner of the Planet of Phoenix.

'We must head directly south-west across the Grass Terrain Fields. I can't see any obstacles that will get in our way on this route, although, I'm not sure what we will experience upon entering the Realm of Deserted Lands,' states Raven gloomily as he now folds up the map of the Planet of Phoenix and puts it back in one of the pockets of his brown coat. The sun glistens slightly, and the air breezes over the clouds within the sky of the Planet of Phoenix; without hesitation, Raven and Parrot both kick their heels into the sides of Felix and the black horse. They are required to hold tightly on to the rope reins as the horses begin to gallop swiftly out of the west entrance wooden gate of Pine Villager and continue in the south-west direction, and they begin to undertake their long and epic journey over numerous vast Grass Terrain Fields towards the Realm of Deserted Lands.

Thirty-One

LYNX, BRUCE, AND his 200 Pine guards and men Pine villagers who are riding fiercely with determination upon their various large brown and black horses are currently galloping rapidly and strongly in the west direction towards Willow Village across the long cobbled road built through the Grass Terrain Fields. They all ride without a pause, allowing their journey to just take under an hour. They now reach the west entrance wooden gates of Willow Village. The sun is now at its highest point in the sky of the Planet of Phoenix, and it streams bright and sweltering sun rays that cause sticky heat upon the Pine guards and men Pine villagers and makes them sweat from their foreheads.

'Halt, Pine guards and men Pine villagers, we have made it to Willow Village. The battle of Willow Village was just like the battle of Pine Village in that it caused devastation and many grievances to all of the Willow villagers. Please approach the village with care and consideration to avoid startling the remaining Willow villagers,' says Lynx, who is currently at the front of the group of 200 Pine guards and men Pine villagers.

'Of course, Lynx, I will rally the men in a poised manner as you confer with Panther,' replies Bruce as he nods at Lynx. Lynx slowly turns around and trots upon his white horse through the west entrance wooden gates of Willow Village. Bruce climbs down from his large black horse and starts to hand signal the Pine guards and men Pine villagers to also steadily trot or walk their horses through the west entrance wooden gates of Willow Village.

The 200 Pine guards and men Pine villagers now enter through the west entrance wooden gates of Willow Village in a respectful manner; they are prudently watched from a distance by some of the remaining forty-seven Willow villagers within Willow Village. These Willow villagers either continue cleaning away the broken pieces of wood from the grassy paths and the from within the broken small wooden flats and shops of Willow Village or begin to visit their deceased loved ones who were killed during the Willow Village battle and have now been laid to rest within Willow Graveyard. The Willow villagers, who notice the army of Pine guards and men Pine villagers entering into Willow Village, gaze over them in astonishment on seeing so many Pine guards and villagers along with their horses eagerly ready to battle in the great war against the creatures.

As Lynx passes across the grassy paths of Willow Village in the east direction, he quickly sees Panther and his twenty Willow guards, who are at present in the middle of Willow Village as they also continue to clean up the rest of the main broken wooden debris from the destroyed small wooden flats and shops where the Willow Village battle had been at its most foulest point due to the giant size of Vulture causing a horrific impact upon his immediate surroundings. Lynx kicks the back of his white horse with his heels and gallops speedily upon his white horse up to Panther and his twenty Willow guards; the 200 Pine guards and men Pine villagers are still quite far back from Lynx, and they remain walking or riding upon their horses progressively across the grassy paths of Willow Village.

Lynx continues riding on his white horse until he pulls the rope reins of the white horse tightly, enabling the white horse to halt right next to Panther. Panther looks up and sees his nephew Lynx mounted worthily upon his white horse. He was looking at Panther with an emotional expression of vengeance in his eyes. Lynx carefully climbs down from the large back of his white horse due to his ankle still being sprained and bruised from the injury he had suffered in his fight against Vulture during the battle of Willow Village, although, Lynx's ankle has now become a bit better, permitting Lynx to walk more properly as he walked before he sprained his ankle.

LYNX TURNS TOWARDS Panther, and they grab each other's forearm strongly as a sign of respect for one other.

'Glad to see you're still alive, Uncle,' smiles Lynx.

'Yes, well, you know that no creature will get the better of me.' Panther chuckles as he and Lynx now let go of the strong grip they had upon each other's forearms.

'How are the Willow villagers bearing after that ghastly battle of Willow Village?' Lynx asks with empathy.

'Most of the Willow villagers are not coping too well as they have never seen the likes of blood and death before due to Willow Village normally being a peaceful and uneventful place, but the strong hearts of the villagers will support their survival through this treacherous time. I'm also very glad to see that you are unharmed, my nephew. What has happened in Pine Village? We saw cruel black smoke arising from the distance?' asks Panther in a concerned manner.

'Yes, I am fine. Thank you, uncle, and my ankle has also healed a bit better now from that fall I endured by the blow of that revolting giant creature. But after I had left Willow Village yesterday to return to Pine Village, upon my arrival I was in the midst of being attacked by hundreds of Potorians along with that fire-breathing creature who had also attacked Willow Village. My Pine guards and Pine villagers displayed a valiant effort in defeating these creatures and protecting Pine Village from a fate that Oak Village unfortunately endured last year.

'I found myself accompanied with one of my most trusted Pine guards Bruce in the heat of the battle. We did, however, lose the innocent lives of many Pine guards and Pine villagers who suffered an untimely and atrocious end. Many of these Pine guards and Pine villagers were dearly loved by their remaining families and friends. Pine Village also had many of the buildings and defences severely destroyed during the battle, which Pine Village might never properly recover from,' explains Lynx with much heartache.

'My ears bleed on hearing about the devastation caused at Pine Village, which is just like that suffered by Willow Village and Oak Village. It does please me to know that those creatures that attacked both our villages have now been completely removed from the Planet of Phoenix. But their cruel masters, Triton and Venus, along with Viper, are still alive and are a threat to us, where they possess the creatures' abilities to cause undisputable damage to all of the humans who still exist upon the Planet of Phoenix,' remarks Panther.

'The time has now come for our villages and guards to join forces and seek aid from King Exodus and the royal Falcon guards within Falcon City, residing within the Kingdom of Humans. This global unity of humans will help us all to survive the long-awaited great war that is inevitably about to occur and will indeed change the Planet of Phoenix along with the inhabitants that survive through it forever. It will also shape the future lives or our family generations,' states Lynx as he pauses a moment and thinks about his father Saber and mother Lunar, who were killed by Viper in a battle that occurred in Falcon City eight years ago. The circumstances during the battle had impacted upon the rest of Lynx's life and had caused it to change in a way that his life would never be the same. Panther intuitively realises Lynx's change of emotions in his face, and Panther places his right hand on Lynx's left shoulder.

'Your parents always knew that you would become a great leader, but more importantly an honourable human. Both of them would be so very proud to see the man that you have become, along with the vast wisdom, knowledge, and compassion you possess. Your mother's kind love and caring attributes, matched with your father's determination and leadership skill set, have enabled you to be moulded into an impeccable human who will make a great impact within the great war of our time that we are all about to experience. Your father and my brother Saber spoke countless times with me about how he had dreams of you becoming a great guard. This was the reason why he, along with me, spent all those long years and resources training you to become the next royal Falcon captain. Saber didn't expect to leave you his succession at such a young age though, but unfortunate events sometimes happen beyond our control and carve out the rest of our lives for us, where we can either embrace these situations or crumble within them,' wisely says Panther.

'Yes, I remember how much support my father and you gave me in my training. That indeed empowered me to initially become part of the royal Falcon guard. It was originally even against my mother's wishes she wanted me to pursue my education and gain a degree at Falcon University. But my father was very persistent, and, although, I was put through countless hours of hard physical endurance and coaching, I remember him telling me how proud he was when King Exodus knighted me into becoming a part of the royal Falcon guard army.

'After my parents were sadly killed by Viper, my father's belief and faith in me was the reason why I agreed to be made the royal Falcon captain by King Exodus, which was also requested by you. I wanted my parents to watch over me from the heavens and be proud of their only son. However, the constant reminder of my old home where my parents had been killed within Falcon City was just too much pain for me to bear. These unstoppable haunting feelings pushed me to plead with King Exodus to permit me to resign and pronounce a new royal Falcon captain. I influenced this decision to be for one of my greatest royal Falcon guards who had also taken over from your title as the main royal Falcon captain guard, when you left Falcon City to become the leader of Willow Village. This man is known as Clang, and with him being the new royal Falcon captain, King Exodus allowed me to become the leader of Pine Village, where at the same time due to untimely events of the previous Pine Village leader Igon being killed by the nomad warriors in the Wastelands left Pine Village leaderless.

'It did indeed break my heart to leave my home and a lot of my childhood memories within Falcon City behind me as well as have to unhappily part ways from Princess Lily, where at this point we had become very close due to the many years we had spent associating with each other. But I felt a fresh start was needed, and it was the best option for me to help my damaged life repair itself and facilitate me to become the leader I was predestined to be and hopefully one day end the great war between the humans and the creatures once and for all, along with especially eliminating that malevolent creature Viper from the Planet of Phoenix as I would not have any other human suffer from the devastation his black venom causes,' states Lynx.

'WHATEVER HAPPENS TO us in the great war, know that your leadership and noble efforts in maintaining and developing Pine Village over these past few years has made a major difference to many human lives, especially in the countless times you saved these villages from being attacked by the nomad warriors. Along with the technology and plans you have put in place during your time as the

Pine Village leader, it will preserve our human heritage and ancestry for hundreds of years to come,' replies Panther modestly.

'Thank you for your warm words, Uncle, they are much appreciated and will provide me with hope in the forthcoming days. We must now journey to the grand Falcon City to seek advice and aid from the wise King Exodus as well as the royal Falcon guards,' remarks Lynx.

'Will King Exodus be willing to risk the lives of the many innocent humans that reside within Falcon City to face these creatures we have been battling with during the great war?' ponders Panther.

'You have been friends with King Exodus along with the late Barious for a very long time, and I used to be his captain of the royal Falcon guard. King Exodus will listen to the tragic information regarding our village battles we'll share with him, and he will see our purpose and reasons for asking for the aid of the humans living in Flacon City. He will also understand that the great war is now upon us all, and this great war will eventually consume the whole Planet of Phoenix. Whether we leaders risk the lives of our village humans or not, the great war will spread throughout our homes, nonetheless.

'I also think now that after persuasion, Viper and his Serpents may have joined forces with Triton and Venus due to our villages having destroyed Triton's Potorian army during the Pine Village battle. This will mean that once again Viper and his Serpents will certainly attack Falcon City during the great war. This is also what we need to warn King Exodus about, where he will see it necessary to prepare Falcon City's humans and Falcon City defences for an epic battle during the great war,' says Lynx.

'That you are right, Lynx. King Exodus is also a very sensible and honourable king. He has taken part in numerous previous battles himself and has seen many changes to the Planet of Phoenix during in his long stretch as king that has consisted for many decades following the death of his farther King Sharkus. King Exodus and I have kept in contact consistently via carrier pigeons ever since the time I left Falcon City to become the Willow Village leader, although, for us sharing words in present times has been most difficult due to the creatures intercepting our messages that we send to one another by carrier pigeons. It will be good to see King Exodus in person once again as we used to do every day when I was the main royal Falcon guard to my brother Saber and you, when you were both the royal

Falcon captain. I'm not sure how aware he is of all these disastrous events that have occurred with the creatures and what is happening with regards to the anomaly crystal, but I know we can count on him and Falcon City for their support. Do you know where the anomaly crystal currently is, Lynx?' replies Panther.

'Barious's grandson Raven, my best friend Parrot, and his girlfriend Sapphire are currently travelling across the south-west of the Planet of Phoenix, heading towards the Realm of Deserted Lands as we speak. Their aim is to seek and destroy Triton and Venus in the hope of bringing Raven's recently killed wife Emerald back from the afterlife. They are attempting to do this unheard of act by using a magic curse known as the curse of death that the leader of the Hawk Tribe within Eagle Forest called Hake has just told them about.

'They believe they will perform this uncertain act with the anomaly crystal by utilising its astonishing elemental powers, and then we will have the magical advantage in leading us to victory in the great war, but this can only happen if they find Triton and Venus quickly and find a way to take the anomaly crystal from them. We must all do our parts in this most pertinent time of human need. We should do our very best to help or sacrifice our resources in order to provide Raven, Parrot, and Sapphire the time they need to be undisturbed by creatures or mitigating situations they might experience in their journey across the Planet of Phoenix along with the fight they could experience against Triton and Venus. Once we have gained the support from King Exodus, I promised Raven that I would also meet up with them and assist with the slaying of Triton and Venus once and for all as their quest is going to be extremely challenging and dangerous due to these types of powerful creatures they have to fight against. Will you also come to their aid along with me, Uncle?' asks Lynx.

'Yes, of course I will, Lynx. Not only would I want to protect the blood generations of Barious's family, but the time has indeed come for an old man like me to play his final calling in saving the Planet of Phoenix from the evil creatures that roam its precious lands by whatever means necessary. Even if it means that it will be the end of my time upon the Planet of Phoenix, I would like my final deed to be known for the saving of the entire human race. I will now leave six Willow guards here at Willow Village to protect the remaining villagers that still remain here. I will travel with you and your Pine guards, along with fourteen of my best Willow guards that are masters of archery and will come in great use during battle situations. Willow Village will do our upmost duty in this great war between humans and creatures,' states Panther humbly.

'You are very righteous, one of a kind, Uncle, and a glorious leader with a much deserving title and name. We ride and fight together for the first time since we left the royal Falcon guard within Falcon City. The stories of the actions we inflict within the great war will remain forever within our families' history and will continue to be told as great tales for many future generations to come,' mentions Lynx with passion in his eyes and enthusiasm within his voice.

'And these great stories will remain for eternity for all of the humans who come to live on the Planet of Phoenix. They will always remember how their peaceful lives were created by the honourable action of those humans who existed before them,' replies Panther.

DURING THE CONVERSATION that was taking place between Lynx and Panther, many of the remaining forty-seven Willow villagers gather near Panther and his twenty Willow guards to find out what will happen to Willow Village next. Bruce, along with the 200 Pine guards and men Pine villagers also now walk or trot up to Lynx and Panther who are at present with Panther's twenty Willow guards, standing in the middle of Willow Village. As the Pine guards and men Pine villagers interact with the Willow guards, they all begin shaking forearms with one another as a sign of respect.

As Lynx finishes his conversation with Panther, he looks around him and sees Bruce, accompanied by 200 Pine guards and men Pine villagers, along with Panther's twenty Willow guards who were all standing together with pride and desire in their eyes.

'All men of honour, join us now as we ride south for the grand Falcon City,' shouts Lynx as he raises his arm up high in the air and points in the south direction of Willow Village. All the Pine guards, men Pine villagers, and Willow guards cheer loudly in excitement and bang their metal swords against their metal shields.

'For all of the humans living or dead, we will honour or avenge them by abolishing every creature from the Planet of Phoenix,' shouts Bruce during the chanting of the Pine guards, men Pine villagers, and Willow guards. Lynx now climbs back on top of his white horse as does Bruce, along with many of the other 200 Pine guards and men Pine Villagers who had been standing up the grassy paths of Willow Village. Lynx and Bruce manoeuvre their horses to ride to the front of the group of 200 Pine guards and men Pine Villagers as they all begin cantering upon their horses across the grassy paths of Willow Village in the east direction that will lead them out of the east entrance wooden gate. Upon leaving Willow Village, Lynx and Bruce, along with the 200 Pine guards and men Pine villagers, will change direction to the south perimeter of Willow Village, enabling their journey to be taken in the direct south direction towards Falcon City at the far south-east corner of the Planet of Phoenix.

'Willow guards, listen. As stated before, I wish for you six guards to stay here. Barricade the village and protect the Willow villagers in case the great war unfortunately ends up upon our village again. You other fourteen of my best archers will be required to battle alongside me during the great war,' states Panther as he firmly mounts upon his horse. 'My loyal Willow villagers, you will be safe here, for I will fight these evil creatures until my very last heartbeat to make sure that the great war ends in the south of the Planet of Phoenix, so that no Willow villager will suffer no more grievances. I now bid you all farewell, for I may not return. If this is what is meant to be, King Exodus will make sure that Willow Village is provided with another amiable leader and looked after in the future years to come. It has been a great pleasure leading you all.' The Willow villagers, who were listening attentively to Panther's words, either cheer or cry in tribute to their leader Panther.

Six of the twenty Willow guards who were to remain in Willow Village, quickly began assisting the other fourteen Willow guards in suiting their armour upon their bodies as well as passing them their weapons that mostly consisted of wooden bows and wooden arrows. Some of the Willow villagers also went to collect and bring several horses to the Willow guards, along with saying goodbye. The Willow guards who were leaving Willow Village and other Willow villagers had gathered provisions and supplies for these Willow guards and placed them within leather bags, which included food such as bread, vegetables, and salted meat as well as medical supplies like wool bandages and stitching needles.

Once the fourteen Willow guards have their full armour fixed upon their bodies, they mount upon their horses, and led by Panther, they gallop swiftly along the grassy paths and out of the east entrance wooden gate of Willow Village, where they catch up with Lynx, Bruce, and the 200 Pine guards and men Pine Villagers. As Panther and the fourteen Willow guards leave the east entrance wooden gates of Willow Village, they were waved at and cheered by the tentative Willow villagers that were left within Willow Village.

Lynx, Panther, Bruce, 200 Pine guards including men Pine villagers, and the fourteen Willow guards all continue to gallop rapidly in the south direction across the Planet of Phoenix's Grass Terrain Fields. The journey from Willow Village to Falcon City is long, tough, and exhausting for all the guards involved, especially with the heat of the sun blazing upon their covered bodies. As they all continue to swiftly ride in south direction, the leader Lynx and Panther make sure that they all keep riding a far distance away from coming in close perimeter to the treacherous and stretched Komodo Jungle that is located towards the middle section of the Planet of Phoenix. Lynx, Panther, Bruce, 200 Pine guards, including the men Pine Villagers and fourteen Willow guards, continue for many hours on their long ride south towards the magnificent Falcon City that resides within a large fertile area that covers the south-east corner of the Planet of Phoenix that is known as the Kingdom of Humans.

Thirty-Two

AFTER SEVEN HOURS of hard trekking very quickly across the Grass Terrain Fields over the middle section of the Planet of Phoenix as well as the blistering sprinting through the tough rocky ground of the unforgiving Realm of Deserted in the south-west direction of the Planet of Phoenix, Viper and his 800 Serpents finally reach Triton's Underground Dungeon. During this time, the Planet of Phoenix's core mysteriously changed in mass, causing the Serpent's journey to the Realm of Deserted Lands quicker than anticipated. To travel through the Realm of Deserted Lands, Viper and the Serpents forcefully pushed forward through the freezing gusts of winds that carried tiny dirt, rock, sand, and gristle particles in the gloomy and darkened sky above the Realms of Deserted Lands. Viper and his 800 Serpents now find themselves at the entrance to the passageway that leads directly below the rocky surface of the Realm of Deserted Lands into Triton's Underground Dungeon.

Without hesitation, Viper and his 800 Serpents continue running straight through the rocky and narrow passageway that leads into the main room of Triton's Underground Dungeon, below the surface of the Realm of Deserted Lands. On entering into the main room of Triton's Underground Dungeon, Viper and his Serpents see Triton and Venus sitting down upon big wooden chairs next to a big wooden table at the opposite side of the main room.

Triton and Venus are currently looking at a map of the Planet of Phoenix laid out across the big wooden table; they had retrieved the map of the Planet of Phoenix earlier from their bedroom along with Triton's golden chain with the iron spiked ball at the end of it. Viper hurries over to the big wooden table and quickly sits down upon another big wooden chair as the 800 Serpents wait at the entrance of the main room. As the Serpents wait in stillness at the entrance of the main room, they all pant and cough, attempting to catch their breath from experiencing the long journey that they had just endured across the Planet of Phoenix.

'That was a very lengthy journey to reach your hideout, Triton. It better be worth it,' hisses Viper as he also takes a big gasp of air.

'It will be, Viper. You will have your deserved rewards soon enough. Besides, you have lived long enough. Your hard and scaly body must be used to these long journeys and fighting battles,' states Triton as he continues to examine the map of the Planet of Phoenix.

'Unless it appears that age has finally caught up with you and your Serpent warriors,' laughs Venus, turning around and looking at the Serpents still breathing deeply and noisily from the long journey.

'Impossible, my Serpents and I, with my perfect and strong reptilian skin, never weaken or deteriorate unlike some creatures,' hisses Viper, noticing Triton's infected leg that had been covered with a cloth. Due to the sword of Grackle's infectious power against evil creatures, this stab wound has rotted more away of Triton's skin, and the infection has now spread beyond the cloth wrapped around his right leg. Triton snarls at Viper and points back on the map of the Planet of Phoenix to an image representing Falcon City.

'King Exodus in Falcon City will probably position his royal Falcon guards within the north areas of the city's walls, probably near the iron portcullis and also protecting the region around Nautilus Lake as he usually does due to these points being the only entrances into Falcon City's resilient walls. As of this moment, no human knows about my Underground Dungeon being located within the Realm of Deserted Lands, so he wouldn't expect an attack coming from the south-west direction from within the area known as the Kingdom of Humans.

'I reckon the best approach would be to launch a surprise attack from the far south-west and destroy the outer stone walls of Falcon City with the anomaly crystal's outstanding powers and then once we have all entered inside the walls of Falcon City, we will quickly slaughter all of the humans in our path before we reach Falcon Castle to then exterminate King Exodus and the rest of his royal Falcon guards. The panic and terror that will be caused from the south-west area of Falcon City will disrupt King Exodus's plans to regroup his royal Falcon guards in order for them to have a real chance in defending or defeating us. It will still be a great and fierce war on both sides, but with this plan we will have the upper hand, especially with all of our unique creature abilities and of course the almighty anomaly crystal,' declares Triton.

'King Exodus and his pathetic humans have for too long ruled over the Planet of Phoenix's land and precious resources. This planet was originally inhabited first by the ancient creatures such as my mother Mamushi. It's inevitably time for the kings of the humans to fall hard and pitifully. King Exodus and his royal Falcon guards will not stand a chance against me or my violent 800 Serpent army,' hisses Viper.

'Then how come you have not managed to defeat King Exodus and his royal Falcon guards before in the previous battles you have enforced upon Falcon City?' snipes Venus.

'Yes, we have battled Falcon City several times in previous years, and, although, we have not been successful, we have indeed killed many humans, reducing their overall numbers, along with eliminating important humans of the city. For example, a few years ago, I used my black venom to annihilate one of the previous royal Falcon captain called Saber, along with his wife. Since then I have also increased the numbers of my bred Serpent army, and this time King Exodus and Falcon City will fall in unbelievable pain and terror,' laughs Viper.

'Do not underestimate the strength, loyalty, and union of the humans. They have obviously survived this long upon the Planet of Phoenix, along with being quite successful in previous battles before. The great war will, however, be a promising turn of events for us creatures, but to ensure victory we must be prepared to fight swiftly and for a long time as we will still be outnumbered if all of the humans from the surrounding villages across the Planet of Phoenix mange to join forces together. These circumstances may have already begun to start now,' states Venus.

'You are correct, my love, but we possess something that the humans do not, the unstoppable anomaly crystal that will match any obstacle within its way,' says Triton excitedly.

'Yes, but we are still unsure of how to precisely wield the wondrous powers of the anomaly crystal. It has aided us so far, but if the time comes where we can't rely upon it, we must still need to make sure that we will obtain the upper hand during the great war and crush all of the humans with an iron fist,' remarks Venus with passion in her voice.

'Your woman speaks wise words, Triton,' hisses Viper.

'As always you are right, my love. What of Raven? He also possesses the bloodline of Grackle inside of his puny body. He must also be slayed immediately before he gets his chance to use the anomaly crystal against us,' remarks Triton, looking at Venus.

'Yes, I was pondering upon that in my thoughts, my love. Our best offence plan would be to quickly go to Eagle Forest first and destroy Hake and his remaining Hawks, before they have any opportunity to interfere within this great war.'

'That bizarre bird creature Hake would be too scared to leave his precious Eagle Forest,' hisses Viper.

'Although, Hake will not abandon Eagle Forest, if he foresees the humans losing the great war, he may interfere somewhat with his vast range of sorcerous powers, and I will not tempt this fate. Hake must be killed for us to have any high probability in succeeding within the great war. While we are back in Eagle Forest, we will also kill Raven and his friends as they may also still be there due to them all grieving over Raven's dead wife. Now would be the perfect time to defeat them all as they will not be much of a challenge to us due to the devastated emotions they will be experiencing from that human Emerald's death. Emotions are the one main weakness of humans that will always be their downfall, unlike us creatures' laughs Venus.

'Yes, that sounds like the best plan of action. Viper, you must also journey back east to the far south of the Planet of Phoenix with your Serpents, where you will launch a surprise attack on Falcon City from the south-west wall. Venus and I will annihilate Hake and the Hawks along with Raven and his friends at Eagle Forest, and then afterwards we will join with you at the south-west corner of Falcon City as you would probably just reach the Kingdom of Humans by the time are finished with our evil-doings within Eagle Forest.

'However, if we have not reunited with you before you approach Falcon City, wait for us first to strengthen each other's forces, unless you need to attack immediately if you feel that your presence is noticed by any of the royal Falcon guards who will be on watch duty upon the top of Falcon City walls and watchtowers. We will indeed come to Falcon City at some point and join forces with you during the great war in all of our times and in the history of the Planet of Phoenix,' states Triton. Viper looks peculiarly back at Triton before standing up from his big wooden chair that was besides the big wooden table and starts to walk towards the exit for the main room within Triton's Underground Dungeon. Viper turns around quickly just before he exits the main room with his 800 Serpents.

'Don't take too long in joining me and my Serpents for the great war, Triton,' Viper shouts as he sturdily leaves Triton's Underground Dungeon followed by his 800 Serpents. Viper and the Serpents march up through the rocky and narrow passageway that leads out above the rocky ground at the surface of the Planet of Phoenix within the Realm of Deserted Lands. Upon exiting the rocky and narrow passageway, Viper looks around at his army of Serpents, who look hungry for blood and flesh. 'It's time to feast on human bones, my Serpents!' The Serpents roar in hunger and excitement. Viper and his 800 Serpents now begin to sprint swiftly in the south-west direction across the rocky surface of the Realm of Deserted Lands and towards Falcon City in the south-east direction of the Planet of Phoenix.

VENUS STANDS UP from her big wooden chair against the big wooden table within the main hall of Triton's Underground Dungeon; she stands still for a moment and utilises her Animagus abilities that enable her to turn her red eyes into pure white and then magically turns her entire physical body back into her Quetzalcoatlus form. In her Quetzalcoatlus form, Venus flaps her large scaly wings powerfully to hover in the air just above the ground. Triton also stands up from his big wooden chair, but as soon as he stands upon his large feet, Triton feels intense pain from the wound that he has received from the sword of Grackle. Triton bites his lip hard to forget about the excruciating pain he is currently experiencing in his right leg. He grabs the anomaly crystal and his golden chain with the spiked iron ball at the end of it that had been laid out over the big wooden table.

Venus uses her Quetzalcoatlus feet claws to grab firmly upon Triton's bulky shoulders in order to lift him up off the ground and into the air within the main room. Venus now flies briskly out of Triton's Underground Dungeon via the main room and through the rocky and narrow passageway, until she is able to fly high up in the air of the Planet of Phoenix's darkest skies in the south side of the Planet of Phoenix over the Realm of Deserted Lands. Venus furiously and rapidly flies through the skies, swerving through the cold, gusty, and infested winds of the Realms of Deserted Lands to quickly reach the lighter and calmer sky above the Swamp Fields near the Mountains of Doom in the north direction of the Planet of Phoenix.

Venus flies rapidly for a few hours until she enters the vast perimeter of Eagle Forest from the air above it. Venus continues flying strongly while holding tightly on to Triton towards the middle section of Eagle Forest, where she circles around the area high above the tall and thick trees until she spots the Hawks' Tribe Camp below on the ground with her heightened bird-like vision. Venus now flaps her large scaly wings sturdily to manoeuvre and steady herself, enabling her to fly directly down gradually through the tall and thick trees of Eagle Forest, and she soon reaches the ground of Eagle Forest just outside the Hawks' Tribe Camp.

Upon reaching the ground of Eagle Forest, Venus puts Triton down upon the ground first, and then after she touches the floor, Venus uses her Animagus abilities to turn back into her normal physical appearance and her eyes turn back to their normal red colour again. After Venus has changed completely back into her human physical form, she stands fiercely next to Triton while deviously looking through the tall and thick trees at the Hawks' Tribe Camp. As Triton and Venus flew down through Eagle Forest's thick and overgrown trees, they were fortunately spotted by some of the Hawks who were hiding within the tall and thick trees as lookouts.

The Hawks who had spotted Triton and Venus from high up in the tall and thick trees, along with other Hawks who had just witnessed Triton and Venus land upon the ground just outside of the Hawks'

Tribe Camp, all begin to screech out loudly in their high-pitched alarm sound from their small beaks, which instantly alerts Hake and all the rest of the Hawks residing throughout the Hawks' Tribe Camp and within Eagle Forest. Within moments, all the remaining twenty-six Hawks softly rush by their bird-like feet or flying with their feathered arm wings from wherever they were initially within Eagle Forest and head straight to the area where Triton and Venus had landed upon the ground just outside the Hawks' Tribe Camp.

As all the Hawks approach Triton and Venus, they quickly begin to shoot their green, sharp, powerful laser beams from their green eyes directly at Triton and Venus. Upon seeing the green laser beams being shot at them, Triton and Venus quickly hide behind a couple of tall and thick trees; the green laser beams do indeed pierce straight through these tall and thick trees but narrowly miss Triton's and Venus's bodies. Triton quickly becomes furious and is overwhelmed with emotion, wanting to protect Venus from being shot again by the Hawks' green laser beams. Triton squeezes the anomaly crystal within his large hands, and suddenly the anomaly crystal mysteriously stops swirling with all the colours of the rainbow and the shades of white and black; it now turns into a pure violet colour that covers the entire anomaly crystal.

The anomaly crystal mystically releases a violet bubble force field that covers the area where Triton and Venus are currently standing behind a couple of the tall and thick trees; this purple bubble force field stops the Hawks' green laser beams from penetrating through it and as the Hawks' green laser beams bounce back off the purple bubble force field, they are sent back in an opposite direction and hit into some of the Hawks, causing small holes being burnt straight through the Hawks' bodies or in the bark of some of the tall and thick trees.

The Hawks that were shot by the green laser beams either screech out in agonising pain from their feathery bodies being burnt by their own green laser beams or stand still in panic and shock at the sight of the anomaly crystal's astonishing powers. All the Hawks now decide to stop shooting their green laser beams from their green eyes to avoid further damage to themselves or the tall and thick trees within Eagle Forest. Triton now becomes full of lust and voracity from the achievement of creating the violet bubble from the anomaly crystal and applying it to protect Venus and himself. Triton holds the anomaly crystal back out again within his large hands, where it magically changes the violet colour that covered the whole of the anomaly crystal rapidly back into the swirling colours of the rainbow and the shades of black and white. The violet bubble force field suddenly disappears from covering Triton's and Venus's bodies.

Triton focuses his intensified energy upon the anomaly crystal; as some of the blood from Grackle races through the arteries deep inside his bulky body, the anomaly crystal magically turns its swirling colours of the rainbow and the shades of white and black into a wavy blue colour that ripples continuously across the anomaly crystal. The supernatural powers of the anomaly crystal cause it to release a large tsunami that quickly pours out of one edge of the anomaly crystal and engulfs all the twenty-six remaining Hawks in the immediate surrounding area upon the ground of Eagle Forest, along with those Hawks that had been positioned high up in the tall and thick trees.

The large tsunami swirls and spins around high up in the air that even towers above the tallest and thickest trees of Eagle Forest. The tsunami could be seen by even some remaining wild animals from the Swamp Fields and the Wastelands. The overpowering water within the tsunami is filled with drowning Hawks, along with tall and thick trees as well as shrubs, bushes, and small animals that are being wildly thrown about within the water of the large tsunami and are being bashed into one another.

The large tsunami reaches its peak where it's small in width, but the height of it towers further beyond the tall and thick trees of Eagle Forest. The very top of it is noticed in the very far distance by shocked Raven, Parrot, and Sapphire, who are currently travelling upon Felix and another black horse in the south-west direction across the Grass Terrain Fields towards the Realms of Deserted Lands. As the loud and domineering tsunami continues to spin around powerfully, all the Hawks engulfed within the potent swirling waters of the tsunami attempt to gasp for breath desperately until they all unfortunately die from the strong deadly water gushing through their small lungs.

ONCE ALL THE twenty-six remaining Hawks are killed in the tsunami, the anomaly crystal starts swirling the colours of the rainbow and the shades of white and black again, and the large waters of the tsunami get sucked quickly back into the anomaly crystal until it all completely disappears. As the tsunami is removed from Eagle Forest by the anomaly crystal, it leaves the dead bodies of the Hawks along with the small animals as well as the bushes, shrubs, tall and thick trees to all fall briskly to the ground of Eagle Forest, where the dead bodies, shrubs, and trees all land upon it with a loud and hard thump. Triton looks and grins at Venus as they both start walking, holding hands together, directly into the Hawks' Tribe Camp.

Triton and Venus look around and see a quiet and empty half-destroyed Hawks' Tribe Camp, where the camp had either been destroyed by the large tsunami as well as the Spinosaurus dinosaur that Venus had created with her creature abilities last night during the battle of Eagle Forest. Triton and Venus look ahead and perceive the big wooden hut against the large kapok tree located in the middle of the Hawks' Tribe Camp, which they assume to be where Hake lives. Without hesitation they both walk forcefully towards Hake's big wooden hut.

Upon reaching the big wooden hut against the large Kapok tree, Triton and Venus both push aside the thick colourful cloth that covers at the entrance to Hake's big wooden hut, and as they enter it, Triton and Venus see Hake sitting upon the floor of his big wooden hut. Hake is sitting cross-legged in the opposite direction to the entrance. He has his eyes closed and is sitting behind the black cauldron that has the bubbling green liquid within it in the middle of his big wooden hut. Hake doesn't even move or flinch as Venus and Triton walk slowly around his big wooden hut and look suspiciously at all of Hake's potions and herb plants residing upon the wooden shelves within his big wooden hut. Out of spite, Venus kicks with her right foot at the black cauldron that knocks it over in the middle of the big wooden hut, where the green bubbling liquid within it now pours out slowly on to the floor of Hake's big wooden hut.

'We meet at last, Triton and Venus,' states Hake, realising that the black cauldron had been turned upon its side.

'And this will be the only time we meet,' laughs Venus, watching the hot green liquid disintegrate within the wood and the mud that is upon the floor of Hake's big wooden hut.

'You are right about that, Venus. Our souls will not coexist in the same destination in any afterlife,' remarks Hake calmly as Venus turns to snarl at the back of Hake's head.

'It will be a long time before either of us end up in the afterlife,' states Triton while manoeuvring around the inside of Hake's big wooden hut towards Hake.

'All good things come to those who deserve it, especially when their fate comes to pass,' remarks Hake.

'You talk in riddles, old sorcerer, but do nothing within your vast spectrum of sorcerous powers to stop us. You are more of a pathetic fool then I took you for,' snaps Venus.

'There are many situations and events that have happened just as they were meant to upon the Planet of Phoenix that have led us to meet at this very precise moment. Most of what has happened was unavoidable due to mitigating circumstances, whereas for some of those humans or creatures, it was indeed their own choices and decisions that may haunt their souls for eternity. Whatever the cause, this moment was predetermined by those entities higher than any of us who has ever existed on the Planet of Phoenix or indeed within the other planets of our universe. They alone have decided our fate, and as I have interacted spiritually with the gods recently, I have realised that I don't need to use my sorcerous powers to defeat you as that fate of you and I has already been decided.' Hake spoke in a mystical manner.

'Where are Raven and his friends? If you will tell us, we will not end your precious life this day,' states Triton, getting irritated by Hake's confusing words.

'Poor Triton, the abuse and humility you took from Lord Scartor in all of those years as his lieutenant has now made you empty and cruel inside,' replies Hake.

'We didn't come here to hear your insights, wise one. We have come to end your life this day, and soon after we will end the lives of the race of humans that resides upon our Planet of Phoenix like a disgusting and revolting plague,' shouts Venus.

'I foresaw you two coming here to kill me several months ago, yet I am still sitting here calmly and waiting for my destiny to fulfil itself as we all need to play our part in this great war. I'm willing to sacrifice myself for the greater good,' states Hake contently.

'Then you're a fool, old sorcerer, as you have sacrificed yourself for the wrong destiny and the wrong species. We will not be defeated in the great war for we possess the anomaly crystal, which is the most powerful artefact in existence. At last the creatures will rule the Planet of Phoenix as it was always meant to be,' remarks Triton just as Triton positions himself to stand right next to Hake, who was still sitting closed-legged upon the floor with his eyes closed.

'Triton, you are blinded from reality and will not be victorious in this great war. Venus, you have too much power and pride that cannot be controlled. You will also fall at the hands of those honourable and righteous humans.' Hake now opens his eyes to look mysteriously at Triton and Venus, who both stood on either side of him. Triton becomes furious with revulsion from what Hake has just said about Venus and his demise in the great war.

In his intense anger, Triton quickly swings his golden chain with the spiked iron ball at the end of it around his head and crashes it right through Hake's head. The spikes of the iron spiked ball plunge deep within Hake's small dwarf and bird-like head as pure red blood splatters from the newly cut holes within Hake's head and sprays across the inside wooden walls of Hake's small wooden hut. Hake's eyelids close softly as darkness impacts upon Hake's vision. Triton pulls his golden chain with the spiked iron ball at the end of it away from Hake's tender head, which yanks Hake's head from his body. Hake's head falls awkwardly upon the floor of his small wooden hut. After thousands of years of life, the sorcerer Hake is now dead.

TRITON AND VENUS look down with satisfaction upon Hakes' dead body that is now lying on the floor of his big wooden hut within the wondrous Eagle Forest. Triton bends over and picks up his iron spiked ball that is attached to the end of his golden chain; he brings the iron spiked ball to his mouth and licks Hakes' blood from one of the iron spikes that had just plunged through Hake's fragile bird-like head. Venus laughs and then also walks over to Triton and slowly licks Hake's blood from another one of the other iron spikes. As Venus licks the iron spike with her tongue leisurely, she looks at Triton in a seductive manner with her devious eyes.

'Hake's untactful words of wisdom are of no concern to us dominant creatures that are indeed worthy of ruling the Planet of

Phoenix. Just as it always should have been since the beginning of life upon the Planet of Phoenix, because us creatures existed first on this planet,' remarks Venus as she stops licking one of the iron spikes from the iron spiked ball that was attached to the golden chain that Triton was holding.

'It does confuse me, however, that Hake, who is one of the most powerful sorcerers that ever existed upon the Planet of Phoenix, didn't even attempt to use his sorcerous powers to try and stop us in anyway. It's almost like Hake wanted me to kill him at this precise moment,' replies Triton in a concerned manner.

'I wouldn't ponder upon these thoughts, my love. Hake has lived for far too long, and he probably forgot how to conjure up magic to stop us or even use the powerful sorcery knowledge and skills that he used to be able to evoke upon his enemies. A new age has come where the most powerful creatures will take over from the previous ancient creatures that once roamed this planet.' Venus smiles excitedly at Triton. Venus holds on to one of Triton's hand as they start to leave and walk out of Hake's big wooden hut, when suddenly the excruciating pain in Triton's right leg causes him extreme discomfort and makes Triton fall directly to the floor of Hake's big wooden hut. Triton grabs tightly on to the cloth bandage that was wrapped around his right leg in order to try and numb the intense pain caused from the wound that Raven had inflicted upon Triton, using the sword of Grackle during the battle of Eagle Forest.

'Triton my love, what is happening to your leg?' says Venus anxiously as she is shocked to see Triton fall upon his knees to the floor.

'It must be that bastard sword of Grackle's mystical energy spreading through my whole leg, and now I can feel it infecting the rest of my body. I can barely feel the strong power within my muscles in my leg now. Instead, it feels like my leg is being ripped apart from the inside,' groans Triton loudly.

'Hold on, my dear, I will help you with this unfortunate discomfort,' states Venus as she hurries over to the wooden shelves that were fixed upon one of the wooden walls within Hake's big wooden hut. Venus moves her hands around the wooden shelves and quickly moves the herbs and potions that were in glass containers around in order to look for something to soothe the pain within Triton's right leg. Venus notices a small glass container that has an orange liquid within it.

'This might help diminish some of your pain, my love,' says Venus as she picks up the small glass container that contains the orange liquid from the wooden shelf. Upon this glass container there was a marking in the ancient Phoenix language that stated this orange liquid to be a healing potion. Although Venus couldn't really read the ancient language of Phoenix, she remembered some words of items that she had read previously in a couple of the ancient books that she occasionally uncovered from different and hidden areas of the Planet of Phoenix, when she used to fly around in her Quetzalcoatlus form a few years ago in an attempt to understand more about the war between the creatures and the humans.

Venus runs back over to Triton who is now lying straight out upon the floor of Hake's big wooden hut. Venus grabs both of Triton's hands and pulls them away from his leg. Triton moans loudly again in pain. Venus quickly rips off the cloth bandage wrapped around Triton's leg and pours the orange liquid from the glass container into the middle of the stab wound in Triton's right leg. Triton's right leg had turned a yellow mouldy colour especially around the outside of the wound, and the colour of his entire right leg had also turned quite a bit paler. As Venus rubs the orange liquid smoothly within and around Triton's stab wound, the colour around his right leg begins to turn back to its normal black colour again, and the yellow mould around the outside of the stab wound within Triton's right leg also begins to disappear and fade away.

'Does that feel better now, my lover?' asks Venus as she holds firmly on to Triton's hands and helps him stand back to his large feet.

'I can still feel slight tingly pain within my right leg through some part of my body, but yes, it has got a lot better very quickly, and the colour and feeling in my right leg has greatly returned,' smiles Triton in relief.

'Well, at least Hake's knowledge and his practice of diverse sorcerous potions were actually good for something as you are surely going to need your fullest strength to ensure that us creatures will succeed in the much-anticipated great war,' remarks Venus. Triton takes a deep breath and clenches his fist tightly as he feels the blood flowing through his body and his muscles tensing strongly within his right leg as he stands upon the floor of Hake's big wooden hut.

'Yes! And I feel my immense strength returning back to me now as my thick blood flows through my veins and my leg again,' states Triton confidently.

'Then let's end the human race once and for all.' Venus cackles as she grins widely at Triton's reaction. Venus holds Triton's hand again as they walk towards the entrance of Hake's big wooden hut. Triton lifts up the colourful cloth of Hake's big wooden hut, and they both walk out through it, leaving Hake's broken and dead body lying on the floor behind them. Triton and Venus continue walking strongly through Hawks' Tribe Camp until they reach the edge of it in the south-west direction.

'Quick, let's meet up with Viper and his Serpent warriors in the far south of the Planet of Phoenix. They will probably be approaching the Kingdom of Humans and Falcon City soon. It's time for King Exodus to plummet at the hand of creatures!' shouts Triton.

'Of course, my love. Let us enforce the start of this great war and end it with a glorious victory, making us the dominant rulers of the Planet of Phoenix,' replies Venus as she turns her eyes quickly into a pure white colour.

'We have waited for this day for far too long,' comments Triton as he watches Venus getting ready to use her Animagus abilities. Just as Venus is about to use her Animagus abilities to turn her physical body back into her Quetzalcoatlus form, her Animagus abilities subconsciously connect with the eyes of the white dove's eyes that Venus had created several days ago at Ruby's house in Oak Village when she sent Emerald a message in order to make Emerald return back to Ruby's house, when Venus stole the anomaly crystal from her.

'Wait!' pronounces Venus. As Venus looks through the white eyes of the white dove that she has just connected with, she sees the white dove currently flying in the south-west direction over the Realm of Deserted Lands on the Planet of Phoenix. Venus angrily sees Raven, who was holding on to Emerald's body and riding upon Felix, accompanied by Parrot and Sapphire, riding on another brown horse, and all heading in the direction towards Triton's Underground Dungeon. Venus subconsciously controls the white dove's brain and forces it to fly closer in the sky to circle around Raven, Parrot, and

Sapphire that are galloping swiftly upon their horses over the rocky surface of the Realm of Deserted Lands. Venus focuses the white dove's vision more and notices that Sapphire is carrying the sword and shield of Grackle.

'What is it, my lover?' asks Triton suspiciously, looking at Venus's pure white eyes that were shaking. 'I see Raven and his friends heading close towards the entrance of your Underground Dungeon. They also have the sword of Grackle with them, and I fear that the shield the woman carries could possibly be the shield of Grackle as it is crafted in a similar way as the sword of Grackle is designed. We must take the sword and shield of Grackle for ourselves as they are too much of a threat to us creatures during the great war. And for some strange reason, Raven is also carrying Emerald's dead body with them,' says Venus apprehensively.

'Why are they carrying Emerald's dead body on their journey to seek and fight against us?' asks Triton, confused.

'I'm not sure, but we must now be very cautious as they had been interacting with Hake within Eagle Forest. Who knows what unworldly information he has shared with them. Raven also now possesses the shield of Grackle that Hake must have supplied to him as before he only carried the sword of Grackle. Before we aid Viper and his Serpents in attacking King Exodus at Falcon City in the great war, we must defeat Raven and his friends once and for all as we need to finally end the bloodline of Grackle so that this bloodline will never cause a menace to us creatures ever again, it being the only bloodline that can yield the elemental powers of the anomaly crystal,' states Venus as she stops her subconscious from connecting with the white dove, but her eyes still have their pure white colour.

'Yes, you are right, my woman. We must get back to my Underground Dungeon now and quickly slay Raven and his companions before we go to aid Viper in the great war between us creatures and the humans, for we cannot have those insignificant humans of the last bloodline of Grackle interfering in any form with our refined plans of eternal victory,' says Triton as he kisses Venus hard upon the lips without her noticing as Venus is preparing herself to utilise her Animagus abilities.

VENUS USES HER Animagus abilities that enable her to turn back into her Quetzalcoatlus form; she flaps her large scaly wings furiously to lift herself above the ground and into the air. Venus screeches loudly in a high-pitched sound with her long beak and then picks Triton up by his muscular shoulders via her tough feet claws. Triton holds the anomaly crystal and his golden chain with the spiked ball at the end of it firmly within his bulky hands as Venus flies hastily higher in the air and straight upwards through the tall and thick trees of Eagle Forest until she reaches the sky that lies above Eagle Forest. Venus flaps her large scaly wings in a fast and firm motion to permit her to change the direction of her body, where she continues to fly swiftly in the sky across the top of Eagle Forest in the south direction and continues over the Swamp Fields, heading towards the Realm of Deserted Lands in the furthest south-west corner of the Planet of Phoenix.

Venus continues holding on to Triton's shoulder tightly, and in just less than an hour of rapid flying through the open and clear skies of the Planet of Phoenix, they now approach the sky above the Realm of Deserted Lands, where the skies drastically change into a darker and more hostile environment. Venus flaps her large scaly wings harder in order to go higher above in the sky as she aims to avoid most of the freezing gusty winds that are littered with tiny dirt, rock, sand, and gristle particles. Venus also flies higher in the sky in an attempt not to be spotted by Raven, Parrot, and Sapphire who are still riding hastily across the rocky surface upon the Realm of Deserted Lands and are currently closing ever more towards the south-west direction where they assume Triton's hideout could potentially be.

After another hour of fast flying, while still holding on to Triton's muscular shoulders, Venus flies a little more higher up in the sky as they pass on the ground below Raven, who is holding securely on to Emerald's dead body while riding exhaustedly upon Felix, as well as Parrot and Sapphire, who are also out of breath but are still riding heatedly upon the other brown horse.

Venus and Triton go unnoticed by Raven, Parrot, and Sapphire; however, Venus and Triton get caught up in some of the freezing gusty winds that carry the tiny dirt, rock, sand, and gristle particles. Venus continues to flap her large scaly wings more firmly; she creates more power within the wings in order to hastily fly across the rest of the Realm of Deserted Lands in the south-west direction without being hampered too much by these powerful and hostile gusty winds. Venus now changes her flight direction and heads quickly towards the ground and straight into the entrance below the Realm of Deserted Lands' rough, rocky surface; she flies through the narrow and deep passageway that leads into the main hall within Triton's Underground Dungeon.

As Venus in her Quetzalcoatlus form, holding on to Triton's shoulders, hurriedly dives down towards the ground in the far south-west distance, Sapphire gets a glimpse of a quick dark animal-shaped figure just as she is squinting her eyes through the thick gusty winds swarmed with tiny dirt, rock, sand, and gristle particles.

'Did you see that, Raven?' Sapphire shouts loudly to Raven, who was riding upon Felix just in front of Parrot and Sapphire, who were still riding on top of their brown horse. Raven hears the sound of Sapphire's voice from behind him, and he pulls hard on Felix's brown rope reins in order to bring him to a stop. Parrot also does the same to the ropes of his brown horse and then guides the brown horse to stand next to Raven and Felix.

'What did you see, Sapphire?' asks Parrot, turning around to look at a concerned Sapphire.

'I saw in the far distance a large dark figure that looked a bit like a bird creature, but the creature was also holding on to something that was quite bulky,' says Sapphire in a confused manner.

'Who knows what creature or mysterious being that could have been as there are many unknown creatures lurking throughout the Realms of Deserted Lands,' says Raven, breathing deeply due to being exhausted from the long ride they had experienced through the Realm of Deserted Lands.

'It does seem quite suspicious though that we recently saw that unworldly tsunami appear from nothing out of the top of Eagle Forest, and now I see that strange creature flying extremely fast inwards to one of the furthest and darkest parts of the Planet of Phoenix,' remarks Sapphire intuitively.

'It could indeed be Triton and Venus returning to their hideout I suppose. There has never been any other human that has ever ventured this far within the Realm of Deserted Lands. This is why Triton and Venus may have built their hideout around this location, making it more difficult for us humans to discover it,' replies Parrot as he turns around to look at Raven, who was looking down at Emerald's body that he had still securely grasped within his arms upon Felix's back.

'You could both be right, but Sapphire said that the dark figure looked like a bird creature shape? Surely that couldn't be Triton or Venus?' asks Raven suspiciously as he strokes Emerald's blonde hair with one of his hands.

'Venus is known to be a Metamorphmagi as she turned into Emerald's mother Ruby previously as well as Venus possesses that creature ability to create those God-awful dinosaurs that we unfortunately encountered during the battle of Eagle Forest. She might have other creature abilities that we are unaware of, and maybe she can also change into other types of creature beasts,' explains Sapphire.

'Yes, that could be quite possible. It's best that we catch our breath quickly now and brace ourselves for the battle we will soon face against Triton and Venus. This battle will be a challenge that none of us have ever experienced before or are likely to forget for the rest of our lives,' says Parrot nervously as he turns his head back around to kiss Sapphire passionately on the lips. Raven takes a deep breath and remembers all the passionate moments that he had shared with Emerald during all those years that they grew up together in Oak Village.

'Let's once and for all end this great war for Emerald and all those other humans who have suffered the evilness of creatures,' shouts Raven, still looking at Emerald's dead body. Raven takes another deep breath before he kicks his feet into Felix's backside and holds tightly on to Felix's brown rope reins as Felix's quickly gallops again in the far south-west direction across the rocky surface over the Realm of Deserted Lands. Parrot grabs on to the rope reins of his brown horse and also kicks his feet into the backside of his brown horse. Sapphire holds on to Parrot's waist tightly as they both also gallop upon their brown horse and follow Raven galloping upon Felix.

Venus has now flown into the main hall of Triton's Underground Dungeon and travels near to the big wooden table that was towards the back of the main hall opposite to its entrance. Venus places Triton down upon the ground carefully, being cautious of his recently healed right leg. After Venus places Triton upon the ground in the main hall of Triton's Underground Dungeon, Venus herself lands upon the ground, where she employs her Animagus abilities at the same time to turn back into her normal physical body before her normal feet touch the ground. Her eyes now turn back to their normal red colour again. Both Triton and Venus stand side by side and look at the entrance of the main hall within Triton's Underground Dungeon, where they wait eagerly for Raven, Parrot, and Sapphire to come and fight against them.

'You take the anomaly crystal, Venus, and use its incredible powers to protect yourself against the humans just in case anything happens to me. But always remember that you're the only woman for me and that we will reunite again in whatever afterlife we end up in,' mentions Triton as he passes the anomaly crystal into Venus's petite left hand and then confidently holds his chain with the spiked iron ball at the end of it in front of him in preparation for battle.

'Don't worry, my love, nothing will happen to us, especially from these puny humans. Even if they have the sword and shield of Grackle now, they will be no match for us. I have extremely powerful creature abilities, and you're as strong as a dragon now due to your leg having recovered. The anomaly crystal will also unleash the full extent of unimaginable powers to protect us against these humans and will allow us to be victorious this day in the destined great war,' replies Venus as she holds on to one of Triton's hand left hand with her right hand and then turns to kiss him passionately and seductively upon his rough lips.

Thirty-Three

LYNX IS RIDING swiftly upon his white horse along with his 200 Pine guards and men Pine villagers upon on their horses, including Bruce, who is still carrying Flame's sword, and Panther and his fourteen Willow guards upon their horses. They continue travelling for many hours across the Grass Terrain Fields around the outer perimeter in the far east direction of Komodo Jungle. After a fast pace and heated ride, they all now eventually reach the Kingdom of Humans zone located at the far south-east of the Planet of Phoenix. The Kingdom of Humans is a vast area of environment located in the far south-east direction of the Planet of Phoenix. It's filled with an abundance of Grass Terrain Fields, trees, plants, vegetation, farm fields, and farm animals that surround the grand and historic Falcon City.

The Kingdom of Humans zone was claimed by King Primus, being the original king of Falcon City. He developed the city by taking advantage of the plentiful environment that the Planet of Phoenix had to offer. Lynx, Panther, Bruce, the 200 Pine guards and men Pine villagers, and the fourteen willow guards ride promptly through the Kingdom of Humans, where in the sunlight they all gaze upon the Kingdom of Humans' flourishing and prosperous Grass Terrain Fields that are full of various different plants, livestock, and crops adjacent to Nautilus Lake.

As they all approach the renowned Falcon City, the Pine guards, men Pine villagers and the Willow guards quickly admire the large, solid grey-and-white stone wall that surrounds the outer perimeter of Falcon City, as they had never laid eyes upon this magnificent architecture before. The large grey-and-white stone wall is over fifty foot in height and has a passageway at the top of the stone wall, where the royal Falcon guards can walk across to patrol and keep watch for any intruders that may attempt to approach Falcon City from within the Kingdom of Humans zone.

As Lynx, Panther, Bruce, the Pine guards, men Pine villagers, and Willow guards ride closer to the large grey-and-white stone wall, they appreciate the grand aspects of Falcon City, and from a distance, they manage to just see the top section of the grand and elegant white brick Falcon Castle deep within Falcon City in the south-west direction, where the gold crucifix located at the top of Falcon Castle glistens in the bright sunlight. Led by Lynx, Panther, and Bruce, the Pine guards, men Pine villagers, and Willow guards ride in formation right up to the big iron portcullis that is located within the middle of the large grey-and-white stone wall, but they are briskly stopped by a couple of royal Falcon guards that were guarding at the front of the big iron portcullis.

'State your purpose, villagers,' states a royal Falcon guard in a suspicious manner. All of the royal Falcon guards within Falcon City wear knighthood metal armour that is made of the finest metal crafted by stone masons within Falcon City. The royal Falcon guards also carry silver swords and silver shields that are crested with a Falcon bird upon the metal weapons to represent that they belong to the royal Falcon guards of Falcon City.

'My name is Lynx, leader of Pine Village and ex-captain to the royal Falcon guard. I am accompanied by my Pine guards and men Pine villagers, along with Panther, leader of Willow Village and his Willow guards,' states Lynx in a direct fashion.

'Oh, I do apologise, Lynx. I didn't recognise you for a moment due to my quick reactions as we do have to make sure that we are more cautious and careful in these ghastly dangerous times. Falcon City welcomes you back and permits entry for the company you travel with, please enter,' replies the royal Falcon guard with slight embarrassment as he puts one of his hands high up in the air, which is then seen by another Royal Falcon guard who was guarding the top passageway of the large grey-and-white stone wall and was watching over the area below the big iron portcullis. This royal Falcon guard also raises his hand to signal to another royal Falcon guard who was on the inside of Falcon City's large grey-and-white stone wall in order to open the big iron portcullis. This royal Falcon guard inside Falcon City's large grey-and-white stone wall now spins a big metal chain via a wooden lever that is attached to the large grey-and-white stone wall. This big metal chain enables the big iron portcullis to slowly lift up from the ground, where Lynx, Panther, Bruce, 200 Pine guards and men Pine Villagers, as well as the fourteen Willow guards now enter into Falcon City through the big iron portcullis and begin trotting across the stone paths that are laid throughout Falcon City.

Falcon City is the largest human establishment that resides upon the Planet of Phoenix, and it's mainly where the richer or more intelligent humans live. Falcon City has just over 2,000 human inhabitants living within the large grey-and-white stone walls; this includes the 500 royal Falcon guards that are sworn to protect Falcon City from any danger. When the humans originally came into existence upon the Planet of Phoenix, the humans were located in two different places of the Planet of Phoenix. There were those humans who lived in the far north-east direction in the first developed village known as Alder Village and those humans who were located in the south-west direction and at first also developed and lived in small villages.

After many generations, a human called Primus was born and eventually grew up to become a very ingenious and imaginative human. Primus's innovative ideas and vision led him to become the first king of the humans followed by a unanimous decision. King Primus's responsibility was to lead these humans to a superior future. Shortly after being named king, Primus's first commands were to begin the construction of a grand city to be a home or refuge for any of the human species that resided upon the Planet of Phoenix; this city was called Falcon City.

Falcon City was developed after countless years of hard work and determination; it was mostly crafted from the large grey-and-white stones and rocks that were forged from the Realm of Deserted Lands that was located not too far from Falcon City; although, it was still a challenging mission to transport these large grey-and-white stones and rocks across the vast open Grass Terrain Fields. After the first parts of Falcon City were moulded, Falcon City was able to sustain a vast population of growing humans by exploiting the unusual resources that they had located within Komodo Jungle.

When Mamushi, who was Viper's mother, realised that the humans from Falcon City were utilising Komodo Jungle's resources, she saw this as an invasion of her territory and began attacking the humans to defend her home. But eventually Mamushi was killed by these Falcon City humans. That is the reason why Viper has an intense hatred for any human who is born upon the Planet of Phoenix. By the time of Mamushi's death, the Kingdom of Humans was further established, which enabled the harvesting of crops and upkeep of livestock. This increased the prosperity of Falcon City, although there was a threat that would last forever from Viper and his Serpents.

As time went on, King Primus's legacy was also continued by his son King Zunus; he established contact with the humans who lived in the villages located in the north direction of the Planet of Phoenix. These developing relations enabled trade and alliances to be formed between all of the humans upon the Planet of Phoenix.

At present, Falcon City has an extensive amount of brick and stone houses located within Falcon City as well as various kinds of shops such as weapons, foods, pets, clothing, and jewellery shops; it also has pubs, libraries, schools, Falcon University, Falcon Church and Falcon Graveyard matched with a crematorium, Grand Falcon Tomb, combat training centres, vehicle and boat building factories, along with the grand white castle where the King of Falcon City lives; it is known as Falcon Castle.

Located outside the north-west of Falcon City's large grey-and-white stone walls is a lake called Nautilus Lake. Nautilus Lake had been formed thousands of years ago when the original materialising of the Planet of Phoenix took place. Nautilus Lake supplies Falcon City with the valuable resource of water, which played a pertinent role in helping Falcon City to prosper and generate the rich area of Grass Terrain Fields that are located within the Kingdom of Humans. Nautilus Lake had ancient sea creatures existing within it like the sea lion creature; these ancient creatures were initially seen as a threat to humans, though there was no history of the sea lion creature ever attacking the humans from Falcon City.

King Pinus felt it necessary to build the large grey-and-white stone wall to cover a small part of Nautilus Lake with the intention of allowing an entrance for the water to flow within Falcon City. This entrance is useful for wooden boats used by the royal Falcon guards to get in and out of Falcon City and on to Nautilus Lake, if they were required to patrol that area for any risks as well as to hunt for food such as fish, which was a valuable source of protein for the growing human population of Falcon City.

As Lynx, Panther, Bruce, 200 Pine guards and men Pine villagers, and the fourteen Willow guards continue to trot upon their horses across the various interconnecting stone paths through Falcon City, they are watched keenly by Falcon City humans as these Falcon City humans pass beside them while travelling between the shops or friends' homes within the cobbled streets of Falcon City. After a long ride up on of the stone paths over a slight hill in the south-west direction within Falcon City, they now approach the grand white brick Falcon Castle that is magnificently decorated with stone monuments of the previous kings of Falcon City as well as warfare and human and animal symbols.

At the very top of Falcon Castle is a gold crucifix that has a golden coloured Falcon animal fixed upon it. Falcon Castle is large in height and stretches far in width, facilitating many different rooms and chambers that are used for the living quarters of the King's family, along with his trusted and loyal advisors. The other rooms and chambers within Falcon Castle include a royal Falcon School, the royal kitchen, and various combat places that are used for the training and coaching of the royal Falcon guards. There's also a large courtyard that is full of trees, herbs, fruits, monuments and statues, candles, and stone seats for guests that reside at the back of Falcon Castle.

AT THE FRONT of Falcon Castle, Lynx climbs down from his white horse, being cautious of his bruised ankle. As he steps upon the stone paths that lead to up to the big bronze entrance doors of Falcon Castle, Panther also does the same.

'Pine and Willow guards, wait here for now. We will be back shortly after we have conversed with King Exodus. Bruce, I will leave you in charge of these humans. Assist these men in gathering their essential rest and prepare their focus for the great war,' orders Lynx.

'Yes, your wish is my command, Lynx,' replies Bruce as he also gets down from his horse to hold on to the rope reins of Lynx's and Panther's horses. Lynx and Panther walk right up to the front of the big bronze entrance doors of Falcon Castle.

'It's good to be back again,' says Panther to Lynx and smiles. Lynx grins back at Panther and then knocks hard upon the big bronze entrance doors. After a moment of knocking upon the big bronze entrance doors of Falcon Castle, a royal Falcon guard unhooks the wooden barrier that was installed to lock the inside of the big bronze entrance doors; upon opening the big bronze entrance doors, he sees Lynx and Panther standing respectfully in front of it.

'Lynx! What a splendid surprise to see you back here in Falcon City again. What is the nature of your visit? I will aid you as best as I can with it,' says the royal Falcon guard who had previously known Lynx from when he used to be the royal Falcon captain.

'It's good to see you again too, my fellow royal Falcon guard, and it feels like only yesterday that I was putting you and all the other royal Falcon guards through all those hours of war training and preparation. Panther and I would like to request a meeting with King Exodus. I do understand he may be currently in progress of dealing with other matters of Falcon City, but if it's at all possible, we would like to meet with him now as our time is unfortunately very precious at present,' answers Lynx directly.

'Yes, I understand. You would not request a meeting if it wasn't urgent. Of course King Exodus will make this time for his ex-royal Falcon captain. Please come in Falcon Castle and follow me. King Exodus is currently in the main chamber meeting room along with the new royal Falcon captain Gaius, some of his royal Falcon guards, his daughter Princess Petal, and her handmaid Lily. They are already discussing the preparation plans for Falcon City in case of the great war commencing,' says the royal Falcon guard. Lynx smiled back at the royal Falcon guard at the thought of seeing Princess Petal again.

'I thought as much. King Exodus would be aware of this forthcoming great war and would have been doing everything within his power to minimise the impact of it affecting any of the humans that lives upon the Planet of Phoenix,' Panther remarks sagely. Lynx, Panther, and the royal Falcon guard walked courteously through the great hall of Falcon Castle, the part of Falcon Castle where King Exodus' magnificent golden throne resides at one end of the great hall. The great hall is also decorated with various colourful pictures, paintings, and statues that represent the image of King Exodus as well as previous the kings of Falcon City, which include King Zunus, who was King Exodus's father, and King Primus, who was King Exodus's grandfather. Also positioned within the great hall is a grand organ that is located near King Exodus's magnificent golden throne. In the middle of the great hall, there are big wooden tables accompanied with wooden chairs that are positioned in a symmetrical order as well as many church artefacts such as crucifixes, candles, and holy artefacts.

The royal Falcon guard continues to lead Lynx and Panther down one of the passageways connected to the great hall, towards the main chamber meeting rooms within Falcon Castle, where King Exodus was currently having the great war preparation meeting with his loyal advisors. As Lynx and Panther walk into the main chamber meeting room that was opened by the royal Falcon guard, Lynx and Panther see King Exodus, his daughter Princess Petal, his royal Falcon captain Gaius and twenty other royal Falcon advisors and guards all sitting around a big wooden table.

A map of the Planet of Phoenix was laid across the big wooden table that had areas in the middle north direction of Falcon City highlighted with orange markings. Also upon the big wooden table were plans of alterations of wooden boats, metal weapon designs, as well as written demonstration plans on how to best protect Falcon City from an attack during times of battle or war. Lily, who is Princess Petal's handmaid, is at present walking around the big wooden table to bring everyone glasses of red wine.

King Exodus is sixty-four years old and has long grey hair and brown eyes. King Exodus is very tall in height and possesses a muscular build. He has been the king of Falcon City for twenty-seven years now, ever since his father King Zunus passed away due to his old age. King Exodus wears a marvellous golden crown that has a symbol of the Falcon crested upon it, along with his name written in the ancient language of phoenix upon the middle of the golden crown in silver writing. King Exodus carries with him a gold sword and gold shield; these special weapons had been passed down the through bloodline generations right from the start of Falcon City's first king when the city was initially developed. This was King Exodus's grandfather, King Primus. King Exodus also wears gold-plated knighthood armour that covers him from shoulders to feet, accompanied with chainmail and leather boots. King Exodus is an inspirational human who has had a worthy and prestigious rule over Falcon City for numerous years; he is much loved by all of his 500 royal Falcon guards, along with the other 1,500 humans who currently live within Falcon City.

King Exodus is opinionated and proud, but he also listens and considers all points of view during a predicament or deliberation. King Exodus is also a very honourable, kind and a courageous human. King Exodus loves Falcon City and puts the safety of his people before all other concerns and most importantly he cherishes his daughter Princess Petal. King Exodus was trained and moulded to being a great king by his father King Zunus, just as his father King Zunus was also groomed to be king by his father King Primus. King Exodus fulfilled his father King Zunus's wish by making him very proud of the prince he had come to be just before King Zunus died of old age twenty-seven years ago, when King Exodus took his place to become king of Falcon City. King Exodus has also been friends with Panther for many years due to Panther being the son of the previous royal Falcon captain Sharkus. This is why Panther's brother and Lynx's father Saber inherited the position of royal Falcon captain after Sharkus's death, which was caused by illness and infection from a battle wound.

King Exodus also developed a strong friendship with Lynx after Lynx undertook the position of the royal Falcon captain following his father Saber's untimely death that was caused by Viper's deadly venom during one of the battles within Falcon City, which occurred eight years ago. King Exodus had also been a great friend of Barious just as Panther was also; this friendship had developed because Barious's father Trogon was also greatly associated with King Exodus's father King Zunus via one of the previous leaders of Oak Village, who was Wolf's father and was named Jackal.

King Exodus's daughter Princess Petal is now twenty-two years old. She has long, wavy, shiny blonde hair and blue eyes. Princess Petal is slim in weight, curvy in body physique, and also tall in height like her father. She is wearing a small and specially designed golden tiara and a purple elegant princess dress with many small sparkly diamonds upon it that covers her entire body. She is also wearing her mother's sophisticated royal jewellery that includes rings, earrings, and bracelets all shaped to represent images of the falcon bird.

Princess Petal's mother and King Exodus's wife, who was the queen of Falcon City for seven years, ruled alongside King Exodus following the death of King Zunus. Princess Petal's mother was called Eclipse. Before her death, Eclipse enjoyed the arts and culture of their human ancestors and also had a strong passion for music, which she very much wanted to share with her unborn daughter. King Exodus and Eclipse had been in love for all of their lives ever since they had met at the Royal Falcon School during their childhood. They spent many years together being happy and creating special memories for themselves, which included the birth of their only child Princess Petal. Unfortunately, the birth of Princess Petal led to ill-fated circumstances that caused Eclipse to eventually die from a virus that she caught shortly after giving birth to Princess Petal, due to the complications she had endured during childbirth. The death of his wife Eclipse broke King Exodus's heart into a million pieces, but he brought up Princess Petal just as Eclipse would have wanted him to, and was aided by Eclipse's handmaid named Lily.

Princess Petal is well educated in academic subjects such as maths, English, science, history, and philosophy; she also has been trained in combat as her father King Exodus felt it necessary for his daughter to be able to protect herself during any unfortunate contact with the creatures of the Planet of Phoenix like Viper and his Serpents. Princess Petal was taught these combat training classes alongside Lynx, when Lynx was also training to be a royal Falcon guard by Lynx's father Saber. Princess Petal was also taught to play musical instruments like the grand organ and a large harp; she was taught music by the very best musicians who lived within Falcon City. Princess Petal grew up quickly with maturity, kindness, and a sense of humility towards humans and the good creatures that existed on the Planet of Phoenix. Princess Petal loves harmony and nature and takes the time to appreciate and admire beautiful sights on the Planet of Phoenix's luxurious environment.

Princess Petal is still a virgin as she never wanted to have intimate relations with another man, her heart being given to Lynx, with whom she had spent much time in her childhood during their education lessons at the royal Falcon School, along with their classes for the combat training. As Princess Petal became of an older age, her feelings for Lynx grew more deep and they enjoyed numerous dates and memories together; their feelings for one another were greatly received by all the humans who lived within Falcon City.

The relationship that had been developing for many years between Princess Petal and Lynx was, however, prematurely reduced due to Lynx making a difficult decision to leave Falcon City to become the leader of Pine Village, due to the heartache he was suffering from his parents' death that was caused by Viper in a battle of Falcon City. Princess Petal knew that her father King Exodus would not let her leave Falcon City to be with Lynx in Pine Village, because her mother Eclipse had died and King Exodus never remarried to produce a male heir. Thus Princess Petal would have to become the queen of Falcon City when her father King Exodus dies and would need to produce an heir to maintain their family bloodline. Princess Petal felt much sorrow and sadness when she said her goodbyes to Lynx, but they remained in contact through heartfelt messages they passed to each other often via carrier pigeons. Princess Petal waited within Falcon Castle very patiently for the day that Lynx would finally return to Falcon City.

GAIUS IS FORTY-EIGHT years old; he has short and straight brown hair and blue eyes with a clear face, but has hairy arms and legs; he is medium-sized in height with a muscular build. Gaius wears silver-plated royal Falcon captain knighthood armour and carries a gold-plated sword and shield that were specifically created for the royal Falcon captains. The armour and matching weapons are crested with a falcon bird and royal Falcon captain symbol. From a young age, Gaius had been mischievous and undisciplined; he got into many fights and other trouble with the other young human men who attended one of the normal Falcon Schools within Falcon City. Gaius lived with his parents; his father, called Nerolus, owned a cloth shop within Falcon City, where Gaius's mother Tameka made various different clothing and accessories for Nerolus to sell in his cloth shop. As Gaius grew in age, Nerolus wanted Gaius to help him by working at the cloth shop as a store assistant, with the view of Gaius taking over ownership of this cloth shop when Nerolus would seek to retire.

Gaius, however, showed no interest in being a cloth shop assistant or owner and he continued getting into disputes around Falcon City, where he would cause trouble by cheating on females by dating more than one girlfriend at the same time or he would be again fighting with the men whom he had disliked from Falcon School. To much displeasure of his wife Tameka, Nerolus paid one of his cloth traders named Ruthus, who was Raven's father, to help Gaius sort his life out, by allowing him to start a fresh life back in Oak Village, where he would be far away from the trouble he had got himself into within Falcon City. Nerolus persuaded Tameka that Gaius moving to Oak Village with Ruthus would also be beneficial for him as he could also learn the trade of a trader that would suit his characteristics better. Tameka eventually agreed but was not happy to see her only son Gaius leave their family home in Falcon City to live in a different location upon the Planet of Phoenix, especially as it was located near the notorious Wastelands, where, it was rumoured, the nomad warrior criminals lurked.

Gaius and Ruthus instantly became good friends, as they were of similar ages as well as shared similar interests. Both Gaius and Ruthus also possessed enthusiasm and passion for the trading industry, where Ruthus was happy to promote Gaius to become a partner with him for his trading business. After living in Oak Village for a while and being good friends with Ruthus and Ruthus's wife Jewel, Gaius was introduced to Jewel's best friend from school, Ruby. Gaius and Ruby developed a connection with one another, where they ended up getting married and having a daughter called Emerald quite early in their relationship.

Although Gaius did love Ruby and his new daughter Emerald, he felt extremely engulfed by the responsibilities he now had, where he was used to not having any commitments or responsibilities before. Gaius continued to work long hours besides Ruthus in order to provide a good lifestyle for his wife Ruby and daughter Emerald; although, he occasionally had urges to break away from Ruby and the responsibilities he now had. The situation ended up changing due to Ruthus's and Jewel's unfortunate death by Viper that occurred twelve years ago now. Gaius didn't cope well with the death of his only good friend in Oak Village, and he couldn't manage running the entire trading business by himself as well as raising a family and a home.

Gaius and Ruby therefore ended up having many disagreements as time went on due to them both coping with their beloved friends' deaths and continuing to always mend and repair their relationship, following continuous arguments they would have with each other. Gaius found it difficult to cope with these circumstances he was experiencing with Ruby. Hence he started to undertake more visits back home to stay with his parents in Falcon City. Gaius's parents Nerolus and Tameka tried to reason with Gaius about continuing his relationship with Ruby, especially since they had their daughter Emerald's life to consider; however, Gaius was never really good at listening to the advice from his parents. On one of these many visits to Falcon City, Gaius bumped into a woman called Lily in Nerolus's cloth shop as Lily was in there to buy a new dress for Princess Petal, Lily being Princess Petal's handmaid.

Gaius and Lily suddenly felt a connection with each other, and they found themselves spending more and more time and intimate moments with each other on the occasions Gaius was in Falcon City following his trade travels from Oak Village. Ruby felt that something was going wrong with Gaius and her marriage, but she kept herself busy with her religious education teaching at Oakus School in Oak Village and assured Emerald that everything would be fine between her and her father, and that sometimes they just needed a break from each other. On many of his journeys to Falcon City, Gaius noticed the royal Falcon guards that were on patrols throughout the stone paths and streets within Falcon City as well as outside the perimeter of the large grey-and-white stone wells in the Kingdom of Humans.

After a further three years, Gaius became more restless because of working by himself as a trader as well as the negative situation Ruby and he were experiencing with one another. Gaius also discovered that the royal Falcon guards got to learn and train in combat inside Falcon Castle, which was where Lily also lived due to her being Princess Petal's handmaid.

On several of his long travels from Oak Village to Falcon City, Gaius had abundant time to think and consider what his options were or what he wanted as a career for the rest of his life. Thus after much thought, Gaius decided he wanted to leave Ruby due to his feelings for Lily being stronger as well as give up his job as a trader and join the royal Falcon guard as he also thought this would aid in developing better characteristics in himself that his parents had complained about for many years. Gaius decided he couldn't build up enough courage to explain this awkward situation to Ruby or his daughter Emerald; this was the reason why he had just left a note to Emerald, when he left his family and Oak Village for good. That was now three years ago.

Once Gaius had finally moved back home with his parents at Falcon City, he convinced his parents Nerolus and Tameka not to reply to any of the letters that Ruby sent to their cloth shop via carrier pigeon as he didn't want her ending up travelling to Falcon City to try and persuade him to come back to live in Oak Village again. Although Gaius's parents weren't pleased about the situation, especially since it meant losing contact with their granddaughter Emerald, they said that it might have been the right decision for their son Gaius as he quickly joined the royal Falcon guard, which changed his life for the better. Shortly afterwards, they became lovers, and moved he in with Lily.

Gaius had to become very tenacious, and he worked hard to prove himself within the ranks of the royal Falcon guards, which he did in honour of his relationship with Lily. The royal Falcon captain known as Clang took over from Lynx after Lynx left Falcon City to become the new leader of Pine Village. Clang was killed a year ago by one of the Serpents who was attacking Falcon City humans who were walking through the area within the Kingdom of Humans. It was a very sad situation that the new royal Falcon Captain Clang was recently killed. Lily saw this opportunity to persuade Princess Petal to speak with her father King Exodus about now making Gaius the royal Falcon captain to replace Clang due to the amount of effort Gaius had put into being a royal Falcon captain.

King Exodus was slightly dubious regarding this decision of letting a newish royal Falcon guard become the new royal Falcon captain. He had seen a huge change and extensive potential within Gaius and decided to take a risk and gave him this chance, particularly at the request of this wish by his daughter Princess Petal. After a short time of only a couple of years, Gaius became a successful royal Falcon captain with his leadership and combat abilities. Lily and Gaius also have a very solid relationship, and they both live at Falcon Castle.

Lily is thirty-nine years old and has shoulder-length black hair and green eyes. She is of medium height and weight and has pale skin with many freckles upon her body. Lily is a very calm and considerate human and seeks to please others before herself. Lily was brought up from a child to become a handmaid, in order to follow in her mother Cassandra's role. Cassandra was also the main handmaid to Queen Eclipse, who was Princess Petal's mother. Cassandra served Queen Eclipse wonderfully for many years until Cassandra herself died of old age, which led her daughter Lily to become Queen Eclipse's handmaid in lieu of her mother Cassandra. When Queen Eclipse also died of a virus shortly after giving birth to her daughter Princess Petal, Lily became Princess Petal's handmaid and has remained so now for twenty-two years. Lily was very happy to look after Princess Petal and serve as her full-time handmaid as Lily was unable to have any children of her own.

Lily is a very devoted handmaid to Princess Petal and has helped her grow up to become a delightful princess, especially after her mother Queen Eclipse died when she was a baby. Due to Lily being like an actual mother to Princess Petal, Lily rarely found any time to find a man of her own. That all changed though when she first met with Gaius, and since Princess Petal had now become a young woman herself, Lily felt that Princess Petal wouldn't need Lily to look after her as much as she had in the past. Princess Petal was indeed a young woman now and wanted more of her independence; she also wanted Lily to find true happiness, and so Princess Petal gave Lily her blessing and encouragement to pursue her affections for Gaius.

Princess Petal also wanted to repay her gratitude to Lily for all the years of service Lily had given to Princess Petal. That is why she wanted to also persuade her father, King Exodus, to promote Gaius as the new royal Falcon captain due to his motivation and ability, which would assist both Lily and Gaius to have a very comfortable life together. Lily and Gaius have now been together for just over two years, but are currently unable to marry one another due to

Gaius still being legally married to Ruby. King Exodus is not aware of Gaius's history with regards to being married to Ruby; otherwise he wouldn't have given his blessing for Gaius and Lily to live together within Falcon Castle.

Lily and Princess Petal are aware of Gaius's marriage to Ruby, and although they are not pleased with the situation, they understand what has happened in the past sometimes can't be changed. Gaius has confirmed to Lily that he will soon look into being divorced from Ruby, so Lily and he can get married; although he wants this situation to be handled delicately, taking into consideration the feelings of his daughter Emerald.

AS LYNX AND Panther enter through the wooden door of the main chamber meeting room; everyone stops talking with one another to have a look and see who had entered.

'Lynx, what a pleasure it is to see you and Panther at Falcon Castle. It has been far too long!' says King Exodus as he notices that it was Lynx and Panther that walked through the wooden door of the main chamber meeting room. King Exodus stands up from his wooden chair and grabs Panther's and then Lynx's forearm as a sign of respect for one another. When King Exodus grabs Lynx's forearm, Lynx kneels to the ground in front of King Exodus.

'The pleasure is all mine, my splendid and wise King,' replies Lynx respectably.

'Stand back up, my lad. How are things in Pine Village?' asks King Exodus as he sits back down in his wooden chair and drinks some of the red wine from a glass that Lily had just brought to him. Lynx and Panther now also sit down on two wooden chairs that were vacant around the big wooden table next to a few of the royal Falcon advisors and royal Falcon guards. Lily continues to bring glasses of red wine to everyone sitting around the big wooden table, including Lynx and Panther. Princess Petal smiles softly at Lynx as he sits down upon his wooden chair opposite to her around the big wooden table, and Lynx smiles shyly back at her.

'My King, Pine Village was recently attacked by Triton's henchman and Potorian army. Another horrific battle also occurred in Willow Village. Many innocent villagers have now died from this atrocious deed, and numerous homes, shops, and resources have been destroyed or depleted from our villages,' explains Lynx as everyone gasps in shock at this information. There is a moment of silence in honour of the humans who had been killed during these battles by the creatures.

'Sorry to hear about your villages Lynx and Panther as well as those poor innocent humans who have suffered from these evil-doings. I was unaware that these battles were taking place in your villages. Otherwise I would have sent much-needed aid and resources to you with regards to these battles. We have all lost many great human lives and resources during the battles we have had to suffer with the evil creatures that exist upon the Planet of Phoenix. Panther's and my grand old friend Barious was also killed at the hands of that formidable creature Triton in the battle of Oak Village that occurred just over a year ago. We have also had frequent battles ourselves over the past hundred years with Viper and his Serpents from Komodo Jungle. It's now the time for us to rid these creatures and regain the Planet of Phoenix for the peaceful humans!' states King Exodus as all of his royal Falcon advisors and guards around the big wooden table cheer at King Exodus's words.

'We had received word from Panther last year about the tragedy that had happened within Oak Village, and since then we at Falcon City have been preparing for the inevitable great war as we also assumed that Viper and his Serpents would join with Lord Scartor and Triton in their last attempt to destroy the race of humans from the Planet of Phoenix,' mentions Princess Petal.

'Did you also not receive a note from my carrier pigeon a few days ago?' asks Panther curiously.

'No, we haven't, the royal Falcon guard has not received any word from your villages recently. That has grown to be a concern of ours,' replies Gaius to Panther.

'Lynx and I had sent a carrier pigeon with a message to King Exodus about Lord Scartor having now been killed on Cadaver Rock within the Realm of Deserted Lands. We assume that Triton has now taken over command of the creatures and will enforce the great war upon us humans,' exclaims Panther.

'Triton and his mistress Venus have already attacked my friends, Raven, Parrot, and Sapphire at Eagle Forest in the far north-west direction of the Planet of Phoenix. At present, Raven, Parrot, and

Sapphire are searching for Triton and Venus's location assumed to be within the Realm of Deserted Lands. Their desperate but brave actions are in hope of Raven bringing his wife Emerald back from the dead, using the powerful artefact called the anomaly crystal accompanied with an ancient magic curse that a sorcerous creature named Hake from the Hawk Tribe of Eagle Forest educated them about.' Spoke Lynx elaborately.

'Emerald from Oak Village is dead?' interrupts Gaius.

'Yes, unfortunately she is. Did you know her?' asks Panther.

'Emerald is my daughter,' replies Gaius quickly as tears start to fall from his eyes, and he covers them with his hands. Lily walks hurriedly over to Gaius and puts her arms tightly around him to give him a hug.

'I'm very sorry for your loss, Captain Gaius,' says Princess Petal soothingly due to the dramatic and emotional moment Gaius is experiencing.

'As am I,' echoes King Exodus.

'Wait, you said there may be a chance in bringing Emerald back to life, how is this possible?' questions Gaius in an upset but intriguing manner.

'I'm sorry, Gaius, but I'm not exactly sure of all the elements of this venture, but I promised that I would meet up with Raven and Parrot at the Realm of Deserted Lands in an attempt to aid them with their quest. I explained I would do this, once we had sought advice and support from King Exodus in this forthcoming great war. King Exodus, will you help us?' humbly asks Lynx, turning to look at King Exodus.

'Of course! Falcon City and I will support you, Lynx. You've helped Falcon City abundantly when you were the royal Falcon captain a few years back. Falcon City is in your debt for that great service for which you sacrificed your time. I want to reunite the race of humans once again for the main purpose of protecting our entire and unique species. Falcon City has already been preparing for this unavoidable great war, and we have already sent royal Falcon guards out on boats across Nautilus Lake to guard and defend Falcon City from the north-west direction that overlooks Komodo Jungle just to the north of Falcon City. Unfortunately, we will not be able to send any royal Falcon guards at this time to protect your villages in the far north of the Planet of Phoenix as I predict that the great war will be at its peak within Falcon City. We will need to diminish it here first before we can spare the manpower to leave to help defend the other human settlements across the Planet of Phoenix,' explains King Exodus realistically.

'That's all right, my King, as yes, I agree that the great war will now be forced upon Falcon City due to our villages already having been attacked in devastating battles. Panther and I have therefore travelled accompanied with 214 Pine guards, Pine villagers, and Willow guards to assist Falcon City with its great war,' indicates Lynx.

'That's very kind of you both to bring your human and resources' aid to our city as I fear that we will all be facing the greatest of wars that none of us humans will have ever experienced upon the Planet of Phoenix before,' sadly says Princess Petal, although, Princess Petal also blushes red slightly as Lynx gazed upon her as she spoke.

'I would like very much to come with you, Lynx, to the Realm of Deserted Lands in order to help Raven, Parrot, and Sapphire bring Emerald back to life and finally destroy that treacherous creature Triton,' angrily states Gaius.

'I feel your grief, Gaius, but I will ask you to stay within Falcon City during the great war. You are the royal Falcon captain and possess the knowledge of all the preparation and emergency plans for protecting Falcon City that we will indeed need during the great war. I'm sorry, Gaius, but we won't survive this great war without you. However, in your place, I feel Lynx could handle such a mission. Although you wanted to help us in the great war, Lynx, you are more than competent in aiding Raven and the others at the Realm of Deserted Lands who are in desperate need of assistance,' proclaims King Exodus.

'I am aware of my duty, my King, but my daughter . . .' says Gaius, but he is interrupted by King Exodus.

'And your emotions, Gaius, may cloud your judgement in this quest, and that will be more of a hindrance then a support. Lynx, take as many of your men and also our royal Falcon guards that you feel you might need to help your friends defeat Triton and Venus and bring Gaius's daughter Emerald back to life. Triton, Venus, Viper, and his Serpents may already be on their way to attack Falcon City as we speak. We must prepare for the great war immediately. I wish luck and confidence to us all, wherever we find ourselves during this greatest of wars. The creatures can indeed take our human lives, but our souls will unite with one another in the afterlife, that will always remain separated from those souls of the creatures,' declares King Exodus vibrantly as he stands up from his wooden chair and nods at his royal Falcon advisors and the royal Falcon guards before leaving the main meeting chamber room, where he is followed by a couple of his royal Falcon advisors.

Upon leaving the main chamber meeting room, King Exodus goes to his royal bedroom that was down a couple of hallways within Falcon Castle. In his room, King Exodus collects his gold-plated sword and gold-plated shield that were crested with a falcon bird and golden crown upon it. After King Exodus is dressed for battle, he begins preparing Falcon Castle to be protected from any type of attack with the aid of his royal Falcon advisors. A few of the royal Falcon guards have now also left the main chamber meeting room to follow and assist King Exodus with barricading the entrances and windows of Falcon Castle.

'Royal Falcon guards, you know what requires to be done, protect the innocent humans and slaughter these cruel creatures and finally resolve the long-standing war that we have had with these creatures since the time of our existence upon the Planet of Phoenix. On contact with the other 500 royal Falcon guards within Falcon City, along with the newly recruited 900 Falcon City men, advise them to quickly suit up in their armour and weapons and position themselves in their specified and designated areas, especially around the northern middle section of Falcon City.

'The race of humans and Falcon City will survive this night and will then forever bask in this glorious victory we will have during the great war of our time,' states Gaius as he also stands up from his wooden chair but with tears still upon his sore eyes at the thoughts of Emerald's death. Gaius turns and kisses Lily passionately on the lips and then one last time on her forehead, before leaving the main chamber meeting room with the remaining royal Falcon guards. As Gaius and the royal Falcon guards leave Falcon Castle, they quickly give the battle preparation orders to the rest of 500 royal Falcon guards and 900 Falcon City men who are required to participate within the great war. The remaining 600 Falcon City women and children are also given instructions for where to hide, survive, or aid with health care and clean-up for the aftermath following the end of the great war.

LILY BEGINS CLEANING up the empty wine glasses from the big wooden table.

'Come on, Lynx, we should go get our men ready to either travel to the Realm of Deserted Lands or prepare them for helping the royal Falcon guards should Falcon City be the host of the great war,' says Panther to Lynx, who was sitting beside him around the big wooden table. Panther and Lynx now both stand up from their wooden chairs and calmly walk towards the wooden door of the main chamber meeting room. Panther is the first to walk outside of the wooden door, and just as Lynx was also about to leave, Princess Petal stands up from her wooden chair and looks over at Lynx.

'I remember the days when you used to make me blush instantly with just a deep gaze from your valiant eyes,' remarks Princess Petal. Lynx stops himself from walking out of the wooden door to follow Panther. He turns around courteously and walks slowly back towards Princess Petal.

'I remember the times when you would make me speechless with a glimpse of your elegance and beauty, where usually I am filled with expressive words,' replies Lynx softly as he stops in front of Princess Petal and gazes into her endearing eyes.

'Time has sadly quickly moved on since we spent those enjoyable and precious times with each other a few years back. Although, I am indeed a younger age than you, now in my mind and body I am far beyond my years, and after the plentiful time I've had to think over these past few years, I have decided what kind of man I want to spend the rest of my life with, along with the future I want to provide for my family and Falcon City. You've always been and always will be the man I love, Lynx, and I think it's time we start building our future together. Why don't you stay and help us in Falcon City should the great war commence? Then we may still have some more little moments to finally spend some intimate time with one another before our lives may change forever if the great war does not to end as we all hope it will,' softly says Princess Petal while touching Lynx's shoulder slowly with her tender hand.

'Of course, you know that I feel the same way towards you and that I always have felt so. It broke my heart even more so, knowing that I couldn't spend every second with you no more once I felt I had to leave Falcon City due to the tragedy that had happened to my parents. I pray that we have the chance to renew the time we have lost during these past few years, and I would have liked nothing more than to stay with you and Falcon City during the great war, but I have made a promise to my friends that I will help them also in their time of need. I will, however, come back to Falcon City and to you as soon as my duty has been fulfilled, and hopefully, our time will be granted to us as long as King Exodus is happy to permit it,' replies Lynx while gently grabbing and holding on to one of Princess Petal's hands.

'Honourable Lynx as always. I should have known you will require carrying out your promises and duties, but this is why you are respected so much by everyone including me. Yes, my dear, I will always wait for you to at last return to me where you belong, and of course my father would permit us time together. He would be very happy that I have found such a magnificent and remarkable human to love and continue our family bloodline with,' responds Princess Petal as she kisses Lynx softly upon his lips. Lynx and Princess Petal experience a very intimate and passionate kiss together that reminds them both of the romantic moments they used to experience with one another when they were younger. Lynx blushes and looks deep within Princess Petal's eyes for a moment. Lynx smiles vibrantly at Princess Petal, before letting go of her hand, and then leaves through the wooden door to the main chamber meeting room, where he meets back up with Panther and Bruce outside Falcon Castle's big bronze entrance doors. Panther and Bruce are currently organising their 200 Pine guards and men Pine villagers as well as the fourteen Willow guards upon their horses for duty during the forthcoming great war.

Princess Petal sits back down in her wooden chair in a thrilled manner with a vibrant smile upon her face.

'I've always thought you and Lynx would end up being soulmates with one another,' says Lily as she smiles at Princess Petal while finishing the cleaning up of the last of the empty wine glasses from the big wooden table. Lily places the empty wine glasses upon a wooden tray to take them into Falcon Castle's kitchen that is in another room near the main chamber meeting room.

'Yes, as did I, and I was extremely gutted when Lynx had to leave Falcon City to become leader of Pine Village. I was hoping to visit him in Pine Village soon after this creature threat had passed as father wouldn't let me undertake the long journey to Pine Village, possessing the knowledge of a great war due to occur soon. That meant it has been far too long since Lynx and I got to see each other physically,' replies Princess Petal with a slight touch of heartache in her voice.

'It seems that fate has brought you both back together now, my Princess, as it was always meant to be,' says Lily in a comforting fashion.

'Poor Gaius and yourself, I genuinely hope Emerald can be brought back to life,' remarks Princess Petal, looking up at Lily as she walks around the big wooden table towards her.

'Yes, I feel really upset for Gaius. Although I've never met Emerald myself, Gaius has spoken of her to me on several occasions. I also hope Emerald is revived from the afterlife too. It's such a tragedy for death to happen to such a young and innocent girl. I've never heard of such a magic curse that can bring someone back from the dead ever before though, and it makes me feel a bit reluctant to give Gaius hope regarding this endeavour,' replies Lily as she sits down upon a wooden chair next to Princess Petal.

'There are many things in this world we do not understand or have never experienced before, but as long as we believe in our hearts and the hearts of those humans we care for, anything can be possible,' says Princess Petal, holding on to one of Lily's hand.

Thirty-Four

THE GREAT WAR between the humans and creatures has inevitably started at the grand Falcon City within the remarkable Kingdom of Humans. After a long and tough run from the Realm of Deserted Lands and across the Grass Terrain Fields in the south direction of the Planet of Phoenix, Viper and his 800 Serpents have now arrived at the far south-west large, solid grey-and-white stone wall of Falcon City. Upon approaching the large, solid grey-and-white stone wall, the Serpents broke formation and ran in smaller groups. The Serpents ran by using their arms and legs just like a horse would as they wanted to stay closer to the ground in attempt to go unnoticed by the patrolling Royal Falcon guards that walked up and down within the middle of the large, solid grey-and-white stone wall.

King Exodus's royal Falcon advisers assumed that an attack was more likely come from the front of Falcon City at the big iron portcullis, just as it usually always had from Viper and his Serpents, especially since the surrounding large, solid grey-and-white stone wall is known to be impenetrable. The royal Falcon advisers advised Gaius to position the majority of the royal Falcon guards in the middle of northern section of Falcon City. This meant leaving the outer areas to the south-west direction of Falcon City having limited number of royal Falcon guards patrolling the area.

Due to the south-west area of Falcon City, which overlooked the Grass Terrain Fields from the large, solid grey-and-white stone wall, being guarded by only a few royal Falcon guards, Viper and his 800 Serpents managed to make it up to the large, solid grey-and-white stone wall unnoticed. As soon as the Serpents reached the large, solid grey-and-white stone wall, they pressed their reptilian bodies flat against the large, solid grey-and-white stone wall at the south-west direction of Falcon City. The few royal Falcon guards that did patrol past these areas were not be able to see them at all due to the manner in which the large, solid grey-and-white stone wall was built in a towering vertical construction but with the top of the large, solid grey-and-white stone wall curving and making it difficult to see directly below it.

'Let's attack now,' says one of the Serpents who had been standing against the large, solid grey-and-white stone wall for several minutes, waiting for the rest of the Serpents to press their reptilian bodies against the large, solid grey-and-white stone wall, and this Serpent was at present standing near Viper.

'No, we should wait for Triton and Venus to reunite with us here as they also have the anomaly crystal with them, and we will need that incredible elemental artefact to make a hole through this unbreakable solid wall of Falcon City. We can then enter through it in order to spring a surprise attack from the south-west direction of Falcon City as we had planned,' hisses Viper back to the Serpent.

'Triton said that they would be here by now, and the longer we wait to break into Falcon City, the more chances we give to those guarded humans above to spot us and then prepare the rest of Falcon City to defeat us in the great war. Besides, how do we know that Triton and Venus have not been killed already by Hake in Eagle Forest or have their changed plans and stitched us up? These devious creatures should not be trusted,' says the Serpent. Viper pauses a moment to question Triton's and Venus motives and loyalty in this great war.

'We should stay close to this wall but walk along it until we get to Nautilus Lake. If we attack the royal Falcon guards from within that lake, they won't stand a chance against our powerful claws and stinging tails. We will also be able to attack from within the waters, and they will not expect us to do that. After we destroy the guards there, we can go straight through the lake entrance that leads directly into Falcon City and launch a surprise attack from that area, which will also give us the advantage during this battle,' says another Serpent quietly while looking up to see if any of the royal Falcon guards were bending over the top of the large, solid grey-and-white stone wall in attempt to look straight down to the ground.

'Yes, that does sound like another good plan. I don't see we have another choice in the matter now as Triton and Venus should have joined up with us already, and we won't be able to break through this wall without the anomaly crystal's magnificent powers. We shall be the dominant creatures at the start of this great war, and then if Triton and Venus eventually join up with us during the great war, then all of us creatures combined will possess not only the strength but also the numbers to once and for all see the demise of that revolting King Exodus, along with all the other humans that exist upon the Planet of Phoenix,' eagerly hisses Viper.

Viper manoeuvres to the front of a few Serpents that were in front of him against the large, solid grey-and-white stone wall, and he leads the rest of his 800 Serpents as they all begin to creep alongside the large, solid grey-and-white stone wall of Falcon City towards the north direction within the Kingdom of Humans that leads to the enigmatic Nautilus Lake.

The sun shines down strongly upon Falcon City and glistens upon the numerous tall brick buildings that reside within the city. The air also brings warmth across the scaly dry skins of the Serpents, which causes them to get slightly agitated as their scales become itchy. As the Serpents approach Nautilus Lake, the thought of quenching their thirst for blood and cold water upon their dry skin quickly energises them with rage and fury, which they will require to kill all of the royal Falcon guards upon Nautilus Lake, along with the rest of the humans nervously waiting within Falcon City.

Gaius had already given out earlier the final orders for the majority of the royal Falcon guards and Falcon City men throughout Falcon City to swiftly go to their designated areas and places where they would guard and protect the humans within Falcon City during the great war; these designated areas included the Nautilus Lake, and a few of the royal Falcon guards were to be positioned on wooden boats upon Nautilus Lake to watch for any suspicious activity from

Komodo Jungle in the middle section of the Planet of Phoenix, which was just north of Nautilus Lake.

After approximately twenty minutes, Viper and his 800 Serpents now reach the edge of Nautilus Lake, against the large, solid grey-and-white stone wall; they immediately notice in the far distance five big wooden boats that were currently patrolling Nautilus Lake. Several armed royal Falcon guards were upon the big wooden boats. These five big wooden boats were equipped with a sail that had the royal Falcon guard symbol upon the middle of this big white cloth material, and the royal Falcon guard symbol was in the shape of a Falcon bird.

These big wooden boats also had cannons fixed upon the surface of the wooden decks, and the big wooden boats were steered by the royal Falcon guards as they rotated wooden oars within the waters of Nautilus Lake. Viper waves his scaly arm in the air and points into the dark waters of Nautilus Lake. Viper, along with his 800 Serpents, quickly slithers close to the ground and straight into Nautilus Lake from the south-east part of it that was bashing against the large, solid grey-and-white stone wall. Viper and his 800 Serpents now all quickly enter deep within Nautilus Lake and dive straight down below the surface of the water, where they would not be seen by the royal Falcon guards upon the five big wooden boats that were at present circling around the jagged waters upon the surface of Nautilus Lake.

With anxious thoughts, the royal Falcon guards upon the five big wooden boats are quietly watching the surrounding areas of Nautilus Lake as well as the far north region close to Komodo Jungle. The water of the Nautilus Lake is quite calm, but due to the breeze, some of the water is chopping around a bit below the bottom of the wooden oars. The air is strangely quiet with the occasional bitter breeze that brushes against the royal Falcon guards' faces. Suddenly some of the royal Falcon guards upon one of the five wooden boats have their attention quickly drawn to another wooden boat in the distance where they see another wooden boat being abruptly turned over into the water; all of the royal Falcon guards that were on top of this wooden boat also fall straight into Nautilus Lake while shouting and trying to grasp on to the now turned over big wooden boat.

As the royal Falcon guards upon other big wooden boats watch this incident in horror, they also see in concern that some of the royal Falcon guards who were on the turned-over big wooden boat and now in the water quickly disappear below the surface of Nautilus Lake without a plausible reason. The big wooden boat that had been turned over and the shouts from the royal Falcon guards who were dragged into the water from this big wooden boat alerted the entire royal Falcon guards upon the other four big wooden boats that were spread throughout Nautilus Lake. All the royal Falcon guards upon the other four big wooden boats quickly grab their metal swords and shields and anxiously look overboard into the deep swaying water of Nautilus Lake in an attempt to fight of the creatures that had caused the other big wooden boat to be turned over.

The Serpents swiftly attack the royal Falcon guards in vast numbers; they easily turn over one of the big wooden boats swiftly over into the water and hastily drag the royal Falcon guards upon this big wooden boat from its surface deck and then harshly drown these royal Falcon guards deep into the cold waters of Nautilus Lake. One more big wooden boat also gets turned over immediately after, and all these royal Falcon guards who were upon it perish in the abysmal waters of Nautilus Lake.

The royal Falcon guards upon the other two big wooden boats witness the dramatic scenes of their fellow Royal Falcon guards being dragged into the waters of Nautilus Lake; these royal Falcon guards start to turn their big wooden boats hastily around by heavily pushing their wooden oars within the waters to hurriedly sail back towards the lake entrance near the large, solid grey-and-white stone walls in the north-west direction of Falcon City. However, the Serpents begin to swim without hesitation towards these two big wooden boats that are trying to escape. The Serpents swim incredibly fast up to the surface of the water in Nautilus Lake, which enables them to gain enough speed to jump straight out of the water, where they grab some of the royal Falcon guards with their clawed hands from their big wooden boats and also drag these royal Falcon guards viciously back into the water of Nautilus Lake.

Before the last two big wooden boats have a chance to make it back to the lake entrance near the large, solid grey-and-white stone walls in the north-west direction of Falcon City, all the unfortunate royal Falcon guards are dragged overboard their big wooden boats. They are either drowned at the bottom of Nautilus Lake or are brutally stung with the Serpents' scorpion tails while fighting for their lives at the water's surface, where the sting from the Serpents' scorpion tails kills the royal Falcon guards painfully as the poison of the sting is quickly transferred through the arteries of the royal Falcon guards' bodies and the poison is carried straight towards their vital organs and causes these vital organs to stop working almost instantly. This poison from the Serpents' scorpion tails causes an excruciating death for the royal Falcon guards that are stung by the Serpents' tails.

Some of the royal Falcon guards from above the large solid grey-and-white stone wall that surrounds the perimeter of Falcon City curiously happened to gaze over the wide Nautilus Lake. These guards unbearably witness the other royal Falcon guards being attacked and then killed from their big wooden boats by the Serpents who were swimming in Nautilus Lake. The royal Falcon guards who witnessed this terrible sight of many royal Falcon guards being viciously slaughtered quickly begin blowing the loud brass horns that they had been carrying with them, which sounds the alarm for the start of the great war between the humans and the creatures. Viper grins at the sight of his first victory against the royal Falcon guards; he then swims through the rest of Nautilus Lake placidly, where he starts directing his 800 Serpents towards the lake entrance near the large, solid grey-and-white stone walls in the north-west direction within Falcon City.

VIPER AND HIS 800 Serpents sneakily enter through the lake entrance near the large, solid grey-and-white stone walls and swim within a smaller lake river that travels through a docking area, where the royal Falcon guards' big wooden boats are kept, and then it leads out into a large open fountain built upon one of the streets of Falcon City in the north-west direction that will lead the Serpents to travel in an east direction through Falcon City. One after another the army of Serpents enter through the lake entrance and climb out of the large fountain that then leads them on to the stone paths of Falcon City.

Falcon City women and children in this area had already begun to panic hysterically upon hearing the great war alarm sounds from the brass horns that were blown by the royal Falcon guards that were patrolling upon the large, solid grey-and-white stone walls. As some of the Serpents come out of the large fountain, they see some of these frantic Falcon City women and children scattering all over the place; these Serpents quickly grab some of these Falcon City women and children and bite their heads off their bodies with their pointed teeth. The rest of Serpents also continue to run wildly, attacking any humans they immediately see in this north-west area by using their stinging scorpion tails or sharp scorpion claws like a malicious plague.

Falcon City women and children sprint desperately to hide within their designated Falcon churches and sanctuaries that were barricaded from the inside to stop creatures getting within it. As soon as these Falcon City women and children made it to one of the designated sanctuaries, they would knock upon the door in a unique manner, permitting them to be let within the sanctuary and luckily escape the brutal fights upon the stone paths throughout Falcon City. The royal Falcon guards and Falcon City men that were in the north-west area within Falcon City and were near the lake entrance quickly begin to battle against the plague of Serpents that had just entered into Falcon City. The royal Falcon guards and Falcon City men hastily attack the Serpents using their metal swords and shields; the royal Falcon guards fortunately manage to inflict minor wounds upon some of the Serpents, but the less-trained Falcon City men get killed quickly by the Serpents' large scorpion claws.

Lynx is currently outside of Falcon Castle with Panther and Bruce and was only moments ago planning and instructing his Pine guards, men Pine villagers, and Panther's Willow guards whether to accompany him to meet up with Raven, Parrot, and Sapphire at the Realm of Deserted Lands or indeed stay within Falcon City to the fight against the creatures in the great war. The deep sound of brass horns that were blown by some of the royal Falcon guards upon large, solid grey-and-white stone walls just recently has travelled throughout Falcon City, where it reaches Lynx's ears; he instantly becomes shocked at the alarm for the great war that has now already started somewhere within Falcon City.

'That's the great war alarm sound,' states Panther heatedly.

'Those foolish creatures dare to attack the grand Falcon City! They won't even make it through its unbreakable walls,' remarks Bruce.

'They have come to battle against us humans in a great war
that will never be forgotten. Come quickly! We must travel to the
entrance of Falcon City and aid those royal Falcon guards there by
defeating the creatures that have entered and attacked within here.
We will seek to help Parrot and Raven after this great war has ended.
My fellow humans, follow me and let's send these evil creatures to
their own hell!' shouts Lynx as he quickly climbs on top of his white
horse. Bruce and Panther also jump upon their horses, and along
with Lynx, without hesitation, they swiftly begin charging down the
stone path hill and continue along many of the interconnecting
stone paths through Falcon City to find the creatures that had just
started attacking it. The 200 Pine guards, men Pine villagers, and
fourteen Willow guards also charge upon their horses, following
Lynx, Panther, and Bruce to fight in the great war.

In another part of Falcon City on one of the stone paths in the
south-west direction, there resides the cloth shop where Gaius's
father Nerolus and mother Tameka are currently living in. Nerolus
and Tameka hear the great war alarm sound and quickly begin
barricading their wooden entrance door with all their wooden chairs
that were placed around their wooden table within the kitchen at the
back room of their cloth shop. Nerolus is currently sixty-one years
old; he has green eyes and is tall in height and thin in weight for a
human; his face also has many wrinkles. Nerolus has always generally
been a happy and loyal human to his wife Tameka and son Gaius,
but he could also be set in his views, opinions, and traditional ways.
That is why he enforced a strict upbringing upon his son Gaius before
Gaius left Falcon City and moved to Oak Village with Ruthus many
years ago.

Nerolus's wife Tameka is currently fifty-eight years old. She has
short curly black hair, brown eyes, and also wrinkles and freckles
upon her face too. Tameka is a very caring human, but she also
becomes easily worried and stresses about the changing life situations
she has experienced, such as when Nerolus sent Gaius away to Oak
Village with Ruthus to learn to be a tradesman in order to avoid
getting into any further trouble within Falcon City. Nerolus and
Tameka had got married early in their lives; they have been together
ever since they first met each other during their teenage years at one
of the libraries within Falcon City.

'I think that should do it,' says Nerolus as he places their last wooden chair up against the wooden entrance door to their cloth shop.

'It's best if we also put more objects against our door as I'm not sure if this barricade will be strong enough to stop any creatures breaking through it,' says Tameka worriedly, looking at the stacks of wooden chairs lodged against the wooden entrance door to their cloth shop. Suddenly two Serpents use their mighty scorpion claws to shred apart Nerolus and Tameka's wooden entrance door into pieces after these Serpents hear voices from within this cloth shop when they were running past it during their attack upon Falcon City. Tameka screams at the sight of the two Serpents forcing their way through their wooden entrance door and into the front part of their cloth shop. Upon entry, one of the Serpents easily rips off Nerolus's head with both of its scorpion claws; the other Serpent swiftly pierces its scorpion tail directly into the back of Tameka as she attempts to run away from the Serpents. The sting from the Serpent's scorpion tail sends a deadly poison straight into Tameka's bloodstream; the poison reaches her body's vital organs within seconds and quickly stops her vital organs from working. Tameka gasps intensely for her last breath as she falls harshly to the ground in intense pain until she dies.

FIVE HUNDRED OF Viper's Serpents break off from the large Serpent army and begin attacking other areas throughout Falcon City; these Serpents spread through Falcon City with ease and forcefully devour Falcon City humans and historic buildings in different directions within Falcon City. Panic and terror consumes Falcon City humans as they are brutally attacked by many Serpents at once; these Serpents show Falcon City humans no mercy, and within a short period of time, many Falcon City humans are murdered, their dead bodies left helpless upon the spot they were killed.

One large group of Serpents who were heading in the southern-middle direction of Falcon City now manage to come in contact with Gaius, who was at present with the majority of his 500 royal Falcon guards accompanied by most of the 900 Falcon City men. Since the start of the great war within Falcon City, Gaius had regrouped and instructed his royal Falcon guards and Falcon City men to join with him as soon as he had heard the great war alarm sounds from the patrolling royal Falcon guards blowing the brass horns.

Gaius and the majority of his 500 Royal Falcon guards and 900 Falcon City men were also sprinting on foot towards the north-west direction of Falcon City where the great war had initially started. As Gaius is sprinting quickly and leading his royal Falcon guards and Falcon City men, they also see this large group of approximately 500 Serpents scurrying spitefully towards them. Gaius takes a deep breath and quickly charges onwards, leading his royal Falcon guards and Falcon City men to fight fiercely with their metal swords and shields against these Serpents upon the stone paths in the southern-middle area of Falcon City.

Upon contact, the Serpents rapidly use their powerful scorpion tails and claws to attack the royal Falcon guards and Falcon City men in a forceful manner, and they kill many of these humans quickly and without hesitation. The royal Falcon guards and Falcon City men retaliate by stabbing the Serpents back with their metal swords in the Serpents' scaly faces and bodies. The royal Falcon guards and Falcon City men's metal swords pierce into the Serpents' tough but tender skin, which causes some of this large group of Serpents to also be killed and injured. The constant attacking of the Serpents by both the royal Falcon guards and Falcon City men continues swiftly and loudly with many of these humans and Serpents striking an opponent down or also getting their bodies sliced into pieces.

In rage, the Serpents push back the royal Falcon guards and Falcon City men and instantly kill plenty of these humans by stinging them with their large scorpion tails, enabling their poison to stop the vital organs of the humans from functioning as the poison stops the flow of blood being circulated through the rest of these humans' bodies. The Serpents also slice some of the royal Falcon guards and Falcon City men's bodies into halves by digging their forceful scorpion claws in to the skin of these humans. The royal Falcon guards and Falcon City humans who are injured or killed during this fight shout and scream loudly in pain and agony as their blood pours out from their body and their bones shatter like broken glass.

Gaius, who is at present in the midst of this fight, manoeuvres swiftly between the big and horrible Serpents to snappishly cut and sever some of the Serpents' heads off with his mighty sharp silver swords. As Gaius continues to kill as many Serpents as he can, he constantly dodges between the fight, being careful not to get stung by any of the Serpents' large scorpion tails. The fight continues on in a brutal fashion for many hours between Gaius, the royal Falcon guards, Falcon City men, and the Serpents; the stone paths quickly get covered with blood and bodies of the dead humans and Serpents.

As the sun continues to shine heatedly down upon Falcon City, the windy breeze carries the loud noises created from the smaller fights that are currently occurring within different areas of Falcon City, along with the ear-piercing shrieks of those Falcon City women and children that are being innocently killed by the plague of Serpents that are sweeping through most of Falcon City very quickly. Falcon City is in complete chaos and anarchy from the great war that has only just recently begun upon the Planet of Phoenix.

Many of the royal Falcon guards along with Falcon City men, women, and children have already died brutal and cruel deaths from the Serpents who still remain piled up across the top of the stone paths through Falcon City. Most of the royal Falcon guards and Falcon City men fight back against the Serpents with all their strength and heart, but sometimes this will of these humans to succeed was quickly diminished by the ultimate might of the Serpent warriors' physical bodies. Some of Falcon City women cry hysterically in fright and helplessness as they grasp their children within the designated Falcon City churches and sanctuaries, hoping they will not be discovered and then killed by the malicious Serpents.

Lynx is currently riding upon his white horse along with Panther and Bruce riding upon their horses, while being followed by the 200 Pine guards, men Pine villagers, and fourteen Willow guards. They have all now galloped down the stone path hill from Falcon Castle in the north direction towards Falcon City's big iron portcullis. As they continue riding upon the stone paths towards the big iron portcullis of Falcon City, they become surprisingly involved in a brutal battle against Viper and 300 of his Serpents who have also reached these stone paths that lead up to the big iron portcullis at the entrance of Falcon City, following their attack that started in the north-west direction of Falcon City.

Lynx, Panther, Bruce, the 200 Pine guards, men Pine villagers, and fourteen Willow guards riding gallantly upon their horses, immediately begin attacking by stabbing these Serpents in their heads as well as chopping their heads off with their metal swords. The Willow guards are experts at archery. From the back of their battle formation behind the Pine guards and men Pine villagers upon their horses, the Willow guards start shooting their wooden arrows from their wooden bows high up in the air; these wooden arrows fly quickly through the air and are targeted to land in the eyes and heads of the Serpents, which enables some of them to be killed in a fierce manner.

A small group of Serpents begin to swerve from side to side and between the flying wooden arrows fallen from the air and quickly charge away from the middle of this battle. They head down another one of the stone paths in the south-east direction of Falcon City with the aim of causing more havoc to Falcon City humans in other areas of Falcon City. Bruce had just brutally killed several Serpents while being on top of his horse. He used both his metal sword and Flame's sword that had Flame's named carved upon the handle of it straight in to the Serpents' faces and chests. Bruce's attention is distracted from the fight on seeing this small group of Serpents break away from the fight to charge down another stone path. Bruce makes a quick decision to also leave this fight and wavers to several of the other Pine guards who were still upon their horses to follow him and chase after these Serpents down this stone path.

Lynx rides firmly upon his white horse and quickly swerves between the huge numbers of Serpents in this fight that is occurring upon the stone paths near the big iron portcullis entrance of Falcon City. While stabbing many Serpents in their heads and chests with his sturdy silver sword, at the same time, Lynx notices Viper dashing through many of the Serpents upon the stone paths and heads straight towards him. With fast reaction, Lynx sticks his silver sword straight down in front of him in order to pierce right through Viper's heart; however, as Viper approaches closer to Lynx, Viper successfully dodges Lynx's silver sword's blow. Viper turns his neck speedily to his right and evilly spits his pure black venom from both of his big white fangs; in a split second the black venom squirts from Viper's big white fangs and into the air where it hits Lynx upon his sweaty face. Lynx frantically tries to remove this black venom from upon his face, but unfortunately it is too late. Lynx falls off from his white horse and lands hard directly on to the stone path below him. He drops his silver sword and silver shield from both of his hands as he falls to the stone paths just as his silver Pine crown falls from the top of his head and tumbles across the stone path. Viper's black venom is extremely poisonous. It disintegrates Lynx's whole body, including all of his flesh and bones, and Lynx dies quickly but also in excruciating pain.

'No! Lynx!' shouts Panther unbelievably as he sickly witnesses Lynx's death through the fight upon the stone paths of Falcon City. Viper sniggers cunningly and also continues spitting his poisonous black venom out of his big white fangs, which also lands upon the flesh of Lynx's white horse and other Pine guards and men Pine villagers and their horses in the immediate vicinity of this fight. Again, Viper's poisonous black venom quickly disintegrates the bodies of these Pine guards, men Pine villagers, and horses effortlessly; also it is an agonising experience for these humans and animals.

The remaining Serpents who are still fighting against these humans in this battle now quickly sting with their sharp and powerful scorpion tails just about all the Pine guards, men Pine villagers, and Willow guards who are still saddled upon their horses. The horses that were stung by the Serpents' scorpion tails quickly crash-land on top of the stone paths, which also causes the Pine guards, men Pine villagers, and Willow guards to be thrown from their horse backs. The Serpents then take this opportunity to sting the fallen Pine guards, men Pine villagers, and Willow guards directly on their faces and backs with their scorpion tails as well as to slice these humans into pieces by tearing their limbs apart with their gargantuan scorpion claws.

This hard fight between these Serpents and the Pine guards, men Pine villagers, and Willow guards continued for another forty minutes. These humans attacked forcefully with their metal swords and wooden arrows as well as defended themselves with their metal shields, but as the numbers of the Pine guards decreased, the Serpents attained the control of this fight, which made it easier for them to kill these humans with more simplicity. After approximately forty minutes of crucial time, Viper and his Serpents compellingly massacre all the Pine guards and men Pine Villagers who were still present in this fight, along with the fourteen Willow guards.

During the remaining minutes of this brutal fight, Panther had also been killed by an agonising sting to his brain from one of the Serpents' scorpion tail that caused Panther's vital organs to stop working. As the bodies of the Pine guards, men Pine villagers, and Willow guards, including Panther's body, now piled upon one another on the stone paths of Falcon City near the big iron portcullis entrance, Viper, along with the remaining 116 Serpents who had survived this battle, leaves this area and charges up the stone path hill towards Falcon Castle in the southern-middle direction of Falcon City.

IN ANOTHER PART of Falcon City, Bruce and some of the remaining Pine guards upon their horses were still galloping hastily after the small group of Serpents that were currently charging down another stone path in the south-east direction of Falcon City. As Bruce and these Pine guards catch up with these Serpents due to their horses being faster than Serpents, Bruce and the Pine guards quickly stab their metal swords into the back and the heads of all these Serpents, which killed them, but some of these Pine guards also get killed during this fight by the Serpents who quickly reacted to being stabbed by stinging these Pine guards with their powerful scorpion tails causing the vital organs of the Pine guards to rupture and not work no more. Bruce stabs Flame's sword deep into the last of the Serpent's brains, which kills this Serpent instantly. As the Serpent's dead body flops to the stone path beneath it, Bruce looks ahead of him, and in the distance, he sees a large noble building that had 'Falcon University' written above the big wooden entrance doors.

'Nia,' says Bruce aloud as he remembers that Nia would still be a student at Falcon University as she was currently training to become a lecturer of history. Without pause, Bruce kicks his heels into the sides of the horse he is riding, which makes the horse gallop quickly towards Falcon University building that was straight in front. After approaching the front of the building, Bruce jumps down from his horse and quickly bangs loudly upon Falcon University's big wooden entrance doors. The remaining few Pine guards that had accompanied Bruce also ride up to these big wooden entrance doors.

'Leave us alone!' shouts Nia alarmingly from behind the big wooden entrance doors, thinking it was the attacking creatures.

'Nia, is that you?' asks Bruce, as he slightly remembers the sound of her voice.

'Yes, it's Nia. Who's asking for me?' asks Nia curiously, looking at one of her fellow students in slight hope.

'It's me Bruce from Pine Village. Quick, let me in, and I will protect you from these Serpent creatures that are out here,' states Bruce directly.

'Bruce! What are you doing here at Falcon City?' asks Nia as she quickly removes the wooden barricades that were lodged against the big wooden entrance doors from the inside of Falcon University. She is helped by Falcon City priest and other Falcon University lecturers and students who were currently hiding within Falcon University from the great war. As the big wooden entrance doors are opened for Bruce, Bruce is just about to walk into Falcon University and explain to Nia how they had now come in contact with each other again, when suddenly Bruce's body receives one of the Serpents' solid scorpion claws stabbed right through his back. It punctures straight through his body and appears through the other side of it and out of his chest. A Serpent had quickly snuck up behind the back of Bruce, just before any of the Pine guards could have stopped it as they had only just made it up to the big wooden entrance doors of Falcon University. Nia screams loudly as she watches her ex-boyfriend Bruce fall directly to the ground in front of him, while also dropping both his metal sword and Flame's sword that had Flame's name carved upon the handle of this sword.

The Pine guards behind Bruce jump down from their horses and attempt to stab this Serpent in revenge for Bruce's death. They do not notice another couple of Serpents charging up behind the last of these remaining Pine guards and biting their heads off their bodies with their sharp teeth. The Serpent who had killed Bruce now barges inwards into the big wooden entrance doors of Falcon University and quickly stings Nia, the Falcon priest, and the other Falcon University lecturers and students with his deadly scorpion tail. Within minutes, the poison from this Serpent's scorpion tail reaches the vital organs of these humans and ruptures the vital organs from the inside of their bodies, which kills all these humans within Falcon University grotesquely.

The great war within Falcon City continues outrageously for approximately another three hours. The tough and ruthless fights throughout Falcon City occur either upon the stone paths or within numerous Falcon City buildings. Hundreds of royal Falcon guards, Falcon City men, women, and children get brutally killed along with all the Pine guards, men Pine villagers, and Willow guards. However, plentiful Serpents also get murdered by the humans. During the fight that incorporated Gaius and his remaining royal Falcon guards and Falcon City men against the Serpents upon the stone paths in the middle-south direction of Falcon City, Gaius and these Falcon City humans end up being victorious in killing the large group of approximately 500 Serpents that they had initially come into contact with following the start of the great war.

Gaius and his now remaining 144 royal Falcon guards and 273 Falcon City men gather their breath and stamina following the long and brutal fight they had just experienced with this Serpent army. Gaius wastes no time in trying to recuperate from this fight; he immediately sprints towards Falcon Castle where he is followed by most of the surviving 144 royal Falcon guards and 273 Falcon City men who were not too injured during their recent fight against the Serpents. Gaius and these Falcon City humans continue sprinting towards Falcon Castle in the south-east direction. From a distance and looking up at the stone path hill, Gaius spots Viper and his remaining 116 Serpents also charging towards Falcon Castle.

Within Falcon Castle, King Exodus wore his golden-plated knighthood armour and held his golden sword and shield, whereas Princess Petal held tightly on to her golden sword and shield. Lily also grasped a silver axe in one of her hands. Eleven royal Falcon guards accompanied King Exodus, Princess Petal, and Lily; these royal Falcon guards were suited in their metal knighthood armours and metal swords and shields. The royal Falcon guards had barricaded Falcon Castle's big bronze entrance doors from inside of Falcon Castle with large wooden tables and chairs, as soon as they heard the great war alarm sound that was blown over three hours ago by the patrolling royal Falcon guards upon the large, solid grey-and-white stone wall in the north-west direction of Falcon City. King Exodus, Princess Petal, Lily, and the eleven royal Falcon guards stand firm and ready to protect one another; the royal Falcon guards' main responsibility is not let anything happen to the heiress, Princess Petal, who was the next in line to rule Falcon City.

'Stay strong and hit them hard, my lovely daughter. I will protect you with all my strength against whatever creature attempts to break into Falcon Castle. If I were to be killed this day, however, you must live on to continue our ruling over the humans within Falcon City. With the intention of one day finally ridding the Planet of Phoenix from this plague of evil creatures,' fervently says King Exodus to Princess Petal as he places his right hand upon her left shoulder in loving comfort.

'Don't worry, Father, you have trained me well to protect myself, and I also won't let anything happen to you either as you will be much needed to help those humans who have suffered during this terrible great war,' replies Princess Petal, nodding and smiling at her father King Exodus.

'Both of you noble humans will survive this great war, and I will make sure I do all I can to protect you both. Make sure you stay close to me, my Princess,' states Lily as she smiles at King Exodus and Princess Petal.

Viper and his remaining 116 Serpents now reach Falcon Castle at the top of the stone path hill. Several of the Serpents quickly make multiple cuts with their impenetrable scorpion claws against the big bronze entrance doors. Even after numerous attempts, the big bronze doors are not broken by the Serpents' scorpion claws; thus these Serpents constantly barge into these big bronze entrance doors until they manage to break them. As the Serpents enter forcefully through the big bronze entrance doors, they immediately begin attacking King Exodus, Princess Petal, Lily, and the eleven royal Falcon guards who were just inside of Falcon Castle. King Exodus quickly uses his golden sword to stab a few Serpents in the heart as they are running through the big bronze entrance doors of Falcon Castle, which causes them to die.

Princess Petal swings her golden sword swiftly out in front of her and manages to cut some Serpents' heads off. The royal Falcon guards protect themselves as well as Princess Petal by utilising their metal shields to stop themselves from getting stung by the Serpents' large scorpion tails. As some of the royal Falcon guards swiftly dodge the stinging attack from the Serpents' scorpion tails, some of the other royal Falcon guards stab these Serpents in the chests and heads with their metal swords. Lily also manoeuvres around this newly started fight and smacks several Serpents in the face with her silver axe. As more Serpents begin to enter through the big bronze entrance doors and pile into the great hall of Falcon Castle, King Exodus, Princess Petal, Lily, and the eleven royal Falcon guards hurriedly retreat straight to the back of Falcon Castle's great hall as they soon begin to become hugely outnumbered.

Viper also now enters through the big bronze entrance doors into the great hall of Falcon Castle with the remaining Serpents. Viper drives forward deeper into the great hall and harshly attacks and kills most of the eleven royal Falcon guards by breaking their necks with his strong scaly hands or stealing the metal swords from the royal Falcon guards. As they attempt to attack Viper, the Serpent stabs the royal Falcon guards' metal swords back into the faces of these royal Falcon guards. King Exodus, Princess Petal, and Lily continue to fight honourably against a huge number of Serpents as best as they can, but they become very exhausted, overwhelmed, and slightly injured due to receiving bumps and knocks to their bodies from some of the Serpents' strong scorpion claws.

As Viper joins the heart of the battle near the back of the great hall within Falcon Castle, he starts spitting his black venom from his big white fangs out of his reptilian mouth, which disintegrates and kills the rest of the eleven royal Falcon guards. When all hope seems lost for the last of the royal humans that ruled over Falcon City, Gaius and most of his remaining 144 royal Falcon guards, accompanied by 273 Falcon City men, arrive at the big bronze entrance doors of Falcon Castle. With furious emotions, the royal Falcon captain Gaius and the surviving Falcon City humans quickly charge through the big bronze doors and join this heated fight towards the back of the great hall within Falcon Castle. The great war continues to be fought maliciously and harshly for another forty minutes between the remaining humans and creatures within Falcon Castle of Falcon City. Countless Serpents, royal Falcon guards, and Falcon City men are either stabbed to death or their body limbs are sliced and ripped apart, or are stung or poisoned to their demise.

As the great war continues within the great hall of Falcon Castle, the number of humans and Serpents continues to decrease on both sides, but the Serpents are now outnumbered by the royal Falcon guards and Falcon City men. King Exodus and Gaius valiantly lead the royal Falcon guards and Falcon City men to attack the Serpents harshly, and fortunately for these humans, a large number of the Serpents die rapidly. Lily finds herself in the midst of this fight within the great hall in Falcon Castle, where she is currently standing behind Viper.

Lily heroically attempts to end Viper's life and stop this great war by hitting Viper on his tough scaly back with her sharp silver axe. Lily manages to quickly get close enough and forces her silver axe into the scaly back of Viper; Viper quickly feels the pain of the silver axe digging into his scaly back; before this silver axe could do any irreversible damage to Viper's scaly back, he swiftly turns around and grabs Lily's neck. In shock, Lily drops the silver axe, which falls from Viper's scaly back and lands on the floor beneath them. Viper then breaks Lily's neck with his strong snake-like hands. The breaking of Lily's neck kills her instantly; Viper releases his grip from Lily's neck, which makes Lily's dead body fall directly to the floor.

From another side of this fight within the great hall of Falcon Castle, Gaius is devastated to see that Viper had just killed his partner Lily. Gaius becomes distraught and furious within a split second of seeing Lily being killed by Viper. Gaius uses all his remaining energy to charge at Viper at full speed, but physically he crouches low to the floor between the lingering fight between the royal Falcon guards, Falcon City men, and remaining Serpents. Gaius quickly sees just in front of him a dead Serpent's body that was laid upon the floor of the great hall, and this dead Serpent's body was directly in front of Viper, who was unaware of Gaius charging towards him, because Viper was smirking at Lily's dead body upon the ground next to Viper's snake-like feet. Gaius sprints faster, and he leaps off the floor on to the dead Serpent's body, and then he jumps off the dead Serpent's body, which enables Gaius to gain more height in the air. Gaius lunges his silver sword far out in front of him and plunges it right into Viper's face as he flies momentarily through the air. The sharp blow from Gaius's silver sword shatters the bones and brains within Viper's snake-like head. This furious wound finally kills Viper instantly. Viper's dead body now falls to its knees; as Gaius flies past Viper's dead body, he releases his grip from his silver sword that is stuck in Viper's head, in order to fortunately land upon his feet on the floor within the great hall.

Gaius stands up tall next to Viper's dead body that was currently kneeling upon the floor; he places both of his hands back on to this silver sword again, and Gaius rips his silver sword out from Viper's scaly green face, which causes large volumes of green blood to spray over the floor everywhere. Gaius kicks Viper mightily in his scaly chest with his right foot, which causes Viper's dead body to fall compellingly upon the floor of the great hall within Falcon Castle. King Exodus, Princess Petal, Gaius, and the remaining sixty-three royal Falcon guards and fifty-four Falcon City men now make their final resilient stabbing blows and wounds to kill the last of the Serpents that were left remaining within the great hall of Falcon Castle. After another ten minutes of fighting these creatures, the humans of Falcon City finally end the great war.

Thirty-Five

DURING THE TIME that the great war was currently taking place within Falcon City in the Kingdom of Humans in the south-east area of the Planet of Phoenix, Raven, who was holding on to Emerald's dead body while riding on top of Felix, along with Parrot and Sapphire, who were riding upon their black horse, has galloped quickly in the far south-west direction across the Realm of Deserted Lands. Along Raven, Parrot, and Sapphire's challenging and far-reaching travels, they endure the dark, misty, and gusty sandstorms, along with the sharp and rocky terrain until they fortunately discover the location of Triton's Underground Dungeon that is deep beneath the rocky surface of the Realm of Deserted Lands in the furthest south-west corner.

Upon approaching the furthest south-west corner of the Realm of Deserted Lands, Parrot notices a big rock-shaped archway that had a dark opening within it and seemed to go underneath the rocky surface of the Realm of Deserted Lands. Parrot manoeuvres his black horse towards this big rock-shaped archway; shortly after pulling the rope reins of this black horse tightly in order to stop its fast pacing, Parrot climbs down from his black horse near the passageway that leads beneath the rocky ground to the inside of Triton's Underground Dungeon. Parrot also smoothly helps Sapphire down from the black horse due to Sapphire holding on to most of everyone's weapons, and then both Parrot and Sapphire walk over to Raven, who had just halted Felix next to the black horse.

Both Parrot and Sapphire place their weapons on the rocky ground and hold gently on to Emerald's dead body to allow Raven the space to climb down from Felix's large back. Once on the rocky surface of the Realm of Deserted Lands, Raven grabs the brown rope reins of Felix and the other black horse's rope reins. Raven pulls both horses over to a small pile of hard rocks that was near the entrance to Triton's Underground Dungeon, and he fixes the rope reins of both the horses underneath a couple of rocks to secure them.

Raven carefully takes Emerald's dead body from Parrot and Sapphire, who are holding on to her. He puts Emerald's dead body over his shoulder and starts to walk cautiously down into the long and narrow passageway that went beneath the rocky ground of the Planet of Phoenix. At the same time, Parrot and Sapphire pick up their weapons from the rocky ground. Parrot carries his wooden bow and wooden arrows with the metal spikes at the end of them, his fury raptor throwing stars, along with Raven's sword and shield of Grackle. Sapphire holds on to her small silver dagger, the book of curses, and the blue potion within the glass container that were placed within the brown leather bag. They also follow Raven down into this long and narrow rocky passageway.

'Are you sure about this, my family? You both don't have to come with me as you have so much to live for back at Pine Village. Think of your son Tigra,' says Raven quietly to Parrot and Sapphire as Raven turns around to see Parrot and Sapphire also walking down into the dark and deep passageway guardedly behind him.

'Don't be silly, Raven. We all will survive this great war, and there's nothing I want to do more right now than to send those evil creatures Triton and Venus to the deepest and darkest depths of hell for all the suffering they have caused so many of us humans over the years,' replies Sapphire, also in a quite tone of voice.

'If we don't end these most evil of creatures' lives now, they will never stop torturing the humans existing upon the Planet of Phoenix. Besides, life back in Pine Village wouldn't be the same to go back to if you and Emerald aren't also there to share it with me, Sapphire, and Tigra. Sapphire and myself are always here for you no matter what, my cousin,' states Parrot as he looks at Raven, who smiles back at Parrot and Sapphire softly before he turns back around.

Raven is still holding firmly on to Emerald's dead body as Parrot, Sapphire, and Raven continue walking steadily through the long and narrow passageway for a further ten minutes until they all end up entering through an entrance that leads straight into the main room of Triton's Underground Dungeon. As soon as they pass into the main hall, Raven, Parrot, and Sapphire notice heartless Triton and Venus, who were standing still at the other end of the main room near a big wooden table. Raven, Parrot, and Sapphire feel an abundance of negative emotions on seeing Triton and Venus and also experience the intense heat within the main hall due to it being really hot and steamy from the several lava pits that were embedded within different sections of the ground throughout the main room. This volatile environment was something that Raven, Parrot, and Sapphire had never experienced or seen before.

'The time has come for us to end this great war between us creatures and them humans, where we will fulfil our destinies in becoming the only rulers over the Planet of Phoenix!' shouts Triton loudly in a husky voice as he stares nastily at Raven, who had just walked into the main room of his Underground Dungeon.

'The only destiny you will fulfil will be decided by the end of my sword of Grackle!' shouts Raven back at Triton after hearing what Triton has just said. Raven carefully lays Emerald's dead body down upon the ground of the main room; he takes his sword and shield of Grackle from Parrot as Sapphire also puts the brown leather bag down upon the ground of the main room next to Emerald's dead body. Raven, Parrot, and Sapphire start walking intensely through the main room while holding their weapons out in front of them as they head towards Triton and Venus, who are still standing by the big wooden table at the other side of the main room.

'Stupid humans, you are walking to your deaths,' says Venus bitterly as she lets go of Triton's hand and uses her creature instincts to turn her eyes into a pure white colour. Venus puts one hand above the other hand out in front of her with both of her hands facing towards the ground; Venus applies her Animagus abilities to magically create three ferocious dromaeosaurus dinosaurs. Within a few moments, Venus supernaturally creates all three small dromaeosaurus dinosaurs between the middle of her hands; at the same time, she moves her bottom hand to the side and levitates the three small dromaeosaurus dinosaurs towards the ground of the main room. Venus then raises her top hand in the air, and the three small dromaeosaurus dinosaurs enchantingly grow into their full physical size, which was larger than the humans.

The three full-sized dromaeosaurus dinosaurs have long, powerful, and whipping tails that are attached to their cold-blooded tough-skinned bodies, and their rounded mouths are full of sharp snapping teeth. Attached to their rough and turquoise-coloured backs with numerous black stripes are also severe striking claws, especially upon the two smaller arms they have at the top half of their body. They all run on two powerful hind legs. As soon as these three dromaeosaurus dinosaurs' clawed hind legs touch the ground, they instantaneously make loud high-pitched shrieking noises, and without warning they begin to spring upon their two strong hind legs towards Raven, Parrot, and Sapphire who are presently walking from the other side of the main room within Triton's Underground Dungeon.

Parrot invigorates his legs and runs straight out in front of Raven and Sapphire in an attempt to distract two of the three dromaeosaurus dinosaurs; Parrot leads both of them in a different direction within the main hall. Sapphire also quickly turns around and runs behind and away from Raven, which distracts the other dromaeosaurus dinosaur to follow Sapphire directly past Raven and back towards the passageway entrance at one side of the main hall. Raven takes this opportunity of being avoided by all of the three dromaeosaurus dinosaurs, and he hastily sprints towards Triton and Venus near the big wooden table. Triton clenches his bulky fists and grasps tightly on to his golden chain with the iron spiked ball at the end of it and charges fiercely towards Raven.

As Triton charges forward, he briskly swings his golden chain with the iron spiked ball at the end of it around his head and slams it towards Raven's chest. Raven thrusts the durable shield of Grackle swiftly out in front of him, which fortunately stops the heavy blow from the iron spiked ball from hitting him in the chest; the powerful hit of the iron spiked ball, however, indents a mark within the shield of Grackle that was made of silver. Raven now lunges the sword of

Grackle directly in front of him, and it pierces and slices straight through Triton's muscly left shoulder. Triton shouts loudly in agony as thick red blood pours quickly out from Triton's left shoulder wound that still has the sword of Grackle lodged in it.

As Parrot keeps dashing in another direction away from the two dromaeosaurus dinosaurs that were chasing ferociously after him around the main room of Triton's Underground Dungeon, Parrot quickly grabs two wooden arrows with metal spikes at the end of them from his back pouch and positions both of these wooden arrows with the metal spikes at the end of them into his wooden bow at the same time. Parrot swiftly manoeuvres his feet to quickly turn his whole body around, and he accurately shoots both the wooden arrows with the metal spikes at the end of them speedily form the wooden bow. Both the arrows fly through the air and they harshly hit one of dromaeosaurus dinosaurs in its head right between its eyes. These two wooden arrows with the metal spikes at the end of them pierce straight through the dromaeosaurus dinosaur's dry skin and lodge themselves through the dromaeosaurus dinosaur's brain; this dromaeosaurus dinosaur falls unintentionally from its two strong hind legs and crashes hard upon the ground as it's now dead.

The other dromaeosaurus dinosaur that was also chasing after Parrot screeches sharply at the sight of one of the other dromaeosaurus dinosaurs being murdered. This dromaeosaurus dinosaur rapidly swings its thick and powerful long tail to one side and smacks Parrot in the stomach and knocks him flying back in the air. Parrot flies backwards and falls back down to the ground with a thud in another part of the main room within Triton's Underground Dungeon.

Sapphire stops dashing suddenly near one of the hot and steamy lava pits that were embedded within the ground of the main room. She speedily turns around and is troubled on seeing one of the dromaeosaurus dinosaurs sprinting irately towards her and biting its sharp teeth in its rounded mouth. Sapphire quickly jumps to her left side and dive-rolls out the way as the dromaeosaurus dinosaur approaches her. Just as Sapphire rolls out of the way, the dromaeosaurus dinosaur tries to stop his strong hind legs from sprinting, but it unintentionally slides into this lava pit embedded within the ground and burns quickly and painfully to its death. As the dromaeosaurus dinosaur dies within the embedded lava pit,

Venus experiences an overwhelming sensation within her body due
to one of the creatures she had made being killed. This causes Venus
to become livid.

Sapphire staggers back up from the ground after rolling on to
it, and she hurriedly runs back towards Emerald's dead body at the
entrance to the main room that was located in the long and narrow
passageway. Sapphire quickly places her silver dagger on the ground
near Emerald, and then she kneels to the ground and grabs the
blue potion in the glass container from the brown leather bag and
carefully opens Emerald's mouth. Sapphire pours some of the blue
potion into her mouth, and it trickles down her throat.

At this same moment, Triton drops his golden chain with the iron
spiked ball at the end of it from his right hand, which lands on the
ground, and then he uses his right hand to forcefully pull the sword
of Grackle out of his left shoulder, which still lodged inside his left
shoulder. Triton applies his immense strength to yank the sword of
Grackle out of his left shoulder and away from Raven's hands, and
then Triton drops the sword of Grackle to the ground. Triton now
begins to punch Raven strongly and fiercely in his face with his huge
fisted hands. Raven tries to block Triton's powerful punches with the
resilient shield of Grackle; however, Raven stumbles back over hard
to the ground behind him from the constant colossal punches that
he was receiving from Triton.

VENUS LAUGHS CRUELLY as she sees Raven fall backwards to the
ground from being punched by Triton, but out of the corner of one
of her white eyes, she angrily notices Sapphire pouring a blue potion
from a glass container into Emerald's mouth. Venus's attention is
now drawn to Sapphire at the other side of the main room. Venus
witnesses Sapphire pulling away the half-empty glass container that
still had some blue potion within it and quickly grabbing an old book
from her brown leather bag.

Suddenly Sapphire stands up upon the ground and rapidly
runs towards Venus, dashing through the hot and steamy lava pits
embedded within the big main room of Triton's Underground
Dungeon. Sapphire carries the old book and some of the blue
potion within the glass container. Venus quickly becomes anxious as
Sapphire runs towards her with this old book, and Venus holds out

in front of her the anomaly crystal that currently has all the colours of the rainbow and shades of white and black are swirling frantically around the centre of it.

Parrot is currently experiencing pain in his back and thighs from hard landing he had on the ground of the main room when he received the strong blow from the dromaeosaurus dinosaur's powerful tail. Parrot strains himself to his feet and grabs three of his silver fury raptor throwing stars from one of his big brown coat pocket; he quickly examines his surroundings and takes aim for the last dromaeosaurus dinosaur that was sprinting hungrily towards him. Parrot launches the three fury raptor throwing stars into the air one at a time. The three fury raptor throwing stars fly speedily and accurately across the air straight towards the dromaeosaurus dinosaur. The dromaeosaurus dinosaur swerves his whole body swiftly by manoeuvring his strong hind legs to the side, which enables the dromaeosaurus dinosaur to miss the first fury raptor throwing star that was flying at it, and this fury raptor throwing star now falls on to the ground.

The second fury raptor throwing star that is thrown by Parrot, however, hits the dromaeosaurus dinosaur in the side of its large body, and this fury raptor throwing star pierces through its tough skin. The dromaeosaurus dinosaurs squeals as it feels the sharp pain from the spiky edges of the silver fury raptor throwing star as it digs inside its body. The third fury raptor throwing star is thrown by Parrot more precisely, and this fury raptor throwing star flies straight into the middle of the dromaeosaurus dinosaur's rounded mouth as it squeals from the wound it had just received to the side of its body from the second fury raptor throwing star.

As the third fury raptor throwing star enters the dromaeosaurus dinosaur's rounded mouth, it shatters some of the dromaeosaurus dinosaur's sharp teeth. The piercing silver spiky edges of the fury raptor throwing star also cut through the dromaeosaurus dinosaur's inner throat and windpipe, which causes the dromaeosaurus dinosaur to stop breathing. The dromaeosaurus dinosaur soon dies from a lack of oxygen to its lungs, and it also falls to the ground and dies.

In the middle of the main room of Triton's Underground Dungeon, Triton kicks the shield of Grackle out of Raven's hand, which Raven was still holding securely when he fell backwards on the ground. As Triton strongly kicks the shield of Grackle out of Raven's hands with his bulky left foot, the shield of Grackle is knocked over on to the ground next to Raven. Raven turns his attention back to Triton after losing the grip he had on the shield of Grackle and now sees Triton lifting his huge and bulky left foot in the air and move it to crush Raven's face. Raven quickly reaches down his body and grabs the small silver dagger that Parrot had previously given him from one of his brown boots. Raven snappishly stabs this small silver dagger straight into the wound of Triton's right thigh from when Raven had stabbed Triton with the sword of Grackle during the battle of Eagle Forest. The small silver dagger slices through the wide skin; it gets stuck right in the centre of the wound within Triton's right thigh. Triton yelps loudly in agony and stumbles back as his lifted left leg drops straight back down to the ground in order for Triton to try and steady his large body. Raven hastily rolls across the ground to grab the sword of Grackle from the ground that Triton had just dropped upon it.

Venus, who was just preparing herself to fight against Sapphire as she was running towards her, now becomes unintentionally distracted by Triton's painful yelp because of his new wound to his right thigh. Venus draws her vision to look over at Triton. But at the same time, Venus doesn't see another fury raptor throwing star that Parrot has just thrown swiftly through the air at Venus. This fury raptor throwing star hits Venus directly into one of her pure white eyes, and the fury raptor throwing star gets stuck within the left eyeball. Both of Venus's eyes now instantly turn back to their normal red colour again as her creature abilities are affected by this horrible wound.

Venus screams abruptly in intense suffering and falls straight on to her knees upon the ground and accidentally drops the anomaly crystal from her hand. This causes the anomaly crystal to roll along the ground of the main room. Sapphire had by now run across the main room to the big wooden table. She grabs Venus quickly in a tight headlock with her right arm as Venus is currently kneeling upon the ground and covering both of her eyes with her hands, although she was being careful with holding her left eye due to the fury raptor throwing star still being stuck within the left eyeball.

As Venus is experiencing loads of discomfort and excruciating pain from her injury in her left eyeball and is fixed within Sapphire's headlock, with her left hand, Sapphire forces Venus to drink the remaining half of the blue potion that was within the glass container. Parrot also sprints across the main room and over to Sapphire and Venus near the big wooden table. Parrot leans over to pick up the anomaly crystal from the ground and holds it out in front of him as all the colours of the rainbow and shades of white and black swirl around the anomaly crystal; the anomaly crystal suddenly turns to a deep black colour as Parrot also has the blood of Grackle inside his body. Sapphire places the empty glass container on the ground, and with her left hand she hurriedly turns the book of curses that she had also put on the ground beside her. Sapphire quickly flickers through the pages within the book of curses until she reaches the page that possessed the curse of death spell written in animal's blood upon it. Sapphire now applies her knowledge from her PhD in ancient language and literature to understand, translate, and read the curse of death spell's text.

Raven manages to stand back on to his feet, and with the sword of Grackle firmly in his right hand, he thrusts the sword of Grackle into Triton's thick, strong chest, and then Raven pulls the sword of Grackle quickly back out of Triton's chest. Triton's lung becomes pierced from the sword of Grackle stabbing inside of his chest; Triton grabs his chest with his right arm as he gasps for breath. Raven compellingly kicks Triton in his chest where it was wounded by the sword of Grackle. Triton falls straight down to his knees. As Triton's sturdy knees fall downwards, it makes the ground beneath his knees crumble because of Triton's enormous physical strength in his muscles. Venus can barely see through her blurred vision out the corner of her right eye, although the right eye didn't have the fury raptor throwing star stuck in it. Venus's sensory perception is affected massively due to the excruciating pain she is still experiencing from her left eyeball being stabbed by the fury raptor throwing star.

Venus's heart now breaks into a million pieces as she observes Raven from her right eye's blurred vision. Raven swings the sword of Grackle out in front of him and chops off Triton's head with one stiff blow from the remarkable sword of Grackle. Triton's head is detached from his body and falls to the ground of the main room. Triton's detached head now spins across the ground as his headless strong muscular body also slowly falls on to the ground in front of him. Sapphire begins reading the curse of death spell aloud from the book of curses in the ancient Phoenix language, Sapphire speaks:

> Soul, Force, Energy, and Aura of Life,
> Creature, Human, or Nature's Sacrifice.

Parrot holds out the anomaly crystal steadily in his hands in front of him as Sapphire quickly releases Venus from the headlock of her arms. The anomaly crystal miraculously turns into a pure black colour all over, and it releases a thin pure black smoke from one edge of the anomaly crystal, which swiftly covers Venus entire body.

After the thin pure black smoke engulfs Venus's body, it inexplicably sucks her life force and soul from Venus's body, and then the thin pure black smoke filters away from Venus's body and returns to the anomaly crystal, where it also brings Venus's life force and soul deep inside it. As Venus's life force and soul are taken from her body, the white dove that Venus had also created previously by utilising her Animagus abilities, where the white dove was currently flying unassumingly over the Grass Terrain Field area that was located nearby Oak Village, also suddenly loses its life force and subconscious connection with Venus, which causes this white dove to fall harshly to the ground below to its death.

Venus's soulless body now falls in a lifeless manner to the ground in the main room; At the same time, another thin pure black smoke is wondrously released from the anomaly crystal again, and it expeditiously travels in the air across the main hall of Triton's Underground Dungeon. The pure thin black smoke travels to the other side of the main room where Emerald's body is currently laid on the ground; the thin black smoke now covers Emerald's entire dead body. As the pure thin black smoke finishes covering Emerald's dead body, Emerald's life force and soul is now passed from the pure thin black smoke and returned back into Emerald's dead body as the thin pure black smoke disappears within Emerald's body. Emerald feels a jolt of energy back in her body, and she starts to cough and breathe heavily and shockingly while attempting to sit up from the ground.

RAVEN DROPS THE sword of Grackle to the ground beneath him in shock and amazement after seeing the thin pure black smoke bring Emerald back to life from the dead. Raven rapidly sprints across the main room of Triton's Underground Dungeon over to Emerald, who is near at the entrance of the main hall. After reaching Emerald, Raven crouches to the ground and holds Emerald tightly within his arms once again upon the ground. Raven now sees Emerald's blue sparkly eyes looking back into his.

'I never thought I would see your beautiful eyes again,' says Raven with tears streaming down from his eyes.

'It's the will of the gods and our fates that have brought us back to each other, and we will always remain together, my dear Raven. Thank you for rescuing me again,' smiles Emerald as she draws a deep breath while feeling more relaxed, being held within Raven's arms. On the other side of the main room in Triton's Underground Dungeon, Parrot and Sapphire quickly pick up Venus's dead body together from the ground; Parrot carries Venus's head as Sapphire picks up Venus by her small feet. Parrot and Sapphire both carry Venus's body hurriedly to the closet lava pit and throw Venus's dead body to burn within this lava pit, which was embedded within the ground of this main room.

Parrot and Sapphire also dispose of Triton's chopped off head, golden chain with the spiked ball at the end of it, and dead body in the same way as Venus's body, especially as they wanted to give Raven and Emerald a moment to spend time with one another. Parrot disposed of Triton's chopped-off head and his golden chain with the spiked ball at the end of it in the embedded lava pit first. Parrot and Sapphire then struggle to carry Triton's bulky and muscly dead body over to the lava pit, but they eventually manage to roll Triton's huge dead body into this lava pit, and as the hot and steaming lava burns through Triton's dead body, fragments of fire spit out from the lava pit in front of Parrot and Sapphire. Parrot wipes his forearm across his hot and sweaty forehead; then Parrot and Sapphire walk across the main room of Triton's Underground Dungeon and over to Raven and Emerald who now have just managed to stand upon their feet while holding on to one another. Sapphire smiles brightly and squeezes Emerald tightly with a loving hug.

'I've missed you so much, Emerald. I knew Hake's curse of death spell would work in bringing you back to life. The bond and love between us humans is far too strong, and I think Hake knew that all along. Maybe Hake knew all of this would happen even from the beginning of time when Grackle, he, and all those other mystical creatures originally created the book of curses,' mentions Sapphire breathlessly, glistening with joy at the thought of Emerald living again.

'It's good to have you back with us again, Emerald. Fighting evil creatures hasn't been the same without you,' remarks Parrot as he also hugs Emerald and Sapphire at the same time.

'Thank you all so much for saving me as you have all risked your lives and those closest to you in a nearly impossible attempt to bring me back to life. I thought my soul would have been lost in that timeless and empty dark place for eternity,' cries Emerald, thinking back to some of the emotional and weird feelings she had subconsciously experienced when her soul was trapped within the anomaly crystal.

'You don't need to think about that again, Emerald. We're all safe now, and it will remain that way as soon as we make sure that the great war has ended in favour of us humans,' states Raven, kissing Emerald passionately upon her lips after Sapphire and Parrot release Sapphire from hugging her.

'We must hurry back to Falcon City, so we can try and help Lynx, Panther, Bruce, King Exodus, and all the other humans to become victorious in the great war,' remarks Parrot.

'Do you think they are fighting against Viper and his Serpents now?' asks Sapphire worriedly.

'Viper, that evil creature that killed your parents, Raven?' asks Emerald with an angry expression as Parrot and Sapphire stop kissing each other.

'Yes, we think that Viper joined forces with Triton and Venus recently and has now enforced the great war against the humans at Falcon City,' replies Raven, looking at Emerald.

'We must go and destroy Viper at Falcon City and forever rid the Planet of Phoenix from his sinful presence,' comments Emerald feistily. Parrot opens his hand to look at the anomaly crystal that currently had all of the colours of the rainbow and the shades of white and black frantically swirling around it.

'What of the anomaly crystal? This could come in considerable use to us against Viper and his Serpents during the great war,' says Parrot.

'We should destroy the anomaly crystal! We can't allow another great war to ever be caused again by such a powerful artefact,' suggests Sapphire as she grabs the anomaly crystal from Parrot's hand, and without hesitation she chucks it into the closest lava pit that was embedded within the main room of Triton's Underground Dungeon. As the anomaly crystal lands in the embedded lava pit, the lava's intense and ferocious heat burns through the anomaly crystal. Nothing happens for the first few seconds of the anomaly crystal being within the lava pit, but then the overpowering heat of the lava manages to disintegrate the anomaly crystal's resilient crystal.

As the anomaly crystal begins disintegrating because of the intense temperature of the lava, the anomaly crystal releases bright and sparkling flashes that consist of all the colours of the rainbow and the shades of white and black; these colourful bright and sparkling flashes shine in the air within the main room of Triton's Underground Dungeon, where Raven, Emerald, Parrot, and Sapphire watch on in astonishment this supernatural spectacle. The colourful bright and sparkling flashes continue lighting up the main room of Triton's Underground Dungeon in different colours for a few moments, until the entire anomaly crystal is completely destroyed from the Planet of Phoenix.

'You're right. We will defeat these creatures not by magic and curses, but by the human love, strength, and honour,' states Raven as the remaining colours of the rainbow and the shades of black and white stop lighting up the main room.

Raven and Parrot hurry through the main room of Triton's Underground Dungeon to collect the weapons that they had used and left in different locations while battling against Triton and Venus. After Raven and Parrot collect all their weapons, they return to Emerald and Sapphire near the main entrance of the main room. Raven holds one of Emerald's hand, and in the other hand, he holds both his sword and shield of Grackle. Parrot carries his wooden bow and wooden arrows with the metal spikes at the end of them around his back and pouch attached to his back as well as a few remaining fury raptor throwing stars left within his big brown coat pocket.

Sapphire is still holding on to the brown leather bag that has the book of curses and her silver dagger left within it. Raven, Emerald, Parrot, and Sapphire all find the energy within themselves to swiftly run out of the entrance to the main room and straight up through the long and narrow passageway that led above the ground to the rocky surface of the Realm of Deserted Lands located above Triton's Underground Dungeon.

As Raven, Emerald, Parrot, and Sapphire make it out of the long and narrow passageway in the Realm of Deserted Lands, Felix kicks his large black hooves high up in the air as he sees Emerald alive again and running out of the passage that connected to Triton's Underground Dungeon. Emerald happily runs straight over to Felix and pats him softly on the back of his black neck hair as Felix places his hooves back upon the rocky ground over the Realm of Deserted Lands. Raven also runs up to Felix, and he helps Emerald climb back on top of Felix's large black back. Raven also climbs on top of Felix's back; at the same time, Parrot and Sapphire unfix the brown rope reins of Felix and their black horse that were lodged underneath the small pile of hard rocks where they had left the horses earlier.

After removing Felix's and the black horse's rope reins from the small pile of rocks, Parrot passes the brown rope reins for Felix to Raven's hand as Raven and Emerald were now sitting firmly upon Felix's large back. Sapphire had also climbed on to their black horse, and Parrot passes Sapphire the rope reins of their black horse to hold before he climbs on to this black horse's big back. Parrot takes the rope reins back from Sapphire's hands. Raven and Parrot now kick their feet into the sides of both their horses, which makes Felix and the black horse find the power in their muscly legs to start galloping swiftly in the east direction in order to leave the Realm of Deserted Lands and head towards the Kingdom of Humans in the south-east area of the Planet of Phoenix, where Falcon City is located.

Thirty-Six

FALCOLN CITY IS now covered with black dust, broken brick and stone rubble, along with an abundance of dead bodies of the royal Falcon guards, Falcon City humans, Pine guards, men Pine villagers, Willow guards, and the Serpent creatures everywhere, especially over the various stone paths that interlink the enormous Falcon City. During the epic battle in the unforgettable great war, all the 200 Pine guards and men Pine villagers including Lynx and Bruce were killed. Panther and his fourteen Willow guards were also killed during the great war, along with 437 royal Falcon guards, 700 Falcon City men, as well as 500 women and children Falcon City humans. Princess Petal's handmaid and Gaius's partner Lily was killed. Due to the large number of humans being killed during the great war, the number of survivors that were left within Falcon City were sixty-three royal Falcon guards and 800 Falcon City men, women, and children. King Exodus, Princess Petal, and the royal Falcon Captain Gaius also survived the fierce battle that occurred during the great war.

All the 800 Serpents, along with the obnoxious leader Viper, were completely destroyed during the great war, which meant that the last remaining army of creatures that resided upon the Planet of Phones was now extinct. The remaining men, women, and children that survived the great war within Falcon City were happy to have not been murdered by the Serpents, but they will also be tormented for the rest of their lives by some of the awful experiences they had to endure during the great war.

Although these Falcon City men, women, and children remain devastated due to mourning for their recently murdered family, friends, and fellow humans, they follow the orders by King Exodus that is to start helping to clean up Falcon City in case any Serpent warriors were not completely dead as well as to make sure that none of the broken rubble could cause accidents for any of the surviving Falcon City children. These Falcon City humans immediately begin to remove the broken rubble that is currently upon the stone paths throughout Falcon City. To clean the entire amount of broken rubble throughout Falcon City it will take numerous hours and will require all the humans to help one another in lifting up the heavy pieces of rubble and place them into large metal containers in order for the stone masons and builders to rebuild the broken houses and shops. Also, Falcon City humans start searching the broken-down houses, shops, and wooden boats near Nautilus Lake and other locations to salvage weapons and resources that were involved or used during the great war within Falcon City.

The remaining 437 royal Falcon guards also begin helping to sort out the chaos that was created by the great war that occurred within Falcon City. Most of the royal Falcon guards congregate at the magnificent Falcon Castle to either collect the dead bodies of Viper and the Serpents or the royal Falcon guards that lie lifeless within the great hall of Falcon Castle. These creatures' corpses and the dead bodies of royal Falcon guards were placed upon medium-sized metal carts attached to four metal wheels that were pulled by strong ropes that were attached to horses. The bodies of Viper and the Serpents are quickly burnt to ash in large, deep ditches that had been newly dug by some of Falcon City men just outside of the large, solid grey-and-white stone wall of Falcon City in the north-east direction, which was ordered by Gaius in order to get rid of numerous creatures' bodies that lay rotting within Falcon City.

As the Serpents' corpses were being burnt, other royal Falcon guards carefully and sympathetically gather the dead bodies of royal Falcon guards from the great hall within Falcon Castle and place these dead bodies on to separate metal carts upon metal wheels and pulled by horses. Just as the royal Falcon guards' dead bodies from the great hall of Falcon Castle are being collected by the surviving royal Falcon guards, the bodies of all the dead humans throughout Falcon City's plentiful brick buildings and stone paths are gathered and placed on to metal carts attached to metal wheels and pulled by horses. These humans were countless other royal Falcon guards and Falcon City humans including Bruce, Nia, Falcon City priest, and Falcon University lecturers that were also murdered by a couple of the Serpents at Falcon University during the great war.

It takes many hours in the hot and bright sun at its peak in the sky of the Planet of Phoenix for the surviving royal Falcon guards and Falcon City humans to carefully gather all the dead humans throughout Falcon City. Most of these humans' dead bodies are transported and buried within the main Falcon Graveyard and Crematorium that resided next to the prodigious Falcon Church located inside the large, solid grey-and-white stone wall of Falcon City in the furthest east direction.

Falcon City had other smaller graveyards and crematoriums adjacent to smaller Falcon City churches in different areas of Falcon City where many other Falcon City humans that were of a low status were buried, but Falcon City Graveyard and Crematorium that was located in the furthest east direction of Falcon City was the main one and was the final resting place for all of the royal Falcon City guards and other Falcon City humans who were of a high status, which also included Falcon City priest and university lecturers, along with Bruce and Nia. The dead bodies of these brave and honourable Falcon City royal Falcon guards and humans that were of high status who had untimely lost their lives during the great war are transported across the long stone paths throughout Falcon City by royal Falcon guards riding upon the strong horses that pulled the metal carts upon the metal wheels towards Falcon Graveyard and Crematorium in the far east direction.

The surviving humans respectfully place various types of flowers, clothing, and jewellery upon the dead bodies of family and friends that lay on these metal carts upon metal wheels as a sign of respect and sorrow for their departed loved ones. The collating, transporting, and spiritually burying of the royal Falcon guards and all types of Falcon City humans at these Falcon City graveyards and crematoriums throughout Falcon City takes numerous heart-whelming hours and is a tragic sight for any surviving human to witness.

During the clean-up of Falcon City and the search for the dead humans' bodies, the royal Falcon guards find only Lynx's silver crown, silver sword, and shield from one of the stone paths at the bottom of the stone path hill that was located near the big iron portcullis in the middle of Falcon City. They are shocked to not discover Lynx's human body but realise sadly that his entire body was completely disintegrated by Viper's intoxicating black and deadly poisonous venom. These royal Falcon guards collect Lynx's remaining belongings as well as Panther's dead body that was laid across the stone path in the same location as Lynx's belongings, along with Nerolus's and Tamika's dead bodies that were found within their home in the south-west direction of Falcon City, and also Lily's dead body, which was transported earlier from Falcon Castle. These are all brought pragmatically to wait outside Grand Falcon Tomb, accompanied by some of the royal Falcon guards.

It was decided that Flame's sword that had Flame's name carved upon the handle and was found lying on the floor within Falcon University should also be buried in the same limestone tomb that Lynx's belongings were going to be placed in within Grand Falcon Tomb, because Flame was one of Lynx's most trusted Pine guards. Grand Falcon Tomb was located in the far south direction of Falcon City behind Falcon Castle and Falcon University. The dead bodies of Lynx, Panther, Lily, Nerolus, and Tamika were specially brought to Grand Falcon Tomb to be laid within Grand Falcon Tomb as their final resting place as they were related to or involved with the royal kings and queens of Falcon City.

KING EXODUS, PRINCESS Petal, and Gaius took some time to clean themselves up after fighting in the great war within the great hall of Falcon Castle due to them all being covered in blood from their killings of the Serpents they had fought against. Their energy was also depleted. King Exodus and Gaius had also given appropriate orders to the royal Falcon guards and Falcon City humans directing them how to recover and tidy up Falcon City efficiently and rationally. During the clean-up period of Falcon City, which took several hours, King Exodus, Princess Petal, and Gaius also required some personal moments in order to deal with their grief and thoughts of losing countless fellow humans and friends that also included those that they loved such as Princess Petal's handmaid and Gaius's partner Lily as well as Gaius's parents Nerolus and Tamika, along with King Exodus's loyal friend Panther and Princess Petal's affections for the leader of Pine Village, Lynx.

The news with regards to the deaths of Lynx, Panther, as well as Nerolus and Tamika had come to King Exodus, Princess Petal, and Gaius from some of the royal Falcon guards who had found their dead bodies and sent this information via other royal Falcon guards to Falcon Castle. After hearing such tragic and heart-rending information, King Exodus, Princess Petal, and Gaius were deeply devastated and spent some time comforting one another.

After about an hour of hearing this tragic news, they decided to leave Falcon Castle and travel together on horseback across the stone paths in the furthest south direction of Falcon City towards Grand Falcon Tomb. The news from the royal Falcon guards explained that the dead bodies of Lynx, Panther, Nerolus, and Tamika would be taken to Grand Falcon Tomb, and Princess Petal felt it would be appropriate to say their heartfelt goodbyes now to Panther's, Nerolus's, Tamika's, and Lily's dead bodies that were waiting and accompanied by royal Falcon guards outside Grand Falcon Tomb, along with Lynx's silver crown, silver sword, and shield.

Grand Falcon Tomb had been specifically constructed with white limestone in the shape of a large cave that was separated inside into different chambers; it was initially built over 150 years ago when King Primus first ruled over Falcon City and wanted a special memorial place for when the death of his ancestors unfortunately occurred. Thus King Primus's royal Falcon guards built this Grand Falcon Tomb only for bloodline royalty or extended related family and lovers to the royal kings and queens that ruled over Falcon City. Certain sections of Grand Falcon Tomb were also used for high-status humans such as royal Falcon captains, councillors, and advisors; these humans were also entitled to be buried within Grand Falcon Tomb.

King Primus and his wife Queen Solar, along with their extended family ancestors and close councillors and advisors, had been already buried within one of the sectioned resting chambers inside Grand Falcon Tomb. This was also the case for King Zunus, his wife Queen Rainbow, and extended family ancestors that included Lynx's great-grandfather Dominous as he was the main councillor to King Zunus and Dominous's wife Cosmika was also King Zunus's cousin. Lynx's grandfather Sharkus and his wife Melody were also buried in another sectioned resting chamber within Grand Falcon Tomb, because previously Sharkus was a royal Falcon captain to King Zunus, and within Sharkus and Melody's sectioned resting chambers were the ashes of Lynx's parents Saber and Lunar as Saber was also another royal Falcon captain to King Exodus as well as being related to Sharkus and Melody, who were already buried there.

King Exodus, Princess Petal, and Gaius now arrive at the front of the marvellously designed Grand Falcon Tomb; as they approach the entrance of Grand Falcon Tomb, their hearts become overwhelmed on seeing the dead bodies of their family, friends, and loved ones lying within one of the metal carts upon metal wheels. After some moments of overwhelming emotions and gloomy silence, King Exodus, Princess Petal, and Gaius climb down from their horses and are escorted by nine of the royal Falcon guards that were kindly carrying Lynx's silver crown, silver sword, and shield as well as Flame's sword. They are holding the heads and feet of Panther's, Lily's, Nerolus's, and Tamika's dead bodies at a big white limestone door positioned at the front of Grand Falcon Tomb that has the symbol of a falcon bird engraved upon it.

King Exodus holds Princess Petal's hand as they enter through a big white limestone door and continue down a long, dark, and narrow passageway that is lighted by candles and lanterns of various sizes located throughout the entire network of passageways within Grand Falcon Tomb. King Exodus, Princess Petal, Gaius, and the royal Falcon guards that were carrying the dead bodies walk slowly along these narrow passageways. Grand Falcon Tomb has different sections that break away into other narrow passageways that lead down to different sectioned resting chambers within Grand Falcon Tomb. The sectioned resting chambers were designed as a large chamber that would be the resting place for each of the Falcon kings and queens that ruled over Falcon City, along with their extended family ancestors, lovers, royal Falcon captains, close councillors, and advisers.

The royal Falcon guards continue carrying Lynx's silver crown, silver sword, and shield as well as Flame's sword and dead bodies of Panther, Lily, Nerolus, and Tamika as they follow King Exodus, Princess Petal, and Gaius through one of the narrow passageways until they all reach the sectioned resting chamber room for King Exodus, which was located deep within Grand Falcon Tomb in the right area at the end of the Falcon Tomb. King Exodus's sectioned resting chamber room displayed large colourful wax candles and dried rainbow roses in marble vases as well as Queen Eclipse's dead body who was King Exodus's wife and Princess Petal's mother, which was already laid to rest within one of the big limestone tombs that was closed by a limestone lid.

Lynx's silver crown, silver sword, and shield as well as Flame's sword, along with Panther's, Lily's, Nerolus', and Tamika's dead bodies are all softly placed by the royal Falcon guards into the individual different empty limestone tombs within King Exodus's sectioned resting chamber. Nerolus's and Tamika's dead bodies are buried together within the same limestone tomb and closed with the limestone lid by Gaius. After the royal Falcon guards had placed all of these humans' dead bodies inside of the limestone tombs and closed the limestone lids of these tombs, the royal Falcon guards leave King Exodus's sectioned resting chamber and exit Grand Falcon Tomb through the narrow passageways that they had just walked through.

'Goodbye, Lynx, the renowned leader of Pine Village and ex-captain to the royal Falcon guard. Your leadership, courage, and bravery will always be remembered and admired. Although your physical body is not resting within Grand Falcon Tomb, your soul force and spirit will physically exist in the afterlife where you will be finally reunited with your much-loved parents Saber and Lunar. Farewell, Panther, the noble leader of Willow Village. Your reign as the leader of Willow Village was gallant and will never be forgotten. You were also very honourable and loyal during the time you served me in the royal Falcon guards, and we shared many cheerful and adventurous memories together. You will now join your dearly missed brother Saber, along with your family of admirable humans who had served my king fathers of Falcon City before me. I'm sure your father Sharkus and his wife melody, along with your grandfather Dominous and his wife Cosmika, will be very glad to see you again in heaven,' states King Exodus as he begins lighting three large colourful wax candles by positioning another already lighted wax candle that he had taken from a golden stand in the middle of his sectioned resting chamber on top of these three unlit wax candles. Once King Exodus has finished lighting all three wax candles, he places the already lighted candle back upon its golden stand in the middle of his sectioned resting chamber.

One of these large colourful wax candles is for Lynx, and this large colourful wax candle was already placed at the top end of his big limestone tomb; the other colourful wax candle is for Panther, which was again already placed at the top end of his big limestone tomb. King Exodus now sadly leaves his sectioned resting chamber after lighting the third colourful candle that was at the top end of another limestone tomb that was for his late wife Queen Eclipse. King Exodus also picks and places a few dried rainbow roses' petals upon the top of Queen Eclipses' limestone tomb lid as the rainbow roses were her favourite when she was alive.

'Goodbye, Lynx. I hope you are blessed with much-deserved eternal happiness in the blissful peace of heaven as your time living upon the Planet of Phoenix had sometimes been filled with unfortunate sorrow. I will seek to find you one day in heaven when we are reunited again, for our time on the Planet of Phoenix with one another was too brief, although it had so much meaning within my heart as I hope it did in your heart too,' says Princess Petal tearfully as she puts her right hand upon Lynx's limestone tomb lid. Princess Petals now also takes the already lit wax candle from the golden stand in the middle of the sectioned resting chamber and lights another spare colourful wax candle for Lynx and then places this colourful wax candle at the top end of Lynx's limestone tomb next to King Exodus's recently lit colourful wax candle. Princess Petal then passes the already lit colourful wax candle to Gaius. Princess Petal pauses for a moment and looks behind her as she also leaves King Exodus's sectioned resting chamber and then holds tightly on to King Exodus's hand as they continue walking back through the narrow passageway until they exit through the big white limestone door of Grand Falcon Tomb.

'My loving parents, you had kindly put up with my negative behaviour while I was growing up. From your advice, support, and guidance you have aided me to becoming the developed human I am today. I will always be very thankful to you both for all you have done for me, and of course I will miss you dearly,' says Gaius at his parents' limestone tomb before he turns to face Lily's limestone tomb that was next to Nerolus and Tamika's. 'Lily, my sweetheart, we found love when my life and mind was broken. From your kind, compassionate manner and characteristics you also helped me change from the human I was to who I am now. You mean the world to me, and now my heart is broken since we have been parted from one another too early in our relationship. I will continue to make you proud, until we are reunited again in heaven. My thoughts and love are with you always,' cries Gaius softly as he also lights two colourful wax candles, one for Nerolus and Tamika and the second for Lily; these colourful wax candles were already positioned at the top end of their limestone tombs. Gaius places the already lit colourful wax candle back upon the golden stand within the middle of King Exodus's sectioned resting chamber, and then Gaius continues walking despondently until he also exits Grand Falcon Tomb.

RAVEN AND EMERALD are currently riding speedily on top of Felix's large black back. Raven is controlling Felix's journey towards Falcon City in the east direction via his brown rope reins, and Emerald is holding on tightly to Raven's waist as well as grasping on to the sword and shield of Grackle. Raven and Emerald are travelling with Parrot, who has his wooden bow and wooden arrows with metal spikes at the end of them around his back, along with Sapphire, who also has the book of curses and her silver dagger securely inside of the brown leather bag, which she carried around her neck as they both are riding on their black horse swiftly across the Grass Terrain Fields in the east direction of the Planet of Phoenix. After three hours of rapid travelling in the heat of the sun and humid atmosphere, they eventually reach the splendid Kingdom of Humans that covered the massive area in the furthest south-east direction of the Planet of Phoenix, which also had the grand Falcon City located within it.

As Raven, Emerald, Parrot, and Sapphire approach the Kingdom of Humans, they all quickly and shockingly notice from a distance some of the destruction at Falcon City, especially the overturned big wooden boats at Nautilus Lake that had all occurred during the great war. Parrot grinds his teeth and kicks the sides of his black horse to gallop faster, just as Raven does to Felix, and both of these horses utilise the immense power within their leg muscles and stride furiously around the Kingdom of Humans in the north-east direction, heading towards the front of Falcon City where the big iron portcullis entrance is located.

After another thirty minutes of speedy galloping, Raven and Emerald on top of Felix, along with Parrot and Sapphire on top of their black horse, come close to the big iron portcullis that had already been lifted up from the ground as the royal Falcon guards needed to continuously enter in and out of Falcon City when they were disposing of the Serpents' corpses inside the large deep ditch that had recently been dug outside the large, solid grey-and-white stone wall in the north-east direction. Raven and Emerald continue riding upon Felix up to one of the royal Falcon guards who was at present with another royal Falcon guard and they were both sitting on top of two white horses that were pulling one of the metal carts upon metal wheels with several Serpents' corpses within it towards the large deep ditch.

'Where can we find King Exodus of Falcon City?' asks Raven while anxiously looking at the Serpents' corpses that were covered with numerous stab wounds and smeared with blood within the metal carts attached to the metal wheels.

'I believe King Exodus is currently at Grand Falcon Tomb laying to rest some of his cherished humans that were regrettably killed during the great war,' replies the royal Falcon guard who also had bloodstains upon his face.

'The great war has already happened at Falcon City? Has the great war now ended in the humans' favour?' asks Parrot eagerly as he rides up with Sapphire upon his black horse and stops the black horse next to Raven and Emerald sitting upon Felix and faces these royal Falcon guards.

'Yes, fortunately the great war has now finished, and the humans were indeed victorious, but this victory comes with the cost of losing countless innocent human lives. The great war lasted for many hours and was extremely tough and brutal, but the glorious gods were watching over us during our greatest hour of need, and they mercifully helped us prevail against such evil creatures,' remarks the other royal Falcon guard that was also upon one of the white horses that had just stopped pulling the metal cart with the metal wheels attached to it.

'Those poor Falcon City humans have lost their lives,' mentions Sapphire while thinking about how many humans had to suffer a terrible death during the great war that happened at Falcon City.

'Finally the demise of creatures has rightfully come to pass. No longer will any humans suffer horrible fates from those treacherous beasts,' states Emerald with fury in her eyes, thinking about all the harm that the creatures who existed upon the Planet of Phoenix had caused the humans for many centuries.

'Where can we find Grand Falcon Tomb?' asks Parrot.

'Head south-east down the stone paths of Falcon City, and you will see Grand Falcon Tomb along your way. Once you have reached Falcon University, it's behind this building and Grand Falcon Tomb is in the shape of a big white limestone cave,' replies one of the royal Falcon guards.

'Yes, I remember Grand Falcon Tomb being behind Falcon University. Maybe we could also go to Falcon University so that I might be able to see my friend Nia there again as it's been a long time since we have spent valued time with one another,' says Sapphire, smiling slightly at the thoughts of seeing Nia again.

'Yes, of course we can go visit Falcon University after we go to Grand Falcon Tomb as it will also be nice for me to see Nia again after all these years,' replies Parrot.

'Thank you for your help. We must go to Grand Falcon Tomb now and catch up from what we have missed with regards to the great war during our absence,' mentions Raven.

Raven taps his heels into the sides of Felix and begins riding with Emerald upon Felix again, just as Parrot and Sapphire also do upon their black horse. Raven, Emerald, Parrot, and Sapphire ride past the two royal Falcon guards upon their white horses that just starts pulling the metal cart attached to the metal wheels again and continue trotting through the big iron portcullis that leads on to the stone paths of Falcon City. As they all continue trotting further within Falcon City across the stone paths in the south-east direction towards Grand Falcon Tomb, Raven, Emerald, and Parrot admire the large stylish and developed brick buildings as well as the monumental royal statues that are fixed upon the stone paths in several different areas of Falcon City, having never visited Falcon City before.

As they trot further into Falcon City on their way to Grand Falcon Tomb, they also excitedly notice the elegant and Falcon Castle they see in the distance; although they are in wonder with regards to the splendid sights within Falcon City, they quickly become saddened after seeing some of dead Falcon City humans that were still being carefully picked up from the stone paths by some of the royal Falcon guards and were placed inside of the metal carts on metal wheels, ready to be transported to one of the smaller Falcon graveyards and crematoriums within Falcon City. Emerald and Sapphire become sensitive after witnessing the expressive emotions from some of Falcon City women and children, who were currently kneeling on the stone paths of Falcon City to mourn their loved ones or pray to the gods in remorse.

After roughly fifteen minutes of trotting down the interlinking stone paths in the south-east direction of Falcon City, Raven and Emerald trotting upon Felix, Parrot and Sapphire trotting upon their black horse now reach Grand Falcon Tomb behind Falcon University. In the near distance, they see King Exodus, Princess Petal, and nine royal Falcon guards now standing outside the big white limestone entrance door of the Great Falcon Tomb, where they were all waiting in morbid silence. Once they trot closer to King Exodus, Princess Petal, and the nine royal Falcon guards, Raven and Emerald climb down from Felix's big black back as Parrot and Sapphire also climb down from their black horse's strong back. Raven holds on to the rope reins of Felix and the black horse, while Parrot walks up to King Exodus, whom he recognises as being the King of Falcon City due to King Exodus wearing a gold crown and gold-plated knighthood armour. Parrot kneels in front of King Exodus before he stands back up and respectfully speaks to him.

'King Exodus of Falcon City, my name is Parrot. I am accompanied by my partner Sapphire, cousin Raven, and his wife Emerald. We are very sorry and shaken to see what has happened to Falcon City during the great war and offer our deepest condolences to those worthy humans that have lost their lives this day. Have you spoken with my best friend Lynx who is the leader of Pine Village and his uncle Panther who is the leader of Willow Village? We received no words nor were we met by them at the Realm of Deserted Lands as arranged previously,' asks Parrot humbly. King Exodus pauses for a moment while looking forlornly at Parrot, Sapphire, Raven, and Emerald.

'Parrot, Sapphire, Raven, and especially Emerald, we gladly welcome you all to Falcon City. We are all very pleased that you have also indeed survived the great war and have now made it back here safe. Yes, Parrot, I spoke with Lynx and Panther earlier this day after they arrived in Falcon City, where they informed me about the recent battles you had endured at your villages in the northern side of the Planet of Phoenix. That came as a great shock to Falcon City. I certainly granted Lynx's and Panther's desire to aid you in returning Emerald's life back to her by destroying Triton and Venus at the Realm of Deserted Lands, but just as they were leaving Falcon City to meet up with you in the Realm of Deserted Lands as planned, we were lamentably attacked by Viper and his Serpents, who initially started the great war within Falcon City.

'All my royal Falcon guards, Falcon City humans, and the brave Pine and Willow guards and villagers fought their hardest and most gallantly against those evil creatures in an uncontrollable battle that lasted for many hours. Unfortunately, hundreds of humans did not survive and are now not able to finally see the unity of humans upon the Planet of Phoenix being victorious in the great war of our time. Including those humans that did not survive the great war, I'm tremendously sorry to speak that Lynx and Panther were also killed. We have placed their bodies in my family's resting chamber within Grand Falcon Tomb to be reunited with their ancestors, where they will also always be remembered throughout the ages for their bravery and courage during these dark days upon the Planet of Phoenix we have experienced against the creatures,' explains King Exodus with much sympathy in the tone of his voice. After hearing the upsetting and shocking news with regards to Lynx's death within the great war, Parrot begins to shed tears down his cheeks. Parrot turns to hug Sapphire firmly.

'I'm very sorry, Parrot. Lynx was one of those admirable and moral humans that has ever lived upon the Planet of Phoenix. He will be deeply missed by every human. We will share much-needed comfort in our friends Nia and Bruce, who will help us through this difficult situation,' says Sapphire softly into one of Parrot's ear.

'Hello, Parrot and Sapphire, my name is Princess Petal, and it's wonderful to meet you both, although under unfortunate circumstances. I'm deeply upset to understand that you were also very close to Lynx and now will have to endure and suffer at the knowledge of his death, just as I will also have to bear myself. I can see how devastated you both already are, and this would certainly not be the best time to share more knowledge with you, but then again I don't think that there will ever be a good time for this kind of information to be shared. Am I right in saying that I heard you mention the names of Nia and Bruce?' asks Princess Petal caringly.

'It's also nice to finally meet you, Princess Petal. Lynx had mentioned about you to us on several occasions, and thank you for your kind-hearted words. Lynx's death will indeed take a very long time for our hearts to recover from. Yes, Bruce and Nia our also our childhood friends,' replies Parrot while tears still keep rolling from his eyes as he stops hugging Sapphire and turns back around to look at King Exodus and now Princess Petal.

'Bruce had travelled from Pine Village along with Lynx and Panther to fight in the great war, and my friend Nia would still have been living at Falcon University. I also used to attend Falcon City with Nia but haven't managed to speak with her in the last couple of months. Do you know where they are now? Are they both all right?' asks Sapphire nervously while looking at Princess Petal with concern in her eyes.

'My heart bleeds for you both with regards to the information that I have to share with you now, but I was looking at the list made by the royal Falcon guards of those humans that were killed during the great war. I remember seeing Bruce's and Nia's names in the list of the deaths that occurred at Falcon University. From being on this list, both Bruce and Nia would have been taken to be buried at Falcon Graveyard attached to the main Falcon Church located in the furthest east direction of Falcon City. My deepest sympathies go out to you both,' unhappily mentions Princess Petal to Parrot and Sapphire.

'Oh dear God, to hear of Lynx's passing and now the knowledge of my best friend Nia and Parrot's childhood friend Bruce, along with the loss of both of our parents from the battles within Pine and

Willow Village, I don't know how I will be able to cope with all this,' cries Sapphire hysterically.

'Why has such cruel fate happened to those kind people who were the closest in our lives?' weeps Parrot as he turns to hug Sapphire strongly again. King Exodus and Princess Petal stay silent as they couldn't find the words to express how sorry they truly felt for both Parrot and Sapphire. Raven and Emerald quickly walk up behind Parrot and Sapphire and touch them both on the shoulders in comfort as Parrot and Sapphire continue hugging each other.

'I'm truly sorry, Parrot and Sapphire. I just only wish that so many bad things didn't happen because of the great war against the creatures from the Planet of Phoenix. Emerald and I will always be here to help you through this awful situation, just as you have been there for us,' calmly says Raven as he grabs hard on to one of Parrot's shoulder in security.

'Yes, you can always count on us as we had done on you. We are all the closest of family members now, and our love and care for one another will provide us with the strength to carry on living through these most darkest of situations,' softly whispers Emerald as she also hugs Sapphire from behind and then turns to look at Princess Petal as Princess Petal just makes eye contact with her.

'Although, we have had so much devastating news this day, my heart warms to see that you, Emerald, you have now been restored back to being alive. Lynx spoke to us about what happened to you during the battle of Eagle Forest. It's incredible to see that the curse of death spell that sorcerer Hake told you about from the book of curses has favourably worked in bringing Emerald back from the dead. That is something that I am most thankful to our gods for,' smiles Princess Petal as she moves over to hug Emerald. After a few moments of respectful silence, King Exodus feels it is best to ask further questions with regards to what Raven, Emerald, Parrot, and Sapphire experienced at the Realm of Deserted Lands.

'Triton and Venus, do you know where they are now?' asks King Exodus patiently.

'I finally killed that beast creature Triton at his Underground Dungeon located deep in the south-west direction in the Realm of Deserted Lands. I sliced off Triton's head with the almighty sword of Grackle. Parrot and Sapphire then utilised the anomaly crystal to take Triton's mistress Venus's life force that fortunately brought Emerald's soul back from the afterlife and returned her to me. That was what Hake said the curse of death would do,' answers Raven as he bows in front of King Exodus.

'The knowledge of Triton's and Venus's death is also very pleasing to be shared,' says Princess Petal as she stops hugging Emerald.

'You all are worthy of being made lords of the Planet of Phoenix. You four have once and for all stopped those most evilest of creatures that had threatened the existence of us humans for many decades,' states King Exodus as he smiles at Raven and Emerald.

'The wondrous anomaly crystal that I have only recently learnt about and has so many strange and extraordinary things, what has happened to it?' asks Princess Petal curiously.

'I destroyed the anomaly crystal in one of the lava pits inside Triton's Underground Dungeon so no creature or human will ever be able to wield such strong magical and elemental power again,' says Sapphire, still sobbing and holding tightly on to Parrot.

'Yes, that does sound like the right thing to have been done to the anomaly crystal. Let's hope that peace and fortune will be restored to all of us humans now that the great war has finally passed. I am still truly sorry about your friends, Parrot and Sapphire, as well as for Lynx and Panther as I understand how much they all meant to you, just as they did to my father and me. There's one other thing that you should also know about Lynx,' mentions Princess Petal.

'I don't think I could take hearing no more distressing news at this time,' comments Parrot.

'I know it's tough for all of you to hear, but unfortunately, Lynx's physical body was disintegrated completely from what we believe to be Viper's poisonous venom. So only his belongings of his Pine Village crown, sword, and shield could be placed within one of the limestone tombs inside of Grand Falcon Tomb,' mentions Princess Petal gently.

'Yes, indeed that evil creature Viper's venom that could have disintegrated Lynx's physical body as the same thing happened to both of my parents in the past,' remarks Raven.

'It's a horrible end to the physical human body, but we know that Lynx's soul and life force will indeed exist eternally in heaven. You all have our permission to visit Lynx and Panther for as long as you like within Grand Falcon Tomb, just as soon as the royal Falcon captain leaves my father's resting chamber. I hope Emerald will also be glad to see the royal Falcon captain,' reveals Princess Petal as Emerald looks at Princess Petal in a curious manner, while Princess Petal smiles back at Emerald.

A second passes, and then the royal Falcon captain Gaius walks out of the big white limestone entrance door of the Great Falcon Tomb, and as he looks straight out in front of him in sparkling sun light, Gaius fortunately sees his daughter Emerald for the first time in three years. Gaius gazes at Emerald's beautiful and elegant appearance and smiles happily at her; although Gaius is still very upset from the recent loss of his partner Lily, he's exceedingly glad to see his daughter alive again. Gaius stops walking just in front of Emerald as Gaius becomes unsure of how Emerald will react to him due to the manner in which Gaius had left Emerald and Ruby back in Oak Village three years ago. After a moment's pause, Emerald hurries up to Gaius and gives him an excessive hug.

'Father, it's so good to see you again. It felt like forever that we've seen one another, and I have been so upset ever since that day that you left Oak Village,' remarks Emerald with both joy but also sorrow, as she stops hugging Gaius and looks at him.

'Emerald, I can't believe that you have turned into such a wonderful young lady, and I thought that I would never get to see you again, especially after what Lynx told us about what had happened to you during the battle of Eagle Forest. That information broke my heart to a million pieces as I never stopped loving you or being your father, although we did indeed live in different locations for a few years. It overwhelms me that you are pleased to see me as I am truthfully sorry for the pain that I caused to you when I left Ruby in the past. It's a complicated story that I will explain to you another time. How is your mother?' asks Gaius.

'Ruby was regrettably killed by Venus back in Oak Village just more than one day ago,' cries Emerald as thinks more about her mother's death and then continues to hug her father Gaius again for comfort.

'That's terrible news about Ruby. My heart, just like so many of us humans' hearts, is filled with so much hurt and grief this day. I promise I will now be here to help you, my daughter, through whatever comes next,' miserably responds Gaius as he holds on to Emerald caringly.

'Come, Raven, Parrot, and Sapphire, I will show you to the sectioned resting chamber where Lynx's belongings as well as Panther's dead body now rest in peace within the limestone tombs inside of Grand Falcon Tomb. You will be able to pay your respects and say your goodbyes to them both. That I think will help to give a little bit of closure.' says Princess Petal as she starts to lead Raven, along with devastated Parrot and Sapphire, through the big white limestone entrance door into Grand Falcon Tomb. Emerald and Gaius remain outside of Grand Falcon Tomb hugging each other, while King Exodus and the nine royal Falcon guards slowly saddle upon their horses and begin travelling back across the stone paths in the north direction towards the middle of Falcon City in order to continue with the restoration of Falcon City following the anarchy caused by the great war.

Thirty-Seven

TWO WEEKS HAVE now passed since the epic great war that occurred between the humans and creatures within the magnificent Falcon City residing in the south-east corner of the Planet of Phoenix. In these past two weeks, King Exodus, Gaius, and his remaining sixty-three royal Falcon guards and 800 Falcon City humans, along with Princess Petal, Raven, Emerald, Parrot, and Sapphire have all been very busy in helping in the clean-up of the stone and brick rubble that was laid upon the stone paths throughout Falcon City.

During the restoration of Falcon City, King Exodus and Princess Petal organised the burying, cremating, and laying to rest with a well-deserved send-off to the heavens for those close family and friends of Falcon City humans that were killed during the great war by Viper and his Serpents. The dead royal Falcon guards and Falcon City humans were either buried or cremated within the various Falcon City churches' graveyards or crematoriums that were located in different sections of Falcon City. Also in these two weeks, the royal Falcon guards and Falcon City humans fixed most of the broken and destroyed buildings throughout Falcon City, including mending the collapsed big wooden boats that once sailed across the marvellous Nautilus Lake.

Not only did the restoration of Falcon City take place in the past two weeks, but also many relationships between the humans were strengthened or developed. Emerald spent quite a bit of her time getting to know her father Gaius more since they had not seen each other or spoken with one another during the last three years. Emerald and Gaius shared much laughter while getting to know each other again as well as enjoyed learning about one another's adventures, such as Emerald being involved in the gymnastic competitions at Oakus School and Gaius's personal development during his time being a part of the royal Falcon guards within Falcon City. Emerald and Gaius spent some emotional moments discussing the situations that had happened during their interactions with the creatures from the Planet of Phoenix and some of the suffering and distress they had to endure.

Gaius also spoke respectfully and sincerely to Emerald with regards to his relationship and love story with Lily along with his rise within the ranks of the royal Falcon guard and ending up becoming the royal Falcon captain. As Emerald and Gaius appreciated learning more about one another's life's, they also spent much time in grieving for the loss of Emerald's mother and Gaius's ex-wife Ruby, along with the recent death of Gaius's new partner Lily, where both Emerald and Gaius visited Lily's dead body several times within Grand Falcon Tomb situated in the south of Falcon City.

Emerald also spent some much-needed quality time and shared intimate encounters with her husband Raven as they had only just come to be together again following Emerald's death. Raven and Emerald also wanted the time to support each other properly through the sorrow and anguish that they had both unfortunately experienced within the last year such as the loss of Raven's grandfather Barious and Emerald's mother Ruby, along with coming to terms and trying to understand the death and revival of Emerald during the great war at Triton's Underground Dungeon. Raven and Emerald's reunited love for one another grew forever stronger, and they spent many romantic and passionate evenings in their grand bedroom at the royal Falcon Castle. Raven was also requested by King Exodus to enjoy some valued time together during some of the big royal gatherings King Exodus and Princess Petal hosted at the royal Falcon Castle, where an abundance of sumptuous food and drink was served to the guests to celebrate the victory of the humans in the great war. These gatherings were also meant for remembering those humans who were sadly killed during the great war.

During the time King Exodus spent drinking with Raven at these big royal gatherings at the royal Falcon castle, King Exodus shared with Raven the prodigious adventures that he had shared with his grandfather Barious and their friend Panther during their younger years. For example, King Exodus spoke to Raven about the battle King Exodus, Barious, and Panther experienced against the gigantic sea lion creature at Nautilus Lake. King Exodus also wanted to hear from Raven more about Barious's last few years of living upon the Planet of Phoenix as Barious was a cherished friend of King Exodus, although in recent years they were unable to spend as much time with one another as they had done in the past.

Also during the past two weeks, Parrot and Sapphire had spent numerous moments mourning and grieving for their great friends Lynx, Bruce, and Nia, and although, they missed their son Tigra dearly, they both decided to stay in Falcon City for a couple of weeks more. During this team, Parrot and Sapphire repeatedly visit Nia's and Bruce's beautiful graves that were located within one of Falcon graveyards that were situated in the furthest east direction of Falcon City. Parrot and Sapphire wanted to spend time at Nia's and Bruce's graves, where they would both openly talk about the wonderful memories they had all shared with each other while growing up within Pine Village. As a sign of respect for Nia's life, Sapphire chose to display the book of curses that Hake had given her previously at Eagle Forest within Falcon University's large library, so that the new students who joined Falcon City University could analyse and research the magical and mystical information, spells, and curses written inside this phenomenal and ancient book.

Sapphire also requested a special tribute to be created and displayed for Nia to honour their loyal friendship as well as Nia's hard work in her studies when she was training to be a history lecturer at Falcon University. Princess Petal thought this was a fitting idea and granted Sapphire's wish, especially since Sapphire had donated the book of curses to Falcon University. Thus Princess Petal proclaimed that the history section within Falcon University's large library would be named after Nia.

SAPPHIRE AND PRINCESS Petal became very good friends during the past two week as they got to know each other very well. Sapphire and Princess Petal spent quite a bit of time with each other at Falcon Castle within Falcon City, especially since Sapphire, Parrot, along with Raven and Emerald, were granted permission by King Exodus to stay within the splendid Falcon Castle for as long as they wanted to stay at Falcon City following the victory of the great war. Sapphire and Princess Petal shared many interests including their academic education, love of music, and interest in nature. Sapphire and Princess Petal realised they had a lot in common with each other and quickly bonded together; they shared much laughter and storytelling with one another. Princess Petal also asked Sapphire to help her host and entertain guests during the big royal gatherings that were held within Falcon Castle.

In their spare time, Raven, Emerald, Parrot, Sapphire, Gaius, King Exodus, and Princess Petal visited Grand Falcon Tomb together on many occasions, where they mostly spent their time within King Exodus's resting chamber room within Grand Falcon Tomb so they could mourn and give worship to the loss of Lynx, Panther, Lily as well as Queen Eclipse, who had previously died and was laid to rest there. On these occasions journeying to Grand Falcon Tomb, they all shared previous happy and cherished memories with one another with regards to their interactions with Lynx, Panther, Lily, or Queen Eclipse as well as stories of their past when growing older upon the Planet of Phoenix. When Princess Petal visited Grand Falcon Tomb with everyone, but also by herself, she spent some time alone next to the resting place for Lynx's silver crown, silver sword, and silver shield that were crested with the royal Falcon guard symbol upon it. Princess Petal prayed to the gods to ask them to send her words of love and thoughts to Lynx and her ancestors that she believed were now in heaven.

Towards the end of the two weeks that Raven, Emerald, Parrot, and Sapphire decided to stay at Falcon Castle within Falcon City, Parrot and Sapphire decided to take the opportunity to get married in order unite their endless love for one another in a bond for eternity as well as use this special occasion to pay homage to their cherished friends that were killed during the great war. Parrot and Sapphire were married by King Exodus because no other priest or vicar is currently living on the Planet of Phoenix to perform this marriage ceremony, as all of them were killed in the great war. With the help of Emerald, Princess Petal quickly planned and arranged Parrot and Sapphire's wedding and ceremony within Falcon Castle as Princess Petal felt that holding their marriage ceremony within Falcon City after the great war would bring a cheerful and joyful occasion for the surviving humans to celebrate.

Parrot and Sapphire's wedding was conducted in the great main hall of the glorious Falcon Castle. Raven was Parrot's best man, and Emerald was Sapphire's maid of honour. All the royal Falcon guards and all Falcon City humans were invited to Falcon Castle to attend their dreamlike wedding, and all these humans from Falcon City wore their smartest suits and dresses. Parrot wore a specially made grey suit-style clothing and Sapphire also wore a beautiful elegant purple wedding dress that had previously been made by Gaius's mother Tamika and was left at Nerolus's cloth shop within Falcon City. Princess Petal played glorious music on her harp as Parrot and Sapphire walked down an aisle within the great hall. The aisle was made of a long red carpet that was laid out between the numerous seats where Falcon City humans sat on either side of the great hall. The great hall was also decorated with an abundance of flowers and wedding ceremony items and silver crockery.

At one end of the great hall, where the golden thrones were, Parrot and Sapphire emotionally spoke their personally written vows while facing each other just in front of a specially designed golden altar. King Exodus stood behind this altar. During their wedding ceremony, Parrot and Sapphire placed gold rings upon each other's fingers. King Exodus conducted his duty that was bestowed upon him, as he was the King of Falcon City, and he favourably pronounced Parrot and Sapphire husband and wife. A huge party within the great hall of Falcon Castle was then thrown after Parrot and Sapphire's wedding, and this huge party was organised by Princess Petal with the help of Emerald, Raven, and some of the royal Falcon guards.

At Parrot and Sapphire's wedding party, plenty of sumptuous food and wine was severed; various types of musical instruments were played like harps, organs, and trumpets; as well as different styles and variations of dances were performed by some of Falcon City guests. At the main feast of this party, many amusing speeches were given by Raven in honour of his cousin Parrot as well as by Emerald in honour of her new sister-in-law Sapphire. An enjoyable time and merriment was shared by all the humans that attended Parrot and Sapphire's wonderful wedding within Falcon Castle, and this pleasurable enjoyment continued in the late hours of that night.

THREE DAYS AFTER Parrot and Sapphire's wedding celebrations, the time had now come for Raven, Emerald, Parrot, and Sapphire to return back home to their villages in the north direction of the Planet of Phoenix, as they wanted to be reunited with Tigra and Rexus again. King Exodus and Princess Petal would continue to rule Falcon City along with Gaius, who remained as the royal Falcon guard captain. Although, Gaius was very sad to see Emerald go back to Oak Village, he wanted to remain close to Lily's dead body that was peacefully resting inside of Grand Falcon Tomb.

Gaius also felt that he wanted to continue being the royal Falcon captain to remain loyal to King Exodus and Falcon City in an attempt to make up for all the wrongdoings he had done in the past. Gaius wanted Emerald to finally be proud of her father, and he promised Emerald he would visit her and Raven in Oak Village as much as he could. King Exodus also initially requested Gaius to help rebuild Falcon City following the great war to make it thrive and flourish again in order to share this prosperity with all the humans throughout the Planet of Phoenix; this would also eventually benefit the other main villages that included Oak Village. That is what Gaius wanted to do for his daughter Emerald.

At Parrot and Sapphire's recent wedding within Falcon Castle, King Exodus declared to the royal Falcon guards and the humans within Falcon City that he felt it appropriate to make Raven the new leader of Oak Village as well as Parrot to be made the new leader of Pine and Willow Villages in honour of his best friend Lynx and Lynx's uncle, Panther. This great news came as a bit of a shock to Raven and Parrot, and they took some time to discuss this with King Exodus as well as their wives Emerald and Sapphire. After having a very transparent conversation with regards to the future of all the humans on the Planet of Phoenix with the hope of maintaining a unified peace among the humans living upon the Planet of Phoenix,

Raven and Parrot agreed that it would be the right thing for them as individuals, along with their family.

Raven and Parrot were now more confident as both of them had recently acquired some essential knowledge, character, and skill sets during the events of the great war that would be important when ruling over a village. King Exodus also wanted to reward both Raven and Parrot greatly for their bravery, courage, and actions they had done during the great war that indeed protected all of the humans' survival. The royal Falcon guards and Falcon City humans took this news with regards to the main villages' new leaders with much joy and were very pleased for Raven and Parrot.

On the same day of Parrot and Sapphire's wedding, King Exodus proclaimed that a coronation ceremony will be conducted on the day that Raven, Emerald, Parrot, and Sapphire decide leave Falcon City, especially since all the main villages now had no leaders, and it would need these humans who had demonstrated so much commitment and initiative to further the development of these main villages to be more like Falcon City in the future.

After King Exodus's wishes were announced on Parrot and Sapphire's wedding day, the royal Falcon guards sent three carrier pigeons with messages written upon wool cloth and tied to the three pigeons' feet from Falcon City to travel to Oak, Pine, and Willow Villages in order to let the villagers in these main villages know the information with regards to Lynx's and Panther's unfortunate recent deaths. Princess Petal thought it would be a good idea to let the villagers know about this devastating news now so that the villagers could mourn Lynx and Panther respectfully with expressive prayers. It was also important to decree to the villagers about Raven being made the leader of Oak Village and Parrot being made the leader of Pine and Willow Village, so that the villagers would be aware of the new regime upon their return and could welcome their new leaders with much pride and honour.

On the day of Raven's and Parrot's coronation ceremony that is three days after Parrot and Sapphire's wedding, the sun shines brightly and warmly and glistens upon Falcon City, along with the numerous royal Falcon guards and Falcon City humans that are joyfully walking along the stone paths of Falcon City that lead up the stone hill to the famous Falcon Castle. The royal Falcon guards are suited in the full and clean uniforms and Falcon City humans were dressed in their smartest outfits. Upon entering Falcon Castle, the royal Falcon guard and Falcon City humans make their way to sit down upon loads of metal chairs positioned in straight lines on either side of a red silk carpet in the great hall, where they wait patiently in admiration for Raven and Parrot to be crowned the new village leaders.

King Exodus is currently standing in front of the golden throne placed at the furthest end of the great hall from the big bronze entrance doors. King Exodus is dressed in his golden-plated knighthood armour just as many of his royal advisors and councillors are, and they also now start to position themselves on either side of the golden throne. At present, Raven and Parrot are kneeling upon the red silk carpet in front of King Exodus, where they also wait humbly for the coronation ceremony to begin. Emerald is standing up next to Raven, who is kneeling, and Sapphire is also standing beside Parrot kneeling upon the red silk carpet. Raven and Parrot were given specially designed royal knighthood armour to wear for this coronation ceremony, and Emerald and Sapphire were given long silver silk dresses to wear in recognition of the coronation ceremony for their husbands to be crowned the village leaders.

Princess Petal is dressed in a light blue dress that had overlapping folds down the bottom half of the dress, and she is currently holding the joint Pine and Willow Village silver crowns as she stands next to King Exodus at the golden throne, just in front of Parrot and Sapphire. Gaius is currently holding the Oak Village silver crown and is standing on the other side of King Exodus at the golden throne, just in front of Raven and Emerald. Some of royal Falcon guards at the sides of the great hall within Falcon Castle begin to blow loudly on their brass trumpets as King Exodus moves forward from his golden throne and lifts his golden sword up in the air and taps it gently upon Raven's shoulder and then does the same to Parrot's shoulder.

'I humbly stand before two heroic, honourable, and courageous humans who were born and raised in Oak and Pine Village. These outstanding humans fought bravely with unity and passion against those vile creatures and aided us all to become triumphant against the purest of evil during the great war of our time. Their worth as humans has far exceeded all expectations that could have ever been placed upon any human residing on the Planet of Phoenix, no matter of status. The survival of us humans wouldn't have been possible against such destructive creatures, if it wasn't for the tenacity and purity of the souls of these two humans. Thus on this beautiful and glorious day, we will now show our appreciation to their accomplishments.

'Raven, I declare you the new leader of Oak Village. May Oak Village succeed once again under your rule, just as it did when Wolf and his noble ancestors were the leaders of Oak Village. Parrot, I declare you leader of Pine Village. Let Pine Village become strong and fearless under your command, just as it was when Lynx was its spirited and magnificent leader. Parrot, I also declare you leader of Willow Village. Bring peace and wealth back to Willow Village, just as Panther had conveyed to this newly developed village upon the Planet of Phoenix. We now must say goodbye to two valiant humans and their wonderful and praiseworthy wives, but we will always remain in close allegiance, unity, and connection with these new leaders and their villages as the humans will remain favourably for eternity over the Planet of Phoenix. Stand, Raven, leader of Oak Village, and Parrot, leader of Pine Village and Willow Village,' declares King Exodus loudly and assertively.

After hearing King Exodus's humble words, Raven stands up slowly from kneeling upon the red silk carpet, and Gaius places the Oak Village silver crown upon Raven's head. The Oak Village silver crown had the word 'Oak' written in gold in the ancient language of Phoenix across the front middle part of the silver crown. A royal Falcon guard also brings over and gives Raven his sword and shield of Grackle. Parrot also stands up from the red silk carpet, and Princess Petal gently places the Pine and Willow Village silver crown upon Parrot's head. Like the Oak Village silver crown, the Pine and Willow Village silver crown had the words 'Pine & Willow' written in gold in the ancient Phoenix Language across the front middle part of the silver crown. Usually the 'Pine' and 'Willow' words written in gold would have been written on two different silver crowns, but as Parrot is now the leader of both Pine Village and Willow Village, these village names specifically were written across the same silver crown. A royal Falcon guard also walks up to Parrot and gives him his wooden bow and wooden arrows with the metal spikes at the end of them, along with several of his remaining fury raptor throwing stars.

The royal Falcon guards and Falcon City humans within Falcon Castle stand up from their metal chairs and clap and cheer loudly and enthusiastically for Raven and Parrot who have now just been crowned the new village leaders. Some of the royal Falcon guards also play musical instruments, which include brass trumpets and horns, along with also letting go into the air various types of small birds including white doves and red robins that rapidly start flying high in the air within the great hall of Falcon Castle. The royal Falcon guards and Falcon City humans then start to chant aloud both Raven's and Parrot's names as they happily watch Raven and Parrot grab forearms with King Exodus and then Gaius as a sign of respect for one another. Raven and Parrot both bow together in front of King Exodus, Princess Petal, Gaius, and the royal advisors and councillors that are standing in front of them by the golden throne.

Raven and Parrot smile brightly, before turning around and walking slowly down the middle of the great hall upon the red silk carpet and continue walking across the red silk carpet while waving at the royal Falcon guards and Falcon City humans until they end up just in front of the big bronze entrance door of Falcon Castle. Sapphire hugs Princess Petal warmly and smiles and curtsies to King Exodus and Gaius before also turning around and walking over the red silk carpet to follow Raven and Parrot towards the end of great hall by the big bronze entrance doors within Falcon Castle. Emerald now also firmly hugs her father Gaius.

'Remember you can come back and visit me any time, my miraculous daughter, as well as I will also journey to Oak Village more often to see you, especially as I would like to share more of Falcon City's resources, wealth, technology, and knowledge with the other humans upon the Planet of Phoenix including Oak Village,' says Gaius unhappily to Emerald as he realises she is just about to leave Falcon City.

'Raven, Parrot, Sapphire, and I really appreciate you wanting to share and provide more for the other humans within our villages. This is very much appreciated and will not be forgotten by our future generations. It has truly been wonderful spending time with you,

Father, just a shame we have missed so many years together,' sobs Emerald as she looks down at the floor in sadness.

'You always remained in my heart during those years apart. You have turned out to be a lovely daughter as well as an inspirational human. I'm so proud of you, just as Ruby and Lily are, and they both will continue to be your guardian angels when watching over you from heaven. I wish you and Raven a wonderful family, where I hope you will share many happy times together that you both greatly deserve, just as Parrot and Sapphire also do. My love for you will last in this world and the next, no matter where we are located or how long we are apart from each other,' remarks Gaius as he kisses Emerald on the forehead. Emerald looks back and smiles at Gaius.

'It has been a grand pleasure having you here with us, Emerald. You are welcome to return and stay with your father any time. We will all miss you dearly,' says Princess Petal.

'Thank you for everything that you have done for us,' replies Emerald as she turns to hug Princes Petal, and then she smiles and curtsies to King Exodus, who smiles back at Emerald. Emerald hugs Gaius one last time, before she quickly turns around also walks down the red silk carpet in the middle of the great hall until she meets up with Raven, Parrot, and Sapphire at the big bronze entrance door. King Exodus, Princess Petal, Gaius, the royal advisors and councillors, the royal Falcon guards, and Falcon City humans all wave happily but sadly as they watch Raven, Emerald, Parrot, and Sapphire now leave through the big bronze entrance door of Falcon Castle, which Emerald closes behind her as she hears the brass trumpets and horns continue playing music.

Outside of Falcon Castle, Raven and Emerald are helped by a few royal Falcon guards to climb back on top of a well-groomed Felix. Emerald is also handed Raven's silver sword and shield of Grackle to carry on their journey back to Oak Village. Parrot and Sapphire are also assisted by a few royal Falcon guards to climb on top of their well-groomed black horse. Parrot has fixed his wooden bow and arrows with the metal spikes at the end of them around, having placed his remaining fury raptor throwing stars within his knighthood armour compartments. Sapphire is handed her brown leather bag by a royal Falcon guard to hold on to during their journey back to Pine Village.

The brown leather bag has Sapphire's silver dagger inside of it, along with some sumptuous food and water provisions that Princess Petal had prepared for their long journey home.

'Thank you for your assistance and the hospitality we have received during our stay in Falcon City. We promise to return the favour to any Falcon City humans who may travel to our villages in the future,' mentions Raven to one of the royal Falcon guards who had helped him back on top of Felix.

'We hope to return back to Falcon City to see you all again soon,' remarks Parrot as he nods at these royal Falcon guards.

'You are all most welcome and deserve the honour that has now been bestowed upon you. Let the humans within all the villages and locations of the Planet of Phoenix now finally live a peaceful and affluent life with another,' replies one of the royal Falcon guards.

'May the gods bless you and all the humans living upon the Planet of Phoenix for eternity,' states Sapphire happily as she looks up at the blazing sun in the sky of the Planet of Phoenix.

Raven, Emerald, Parrot, and Sapphire all now smile and nod at the royal Falcon guards that had helped them all back on top of their horses. Raven gently kicks his heels into the sides of Felix as does Parrot to his black horse, which enables Felix and the brown horse to begin trotting down the stone path hill and the other interconnecting stone paths in the north direction of Falcon City until they reach the big iron portcullis in the north middle section of Falcon City. As Raven, Emerald, Parrot, and Sapphire upon their horses reach the big iron portcullis, it is slowly opened by a couple of the royal Falcon guards at the big iron portcullis for them all to exit Falcon City.

'Safe journey home, our lords of the main villages,' states one of the royal Falcon guards who had just spun the big metal chain attached to a wooden lever that raised the iron portcullis up.

'It's time to return home,' says Emerald to Raven, Parrot, and Sapphire. Raven and Emerald, riding upon Felix, and Parrot and Sapphire, riding upon their black horse, start to gallop swiftly in the north direction across the marvellous Kingdom of Humans and over the Grass Terrain Fields that takes many hours travel through. Raven, Emerald, Parrot, and Sapphire all continue their journey north across the Planet of Phoenix to head directly towards Pine

Village to at last be reunited with Raven and Emerald's dog Rexus and Parrot and Sapphire's son Tigra.

RAVEN AND EMERALD are riding upon Felix's strong and healthy black back. Parrot and Sapphire are also riding upon their black horse, and after numerous hours of travelling across the vast Grass Terrain Fields in the north direction of the Planet of Phoenix from Falcon City, they all happily return to the east entrance wooden gates of Pine Village. As Parrot trots steadily upon his black horse first through the east entrance wooden gate, he gazes across the whole of Pine Village's marvellous small wooden houses, flats, and shops, along with the monument statues and plentiful vegetation, including many pine trees, and it takes a moment's thought for him to fully realise that he is now the Pine and Willow Village leader.

Parrot and Sapphire, riding upon their black horse, begin trotting down the cobbled paths of Pine Village in the east direction towards Pinus Tavern. Raven and Emerald, riding upon Felix, follow Parrot and Sapphire. As Raven, Emerald, Parrot, and Sapphire continue trotting upon their horses down the cobbled paths of Pine Village, they are amiably cheered, greeted, and waved at by the Pine villagers passing by. Many of these Pine villagers also kneel or lay down various types of flowers and baskets of fruit and vegetables upon the cobbled paths in honour of the new Pine Village leader Parrot. Parrot manoeuvres his black horse around the flowers and baskets of fruit and vegetables, being careful that the horse does not to step on anything. Parrot nods back at the Pine villagers. He also now wears the silver Pine and Willow Village crown upon his forehead. Raven, Emerald, and Sapphire also smile and wave back to the Pine villagers who now start to congregate on the cobbled paths of Pine Village.

Pine Village's small wooden houses, flats, and shops have now all mostly been rebuilt after the devastating battle it endured against Vicious and the Potorians during the battle of Pine Village. The cobbled paths are now also completely cleaned from the dead bodies of the Potorians and any of the Pine guards and Pine villagers who had lost their lives during the Pine Village battle, where the Potorians' bodies were burnt in a deep mud pit outside Pine Village and the Pine guards and Pine villagers were either buried or cremated within Pinus Graveyard. The surviving farm animals and livestock have also now returned to happily graze in the Grass Terrain Fields that surround the perimeter of Pine Village. The general emotions of all the Pine guards and Pine villagers within Pine Village have risen a bit since their recent mourning of the previous Pine Village leader Lynx, along with their family and friends who had died during the Pine Village battle or in the great war.

The reason why the Pine guards' and Pine villagers' outlook on life is more positive, is that their new Pine Village leader Parrot and his wife Sapphire have returned to rule over Pine Village and will make Pine Village the great village it once was before the attack by the creatures that used to reside on the Planet of Phoenix. Raven, Emerald, Parrot, and Sapphire are helped down from their horses by some of the men Pine villagers just outside Pinus Tavern, and another couple of men Pine villagers take and hold the sword and shield of Grackle from Emerald, along with any other weapons or items carried by Parrot. Sapphire remains carrying the black leather bag around one of her shoulders. After Raven, Emerald, Parrot, and Sapphire have got down from their horses, these men Pine villagers hold on to the brown rope reins of Felix and the black horse, while women Pine villagers give wooden buckets of water and big bunches of hay to Felix and the black horse. Raven, Emerald, Parrot, and Sapphire enter into Pinus Tavern through its big wooden entrance doors.

Pinus Tavern is currently filled with many Pine villagers who are drinking ale and talking enthusiastically with one another, although they are also still mourning but celebrating the lives of Lynx, Panther, Bruce, the 200 Pine guards, and men Pine villagers as well as any other Willow villagers who had unfortunately been recently killed during the great war. In honour of these brave humans that had fought during the great war, the Pine villagers created a special memorial display upon one of the wooden walls inside of Pinus Tavern, where the names of all these dead humans is carved upon the wooden wall. Lynx's name is at the top of this special memorial display and his name is written in gold paint and all the other humans have their names written in silver paint.

Bella is at present sitting down upon a wooden chair next to the big wooden table on one side of Pinus Tavern; Bella is sitting with some of her Pine villager friends and is currently holding on to

Tigra, while Rexus is sitting upon the wooden floor next to Bella. As Raven, Emerald, Parrot, and Sapphire enter through Pinus Tavern's big wooden entrance doors, all the Pine villagers look towards the entrance and quickly notice that their new Pine Village leader has returned home to Pine Village. All the Pine villagers within Pinus Tavern stand up and cheer and clap for the Raven, Emerald, Parrot, and Sapphire and then they kneel in honour of Parrot, especially as they know that Parrot is now the new leader of Pine and Willow Village due to Pine Village having received a letter from one of King Exodus's carrier pigeons a couple of days ago with regards to the recent events and situations that had occurred during and following the great war.

Sapphire gratefully notices Bella standing up from her wooden chair while holding on to Tigra at one end of Pinus Tavern by the big wooden table. Sapphire quickly rushes over to Bella and Tigra in excitement. Sapphire places the brown leather bag that she had borrowed from Bella upon the big wooden table and then gives Bella and Tigra a firm hug; afterwards Bella passes Tigra over to Sapphire's loving arms.

'I've missed you so much, my gorgeous baby Tigra. Your parents have married now, and by the God's will, we have been returned to you for us two and Parrot to remain a true and blessed family for the rest of our futures,' says Sapphire happily as she hugs and kisses Tigra vibrantly. Parrot also walks through the middle of Pinus Tavern; as Parrot passes by some of the kneeling Pine villagers, he helps these Pine villagers stand back on their feet and hugs or shakes their hands for the respect they have just shown him. As Parrot comes over to Sapphire who was now holding Tigra next to Bella, Parrot also hugs Tigra devotedly and smiles thankfully at Bella.

'Our fullest gratitude for taking care of Tigra and Rexus during our absence, Bella,' says Parrot in an appreciative manner.

'You are most welcome, my Pine Village leader. Many congratulations also to you both on your marriage. I wish I could have seen you enjoy that well-deserved special occasion. I can't think of a more honourable human that deserves to be the new leader of Pine Village as well as Willow Village, although I can image how heartbroken you must be feeling from the devastating news of Lynx's death, just as I am. I do know, however, Lynx would have wanted you to have taken his place as the Pine Village leader, and he would be looking at you from heaven with much pride. May Pine Village and Willow Village be blessed by the gods by the return and start of a new reign of their valiant leader Parrot,' states Bella as the Pine villagers in Pinus Tavern clap and cheer again for Parrot.

'Thank you for your kind words, and I aim to make Lynx proud and will try to become the brilliant leader that he was, although my heart does indeed bleed that Lynx, along with many other remarkable humans, is no longer with us now,' replies Parrot.

'Apologies, Bella, as we would have also wanted you and our little Tigra at our wedding. It was a spontaneous moment that fortunately was granted by King Exodus,' mentions Sapphire. Just as Bella is about to reply to Parrot and Sapphire, her attention is suddenly grabbed when she notices Emerald standing gracefully behind Parrot as Raven and Emerald had also now walked through Pinus Tavern and up to Parrot, Sapphire, Tigra, and Bella. Bella smiles colourfully and gives Emerald a strong hug.

'I can't believe my eyes! It's so good to see you again, my precious angel. It's truly a blessing from the gods to have your soul returned to you and for you all to have now returned safely back to your homes within our villages,' mentions Bella delightedly and with much admiration in her voice.

'Yes, it's a blessing indeed, and it will never be forgotten how lucky I was to survive such a horrible situation. It's also very good to see you again, Bella,' replies Emerald as she is about to hug Bella. But then Rexus stands up from the wooden floor and runs joyfully up to Emerald, wagging his tail frantically. Rexus jumps up to Emerald's chest as Emerald kneels down to stroke and kiss Rexus on his head. Raven also bends over to stroke Rexus affectionately.

'We really appreciate you watching over Rexus for us, Bella,' says Raven thoughtfully.

'You're both most very welcome,' replies Bella as she smiles at Raven and Emerald being back together again.

'I'm sorry we did not return back here sooner, Bella, but you have really done a splendid job in looking after Tigra and Rexus as well as maintaining Pinus Tavern, along with assisting in bringing back a jubilant atmosphere to Pine Village again, especially after the unfortunate things that happened to Pine Village and the rest of the humans on the Planet of Phoenix recently. Are my parents still resting within the guest room of Pinus Tavern?' asks Sapphire with a tear rolling down her cheek as she thinks back to the awful sight when she witnessed her parents' body in the wooden coffins in one of Pinus Tavern guest rooms.

'It has been my pleasure to watch over Tigra and Rexus while you were gone. They both behaved very well and have already grown up more in such a short time. Yes, just after the battle of Pine Village, the Pine villagers were distraught and even more devastated when we all heard about what happened during the great war with regard to Lynx, Bruce, and the Pine guards and men Pine villagers who all lost their lives in the great war. We mourned for these brave souls properly, and then we rejoiced at the news of Parrot being crowned the new leader of Pine Village. We also felt that the humans who had fought for Pine Village during the great war would have wanted the rest of us to celebrate their lives and live the rest of our lives to the fullest as they would want us to be happy that the great war between humans and creatures has finally now come to an end.

'Unfortunately, Sapphire, due to the length of time you were away from Pine Village, and I wasn't sure exactly when you would return or even if you were able to return back to Pine Village, we had to bury Sirius and Aura together within Pinus Graveyard to enable them to rest in peace in order to undergo their blissful journey to heaven. We gave them a lovely send-off during their funeral, and I have decorated their grave with beautiful flowers and some of Tigra's toys. Some of the other Pine villagers and I said prayers and sang hymns for Sirius and Aura and also sent loving thoughts from you and Parrot during their burial. I hope this is all right with you?' says Bella softly.

'Yes, that's fine, as I understand that my parents required to be buried for their send-off to heaven. Thank you so very much for all that you have done, Bella. You are truly a rare breed of diamond. My parents always wanted to be buried together as they had loved each other all of their lives, and I'm sure that the funeral was very peaceful and respectable,' replies Sapphire while another tear rolled down one of her cheeks.

'We will go visit your parents' grave at Pinus Graveyard shortly, Sapphire, and we will then spend a lot of time there telling your parents about everything that has happened in recent times as well as reminiscing over the memories that we had shared with them and Tigra before their unfortunate passing,' smiles Parrot while he turns and hugs Sapphire and Tigra contently. Everyone within Pinus Tavern pauses their conversations for a few moments in honour of Sapphire's parents Sirius and Aura, along with showing their respect for Lynx, Panther, Bruce, Pine guards, Willow guards, Pine villagers, Willow villagers as well as the royal Falcon guards and Falcon City humans that were killed during the great war.

'I'm really sorry, Cousin, but it's time for us to get back to Oak Village now as we would also like to arrange suitable plans for what will need to be done about Ruby's body,' says Raven quietly. Parrot stopped hugging Sapphire, and Raven grabbed Parrot's forearm as a sign of gratitude for all the aid Parrot had given Raven during this great war. Parrot also grabbed Raven's forearm and then hugged Raven strongly.

'Of course, Cousin, you go do what needs to be done for Ruby and also for your Oak Village. Do come and visit us as much as possible though, and we will work together to rebuild all of our villages to regain their magnificence again,' replies Parrot as he smiles at Raven after he stops hugging him.

'Thank you for everything, Parrot. I couldn't have survived the great war without you and Sapphire. You have also looked after me and all of us right from the beginning of this great war. Our lives would also not be the same now, if you both weren't here to share it with us,' smiles Raven at Parrot and Sapphire, and then Sapphire and Emerald hugged each other tightly and caringly.

'I missed you so much when you had passed from this life, Emerald. Don't ever leave me like that again as I really couldn't bear to lose another loved one from my life,' remarks Sapphire, looking at Emerald and then Tigra, who was still held within her arms.

'Don't worry, I will always remain in your life, Sapphire, as a true friend and now also as a family member. I will come back to Pine Village soon and help you to raise Tigra as promised. Also, I would like to thank you for all you have done for me and Raven. We really appreciate it, and our love and thoughts are with you both always,' mentions Emerald meaningfully as Sapphire and Emerald now stop hugging each other.

'Goodbye, Bella,' says Emerald as she turns to hug Bella.

'Come back soon, both of you. This place would also not be the same without your faces lighting up the place,' says Bella favourably as Emerald and Bella also stop hugging one another. Raven and Emerald smile brightly at Parrot, Sapphire, Tigra, and Bella, and then along with Rexus, they begin to walk out of Pinus Tavern as all the Pine villagers within Pinus Tavern, including Parrot, Sapphire, and Bella, cheer and clap for Raven and Emerald. As soon as Raven and Emerald exit the big wooden entrance doors of Pinus Tavern, the Pine villagers outside politely help Raven and Emerald back on to Felix's big black back, and Emerald is then given the sword and shield of Grackle back to hold on to during their journey to Oak Village.

'Thank you for your assistance here, Pine villagers, take care and carpe diem,' says Raven to the Pine villagers that had just helped Raven and Emerald on top of Felix's back. Raven now taps his feet into the sides of Felix, and along with Rexus, who was running along the cobbled paths, Raven and Emerald both trot upon Felix across the cobbled paths of Pine Village that lead towards and finally out of the west entrance wooden gate of Pine Village.

RAVEN AND EMERALD continue riding upon Felix's big black back, accompanied by Rexus, who is walking upon the ground as they all journey across the long cobbled road between Pine Village and Oak Village. Raven, Emerald, Felix, and Rexus travel calmly over the cobbled road in the west direction for about an hour in the heated sun until they reach the east entrance wooden gate of Oak Village. The sun glistens brightly, and the wind is calm; many various birds tweet and twerk as they fly around in the air in clear blue sky above the pleasant Oak Village. Upon arrival at the Oak Village's east entrance wooden gate, Raven and Emerald are greeted warmly by many Oak villagers. These Oak villagers had also set up a small celebration festival within the Oak Village square for the return of their new Oak Village leader Raven.

The small celebration festival also continues throughout the wooden and cobbled paths that lead towards the east entrance wooden gate of Oak Village. Within the Oak Village square and over the wooden and cobbled paths, some of the Oak villagers were playing music on brass instruments like trumpets and horns as well as serving specially made broth, pies, and sandwiches to the other Oak villagers, and the Oak Village children were playing different games with one another. Colourful banners and flowers were also displayed throughout Oak Village in honour of Raven's and Emerald's return home.

Raven and Emerald smile brightly and wave back at the Oak villagers as they pass through the east entrance wooden gate of Oak Village. All the Oak villagers are full of excitement and joy; they clap and cheer for Raven, Emerald, Felix, and Rexus, as they know all that they have suffered and endured has now led to peace for all the humans that reside on the Planet of Phoenix.

Raven and Emerald are gently helped down from Felix's big black back by a couple of the men Oak villagers; the silver sword and shield of Grackle are taken to hold from Emerald by the men Oak villagers as Emerald is helped down to the ground from Felix's back. The men Oak villagers then hand back the silver sword and shield of Grackle to Raven. Raven stands upon the wooden and cobbled path of Oak Village, and most of the Oak villagers now begin to crowd around Raven and Emerald. Other Oak villagers quickly gather fresh hay, ripe green apples, and clear water to bring to Felix. These Oak villagers pat Felix tenderly over his long rugged black neck hair; some of the Oak Village children also bring water and some bones for Rexus to feast upon, Rexus becomes very excited and wags his tail vibrantly as he runs around and in between the Oak Village children.

'Welcome back, Raven, our new and glorious leader of Oak Village, along with Emerald, our prestigious queen of Oak Village,' graciously remarks the old woman Oak villager named Edna as she bows in front of Raven and Emerald; the other Oak villagers also bow and share merriment with Raven and Emerald as well as with one another.

'Three cheers for our magnificent leaders Raven and Emerald!' shouts another man Oak villager as all the Oak villagers start shouting Raven's and Emerald's names loudly for three times in enthusiasm and elation.

'This warm welcome is very much appreciated, and it's good for us to finally be back home and see our fellow Oak villagers again, who all look healthy and full of life. We all shall enjoy this celebration festival for many days in gratitude of how much we have all had to undergo to experience this very moment. We will also hold some religious rituals in honour of the gods for aiding us during the great war as well as hold ceremonies to mourn for all of our loved ones that we have sadly and untimely lost on the Planet of Phoenix during the great war. After these days have passed and along with the new leader of Pine and Willow Village, who is now my cousin Parrot, as well as King Exodus and Princess Petal of Falcon City, we shall all continue to make the Planet of Phoenix flourish in resources as well as create a peaceful and blissful place for all of us humans to live the rest of our lives in happiness,' announces Raven as he punches and lifts the sword of Grackle high up in the air, and all the Oak villagers continue to cheer for Raven.

'Thank you, everyone, for your kind gestures upon our return to Oak Village and for your loyal support to your new leader of Oak Village. We have never been happier to see so many smiling faces and for Oak Village to turn back into the fun-loving place that it once was. I want you all to enjoy this celebration festival to the fullest as Raven and I will soon join with you in the enjoyment of the celebration. But first, I must attend to a matter of my heart. I was wondering if anyone found the dead body of my mother Ruby?' asks Emerald sadly and with watery eyes. The Oak Village crowd stop cheering and pause for a moment in honour of Ruby and to appreciate Emerald's loss of her mother.

'Yes, Emerald, we found Ruby's body in the compartment underneath the wooden staircase of her house when we were cleaning up the broken wood and glass from the wooden and cobbled paths in front of Ruby's house following the explosion that had happened there a few weeks back. We are deeply sorry for your loss, and we all give you both our condolences for all that you have both lost during the great war. We weren't sure of when you or Raven would return to Oak Village, so we buried Ruby next to Barious's grave within Oakus Graveyard next to Oakus Church. We gave Ruby a wonderful send-off to heaven and have made their graves beautiful for you both to visit,' answers a woman Oak villager sadly in response to Emerald's question. Emerald smiles back softly at the woman Oak villager as she is glad that Ruby's body has been found and buried properly.

'Thank you again, Oak villagers, for taking care of our families as well as Oak Village in our absence. I promise to continue to looking after all you Oak villagers and maintaining Oak Village's pleasant environment as well as do everything I can to make sure I am as good a leader as Wolf was to us all. At present, Emerald and I would like a quiet moment alone at Oakus Graveyard with our family. Afterwards, we will return to the Oak Village square and celebrate with you all our victory and the final end to the great war between the humans and the creatures of the Planet of Phoenix,' says Raven. The Oak villagers in the crowd nod back at Raven, and then a couple of the men Oak villagers take the silver sword and shield of Grackle from Raven, and they eventually place the silver sword and shield of Grackle back in Barious's small wooden tool shop.

Raven and Emerald have decided to live in Barious's small wooden tool shop and rule Oak Village from this building. Raven also wanted to keep the silver sword and shield of Grackle as remembrance artefacts of his ancestry heritage right from the beginning that started with the almighty wizard Grackle and Raven's great-great-grandfather Sparrow, along with Barious's and Ruby's things for Raven and Emerald to reminisce about them. A man Oak villager takes the brown rope reins of Felix and leads him over the wooden and cobbled paths of Oak Village to the small grass field at the back of Barious's small wooden tool shop for Felix to rest up after his long journeys across the Planet of Phoenix.

Raven, Emerald, and Rexus now walk slowly on the wooden and cobbled paths through Oak Village in the south direction until they reach Oakus Graveyard in the south-east side of Oak Village. Along their way to Oakus Graveyard, Raven and Emerald shake hands or hug Oak villagers they pass by along the wooden and cobbled paths. Upon approaching Oakus Graveyard adjacent to Oakus Church, Raven, Emerald, and Rexus enter calmly through the black metal archway entrance of Oakus Graveyard. Once within Oakus Graveyard, Raven, Emerald, and Rexus continue to walk gradually up the small grass hill until they get to halfway up the small grass hill, where they reach Barious's and now Ruby's graves that lay next to each other.

After a deep emotional breath, Raven, Emerald, and Rexus position themselves to stand at the front of Barious's and Ruby's graves that were decorated elegantly with bountiful red roses on top of the graves. White wax candles that were lighted surrounded the edges of the graves. Emerald looks over and sadly notices Ruby's wooden crucifix attached at the top part of her grave. Emerald devastatingly reads Ruby's wooden crucifix to herself. Ruby's wooden crucifix reads:

> Ruby remains an inspirational human, mother, and teacher who cared deeply for Oak Village. Ruby's love for Emerald and Raven will remain forever.

Emerald cries expressively after reading Ruby's wooden crucifix, and she hugs Raven tightly, when suddenly she feels a strange pounding inside her stomach. Emerald grabs her stomach quickly with her right hand and stops crying.

'What is it, Emerald? Are you all right?' asks Raven curiously after he stops hugging her and looks down at Emerald's stomach.

'Raven, I think, it feels like I'm pregnant.' Emerald smiles back at Raven's eyes as Emerald lets go of her stomach and grabs on to Raven's and passionately kisses Raven upon his lips.

'That seems strangely quick as we have only made love again within the last two weeks since your death back at Eagle Forest,' mentions Raven in a surprised manner after Emerald and Raven stop kissing one another passionately.

'We have been truly blessed by the gods,' replies Emerald ecstatically with a wide smile upon her face, while Raven smiles back at Emerald, confused as a thought begins to wander deep within his mind about how Emerald had become pregnant so quickly and just after her soul has been returned to her after they had sacrificed Venus's life force into the anomaly crystal back at Triton's Underground Dungeon. Emerald grabs Raven's hand and places it upon her stomach, and Raven also feels a slight movement within Emerald's stomach that makes Emerald smile radiantly at Raven with much gladness.

'If it's a girl we will call her Ruby, and if it's a boy, we will call him Barious,' smiles Raven back as he understands Emerald's vibrant delight with regards to the news about their baby. Raven holds Emerald firmly within his arms.

'I love you Raven with all my heart. Don't ever let me go again,' remarks Emerald happily as she firmly holds on to Raven.

'I'll never do that Emerald. Our love is for eternity. Life is only the beginning,' says Raven.